The GREEN Phantasm

GEORGE ROBERT COATES

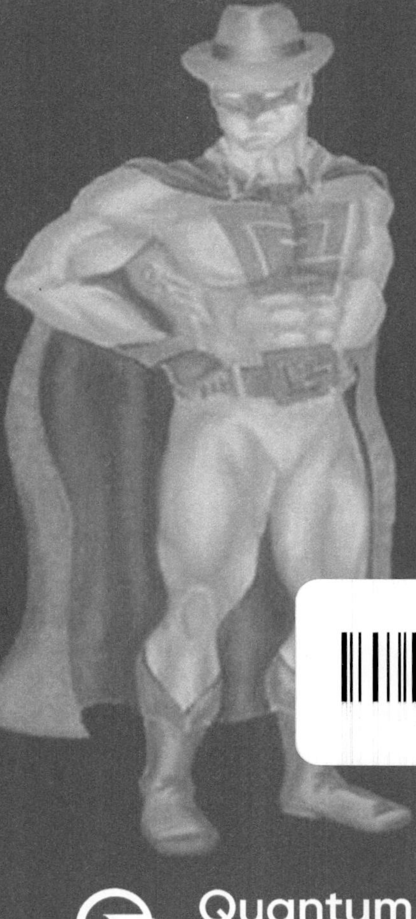

ISBN
978-1-963254-52-5 (Paperback)
978-1-963254-53-2 (eBook)
978-1-963254-51-8 (Hardcover)

Table of Contents

The GREEN Phantasm

Scott Mark MacNicholl
age: 24
height: 5'9
weight: 180lbs

Eric Austin Thomas
age: 26
height: 5'10
weight: 170lbs

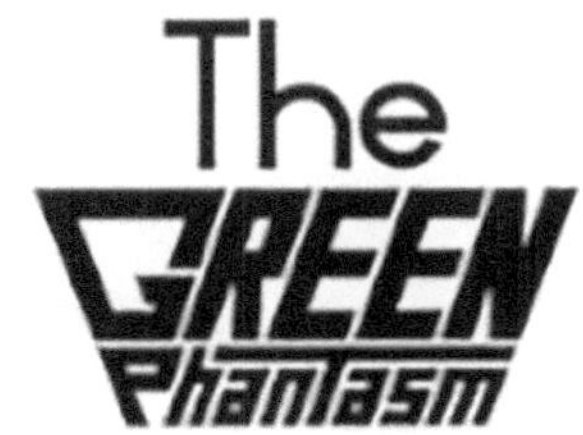

(James Paul Clifton)
age: 25
height: 6'3
weight: 290lbs

Amanda Lee Taylor
age: 26
height: 5'9
weight: 155lbs

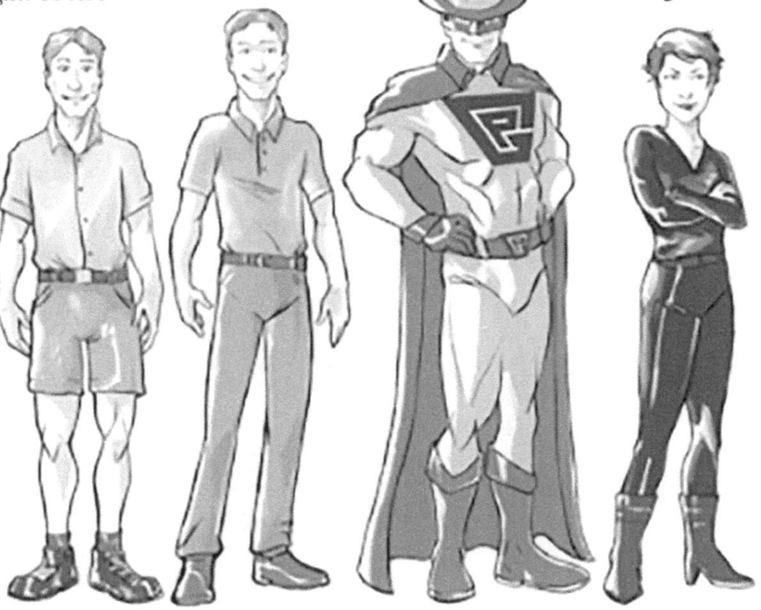

X-TERMINATION

(John Perry
Perone)
XTE
age: 52
height: 6'0"
weight: 200lbs.

ZAPPER
(Axel Jerome Axtel)
Senior Lieutenant
age: 42
height: 6'2"
weight: 265lbs

ZINGER
(Nicholas Devin
Jarrett)
Junior Lieutenant
age: 26
height: 5'7"
weight: 235lbs

D.D.T
(Anselm Jerad
Nielsen)
Premier Associate
age: 35
height: 7'0"
weight: 650lbs.

CHAPTER ONE

Enter James Clifton

James Paul Clifton was a young bachelor who lived in the Mayfair subdivision in Philadelphia, Pennsylvania. Philadelphia was also Clifton's place of birth. He was the chief engineer at a company called Ace Nuclear Supply and had recently been promoted to that position after having worked for the company for two years. But Clifton was currently only twenty-five years old. He had achieved a PhD in nuclear engineering by the age of twenty-three.

James Clifton was a white male. He stood six feet three inches tall and weighed about 290 pounds. He had a fairly good build and slightly darker skin than *most* white people. He also had black hair, which he always kept cut very short, and hazel eyes.

Clifton's appearance and personality helped him earn a great reputation. He always tried to do his best in personal hygiene. For instance, he always kept his teeth brushed, and kept himself clean-shaven. James also made it a point to have at least one bath or shower each and every day. Plus, whether at work or anywhere else, he made certain to be dressed nicely, neatly, and appropriately. In addition to all that, James was generally friendly, easygoing, and able to get along with anyone with whom he interacted. He undoubtedly felt that these things were important to the way others would perceive him as a chief engineer.

Perhaps James's greatest strength was his desire to do what was right. He usually forced it to override any other desires he may have had. Because of this, he currently had no criminal record and had never been to jail. Clifton had also never been the type to smoke, drink alcohol, or take illegal drugs. Occasionally, he did have to get tough with himself in order to do what was right. For instance, he may have occasionally felt tempted to get involved in gambling or prostitution but stubbornly refused to do so.

Although not perfect, James Clifton had a very good heart and conscience. He even tried to be fair to people he really did not like and sometimes gave a helping hand to those less fortunate. However, he was unwilling to become a complete pushover and sometimes tried to encourage others to do what was right. He also always showed politeness, courtesy, and respect to other people and that respect included their property. James Clifton was loved, respected, and truly appreciated by those who knew him well. Even though a few individuals hated him for doing the right thing, he still made certain that the desire to do so was stronger than any other desire of his.

He was born and raised two streets east of where he now lived. That was the home of his parents, Melburn and Diane Clifton. He was their only child. Melburn was a chemical engineer, and Diane was a high school geography teacher. Fortunately for James, they loved and treasured him so much that they wanted only the absolute best for him. So they always did what they could to make sure that he had a great life. As a result, he ended up having a great life indeed.

Even while they gave him the very best provisions and treatment that they could, his parents made sure to teach him to distinguish right from wrong. In turn, because of the lessons and discipline he received, James usually conducted himself in an excellent manner and seldom had to be punished. He had received much guidance in making good decisions. As a result of all that, young James was always very mature for his age. He even brought in lots of compliments from strangers on his behavior and manners. Before very long, he had come to understand and appreciate everything his mother and father had tried to get across to him.

In addition to teaching him how to make good decisions and behave himself, Melburn and Diane tried to encourage their only son to give his all and do his absolute best in everything he was trying to do. This included what he did for school, work, or any other activity in which he was involved.

One of these activities was getting through school. All the way from kindergarten to twelfth grade, James Clifton was always determined to do nothing short of outstanding schoolwork. In effect, he always made straight

A's in all of his courses. Also, on two occasions, between kindergarten and eighth grade, James earned the privilege of skipping a grade. In the end, he graduated from high school when he was only sixteen years old.

Even though Clifton did excellent in all school subjects, the two he actually liked best were math and science. After all, they had the most to do with what he intended to do when he grew up. His father inspired him to find out more about different branches of engineering. So James wanted to become an engineer too. From grades eight to twelve, he was one year ahead of most other students in his math and science courses. The two sciences he enjoyed most were chemistry and physics. But he had already been through both of them by the time he became a high school senior. James had also been through all of his required math courses by his senior year, and during his senior year, he was enrolled in calculus.

High school graduation eventually came along for him. Though he was not the valedictorian, he was still one of the top three in his class with his grade point average. He was also the youngest graduating senior. Next, of course, the time came for James to proceed to college. He decided that he wanted to become a nuclear engineer. So, following his high school graduation, he enrolled at Pennsylvania State University, for he had received an academic scholarship there. He majored in nuclear engineering. He certainly had two proud parents because of his outstanding grade point average and his high school degree by age sixteen. Both parents, but especially his father, were very confident that their son could become whatever he wanted.

Although James got to attend Pennsylvania State by means of a scholarship, he opted to live at home with his parents. He felt that this would help him to focus on his studies a lot more. After all, just like through high school, he wanted to do nothing less than outstanding work. Fortunately, James also wound up making straight A's in college. Much like in high school, he was ahead in his math and science courses. This was due to advanced placement tests he had taken in the areas of calculus, chemistry, and physics, on which he had earned credit before beginning his first semester at Pennsylvania State. Then, while trying to achieve his bachelor's degree, James did so well in those areas that he made them look easy. He even helped other students who asked him for it. This advanced placement, along with the desire to get through college, enabled him to achieve a bachelor's degree by the age of nineteen. Of course, his parents were very proud of his achievement, and so was James himself. Just like with high school, he was one of the top few graduates from Pennsylvania State.

Even after getting a bachelor's degree, he wanted to better himself. He would do so by furthering his education in graduate school. Because he had little trouble obtaining a bachelor of science, James wanted to go for a PhD in nuclear engineering. For the time being, he continued to stay with his parents, for he wanted to take his studies seriously. He also did something else to work toward becoming a nuclear engineer. Soon after graduating from Pennsylvania State University, James got a job at a nuclear power plant north of Philadelphia. He continued to work there while attending graduate school. Although he had yet to earn his PhD, this job at the power plant gave him excellent pay and allowed him to obtain some hands-on experience that was very relevant to a nuclear engineer. But, because he was going to school full-time and working full-time, James almost never had time for fun or enjoyment, except on the weekends.

Fortunately for James, his pay at the nuclear power plant was good enough that he was able to move out of his parents' house before too long. At age twenty-one, Clifton moved into the house in which he now lived. It was slightly larger than his parents'. It consisted of two stories, as his parents' house did. However, it had four bedrooms instead of three and a somewhat larger kitchen, living room, and dining room. Although James actually loved his parents and had stayed with them to get himself through school, he felt the need to move into his own place. After all, he was eager to become independent and move forward with his life.

Finally, at age twenty-three, James earned his PhD. With very little doubt, this was his greatest accomplishment up to that point. Melburn and Diane had to be more proud of their son than ever before. However, James still wanted to do better.

Before too long, he found a possible way to make himself better off in quite a few ways. He felt that this opportunity would help him financially, as well as make him more valuable, functional, and practical. This was the chance to go to work for the employer by which he was now employed, Ace Nuclear Supply.

Ace Nuclear Supply was located in a large building a couple of miles northwest of the Northeast Philadelphia Airport and a few miles west of the state hospital. The building was five stories high and took up the space of six football fields. The south end, which was considered the front of the building, was like a five-story office building. But behind that was a vast warehouse, in which manufacturing and a lot of other work took place. This warehouse took up two-thirds of the building's area.

Just as the name suggested, Ace Nuclear Supply produced and manufactured nuclear devices and equipment and supplied them to companies that needed them. This included vital parts and equipment for nuclear power plants. Ace also constructed nuclear engines and nuclear weapons. They even dealt with nuclear reactors and particle accelerators. They also frequently developed uses for radiation and radioactive materials. Ace Nuclear Supply even produced nuclear fuels and other necessary chemicals.

James soon felt that he was as ready as he would ever be to go to work for Ace Nuclear Supply. After all, he had become very familiar with how a nuclear power plant was built and how it worked. Other than that, he found a lot of other nuclear devices to be very interesting. This triggered a desire to become more versatile in nuclear engineering. This desire for versatility was also a reason that Clifton had taken a minor in mechanical engineering. After all, the work of a nuclear engineer often overlapped with that of certain other kinds of engineers. James had used some of his spare time to read and study about other engineering branches. They included, but were not limited to, chemical, industrial, and electrical engineering. James was anxious to go to a more advanced level in engineering and get involved in designing and creating nuclear devices, supplies, and equipment.

James went on to put together a résumé and send it in to Ace Nuclear Supply. He soon received a call from the chief engineer, who set up an interview with him. The chief engineer had been very impressed with Clifton's background;. This was because James had always been a straight-A student, now had a PhD, and even had a few years of hands-on experience at a power plant under his belt. The interview went extremely well. The chief engineer greatly admired James's desire to learn a lot more, as well as his interest in making Ace a growing company. He was confident that James could become an asset to them and hired him for an entry-level position.

James began his career as an engineering assistant. Understandably, he was a little intimidated during his first few days on the job, as he had been before at the nuclear power plant. However, he had more determination than anyone else at Ace Nuclear Supply and turned out to be a relatively fast learner. James was especially helpful as an assistant once he better understood how nuclear equipment was designed and built. Ace soon developed new versions of a few existing devices. This had a little something to do with some helpful suggestions that James had passed on to the engineer he was assisting. That particular engineer was very happy to have James Clifton as his assistant.

Before too long, advancement within the company came along for him. His productivity as an engineering assistant allowed for a slight increase in the business of Ace Nuclear Supply. Of course, he also had a very positive effect on the engineer to whom he was an assistant. However, by the time he had been employed by Ace Nuclear Supply for six months, he was made a full-fledged engineer. He even came to have his own office.

Acquiring the status of a full engineer brought James much success. For instance, he developed a lot more versatility in the field of engineering, for he picked up on other branches besides nuclear. This allowed him to develop designs and other ideas that led to Ace Nuclear Supply's output of several new inventions. In addition, he was named employee of the month on several occasions. Within a year of being a full-fledged engineer, he became one of the highest paid engineers at Ace Nuclear Supply. But his advancement within the company did not stop there.

Shortly after becoming practically the top engineer, James obtained a major promotion. At the beginning of the next year, the chief engineer who had hired him retired, creating a vacancy. Therefore, the operations manager had to put someone else in that position. Although the decision was not easy, he chose James Clifton for a number of reasons. For instance, during the previous year, James had been the employee of the month more times than any other engineer. In addition, during his employment, Ace had an increase in business like never before. This had something to do with his ideas and positive influence on other engineers. Besides, both the company's owner and operations manager could see that he was the most determined and most put together of all the engineers at Ace Nuclear Supply. So the new chief engineer was none other than the one and only James Paul Clifton.

At age twenty-five, he was the youngest chief engineer that Ace had ever had. What an achievement he had made in such a short time. James even came to have a salary of over a hundred thousand dollars per year. Everyone at Ace Nuclear Supply was happy to have him as the chief engineer. In addition, his parents were prouder of him than ever before. They even threw him a huge party to celebrate his promotion. James was able to buy almost everything he had ever dreamed of owning. This included not only his two-story home, but also one of his dream vehicles. It was a black Chevrolet Suburban. His vehicle was now paid off, and his home was nearly so. James was actually more prosperous than his father.

As chief engineer, James was the absolute head of Ace Nuclear Supply's engineering department. He supervised all of the other engineers, as well as various technicians. It was his job to approve and/or recommend changes to the designs of all the engineers. James himself still continued to come up with ideas for new technology and changes to existing products. He frequently held meetings in a conference room. At each meeting, he would go over a major project with a whole crew of engineers and technicians. He would also tell each individual on which part to focus. As chief engineer, James spent more time in his office and less time in the huge warehouse. But sometimes, he would walk through the warehouse to make sure that his men were doing their jobs correctly. James Clifton made an excellent chief engineer, and Ace Nuclear Supply was now doing better than ever before.

Even though he had some interest, another promotion was going to be rather difficult to come by. Not too many people at Ace Nuclear Supply were ranked above him. They included the operations manager and the owner, Sherman Acey, who had started the company fifty years earlier. However, James did not want to take a position that did not belong to him. So for the present, he decided to try to be the best he possibly could as the chief engineer. He wanted to help Ace Nuclear Supply increase their business, as well as make better money for himself.

In spite of his success and good fortune in his career, James Clifton remained down-to-earth and kept striving to be good and do right. For one thing, he found contentment with his assigned position at Ace Nuclear and only wanted to make an honest living. Therefore, he never felt the need for a scam, and did not want to take money that was not rightfully his. Also, although he was doing better than either of his parents, he still tried to maintain love, honor, and respect toward them.

James even made it evident that Melburn and Diane had done a great job raising him and teaching him how to make good decisions based on what was right or wrong. As much as Clifton wanted to improve himself and his living situation any way he could, he refused to do anything by which he could be corrupted. For instance, he did not want to become part of a crime syndicate or do anything illegal. So he was stubbornly determined not to get involved in such activities as gambling or drug-dealing, for he felt that they were not worth doing. He was also not the type of person to accept a bribe. Instead, he was very happy to have things that could not be taken away from him, such as his PhD degree and his work ethics.

In addition to doing what he could financially, James also strived to take care of himself and improve himself physically. He enjoyed weight lifting and did other kinds of exercises as well. James usually worked out at a health club four or five times per week. In regards to eating, he always put proper nutrition first. Plus, in taking care of himself, James did very few things that were unhealthy. He never smoked or drank alcoholic beverages and seldom consumed sodas or anything with caffeine. In addition, he tried to keep his anger and stress under control.

Throughout his high school and college years, James also did other things to promote physical activity. Of course, he always put his schoolwork first. However, every spring in high school, he competed in several track and field events, as a member of his school's team. He proved to be a valuable team member and always made it to the state finals in a few events, winning one or two of them. For his numerous achievements, James had medals, trophies, and other awards, as well as a letterman's jacket.

While working on his bachelor's degree at Pennsylvania State, James went to a local sports academy two or three nights per week. At that academy, he received training in amateur boxing. The main reason James went through that training was for physical fitness; he thought it to be one of the best ways to get in top athletic condition. But, occasionally, he competed in a tournament or fought in an exhibition bout. Clifton won a few awards from all that as well. But as good as James may have become, he did not elect to try to become a professional. After all, he did not want to become corrupt, violent, or aggressive. Besides, he chose to stay focused on his college education. So, soon after James achieved his bachelor's degree, he stopped going to the sports academy but still continued with some of the kinds of training he had been taught.

Two evenings per week, James took lessons from a karate club at Pennsylvania State. He was trying to pick up on Shotokan karate, a Japanese self-defense method. The two main reasons that Clifton went into this were to take advantage of the physical exercise involved and to learn techniques he could use for self-defense, though he would fight only when and if absolutely necessary. James discontinued this course whenever he achieved his bachelor's degree. However, at that point, he had become a second-degree black belt. Regardless of that or his boxing achievements, Clifton never used any of his knowledge or training to look for trouble or start fights. His good conscience would not allow that. He only intended to protect or rescue himself, a loved one, or anyone else he came across who needed help. But for some reason, up to the present, James had not ever had the opportunity to do so.

In addition, James learned a lot of other techniques to defend himself and to take down enemies in order to survive. These techniques included different ways to attack an opponent's pressure points, as well as ways to deal with more than one attacker simultaneously. James also picked up on ways to defend against someone who had a knife, club, or other weapon. He even found out a possible way to take a handgun from someone who was holding him at gunpoint. In order to learn these things, James had purchased numerous books and videos.

Although James had picked up on so many ways to fight and defend himself, he was still undecided about one thing. That was the question of whether to purchase a handgun. The only reason he would have would be to protect himself. But he did not want to get himself into trouble with the law, or risk anyone else who was innocent getting hurt or killed. Besides, James always tried to avoid dangerous situations to begin with. Up to the present, no one had ever tried to attack, threaten, or provoke him. So James still had not yet bought a gun.

Although James did not continue his boxing or martial arts training through graduate school, he still kept working out with weights and exercising, even to the present. He discontinued being an amateur boxer but eventually set up a few punching bags in his garage, which he still sometimes used for practice. Plus, though he was no longer enrolled in karate, he occasionally practiced his techniques to make certain he remembered them. Other than that, James studied various kinds of martial arts and self-defense and was still interested in adding to his present knowledge. He also wanted to keep striving to better his physique and physical strength through weight lifting. James was not going to quit those things altogether by any means.

Even with as much as James had accomplished in his life and though he had never gotten into trouble with the law, he was by no means perfect. He had a lot of faith in always doing the right thing but perhaps took it too seriously from time to time. He occasionally got angry and walked off if something did not go the way he wanted it to. But that was because he was trying to stand up for what he believed was right. However, James's behavior on a couple of occasions created a very disturbing scene. Fortunately for him, he did not go as far as getting arrested. He was usually easygoing and understanding about a lot of things, but occasionally, he got out of line if he did not understand something at all, or strongly disagreed with something.

Of course, James Clifton had his faults, as everyone did. However, a few great qualities seriously stood out. One was the fact that he could be trusted. Another was his ability to get along with anyone, for James was always polite and courteous toward others. Also, whenever James set himself a goal, nothing would keep him from pursuing it. Even occasional periods of being sick or in pain did not diminish his determination.

Furthermore, as great of a life as James Clifton had, he did not have everything. Of course, he had an excellent career with a bright future. He also owned a home that was very close to being his dream home. He even had one of his dream vehicles, as well as many other spectacular possessions. But he was seriously lacking a social life. He had never had many friends. It had always been few or none up to the present. This was chiefly because he was trying to remain focused on his goals, mainly getting through school and obtaining an outstanding career. But perhaps the sacrifice of a social life paid off for James. However, in addition to almost never having any friends, Clifton had never had a girlfriend or dated a woman up to the present. Neither had he ever gone to a dance in school.

But in spite of all that, Clifton now had two close friends. After all, he normally worked from 8:00 a.m. to 5:00 p.m. five days a week. He no longer had to study for school or do any other work besides that. He had had those two great friends for much of his employment with Ace Nuclear Supply. Their names were Eric Austin Thomas and Scott Mark MacNicholl. James had first met them at a local pub in downtown Philadelphia. Presently, Clifton had a weekend camping trip planned with his two buddies. The three of them were planning on camping and hiking in the Allegheny Mountains, and they wanted to explore Mount Davis, the highest point in Pennsylvania.

Eric Thomas was a twenty-six-year-old white male. He stood five feet ten inches tall and weighed one hundred seventy pounds. He had dark-brown hair and brown eyes. Eric lived in the same subdivision as James but one street east of him. Eric worked as an electrician. His personality was much like Clifton's, except that perhaps he was slightly friendlier and more laid-back than James was. Regardless, he was still James Clifton's best friend.

James's other close friend was of course Scott MacNicholl. He was a twenty-four-year-old white male. He stood five feet nine inches tall and weighed one hundred eighty pounds. Scott had medium-brown hair and brown eyes. He lived on the same street as Eric Thomas. Scott had been friends with Eric for about four years before James Clifton came along and became his new best friend. Whatever the case was, all three were still very good friends and often did things as a group. Also, like James and Eric, Scott was a good person who had never been in trouble with the law up to the present. However, he tended to be more eager and anxious than the other two and sometimes made decisions impulsively.

Scott had also graduated high school, as his two best friends had. However, he did not go to college like James or go to trade school like Eric. For a career, Scott went into the trucking industry. He was currently a dispatcher at a trucking company. Shortly after his high school graduation, Scott began as a dock worker. He loaded and unloaded trucks and helped keep the premises clean. Like James Clifton, he was determined to better himself only by moving up or forward. So, by the time Scott was twenty-one years old, he had acquired a commercial driver's license. Then before too long, he was promoted to the position of a pickup-and-delivery driver. Finally, after doing that for a couple of years, Scott received another promotion. Of course, that was to his current position of dispatcher. Scott did that job very well and made very good money, much like his buddy Eric, who was an electrician. But neither Scott nor Eric made the kind of money that James made as an engineer.

Despite all the different kinds of work they did, James, Eric, and Scott enjoyed a lot of the same things. For instance, they often went out to bars and dance clubs on weekends. In addition, James frequently invited Eric and Scott to his house for barbecues, pool tournaments, just hanging out, or any of a few other things. Also, the three of them sometimes watched sporting events together, whether on television or live at the arena, or wherever it was taking place. The three of them were so close that James's parents and other family members had gotten to know Eric and Scott well. Eric and Scott both had family members who had gotten to know James as well.

It was approaching 5:00 on a Friday evening in September. James was trying to finish wrapping up another week's work at Ace Nuclear Supply. Afterward, he planned to run home and get ready to meet Eric and Scott for their weekend camping trip. At 5:02, James closed up his office and began making his way to the front of the building. Once he got there, he spoke to the receptionist. She was a twenty-eight-year-old woman named Jenna Daniels, who had short blond hair. "Have a nice weekend, Jenna," James told her.

"You too, Mr. Clifton," she replied.

Very shortly, James got into his Suburban and began driving toward home. While heading south on Bustleton Avenue, he was talking and thinking to himself about his upcoming camping trip. "Oh man," he said, "I can't wait to go hiking in the Alleghenies. I'm so eager to see what I'll find. I even wonder what new discoveries I could possibly make."

All of a sudden, James began slowing down, for something had caught his eye. "Talk about new discoveries," said a somewhat surprised James Clifton. "Who is that?" He was referring to a young woman walking through a parking lot to the right. "You know, I think I'm gonna go find out, because she's hot," James said to himself. That very moment, he drove forward a little more and turned right into the parking lot.

The lovely young woman James had spotted was twenty-six-year-old Amanda Lee Taylor. Amanda was a loan officer at a company called Stanley Financial, which was a large business that provided banking and financial services. These services included trust funds, mortgages, and loans, of course. They did other banking as well and even provided tax services. James happened to be pulling into the parking lot of their Philadelphia location, which was on the west side of Bustleton Avenue.

Amanda Taylor was a white female with dark-brown hair, which she cut relatively short, and brown eyes. She was five feet nine inches tall and weighed about 155 pounds. She too was an only child. Amanda was the daughter of Warren and Linda Taylor. She now lived in a two-bedroom apartment in the Lawndale subdivision of Philadelphia, but was not originally from Philadelphia. Amanda was raised in the city of Camden, New Jersey. Her parents still lived there.

Camden was also the city where Amanda had attended high school, as well as elementary and junior high, of course. But then, after graduating high school, Amanda enrolled at the University of Pennsylvania in Philadelphia, where she majored in accounting. Also, while attending the University of Pennsylvania, she worked at a bank as a teller. She continued both her employment and education until she received a bachelor's degree in accounting.

It was soon after graduation that Amanda obtained employment with Stanley Financial. This happened when she was twenty-two years old. Her degree in accounting in combination with her previous employment with a bank, were very helpful in getting her hired at Stanley Financial. She received training to become a loan officer, whose job it was to arrange and set up loans for people and businesses. Amanda had now been a loan officer for the company for about four years.

Amanda Taylor was a law-abiding citizen and was very friendly and courteous toward others, much like James Clifton was. Also, like James, she had a really good conscience, which moved her to try to do the right thing and keep out of trouble. However, her sweet and beautiful outward appearance concealed something about her that no one ever suspected. Both mentally and physically, Amanda was one tough cookie, tougher than most women, as well as a lot of men. She was not the type to be easily upset by others or to cry easily. She was also super tough as far as being able to fight and defend herself physically.

It was mostly while going to college that Amanda had gained knowledge and skills in different self-defense techniques and ways to fight. For instance, she eventually became a black belt in karate like James. Amanda also underwent training in judo and kickboxing. She learned many other ways to defend herself and disable opponents as well. However, opportunities for her to apply the things she learned were few and far between. Amanda was not the type to try to start a fight with anyone. Fortunately for her, she had never been attacked.

In addition, Amanda did a few other things to keep herself physically fit and active. In high school, she was a valuable athlete on her school's track and field team, also like James. But Amanda played softball as well. Besides the sports she played in high school, Amanda worked out with weights and did other various conditioning exercises as well. She still continued to exercise and lift weights up to the present.

In regards to Amanda's social life, she had always had a couple or a few friends at any and every point in time throughout her life. Currently, the names of her two best friends were Erin and Michelle. In high school, Amanda had three different boyfriends, but not one of those relationships ever lasted beyond a school year. Then in college, Amanda never actually had any boyfriends. One reason was that she wanted to focus a lot more on her studies. Other than that, although a lot of young men tried to hit on her, Amanda never felt that a single one of them seemed like her type. Perhaps things were about to be different with the opportunity to meet James Paul Clifton.

Also, since James had never had a girlfriend before, he was undoubtedly very eager to meet a woman. Because of his lack of experience, he was unsure of what to do and a bit nervous but still wanted to try something. So shortly after pulling into the parking lot, James parked and shut off his Suburban. He then got out and began slowly jogging toward Amanda. By the time he had made his way over to her, she was about to get into her vehicle, which was a purple Ford Explorer. Just when Amanda was about to unlock her Explorer, James appeared to her left and said to her, "Hey, excuse me."

At that, Amanda looked to her left and said, "Yes, can I help you?"

Not sure of what to say, a nervous James Clifton began to stutter, "Well, uh, I, um… I'm… not really sure where to begin." This caused Amanda to roll her eyes and shake her head in confusion. But then, James went on to tell her, "You see, I just happened to be nearby, and I saw you. So, I just um, thought it might be nice if I, uh, you know, came and said hello."

"Okay," replied Amanda, who was still confused. "Well, hello."

"Oh yeah," said James. "Anyway, I'm James, James Clifton." As he spoke, he reached out to shake her hand.

Reluctantly, Amanda proceeded to shake his hand and said, "Well, good to meet you, James. I'm… Amanda."

"Amanda," he said right back to her. "So, Amanda, where are you from originally?"

"Originally, I'm from Camden in New Jersey," she answered him.

"So you're from Camden," James said in reply. "I think I've heard of that. So, anyway, I take it this is where you work?"

"Yes," Amanda said while nodding, "it certainly is."

"This ought to be a pretty good job for you, right?" asked James.

"Yes, it is," Amanda told him. "I'm a loan officer. I went to college for this."

"Why, that's great," James told Amanda, "and it just so happens that I work at Ace Nuclear Supply, which is north of here. I'm their chief engineer."

"Wow!" Amanda exclaimed with a little enthusiasm. "So, you work for them?"

James responded affirmatively by saying, "Oh, yes, I most certainly do. By age twenty-three, I got a PhD in nuclear engineering. Then, in a couple of years, I worked my way up to chief engineer."

"Well, that sounds great," Amanda told James.

"Other than that," James continued, "I don't mean to brag, but as far as I know, this is my dream job. I couldn't possibly ask for better. I think it's allowing me to live a great life."

In response to all that, Amanda said, "Oh, so what you're saying is, if you were any greater, then I guess you'd be a superhero or something?"

Not knowing what to think, James said, "Uh, well, I, uh, never really thought about it that way. However, if you say so, then yeah, I guess so."

At that, Amanda just nodded.

Next, James said, "So, what are you up to this weekend?"

"I'm going somewhere with two of my friends," answered Amanda.

"Me too," James replied, "but actually, we're going on a camping trip. We're going to the Allegheny Mountains to try to get to Mount Davis, and we want to see what else we can find as well."

"Really!" said Amanda. "Well, good luck. You just might find the thing you need."

"The thing I need?" questioned James, "Uh, for what? What thing?"

"You know," Amanda responded, "to make you a superhero. Who knows? You just might find the source of your super power right there in those mountains, like if a meteorite strikes or something."

"Oh yeah, right," James replied most affirmatively while nodding.

Finally, Amanda said to James, "Anyway, I gotta go."

"All right," James responded, "no problem. It was nice talking to you. You have a great weekend, okay?"

"Yeah, you too," said Amanda.

"I hope to see you again," James told her. At that, they parted company. But then, shortly after James started heading back toward his Suburban, he stopped for a moment; he'd had an afterthought. "Ah, doggone it!" he exclaimed in frustration. "I forgot to ask for her phone number!" But after that, he immediately calmed down and said to himself, "Well, at least I know where she works. Maybe I'll get it next time." Finally, he continued to walk back to his vehicle.

While James was doing that, Amanda was having some thoughts of her own. As she got ready to climb into her Explorer, she stopped and turned her head momentarily to watch James Clifton. Perhaps she had some sort of interest in him. In fact, she shortly began thinking, *Well, hmm, you know, I've had guys try to hit on me before, but this one seems different from all of them. I mean, after all, he's got a great job that he really worked for. That might indicate some maturity and stability. Other than that, he is kind of a handsome hunk. But, I wonder why he didn't ask for my phone number. Well, he did seem nervous; maybe that was it. Who knows? He could also be inexperienced with dating and relationships. But, at least he was interested enough to come and try to meet me. Maybe I would like to see him again.*

At last, they both got into their vehicles and began driving home. James, of course, was trying to get home to finish getting ready for his camping trip with Eric and Scott. Amanda was now driving home as well to her two-bedroom apartment in the Lawndale subdivision, where she had lived for much of her employment with Stanley Financial. Most of all, this wrapped up another week of work for James Clifton, who now had a weekend to which to look forward.

CHAPTER TWO

A Remarkable Camping Trip

It was now past 5:30 p.m. James Clifton was home from work. He had to start preparing for the camping trip to the Allegheny Mountains with his two friends, Eric and Scott.

James began gathering and preparing all the equipment and supplies that he needed for the trip. However, he did not seem to be in a big hurry. That was because he was also doing some daydreaming at the same time, which really slowed him down. One of the things on Clifton's mind was the young lady he had met earlier that afternoon. Also, James was imagining himself making a brand-new discovery in the Allegheny Mountains and thinking of how that could possibly make him rich and famous.

Unfortunately, all the daydreaming caused James to lose track of time, and it soon came to be 6:30 p.m. An hour had passed. He noticed this, gasped in surprise, and said, "Oh no, I was not paying attention to the time. I did not realize it was this late. I still have to call Eric."

So now, James finally called his friend, Eric to notify him that he was ready to come and meet them.

"Hello," answered Eric on his cell phone.

"Hey, Eric," said James, "It's me, James."

"James, what's up?" replied Eric. "I'm glad you called. I was starting to get worried. What's going on?"

"Oh, well, Eric, I just called to let you know that I'm finally ready and fixing to be on my way to meet up with you and Scott at your house. I mean, this camping trip is still on, right?" James asked nervously.

"Of course it is," said Eric. "Is everything all right with you, James?" Eric asked this because of the way James was stuttering and the fact that he had taken a little while to call. He began to wonder if James was holding back, not telling him something.

James realized that he should let Eric know what was really going on. However, he was too embarrassed to do so. So he just went on to say, "Oh, of course, absolutely, there's no problem. Anyway, Eric, have you talked to Scott?"

"I most certainly have," said Eric. "He is already on his way over here. In fact, he should be here any minute. When are you going to get here, James?"

"Oh, well, I should be there in about twenty minutes or so. I'm fixing to be on my way."

"Well, then," said Eric. "We will most definitely be waiting for you when you get here."

"All right, I will see you and Scott when I get there, okay?"

"Okay."

"All right, bye," said James. At that, both James and Eric hung up.

James just had to double-check one last thing to make sure that he was not missing a single necessity for the camping trip. After that, he put his backpack and other supplies in the back of his truck. Then, he left on his way to Eric's house.

So, the thing that James had to do now was make his way over to his friend Eric's house one street east of his home. Of course, James had no problem finding his way to Eric's house, since he had gone there many times before. However, he had another thing on his mind besides meeting with Eric and Scott. Without a doubt, it was Amanda, the woman he had said hello to earlier that evening. So once again, he focused all his thoughts on her. Once James started thinking about Amanda again, he started to imagine her sitting in the passenger side in his truck beside him. The next thing Clifton could see and feel in his mind was Amanda showing affection by talking sweetly, running her hands all over him, and even kissing him. Consequently, he asked himself, "Why can't I just go to the mountains to be alone with her, instead of those two lunkheads?"

Before his thoughts persisted any further, he stopped himself and said, "Wait a minute, what did I just say? Did I call them lunkheads? Why, they're not lunkheads; Eric and Scott have been my friends for a long time, right? Right!"

Clifton now realized that he had just gotten too carried away with his feelings for Amanda. He also knew that it would not be right to allow her to come between him and his friends. So he said, "I guess I was just thinking too much about Amanda again. But I have to admit that I'm really attracted to this girl. She caught my eye this afternoon, and now I just can't seem to get over her. It's already been twice in the last hour and a half that thinking of her has made me lose control of myself."

While James was thinking about Amanda and reasoning with himself, he was not paying full attention to where he was on the way to Eric's house. Naturally, he was able to make his way over to Eric's place without even thinking about it. But when he was finally on Eric's street, his thoughts distracted him and caused him to pass it. As James was passing, he saw his two best friends standing in front of Eric's house. When he did, he said to himself, "Well, that looks like Eric and Scott."

Upon saying that, James stopped all his thoughts that very minute and exclaimed, "What! Eric and Scott!" He quickly took a look around at his surroundings. In the instant James realized he was actually on Eric's street, he slammed on his brakes, pounded the steering wheel with his fist, and hollered out in frustration. "Aw shoot! Doggone it!" he cried. "What on earth have I just done? For the first time in my life, I paid no attention whatsoever and passed his freakin' house by three doors!"

That vision Clifton had seen was not merely a vision. It was in reality none other than his two good friends, Eric Thomas and Scott MacNicholl, who were actually standing outside in front of Eric's house waiting for him.

James just went on, turned his truck around, and headed back to Eric's house. It was now approaching 7:00 p.m. Once James pulled into Eric's driveway, both Eric and Scott came over to greet him.

James got out of his truck. "Hey Eric! Hey, Scott! How's it going?" he said greeting them and shaking hands with both of them.

"Not bad James. Is everything all right with you?" replied Scott, with a concerned look on his face.

Eric agreed with Scott and said, "Yeah, James, we were rather concerned when you passed us up and skidded to a stop."

James understood their concern and thought that maybe he should tell them what was really on his mind. However, he was too ashamed, embarrassed, and afraid to tell those two that it was a girl named Amanda.

So, startled by their questions, after holding his breath momentarily, James answered, saying, "Oh yeah, I'm fine; it's nothing serious."

"Well, okay," Eric replied doubtfully. "It just got me really worried when you just now passed me up and when you called me a little while ago."

James knew that he should let them know the truth. However, he took a few more seconds and made up another excuse. He went on to say, "Oh, well, you see, I just had a rough day at work. A couple of guys just did not come in, and we got really backed up."

"Well, we can understand," said Scott.

"Yeah, we certainly can," said Eric. "I just haven't ever seen you like this before."

James grew a little more nervous; he was trembling and holding his breath with a guilty feeling, because he had not told the truth. However, the three friends went on about their business to get ready to leave for their camping trip.

"So, anyway," said James, "have we got everything ready to go?"

"We sure do, James," answered Scott.

"Yes, James," confirmed Eric. "Would you mind coming to give us a hand, please?"

"Certainly," agreed James.

The three of them then walked inside Eric's home. They went into his living room, where both Eric and Scott had their backpacks and other supplies ready. Each of his friends grabbed his own backpack. James picked up both of their canteens and the lantern that Eric was bringing.

Next, James, Eric, and Scott carried everything over to the back of James's truck to load it. When James opened the back of his truck, the things he had brought were sitting before them, including his backpack, canteen, lantern, ice chest, and stove.

Scott said, "Well, it looks like we'll have to make an extra trip to carry all this to our campsite."

"Oh, it's all right, Scott," said James. "Hopefully, we won't be too far into the mountains. Anyway, come on, guys; let's load up." Scott and Eric took turns handing their supplies to James, who in turn, put them in his truck.

"You know what? I almost forgot something," said Eric, when he noticed they needed extra containers of propane for James's lantern. He went back inside to get the extra cans and also took a few minutes to double-check and make sure he had not forgotten anything.

Scott also had to get something out of his pickup. "Excuse me, James," he said, "I got to grab something else too."

"Okay, that's fine," said James. He waited a few minutes.

Soon, Eric and Scott returned with the things they had gone to retrieve. Eric had the extra propane for his lantern, and Scott had gone to get some music to listen to on the drive. James allowed Eric to put his propane in the truck and then asked Scott, "Hey, what sort of music you got there?"

Scott answered, "Oh, you know, just some classic rock and hard rock."

"Well, that'll work," said James. "Anyway, guys," he continued, "I guess that's it, huh? Are we ready to roll?"

"Oh yeah, sure, I'm all fired up," replied Scott.

"Let's hit the road," agreed Eric.

"Okay then," said James, "let's roll."

It was now 7:12 p.m. James, Eric, and Scott got into James's truck to start their trip. They had about a four-hour drive ahead of them.

James started his truck, backed out of Eric's driveway, and headed toward the interstate.

Before too long, Eric and Scott began talking. Eric started out by saying, "So anyway, Scott, anything extraordinary or unusual happen at work today?"

"No, not really, Eric," replied Scott, "not too much happened. We all got out of there in decent time. How about you?"

"Well Scott," said Eric, "I had a major project today that made me work over a little bit. I had a two-story house being built, in which I had to install wiring and other electrical equipment."

"Wow!" said Scott. "I bet you were glad to get done with that."

"Yes, I was," agreed Eric, "but now that that's over with and the weekend is here, I want to forget about all that and enjoy my trip to the mountains. So what I now want to know is, is anybody having fun yet?"

"I sure am," answered James, "and one reason is that I now get to enjoy a nice ride."

"Yeah, me too," said Eric, "but by any chance, is there a way to make this ride a little more fun?"

"You know," responded Scott, "I've got a tape here we can listen to. It has some hits I personally put together to enjoy. It's got both classic rock and hard rock."

"Well then," said Eric, "don't be so selfish and keep it all to yourself. Why not share it with James and me?"

"All right then," said Scott, "you asked for it."

Scott passed his tape to Eric, who inserted it into the cassette player. Almost immediately, both Scott and Eric started dancing and moving to the music. James, however, was not too captivated by it.

Now, why was James not into the music as much as his two best friends were? Well, it just so happened that he had other things on his mind, so much so, that he practically did not hear a single note from the songs being played. Although he had no trouble getting himself and his two friends to the mountain range and could see where he was going, in his mind, he was staring into space and daydreaming. One of those was the possibility that he could find something in those mountains that could bring him wealth and fame and even provide him with powers undreamed of. Why not? After all, new discoveries had to be made at some time, somewhere, and James figured that he didn't know what he might find. The other thing on James Clifton's mind was Amanda, the beautiful young lady to whom he had just lost his heart.

In the meantime, Eric and Scott were getting into their music. Eric soon caught a glimpse of James and noticed that he was not the least bit swayed by what was being played. So Eric stopped and tried to figure out why he was so quiet and practically sitting still. Finally, he said, "Hey, Scott."

Scott said, "Yeah, Eric, whatcha got?"

"What's the deal with James here?" Eric asked. "He doesn't appear to be every bit in the mood for this trip. What's up with him?"

"Well, I really don't know," answered Scott. "Why don't we ask him?"

Eric tried calling his name. "James," he said. Getting no response, he tried again. "James?"

Since that did not work, Eric and Scott decided to try together. They both said a little loudly, "James!"

James stopped his daydreaming and looked around for a few seconds in panic. That was until he looked to his right and saw Eric looking at him; then, he knew who had called his name. He calmed down.

"Oh man, I'm sorry, James," said Scott. "We didn't mean to scare you or alarm you."

"Of course we didn't," agreed Eric. "We were just enjoying this hard rock that Scott brought along and happened to notice that you were all quiet. Other than that, I just didn't hear you respond when I tried a couple of times to call your name. Is everything okay?"

"Oh, of course," answered James, "I was just thinking about our trip to the Allegheny Mountains. I mean, who knows what it could be like?"

James was not really thinking so much of the time he would have in the mountains with Eric and Scott but rather what he could discover for himself. Other than that, he had no doubt tried to imagine how he could win Amanda's love and affection. However, James did not have the courage to admit those things. Scott and Eric were now more concerned than before.

"Well, James," said Eric, "I really don't mean to doubt you or anything, but I just can't help thinking about what happened earlier, when you passed my house, and what happened just now. It just makes me wonder. Are you sure there's nothing bothering you?"

"Why, certainly not," said James, "I'm really sorry if I made you worry. But you know what? Maybe I shouldn't let the pressures of work bother me right now. In fact, I ought to not give work a moment's thought, so that this camping trip can be more enjoyable."

"You know, James," said Scott, "that's probably a good idea."

James still felt somewhat guilty that all the things he'd just said to Eric and Scott were impulsive, senseless, and misleading. He also felt sorry that the things on his mind were starting to produce friction between his two friends and himself. James tried to stop having those thoughts and turn his attention to Eric and Scott in order to have a good time with them.

From then on, the three friends were all able to enjoy the music together and talk about all kinds of fun things. James, Scott, and Eric continued this way for the remainder of the ride up to the mountains. Not a single distracting thought came into the mind of James Clifton. He decided he would ponder those thoughts later on his own time.

James was still driving along the interstate and soon was within a mile of an exit at which a truck stop called Big JD's Truck Stop was located. It was now around 9:45 p.m. The three friends had just finished talking about an embarrassing moment for Eric that had occurred a few months ago at a sports bar. Scott, who was sitting in the backseat, said, "Hey, guys, are either of you hungry?"

"Well, I don't know," responded James. "What do you mean, Scott?"

"Well, I'm asking because we have been riding for a while, and I'm starting to get hungry. I was gonna ask if you could stop at that truck stop," said Scott.

"Well, perhaps," said James, "I just don't know if I want anything that bad, but, uh—"

Scott said, "If you stop, I'll buy us all something to eat. I mean, after all, you're driving us to the mountains. So I'd like to try to repay you somehow."

At that, James stopped hesitating and said, "Well, in that case, let's stop then. I'm all for that. What do you say, Eric?"

"I guess I'll have to say that goes for me too," he agreed.

James took the exit ramp for Big JD's Truck Stop. He then drove into the parking lot and parked. The three of them went inside and sat down in the restaurant.

A waitress came along. She said, "Good evening, guys. My name is Janet. I'll be serving you this evening." She handed them three menus and asked, "Can I start you out with something to drink?"

Scott said, "Sure, bring us each a Coke, please."

"No problem," said the waitress. "I'll go get those while you think about what you want to order." She went off to get the drinks.

After that, Scott turned his attention to James and Eric. "All right, guys," he said, "what are we gonna get?"

"Scott," said James, "is it okay if I get me a double hamburger? That's what I was hoping to get."

"Well," said Scott, "I didn't know you'd want a double burger, but I guess that's okay, sure."

"Hey, Scott," said Eric, "I think I'll get a hamburger."

Scott said, "Okay then." Then, speaking to them both, he asked, "Do y'all want fries too?"

"Yes," James and Eric both said.

Before long, the waitress came back with three Cokes. As she handed them out, she asked, "So, guys, are we ready to order?"

"Yes, uh, Janet," said Scott, "get me and this guy next to me each a hamburger with fries."

"Okay," she said. She then started to look to James, who was across the table from Scott.

But pointing across to James, Scott said, "Oh, and for this guy get a double hamburger with fries. See? I didn't forget you, James."

"Well, thanks, Scott," said James.

"Anyway, that's it," Scott said to the waitress.

"I'll go put this in at once," she said as she turned to go put in their order.

While waiting for their food, the three friends engaged in conversation. Undoubtedly, they talked about things that were enjoyable to talk about, including other fun times that the three of them had had together, as well as other such experiences that any one of the three had without the other two. Other than that, they shared a few embarrassing moments as well. James, Eric, and Scott talked and talked until James noticed Janet coming with their burgers. "Hey, guys," said James, "here comes our food."

Eric and Scott turned their attention to the waitress as well. She put the tray down on the table, and they all took their plates.

"Thanks, Janet," Scott said to her. Then he added, "Oh, Janet, when you bring the check, include all of us. I'm covering it."

"No problem," she said.

After that, the three of them began eating their burgers. Of course, James, Scott, and Eric still talked while eating. But they eventually finished, and it came time to pay the check.

Finally, the waitress came back by. "Are we finished?" she asked.

"Yes, we are," answered Scott. "I think I'm ready for the check now."

"I'll bring it on over," said Janet. She went to print up the receipt soon; she returned and brought it over to collect from Scott. He gave her a twenty and a five, since the total was between twenty and twenty-five.

Then, Janet brought Scott his change, and all three young men pitched in to provide their waitress a tip.

Janet asked, "So, what are you guys up to?"

"Well, Janet," said James, "we're all headed to the Allegheny Mountains to go camping and hiking."

"That sounds like fun," she said. "I hope you all have a great trip this weekend."

"Well, thanks," said James. "Take care now."

Afterward, James and his two friends went back out to his truck in order to continue on their way. It was now 10:20 p.m. They just had about ninety miles left to get to the mountains. That was going to take about an hour and a half.

All the rest of the way, James, Eric, and Scott kept chatting and playing music as before. However, James spoke up and said, "By the way, thanks, Scott. I really, greatly appreciate you buying me supper."

"Oh yeah," added Eric, "I thank you too, Scott."

"No problem whatsoever," said Scott. "It was the least I could do, especially for you, James, since you're bringing us to the Allegheny Mountains."

After that, the three just continued talking and enjoying each other's company for the rest of the ride—that was until they were close to the Allegheny Mountains.

"Say, uh, James is that where we're going?" asked Eric, pointing to a guide sign.

"You bet it is," answered James.

"Oh man," said an anxious Scott. "I can't believe we're already this close. But waiting to go these last few miles is the hardest part for me. It's, like, gonna take longer than how far we've gone already did. I'm ready to get out and set up camp."

"All right, just be cool, Scott," said James. "Just a few more minutes, okay?"

"Okay, okay, I'm sorry," replied Scott. "I just find this the most exciting and interesting of all the things we've done together, and I've always wanted to do this."

"I hear you, Scott," said Eric. "I hope this will be something to remember and tell people about."

Soon, it was about 11:45 p.m. At that time, James got off at the necessary exit. Then, in just four more minutes, he finally pulled into a visitor's parking lot. The three were very happy to finally reach their destination.

"Well, look, you guys," James said to Scott and Eric. "We're here."

"Yes, that's great!" responded Scott. "What are we waiting for? Let's go get camp all set up."

"Okay, Scott," said Eric, "we're coming."

James went to the back of his truck with Eric and Scott. He opened up the back door. "You know what, guys?" asked James. "We might have to make two trips to get everything to our campsite, wherever we set it up."

"That's all right, James," replied Eric.

"Thanks, Eric. I just didn't think about that earlier when we were loading all this," James said.

"Ah, never mind that," said Scott. "Let's just get this stuff over to our camping spot and get camp set up." At that, each person put on his backpack and carried whatever he could with no problem.

"Listen, guys," said James, "we'll walk as far as these two mountains here ahead of us and see how good of a spot we can find. I would like something that'll work for all of us. So I want feedback from each one of you, okay?"

"You got it," answered Eric.

"Sounds good to me too," replied Scott. "Let's start looking."

The three friends started walking toward the closest mountain, which was straight ahead and off to the left. Of course, as dark as it was, each of them carried a flashlight to guide himself.

James would search ahead of the group by shining his light straight ahead and slightly toward either side. Scott was right behind him, searching to the left of the group. Eric followed Scott, looking to the right side. Whoever found a nice spot would notify the other two. James, Eric, and Scott were searching in this divided manner to cover more area.

The three young men continued walking straight ahead from where they parked. They were now making their way around the right side of the first mountain to which they came. Then, Scott found a possible spot.

"Hey, guys," said Scott, "how about this?" The spot that Scott had found was located about three-fifths of the way around the first mountain. It was a patch of land that had little or no grass. Within it, there was also a big log on which they could possibly sit. The spot was about one-third of the way up the side of the mountain, and it was about two hundred feet away from them at the moment.

"Whatcha got there, Scott?" asked Eric, turning his attention to the spot at which Scott was shining his light. James too turned to see it.

"That's not too bad, Scott," James told him. "I like how that big log is lying down, so we can have a place to sit, but I still want to see what else we can find. I'm talking about like perhaps something higher up and not too far from a river or creek. Maybe we'll come back to this if we don't find anything else."

"All right, James," said Scott.

Then, turning his attention to Eric, James asked, "What about you, Eric? See anything yet?"

"Oh, I don't know… I mean, not really," answered Eric. He was rather afraid to suggest anything, for he had doubts as to what James and Scott would like. Eric had seen a few possible great prospects but was afraid to show James and Scott.

"If you see something that you think looks good for us, just tell me," James said to Eric. "Are you quite sure that you've seen no possibilities whatsoever?"

"Oh no, honest, I haven't seen a trace of a possibility," Eric responded.

"All right," James said rather doubtfully. "Let's keep moving."

Soon afterward, James, Scott, and Eric walked on past the first mountain where Scott had found a possible spot. Before too long, they approached another mountain, just a few degrees to their right. The three friends began an upward climb, to try to walk over and past that mountain.

After making their way around the peak, James, being out in front, was the first to see a possibility. It was about thirty feet from them off to their right. "Look at this, guys!" said James.

The area James had just stumbled upon was a wide-open space with little or no grass. One spot had a couple of big boulders to either climb or rest against. Another spot had a fallen tree to make a good place to sit.

"This ain't too bad," replied Eric. "We have plenty of room for ourselves, and those big rocks and that fallen tree keep us from having to sit on the ground."

"I guess I'd have to agree with both of you," said Scott, who could not see any reason to object.

Curiously, James used his flashlight to check out the surrounding area. He went about twenty feet past the fallen tree and boulders, and then he heard the faint sound of rushing water. James searched with his light and found a stream at the bottom of the mountain.

Then, James went back to Eric and Scott, who had remained at the campsite, and said, "Hey, Eric! Hey, Scott! On the other side, way down at the bottom, is a stream where we can get water and wash our dishes."

"That sounds great," Scott said. "Let's just get camp set up right here." At that, they all set down their backpacks and the few supplies they had already brought against the two boulders.

James said, "Well, guys, I guess I'll start setting up our tent. Why don't the two of you get the few remaining items out of the back of my truck? Here's my keys." He handed his keys to Eric.

The time was now 12:15 a.m. James was starting the task of erecting the tent. Eric and Scott were headed back past a couple of mountains in order to get the rest of their camping equipment from James's truck.

In order for James to start his chore, he lit up two of the propane lanterns that they had brought along, in order to give himself whatever light he could. Next, he spread out the tent in the spot in which he would put it. Then, of course, he would put the stakes and poles in their proper places so that the tent could be erected and secured.

Meanwhile, Eric and Scott were getting near James's truck. "Say, uh, Scott," said Eric, "are we going the right way?"

"Of course we are," answered Scott. "All we had to do was go back over the second mountain and back around that first one."

Soon afterward, Eric spotted the parking area with James's truck, which was only about forty feet ahead. "So, we were going the right way after all," Eric said to Scott.

"Of course we were, Eric," Scott told him. "Let's just get what we need out of here, so we can go back and meet up with James."

Eric used the set of keys to open the back of James's truck. All that remained was a cooler, a propane stove, and some extra propane. Scott grabbed the cooler, and Eric gathered the stove and a couple of propane containers. Eric closed the back door. Finally, the two men started walking back toward the campsite, where James was. Soon, as Eric and Scott were heading back to camp, James was pounding in the last stake for the tent. Upon noticing his two friends, James replied, "Hi, fellas, I see you made it back."

"We sure have," said Scott.

"So, is the tent all set up?" asked Eric.

"You betcha," answered James.

"Good," said Scott. "Now we can finally rest after a long, rough day."

"I wonder what time it is," said Eric, who went on to look at his watch with his flashlight. "Whoa! It's 12:45!" he exclaimed.

"Is that right?" asked James.

"Yes, it is," said Eric. "I think maybe it's time for us to call it a night, don't you think so, Scott? What about you, James?"

"I think so," agreed Scott.

"I guess so too," James said. "I mean, after all, it is so very, very late, and I've had all I can take of this long, hard day."

"That goes for me too," replied Scott.

"Well," said Eric, "at least it's on a Friday, because we'll be sleeping late; it will be Saturday morning. Actually, wait a minute; it's already Saturday morning. I told us the time just a minute ago, didn't I?"

"You sure did," answered James. "We've already gone from today to tomorrow, or however you want to look at it."

"No matter how you two want to look at it," said Scott, "I'm ready to go on in and hit the sack." Upon saying that, Scott got his sleeping bag and took it with him into the tent. "Good night, everyone," he said finally.

"I'm with you, Scott," Eric told him. Eric too, went on in with his sleeping bag. But then, he paused, looked back, and said, "Say, uh, James, you coming too?"

"Yeah," James said. "I'll be right there in just a few minutes."

"All right," said Eric, whose eyelids were getting heavier, as he grew sleepier. "Well, good night, James," he said as the last thing for the night.

"Good night, Eric," James responded.

Now that Eric and Scott had gone off to bed, James decided to spend a little time alone. It was the first real chance he had had after the whole busy day on Friday. He now had a full day's work behind him, followed by the rush to meet Eric and Scott. Following that was all the time he'd spent with his two friends—the whole evening really to early morning. But now, he had some real peace and quiet after all that.

James began looking all around in every different direction, but mainly away from where he had parked. He could not help wondering how far he would go hiking and exploring with Eric and Scott. They could not possibly see it all. This made James start to wonder if he should explore just a tiny bit with this peaceful time alone. After all, it had been a long, hard day in which he had gone through the trouble to get his two friends and all the supplies to the mountains. Should he not perhaps reward himself for that? Besides, the three of them could not cover the entire Allegheny Mountain Range. What would it really hurt for James to take a quick, short hike to free his mind for a few moments?

So then, James said, "I think I'll take just a few minutes to do a little exploring, just to get myself some sort of preview of my day tomorrow with Scott and Eric. Wait, what did I just say? It's already tomorrow, isn't it? Well, whatever the case may be, just a short one won't hurt."

At that, he started walking down the mountain on which he was already standing. He just wanted to check out what was on the other side of the two mountains ahead of him. He went around the first mountain and kept going until he was halfway up the other side of the second one, which was behind the first one and almost completely left of it.

When James reached that point, he stopped and took a moment to have a thorough look around at the big, wide area that lay ahead of him. Of course, he could see any number of mountains in whatever direction he would flash his light. But the nearest, most obvious thing James could see was an open valley. It was in the foreground among everything and stretched as far as he could see. James only needed to go the rest of the way down the mountain to get to it.

This valley that James found on his short, little hike was a big, wide open field covered mostly with grass, but no trees. James used his flashlight to examine this valley, perhaps in order to look for any interesting features. Coming from the end opposite from James toward his left was a stream of water, which flowed in serpentine over the far left part of the valley but made close to a U-turn when approaching the halfway point along the left end.

James spotted another interesting feature off to the right of his field of vision. It was a cave in the side of a mountain, and it was not very far above the valley. James now said to himself, "I wonder what's in that cave. Could I possibly discover anything in there? Maybe I ought to check it out real quick and then go on back to camp. James took a few steps toward the cave but stopped himself because he was having second thoughts. "Actually, maybe not," he said reluctantly, "it's after midnight right now, and for all I know, it could possibly be dangerous. I'll go check it out tomorrow with Eric and Scott… Why do I keep saying that? It is tomorrow!"

James then decided to go on back to camp and get some sleep. But before he started back, he took one last look around. As he did, he started to think once again about Amanda, the lovely loan officer who had caught his eye much earlier that day. That was because with the peace, quiet, beauty, and wide-open space of the Allegheny Mountains, he wondered if he would ever possibly get a chance to bring her up there with him. He then went on to say, "I sure wouldn't mind if Amanda was here with me right now. I mean, I don't know of a better person to accompany me in these peaceful mountains, with their complete, beautiful nature. I'd really like to show her the interesting features of this valley and possibly that comet, falling star, or whatever that is up there." At that, he began to head back toward camp.

After taking a few steps and thinking to himself, James stopped and said, "Wait a minute, what did I just say? Comet! Falling star! Huh?" That very instant, he turned around to take another look at the object he had seen in the sky. It was a nearly round, moving object that appeared to be a glowing, radiant, neon yellow. James continued to watch the meteoroid. As he did, it gradually appeared bigger and nearer. This made James wonder if, by any chance, it was headed his way. After a few more minutes passed by, he began to hear a faint sound like a jet or rocket coming from the meteoroid. Then, within another few minutes, the noise grew louder as the meteoroid apparently got nearer. James asked himself, "Is that sound coming from that meteor, comet, or whatever? I don't see an airplane or a rocket."

Then, a few minutes later, the meteoroid was even closer and louder, so much so that it almost sounded to James like it was flying just above him. More concerned than before, James wondered, It's not coming my way, is it? But then, he thought, No way. That's impossible… well, not totally impossible, but not likely either… I wouldn't think… of course not.

However, within the next two minutes, the glowing, neon-yellow meteoroid was dangerously close and roaring so loudly that James could not hear anything else, including himself. It was headed his way after all.

In fear, he started running back over the mountain and continued down the other side toward his campsite, where Eric and Scott were still asleep.

Shortly, a very loud sound, like a tremendous explosion, shook their campsite. It was the sound of the meteorite that had finally landed in the valley over which James had been looking. Now that the meteorite had finally landed, James wanted to go back over the mountain and look one more time to see the effects of the impact.

When James got to where he could see the big valley again, he stopped momentarily to take a look around. In the midst of everything was a huge, radiant, glowing meteorite. It was about twelve feet in diameter. It was located off the center of the valley, to the right of James's field of vision, about twenty-five feet away from the cave that James was seeing at the far right. The impact of the meteorite's landing had engraved a crater in the earth, which was about four feet deep at its deepest point. The meteorite seemed to be made of a material from an unknown, maybe undiscovered planet. Surrounding it were much smaller glowing pieces that had broken off and scattered when it landed. A couple of little pieces were even located a few feet from the cave.

James decided to go get a better look at the fallen meteorite and some of the scattered fragments. He did not know how long the radiant glow would last or if it would still be glowing in the morning. So he wanted to check it out while he could. James began running down the mountain to get to the valley where the meteorite was. However, he slowed down and restrained himself as he got close because he did not know how hot it was. He forced himself to be cautious.

Next, James began slowly walking in a circle around the meteorite, checking out its structure and details, as well as whatever pieces he came across, which varied somewhat in shape and size. Every fragment was glowing in a bright, neon yellow, just like the remainder of the grounded meteorite. He then said, "I wonder what sort of stones these are. Moreover, I wonder what this can possibly mean for me. I've never seen rocks that glow bright yellow like this. Could this be a new discovery that I just made?"

James continued in a clockwise direction around the meteorite. When he got to the point at which the cave was to his left, he took a quick glance to his left and barely noticed a faint, green flash of light in the cave. Still focused on the scattered neon-yellow pieces, James mumbled, "What do you know? I thought I saw some green light coming from the cave. Oh well, what's the meaning of this neon-green light coming from the cave?"

He suddenly stopped and asked himself, "What? What did I just say? A neon-green light coming from… huh?" He then turned toward the cave to get a better look at it. "Wow!" said James. "I don't believe this. This just gets better and better. It's already been an amazing trip for me with this glowing yellow meteorite, but now, what on earth is doing that?" He stopped what he was doing and started walking slowly toward the cave. James was moving carefully in case the source of radiation was dangerous.

When James finally made it over to the cave, he used his flashlight to examine all the surroundings in front and to the sides before he dared to take a single step inside. He found nothing dangerous in the space into which he was getting ready to step, but the radiant, neon-green glow he had spotted a few minutes before was no doubt brighter and more obvious. It was coming from about eighteen feet ahead of where James was standing, from behind a piece of sedimentary rock that was about sixteen inches high. Still moving slowly and carefully, James advanced toward the source of the bright-green light. When he made it to the rock from behind which it was coming, he stopped himself. Then, he slowly bent forward to peer over the rock, trying to be cautious, because there was no telling what could happen. Once he caught a glimpse of the source, he suddenly and quickly stepped backward, turning his head aside and putting up his hands in front of himself. "Oh my!" cried James. "That was so doggone bright! I was in no way prepared for that. It seemed to be a very, very bright green piece of crystal, quartz, or something. Maybe I'll take a moment to recover and then try to approach it more carefully. I don't want to get blinded."

Then, a couple of minutes later, when his vision had recovered, James tried a different approach. This time, he walked around the left side of the rock that was in front of the material. Still stepping slowly and carefully, he kept his hands ready to block some of the glare. Once he got to where he could look down at it, he put his hands between his face and the mineral, but it was nearly impossible to keep looking straight at it; every time James caught a peek of the neon-green, radiating mineral, he immediately put his hand back in place to protect his eyes.

Although James had trouble looking at this incredible, glowing mineral, he took a minute to check out the ground surrounding it, since the bright, neon-green light practically lit up the whole inside of the cave. James noticed several pieces of clear, coarse crystalline quartz of somewhat various shapes and sizes. He then said to himself, "Was this really supposed to be a quartz crystal just like these other ones? I mean, none of those other crystals are bright, radiating green like that. Say, I wonder if that unusual meteorite has anything to do with this. After all, these are two things I've stumbled upon that I've never seen before."

Immediately following that, James went back out of the cave to look again at how the smaller meteorite pieces were scattered. When he got there, he noticed that the circle of fragments thinned out, with the pieces getting smaller, as it advanced farther from the big boulder that was in the very center. One small piece was about a foot and a half from the entrance to the cave. A few pieces were a couple of feet farther from the circle's center than from the entrance to the cave. The few that had shot out the farthest were each no more than an inch in diameter. All the other pieces of crystalline quartz inside the cave were clear in color unlike the neon green one with the blinding glare. Perhaps a speck of the neon-yellow meteorite had actually flown off and hit a piece of crystalline quartz, with which it chemically reacted to make it neon green.

Next, James went back to the glowing, neon-green piece of quartz. Of course, as he approached it, he shielded his face so that he would not look directly into it and be blinded. He knelt down next to it. But he was afraid to touch it, because for all he knew, something that bright could be way too hot to touch. So then, James took off his flannel shirt. He used it to protect his hands while picking up the radiating piece of quartz. After gathering it up with his shirt, he started walking back toward camp, where Eric and Scott were still asleep.

As James was walking back over and around the two mountains that he had gone over to get to the valley, he said to himself, "Oh man, I'll never forget this. I feel like I've seen everything now. Tomorrow, I need to show that meteorite to Eric and Scott. What did I say? It is tomorrow. I got a real problem with that, don't I? Well, anyway, I think I'll keep this crystal to myself for the time being, because it's the only one I got and I don't want to stir up too much commotion. However, I sure can't wait until we all go check out that most awesome, spectacular meteorite. After all, there are plenty of pieces to share. So that's what we'll all go do when we get up. But right now, I don't want to wake them. Besides, I'm ready to hit the sack myself."

Shortly thereafter, James finally made it back to his campsite, where Eric and Scott were sound asleep. Before entering the tent, James took the glowing quartz crystal he had found, which was buried and hidden in his shirt, and placed it in a compartment halfway down the right side of his backpack. Then, he said softly to himself, "I might try to examine this crystal on my own time, the next chance I get, and I'm not going to say anything about it just yet. I just can't help wondering if this could mean anything wonderful or special for me. Well, anyway, right now, I only feel like sleeping." At that, he quietly entered the tent, removed his hiking boots, and lay down in his sleeping bag.

The time was now approaching 1:30 a.m. What a night it had been for James Clifton! After all, the way it had ended up was most unexpected. Who would have thought that what started out as an ordinary camping trip would become this remarkable. James had witnessed a meteorite and discovered something that no one had ever seen before. What a remarkable camping trip!

Now that James was in his sleeping bag, he was no doubt getting sleepier, on account of the long, action-packed day behind him. Even as he was gradually falling asleep, he continued to think about the radiating quartz crystal that he had found. Mumbling and whispering, so as not to wake Eric and Scott, James was saying, "Oh, man, man, man, that was the brightest, most radiant, most colorful, most awesome mineral I have ever seen. What on earth could it possibly get me or do for me?" Then, once his eyelids were too heavy for him to stay awake any longer, he said one last thing as he was falling asleep. It was, "Wouldn't it be something if it could keep Amanda united with me for always?" At that, James was fast asleep.

Immediately following that, James began to dream. At the very beginning of his dream, he was at home in his bedroom, holding and looking at the glowing, neon-green quartz crystal that he had found. He then took a few more moments to examine it carefully and thoroughly. After that, James said, "I think I've looked at it long enough. I'm going to go out and maybe catch some action, and I hope I'll meet up with Amanda. Of course, I better not tell anyone about my new discovery. This crystal could be extremely valuable to me, for all I know. But otherwise, I wonder if it could possibly keep Amanda and me together. Well, just in case, I'll wrap it real good in a handkerchief and put it deep down into my left pocket to conceal it as much as possible." James wrapped a handkerchief around it and put the crystal into his left front pocket. Next, he put an extra handkerchief on top and then his wallet.

James left his house and went walking into downtown Philadelphia. He passed many restaurants and clubs, wondering which one to go to and if he could even find Amanda at one of them.

Finally, James came to Sixty-Third Street, where by the pay phone stood none other than Amanda. James walked up and said, "Hi, Amanda!"

She took a moment to look around in wonder, until she saw the familiar face of James Clifton. Then, looking away and rolling her eyes, she said doubtfully, "Oh, hey, um…"

"James," he reminded her. "James Clifton."

"Well, of course," Amanda replied. "So what are you doing here?"

"Well, um," said James, "I've been thinking about you since I met you, and I wanted to show you something."

"Oh, really!" said Amanda, shaking her head in disbelief. "And just what would you like to show me?"

Keeping his voice down, James said, "It's a real special mineral, a rather unique piece of coarse crystalline quartz. Just come between those two buildings there for a moment. If you don't like it, I'll never bother you again."

"All right," said Amanda reluctantly, "if I take one quick look at it, will you leave me alone?"

"Sure," agreed James.

"My goodness, why am I doing this?" Amanda whispered to herself as she went with James into the alley between the two nearest buildings.

As soon as they got there, James reached into his left pocket and took out the handkerchief-wrapped, glowing piece of quartz. "Here it goes," he said. "I'm fixing to open it up."

When he did, they both looked upon the crystal. After a few seconds, James looked up and saw that Amanda was staring at it while standing completely still.

Hesitating, James said, "So uh, Amanda? What do you think?" However, she said nothing and held the same position. This was because she was in a trance. "Can you hear me?" James asked, rather worried. Still, he received no answer.

So then, he immediately rewrapped his glowing quartz crystal and placed it back in his left pocket. Amanda, however, was still motionless in the same position. He was really worried now. "Oh no!" he cried. "What have I done? I know I've been wanting to win her over, and I know I was trying to impress her, but I didn't mean to put her in a state of paralysis like this. I should've known better since I had a tough time trying to look at the glare of that crystal myself. Oh, Amanda, say something, anything, please!" James tried shaking her from side to side a little bit, but it did not help. "Oh, this is all my fault," lamented James.

That very instant, he put up his left hand and repeatedly snapped his fingers in front of Amanda's face. While doing so, he slumped his head forward in guilt and frustration. All of a sudden, someone grabbed his left wrist to stop him. James looked up and saw that it was Amanda, who was now free of her trance. "Oh, Amanda," said James, "Are you okay? Thank goodness you're out of your trance. Listen, I can explain this, okay?"

Still holding his left wrist, she said, "Oh, James, there is nothing to explain."

"There isn't?" asked a surprised James Clifton. "I just thought maybe—"

"Oh, forget it," she said happily. She put her left hand on James's right cheek. "It doesn't matter. What matters is that I'm attracted to you, you handsome hunk." She placed her right hand on the left side of his neck and said sweetly, "If it isn't James Paul Clifton. Oh, that name is irresistible."

"Well, thank you so much," said James, now calmed down, but pleasantly surprised.

Then, Amanda said, "So, James, how would you like us to go to a much nicer place than this alley?"

James exclaimed, "Would I ever! I thought you'd never ask!"

"Well then," said Amanda, "just close your eyes for a minute, and I'll take us there at once."

"Close my eyes?" asked James, in wonder about how it would work.

"Just do it," replied Amanda. "You'll see."

"Okay," said James, who then shut both of his eyes in order to please Amanda. Suddenly, Amanda's right hand dug into his left pocket.

Confused, James began to lift his hands from beside himself and started asking, "But what are you——"

"James, please," interrupted Amanda, as she used her hands to restrain his hands. "Put your hands down. Just trust me, okay?"

"Oh, all right," replied James, who then returned to his relaxed standing position.

Amanda removed the handkerchief-wrapped quartz crystal from James's left pocket. She unwrapped it, and using her left hand to hold James's right, she positioned the neon-green crystal in her right hand. She took a firm grip on it, which she held momentarily. During that moment, the glowing radiation of the quartz crystal gradually charged up, until all of a sudden, an enormous flash of neon-green light went off and expanded into the space all around them. That very instant, James and Amanda were teleported to their destination. Amanda said softly, "Okay, James, you can open your eyes now."

When he did, he could not help but notice that he was back in the same valley where he had seen the meteorite strike. It was the valley he had explored when he had gone to that same mountain range with Eric and Scott. James momentarily took a look around. While he was doing that, he noticed the same glowing yellow meteorite on the opposite end from where he was now standing with Amanda. They were close to the serpentine stream. James then said, "Oh man, this is amazing. Thanks so much, Amanda. I've actually been wanting to bring you here."

"Well," said Amanda, "just don't ever underestimate me again. I know you much better than you think I do."

For a few seconds, James was a bit puzzled by this. However, he just stared and smiled back at Amanda, who was already doing the same thing to him. He realized that the green quartz crystal had to have caused her to know all about him.

Next, she gestured for James to follow her, saying, "Come this way, James." She then turned around and walked along the stream with James following behind. They had walked about twenty feet when Amanda stopped, turned ninety degrees to her right, and looked sideways at James, who had also halted. She then put out her left hand to her left side to show what she was leading him to. It was a luxurious table with two ornate chairs. On the table, there were a bottle of champagne and two wineglasses.

"Oh, Amanda," James said, pleasantly surprised, "I got to admit, you've thought of everything."

After that, Amanda took hold of his left hand with her right and walked him toward the table, saying, "Let's go sit down, James." Next, when they got to it, she positioned herself by the chair that had been farthest from them and gracefully guided James to the other one. Then, they both sat down. Of course, James and Amanda were looking into each other's eyes with interest.

"Amanda," James said, "I'm so amazed that I don't know what to say. Furthermore, I don't know how I can thank you enough for all this trouble you went through for me."

"You can thank me later," Amanda replied with a nice, friendly smile. "Right now, let's pour the champagne."

"Well then," said James, "I'd be real happy to do that for us." That very minute, he grabbed the champagne bottle with his left hand, and with his right, he got his pocketknife out and set up the corkscrew feature. He screwed it into the cork and pulled on it while securing the bottle with his left hand and thighs. Ten seconds later, James finally pried the cork all the way, so that it completely popped out of the mouth of the bottle. He set down his pocketknife beside himself on the ground, after which he held up the champagne bottle with his right hand and said, "To us." Immediately, he then poured some bubbly, sparkling champagne into the wineglass that was in front of Amanda and afterward, into the glass that was in front of him. He placed the bottle back on the middle of the table.

After all that, James picked his glass up a bit and said, "Look, Amanda, I don't fully understand how or why you did all this for me, but I am so, so grateful that you did. I just never realized that you cared so much. Other than that, I just want to tell you that I've never met anyone like you. What I see in you is definitely something I've never seen in anyone ever before. So I would like to propose this toast to you." He raised up his glass even higher.

"Oh, James!" Amanda sighed sweetly "That is so sweet and thoughtful of you." Afterward, she started lifting her glass toward James's. Consequently, Amanda said, "Cheers." She gently tapped his glass with her own.

After that, they each took a small sip of champagne and set the glasses down on the table. James and Amanda were pleasantly staring at each other. After a moment of that, James took a few seconds to look around at all the surroundings. But suddenly, Amanda said softly, "Oh, James."

Then of course, James focused his attention back on her. Amanda had placed her left hand halfway across the table, signaling James to take hold of it. He gracefully moved his right hand toward her until they joined hands.

"James," called Amanda.

"Uh, yes, Amanda?"

"Come closer," she told him sweetly, also signaling him with her right index finger. Evidently, she was going for a kiss. Was James up for that? Why, of course! He had been attracted to her since she caught his eye after work that day. Furthermore, she had practically been on his mind constantly. So, with no doubt at all, James was all for it. Therefore, he did not hesitate but went straight for the kiss.

However, when their lips came to within less than four inches apart, Amanda apparently suddenly noticed something in the distance off to her right. Consequently, she said, "Hold it, James. What's that?" as she started pointing past James to the right of her field of vision. James turned around to see what she was pointing at but found nothing unusual. He tried to turn back around to refocus on Amanda. But, by the time he could, she was holding her glass of champagne in her right hand. In the instant that James's attention refocused on Amanda, she threw the champagne from her glass into his face. Unfortunately for him, his dream ended immediately.

As quick as a flash, the entire scene of James's dream was completely gone, and he now lay awake in his tent. The first thing he saw when he looked up was his friend, Scott, who had woken him and was looking down at him. James said, "What happened?"

Scott answered, "Oh, nothing at all, James. I just had to come and get you up."

"Oh, you did, huh?" said James. But then, he had regained his senses and noticed that he was wet. It was not really because Amanda had splashed champagne on him. Instead, it was because Scott had poured water on him from a canteen. So then, he asked, "How did I get all wet?"

"I just threw a little water on you," replied Scott.

Starting to get angry, James said in a firm tone, "Oh, is that right? Well, what did you do that for?"

"Well," answered Scott, "it was getting a little late, and we have a long day ahead of us. Besides, nothing else I tried worked."

Regardless of that, James had just had a most wonderful experience with Amanda, even if only in a dream. He had not really wanted it to end. Therefore, he was really upset that it had suddenly ended the way it had. So next, out of anger, James quickly got back onto his feet, used both hands to grab hold of Scott's shirt, and scolded him. "Let me tell you something, Scott!" yelled James. "I don't care what your problem is! Don't you ever wake me up like that again, you understand me?" At that, he went on to shove him.

However, before he could get any angrier, his good friend Eric, who had heard him yelling, came inside quickly to try to stop the quarrel. Stepping between James and Scott, Eric extended his arms from his sides, signaling both of them to yield. "Hey, hey, guys, hold it, hold it," he said to both of them. "What is the problem here?"

James immediately cooled off and said calmly, "Look, Eric, all that happened was I was having a really wonderful dream, and Scott ended it so abruptly by what he did to wake me up. On top of that, I hate having water thrown on me."

Scott went on to say, "All right, all right, now look, you guys… just listen. I really, really should've stopped and thought about it. Of course, a part of me always wanted to try that but was always afraid to. So I finally did it just now, mainly because no one else was watching, and I didn't think it would bring embarrassment. Also, I didn't know if I should touch you to wake you. But on the other hand, maybe you were right, James. I don't think I would've liked it either. So anyhow, sorry about the water."

Now, James was completely calm again. After all, he did not want to lose a friend that he had known and trusted for a long time over something as silly as a little prank. Besides, his dream had not even been real. James went on to say, "Well, I guess I overreacted. I'm sorry, Scott. Just please don't splash water on me anymore while I'm sleeping, okay?"

"Okay, no problem," replied Scott.

"That's much better," said Eric. "So anyway, James, I've already prepared some breakfast for all of us. Would you care for some? I made some pancakes and sausage."

"Sure," answered James. "I most certainly would. Thank you very much, Eric."

After throwing on his boots, James left the tent. He then proceeded to put three pancakes as well as four patties of pork sausage onto a plate that he had brought along. He also poured himself some orange juice from a jar. James then went on to eat up until he had had enough. It was 10:32 a.m. on Saturday morning. After James had finished eating, he used some water from his canteen to rinse the cup and plate, and then he put them away.

Next, James called his two friends together to tell them something. "So anyway, Eric, Scott," he began, "I don't quite know how to begin this, but I am grateful for what you two did for me ever since we left Eric's house yesterday evening. First of all, Scott, I thank you for buying me a burger at the truck stop last night. Also, I thank you, Eric, for making me breakfast this morning. So anyway, I don't want y'all to think I'm not grateful or appreciative, okay?"

"Why, certainly James," responded Eric.

"Oh, of course, no problem whatsoever, buddy," said Scott.

"All right, all right, so anyhow," James continued, "I got something I think I ought to let y'all know. You see, right after you two went to bed late last night… or early, early this morning, I, uh, kind of wandered off just a little bit out of curiosity."

"Oh, you did?" said Eric.

"Well, okay, all right, so what ended up happening?" asked Scott.

"Well, Scott," James replied, now more eager than before, "I'm glad you asked me that, because that's the point I was trying to get to. You see, I went to the other side of that mountain back there. There was a big valley. A meteorite struck the ground somewhere in the middle of it. But y'all see, it was no ordinary meteorite. It was bright yellow. I mean a glowing bright yellow."

"Oh, come on, no way," Eric said, finding James's story hard to believe. "Are you kidding me?"

"Yeah, man," agreed Scott, "you sure about that?"

"Absolutely, positively sure," answered James. "If you don't believe me, just come see; I'll show you."

"Well, all right then," Scott said anxiously. "I mean, I've never seen a meteorite before, especially not one that can glow bright yellow. So, if what you're saying is true, I gotta see it. Let's go, James. Let's have a look at this thing. You coming too, Eric?"

"Okay, all right," said Eric, "I guess you can count me in too."

"Well, anyway," said James, "just let me go put my shirt back on, and we'll start on our way."

James went over to his backpack, where he had hidden the quartz crystal before going to bed. First, he made sure Eric and Scott weren't looking, and then he quickly and quietly got a handkerchief that he had brought along, transferred the crystal from his flannel shirt, and wrapped it with the handkerchief. At the same time, he momentarily looked away, so he would not be blinded by the glare. Right after that, he checked one more time to make sure his two friends could not see what he was doing. Then, he secretly put the handkerchief-wrapped crystal into his left pocket. After that, James went back over to Eric and Scott, putting his shirt on as he walked. "Okay, guys," James said as he rejoined them. "Are you ready to start?"

"Sure, James, I'm ready," responded Eric.

"Why, of course we are," agreed Scott. "What are we standing around for? Let's go."

"Just follow me," James told them. At that, they all started down the mountain. They just kept going until they finally got past the two mountains that were in their way. That put the three friends in the valley where James had witnessed the meteorite striking.

While they were still a good distance from the fallen meteoroid, James stopped to take a look at it. It was still the same shape and size as the glowing meteorite that he had seen after midnight but did not appear to have the same neon-yellow radiant glow as when James had first witnessed it. So then, he put his hand level to his forehead above his eyes to get a better look. However, he could still only see a big boulder made of some sedimentary rock.

"Hey, James, what's up?" asked Eric, who wondered what James was looking at in the distance.

"Well," James replied reluctantly, "I'm afraid to say that the big rock way ahead up there happens to be the meteorite that I wanted you guys to see."

At that, Scott asked, "You mean the one that you said had a bright-yellow glow to it?"

"I'm afraid so," answered James.

"Are you sure about this?" asked Eric.

"Well," answered James, "maybe it's just harder to see in daylight. Let's go take a closer look." They all walked over to it.

But somehow, even when James, Eric, and Scott made it over to the big boulder that James claimed was the meteorite, they still did not see any sign of radiation being emitted from it. In fact, that big boulder as well as the surrounding scattered fragments on the ground all appeared to be just dark-gray limestone with occasional bits of iron.

"Look, James," said Scott, "I don't mean to argue or to sound ungrateful, but I just want to let you know that this just looks like an ordinary big rock to me. I just can't quite see what it is that you were talking about."

"Well, I understand, Scott," said James, "but I'm quite sure that I wasn't imagining it. At this moment, I can't see any sign of the glow either."

"Listen, James," Eric addressed him, rather politely, "I really thank you for bringing us here to show us this. I know you're not lying to us. Now, you see, James, I really don't intend to doubt you, especially since I've known and trusted you for a long time, but wouldn't you say it was a long day yesterday?"

"Well, no doubt it certainly was," answered James.

"Well, anyway," continued Eric, "I'm not pointing out any fault of yours, or even blaming you the least. I even realize that you probably couldn't wait to see more of the mountains; it's understandable. But the only point I'm trying to get at is that you were perhaps real tired and sleepy and hallucinations could've occurred."

"Well, perhaps," sighed James. "But it's just that at the time, I perceived a whole lot for something I wasn't trying to imagine. But, anyway, I suppose that what you just tried to tell me is not impossible. I mean, I guess it is a possibility after all. Other than that, I'm sorry if this wasn't as exciting as you two hoped."

"It's all right, don't worry," Eric told him. "I'm still really grateful to you, James. That's for all the time and effort you went through to bring us out here on this trip and to try to show us this. I know you meant well."

"Believe me, James," added Scott. "That goes for me too. However, I was just wondering, was there anything else you wanted to show us by any chance?"

"Well, I'm glad you asked me that," replied James, "because actually, there was and still is."

"Oh, really! Well, what is it?" Scott asked.

"Well anyway, the other thing I might've found last night, or this morning, is in that nearby cave," James said, pointing to the cave. "You see, inside that cave, I think I may have possibly discovered some pieces of coarse crystalline quartz."

"Oh, you did?" asked Scott. "I got to see this. Thanks for telling me, James."

"Sure, no problem," said James. "You see, I wouldn't try to keep anything from y'all."

"Well, thank you, James," Eric replied.

"Well then," said Scott, "what are we waiting for? Let's go check this out. You guys coming?"

Eric said, "Okay, Scott, I'm coming." At that, Scott and Eric started walking toward the cave.

But then, when they were about ten feet from the cave entrance, Scott stopped, looked back, and noticed that James was still standing by the boulder, facing away from the cave. He called, "Hey, James, you coming too?"

James answered, "Yeah, I am! You two go on ahead. I'll be there in a minute."

Once Eric and Scott had proceeded on into the cave, James put his left hand into his pocket and pulled out the piece of quartz that he had collected. He unwrapped it and noticed that it had a dark-green color to it but completely lacked the blinding neon-green glare that he had perceived when he had first found it.

James said, "Well, isn't that something? This crystal doesn't have a neon glow anymore either. Maybe Eric's right; maybe I was hallucinating. But I never wanted to try to imagine either the meteorite or the radiative piece of quartz. I mean, this all seems really, really odd, and I just can't quite comprehend it. Oh, and for me to think I made a wonderful, awesome discovery that could get me somewhere, and to have that silly dream about it binding me with Amanda—I've never felt so foolish in my life. But now, so much for those stupid, crazy dreams. This must only be a quartz crystal of another color. There's nothing supernatural about it. Well anyway, I guess I'll still keep it. However, I don't need to show it to Eric or Scott. I already got embarrassed and disappointed trying to show them this stupid giant rock here. I don't care to go through all that humiliation again. But anyway, I'll go ahead and keep this green crystal, since it might be kind of nice to have. I'll just have to find some other way to win Amanda. Well, I'm going to go meet up with Eric and Scott in the cave and see what's going on with them." So then, James went on over to the cave.

Meanwhile, Eric and Scott were looking all over the inside of the cave. "Hey, Eric," called Scott.

"Yeah," replied Eric.

"You see anything?" asked Scott.

"No, not yet," said Eric. All they had seen so far were the limestone sidewalls and a few stalactites and stalagmites.

A few moments later, Eric made it as far back as possible into the cave, to the backside of the rock behind which the crystal James had discovered had been hidden. As Eric was moving toward it, he found several scattered pieces of clear, coarse crystalline quartz. At that, he said, "Hey, Scott! Scott! I found something."

"You did?" said Scott. "Whatcha got there?"

Scott then ran over to Eric to see, and Eric pointed at the ground in front of himself, saying, "Those look like quartz crystals."

"You're right," said Scott.

Just then, James entered the cave and said, "Hey, guys, what's up?"

"Oh, it's you, James," said Scott. "You know, you were right. We found them."

"What are you talking about?" asked James.

"James," said Eric, "don't you remember? You told us about the quartz that you saw in here, right?"

"Oh, that," answered James.

Then, rather concerned, Eric asked him, "Are you feeling okay? You don't seem the least bit thrilled about this. Is something wrong?"

"Well," said James, "I just feel terribly sorry that I got you all excited about some cool-looking meteorite that I saw, and then I ended up showing y'all just a plain, ordinary boulder."

"James," Eric said, "I already told you, it's perfectly okay. We don't need to worry about that anymore."

"Yeah, James," added Scott, "just don't even let it bother you anymore. At least we found something, rather than nothing. This will be one camping trip where I get to bring back a souvenir. So anyway, while we're in here, I say we gather some of these crystals."

"Oh, no, you don't," joked Eric while smiling, "I saw them first." At that, he dashed back over to the quartz crystals, where Scott had begun to gather some up.

However, Scott teased Eric, laughing and saying, "It's too late for you. I already got the first shot at them." Then, he finished gathering up four pieces and said to Eric, "If you got a problem with it, come get 'em from me."

But Eric just went on to see what other crystal pieces he could find and picked up three others that were still on the ground.

After that, Scott and Eric went back over to where James was standing near the cave entrance with their quartz crystals. Wonderingly, Scott said to James, "Say, James, aren't you going to gather some too? After all, you're the one who showed us this."

Eric said, "Well, maybe he gathered some when he found this cave after midnight."

"Yeah, that's right," replied James. "I picked up one or two, but maybe I'll get a couple more."

"Okay, that's fine," said Eric.

"Sure, go on," agreed Scott.

James went to the part of the cave where Eric and Scott had just been looking and picked up one more crystal just for the heck of it. James was really not too overjoyed. That was because he was disappointed that the green crystal he had found was perhaps not as supernatural as he had imagined it to be.

However, it was now 11:45 a.m. James went back over to his two pals and said, "Well, guys, are we ready to move on?"

"Well, uh, sure," answered Eric, "I guess we're finished here."

"It's okay with me," said Scott.

"Well in that case," said James, "let's move on."

"Hey, James," said Eric, "do you think maybe we ought to put these pieces of quartz in our backpacks, so we don't have to carry them with us while hiking?"

"Yeah," added Scott.

"Probably not a bad idea," James responded.

After that, the three of them went back to camp. Once there, each young man put the quartz crystals he had found in a special compartment of his own backpack. James, Eric, and Scott each got his canteen to bring along on the hike, in case he got tired or thirsty.

At that, the three young men started on the hike that they planned between breakfast and lunch. They headed back toward the valley from which they had just come and ended up exploring beyond it. Of course, they would stop to look at interesting rock formations when they came across them. They also stopped to observe any animals that a person would not see every day. After about two hours, James, Eric, and Scott went back to camp for lunch.

Once they got done with lunch, it was around 2:30 p.m. This time, instead of hiking and exploring past the valley, the three friends went off to the right of that direction, to see what they could stumble upon by going a different way for a change. This time, they brought some snacks with them, because they would not be going back to camp until suppertime.

While they were all on their long hike between lunch and dinner, the three of them continuously looked in every direction around themselves, with the goal of seeing everything they possibly could in the Alleghany Mountains. Along the way, James, Eric, and Scott would stop at any flowing stream or brook upon which they stumbled, so that each one of them could top off his canteen with water. On top of that, every thirty to forty minutes, James, Eric, or Scott would take out a cookie or cracker to munch on and maybe even have a sip of water. But the whole time they were exploring, they would always stop momentarily to examine any interesting animals, trees, plants, rocks, or rock formations that they would find.

After nearly an hour and a half of their hike, Scott found an oval-shaped piece of limestone. It was light gray and about nine and a half inches long, as well as three and a half inches in diameter. It was practically a perfect oval, except for one dent along the length of it. Scott said, "This is the most perfectly shaped rock I've ever seen. I'm going to keep this one. With this, as well as my quartz crystals, I know I'll never forget this camping trip. I'll exhibit all this stuff in my home."

"Well, Scott," said James, "I guess I'm not the only one who made a discovery. I believe that's limestone. But I actually wonder if it contains a fossil by any chance."

"Oh, I don't know," Scott told him. "At least it's a souvenir. It'll help me remember that I found it."

"Whatever you say, Scott," replied James.

After hiking for another thirty-five minutes, James, Eric, and Scott stopped to rest near the base of a mountain, at the bottom of a fifteen-foot-high cliff. They sat down in that area. James shared some chocolate-chip cookies with Eric and Scott, and Eric shared some cheese-flavored crackers. They all nearly emptied out their canteens. This amounted to a twenty-five-minute break, during which they ate, drank, and rested.

It was now approaching 5:00 p.m. James said to Eric and Scott, "Look, guys, we've been going at it for a couple hours now, and it will be suppertime before we know it. We definitely don't want to stay out too late, not after dark. So I suggest we start working our way back but take a different route this time, so we don't see too much of the same things."

"That's okay with me," said Eric.

"All right with me too," added Scott.

"Sounds good," James said. "Y'all ready? Let's get moving."

"Yeah, let's go," agreed Scott.

At that, the three friends started walking again. Although facing in the direction of their campsite, they went off to their right in order to get back to camp. They wanted to take a different path and pass different mountains. This time, they did not eat as many snacks, since they were determined to get back to camp and have dinner. However, all three of them stopped at a couple of brooks along the way to fill up their canteens. Just like before, they would occasionally stop for a moment to examine anything they found interesting or unusual.

When James, Eric, and Scott finally got back to camp, it was almost 7:00 p.m. and beginning to get dark. At once, James said, "So, Eric, Scott, you guys ready for supper?"

"Oh sure," answered Eric.

"You bet," said Scott.

"I'll make some at once," James said to them.

"Sounds good," Eric replied.

James went on to put together and cook some potato soup. Soon, they all had some soup and crackers.

After supper, the three friends decided to take one more hike before going to bed. This time, they went off in the direction exactly opposite of the way they had gone between lunch and dinner. However, they were not going as far, because it was almost completely dark, and they did not want to stay out unreasonably late. This time, James, Eric, and Scott all brought along flashlights.

Finally, when they returned to camp, it was 9:05 p.m. and very dark. None of them had gathered up any special kind of find this time around. They all had a bedtime snack before going to sleep. James shared some more of his cookies, and they drank fruit punch that Scott had brought along.

Very shortly, James said, "All right, listen up, Scott and Eric. I just want to briefly go over the plan for tomorrow. After breakfast, we'll take one last hike. After that, we're going to have to start heading home. Y'all follow that?"

"If you say so," Eric answered.

"Oh, okay," Scott added.

"Good," said James. "Well, anyway, it's time for bed now. Let's all hit the sack." At that, James, Scott, and Eric all took off their hiking boots, and each one got in his sleeping bag to lie down and get some sleep. This time, every one of them got a good night's sleep.

The next morning, all three of them woke up at a reasonable time. James was the first to awaken, at about 5:45 a.m. That very moment, he rubbed the sleepiness from his eyes, and then he had a couple of sips of water from his canteen. He started preparing breakfast for Eric, Scott, and himself. He fried some bacon and eggs.

While James was in the middle of cooking, Eric came walking out of the tent. He addressed James, "Good morning, James."

"Oh, good morning, Eric," James responded as he turned around and noticed Eric.

"You making us breakfast, huh?" Eric asked.

"Sure am," James answered. "It'll be ready in a couple of moments."

Next, James and Eric started putting bacon and eggs on plates and pouring some of the orange juice that James had brought along. While they were doing that, their friend Scott came on out of the tent. "Hey, you two," he said to them, "what's going on?"

"Oh, nothing much, Scott," James answered. "Just breakfast."

"Oh, well, just hold up there," Scott told James. "I'm coming." He went on to join James and Eric. At that, the three of them enjoyed breakfast together.

But after breakfast, James had an announcement. "Look, you two," he began, "we're going to be heading home this afternoon. However, we're going to take one more hike before leaving. Now that breakfast is over, let's go ahead and take down camp and put everything in my truck."

"Are you sure about this?" Scott asked.

"Well, yeah," James answered, "I figured it would be better to do it now, instead of when we're exhausted from hiking."

"You have a point," agreed Scott.

"Well then," said Eric, "let's do it."

At that, they all started gathering everything together. All three of them got their sleeping bags and rolled them up. Then, James proceeded to take down his tent and roll it up to put it in the bag that contained it. Afterward, James, Eric, and Scott all made two trips to get all their supplies back to James's truck. But they kept their canteens with them, so they could take one more hike.

Next, James, Eric, and Scott got started on one more exploration through the Allegheny Mountains. They went on past the same valley where James thought he had seen a meteorite strike. This time, they crossed the serpentine stream, which was on the opposite end of the valley from the boulder and the cave into which they had all gone the day before. James and his two friends took a three-hour hike. They did not make any interesting discoveries this time around, but they did finally manage to make it to Mount Davis, the highest point in Pennsylvania. As they all passed back through the valley on the way back, James took one last look at the large boulder that he had once thought was an awesome meteorite. Soon, James, Eric, and Scott had all made it back over to James's truck.

Finally, at the end of their last walk, it was nearly 11:00 a.m. James said, "Well, I guess it's about that time."

"I guess you mean to leave," said Eric.

"Well, uh, yeah, that's like, what I was getting at," James said reluctantly.

"Well, uh, okay," Scott said. "I guess if we have to."

"I think we do," James told him. "Because we all have to work tomorrow, and I wouldn't want to get us home too late."

"That's probably a good idea," agreed Eric.

"Well then," said James, "shall we take one last look around before heading out?"

"Oh, you bet," Scott replied.

James, Eric, and Scott took a couple of moments to stand in front of James's truck and look all around at their surroundings. After that, James said, "Well, I guess that's it. Y'all ready to roll?"

"Yeah, I guess so," answered Eric. "But I want to tell you, James, thanks for the camping trip."

"Oh yeah," said Scott. "That goes for me too. I'll never, ever forget it."

"No problem," James told them. "I know I won't forget it either. But anyway, I guess let's hit the road."

At that, they all got into James's truck. He went on to back out of his parking spot and pull out of the visitor's parking lot. He worked his way back over to the interstate, to be on his way back to their hometown, Philadelphia.

James, Eric, and Scott had now gotten what they were going to get out of this camping trip. A couple of things were supposedly not what James had thought they were at first, as the meteorite and the green quartz crystal; both had seemed to have a blinding neon glow to them when he first saw them. They were perhaps not as supernatural as James had imagined. However, no one left empty-handed without a find. James still had a green quartz crystal, as well as a couple of clear ones. Scott had a practically oval piece of limestone, as well as some quartz crystals. Of course, even Eric had the privilege of a few pieces of quartz. This was definitely a truly unforgettable camping trip for James Clifton.

CHAPTER THREE

An Unplanned Transformation

The time was now close to 4:00 p.m. on Sunday afternoon. James Clifton was still driving along the interstate with his two great friends, Eric Thomas and Scott MacNicholl. They were getting close to Philadelphia. Since the three of them did not have lunch before leaving the mountains, they had stopped along the way at the same truck stop at which they had stopped two nights before. Of course, they had spent a lot of time talking about their trip, as well as other fun things that any of them had ever done while taking a trip.

Since James and his two friends were less than forty minutes from home, James went on to say, "Well, anyway, listen, Eric, Scott. I'm sure you two already know that I'm dropping y'all back off at, well, that's your place, Eric. But I'm afraid one other thing is that once I drop y'all off, I've got to go on home. I mean, we've been together all weekend, I've got a lot to unpack, and I got to go to work tomorrow morning."

"Well, okay," Scott said doubtfully.

"Yeah, I guess you're right," said Eric.

"But at least we had a good time this weekend, right?" asked James.

"That's very true," Eric replied. "Thanks so much for the trip."

"Yeah, thanks a lot," Scott said and smiled. "It was most wonderful, awesome, and spectacular."

"Well," said James, "it's good to see you two being grateful and appreciative. But anyway, look, I'll get in touch with y'all tomorrow evening, okay?"

"Okay," answered Eric and Scott.

"But right now, I need to get y'all home," James said.

So all the while they continued their ride home, they just kept on talking with each other. James finally made it back to Philadelphia and then made his way to Eric's house, where all three of them had met earlier to take the trip. At that, James helped Eric and Scott unload the things they had brought along. They brought Eric's supplies just inside his front door and placed them in his living room. As for Scott's belongings, they transferred them into his pickup. Then, checking one last time, James said, "Well, it looks like that's everything. But anyway, I want to thank you two for coming with me to the Allegheny Mountains this weekend. Maybe some other time we'll do something like this again."

"Sounds great," replied Scott.

"Yeah, you bet," said Eric.

Finally, James went on and said, "Well, I guess I'm going to get home right now. But, look, I'll call you both tomorrow, okay? Well, I'll see y'all later." Then of course, he shook hands with them both.

"Take it easy," Eric told him.

"See you later," said Scott.

James immediately got into his Suburban and headed home. He kept going until he finally pulled into his driveway. Upon arriving home, the first thing James did was get his backpack out of the back of his truck. Then, he went inside and temporarily set it down in his living room. After that, he filled up a glass with water and carried it and his backpack upstairs to his bedroom.

Once in his room, James set down his backpack and turned on the light. He moved the backpack and leaned it against the foot of his bed. He took a sip of water and then set the glass of water down on his desk.

James then went back over to his backpack to start unpacking. He said to himself, "Well, I guess I'm gonna unpack and put everything away. Uh, well, I guess first of all, I'll take out this green piece of quartz and put it in a safe place." At that, he went to that compartment of his backpack and took out that special quartz crystal, which was still well wrapped in a handkerchief. He slowly began to unwrap it.

However, when the crystal was completely unwrapped, all of a sudden, a blinding neon-green flash of light caught James by complete surprise. That very instant, he turned his head quickly to his left and closed his right eye tight so he would not be blinded. James was so surprised and afraid that he exclaimed, "Oh no! Oh my! Oh no, no, no! This can't be happening! Please tell me this ain't happening! Oh no!"

Apparently, the colored piece of coarse crystalline quartz was once again glowing with an extremely bright neon-green glare like it had when he first found it. Maybe it was supernatural after all.

James said, "Oh please, I hope I haven't lost my mind so that I'm seeing things like I was in the mountains when I found this thing. Oh man, man, man. I know I'm not trying to imagine this." He used his left hand to try to rub his eyes and regain his senses. After that, he said, "Okay, I hope now I've gotten ahold of myself. I guess I was somehow just hallucinating again. This has not happened all day today or yesterday, not since after midnight last Friday night. I mean, just now, it was possibly the drive home perhaps that made me just a little weary. Why sure, that's got to be all; it's nothing."

So now that James had regained his confidence and felt that he was in his right mind again, he turned his head to look forward again. However, the quartz crystal still seemed to have a bright-neon glare to it, and almost blinded by it, he quickly looked to his left again.

Rather frightened by the situation, James said, "Oh my, oh no, maybe this is really happening. I mean, I know it's been a long, nonstop weekend, and I know I'm just getting back from a four-hour drive, but I'm not at all trying in any way, shape, or form to imagine this, and it's definitely not my intention to perceive it." Then once more, James began to try to take another peek at the quartz crystal, but it still seemed to be radiating. He had to restrain himself from taking a good look at it.

At last, James decided, "Well, I guess maybe I ought to put it away or something, but I really don't know what to do! I guess at least I should reduce the glare so I won't get blinded. I mean, oh brother, I wish someone could tell me what to do. Heaven help me, please!"

Using his left hand to shield his face, James started to walk over to his desk to put the crystal inside a drawer and hopefully seal off the bright light. However, he could not see very well where he was stepping. As a result, James's right foot landed just to the right of the backpack that was leaning against the foot of his bed. While he tried to proceed past that point, his right foot got caught against his backpack, causing him to trip and fall forward. "Whoa! No! Help! Ahh!" he cried as he was tripping and falling. At some point in the midst of all that, the glowing piece of quartz flew out of his hand.

James did not see where the crystal went. It landed inside the glass of water that he had set down on his desk. Upon landing in the water, that glowing neon-green crystal dissolved, and once again, it stopped glowing. The water retained its clear color even though it was no longer pure water. James did not realize any of that.

He was now lying facedown on the floor along the foot of his bed. He took a moment to try to calm down and catch his breath. Afterward, he got back up onto his feet and rubbed his eyes to try once again to get back into his right mind. But now he saw no sign of the green crystal or the blinding glare put off by it. As he was now looking in the direction of his desk, he said to himself, "Oh man, could someone please tell me what on earth just happened to me? I mean, it seems that maybe I was hallucinating again, and I know I just had my quartz crystal in my hand. But now, I don't even see any sign of either the green crystal that I found or the bright light that I guess I imagined was being emitted from it. Well, hmm, maybe it fell behind my desk or something. I'll go look."

So then, Clifton went over to his desk to see if he could find the piece of quartz. He used a flashlight to help himself look down behind his desk. However, he could not see it. He also tried looking under the desk but could not find it there either. He just stood back up, made a fist with his left hand, tightened up, and exhaled in frustration. "Darn it! Man, man, man, man!" he muttered while shaking his head in disbelief. "This is just impossible. It's got to be around here somewhere."

But then, he calmed himself a little and said, "All right, all right, all right, look, I guess I won't get anywhere losing my cool. So just let me cool off a little, and then I'll resume my search for the crystal." James picked up the glass of water that was on his desk and began to drink the remainder of it; he had no idea that the water was impure. James Clifton was completely unaware that the radioactive crystal had dissolved and combined chemically with the water inside the drinking glass. He had no idea of the transformation that he was about to undergo. He went on and drank until his glass was empty.

After that, James calmly and carefully started to examine the area behind, under, and around his desk to try to find the quartz crystal for which he was looking. Since he did not see it at once, he stood back up on his feet and still remaining calm, began to try to figure out if it had possibly bounced or rolled to another place in his room.

However, after standing around and thinking for a couple of moments, James caught a glimpse of bright neon-green light in the lower left and right corners of his field of vision. He reacted by stopping and turning around to see where it was coming from but saw no sign of it upon turning around. "Huh," James said. " I hope there's nothing wrong with me. I thought I saw something, hmm."

Next, James turned back around to face forward again. But shortly after he tried once again to concentrate, the neon-green flash of light began to reappear. This time, instead of looking behind him, Clifton looked down and got to see it better. The source of light appeared to be his hands. James looked up and away momentarily with a shocked expression on his face. "Oh my! Oh no!" he said in panic. "Somebody please tell me this ain't happening!"

After that, James looked at his hands once again and saw they were still flashing a neon-green light. "No!" cried James. "No way! I know I'm not imagining this; maybe it is really happening! I just hope I'm not in any danger, because I'm so scared right now!" He took off his flannel shirt and went to examine himself in the mirror, and to the greatest shock of all, he could see his whole upper body lit up with a blinding neon-green flash of light, even radiating on through his T-shirt. "Oh no!" James exclaimed, more excited and afraid than ever. "What's happening to me?"

But after a moment, James decided to calm himself and try to think things over. "All right, all right," he said, "just let me take a minute to sit down and think, because panicking and getting overexcited isn't gonna get me anywhere, okay? Just try to relax, James. Hopefully, it'll be okay." At that, he sat down on the side of his bed that was closer to his desk. "All right now," he began, "let's think about what's going on here, all right? Let's see now, if I remember correctly, when I first found that piece of quartz, I thought it had a really really bright flash of neon-green light to it. I also thought I saw a meteoroid come down and land, and it had a bright flash of neon-yellow light, right? Well, I thought so. But the next day, when I went to show Eric and Scott, the meteorite only appeared to be a piece of sedimentary rock with no sign of bright colors, but the piece of quartz was still green, but not glowing so brightly or radiantly like when I first found it. But, none of the other pieces of quartz were green. Besides, I thought I just saw a blinding neon-green flash of light again. Maybe it shines that bright every so often and not all the time. But when I saw the boulder in place of the meteorite, it was not yellow or any other bright color." For a moment, James shook his head and rolled his eyes in confusion.

James went on to say, "But then, I wonder if a little piece of the material that the meteorite was made of continued to be sustained by something in the quartz that it combined with, because maybe without combining with quartz or anything, the big meteorite, as well as the other bits and pieces died and lost their color and their ability to radiate. Yeah, maybe that's it."

James got up and began to walk past his mirror, but he noticed that he was still radiating a neon-green light. He said, "Whoa, whoa, whoa, wait a minute! Wait just a darn minute! I forgot about this the whole time I was sitting there thinking to myself. How could I forget? I mean, because now, I'm so brightly lit up like the crystal was. I wonder how that came about. All right, let me sit back down and think." So he did. Upon sitting back down, James held his two hands in front of himself while shifting his gaze continuously on and off them repeatedly.

Starting to think back on what had happened after he'd gotten home, James said to himself, "All right, I had the quartz crystal in my possession up to a certain point since I got here, right? Right! But now, I can't seem to find it, and next thing I know, I'm a blinding glaring neon green just like it. Did it combine with me somehow? I mean, I had it in my hand, and when I tripped and fell, I thought it flew out of my hand. Also, I didn't see where it landed either. I mean, heck, the only thing I ever did besides hold it or go look for it was to drink that glass of water. Wait a minute, what did I just say? That glass of water? I never really thought that was likely, but I guess it's not impossible. By some chance, the crystal must've flown from my hand, landed in the water, and dissolved in it to combine with it."

So now, James had figured it out. Continuing, he said, "Now, if that's the case, drinking the water is how I got the material into my system."

Still a bit worried, James said, "Oh man, I just don't know whether this good or bad. But fortunately, I don't feel sick. Other than that, I don't even feel dazed, or even a little woozy in the stomach. Man, I hope that means I'm all right. But I also don't know if I should try to say or do something about it; I mean, I don't see how any doctor could get this out of my system."

But then, James began to have a more positive view, and his face both figuratively and literally brightened up. He said, "But you know, this must be a really powerful material. I mean, it just had to be to give that piece of quartz such a powerful flash of blinding light. It made it more powerful, that is, whatever that substance is called. Wait a second, what do I mean by that? I think I discovered it. I guess I'll call it pyxorium, but I don't know if I should tell anyone just yet. How can I? I'm not sure I want to raise too big of an issue and get everybody overeager, overexcited, and so forth. But anyway, like I was saying, that crystal was made more powerful. So I wonder if this, uh, pyxorium made me more powerful." James then took a couple moments to think about it.

After that, he continued by saying, "Now, of course, a small part of me is a bit concerned about any possible side effects. But, oh, what the heck, didn't I say earlier that I don't feel sick or hurt or anything like that? I mean, besides, I got no other negative thoughts, heck no. This is amazing that I'm able to do this. Now, see in the mirror there? Just look at me glow! And a really bright neon green? That is totally cool. Also, I wonder what this could do for me. Could it possibly give me any supernatural superhuman powers? If so, I got to admit, that was definitely by a very long shot the greatest mineral water I have ever had. Of course, I guess it's the only serving of that kind that I'll ever have. Also, I don't have any to share with anyone else, which is also a reason that perhaps I should keep to myself about this. But anyway, right now, I might try to experiment just a little to see if there's anything special I can do."

At least now, James Clifton had practically figured out what had happened. The meteorite that had hit in the Allegheny Mountains was made of an undiscovered material from a different planet of a different solar system. He decided to call this material pyxorium. However, the main portion of the meteoroid, as well as most of the scattered bits and pieces, discontinued radiating neon-yellow light because they had all lost their power and died. That made all of that substance lose its bright color only to look much like limestone. But, by some narrow chance, a very small speck of the new material had hit a crystal of coarse crystalline quartz, of which it had become a part by a chemical reaction. That gave the piece of quartz its green color, as well as its ability to radiate blinding neon light. That particular tiny piece of the meteorite never died because the silicon dioxide of which the quartz consisted was sustaining it.

Also, the crystal would light up, but also stop radiating at certain times. James had first found the piece of quartz when the material from outer space was lit up and radiating. But the next day, it did not appear to be lit up because it had stopped at some point overnight. Then, in his room, it had begun radiating again. But James had not realized that, and that was why he had thought before that he was imagining the radiation of the green crystal. However, no one was aware of all this except James Clifton. Neither did anyone else, besides his two best friends, know about the meteorite that he had witnessed. Anyway, James was going to keep it all to himself for the time being.

Then, when the quartz containing this undiscovered material had fallen into the glass of water, the new material, sustained by silicon dioxide, chemically reacted and combined with the water. But the pyxorium stopped radiating at that point, which was why James went on and drank the water; he did not realize that the new material had made the piece of quartz dissolve in it.

Of course, afterward, the pyxorium, which had now become part of the water, went on to combine with his nervous system. That allowed James to radiate neon-green light. The material from space, which made the quartz more powerful, as well as the water, now made James more powerful. It would allow him the ability to do certain things he could never have done before and use his mind to control it all. That was just what Clifton was getting ready to experiment with and find out.

But in the meantime, James was still lit up with blinding neon light. Not too surprisingly, he continued to look at himself in the mirror for a few moments; he was still wondering what someone that bright and radiant could possibly be capable of doing. After a few moments, James looked wonderingly at the palms of his hands, which he was holding out in front of himself and which of course were also radiating neon-green light.

"Well," he said, "I guess first of all, is there anything I can do with my hands? Let me try something here." At that, James created tension in his right hand by tightening the muscles and tendons of it. As he did so, his right hand lit up even more to become even brighter and more intense, as if it were charging up, which it was. "Whoa!" James said in amazement. "I'm actually charging up my hand. Is it at all possible that I could fire laser beams through my fingers?" So then, he pointed his right index finger away from his desk, in the opposite direction.

He then said, "All right, let's see if I can, uh, actually—wait a minute." James stopped himself to think for a minute. "Hmm," he said, "You know, maybe I shouldn't try it like this. Let's see now, uh, I know what! I'll get an empty soda can to use as a target. After all, I wouldn't want to damage my walls, ceiling, or furniture. I'll be right back."

James then ran downstairs and found an empty soda can. At that, he headed back upstairs to his room. Once there, he placed the can on his desk. He went to the other side of his bed to see if he could hit it with a laser beam. Once again, Clifton contracted and charged up his right hand, which of course got brighter and brighter as it was charging. Next, he lowered his head a bit in order to peer just above his hand and aim his index finger at the can. Also, James tried for a couple of moments to steady his right hand and line it up perfectly, although he was not completely sure that his positioning was absolutely perfect. Still, his mind was definitely and undeniably set on the target that he was to hit. Finally, he released and shot a neon-green laser beam, which hit the soda can in the exact center. His index finger automatically positioned itself accurately. He only had to decide in his mind exactly what to shoot. From there, it was automatically accurate.

The impact of the beam that James fired caused a chain reaction. Instead of standing straight across his bed from the target, he was slightly to the left of that position. So, once the soda can got hit, it briefly shot back against the wall that had the desk against it, but at such an angle that it bounced off and ricocheted into the lamp on his nightstand next to the head of his bed. This caused the lamp to begin to fall over, but it was stopped by the bed's headboard. Next, the can flew past the foot of James's bed and then bounced off the wall against which his dresser was placed. Finally, the soda can came to rest when it landed on top of his bed near the center.

Consequently, James said, "Whoa, I should've been more careful. I could've broken my lamp and my mirror. Maybe I should practice my shooting outside or something."

Right afterward, James went and stood his lamp back up. Next, he looked again at himself in the mirror for a few seconds to see that he was still giving off blinding neon-green light. Still standing to face the mirror, James looked down at his hands for a second or two but then began to examine the rest of his anatomy from his waist down with curiosity. He said to himself, "Well now, I wonder what else I can possibly do." At that very instant, James set his eyes on his feet and once again began to wonder. He said, "I've already tried something with my hands. I wonder if I could somehow utilize my feet by any chance. Now of course, I don't think I'd want to shoot with my feet instead of my hands. But uh… wait a minute! I know what! I wonder if my power will permit me to, like, hover or levitate myself. Hmm, well, let's see here."

James began concentrating immediately. At the same time, he tightened up his feet and lower legs, creating tension. This, of course, caused him to charge up, giving off brighter neon light while charging. This light grew so much brighter that it shone on through even the tiniest cracks, crevices, and openings of his hiking boots, socks, and jeans.

All the while, Clifton's mind was set on levitation. So then, after a moment's concentration, he started noticing something about his reflection in the mirror. His reflection was apparently rising up in the mirror, because his mirror was supposedly slightly tilting forward. "What's the matter with my mirror?" James asked. But then, however, after another moment, his face was no longer visible in the mirror, and the only reflection James could see was from his neck down to just below his knees. "Now, what's happening?" he asked, a little more worried. But then, he managed to notice that the outer frame on his mirror was still standing upright. So he said, "Wait a minute, it's not my mirror. It's—"

Upon interrupting himself, James looked straight down toward the floor. "Oh my gosh!" he cried. "It's me doing that! What's happening? Well actually, never mind; I mean, I was hoping I could levitate like this. I just didn't realize how easy it was."

That was exactly what was happening. James was indeed rising up from the floor. Also, the soles of his boots were now lit up with neon-green light. The pyxorium that was part of James's nervous system was giving off radiant energy which went on through the bottoms of the boots and pushed downward to provide him with a lift that levitated him. Just like before, when Clifton was able to fire a laser beam, he could simply control this levitation with his mind, since the pyxorium was fused with his nervous system.

Then, after a few moments of being captivated by his ability to float in the air, James Clifton began looking down and around himself in every direction he could. "Wow!" he said. "This is amazing. It's unbelievable. I'd have never imagined in all my dreams that I would ever be able to hover or float like this. But of course, I can't describe exactly how I do it. It just seems like all I did was fix my mind on levitating and it happened. I mean, I did it."

However, James was now merely a few inches from touching the ceiling with the top of his head. In the nick of time, he began looking up, and that very second, he noticed how close he was. "Yikes!" James screamed as he quickly leaned backward to avoid hitting the ceiling. "Oh my goodness! That was a close one. Well, maybe I better get down now, and maybe I better practice my new capabilities outdoors. All right now, let's see here. I wonder if I could let myself down from here."

At that, James looked down and saw that radiation was coming on out through the bottoms of his boots. That, of course, was the radiant energy that was enabling him to hover and levitate. "Okay then," James said to himself, "let me try something here." He went on to ease the tension in his feet and calves gradually. At the same time, the radiant energy was subsiding so that Clifton was descending slowly back toward the floor. A moment later, James Clifton was standing on his bedroom floor again. At that, he said, "You know, I think that as long as I'm indoors, I'll keep my feet on the ground."

It was now 5:45 p.m., and James was still radiating bright, neon-green light. After figuring out two totally new abilities, an already amazed James Clifton was more anxious than ever to see what else he could do. So he said, "Well, right now, I think I'll go outside to see what other kinds of powers I have and try them out." He went downstairs and then out the back door into his backyard.

Before starting to do anything, however, James stood approximately in the very middle of his yard to think for a moment. First, he said, "You know something? I got to admit, like I said earlier, that glass of water I had most certainly turned out to be the greatest mineral water I've ever had.

But unfortunately, it looks like it'll be the only serving I'll ever have, and I got none to share with anybody else. I guess that's another reason I can't tell anyone else, not even Eric or Scott, what I went through. I mean, I hate so much to withhold a secret from my two best friends. It's just that I can't help them develop these special capabilities. So for that reason, I think I ought to not bring it up just to raise their hopes and then let them down." Following that, James stood still for a few minutes in silence, having some sort of regret that he was going to have to keep to himself about his most amazing transformation and his awesome, brand-new abilities.

Then, after a few moments, James decided, "Oh well, I'll think about all that later. Right now, let's see what I might try to do next." Once again, he looked wonderingly into the palms of his hands, having put them in front of his face again. "You know," he said, "I wonder, is there anything else I can do with these hands of mine? I can already fire laser beams. Now, could I possibly form some sort of defense mechanism? I mean, you know, like the purpose a shield or a suit of armor serves? Well, actually, I'm not so sure about making something out of metal or anything, but what about, say, a force field or something to put around myself?" After hesitating for a few seconds, he said, "Yeah, that's it! A force field! I might be able to put a force field around myself. I mean, after all, if the energy put off by the pyxorium can provide force to lift me up in levitation, why couldn't it possibly provide the necessary force for a force field to protect me?"

James paused to look at his hands for a few seconds and then up to his left and to his right. He was trying to visualize the outermost extremes of the space that a spherical force field would take up.

After taking a few more minutes to think about it, James eventually decided that he was now ready to try to create the globular force field that he had in mind. So next, an already radioactive James Clifton began increasing the tension in his hands with his mind set and focused on the force field that he would attempt to form. In the meantime, his fingertips were charging and getting brighter. Then, about ten seconds later, James released from his fingertips what were apparently neon-green laser beams, although not as thick as the beams he had shot earlier in his room. These beams were limited in length, obviously stopping at the outer surface of the force field. With little or no effort on Clifton's part, those laser beams appeared to be randomly scattering about, as if the force field was being drawn or sketched.

All the while, James was watching with wonder while constantly looking in all different directions. Then, before he was aware of it, his feet were suddenly elevated a few inches off the ground. James was no doubt scared for a second or two and reacted by looking down. He exclaimed, "Huh! Oh, the bottom of it must be forming. Well, what do you know? Maybe a force field really is forming. If so, it didn't turn out to be that hard after all. Maybe I didn't have to think so long and hard about it." In fact, he did not. With the pyxorium actually being a part of his entire nervous system, it was easier to perform these newly acquired supernatural abilities. It was definitely easier than some people might have thought, including James Clifton himself, who had overestimated the difficulty of handling his superpowers.

But in the meantime, James was still encircled by the force field that he had created. Radiant energy from the pyxorium was pushing outward in all directions to provide protection and keep him in the very center of the force field. James asked himself, "Well, what now?" Then, out of curiosity, he used his right hand to reach out and try to feel the outermost limit of the force field's occupied space. However, something strange occurred. James could not feel anything with his sense of touch, but he himself was somehow moved forward about two feet in a jerky motion, as if something or someone had pushed him. "What was that?" a surprised James Clifton asked as he turned and looked behind himself. He did not see any signs of anyone or anything back there. So he said, "Hmm, that's weird. I thought it felt like I got pushed."

But then, a moment later, James said, "But wait a minute, how could I forget? I'm trapped inside a force field. Maybe I pushed myself by moving it. Yeah, that's it. But anyway, let me try something else here. I wonder if I could utilize my hovering ability and levitate inside this force field." At that, he once again tightened up his feet and calves. Consequently, a surge of bright radiant energy pushed on through the bottoms of his boots, and he began rising straight up although he was encircled by the force field. "Well, what do you know?" he said. "I can float around in this force field. I dare someone to try and shoot me down. I mean, I'm up above that person, and I've got protection. How much better can you possibly do than that?"

Anyhow, James stopped ascending when it got to be about ten feet from the ground to the soles of his boots. "Oh man," said Clifton, "I like the view from up here. I never thought I'd ever be able to look down on people and things like this, and besides, no one on the ground can reach me."

A couple more moments passed, and James had had enough. "Well, I guess I'm gonna come on down and get out of this force field. After all, I don't want to attract too much attention." So then, he eased the tension below his knees and, as a result, descended back toward the ground. But once again, he started looking around in wonder at how he could possibly take down the force field that he had formed. "All right now," he said, "how do I do this? There's got to be a way. I mean, I did manage to form it in the first place, didn't I?" Once again, James looked wonderingly at his hands, trying to think about how he might possibly take down the force field that he had made. He said, "Well, let's try something here." At that, James created tension in his hands while directing them at the outermost layer of the force field. Of course, he was concentrating in his mind on taking it down. So this time, James directed the tightness in his right hand back toward his wrist rather than toward his fingertips, so as to retract rather than force out.

As a result, his right hand began charging and getting brighter. Before James was aware of it, laser beams started forming, coming from the force field's outer surface and heading back into James's right hand. That was the pyxorium in his nervous system, which was now withdrawing the radiant energy that it had put out. Over the next few moments, the force field slowly faded out until it finally disappeared altogether.

After all that, James began to wonder what else the pyxorium empowered him to do. "Well, anyway," he said, "now that I've seen what I can now do with my hands and feet, I wonder what other supernatural abilities I might have. I mean like, since I've got the ability to exert radiant energy and radiate, could I, by any chance, take the form of some sort of radiation?"

James then stood and thought about it for a few more minutes until he had an idea. "You know what?" he said. "I know something I'd like to try. No one seems to be home next door, so I guess I'll go between our two houses and try it." At that, Clifton went over to the fencing that was closest to the neighbor's house to the east of his.

James Clifton was now looking to get over his fence and end up between the two houses. "Let's see here," he started to say, "maybe I would go out my front door, but I don't want to bring about too much of a disturbance. I'd like to be able to utilize my powers to get past such an obstacle as this. Now let's see." Within less than a minute, James said, "Oh, of course! How could I forget what I just taught myself how to do?" Upon saying that, James went on to activate his hovering capability and lift himself up so that his feet were higher than his fence's height. Then, he leaned slightly forward and drove himself past the fence. Finally, of course, James let himself down on the other side of it. "Well, I guess that was all I had to do," he declared.

James was now in the long, narrow space between his own house and the one next door. He went on to say to himself, "Now, a few moments ago, I think I asked myself if I could possibly take the form of some sort of radiation. Since it's over fifty feet or so from here to the front of these two houses, that makes me wonder, could I become like a projectile and simply shoot from one point to another?" So then, he took a moment to think about it.

Next, James decided, "All right then, let's try something here. I guess I'll set myself a destination of about twenty feet from here, all right? All right." James Clifton looked at and concentrated on the point that was located twenty feet closer to his front yard than where he was currently standing. He started tightening all of his muscles, creating tension throughout his whole body, from the crown of his head to the soles of his feet. Consequently, he began charging the pyxorium in his nervous system and progressively lighting up brighter and brighter.

However, James had overlooked one thing. No neon-green light was shining through his jeans or hiking boots. That was because he had not activated them with energy from the pyxorium. James was so focused on what he was preparing to do that he did not notice.

In the meantime, James was practically ready to reposition to twenty feet away. Once he felt that he had built up enough tension, he said, "All right, ready? Now!" That very second, he released himself. Within a split second, he actually turned into a shapeless mass of neon-green radiation and shot over to reappear in the intended spot.

Upon reappearing in his radiating human form, he was a bit dazed and confused momentarily. "Whoa, what happened?" he asked. "Did I make it? Did it work?"

He regained his senses and double-checked for a few seconds to see where he was. He discovered that he actually was at a different point between the two houses. "It must've worked!" an amazed James Clifton exclaimed. "I know I didn't try to run or jump over here; I mean, I can't even recall exactly how I got to this point. I must've shot over here like a comet. Oh man, what an awesome, spectacular transformation I just underwent! This weekend just keeps getting better and better. This is definitely the greatest breakthrough I have ever, ever made in my life. On top of that, I think these new tactics could be very useful for me." At that, he was silent for a few moments and looked up toward the sky with a rather happy, excited, and amazed expression on his face. He looked around in different directions.

After that, he just started looking back down again within the area in which he was standing. He was still feeling happy about having gained his new abilities. As he was gazing around the narrow space between his house and the one next door, he said, "Well, anyway, this was the spot that I wanted to end up in. That's because now, I'm looking back at where I was standing right by my fence. I am about twenty feet from that point like I wanted to be. It's like I just thought about and focused on it, and there wasn't much other effort I put forth besides that. It was so easy that it seems like it just happened by itself."

However, as James was looking back at where he had stood previously, he noticed another thing too. He said, "You know something else? I can definitely tell that I shot over here without too much physical activity like running or anything because I still see my jeans and boots where I just was before. What did I just—huh? My jeans and boots! If they're over there, they must've come off and—" At that, James looked down at himself to see that he only had on a T-shirt, his underwear, and his socks. "Oh my God! Oh no!" he cried.

James said, "Wait a minute. Let me get ahold of myself. Maybe I just pass any radiation or energy on to them. But first of all, let me get over there and put them back on." So, that very minute, he ran back over to where his jeans and boots were lying. Then, he put them back on.

Finally, James said, "All right, there, I believe that does it." Still standing in the spot at which he had started, he took a look down at his pants, wanting to try to activate them with radiant energy so that he would not lose them again. He said, "Let's see if I can make something work here." At that, an already radiating James Clifton once again created tightness and tension throughout his whole body. But of course, he placed more emphasis below his waist, with his mind set on activation of his jeans and boots. Then, less than a minute later, his pants and hiking boots were radiating neon-green light, just like the rest of him.

"Well, what do you know?" James asked himself. "That wasn't hard. In fact, nothing I've tried to do seemed to be. All I had to do was think about it. How could I keep forgetting that?" Somehow or another, James had kept overlooking the fact that the pyxorium was now a part of his nervous system and that made it so much easier to handle his newly acquired capabilities. But, of course, it was only the first night of him having these amazing supernatural powers, and James was still trying to get accustomed to applying them.

However, James was about to try the technique by which he projected himself wherever he wanted once more. "Well, anyway," he said, "let's try that again." Of course, just before beginning another attempt, he took a few seconds to double-check to make sure that his entire self was ready, clothes and all. "Well," said James, "I guess I'm as ready as I'm gonna get. Well, here we go." So then, James once again charged himself up in preparation and focused once more on the same destination that was twenty feet away. He then said, "All right, ready? Now!" That very second, he released and projected himself.

Less than a second later, Clifton reappeared in his human form as himself. At first, he questioned himself, "Did I make it?" Then, he took a look around and asked wonderingly, "Did I get it right this time?" Like before, he looked back at his starting position. But this time, no clothes were left there on the ground. Next, James looked over himself to see that he had kept all of his clothes. "Yes!" he exclaimed happily. "This time, they made it."

Before thinking about what to do next, James gave a little more thought to what had just happened. He said, "Well, anyway, I think I got it down; I mean, I think so. I think I do. I mean, it didn't really seem all that difficult or anything, you know? But maybe I just need to make sure I activate my clothes too. Maybe that's it." As it happened, James Clifton was actually right. It was not too difficult to control the techniques he now had. However, anything that was to be part of the shapeless mass of radiation of which he took the form had to be empowered by the pyxorium from his nervous system.

Now, Clifton wanted to go and try yet another form of movement. He went up to the very front of both his neighbor's house and his own. He then stopped and asked himself, "Well, since I can become a projectile and project myself, you know, like radiantly, radioactively, or whatever, I wonder, could I possibly transfer to another point by some other radioactive means? After all, everything else I've done involved radiation."

James stopped reasoning momentarily and said, "Let's see here now. First of all, let me pick out a spot to transfer to. Like, uh, why not that mailbox right there to my left in front of my neighbor's house? Yeah, I'll try to get right next to it somehow. I mean, why not? After all, I don't think anybody's home." James tried to think in order to decide how he might try to transfer over to the mailbox that was off to his left by the street.

After a couple of moments of trying to think of what other possibilities he had not tried, James finally declared, "I think that's what I'll try. I mean, instead of shooting myself in the form of a cannonball or something, I might want to try to simply teleport over there. Hopefully, I won't risk damaging anything that way, but how will I teleport? Wait a minute; I know how. How could I forget? Didn't I use beams of neon-green light to fire lasers and create my force field? So why couldn't I use one to teleport? Of course, how stupid of me!"

So next, James fixed his eyes and mind on getting to the little paved walkway to the left of the mailbox. "All right then," said a determined James Clifton, "let's see if this works."

But before charging up to begin teleportation, James double-checked to make quite sure that all of his clothes were radiating bright neon-green light; since they were, James was now ready to begin.

Next, James started concentrating, creating tension, and charging with radiant energy. Of course, he was progressively shining brighter and brighter. Then finally, he said, "Ready? Go!" That very second, he disappeared into a long, narrow beam of neon-green light, which stretched between the houses' two front sides to the little walkway by the neighbor's mailbox. As quick as a flash, he teleported through that beam of radiation, which was five feet above the ground, and reappeared by the mailbox at the street like he wanted.

In the instant of his arrival at the intended mark, James said, "Well, did I make it?" Then, of course, upon taking a quick glance around for a couple of seconds, he concluded, "I most certainly did. That wasn't so bad, was it? Somehow, I knew it wouldn't be." In fact, it was definitely not. Understandably, he did not worry or stress as much this time around. That was because although it took a few times to see, he was beginning to remember and understand that handling these capabilities was not quite as tough or complicated as he had imagined it might be.

So now, it was 6:10 p.m., and a still brightly lit, neon-green James Paul Clifton was wondering what he would do next. "Well," he said, "so what now? Should I call it a night? Well, maybe not; I mean, it's still a little early. Besides, I'd kind of like to get a little more practice, you know—that is, to make more certain that I've got my superpowers nailed down. Of course, I think I've got a good handle on them, but I can't wait to put them to good use. Besides, with only the remainder of this evening left of the weekend, I'd like to get out and have a little fun."

James took a minute to think about what he had just said and smiled while thinking about it. After all, anyone should be able to understand how exciting and interesting it must have been for someone like James Clifton to have acquired such amazing superpowers, which he had not even dreamed of having. Besides, with this being the first night for him to realize he had them, it was especially thrilling and exciting.

James then proceeded to say, "You know, it's a good thing I went to the mountains this weekend. I mean, it wasn't a bad idea, was it? Also, on the first night there, it's a good thing I went wandering off in the middle of the night. Otherwise, I wouldn't have found the piece of quartz that became pyxorium. Then also, earlier this evening, it was a good thing I tripped and fell to lose the mineral in my water. Otherwise, I wouldn't have these supernatural powers within me. It's like all these mishaps were meant to happen and for a great reason. As for whoever has been guiding me, thank you so very, very much." James was experiencing so much excitement and happiness that although his weekend was close to over, it felt as if it was only getting started.

Anyhow, James was now ready to go out and try out his new capabilities. But at first, he was not sure where to go or how to go wherever he would go. So he began to try to reason within himself. He said, "All right, where should I go from here? How should I do this? Let's see here." Then, he tried to put his thoughts together to come up with the best route to take.

Continuing to consider different possibilities, James said to himself, "Well, at a time like this on Sunday night, I hate to bring too much disturbance or distraction to those who have to go to work in the morning. So I guess I better not go zooming around the streets in this neighborhood. Now, is there some possible way I can avoid that?"

James continued to think for yet another moment, but then he calmly mumbled, "Maybe I should briefly run through the things that I already know I can do. Let's see... I can teleport. I can shoot myself. Wait a minute, what did I say? Well, I didn't mean kill myself, of course. I only meant project myself, you know? Well, anyway, where was I? Oh yeah, I can also hover, levitate, and float." When James murmured that, it suddenly rang a bell.

"Wait a minute!" exclaimed Clifton. "That's it! Maybe that's what I'll do!" Then, he briefly thought it over once more. After that, he said, "Why, of course! While I'm still in these neighborhoods, I'll just glide up overhead for right now. That's until I figure out what else to do. Of course, I shouldn't create as much distraction up above as I would whizzing through residential areas."

Next, he stopped momentarily to think about how he might get off the ground. "Let's see," said James. "I guess I'll start hovering and slowly ascend until I'm high enough. Actually, people might start watching and become suspicious."

But after a couple of minutes of reconsideration, James decided, "You know what? I think I'm gonna try something else here. I mean, I already launched and projected myself earlier. This time, I'll see if I can shoot myself straight up. Oh, and let's not forget, when I get there, I shall start to hover so I can save myself from falling. I mean, why not? It ought to be worth a try. Heck, with all the supernatural powers I now possess, I should be able to find some way to help myself even if I do start to fall."

James began charging himself up, getting ready to shoot himself off. "All right now," said James, "I think I'll go for about a hundred feet above the ground, and this time, I'll find out if I can project myself vertically and not just horizontally." Still charging, he asked himself, "Are we ready?" At that, James felt quite certain that he was. "All right then," he said. "Ready, set, go!" That very instant, he shot straight upward, looking something like a neon-green comet.

Then, in less than a second, James reappeared as himself, a hundred feet high up in midair like he had intended. However, he allowed a couple of seconds to pass by, during which he fell about fifty feet. But fortunately, before falling any farther, James increased the tension of his feet and activated his hovering ability. He was levitating from that point forward.

After that, James put just a little bit more tension below his knees and ascended back up to approximately where he had reappeared. At that, he took some time to look all around at what he could see of his hometown below him.

After about ten minutes of looking all around, James said, "Oh well, I guess I've looked around from this spot long enough. I guess I might go toward downtown Philadelphia and see what's up." While still radiating blinding, neon-green light and still afloat by means of hovering, James Clifton tilted himself forward until he was in an almost horizontal facedown position. At once, he increased the radiant energy for his hovering in order to push himself toward the downtown area.

In the meantime, at a house in the Richmond subdivision, a five-year-old boy named Alex was getting ready for bed. While walking by his bedroom window, he saw the neon-green figure of James Clifton floating and gliding by in the distance. Of course, little Alex did not know who or what it was. So he ran to his father, hollering, "Daddy! Daddy!"

His father replied, "What is it, Alex?"

"Come see!" exclaimed an excited Alex. "It's a UFO!"

Calmly, his dad said, "Now, Alex, I've told you, there's no such thing as a UFO."

"But it looked like a shiny green man," said Alex.

"That's quite an imagination," replied his father.

"It wasn't my imagination," insisted little Alex. "It was real."

"It's time for bed," said his father. "Good night, Alex." Then, a disappointed Alex just went off to bed.

However, a brightly lit James Clifton continued to glide toward the downtown area. As he was hovering up above, he began to look around and say, "I wonder what's going on down there."

Finally, James made it to downtown Philadelphia. His reason for heading downtown was to get a rather interesting view of all the well-known historic sites, attractions, important buildings, and any other distinguishing characteristics for which Philadelphia was known. But when Clifton made it to the downtown area, he decided to rise up another hundred feet. He was only ascending farther up to cause less distraction or disturbance. Perhaps, he thought, he would get to experience what it was like to look down from a skyscraper without actually being in or on one. That was the same experience that certain other people supposedly enjoyed having; they liked looking down at the many streets, people, vehicles, and more, which appeared to be miniature models from that height. Before too long, James came to a stop and stationed himself in midair above Kennedy Plaza between Fifteenth and Sixteenth Streets. He figured that to be an ideal spot to rest, watch many different happenings in the city, and take a little time to think about something nice.

James said, "Actually, I think I'll put a force field around myself. Of course, it's not that I think something's likely to happen, but it's just to be on the safe side." So he went on to create a force field like he had done earlier in his backyard.

He slowly kept turning to check out every interesting feature he could spot in his field of vision. "You know something?" he asked. "I've never thought about this before, but I can see a lot more different things from up here. I mean, I wonder if I could be the first to see something and notify the police. Huh! I never thought about that either. I might actually prevent more crime that way."

Holding that thought, James stopped to think for a moment. Then, he said, "Actually, you know something else? With these amazing powers I now have, I might be able to stop crimes myself. Why, yes! I'd end up feeling good about myself for not letting something happen to someone so helpless, innocent, and blameless. But first, I'd like to get a little more comfortable with handling my abilities."

Continuing to enjoy the view, James went on to tell himself, "But other than spotting anything unfortunate, I could help someone find something or someone that they're looking for. Also, other than that, I might even spot something I'd like to see myself. I mean, no matter who any of these people think they're hiding around the corner from, I'm looking down at them always. Now, could I possibly ever see Amanda among them?"

Upon asking himself that last question, James stopped himself, saying, "What did I say? Amanda?" Of course, he did in fact say that. "I did, didn't I?" At that, he took his mind off all other thoughts he was having about his powers and began thinking and wondering about Amanda Taylor. As a result, James stopped looking down at the city and looked upward, away from it, concentrating on Amanda. The worst part was that because James was not concentrating as much on where he was or what he was doing, the force he was creating to keep himself in midair began to ease off. Consequently, he slowly started descending toward the ground. However, the force field remained intact because he did not take it down.

James kept thinking about Amanda. He proceeded to say to himself, "Oh man, I wonder where Amanda is and what she's doing right now." With that in mind, Clifton started to imagine further and develop more thoughts. Without a doubt, much like when he was on his way to the Allegheny Mountains, he even visualized her standing inside the force field with him, with her arms placed around his shoulders and midsection. James went on to think to himself, "I never really thought about it all like this, but that is the only thing better than obtaining and possessing these superpowers. With Amanda as the best possible added bonus—or should I consider my abilities the added bonus, with her as the main thing? Well, either way, it's the best possible combination I can think of right now. Also, with this force field protecting both of us, I guess no one could take her from me now."

Now having all those lovely thoughts, James focused entirely on them and overlooked anything else that was going on at the time. His imagination and fantasies went deeper. All the while, James Clifton had been slowly descending toward Arch Street; he was still secured inside the force field. Furthermore, he was still seeing a vision of Amanda Taylor. He thought he saw and heard her say, "Come on, James, how about a big kiss?" Then, he perceived that she was puckering up in preparation for it.

Consequently, Clifton slowly moved his face toward her to try to kiss her back. While doing so, he began to hear a long continuous sound of an air horn as if it was getting near. Worried very little, James rolled his eyes to his right for only a second or two, saying, "Hmm, I wonder what's making that noise. Oh well." Looking back to where Amanda had appeared to be, James thought he was starting to see a big red truck coming up behind her. He looked past her for a second, saying, "Wait a minute, what the—"

All of a sudden, James's vision of Amanda vanished. At that, the big red rig appeared to be drawing closer every second and eventually got dangerously close. James screamed, "Oh no! Whoa!" Then, it felt like the truck had run smack into the force field that contained him and that he was being pushed by it. A startled, surprised James Clifton asked in a panic, "What's happening?"

What had actually happened was that since James had not remained fully focused or concentrated on staying afloat by hovering, he had slowly descended a couple hundred feet before he was aware of it. Other than that, he almost ended up down on Arch Street. The truck James thought he was seeing was real. It actually was a tractor-trailer that consisted of a red tractor pulling a white freight trailer.

In the meantime, the force field containing James Clifton had made it down in front of the truck. It was now being pushed east along Arch Street by that same truck that had run into it. The force of the moving truck practically had Clifton pasted against its windshield. He was face-to-face with the driver. Only the outermost layer of the force field was between him and the truck's windshield.

On the other hand, the driver of that truck had been driving while talking on his CB radio. But that ended very suddenly when the neon-green person of James Clifton suddenly popped up against his windshield. At that, he let out a scream and dropped the receiver. "Oh no!" he cried. "What's *that*?" That very second, he turned his head to his left so as not to look at the frightening image in front of him.

Meanwhile, Clifton, of course, was still pressed against the truck's windshield. He was looking to free himself. Rather scared, he exclaimed, "Oh no! What am I gonna do?" But fortunately, James figured out a possible way out within a few seconds. He would propel himself straight up to get out of the truck's path. So he said, "Of course! I'll just get out of the line of fire." At the same time, Clifton quickly activated his hovering ability and ascended straight up and out from in front of the truck.

Just as Clifton was getting out of the way, the eighteen-wheeler driver was looking ahead of himself again. While doing so, he thought he saw the bright, neon-green image disappear, and everything looked normal to him again. However, he had driven about four blocks along Arch Street. The driver went on to regain his senses and realize where he was. "Oh man," he said, "I don't know who or what that was, but it scared the life out of me. I sure hope that there's nothing wrong with me so that I am seeing things."

The truck driver then got back onto his CB. He said, "I'm sorry to cut you off so suddenly, but somebody or something neon green appeared to smack right into my windshield for a moment. I don't know what it was. Was it someone pulling off a stunt, or some green phantasm that I hallucinated and saw? Well, whatever the case may be, I feel all right now. Now, as I was saying…" At that, the trucker went about his business. But hearing the CB transmission, certain policemen and other truckers started to wonder too.

It was now 6:35 p.m. James Clifton was now between Eleventh and Twelfth Streets, but he was still levitating and hovering inside the force field that he had formed. He was now about four blocks east of where he had been before. Furthermore, James was looking rather angrily toward the truck that had hit him. "Why, that pinhead!" he muttered. "I'll show him a thing or two! Why I'll—"

But before continuing, James restrained himself and calmed down some. "Well," he said, "maybe it's my fault. I guess this wouldn't have happened if I'd have been paying attention more instead of letting those thoughts about Amanda make me lose my head. I mean, what can I say? I guess I was just frustrated like I was at what happened Saturday morning with Scott. But I got to admit, I can't get over this woman. However, I do need to get ahold of myself."

It is understandable why James was angry and upset at the truck. He was having a really lovely and pleasant dream about the young lady to whom he was attracted. It was extremely disappointing when the sudden unpleasant end of the dream took place. First, it was dumped water by Scott MacNicholl Saturday morning, and now it was getting smacked by a truck. Fortunately, it could have been worse. For example, what if James Clifton had not just put up a force field to protect himself? The consequences could have been really tragic, perhaps even fatal. Furthermore, Clifton learned a rather hard lesson not to think too much about Amanda so as not to ruin his concentration on something really important. Fortunately, James began to see that these enjoyable and desirable thoughts with which he had gotten carried away were the root of the problems with his good friend Scott and the eighteen-wheeler. So James decided to be more careful with his desire and like for Amanda Taylor.

James had had enough hovering and gliding around for the time being. "Oh well," he said, "I've had enough of this for right now. I'm just gonna come on down and take down this force field." So then, James descended on downward until he made it to the street. He then put tension in his hands in order to retract the radiant energy by which the force field was established. Thin laser beams were apparently coming from the outermost part of the force field back to him through all of his fingers. At the same time, the force field was disappearing. Finally, James was out of it completely. He was still radiating neon-green light and was now standing in the middle of Arch Street. He stood there momentarily while trying to think of what to do next.

James decided, "Well, I guess I'll call it a night for tonight. Of course, I suppose I could somehow use my powers to get myself home, but no, I'll just get a taxi for right now. Let's see." That very moment, James started walking east on Arch Street. Next, he looked up in the direction in which he was going. He began to cross Eleventh Street at the very next intersection. But unfortunately, before he was aware of it, he had wound up in the way of a gold Mercedes Benz that was headed south on the street. Consequently, James was startled by the car's horn blaring. Immediately, he quickly turned his head to his left and thus came face-to-face with the dangerously close Mercedes. Without the protection of a force field, he was indeed a very frightened James Clifton. What would he do?

Although receiving quite a fright, James quickly discerned a possible way out. Within two seconds, he figured that he might try to teleport underneath the oncoming car. He quickly placed a bit of tension below his knees. In an instant, James Clifton appeared to disappear but actually took the form of the neon-green beam by which he teleported. He reappeared behind the car in his radiant neon-green human form. "Whew!" James uttered in extreme relief. "Oh, thank goodness." Then, with a frightened look on his face, Clifton said, "Oh man, I've received quite a scare a few other times in my life, but never like that. My entire life just flashed before my eyes like never ever before. Oh man!" At that, he stood there inhaling and exhaling heavily for a while.

The driver of the Mercedes Benz had received quite a shock herself. She was about fifty-six years old. Whenever she was dangerously close to running into James Clifton, she panicked, not knowing what to do. Also, since Clifton was radiating neon-green light, the lady probably was not sure whether what she was seeing was real or not. That probably made the situation even more frightening for her.

In the instant that Clifton was no longer visible in front of the car, the woman slammed on her brakes and screeched to a stop. At that, she got out and looked around right by her Mercedes but saw no sign of the one she had supposedly hit. But then, she saw the neon-green James Clifton standing about twenty feet behind her car. "Excuse me, sir!" she said. "Are you all right? I thought I—"

"No, no, no, no!" replied James, who was backing away as the woman walked toward him. "Nothing happened! I swear!"

But still following Clifton, the lady said, "But I saw you in front of me, and then—"

"Stay away from me!" James yelled as he turned to run off. "Leave me alone!" At that, he ran east to the gap between the two closest buildings. He went between them. At once, he charged himself up and then shot all the way down to the other end of that alley. Finally, he came out and reappeared on Tenth Street. James ran from the lady driving the Mercedes Benz so that she would not be able to identify him and know who had those special powers that made him radiate.

So then, the Mercedes driver went to the space between the buildings, into which she had seen him go. But since Clifton had whizzed all the way down the alley at lightning speed, the woman saw no sign of him.

"Oh my goodness," she said, "I just saw, heard, and talked to a guy who was lit up neon green, but now I don't see him anywhere. Is there something wrong with me?"

Before long, a city police car stopped behind the Mercedes Benz that was parked in the road. At the same time, the lady was walking back toward her car.

"Excuse me, Miss?" said the police officer. "Is this your car?"

"Why, yes," the woman replied.

"Well, why is it parked in the road?" the policeman asked.

Not knowing how to begin, the woman said, "Well, uh, I don't know how to say this, but I thought I might've hit somebody. So I stopped to ask him if he was okay."

"Then what happened?" the policeman asked. "Why isn't that person here?"

"Well," she said, "I thought I saw him go between those two buildings there, but now I can't see a sign of him."

"Any memory of what this person looked like?" asked the policeman.

"Well," replied the woman, "I didn't get a real good look at him, but one thing I do remember is—and I know you won't believe it—but he was lit up and putting off neon-green light."

The officer said, "What do you mean? Was it something he was wearing that was doing that?"

"No," answered the woman, "it appeared to be his whole entire self radiating blinding green light."

The policeman hesitated for a few seconds, finding her story hard to believe. After all, what human being could be a blinding neon green? So then, he asked, "Have you been drinking?"

"Why, no," the woman answered.

"Well," the officer said, "I hate to doubt you, but may I suggest that you were somehow hallucinating?"

"But I'm quite all right," she replied. "I not only saw the guy, I actually heard him and talked with him. Furthermore, I know I wasn't trying to imagine him."

"Well," the policeman said, "just to make sure, I'm gonna have you take a breath test."

"Well, all right," the woman said.

After that, the driver of the Mercedes proceeded to take the breath test. But, of course, no sign of intoxication was detected. As a result, the police officer just told her to go on home. Then, he and the woman both just went about their business.

———————— ⌒ ————————

James Clifton was now heading south on Tenth Street; he was between Walnut and Locust Streets. He was feeling rather guilty about the way he had scared the lady in the Benz. He said, "What is wrong with me tonight? I'm causing all kinds of trouble. I mean, I know I'm a little excited about my superhuman powers, but I still need to get ahold of myself and be careful."

After that, James decided, "Well anyway, I think I'll get myself home before something else happens. After all, it's after 7:00 p.m., and I got to get ready for bed and get to work in the morning. The question is, will I take a taxi or the subway?" James started walking along Locust Street while trying to see about a way home.

Although James was earnestly trying to find a way home, all of a sudden, he heard something. It was coming from Mikveh Israel Cemetery, toward which he happened to be walking. It was the scream of a young lady who had been captured by a pair of hoodlums. "Oh no," said James, who was feeling worried, "somebody's in trouble. I hope I've got the power to stop this." He ran over to the south side of the cemetery.

When James finally got there, he saw the young lady who was about to become a rape victim. One of the kidnappers was over six feet tall, wearing a black bandana and a black leather jacket, and his name was Clyde. He had both of his arms around her while holding her in place in front of him. The other guy was about five feet seven inches tall and had a shaved head and a patch over one eye. He was holding out a knife in front of her. The victim was a lovely young woman with reddish-brown hair. She was wearing a nice gray dress. Her name was Kathryn Nicole Brown. "Let me go! Let me go!" she was screaming in fright.

Although James Clifton was on his way home, he did not like what he was seeing. His good conscience caused him to feel terrible pity for the most unfortunate young lady. Clifton had wanted to get home before causing any more trouble, but he could not allow this to happen to her.

James was still radiating bright neon-green light. Before long, he came up with a strategy to save Kathryn Brown. James started charging himself in preparation to take the form of a shapeless mass of radiation, which he would somehow maneuver in order to shoot into both bad guys and knock them away from her so she could escape. All three of them were about sixty feet north of where he was standing along Spruce Street. Kathryn was positioned between Clyde and the other man called Carl. However, James was going to travel in a backward S-shaped pattern to reach them. He was heading straight for Clyde, who was on the left. He was going to make a sudden U-turn around Kathryn to knock Carl away. He was holding the knife on the right. Then finally, James was going to make another U-turn and head toward the north end of Mikveh Israel Cemetery.

James was just about to project himself along the course that he was plotting. In the meantime, Carl was pointing his knife at the girl's genital area while saying, "Come on, sweetheart! Show us what you got!" But fortunately, before any further harm was done, within two seconds, something caused the two young ruffians to be catapulted in opposite directions. It was James Clifton, who had successfully whizzed through at bullet speed, in the manner he had planned. As a result of what had just happened, Kathryn Brown only stumbled backward in order to land on her rear end. But the two gangsters each got projected about twenty feet in a different direction, and both wound up lying flat on their backs. Carl lost his knife in the process.

All three were now in shock, wondering what had just taken place. Consequently, each one said something like, "Where am I?" or "How'd I get here?" or "What just happened?" Otherwise, they all looked around in wonder and concern.

Then, all three people got back on their feet, but they were still a bit confused, not knowing how they had gotten where they were at the time. James Clifton, who was looking on from about twenty feet north of them all, called out to Kathryn, saying, "Hurry, Miss! Flee! Get out of here! Run for your life!" So, on her first impulse, she obeyed and ran in fear and desperation.

However, Clyde and Carl began to wonder who had said that. So then, Carl looked back toward Clifton and said, "Whoa, what the hell is that? Is that the one who said that? Is that guy real, or am I just seeing things? It looks like, uh, some neon-green dude that's bright like the sun?" Not believing what he was seeing, Carl looked away momentarily to rub his eyes and try to set himself straight.

But before he could take another look, Clyde rushed over to him and grabbed his arm, saying, "Come on! Never mind that right now! She's getting away! Let's get her!" They both refocused on the pretty young woman and started to pursue her again.

James Clifton, however, had different ideas for them. He said, "Oh shoot! I can't let them recapture her. I got to do something quick." While trying to see what he might do, James looked down and around in different directions and ended up looking at his two hands, which he was holding up in front of himself. "Hmm," said James, "I wonder if I ought to try to knock them down by firing lasers at them. In fact, could I possibly combine the power of more than one finger to constitute a stronger beam? Well, there's no better time to find out. Heck, I'll combine all five fingers on each hand and even use two hands, one for each of them."

Immediately, Clifton's anger at the two no-good slime balls strongly motivated him to prepare at once. That very instant, he placed a lot of tension on both of his hands as well as all ten fingers. In effect, his hands and fingers grew brighter as they charged themselves with radiant energy. Of course, in the meantime, Clifton had his mind set on the two rogues that he was targeting.

After a moment of charging up, James Clifton tried to stay focused. Then, finally, he released a big laser beam at each of the two gangsters. From each hand, laser beams from all five fingers had fused together to form a huge beam that was five times as thick and powerful as a beam from any one of his fingers.

Fortunately, the two troublemakers were both hit and knocked over forward. They landed on the ground facedown. This happened just when they were about to get out through the south entrance and had almost caught up to Kathryn Brown. Of course, this happened because James had been successful in nailing them.

Upon seeing his success, James Clifton went on to say, "Yes! Bull's-eye! I pegged 'em. Well, anyway, that wasn't so bad. I mean, I've always been worrying too much that something would not work. I mean, you know? I really haven't had to think too hard about anything I would set up as a target."

As soon as Clyde and Carl had fallen forward, they both looked around just a little bit to try to see who or what had made them fall. Carl was more anxious about how it had happened than was Clyde. For a moment, he took his mind off the one they were chasing to look further to see how he had fallen. He said, "Who did that to me? Some pinhead pushed me over. I ought to go knock his head off for this."

However, Clyde restrained him, saying, "That's nonsense, you idiot! We just tripped and fell, all right? Now come on! The girl's getting away; let's go!" So then of course, they began running after her again.

In the meantime, Kathryn had been running for her life. Of course, she was now out of Mikveh Israel Cemetery, running east along Spruce Street. She had made it across Eighth Street. During the past couple of minutes, in desperation, Kathryn had quickly dialed 911 on her cellular phone and stated that two guys were after her and where she was.

Clyde and Carl made it out of Mikveh Israel Cemetery and spotted her. "There she is!" cried Clyde. Determined to catch her, they ran after her along Spruce Street. Of course, they wanted to hurry up and catch her before she had a chance to talk to anybody; little did they know, it was a little too late for that.

All the while, James Clifton had been hovering sixty feet above Mikveh Cemetery. As soon as he had interfered with the culprits' pursuit of their victim, he had risen up above to look on and see that the helpless, innocent girl got away safely.

Kathryn had now made it to Sixth Street. Clyde and Carl had almost caught up to her. She ran across Sixth Street. But before Clyde and Carl had a chance to run across after her, a police car suddenly pulled up in front of them. At that, two cops jumped out, and pointing their guns at the two gangsters, they said, "Freeze!" So, on their first impulse, they stopped running although they were scared and surprised. Then, one of the policemen said to them, "Put your hands up! Keep them up!" Even though the two guys cooperated, they were also stepping back a step or two in view of perhaps turning and running. Before they had a chance, two more police officers came up behind them as if out of nowhere and had them put their hands down behind their backs to get handcuffed.

Also, as soon as Kathryn had heard the cops yelling commands at the two rogues, she stopped running. Was she ever so relieved to see the troublesome twosome get caught and arrested! At the same time, she was also grateful for whoever had helped her escape. She walked back to where the police were making the arrest.

"Are you all right?" one of them asked her.

"Yes, I am," she answered, "and fortunately someone helped me."

"Really? Who?" asked the officer.

"I don't know," said Kathryn. "I didn't have time to see. I had to get away."

But then, the handcuffed Carl said, "You know what? There was someone else involved. I only got one look at him though. He appeared to be lit up with bright neon-green light."

However, no one believed what they heard. "That's enough," said another officer. "All right now, both of you jerks get your butts in this car!" At that, they both got into the back of the police car.

James continued to remain afloat and watched from up above. He just wanted to hang around temporarily to make sure that Clyde and Carl would not get away and his help would not be needed anymore. But then, once Clyde and Carl were cuffed and put into the cops' car, Clifton just moved on to try to get on home.

Kathryn Brown also stopped to think about what she had just been through. She no doubt began to wonder about the one who had come to her aid. She said, "I really wish I knew who it was that helped me. I mean, he really showed that he cared by putting his own life at risk for me. I feel like I owe him for that. Of course, it's kind of a shame that I didn't get to stop and thank him. I was just in danger and had to hurry. But now, I only wish there was a way I could meet him and thank him." After that, she went on about her business.

James Clifton would have liked to meet her too. After all, anyone in his right mind would be happy to receive some form of appreciation or gratitude. But James really did not think that it was a good idea for her to get a good look at him because he did not know how to cope with the possible consequences. Of course, that was the possible result of her getting to know who he was and learning about his superpowers. Furthermore, it might become even more hectic if other people were to get to know too. Clifton was just a little frustrated that he felt the need to keep to himself.

It was now past 7:30 p.m. He refocused his attention on trying to get home. He walked through downtown Philadelphia until he came to the Walnut-Locust station of the Broad Street Line of the subway.

James went down into the station. When he got there, the last few people in line were boarding a subway train. Clifton tried to run over to the train to get on, but he was too late. The doors were shut, and the train was shoving off.

However, something moved James Clifton to do a strange thing. Even after the train took off, he just jumped down onto the railroad tracks and ran after it. He yelled, "Hey, wait! Come back here! I got to get home!" Why would he try to pull off a foolish move like that?

At the time, James was more eager to get home than he had been all evening. Other than that, a lot of exciting things had unexpectedly taken place that evening. Of course from that, James had a lot of mixed emotions, which may have confused him enough to make him run after the train. Otherwise, he might have started to think he could use his powers to somehow catch or stop the train. That too could have possibly confused him and moved him to lose his mind and run after the train. However, since all the happenings and mishaps of the evening were making him crazy, James knew he needed to get home to get some rest.

After a few minutes of running through the subway tunnel behind the train, James noticed more than before that the train was getting too far ahead of him for him to catch it. He was repeatedly glancing in different directions around himself to see that he was going down railroad tracks and that he was somewhere in the middle of a subway tunnel. James decided to slow down and stop running. At the same time, he was regaining his senses from all the excitement. He went on to say, "All right, what's going on? What am I doing here? Where am I? Now, before I do anything impulsive, I need to get ahold of myself. I mean, I've already had a couple of other mishaps today—with the truck and the Mercedes Benz—and now I just lost my mind and ran after this stupid subway train. Well, so far, I'm not getting myself anywhere. Let me think about this." So then, James started walking around in circles, looking down at the ground and trying to think of where to go or what to do.

But at last, James had only one idea after a few minutes of racking his brains for a solution. He said, "Oh well, I guess I'll just go on back to the station and wait for the next train. I know I'm in a hurry to get home, but I got to take my time and do it right." At that, he started walking back toward the previous subway station.

However, before James got very far, he saw a light shining at him that appeared to be getting constantly closer and brighter. He even heard the sound of a train getting closer to him. Eventually, he heard a train's horn blaring at him. He realized that he was facing an oncoming subway train. "Oh no!" he cried. "How did I overlook this possibility? What'll I do?" What in fact would he do? No human being could outrun a speeding train. Besides, even if he shot himself away or sent laser beams at it, he would be no match for the most powerful type of vehicle on land.

After a few seconds of considering possible defenses, Clifton only knew of one other way to protect himself, and that was to put up a force field. So he quickly tightened his hands to sketch and create a force field. It was completed in the nick of time. Less than a second later, James was pasted against the train's windshield with only the outermost layer of the force field between them.

The operator of the train was scared by the sudden appearance of the bright neon-green James Clifton. "Oh my God!" he yelled, taking his hands off the controls and covering his eyes momentarily. That made a few other people look at him wondering what the problem was. However, James used his hovering ability to push himself upward so that he and the train would be out of each other's way. He still got pushed quite a distance before getting out from in front of the train. Then, of course, the operator got back to controlling the train. He said, "Goodness! Who or what on Earth was that? Or was it some green phantasm? Of course, I wasn't trying to imagine anything. I was just trying to do my job."

Once the subway train was gone, Clifton descended back to the ground and took down the force field. With the train gone and out of the way, James focused his attention once again on getting home. This was mainly because he knew he needed to, for all the excitement of the evening was too much for him. It was driving him crazy, especially now, with the frightful experience with the subway train adding to the tension under which he was already operating. James went on to say, "What is the matter with me? First, a truck, then a car, and now a train? If I have just one more mishap,

I will become a demon-possessed psychopath." He stood there inhaling and exhaling heavily from the stress of it.

That was until he had at least one happy thought. "But, you know what?" he said. "At least it feels great that I saved the life of that pretty girl in the cemetery. I mean, because knowing I had the power to save her, I know I'd never forgive myself if she'd have gotten hurt or killed. I'd be even more upset than I am now. But, otherwise, maybe those unfortunate incidents happened because I was not paying attention. I mean, I'm just trying to get used to my new abilities, but I'm not thinking about anything else. However, I still think I've had enough for tonight, and I need to get home and take a rest from all this. I'll try out my new powers another night."

At least James Clifton was now feeling somewhat less tense. That was because he had a bit of pride in how he had managed to help Kathryn Brown a little earlier. But anyway, James was still trying to figure out what to do about getting home.

A couple of moments later, the subway train that had collided with him earlier pulled up and stopped at the next station. James heard the faint sound of it ahead of him in the distance. He said, "That must be the train stopping at its next stop. Maybe I'll go on over to it. Even if I don't catch this train, I'll wait for the next one." At that, James started running toward the station, which was at City Hall. But of course, while Clifton was on his way, the people were getting off at their stop.

In the meantime, a determined James Clifton kept running as hard as he could. Now, why would he not use his supernatural abilities to get there much faster? He had decided to forget about his powers for the night and did not think to do so. However, he kept going and would stop for nothing.

So then, once he was almost at the station, the last of the passengers disembarking were already off. The doors were being closed. When James finally caught up to the train, he was a little too late. For just a moment, he yelled, "Wait!" But he stopped running, for he saw that the train was already leaving. All he was going to do then was just wait for the next one to arrive.

However, something unexpected caught his eye. While he was waiting on the next train, he briefly took a look at all the different people who had just gotten off the previous train. To Clifton's surprise, one of the last few happened to be Amanda Taylor. She was with two of her friends, Erin and Michelle. "I don't believe it!" whispered an amazed James Clifton. "It's Amanda!"

It was indeed a nice surprise to see her too. Now of course, earlier that evening and first thing Saturday morning, merely imagining Amanda had somehow or another thrown James off and made him lose control, but at least this time, she was real. Was it not wonderful for James to see someone he seriously admired after a rough evening? Without a doubt, it absolutely was.

James began to go out to try to talk to her. However, before getting too far, he managed to get a look at himself. He noticed that he was still radiating bright neon green. He had to restrain himself, for he did not feel that he could let her see him like that. So he just backed up to hide in the tunnel.

Understandably, it was rather frustrating for James that he could not go out and talk to Amanda. It was all because of the need he felt to keep his powers a secret. Of course, that became most frustrating when he could not even share it with someone he really cared about and loved. But even as much as James was attracted to Amanda, he figured it was best to keep to himself for the time being. However, he was still determined to win her over somehow. "She will be mine," said Clifton. "Oh yes, somehow or another, I'm gonna get her."

James just kept on watching Amanda Taylor. During the time in which he had his eyes on her, Amanda and her two friends stood around and talked a little bit longer. But about ten minutes later, Amanda finally said, "Good night," to Erin and Michelle. Then, her friends left together while Amanda stayed around a little longer. She was trying to figure out what to do next.

In the meantime, James had kept on looking on from his hiding place. But now, he was under more tension than he had been over ten minutes before. This was because Amanda was by herself without anyone else around to see what was going on. This was an even better opportunity for Clifton to try to talk to her. However, he still did not feel that he could be seen and identified while being lit up with neon-green light. He did not dare try anything for the time being.

However, Amanda Taylor was not the only one at the subway station for very long. This was because a couple of moments later, two guys came downstairs from above, walking side by side. Both stood about five feet ten inches tall, and each weighed around 190 pounds. Each one of them wore black steel-toe boots, black jeans, and yellow T-shirts. Both T-shirts had fairly large black print on the front and back. The shirt worn by the one James saw on the left of his field of vision said: "Ant Killer" and also had the exact same thing printed across the back. The other one read: "Roach Killer." Likewise, he had that term printed on the back of his shirt as well. In addition to all their other clothing, they were both wearing yellow spandex pullover masks that covered their heads except for their eyes and mouths. The opening for each eye and mouth was four-sided and trimmed with black. On each mask, each eye opening was shaped like a rhombus and was slanted away from the other eye opening. Each mouth opening was an upside-down trapezoid.

When James first got a look at the two, he wondered who or what they were out of curiosity. When he looked further to see their masks, he asked himself, "Are they exterminators?"

But then, the mysterious pair started moving closer to Amanda, who did not see them coming. The one who was wearing the "Ant Killer" shirt pointed at Amanda, telling his partner, "Hey, man, check that out."

This made James Clifton more concerned. He asked, "What's the meaning of that? What do they want with her?"

Roach Killer called out to her and said, "Hey, baby, how ya doin', honey?"

At that, Amanda turned around to see who had said that. She was surprised and no doubt a bit frightened.

But next, Ant Killer said, "That's right; what do you say, toots?"

Amanda gradually became more and more afraid. Hesitantly, she asked them, "What do y'all want?"

"I'm so glad you asked," answered Roach Killer, who proceeded to pull out a foot-long Marine Corps fighting knife. He then pointed it at her midsection, saying, "Okay, sweetheart, hand over your purse."

Amanda was now stressed out and in fear for her life. So she slowly but surely handed the purse to Roach Killer, especially since Ant Killer had a knife pulled out as well.

Even after Amanda had given up her purse, both thugs kept her at knifepoint. They only proceeded to harass her further, and Ant Killer pointed his knife at her genital area, saying, "Let's see what you got under there."

In the meantime, Clifton did not like what he was seeing one bit. He said, "I've got to stop them. What do I do?" Then, he suddenly had an idea. "First of all," said Clifton, "I'll try this."

He started charging his left hand in preparation to fire a couple of laser beams. Then, before any further harm was done to Amanda Taylor, he fired two laser beams in succession. One beam hit the hand holding the knife of each thug. As a result, Ant Killer and Roach Killer both dropped their knives.

That temporarily distracted them from Amanda. Both guys started looking around to see what had hit them. "Hey," said Roach Killer, "what was that?"

"Yeah," said Ant Killer, "who knocked the knives out of our hands?"

Fortunately, this distraction gave Amanda a chance to try to escape. While they were looking around, she quickly broke away from Ant Killer's grasp. Then, rather desperately, she stomped hard on the instep of Roach Killer's right foot and got her purse back from him. "Ouch!" yelled Roach Killer.

While Amanda was retrieving her purse, she did so in a manner that threw Roach Killer down to the ground; he landed facedown. Then, with Roach Killer on the ground, and neither one holding a knife to her, Amanda started heading for the stairs to get out of the subway station on the west side of City Hall. However, she did not get very far.

Ant Killer finally caught up with her. He grabbed her left arm and then took out a gun. It was a nine-millimeter semiautomatic. He had Amanda at gunpoint. "Get back over here!" he told her.

Then, Ant Killer said to his partner, "It's all right; I got her. Get up."

Of course, Roach Killer got back up. He too took out his nine-millimeter. At that, Ant Killer pointed his gun at Amanda's head while holding her in front of him. Roach Killer began pointing his gun in every different direction in which he was looking all around, ready to shoot anyone who turned up. In the midst of it all, Amanda was more terrified than before.

"All right now," said Ant Killer. "Somebody in this subway just knocked the knives out of our hands and fouled up our scheme. You better show yourself before she gets it."

After looking all around for a moment, Roach Killer noticed a faint neon-green flash of light coming from the tunnel in which James Clifton was hiding. "Hey, man," he said to Ant Killer, "look! Check it out. You see that?"

"See what?" asked Ant Killer.

"In that tunnel over there," answered Roach Killer. "I can barely see a bit of neon-green light. Can you see it now?"

Ant Killer took a look for himself. He said, "I sure can. Someone or something is obviously doing that. The one making that light must've done it."

At that, Roach Killer aimed his pistol straight at the tunnel, ready to shoot the person once he came out.

"All right, you in the tunnel over there!" yelled Ant Killer. "You better get your ass over here before the girl gets it! You got five seconds."

That definitely put Clifton under stress. The situation had just become more dangerous. Those two were holding out guns instead of knives, and one of the guns was pointed in his direction. Yet, he only had a few seconds to do something without getting Amanda or himself killed. What would he do?

Fortunately, James immediately remembered what he had done earlier at Mikveh Israel Cemetery to save Kathryn Brown. He plotted a similar course to whiz around Amanda, Ant Killer, and Roach Killer. But this time, James planned to shoot up the stairs and out of the station at the end.

James set his course while charging himself up in preparation. Within two seconds, he unleashed himself. At that, he took the form of a shapeless projectile. He shot straight into Ant Killer. The blow knocked him ten feet away from Amanda and sent the handgun flying out of his hand, all before Ant Killer knew what was happening. From that point, he made a quick serpentine maneuver around Amanda and into Roach Killer. This sent him flying and made him lose his gun as well. Finally, of course, James zoomed up the steps and out of the station on its west side.

Amanda and the two ruffians received quite a surprise. Amanda was very relieved, especially after all the stress of having been at gunpoint.

However, Ant Killer and Roach Killer were both stunned from having just been catapulted by the technique that James had used on them.

In the meantime, James Clifton reappeared in his radiating human form just outside the station. He decided to run around the nearest corner and hide somewhere so that no one would have a chance to see him or identify him. James scurried west and turned left onto Fifteenth Street. Then, he went into an alley between the first two buildings to his left.

Down in the subway station, Ant Killer and Roach Killer were beginning to regain their senses. Amanda knew she had to do something to avoid being attacked by them again. So first, she ran over to Ant Killer. As he was trying to push himself up to a kneeling position, Amanda gave him a stomp on the back of his head that shocked and dazed him. Next, she aimed a kick and a stomp at his neck and the base of his head, snapping his neck and knocking him unconscious.

Immediately afterward, Amanda darted over to Roach Killer, who was back on his feet and about to stand straight up. But before he could fully straighten himself, a desperate and determined Amanda Taylor delivered a side kick to his midsection that laid him flat on his back. Then, she stomped him in the genital area, which definitely had to hurt. While Roach Killer was stunned by that, Amanda stomped on the middle of his face and dazed him even further. Finally, one well-placed kick along the right side of Roach Killer's jawbone snapped his neck and rendered him unconscious as well. After that, she rested for a moment and then repeatedly inhaled and exhaled out of relief.

In the meantime, James Clifton was still hiding between the two buildings. He was trying to figure out what to do next. "All right," said Clifton, "what am I gonna do now? I'm not quite certain where to go or what to do, but first of all, I'd like to go check and see if Amanda's okay. I mean, I regret that I had to leave her to come out here, but I just didn't want to risk being identified." James resorted to silence and tried to think things over.

After a couple of minutes, James only had one thought. He said, "I really think I ought to go check on Amanda. I mean, after all, I had something to do with what just happened, and I sincerely do care about her. So I should at least do a little something to show I care."

Clifton then started to walk back to the subway station. But just before getting out of the alley and back into the open, he managed to get a glimpse of himself. He noticed that he was still lit up with neon-green light. "Ah shoot!" James muttered. "I've got to do something about this. I can't be seen like this. Of course, I don't know why I didn't think about that all night, but now, let me see what I can do."

James then started to look himself over to see how he might turn off his neon-green radiation. After looking all over himself, he only had one idea. "Let me try something here," he said. Next, James began increasing tension in every part of his body, from his feet to his crown. In addition, the main feelings on which he concentrated were anger and hate. He held his breath and strained himself further and further with blood rushing to his head. At the same time, he was getting progressively dizzier every second. But the neon-green light he was radiating kept growing brighter and more intense. Fortunately, that made him invincible to any other person or thing that might have tried to affect him, even though it was not good for his brain or circulatory system for him to hold himself like that.

Before too long, James Clifton had been straining so long and hard that he was hallucinating and feeling wooziness in his digestive system. James then knew that he needed to stop straining so that he would not pass out. So he released all the pressure and tension that he had built up, and the brightness of the neon-green light went back down to how it had previously been. James was breathing heavily while trying to regain his senses.

Finally, he felt sane again. "All right," he began. "I think I did the wrong thing. I probably shouldn't have focused on hateful thoughts that make me mad. I was only trying to turn off my radiation. But I got to admit; it was amazing how that really charged me up. I bet no one or nothing could get to me then. At least I discovered something else I can do too. But unfortunately, it was giving me severe dizziness as well as nausea. So I better not do that too much, but only when I have no other choice."

James stopped thinking about that and said, "Okay now, where was I?" Within a matter of seconds, he said, "Oh yes, I was trying to stop radiating, wasn't I?" So then, taking another look at himself, Clifton said, "Well, I still don't quite see what to do here." Then at that, he stopped examining himself and just looked around in different directions feeling puzzled. Next, he tightened up his two fists and said, "Well, like I said, I don't know what to do. I just know I want to stop radiating!" As he finished saying that, he threw both of his fists straight down both of his sides. Then immediately, the neon-green light that he was shining went away. James looked like a normal person again.

Shortly afterward, he managed to catch a glimpse of his hands and forearms and noticed that they were his normal skin color once again. He said, "What do you know? I—Hey, it stopped! Huh, I did it!" So then, James looked himself over to see that his jeans, boots, and T-shirt were all their normal color once more. At once, he said, "Well, that wasn't so bad. Heck, I feel so stupid. I mean, how could I forget? The pyxorium is combined with my nervous system. All I had to do was think about it like I ended up doing just now and all those other times."

But then, he said, "Oh well, no time for that now. I got to go make sure Amanda's all right." At once, he started running back toward the subway station.

In the meantime, once Amanda had knocked out the two thugs, she had gotten her cell phone out of her purse and called the police. She had gone above ground to wait for them, and she was there now.

Soon, James Clifton finally made his way back to where Amanda was waiting. Even after a long, rough, and hectic night, James forgot about how tiring the evening had been for him. That was because he was so happy that he could finally talk to Amanda. Rather excited, he yelled out, "Amanda!"

At that, she looked back wonderingly, saying, "What was that?" But then, she noticed that it was the man who had spoken to her after work on Friday. Although not too thrilled, she said, "Oh, hello."

"Well, hi, Amanda," replied James. "Do you remember me?"

Amanda sighed and said, "Yeah, I remember. You're uh…"

"I'm James, James Clifton," he reminded her.

Doubtfully, she said, "Well, okay, James. So what are you doing?"

"Well," he answered. "I just saw something neon-green shooting by, and I just came over here because I was wondering what just happened. I mean, did you see it?"

Getting a little frustrated, Amanda said, "Look, James, I don't know who or what that was, but someone just did something wonderful and amazing and helped me. That's a lot more than I can say for you. I don't know who did it or how that bright-green flash of light passed through and saved me, but I am going to find out. Right now, I'm a lot more interested in that than I am in you."

At that, James was rendered speechless for a moment, wondering what to say next. Of course, he himself had actually done that. However, he was not sure he could tell Amanda that, because he did not want to risk bringing too much controversy or chaos upon himself. So all James finally said was, "Well, that's understandable. I think it's great that he helped you like that. I just hope you're okay. Are you okay, Amanda?"

Although rolling her eyes and looking away from him, she answered, "I'm fine. Thank you."

At that, James just crossed Fifteenth Street and then continued looking on while Amanda waited for the police. A few minutes later, three police cars pulled up where she was standing outside the subway station. Consequently, six police officers got out and went over to Amanda. One of them asked, "Are you the one who reported the attack in the subway?"

"Yes, I am," answered Amanda. "They both came at me with knives and then guns, and when I escaped, I left them both unconscious. They might still be down there. That's where I saw them last." At that, four of the policemen went on down into the station to find them and arrest them.

Then, one of the two who stayed above ground said to Amanda, "So, you're Amanda Taylor? I'm Lieutenant Wilson, and this is Sergeant Kirk." Then, he shook hands with Amanda. "So, Amanda," he continued, "what happened down there?"

"Well," began Amanda, "I had just gotten off the subway train, and I hung around a little longer. Then, these two guys came up and pulled out their knives. One of them took my purse, and the other pointed his knife at my genitals. Then, somebody knocked the knives out of their hands, and I tried to break loose and run."

"Hold it," said Lieutenant Wilson. "Was there someone else involved too?"

"Yes," she answered, "but I don't know who."

"Well, then what happened?" asked the lieutenant.

"Well," said Amanda. "After I broke free, got my purse back, and started running, one of them grabbed me, and they both pulled their guns on me. But then, somebody or something knocked them away from me, and then I knocked them both out and got out of the subway."

"But you don't know who this other somebody was?" asked the confused lieutenant.

"I couldn't get a good look at him," replied Amanda.

"So, I guess you didn't get a name, huh?" asked Sergeant Kirk. "Do you remember anything about him at all?"

"Well," answered Amanda. "I think at one point, either he or something he had was shining neon-green light. Then, I thought I noticed some neon-green flash of light whiz through when I got free from them, but it was so fast I almost couldn't see it."

"Okay," said Lieutenant Wilson. "Are you sure that what you've told me is true to the best of your knowledge?"

"Honest," said Amanda. "I'm positive."

"All right then," said the lieutenant. "We'll have to investigate further."

The other four officers had gone down the steps to apprehend the two gangsters. Before too long, they had found both Ant Killer and Roach Killer lying unconscious. One of the officers went on to say, "Why don't two of us try to see if we can find any other evidence?"

"Good idea," said another one. At that, two of the policemen put handcuffs on the two bad guys. The other two searched the station thoroughly and eventually found the guns and knives. Then, of course, Ant Killer and Roach Killer were revived and escorted upstairs, where Amanda was talking with Lieutenant Wilson and Sergeant Kirk.

"Look," said Roach Killer. "There was someone else involved in this too. He was neon green."

"All right," said the officer guiding him. "That's enough for now. Get in this car. Come on, both of you." So then, they were put in the back of one of the cars.

After that, Lieutenant Wilson got contact information from Amanda. Then, he said, "We'll be in touch if we need anything from you. Why don't you go on home for tonight?"

Soon afterward, Amanda got ahold of the very next taxicab that she could. Then, she rode it on home.

But right after that, Lieutenant Wilson and Sergeant Kirk talked for a few minutes. Lieutenant Wilson said, "You know something, Sergeant? I think Amanda and one of those thugs said something about a guy or a thing that was lit up neon green. If I remember right, I thought I heard a couple other rumors about someone radiating neon-green light. I mean, there was a lady in a Mercedes Benz. Also, one of those gangsters who attempted a rape in Mikveh Israel Cemetery said something like that. Before all that, I overheard a trucker over my CB who saw a neon-green person or thing, or a green phantasm."

Then, Sergeant Kirk spoke up and said, "You know something else? You just gave me a reminder. I thought I overheard someone talking about a subway train operator who wondered if he saw some green phantasm."

"Well," said the rather curious Lieutenant Wilson. "As much as each and every one of these claims is rather hard to believe, I find it even harder to believe that five people or more all saw some sort of green phantasm or whatever it was and all in the same night. That's even less believable."

"Well," said Sergeant Kirk. "All I can say is, if we've already heard that many rumors, and on the same night like you said, I think maybe there is someone doing that. I don't know who it is or how he's doing it, but I would like to find out about the person or the special effects he created. I'd even like both if possible."

"So would I," added the lieutenant. "I say we notify the *Philosophy of Philadelphia* at once." At that, they left the scene.

However, James Clifton had been watching and listening the whole time. He was a bit worried by what he had overheard from both the lieutenant and the sergeant. He went on to say, "Well, I hope this is a good idea. I mean, I know I made a few mistakes, but I'm really glad I was there for those two ladies in distress. I mean, I sure hate to think about how it would've ended up for them if it weren't for me. I mean, you know? What if I hadn't been there for them? That's terrible to think about, isn't it?"

After thinking a little further, with pity on Kathryn Brown and especially Amanda Taylor, James had yet another thought. He said, "But I got to admit, it will definitely be a responsibility to be a hero and prevent crime and destruction. I know I had those unfortunate mishaps earlier, but hopefully, I can learn from them to better myself. I mean, you know, I'd like to do some more good deeds to cancel them out. Maybe then, it won't be so bad. But then, of course, even as much as no one could identify me, I can't keep running from my problems. I don't want to put myself in too much trouble. But one good thing about taking on responsibility is that you learn from it."

Then, James walked back across Fifteenth Street to where the taxi had picked up Amanda. He said, "Well, anyway, this time, I really think I'd better call it a night. I guess I'll just wait for the next cab that passes. I mean heck, that's especially since I don't feel the need to run my behind off like I've been doing all evening." So Clifton just patiently waited for a cab.

But after about ten minutes of waiting, he grew impatient. He began griping, saying, "I don't believe this. I mean, when's the next one coming, huh? I guess I'll start walking, sheesh!"

But just as James started walking east along John F. Kennedy Boulevard, he heard a horn blaring. He turned around and saw that it was a taxi. "Oh," he said rather happily, "here we go." Then immediately, he signaled the cab, saying, "Hey! Hey!" Consequently, the driver stopped for him. Clifton took it back to his house in the Mayfair subdivision.

It was close to 8:40 p.m. Clifton was just getting home from an exciting, adventurous, and unplanned evening in Philadelphia. He went on inside. Next, he said, "Man, I'm glad I'm finally home. I can find some real peace and quiet now after all the crazy excitement. It's a good thing I'm home too. Now, I can start preparing to be off to bed so I can get to work in the morning. But first, I'll have a little something to eat." James made himself some baked chicken and potato soup, which he fed himself for supper.

After that, James took a shower. Then, he got himself prepared to hit the sack. However, he wanted to take a few more minutes to think about how he might cope with any possible pressures of having his newly acquired supernatural capabilities. He began to say to himself, "Man, I got to tell you, this is definitely the most unforgettable weekend of my life. I mean, there are things I can say about it that I can't say about any other weekend I've ever had. On top of that, this weekend seemed to be a real turning point in my life. That's because before I left to go to the mountains with Eric and Scott, I was like an ordinary, average bachelor. But now, I don't feel normal, not at all. No day at work or anywhere is ever going to feel the same again. Everybody's gonna be wanting to know who that radiant neon-green guy is. I'm gonna have a guilty feeling about not being able to tell them."

Then, he paused and remained silent momentarily, after which he continued by saying, "Heck, to make matters worse, I won't even be able to tell Eric or Scott, two great guys that I've known and trusted for a long time, and maybe not Amanda either. Of course, she's already more interested in him than me. Sharing the secret might be an easy way to win her over, but I still don't know if I can. In addition to everything I've already said, what'll I do if I make some mistakes like the ones I made this evening? That's a lot to think about. Well, I guess until I figure out what I ought to do, I'll just keep to myself. For right now, since it's bedtime, I'll worry more about it later."

Then, for a few more moments, James kept quiet. But soon, he began to smile while thinking about the positive aspects of having a superpower. "But you know," he said, "I got to admit, it felt great when I saved the lives of both Amanda and that young girl in Mikveh Israel Cemetery. If I hadn't prevented them from getting hurt or killed, I'd feel even worse than I do now, you know? Other than that, I'd feel proud of myself if I prevented any sort of crime. I may not be able to go back on where I messed up this evening, but hopefully now, I can make up for that in the future. Maybe I just need to be more careful next time around."

After pausing for a minute, he said, "And just another thing too; right now, Amanda may be interested in that superhero rather than myself. But maybe I'll figure something out about how to get her to love me. Anyway, I think that's enough said for now. Why don't I sleep on it?" At that, James Clifton went off to bed for the night.

It was now the end of the night, as well as the weekend for James Clifton. Who would have expected so much excitement and adventure to rise up so suddenly, especially when he was trying to settle in from a camping trip? Perhaps no one would, not even James. Of course, he had never had such an intense evening as this one, or another weekend like the one he had just had.

CHAPTER FOUR

Enter the Green Phantasm

It was 6:30 a.m. on Monday morning. James Clifton was waking up to the sound of his digital alarm clock like just about everyone else. Amazingly, even after everything he had gone through the previous evening, this Monday morning was starting out much like any other. This was because at the moment, he was mainly concerned about getting ready and going to work. Furthermore, he was going to worry more later about the responsibility of having a superpower.

Anyway, James Clifton proceeded to get his work clothes on and have breakfast like he always did every morning before work. Then, he made sure his briefcase had what it needed for work. James finally had everything ready for another day as the head engineer at Ace Nuclear Supply.

After all that, he just got into his Suburban and started on his way to his job. His drive to work was also much like it was every morning. That was because for the time being, James was keeping his mind off his brand-new abilities and all the occurrences that had so far been associated with them.

Finally, he pulled up into the parking lot of Ace Nuclear Supply and parked his truck. Next, he walked through the front door as usual. He even greeted the receptionist, Jenna Daniels, on the way to his office like he always did.

"Good morning, James," said Jenna.

"Good morning, Jenna," James replied. After that, he went on to his office. Once there, he laid out the plans for a spacecraft engine that the company was about to put together for NASA on his desk. He was now waiting for his workers to report to him so he could tell them all what he wanted them to work on.

Before long, the first guy, Walter Smith, walked into his office. "Good morning, James," he said.

"Good morning, Walt," said Clifton.

"Have a nice weekend?" asked Walter.

"Oh, did I ever! I'll never forget it; that's for sure," answered Clifton. "How about you?"

"Not bad," said Walter. "I took the family out of town. We had a great time at the Gettysburg National Military Park."

"Sounds great," said James, who was not overly impressed, because of all the adventure he had just experienced. He would no doubt never forget it, as he had just told Walter.

But then, Walter pulled out a copy of a newspaper called the *Philosophy of Philadelphia* that he had just picked up that morning. He unfolded it and put it in front of him because he was about to show something to James. "Anyway, James," began Walter, "I just got a paper this morning, and something on the front page really caught my attention. Can I share it with you for a moment?"

"Well, okay," said James. "Whatcha got?"

"Well," Walter said, "I noticed this article here. It's titled: 'Bright Neon-Green Individual Reported.' "

At that, Clifton gasped with surprise. He knew that it was about him.

"What's the matter?" asked Walter.

"Oh, nothing," answered Clifton. "I've just never imagined before that anyone could be neon green."

"Well, neither have I," Walter told him. "I was just wondering why you were all jumpy. You wouldn't know who this was by any chance, would you?"

At that, James hesitated for a few seconds but tried to calm himself at the same time. "Well, uh," he began, "I, uh, can't really say that I do." Now of course, James was not lying about not being able to say that he knew but not because he did not actually know. Instead, it was because he felt the need to keep it to himself. However, Walter Smith did not know that part of it all.

"Oh well," Walter said, "but anyway, it goes on to tell me about this guy, that he was supposedly the same one who helped save a couple of young ladies in trouble, but a few other times, he created a disturbance."

Upon hearing that, James turned and stepped away for a moment. He put his hands in his pants pockets, looked down toward the floor, and started doing a little heavy breathing out of nervousness. He whispered to himself, "Oh my God, what have I done?" He had wanted to try to start out the day and get through it like normal without even worrying about the tension of having a superpower. He became worried when Walter brought that article to his attention.

"James?" said Walter. "What's wrong? Are you all right?"

However, though Clifton was feeling a bit nervous, he was still determined to get through the day like usual. So he decided to end the discussion with Walter. "Walter," James said kindly, "we'll have to talk about this later. Right now, let me show you what we're working on and what I need you to do."

"All right, all right, all right, never mind," said Walter.

"Now look," began James. "Here's the engine that we're building for NASA. This is what it's going to look like. Let me show you what I need you to work on. You see this part right here?"

As Clifton was showing Walter his assigned part of the project, he answered, "Uh, yes."

"All right then," said James, "let's get you started. Here's some drafts of all the different views of it, and here's the other instructions and requirements you will need. Get together with some of our technicians, and get right on it."

"Yes, sir," replied Walter, who then left James Clifton's office with all the papers that he had given him.

After that, James was waiting for the next guy to report to him. He said, "I'll tell you this right now. If the next guy or anyone after him wants to talk about that article in the paper, or even show it to me, I'm not even gonna talk about it. First of all, we've all got work to do. Second, I'd rather worry later regarding my supernatural ability as far as what I've already done and what I'm gonna do now. So I'd rather just get my work done for the day and be pressured about all that later."

Within two minutes after giving Walter his assignment, another associate of his named Jesse Williams reported to him in his office. He said, "Good morning, James. How's it going?"

"Good morning, Jess," he responded.

"Well, James," Jesse began, "now that my weekend's over, I'm ready to get back to work. What we got going on?"

"I'm glad to hear that," James said happily. "Come right this way, and I'll show you."

"But… but, James?" said Jesse.

"Yes, Jesse," replied James.

"Can I talk to you about something for a minute?" asked Jesse.

"Okay," Clifton said doubtfully, rolling his eyes. "What is it?"

"Well," said Jessie, "I was reading the paper this morning, and I saw something on the front page about this guy who—"

"Jesse, Jesse," interrupted James, "you'll have to tell me later. I'm sorry, but right now, I'm trying to focus on this big project we have going on, okay?"

"That's fine," said Jesse.

"Okay then," said James, "let me give you what you need for your part in this, okay?"

After that, James gave Jesse Williams the necessary paperwork to get started on his part of the spacecraft engine. From that point forward, James would not talk about the occurrences from the night before to anyone. Instead, he got all of his associates started on their parts of the project as well. Of course, that was because James remained determined to keep focused on his work and deal with his worries later. So, from then until noon, James just stuck to his job as chief engineer, doing whatever he had to concerning the NASA project.

Later, around noon, it was time for James to take an hour for lunch. He just went to the first place he could find. While he was there, he made a quick order for a burger, fries, and cola and took it back to his office to eat.

While James Clifton was still on his lunch break, he used his cell phone to call Eric Thomas. Fortunately, Eric happened to be at lunch too.

Eric answered. "Hello?" he said upon accepting the call.

"Hey, Eric," James said to him, "it's James."

"Oh, what's up, James?" asked Eric. "What's going on?"

"Not too much," replied James. "Is everything all right? I mean, how's it feel being back to work after the trip this past weekend?"

"Well," said Eric, "mainly just another Monday, but I'll never forget our trip to the mountains. In fact, I think I owe some thanks to you, you know? I mean, heck, you took us there in your truck, and you led me to those pieces of quartz that I found. I can't thank you enough. But anyway, it's good to hear from you. What's going on with you?"

"Well, Eric," James said, "I guess not too too much out of the ordinary. But, um, this week, my company's building a spaceship engine for NASA. Of course, as chief engineer, I've already hit it off to a nice start, and I've gotten everyone else started on it. Anything unusual going on over there?"

"Uh, no big surprises here either," Eric answered him. "We got a decent project going too. We got to install all the wiring and electric devices in a new building on Girard Avenue, but I think I've gotten my workers going as well."

"Not bad, not bad," James said, "but anyway, Eric, have you by any chance talked with Scott?"

"Well, James," replied Eric, "I, uh, can't say that I have, not since you brought us back to my house last night."

"Well, that's cool," said James. "I'll call him later. But anyway Eric, I was just kind of wondering if, uh, you and Scott are still coming Wednesday night, you know, to my company's fiftieth anniversary celebration at the Fairmaine Hotel."

"I sure am," said Eric. "Thanks for reminding me."

"No problem," replied James.

"But anyway, James," said Eric, "while I got you on the line, do you mind if I ask you about something else for a minute?"

"Well, uh, okay, sure, Eric," James answered somewhat hesitantly. "What do you want to ask me?"

"Well, James," Eric began, "I was reading the paper this morning, and I couldn't help notice something unusual on the front page. If I'm understanding correctly, it's about this guy that was lit up neon green. He, like, disturbed a few people who thought they saw him, but at least he supposedly saved a couple of young ladies from some troublemakers. Also, in, like, the latter part of the article, it mentioned something about a couple of similar rumors. It's like this truck driver and subway operator both wondered what it was they saw, or if it was some green phantasm. Well, I personally wouldn't think it likely that four, five, or however many people it was who saw the same green phantasm made it up. That just so happens to be a question that the article goes on to raise. That is, what are the chances that they were all just imagining the same green phantasm? And another thing too, James, by any possible chance, would you happen to know who this guy is?"

It was true that James was very unwilling to discuss any of this with anyone. However, he felt somewhat different when talking with Eric. This was because Eric Thomas was someone he knew well and trusted. Also, James felt more comfortable talking to him about personal matters than nearly anyone else. So this was what Clifton did now. He very kindly said to Eric, "Well, Eric, I can understand why you brought this to my attention. I mean, after all, several of my associates came and told me about the same thing. But anyway, one thing I got to tell you is I can't say that I do know. I'm sorry, Eric."

"Oh well, that's cool," Eric said. "It's just that among the three of us—that is, you, myself, and Scott—you're the most accomplished and most intelligent. Something just told me to ask you."

"Well, in that case," said James, "thanks, Eric."

"Sure, anytime," said Eric.

"Well, anyway," James said, "it was good talking to you. I guess I'd better be getting back to work. Perhaps I should let you go so you can do the same thing."

"All right then, James," Eric replied. "I sure appreciate you calling."

"That's no problem at all, Eric," said James. "If I, uh, get a chance, maybe I'll, um, talk to you again tonight or tomorrow. But, anyway, at least you're still coming Wednesday night, right?"

"I sure am," Eric answered him. "If I don't hear from you or talk to you before then, I guess I'll see you then, okay?"

"That sounds good," replied James.

"All right, James," said Eric. "I'll talk to you later."

"Okay Eric," said James. "Bye."

"Bye," Eric said in return. After that, of course, they both hung up.

It was getting near 1:00. James Clifton decided to go on back to work. After returning to work from lunch, he resumed what he had been working on concerning the engine that the company was making. He made sure that the employees working under him got restarted on their parts of the project as well. From that point on, James and everyone else concentrated on their work until the end of the day.

Later on, at 5:00 in the evening, James situated his computers, papers, and everything else he was using on the project so that he could pick up where he'd left off the very next morning. Other than that, he made sure that all his workers had come to a good stopping point for the day. After that, he left work.

However, James was in no major hurry to get home. So he just decided to cruise toward downtown Philadelphia, kick back, and have a cappuccino while reading a newspaper. He stopped at a newsstand on Broad Street and bought himself a copy of the *Philosophy of Philadelphia*. Of course, he bought himself that particular newspaper because he wanted to see what was written about him on the front page. Regardless, he just placed it on the front passenger seat of his truck and said, "I can't wait to see what it says about me, especially now that my work's done for the day." After that, he continued driving through the downtown area.

Before too long, however, James came upon someone who definitely got his undivided attention. This happened while he was heading south on Broad Street. It was none other than Amanda Taylor. She was walking in front of a nail salon out of which she had just emerged. She had just gotten a manicure, which included the polishing of her fingernails.

Upon spotting Amanda, James pulled over to the first parking space he could find. Of course, immediately afterward, he ran to catch up with her. Upon reaching Amanda, he called out, "Amanda!"

At that, she turned around to see who had called her name. Fortunately, she was in a better mood than she had been the night before after being threatened by those two creeps. Upon seeing James Clifton, she said in a somewhat pleasant tone of voice, "Well, hi, James."

"Hello, Amanda," replied James. "How ya' feeling this afternoon? Is everything okay?"

"It sure is," she answered. "How about you?"

"So far, so good," answered James. "Of course, it was another day at work. But other than that, just now, I saw you walking around out here. So I just wanted you to know that I was thinking about you. That's because I feel sorry about what you went through last night, and I was hoping you were all right after all that."

Then, starting to smile, Amanda said, "Well, thank you, James."

"Oh, no problem," James told her, "but, um, anyway, I don't know if I should bring this up or not, but I kind of wanted to let you know that, um, the guy who came to your aid in the subway… you see, he came around the corner to where I was. As soon as he got there, he told me all about what happened with you. When he did, I felt compelled to come and make sure that you weren't hurt, and everything was all right. But if I upset you or caused you any sort of displeasure, I sincerely apologize. I'm sorry, Amanda. I only came along because I truly care, and I was just really, really worried about you. But, like I said, if I upset you or anything, I'm really sorry."

"Well," said Amanda, "I guess it's okay, James. I'll admit it. That was sweet of you to worry about me, and I'm sorry if I didn't seem too appreciative."

"That's all right," said James. "You don't have to apologize. I mean, it's understandable. You were going through a lot at the time; I understand."

"All right," said Amanda, "well, in that case, thank you for understanding."

"Certainly, no problem," James replied, "but, um, anyway, seeing that you're in a better mood right now, there was something else I thought you might be interested in knowing."

"Really? What's that?" asked Amanda.

"Well," said James, "I wasn't a hundred percent sure, but I thought perhaps you'd like to know more about the guy who saved you. I could probably tell you anything you'd like to know about him. He's a new friend I just made. We seem to be really close, perhaps even closer than you think."

"Oh, really!" exclaimed a rather amazed Amanda Taylor.

"Well, yeah," James Clifton responded. But then, he said, "Oh, oh, um, another thing too, Amanda, did you get to check out the paper today?"

"Well, you know," Amanda said while thinking about it momentarily, "I think I did. Are you possibly referring to what was on the front page about that neon-green guy who was reported?"

James answered, "I think that's exactly what I'm trying to get at."

"Yeah," said Amanda, "and I think I might have read in that article that he was thought to be the same one who saved a couple of young ladies in distress. I can't help wondering if I'm one of them."

"You know," James said, "I was thinking along the same line. But anyway, Amanda, I realize how much this guy means to you—you know, the one who saved you last night? I mean, I realize that he risked his life for you, and you feel that you owe him for that, right?"

"Right," answered Amanda.

James then continued, "So, what I'm trying to say is this. I know I just told you a few moments ago that he's a new friend of mine. But you see, I haven't told anyone else a single thing about him. So… Amanda?"

"Yes?" she replied.

"How would you like to be the first to get to know all about him?" asked Clifton.

"Would I ever!" answered a somewhat excited Amanda. "You'd do that for me?"

"I sure would," he answered, happy with her response.

"I don't know what to say," Amanda said.

"Well, I'll tell you what," James began, "I've got a little free time right now. Of course, I hope you do too. Here's what we'll do. What do you say we ride over to the coffee shop just over on Vine Street and have a cappuccino? I'll tell you all about this new guy. I'll tell you everything."

"Sure," responded Amanda happily. "I don't see why not. I'd love to."

"Well then," said James, "it'll be my treat. This one's on me. Come on. I'll take us."

So, James Clifton and Amanda Taylor started walking toward his Suburban. But about seven seconds into it, Amanda stopped, grabbed James's arm, and stopped him too, saying, "Excuse me, um, James."

"Um, yes, Amanda?" James addressed her.

At that, she said to him, "Listen, James, there's something I feel I ought to tell you."

Upon hearing those words, James became a little worried. When Amanda said that she had something she felt she ought to tell him, James began to think that it might be something not so good. Did she already have a boyfriend? Did any major problems exist within the family? Was she trying to let James know that she really did not like him? Or was it something else that James would not like to hear? Amanda was about to lay whatever she needed to say on the line for him. So Clifton wonderingly and somewhat disappointedly said to her, "Okay, Amanda, what is it you need to tell me?"

Amanda began developing a big smile just before she started to answer. Then, she said, "You know, James, there's one thing I've got to admit; you're kind of cute."

Upon hearing that, James was happily surprised and amazed. He could not believe his ears. He even thought to himself, *did she really say that? If so, I hope it's not just a dream this time.*

But James just continued standing there silently for the time being to give Amanda a chance to say anything else that she wanted to say. She said, "And another thing too, James, I love those eyes. They're pretty."

Consequently, James began gasping in further amazement. He exclaimed, "Why, Amanda! I… uh You really mean that?"

"Come on now," said Amanda, "of course I do, James. You don't think your eyes are pretty? They're beautiful."

"Well, thank you, Amanda," James replied, a bit calmer. He started heading for his truck again.

But before he had even taken two steps, Amanda stopped him once more and said, "Oh, James? One more thing."

"Yes, Amanda?"

"Thank you for last night."

"Well, you're welcome," James replied. "I may not be a hundred percent sure what you mean, but you're more than welcome."

"Well," Amanda began saying, "I never really thought too much about it all until now. You know, it's like you said a few minutes ago, I was going through a lot at the time, and I know I didn't show that I was grateful. But when I really think about it, I am, you know, grateful. Other than that, I do believe that if I had been in your place, I'd have done the same thing. At least now I can see better how much you really did and still do care. And right now, I can't believe you're about to get me a cappuccino. I just never knew like I do now how nice you're being to me… Oh, and James?"

"Yes, Amanda?"

"I just want to tell you one more time: thank you so much for everything."

"Oh, anytime," said James, "and believe me, I know now that you appreciate me. You're much more than welcome." Right after James finished saying that, Amanda and he looked into each other's eyes and smiled at each other for a moment. After that, he said, "So, you ready to go have a cappuccino?"

"Let's go."

"Most certainly," James told her, "I'll escort you across the street." As he finished saying that, he positioned his left arm so that she could grab hold of it. Consequently, Amanda hooked her arm through it, and they walked across to his truck. Once there, James opened the passenger-side front door for her. Amanda got in. James closed the door for her and walked around to the driver's side. He got in, started his truck, and began driving toward the coffee shop.

On the way to the coffee shop, they started talking a little bit. At the start of it, James said, "So, Amanda, where did you say you were you from originally?"

"I'm from Camden, New Jersey."

"Oh, really? That's right; I think you did say that."

"Yes, how about you?"

"Actually, this is where I was born and raised."

"Your parents live around here too?"

"Yes, they're in the same subdivision as me, but I moved out shortly after I got my PhD."

"PhD? Whatcha got a PhD in?"

James went on to answer, "Like I was saying Friday, it's in nuclear engineering. I finished achieving it about two years ago at age twenty-three. Then, I got on with Ace Nuclear Supply at an entry-level position. Then, within the last couple of years, I worked up to being the chief engineer."

"That's terrific, and you know, I think you did tell me that."

"Well, thank you. So, Amanda, how did you end up out here from Camden, New Jersey?"

"Well, after I graduated high school, I had to come over here to go to the University of Pennsylvania and get my accounting degree. That's what moved me here to start with. Then, once I graduated in accounting, I landed a job at Stanley Financial, where I started my training to become a loan officer. But now, I've been there almost five years, and it's still going great."

"Great job, Amanda," James said. "You did something really terrific and amazing yourself."

"Thank you, James."

"So, do your parents still live back in Camden?"

"Yeah, they still do."

Then, he asked, "So, do you sometimes visit them?"

"Yes, I drive over there about every three or four months. What about you?"

"Well," James said, "I hope you won't be ashamed of me, because perhaps it's not as often as it should be. But it's like every other weekend. I mean, anyway, a lot of that's because I can get so busy that I don't remember to do it."

"That's understandable."

"Well, yes, of course, I guess it is. After all, we both probably got other people and other things in life too."

"Exactly."

"You know, that reminds me… when I saw you last night, you hadn't been with any friends, had you?"

"Actually, I had been. Their names are Erin and Michelle."

"That's mighty fine," James said. "There's nothing wrong with that. In fact, over the weekend, I went to the Alleghany Mountains on the camping trip that I told you I was gonna go on. It was with two of my friends whose names are Eric and Scott. We left for it Friday evening, stayed two nights, and got back yesterday."

"Whoa, cool!" said Amanda. "So, you like hiking and camping, huh?"

"Well, yeah."

"Did y'all have fun? See or find anything interesting?"

"Well," James began, "to say the least… I mean, it's like, well, we all gathered up a few quartz crystals that I found in a cave. Other than that, Scott found a real fine sample of limestone. There's only one other possibility. I may have even witnessed a meteorite landing. I'm not a hundred percent sure. It was really, really late."

"That sounds like an exciting camping trip!" exclaimed Amanda.

"Well," James said, "at least I'll never forget it, you know?"

"I'll bet you won't," Amanda assured him. "I wouldn't forget an adventure like that, especially with the striking of a meteorite."

"But, Amanda, I'm not a hundred percent sure I really saw it. I mean, it's like I said, it was really late, you know? I mean, who knows? I might've been hallucinating for all I know."

Then, Amanda asked, "Do you really think you hallucinated or imagined it?"

"Well, no," James replied, a bit puzzled.

"Then maybe you did see it, and there was one," Amanda said, optimistically.

"Perhaps…" James sighed.

Before too long, they arrived at the coffee shop on Vine Street.

After finding a parking spot, James and Amanda both got out and closed the doors. Then, James went around to the passenger side where Amanda was. He opened up his left hand and held it out to his left a little, offering to hold her hand. He said in a friendly tone, "So, Amanda, you ready? Let's go."

"Okay," replied Amanda as she took his hand. They walked hand in hand to the entrance of the coffee shop.

Once there, James opened the door. "Amanda, you first." She walked in with James following behind. Afterward, James and Amanda went to a table not too far inside on their right. First, James made sure Amanda was seated. Then, he sat down directly across from her, facing her.

Soon, a waitress came along and said, "How are we doing? Can I help y'all?"

James told her, "Two cappuccinos, please."

"I'll have them right out," she replied.

Once the waitress went to get the order, James refocused his attention on Amanda and himself. He said, "So anyway, Amanda, when we left off, we were talking about my camping trip over the weekend. But now, I was wondering, what do you like to do?"

"Well," she began saying, "I like to go to the mountains like you. Other than that, I like to play softball. I also exercise; I run and work out with weights. I've also taken a few lessons in martial arts and self-defense. I know I might sound too much like the physical type, but I think it's a really good idea to keep fit."

"Well, you're right," he told her.

Amanda went on to say, "But at least aside from all that, I enjoy other things like visiting national parks, museums, historical sites, and so forth. I even like to go to clubs, have dinner, and go to coffee shops like I am right now. Of course, I don't know if I can tell you everything."

"Oh, well, that's understandable and perfectly okay. But anyway, Amanda, I happen to like and enjoy a lot of the things as you, you know, museums and historical sites, having dinner, and going to coffee shops. But, another thing I might want to mention too is, as far as keeping fit, I like to lift weights, which I guess is similar to you. But other than that, I did track and field in high school. Since then, I've done some amateur boxing on the side. I guess I've even picked up a few self-defense moves as well. The only other thing is, I didn't realize you were into hiking and rock-climbing."

"Well, you know, James, it's a real chance to breathe fresh air, unlike in a big city like this. Other than that, it gets you away from all the noise, air pollution, and other things that drive you crazy. Besides, it's adventurous and an interesting challenge."

"I completely agree," James told her. "But anyway, Amanda, if there's just a few little differences in what we like, I'll understand."

"Of course," replied Amanda, "but, um, look, James, would you mind giving me some input on this new friend of yours? I mean the one who saved me last night and that I read about in the paper. I thought you said you would. Could you please?"

"Most certainly, Amanda," answered James. Of course, he did not hesitate to say that because he was ready and willing to tell Amanda everything he knew about the one who had performed those heroic deeds, including the one in which she herself had been rescued. James still would not tell Amanda that he himself was that guy, because he feared any possible consequences of that. However, he claimed to be a friend of his and offered to tell Amanda what she wanted to know about him, because he thought it would get him as close as possible to having her as his girlfriend. Fortunately, Amanda was already showing some interest in him, and that caused him to see an even better potential of getting her to fall in love with him. "All right," he said, "I'm not quite sure how to begin. Um, let's see."

But suddenly, James was momentarily interrupted when their waitress brought the two cappuccinos. "Here's your two cappuccinos," she said, placing them both on the table.

"Thank you," James told her.

"Enjoy," she said as she turned and walked off.

After that, James resumed his story. "Anyway," he said, "as I was saying, it's like this guy's a new friend of mine. I actually met him while

I was in the Alleghany Mountains with my two pals, Eric and Scott. But I only met him late, late, late Friday night after Eric and Scott had gone to bed. While they were asleep, I wandered off. While I was wandering and roaming for just a little bit, I saw a meteorite coming down; I mean, I thought I did. Then, I thought I heard and felt it land in a nearby valley. So then, I thought I'd go check it out. When I did, it looked like a big boulder that was lit up bright neon yellow. So were the little pieces and fragments that broke off and scattered, supposedly. Now, look, I don't know for sure if what I just told you was real. It was late, and I was tired. So if I were you, I wouldn't take my word for it."

Amanda protested, "But, James, I know you're not lying about that."

"Well, no."

Then, she continued, "So then, maybe it was real. I mean because if this guy was giving off neon light, I wouldn't be surprised if the source of his power did too. I don't see how you simply perceived all that through imagination or hallucination."

"Well, maybe you're right. But anyway, I'll tell you what else happened, okay?"

"Go ahead," Amanda said sweetly with a smile.

"All right," James began. "Next thing I knew, he found a piece of course crystalline quartz that was radiating neon-green light, just like he is now. I think I might know how that piece of pyxorium became able to give off neon-green light—"

"Wait a minute," Amanda interrupted. "*Pyxorium?* What's that?"

"Well, I guess it's a new kind of quartz that he discovered. I mean, that's what he decided to call it."

"Oh, okay," Amanda said doubtfully. "I mean, I know I learn new things all the time, but I've never heard anything like this. Anyway, you can continue your story. I'm sorry, James."

"All right, here's the next thing I was gonna tell you. What I guess might've happened is… a small speck or so of that, uh, bright neon-yellow sedimentary rock perhaps broke off and flew over to that quartz crystal with which it supposedly chemically reacted. Maybe… well, just maybe, that gave it the ability to radiate neon-green light. I mean, I didn't see the chemical reaction take place. But he found that crystal in a cave not too far from the boulder. Anyway, for what happened late Friday night, that's basically it."

"So, when did he acquire his powers?"

"Well," James said, "now, that just happened last night. It was at his home in his room. He was going to examine that piece of green quartz that he found. But before all that, he got himself a glass of water, which he put down on his desk. Then, he tripped and fell. When that happened, the crystal flew out of his hand and landed in that glass of water. But he didn't see where it went."

"So then what happened?"

"Well," James answered, "it's like I said, he didn't see where it went. I mean, he didn't know that it was in the water. That's because once that crystal landed in the water, it dissolved. That pyxorium was then combined with the water. So what ended up happening was, after spending a few minutes looking for the crystal, he decided to cool off. So he drank the glass of water. That allowed the pyxorium to become part of him. Now, I think it fused with his nervous system. That permits him to use his mind to perform all those supernatural abilities, I believe."

"Well, that's really interesting," said Amanda. "So, would you know what any of his abilities are?"

"I sure would," James happily answered. "He told me all about them when I saw him last night. Would you be interested in getting to know more about them?"

"I most certainly would," replied an anxious Amanda Taylor. "Would you mind filling me in?"

"Oh, not at all," he answered. "I'll tell you what I know."

"Thank you, James," Amanda said sweetly. "Go ahead."

"All right then," began James. "For one thing, my friend can shoot neon-green laser beams from each and every finger of his. He can also combine more than one finger to produce as big and powerful of a beam as he would like. There's no burning effect from them. They just have an impact on whatever they hit. He says it's not too difficult. He just has to set his mind on the target, and it all works out as planned. Another thing he can do too is levitate or float in midair because of his ability to hover. That's because of radiant energy that he forces downward out of the bottom of his feet. Just like with shooting laser beams, he controls it with his mind."

"That's really neat," Amanda said. "Is there anything else he can do?"

"Oh yes," James told her, excited. "There's much more. Do you want to hear the rest?"

"You know I do," Amanda answered enthusiastically. "Please tell me."

"All right," replied James, "now I think the next thing I'll tell you about is a kind of defense mechanism of his. You see, another thing he can do too is put a force field around himself."

"A force field?"

"Well, it's like… what he does, Amanda, is like, he has these thin constant continuous beams of neon-green radiation that come out of all his fingers. They appear to be sketching and forming the outer layer of the force field," he explained. "They just keep doing that until it's complete and he's safe inside. It'll protect him from anything."

"Wow," said an amazed Amanda Taylor, "I've never known anyone who could do all that. This guy sounds incredible. I wonder if there's even a way I could be inside the force field with him. I'll bet then, nothing or no one could come between us."

At that, James had a stunned and surprised expression on his face. Because of what Amanda had just said about him, he felt even more tempted to tell her that he was really the man about whom she was being informed. However, he still feared the possible outcome of disclosing the truth about it all. So he did not allow himself to tell her.

When Amanda noticed the surprised look on his face, she asked, "What's that look for?"

James just went on to tell her, "Well, all I can say is, I just wish I could say I was that guy. I mean, I'm sure a lot of ordinary, average guys would like to be able to say that too."

"Yeah, I'll bet," Amanda agreed.

James Clifton had said that because he thought it best not to tell Amanda that it was him. That was what he had meant when he wished he could say he was that guy. He just did not want Amanda to discern the real reason behind his expression. He tried to answer her without lying. Because he had not wanted to lie, he did not directly state, "I am not that guy."

Before telling Amanda more, he said to her, "Look, Amanda, before I go on to tell you more, do you mind if I take a big sip of my cappuccino?"

"Not at all," she answered. "In fact, I think I'll do the same thing."

So at that, James and Amanda both sipped away through their straws until their cups were almost down to half-full. Then, he said, "So, Amanda, are you ready to hear more? There's still more to tell."

"I sure am," she answered. "Go ahead."

James resumed his story. "First of all, Amanda, there's one other thing I want to say before I move on. You see, even when my friend is surrounded by that force field, he can still be moved around or projected by, like, a moving vehicle, or some other powerful force. But, the force field still serves as a cushion against any impact. For example, last night, he was pushed by a truck and later by a subway train while inside the force field. However, he remained unharmed because the protection of the force field did not allow either vehicle to hit him directly. That's why he simply resorted to the force field when he did not know what else to do."

"Oh, I see," Amanda said, nodding her head in understanding. "That's really really clever."

"I'd have to say so too," agreed James. "At least that way, he'll preserve and protect himself as much as possible until he figures out what else to do."

"Absolutely," Amanda replied without hesitation.

"But anyway," James said, "I think I'll go on to tell you what else he is able to do. Is that okay?"

"Sure," answered Amanda, "go ahead."

"All right then," said James, "here's something else that my friend can do too. He can turn into a projectile and shoot himself along any desired path, and end up in the desired spot. He moves along that path at lightning speed. Whenever he is in the form of that projectile, he looks supposedly like a shapeless mass of neon-green radiation, like maybe a neon-green comet? I'm not quite sure. But anyone or most anything that stands in his way will get knocked away."

"Now wait a minute!" Amanda exclaimed. "Maybe that's how he rescued me when those two guys Ant Killer and Roach Killer had me at gunpoint in the subway. I mean, I thought I barely noticed a bright-green flash of light that I couldn't see too well, and something must've sent them flying. Maybe that's what happened."

"By George, it definitely is!" James declared at once.

"How do you know that, James?" asked Amanda.

"Well, because he told me."

"Oh," Amanda replied somewhat doubtfully.

Then, James looked past Amanda for a moment. He had a confused look on his face. She asked him, "What are you thinking about?"

James said, "Oh, uh, I was just thinking about those two guys, Ant Killer and Roach Killer. Those code names just sound like a couple kinds of insecticides used for extermination. I wonder, do they belong to some secret organization by any chance?" But after thinking and wondering for only half of another minute, James said, "Oh well, I'll worry more about it later. But anyway, Amanda, I had, like… at least one other thing to share with you about my new friend."

"Okay, go on."

"All right," James began to say, "you see, Amanda, there's like one other capability that he can perform. It's like, another way he can get from one point to another. Instead of shooting or projecting himself, he can also teleport. Here's how that works. Just like with all his other capabilities, he can use his mind to set up the intended path he will take and the intended destination. Now, once he has designated the point he will reach, he will charge up a little bit, and then release himself. At that, he will disappear into a long, narrow beam of neon-green radiation. Then, in less than a second, he will reappear as himself in the intended spot."

"That's unbelievable!" said Amanda.

"Well," said James, "that's also how he managed to pass underneath a car last night that could've run over him."

"That's really clever," Amanda said. "I mean, that's quick thinking. So I guess he told you about that too."

"He sure did," replied James. "I mean it's like, he says I'm his closest friend. He says that he trusts me more than anyone."

"Oh, really!" Her curiosity was piqued, "Would you know his name by chance?"

"Well," answered James, "it's like, I just met him this past weekend, and I can't say I remember. I'll try to ask him."

"Oh, okay," replied Amanda.

"But look," James told her, "I'm pretty sure I could set things up so you could meet him."

"Well, that sounds great," she answered with a smile.

"And just another thing too, Amanda," said James.

"What's that, James?" she asked sweetly and calmly.

"I have not yet told anyone else any of the information I have just shared with you," James explained, "because you see, Amanda, I just thought I would let you have the privilege of being the first one to get to know all about him. I would not have done this for anyone else, not even my two longtime friends, Eric and Scott."

Understandably, Amanda was very pleasantly surprised. She could not believe what she had just heard. In fact, she was speechless for a matter of seconds. Then, she exclaimed, "Oh, James! Oh my gosh! Do you really mean that?"

"I most certainly do," he answered her.

Amanda was still stunned by the gesture. Trying to say something, she stuttered, "Why, James, I can't believe it… Well, I, uh, I don't know what to say."

James calmly said, "Well, anything's okay with me. I mean, look, I understand how you're feeling. It's all right to tell me when you find the words. I mean, I understand how it can be when you're trying to find the right words for something. Believe me, I understand."

"Thanks," Amanda replied to him. She was still somewhat in shock but had also calmed down some.

"No problem at all," James told her.

After another moment, Amanda said, "Anyway, James, I'm still not completely certain what I ought to say to you. But the least I have to tell you is thank you so much; you're so sweet."

Then, a second later, Amanda took hold of his right hand in both of hers. From that point, she rubbed and massaged his hand. Plus, they both kept looking into each other's eyes and smiling.

After a couple of moments of that, Amanda asked, "So, have you told me everything there is to tell me?"

"I think so," answered James. "I mean, pretty much. Of course, there might be, like, one other sort of defense mechanism of his that I haven't mentioned. But I don't know if you want to hear about it. You know, because he tries to avoid doing it, and he'll only do it when he has to. I just wasn't sure if you wanted to hear about it or not."

"Oh, I do!" exclaimed Amanda. "Of course I want to hear it."

"Well, okay," said James, "here it goes. I'll explain it for you. It's like this. Now, I really can't think of any situations in which he would do this, but anyway, here's another capability of his. In order to make it work, he will tighten up every part of his anatomy from the crown of his head to the soles of his feet, creating tension. He will also hold his breath at the same time. In effect, he will be giving off a lot of radiant energy. That, in turn, will cause the neon-green light he emits to grow brighter and more intense. Also, it will make him invincible to anything and everything. The only bad side is this. In order to make this work, he has to strain himself and, like I said, hold his breath. As he persists in that, he begins to feel side effects like dizziness, nausea, and hallucinations. If he was to keep that up for too long, he could possibly hurt himself, pass out, or something. That's why he only does that when he has to."

"Gee," replied Amanda, "that's really very interesting what you just told me. But of course, I understand why he tries to avoid doing that. I'd sure hate to see someone hurt himself like that."

"Of course, so would I," James agreed. "But anyway, I've told you about everything I can think of about my new friend."

"Well, James," Amanda said, adjusting her grip on Clifton's right hand, "thank you so much for all the insight. On top of that, for letting me be the very first to get to know all this, I still don't know what to say. But you don't know what it means to me, and I'm not sure I can thank you enough. I don't know quite how to say this, but it seems so, um, divine… maybe even beyond that." After that, she kept staring into his eyes, smiling and showing interest.

Then, he went on to tell her, "Well, that's all right, Amanda. If you think of what to say later, you can let me know another time. After all, it's never too late, you know."

"All right," she replied. "Thanks. I'll see what I can do."

"Well, it's no trouble at all," James told her. "And I'd like to thank you for the time we spent this afternoon."

"Oh, you're welcome," said Amanda. "Thanks for the cappuccino."

"Well, no problem at all," said James. "But anyway, Amanda?"

"Yes, James?" she said.

"There was one other thing I wanted to ask you," he said.

"What did you want to ask me?" she asked.

"What are you doing Wednesday night?" James asked her.

"Well, I don't really know," answered Amanda. "Why?"

"Well," he began, "this Wednesday night, my company's having a party at the Fairmaine Hotel. They're celebrating their fiftieth anniversary. It's going to be at a real nice, fancy place, you know, with formal-looking, well-designed tables, chairs, and just about all other structures. There will even be, like, chandeliers and so forth. There will even be a jazz band that well includes someone playing music on a beautiful, expensive grand piano. Of course, I can't quite explain every last detail."

"That's all right."

"But of course," James continued, "you have to dress nice too."

"Okay," she said. "Well, it sounds nice. I've never been there before. What would it cost me?"

He said, "Oh, you don't have to worry about that. You can leave that to me. It's like this. All the employees are welcome to the hotel. But they can invite anyone else they want to come too. However, there is a small extra charge for any guests, whom, of course, we can give passes to. As it happens, I've even got my two friends I told you about, Eric and Scott, coming too. But anyway, let's get back to you and me. Now, with you, I wouldn't give you an invitation if I was going to make you pay. Like I said, you can leave that to me. So I'm asking you, Amanda, will you please go with me?"

"Oh, James," Amanda said kindly with a smile, "you know I will. I can't believe you're not making me pay. You're so kind."

"Well," James said, "it's the least I can do after all the kindness you've shown me. Anyway, I'll pick you up and bring you there."

"Okay."

"As far as the time, I'll come get you, and where you stay, we'll determine that when I bring you back to your truck."

"All right," said Amanda, "but look, James, I've really enjoyed myself with you this evening. Thanks again for the cappuccino."

"Oh, no problem," James replied.

"Well," Amanda said, "I need to be getting home soon."

"Okay then," said James, "let's finish our cappuccinos up, and I'll drop you back off." At that, they both sipped the last of their drinks. Then, James got up out of his seat and stood up. He said, "All right, I just need to find our waitress."

He raised his left hand to try to signal his waitress. Before too long, she noticed him and came over. James said, "I'm ready to pay. Here you go." He gave her the amount due plus two extra dollars. Finally, he said, "Keep the change."

"Thank you," said the waitress. "Come back and see us."

"Okay," answered James.

After that, he looked down at Amanda and said, "So, are you ready to go?"

"Sure," she answered. "Let's go."

Just as Amanda had gotten out of her seat, James put out his left hand, signaling her to take it. She grabbed it with her right hand so that they were side by side holding hands. James and Amanda walked to the doors like that, and James let Amanda exit first.

They walked over to James's Suburban. Before opening the door on the passenger side for Amanda, he said, "Look, Amanda, we'll exchange information when I drop you off, okay?"

"Okay," Amanda said nicely. Then, James opened the door for her, and she got in. He closed the door for her, got in on the driver's side, and started up his truck. He began driving back toward the spot where he had met and picked up Amanda. It was about 6:25 p.m.

While James was giving Amanda a ride back, he said, "So, uh, Amanda?"

"Yes, James?" she replied.

"If you don't mind, there's something else I'd like to share too. Do you mind?" James asked her.

"Certainly not," she answered. "Go ahead."

"All right," said James. "Now, look, do you remember a little while ago while I told you how my new friend found the source of his new powers, I said something about a meteorite that hit?"

Amanda said, "I think so, yeah."

"Well," said James, "it was very late Friday night—or should I say early, early Saturday morning? Anyway, when it was dark, and I wandered off away from camp, I thought I saw that meteorite radiating neon-yellow light. That was even after it landed."

"Okay," said Amanda. "So, what are you trying to tell me?"

"Well," continued James, "the next morning, after Eric made us all some breakfast, I wanted to try to bring them to it and show it to them. Of course, that's Eric and Scott I'm talking about."

"Okay," Amanda replied.

Continuing on, he said, "But when we got to it, there was no sign of any kind of neon light whatsoever. It looked like nothing but a giant boulder made of sedimentary rock like limestone or something. When I tried to tell them what happened, they wouldn't believe me. I even let them convince me that I was really just hallucinating. On top of that, I actually believed them. Wasn't that foolish of me?"

"Now, now, James," she said sympathetically, "don't take it so hard. Maybe they just hadn't ever seen a neon-yellow boulder before. Then, when you tried to show them, there just wasn't any proof. Now, had you ever seen a bright-yellow rock before?"

"Well, no," said James, who had come to have a little more understanding.

"You see?" asked Amanda. "That's all it is. But at least I believe you. Feel any better now?"

"Yeah, I do. You're right," answered James. He briefly looked over at her smiling. Then, he said, "But anyway, at least there might be a couple of positive things about it all."

"Really!"

"At least I got to lead them to the nearby cave where all of us got to collect some quartz crystals. That's something I got to share with them," he explained.

"Well, there you go," Amanda replied affirmatively.

James continued, "Other than that, Amanda, even though Eric and Scott were with me on my camping trip, they still know nothing about what I just told you all about at the coffee shop. But, the only other thing is, even when I brought them to the cave, I didn't go on to tell them about the radioactive neon-green quartz crystal that my new friend found. That's because I didn't think they'd believe me since they wouldn't believe me about the meteorite. Heck, I haven't told them about my new friend either. But, I guess it's a good thing, because then I might've not been able to let you be the first to get to know it all. Besides, there's no one I'd rather reveal special secrets to than you."

"Well, thank you, James," said Amanda, rather pleased. "That's really sweet of you."

"No problem," he replied.

"So anyway, Amanda," James began, "have you gone on vacation anywhere lately?"

She said, "Yes, a few months ago, I spent a week with my parents in Camden."

"That sounds nice," he said. "Y'all do anything fun?"

"Yes," answered Amanda. "We went to the state capitol and every museum and point of interest we could in Trenton. One day, we even went to Adventure Aquarium right in Camden."

"Oh man," responded James, "I don't think I've ever done any of that before. I wish I'd have known you back then so I could've come with you."

"Oh well," she said. She smiled and shrugged her shoulders.

"I think I'd like to take you one weekend to show you that big boulder that's left over from the meteorite I told you about," he said.

"Well, we'll see," she said.

"Yeah, I guess so," said James. "I guess we'll worry more about that and other things after the big party Wednesday night."

"Perhaps," Amanda replied.

Shortly thereafter, James made it back to the point along Broad Street at which he had picked up Amanda. He parked where he had before, and they got out. They held hands again as they walked across the street.

They walked a little bit further to Amanda's Explorer, which was parked along the opposite side of Broad Street. Once there, they stopped and turned so that they were facing each other. Since Amanda was already holding his left hand, she used hers to take his right hand and hold on to it. Then, she said, "James, thank you so much for everything—that is, last night, this afternoon, and for the invitation."

"Oh man, anytime," James replied. "But, look, Wednesday evening, the celebration starts at seven. I'll pick you up around six thirty. Is that okay?"

"That's fine," answered Amanda.

"Well then," he said, "I'll need to know where to pick you up from."

"My apartment is in the first complex to the left of Levick Street in the Lawndale subdivision. I'm at apartment number 1H," she told him.

James stopped to think for a minute. Then, he said, "Okay, I know where you're talking about. That's apartment 1H?"

"That's right," she responded.

"Okay, thanks."

"You're welcome," said Amanda.

"Just one other thing, Amanda," he said. "Can I please get a number to reach you at?"

"Sure," she answered.

"Thanks," he replied. "I'll give you mine too."

"Okay," she said to that and let go of his hands. They wrote down their cell phone numbers and exchanged the slips of paper.

"Well, thank you, Amanda," James said happily.

"Thank *you*, James," she said in return.

"Well, anyway, Amanda," he said to her, "Wednesday night, I'll give you a call before I come to pick you up, that is if I don't see you before then."

"That'll be fine."

"And I look forward to seeing you then," he told her.

"Me too," she said back to him.

"Well, in the meantime," he said, putting his hands on her shoulders, "take care of yourself and be careful."

"You too," she said, smiling and patting James on the left side of his midsection.

They gave each other a big hug followed by a good-bye kiss.

"Good-bye, Amanda," James said, beginning to walk back to his truck.

"Bye, James," she said as she went around to the driver's side of her vehicle. At that, they both left each other for the day and went back about their business. James Clifton got into his Suburban and started for home.

However, before Amanda could get into her Explorer, someone else got out of a vehicle that had just parked in front of her. The vehicle was a full-size, four-door pickup. The one who got out of it was a twenty-eight-year-old man named Mark Thompson. Mark was a doctor of family medicine. He had an office nearby in downtown Philadelphia. He had dirty-blond hair, and his skin had an olive tone, much like James Clifton's, but just a tiny bit darker. He stood five feet ten inches tall, weighed about 230 pounds, and had a good physique. He had blue eyes. Like James Clifton, Dr. Thompson was the very friendly and agreeable type. Perhaps he too had his share of good looks, but at the present, he was still in his doctor's outfit.

It was now less than two minutes after James Clifton and Amanda Taylor had parted company, and Mark was completely unaware that Amanda had just spent a little time with James. He too found Amanda to be attractive. So, once Amanda caught his eye, he said to her in a friendly tone, "Hi, there."

Smiling and chuckling a little, Amanda said in return, "Oh, uh, hi."

"How are you today?" he asked.

"I'm fine," she answered somewhat kindly. "How are you?"

"So far, so good, thank you," the doctor answered. "Another day at the office, but at least there were no problems."

"That's good," she told him.

"So how has your day been?" Thompson asked her.

"It's been great, thanks."

"No problem," said Mark. "But anyway, I just happened to see you here, and I just thought it might be nice if I said hello."

"Okay," she said, nodding. "Well, thank you for doing that."

Extending his right hand for a handshake, he said, "I'm Mark Thompson."

While shaking his hand, she said, "I'm Amanda Taylor."

"It's good to meet you, Amanda."

"You too," she replied.

"So, Amanda," Dr. Thompson began, "where are you from originally?"

"I'm from Camden, New Jersey," she answered. "What about you?"

"I'm originally from around here," responded Mark. "That is, of course, Philadelphia."

"I see."

Mark asked, "So, you just getting off work?"

"Well, actually, just a little while ago."

"Really?"

"Uh, yeah," she answered, "I just had a cappuccino at a coffee shop."

"Oh, okay," he said, "so if you don't mind me asking, whatcha doing now?"

"I'm on my way home," answered Amanda.

"Well, okay," Mark replied. "How's work?"

"It couldn't be better," Amanda said happily.

"So I take it that you like what you do," he said to her.

"I most certainly do," said Amanda, "It's much better than I hoped it would be."

"That's great!" he exclaimed. "You must be uh…"

"I'm a loan officer at Stanley Financial," explained Amanda.

"A loan officer you say, huh?" said Dr. Thompson. "I'm mighty proud for you. You must've worked hard to get that."

"Well," she started, "almost five years ago, I achieved an accounting degree at the University of Pennsylvania. Then, I got on with Stanley Financial where I started my training and eventually became a loan officer, which I still am today."

"Way to go, Amanda!" exclaimed Mark. "That's awesome."

"Well, thank you," Amanda responded.

"But anyway, Amanda," he began, "I'm a doctor of family medicine, and I have an office in downtown Philadelphia."

"Wow, that's very interesting," Amanda said. "I could see that you were some kind of doctor. You know, I've had different sorts of guys try to come up and meet me, but there's never been a doctor. This is a first for me."

"Oh, really?" replied Dr. Thompson. "I'm a bit surprised."

Finally, Amanda said to Mark, "Well, anyhow, look, Mark, it was great meeting you and all, but I need to get on home."

"Oh, okay, it's… no problem," Mark responded. "But, um, Amanda? I just wanted to ask you one last thing."

"Okay, what is it?" she asked.

"Well," began Thompson, "I was just wondering… what are you doing Wednesday night?"

"Wednesday night?" said Amanda. "Um… oh yeah, on Wednesday night, I'm going to a big party at the Fairmaine Hotel. It's to celebrate the fiftieth anniversary of this company called Ace Nuclear Supply."

"Are you serious?" asked a surprised Dr. Thompson. "You know something? I'm going to be there too."

"You are?" asked Amanda equally surprised. "I don't believe it."

"Well," he said, "it just so happens that I have a really, really good friend who's an engineer at that company, and he gave me a pass to this event. I certainly don't want to miss it."

"I'm sure you don't."

"Well, look," Thompson said, "I was just kinda wondering, would you care for us to go together, that is… unless, of course, you're already going with someone. Are you?"

"Actually, Mark…" Amanda sighed. "I am. You see, I already have a date there. I'm sorry."

"Oh no, it's okay," Mark told her calmly. "It's… not a problem."

"Anyway Mark," continued Amanda, "I don't know if you've heard of him, but his name is James Clifton."

"Well, well, well," Thompson replied in amazement, "you're actually going there with James Clifton, their chief engineer?"

"I most certainly am," Amanda answered. "Do you know him?"

"Well," he answered, "I've never met the guy, but I've heard so much about him from my friend that works for him. I guess I might as well say that I know him."

"Wow, what a small world," said Amanda.

"Perhaps," he said, "but you gotta hand it to a guy like that. That James Clifton is quite an accomplished young man. I mean, getting a PhD by twenty-three and becoming the chief engineer by twenty-five, it's just unbelievable."

"Yeah," replied Amanda, "I guess it is. Another thing too is, he's the one I just had a cappuccino with."

He said, "Well, anyway, now that's all been said, I can honestly tell you that I'm very happy for you. You deserve a great guy, and I'm somehow absolutely certain that you got yourself one right there. I wish you both good luck."

"Well, thank you so much," Amanda said in reply.

He had one last thing to say. "Well, look, Amanda, I don't wanna hold you up if you need to get going. But if you don't mind, I'd like to give you one of my business cards. Here you go." At that, he handed her a card.

As Amanda received the card, she said, "Why, thank you."

"You're more than welcome," the doctor told her. "And if you ever need anything at all, then don't hesitate to give me a call."

"Thanks, I appreciate that," Amanda told him. "Well, it was really nice meeting you and nice talking to you."

"You too," Thompson said in return. "I guess I'll see you at the banquet Wednesday night."

"Of course."

"Well, take care, Amanda," said Dr. Thompson.

"You too," she said. At that, Amanda got into her Ford Explorer and started for home.

It was 6:50 p.m., and James Clifton was getting home for the day. He pulled his Suburban into his garage as usual. Then, he took his newspaper with him, went inside, and headed upstairs to his bedroom.

Upon making it to his bedroom, James just sat down on his bed and set the newspaper to his right. For a while, he just kept sitting there and thinking to himself; the events of the previous weekend and the article in the paper were very much on his mind. Not very certain of what to say or think, James just uttered, "Man, what a weekend it's been. On top of that, I'm in the newspaper." He sat on his bed awhile longer in silence.

But soon, he had a somewhat more positive view of the situation. He said, "But at least I'm proud of myself for having rescued those two women, especially with one of them being the one I love. It makes me wonder if my newfound abilities could actually make me a superhero. I just never really gave that any serious thought. Other than that, I'd love to be able to help others like that, but I don't know if I'd want to be identified, and I also wonder what I might call myself as a superhero. I don't know." At that, he just shook his head in confusion and fell silent again.

But before too long, unable to think of anything else, he just picked up his copy of the *Philosophy of Philadelphia* and proceeded to take a look at the article on the front page. Then very shortly, as James was reading the latter part of the article, he began mumbling to himself, "So, these people were wondering if what they saw was real or just some green phantasm." He looked away from the paper momentarily and said more positively, "Oh well, hopefully no one's identified me as James Clifton, and I'm nothing to them but just some green phantasm or something."

All of a sudden, he had a tremendous idea. "Wait a minute!" he exclaimed happily. "You know what? I actually like the sound of that! If I were a superhero with super powers, maybe I could call myself the Green Phantasm." That inspired him to think further.

Momentarily, James had another thought. "Of course, I may need an outfit and a mask to avoid being identified, and maybe even a hat too. I suppose I could do that. But what kind of outfit and what kind of logo would I want to have?"

James thought of something rather quickly. "Why, of course," he said with confidence. "Since I give off green light, then I'll make the outfit green as well. I'll even make it a couple of different shades to make it more interesting. I even know what kind of logo I'd want to put on it. I think it'll be great."

James had one other thought as well. He said to himself, "I might not want to take this lightly. This being a superhero may be a serious responsibility. But if someone's needed to do it, I'm willing. Other than that, I'm willing to take on a challenge and learn from it. Of course, I may need to careful, but I'm definitely more than willing to do that." So James finally decided, "Well, let's do it. For the sake and safety of the innocent ones of Philadelphia, let's get right on it."

That very evening, James drove around town to several stores to find the necessary materials for the outfit that he had in mind. The two main things he gathered while he was out and about were a tight-fitting long-sleeve shirt and a pair of tight pants made of superstretch Lycra. Another major piece was a cape that had a folded-down collar at the top and hung down to his knees. James also gathered a couple of square yards of stretch vinyl. Another piece was a fedora that had superstretch Lycra covering it. James also found a hard rubber mask that was shaped like an upside-down trapezoid and could be strapped on to cover the area of his face from his forehead to above his upper lip. The other three pieces James bought included a shiny leather belt, a pair of gloves, and a pair of boots. Each boot and glove had a cuff at its open end that progressively became a little wider as it slightly slanted up and back. The only other piece that James sought and found was a small piece of hard rubber also shaped like an upside-down trapezoid, but narrower than the rubber mask. James was going to fasten that to the front of his belt.

Eventually, he made it home with all of the supplies that he had picked up while he was out. Almost immediately upon making it home, he set about assembling his suit. From the square yards of stretch vinyl, he cut out two G's and two P's to sew onto the back of his cape and the front of his long-sleeve shirt. Each G was shaped as an upside down trapezoid; like the small rubber piece for his belt, and each P was shaped to fit inside a G. Clifton kept sewing until they were all in place. Other than that, James just carved the small piece of hard rubber so that the front looked like his Green Phantasm logotype with the P inside of the G. Also, the back was carved to fit onto the front of his belt.

The only other finishing touch that James applied to the uniform was to transmit some radiant energy from his nervous system to make sure that it became the two shades of green that he had in mind. At once, he switched on the pyxorium within his nervous system. Then, he placed both hands on each and every piece of his outfit. As James was doing that, he focused his full concentration on his two hands so that some of his radiant energy became part of each respective piece of clothing and changed it to the desired shade of green. As a result, his pants and long-sleeved shirt became a neon green that was perhaps similar to lime green. However, he placed more tension on certain other components to make them a much darker green. These included his cape, fedora, mask, belt, gloves, and boots, as well as the big vinyl logo that was on the front of his shirt. The logo on the back of his cape became the lighter shade of green since the rest of the cape was darker. That completed his Green Phantasm uniform.

After all that, James then thought momentarily about what he would do as the Green Phantasm. After thinking things over a little, he decided that he would still keep his full-time job at Ace Nuclear Supply, for he knew he had to make a living. But he figured that after he made it home from work each day, he would settle in and then venture out at night as the Green Phantasm, who would watch over and protect the city of Philadelphia by breaking up the misdeeds of murderers, criminals, and other troublemakers who threatened the peace and safety of Philadelphia. After staying up a little late to work on his Green Phantasm outfit, James decided to start becoming the Green Phantasm the next night, which was Tuesday.

Eventually, it was getting close to 10:00 p.m. Knowing he had to get to work the next morning, James decided to call it a night. He quickly fixed himself a light supper, after which he showered and got ready to go to bed.

The next day, James went to work and got through the day as he would have done on any other typical day as the chief engineer at Ace Nuclear Supply. Of course, at the end of the day, James went on home from work. Then, by the time it was 6:00 p.m. on Tuesday evening, he had activated the pyxorium within himself so that he was giving off neon-green radiation. Then, he immediately put on his Green Phantasm outfit and was about to go out through the city of Philadelphia.

As the Green Phantasm, James would be able to perform every supernatural technique he had described to Amanda. This included firing laser beams from his fingers, hovering by placing tension in his feet, and forming a globular force field in which he could enclose himself. Fortunately, none of his radiant energy would ever actually be used up or consumed; after it was unleashed, it would return to him as an invisible force, even when or if he ever utilized his invincibility that caused him to radiate even brighter light.

However, even as great as it was for James to have these powers to use as the Green Phantasm, many of them had at least some sort of disadvantage. For instance, as protective as his force field was, he could not attack or shoot at anything while inside it. Also, whenever he was firing laser beams from his fingers or projecting himself as a neon-green projectile, he could knock down, destroy, or penetrate a lot of things. But even with either his shapeless projectile form or his most powerful laser beam, he could not affect some thick, hard barriers made from materials like hardened steel, shatterproof glass, or other such unbreakable material. His teleportation ability also had its advantages and disadvantages. As a teleportation beam, James would be able to pass through narrow openings if necessary and reappear at any point within his field of vision. However, he could only teleport in an absolute straight and unobstructed path, for his teleportation beam form was not as powerful as his shapeless projectile form and could not maneuver in any way other than a straight line.

Finally, even his ability to be absolutely invincible had a serious downside to it. As much as this protected him from anything and everything without trapping him inside the force field, he could not keep it up for very long. In order to activate this ability, James had to increase tension in every part of his anatomy, which raised his blood pressure and stopped him from breathing properly. After even a short period of this, he would begin to experience dizzy spells, hallucinations, and nausea. This put him in danger of either vomiting or passing out. Of course, if either of those things were to happen, James would be a lot more likely to be killed. So, considering the pros and cons of this technique and the others, he knew he would definitely have to be careful and selective as to which he used in any given situation.

Whatever the case, James thought he was as ready as he would ever be to begin his life of heroism as none other than the one and only Green Phantasm. Shortly after putting on his suit, he happily hovered a few feet above the floor of his bedroom for a moment and declared, "Enter the Green Phantasm!"

CHAPTER FIVE

The Green Phantasm
Protects the Streets

It was after 6:00 p.m. on Tuesday evening. James Clifton had just put on his new Green Phantasm outfit. He was trying to decide what to do next. Now that he was in his guise as the Green Phantasm, he asked himself, "All right, what do I do now? I mean, I just put on my new suit, and I've switched on my neon-green radiation. Other than that, I'm wanting to stop and prevent terrible crimes from happening so that Philadelphia would be a safer place to live."

Within ten seconds, Clifton decided, "So, I think I'll venture through downtown Philadelphia and utilize my new supernatural abilities to undo the diabolical schemes of any crooks, criminals, or other troublemakers I come across. I mean, you know? The other night, I didn't have to think or try too too hard to stop those few culprits, even as threatening or intimidating as they might've seemed. Heck, the common crook or criminal doesn't stand a chance with me, the Green Phantasm."

Then, he stopped and thought about it a little more. He continued, "Now, of course, I unintentionally caused a few disturbances the other night, upsetting a few people. Even with those two heroic acts, I've got people wondering who I am and what to think of me. Of course, I can't go back on what I've already done, but maybe now, I can do more good deeds to make up for the little bit of trouble I caused. Hopefully, that'll eventually blot out those mishaps."

James Clifton was almost ready to go out and fight crime in downtown Philadelphia. He had only one more concern. He said, "Now, look, I know

I made a few errors the other night. So I might want to take a moment to think about how I'll avoid making them again. Now, exactly what did cause me to get hit by the truck and the train and to almost get run over by the Mercedes Benz? I mean, they all caught me by surprise somehow. Now, was I being careful?"

After hesitating for a second, he said, "Well, actually, I don't think I was. I wasn't paying attention to what I was doing, was I? Well, it wasn't as much as I could've paid. I mean, whenever that eighteen-wheeler smacked into me, I wasn't focusing on staying afloat. I was thinking too much about something else, and my lack of full attention allowed me to drift down in front of the truck. Even in the incident with that car, I started across the street without watching where I was going. Also, whenever I got smacked by that subway train, I was going along the track like I shouldn't have been. Why? It's because I didn't pay attention to that. Well, anyway, I should be able to be more cautious and pay more attention this time, since I now think I've got a somewhat better handle on my new abilities."

Now that James was finished worrying about all that, he went on to say, "Well, I think it's about that time. I mean, at least to me it is. Of course, other than those few mishaps, it still feels great to have saved those two innocent young ladies. After all, I hate to think how they'd have ended up if it weren't for me. Otherwise, I'm sure the police are doing everything they can to lessen terror. But now, I'm going to get out there and help them, because I too want Philadelphia to be a safer place."

Then, he added one more thing. "Now of course, I've got to work and make a living like everyone else. But I'll just do that during the day. Of course, I can still fight crime in the evening after I get off. After all, I'm sure that in the evening and at night is when I'll be needed the most. And you know something else? I'll even put this crime-fighting before my very own personal fun, pleasures, and other interests. That is because I wouldn't be in the mood to have fun if something horrible was happening to someone I care about. Also, when I really think about it, I'm much happier helping others than helping myself. So, other than my work as chief engineer, crime-fighting must come first, before anything else. After all, I'll have people counting on me. I wouldn't want to disappoint them. Oh, this will be a responsibility. But somebody's got to do it, and they all need someone to count on. So it looks like that will become me, the Green Phantasm!"

As the Green Phantasm, James was now ready to get started on his venture through the city. He now said, "Oh well, any other worries I have will have to be put off until later. Right now, someone could be getting hurt as I speak. So here I go."

He cracked open his bedroom window so that he could teleport through it to get outside. Upon doing so, he set the course he would take from his bedroom to above his subdivision. At that, he began charging himself. Once he was charged up, he proceeded to release himself into teleportation. Just like he had done two nights before, Clifton disappeared into a long, narrow neon-green beam of radiation. Then, in less than a split-second, he reappeared as himself four hundred feet above the Mayfair subdivision. Upon reappearing, he activated his hovering ability to remain afloat while deciding on which course to take next.

While the Green Phantasm was levitating in the same spot, several people in the Mayfair subdivision happened to notice someone or something stationed in midair giving off blinding neon-green light. One of them yelled out, "There he is! That's gotta be the neon-green man reported!"

In the meantime, James Clifton, as the Green Phantasm, was looking toward downtown Philadelphia, trying to determine exactly how he would shoot on over there. Not sure of exactly what part of downtown he wanted to go to, he just decided to dart on over to the middle of it all. That would put him above the approximate location of City Hall.

The Green Phantasm then charged up in preparation to project himself. He soon released himself as a shapeless radiating projectile. Within two seconds, he reappeared, hovering above City Hall. The Green Phantasm began looking around for any kind of violence, suspicious activity, or other signs of trouble.

However, as the Green Phantasm had zoomed downtown, the ones who had noticed him from below stood there baffled. A few of them raised the question of "Where'd he go?" at his sudden disappearance. Unable to understand what they had just seen, they all just went back about their business.

However, in the downtown area, although the Green Phantasm was hovering above a heavily populated area, most people were too busy to look and notice. So, as the Green Phantasm, Clifton remained on the lookout for anything that needed to be stopped.

After a few moments of searching, the Green Phantasm noticed a somewhat beat-up van parked near an ATM machine along Arch Street, not too far from Twenty-First Street. He said, "Hmm, I wonder."

He approached for a better look. He noticed three guys who looked like they were up something. Each one was completely dressed in black. They all wore black boots, jeans, gloves, and black jackets. In addition, they each had on a black ski mask with red trim.

As the Green Phantasm, James decided to move in closer and get more insight in case this threesome needed to be stopped. So the Green Phantasm descended toward the scene. At first, he hid himself from the criminals on the driver's side of their van. He then listened to them for a moment to try to understand what was going on.

In the meantime, one of the crooks was saying, "All right, I got the security camera disabled. Y'all ready to operate?"

Another one said, "Let's go," as he readied a powerful electric drill to begin disassembly. The third guy got ready with a wrecking bar.

However, unknown to them, the Green Phantasm was devising a plan to end the robbery and have a little fun at the same time. The three culprits were all lined up in a row side by side. Before they got too far into their operation, the Green Phantasm teleported underneath their van and reappeared directly behind the threesome without being noticed because they were focusing all their attention on the job they were doing.

Next, the Green Phantasm removed the ski mask from each of the three guys. The crooks still did not take notice right away. However, the one all the way to the Phantasm's right eventually glanced to his left, and noticed that his partner did not have on his mask. At once, he said, "Say, why'd you take off your mask?"

"Wait a minute," said the middle guy. "What are you talking about?"

"I mean, why'd you remove your mask?" the guy on the right asked again. "You want to get identified?"

The middle guy looked at him and said, "Look, I don't know what your problem is, but—Wait a minute! Why'd you take off yours?"

"Ah, come on," he answered. "I didn't take mine off. Now—"

"Hold it, guys," the one to the Phantasm's left said. "What's going on here?" Looking at his two partners, he said, "Hey! Why'd you two remove your masks?"

"I didn't," the middle guy replied.

"I didn't either," said the one to the Phantasm's right. "Why'd you remove yours?"

"What are you talking about?" he asked. "I didn't—" The guy on the left end was now interrupting himself. He was using his hands to feel his bare face and head. "Wait a minute," he said in panic. "Who did this to us?"

The other two then felt themselves and noticed that their masks were actually missing too. At that, they all began looking around in a panic. "Who did this to us?" they all asked, pulling out their handguns.

"Yeah, you'd better show yourself!" demanded the first guy all the way to everyone's left.

However, the Green Phantasm was now hidden behind the front left of their van. He was about to make the situation more interesting for himself. He yelled out to them, "It was the Green Phantasm! The Green Phantasm did it!"

Immediately, the crook on everyone's right said, "Okay then, so it was—Wait a minute! What did you say? The Green Phantasm! Who said that, huh? Where are you?"

The middle guy asked, "Are you that guy in yesterday's paper?"

"That would be me all right," answered the Green Phantasm.

Upon hearing that, the criminal who had originally been farthest left said firmly, "All right, you ugly neon freak! Get your bright-green ass over here now!"

In response, the Green Phantasm told him, "I don't think it's what you want, but, as you wish." Fortunately, the Phantasm already had a game plan. He chuckled, saying to himself, "They have no clue what they're getting themselves into. They're in for it."

In the meantime, the three thieves were anxiously awaiting the Green Phantasm's appearance. Each one was glancing in every direction with his gun held straight out in front of himself, ready to take out the Green Phantasm. However, they were all about to witness something they were not expecting at all.

The Green Phantasm went through with his game plan. He proceeded to teleport in order to reappear by the ATM machine, right behind the second and third thugs who had previously been farthest on his right.

Upon reappearing, the Green Phantasm waited a few seconds. However, he managed to remain unnoticed because the threesome were all focusing their attention away from the ATM. So, after those few seconds, the Phantasm tapped the shoulders of thugs number two and three. Immediately thereafter, he said to them, "Surprise, surprise."

The two crooks looked at each other and said, "*What*?" Then, they looked behind themselves only to see none other than the Green Phantasm. Before they had a chance to aim for him with their guns, the Green Phantasm bashed their two heads together, knocking them unconscious.

Consequently, the one who was still standing turned and looked back to his left when he heard the commotion. Of course, all he noticed was the Green Phantasm, since his two partners were unconscious on the ground. Upon seeing the enemy, the remaining thug began to try to turn himself and point his gun in that direction. At the same time, he yelled out, "Why you—Huh?" The Green Phantasm had just performed another teleportation, and the crook did not see where he had gone. Then, still looking around for the Green Phantasm, he asked, "Where'd you go?"

In the meantime, the Green Phantasm was actually hiding behind him. Every time the thief would look in a different direction, the Green Phantasm would get directly behind him to keep out of his field of vision. This was giving the Green Phantasm a good laugh. However, the thief was only becoming more and more frustrated. He said, "Come on now, this ain't funny! I ain't playing wit' you!"

After a couple of moments, the Green Phantasm had finally had enough fun picking on him. He finally used both of his hands to grab the guy by his right arm. At the same time, he said, "Well, what do you know? Another surprise, eh?"

"What!" exclaimed the shocked criminal. "Why you—"

But before he could finish, the Green Phantasm had lifted his arm up overhead. While doing so, he kept himself out of the line of fire from the gun. The Green Phantasm held the guy's right arm up with his right arm. At the same time, he used his left hand to grab and yank the gun out of the bad guy's hand and throw it several feet away from them, toward the intersection at Twenty-First Street.

"Oh please," the defenseless crook pleaded, "what are you gonna do to me?"

"I'm not gonna kill you," the Green Phantasm answered kindly. "Just remember one thing."

"What's that?" asked the crook.

"I'm the Green Phantasm," he declared. "You got that? Green Phantasm."

"All right," the guy replied.

Then, the Green Phantasm tried to show mercy by letting go of him to give him one more chance because, both as himself and as the Green Phantasm, James Clifton did not like to use any more violence or hostility than necessary. Fortunately, he had a strong desire to do right. That was why he was making an effort to stop and prevent crime. That was also why he wanted to keep his anger, aggression, and violence at the minimum level needed. Once the Green Phantasm released the criminal, the guy was somewhat grateful for not being treated too roughly and being let go. "Thanks, man," he said, breathing heavily and nervously.

"Oh sure," replied the Green Phantasm, "let's just not have any more trouble out of you. As a friend, I just want to tell you, I really think you need to change your ways. You can't continue like this. You'll get caught and taken in sooner or later. Just think about that, okay?"

However, the crook was not happy about what he had just been told. Before doing anything else, he quickly took offense and became angry at the Green Phantasm. Although he may have been grateful for the Green Phantasm's attempt to be fair and just, this piece of advice completely changed his attitude. Consequently, he asked angrily, "What did you say? Why I'll—"

He was now trying to throw a punch at the Green Phantasm with his right fist. However, the Green Phantasm caught it with his left hand and was now holding the guy's right wrist. The Phantasm just pinned him against the wall. At that, he said to the culprit, "You know what? That does it, pal. I tried to be nice to you. Now you're gonna pull this off, huh?"

No answer came from the thug. He just kept glaring at the Green Phantasm. After a moment, he attempted to throw a punch with his left hand, which the Green Phantasm was not holding. However, the Green

Phantasm just blocked the punch and pushed it aside. Then, the man took off his hat and threw it on the ground. At that instant, the Green Phantasm applied three consecutive head butts to his opponent, which. That rendered the victim unconscious along with his two partners.

After all that, the Green Phantasm went looking for a pay phone so he could report the mischievous threesome to the police. He walked until he found one near the corner of Arch and Twenty-first. Once there, the Green Phantasm just dialed 911.

The operator answered, "Nine-one-one Emergency."

The Green Phantasm said, "Yes, I just wanted to report something at the corner of Arch Street and Twenty-First Street. It was three guys that I believe were trying to break into and rob an ATM machine. I just saw them lying there unconscious near their van. Somebody needs to hurry and tend to them before something else happens."

"Who is this?" the telephone operator asked.

"Just a friend," answered the Green Phantasm. "But look, I got to get going. There may be a crime happening somewhere else." Upon saying that, the Green Phantasm hung up.

As soon as he hung up, the operator said, "That's strange."

The Green Phantasm activated his hovering ability and lifted himself up above the city, where he had been before. He was searching for either another sign of trouble or anywhere he might be needed. The Green Phantasm floated and glided around in different directions for a while.

After a few moments of searching, the Green Phantasm noticed something that caught and held his attention. Headed east on Race Street was an armored truck that was being pursued by four city police cars. Upon seeing that, the Green Phantasm decided to try to see whether he could help stop the armored truck.

First, the Green Phantasm drifted down to the part of Race Street that was between Seventh and Eighth Streets. He was trying to come up with a strategy for stopping the truck. Within half of a minute, he had figured out a way to cut it off. However, before he had a chance to do anything, the armored truck turned left and began heading north on Tenth Street, with the four patrol cars following.

Of course, that armored truck was protected by plate armor; it was one of those used by an armored car service to transport money or valuables. It happened to have been hijacked by a threesome. They were presently in control of it. They were armed and dangerous like the three guys that the Green Phantasm had stopped earlier. Each one had on a black jacket, a pair of gloves, and a cap, as well as a black mask that covered his eyes and nose. Other than that, each one simply wore jeans and work boots.

While the police cars were still pursuing the armored truck, the thieves were coming up with a game plan to stop them. As the chase continued heading straight north, the two crooks who were not driving went to the rear of the vehicle. One of them said, "I'll tell you what. Let's toss this safe at the car in front. Then, as two more try to pass him, we'll blast 'em with our machine guns. That ought to make a good chain reaction, eh?"

"I'm with you," replied the other one. "Let's do it."

The two of them then proceeded as planned. Together, they carried a four-foot-tall safe to the doors at the rear. They slowly and carefully opened the doors while making sure to brace themselves so that they would not fall out of the truck. Once they got the doors opened, they planted their feet out in front of them. Then, immediately, they lifted up the safe and hurled it into the patrol car directly behind them. The safe completely shattered the windshield and made an enormous dent across the hood. At that, the police officer driving that car just slammed on his brakes and stopped.

Immediately following that, two other officers went around the first car to continue the pursuit. However, the two criminals who had hurled the safe fired at those two patrol cars with their M-16 rifles. This did a lot of damage to the police cars, including shattered headlights, holes in the body and in the engine compartment, and blown-out tires. Three of the four cars were unable to chase them any longer. The fourth patrol car was stopped behind the wreckage because the three disabled police cars had the street blocked off.

In the meantime, the three in the armored truck just kept going north on Tenth Street, feeling proud of what they had just done. After thwarting the police officers and their cars, the two at the back of the truck just closed the doors. All three criminals gave each other a high five. "We got them! We took them out!" one of them exclaimed excitedly.

"Way to go, boys!" congratulated the driver. "I wonder who's gonna try to stop us now."

However, their celebration did not last long because the Green Phantasm had been watching everything from above. Now, he was going to go down and put an end to this mischief.

The threesome in the armored truck was still headed north on Tenth Street. They were now between Callowhill Street and Buttonwood Street. The Green Phantasm happened to be descending down to the corner of Spring Garden Street; he was now up ahead of them.

In the meantime, the three crooks still had a lot of pride in themselves for defeating the cops who had been after them. The driver was smiling and looking around in all different directions. However, that all stopped when something caught his eye. Without a doubt, it was none other than the neon-green flashing Green Phantasm. The driver saw him looking at them with both hands and arms pointed at them. The Phantasm was apparently charging both of his hands, preparing to open fire at them. At that, the driver of the armored truck yelled out, "Oh my God, no!"

"What is it?" asked one of the other two, who was coming to sit up front.

"Yeah, what was that?" asked the third guy.

But then, those other two got a look at him and said, "Holy shoot!"

The Green Phantasm began randomly firing laser beams from all ten fingers at the armored truck. In reaction, the driver yelled, "Yikes!" and took a sharp left turn onto Spring Garden Street.

While the truck was making that sharp left and the vehicle's weight was shifting right, the Green Phantasm combined the power of all ten fingers into one colossal, gigantic beam. He then fired this one enormous neon-green laser beam at the base and chassis of the armored truck. This caused the vehicle's center of gravity to shift so far right that the armored truck tipped over and landed on its right side. In effect, everyone and everything being transported fell and landed on the vehicle's inside right. The two guys up front landed on the passenger side's door. The third guy in the back had fallen to the right wall along with a heap of money.

Shortly, the crook who had been driving regained his senses and said, "Okay, you guys, that neon-green loser's gonna pay for this!"

Immediately thereafter, the one in the back, who was a bit dazed and confused, said, "Where are we? Who did this to us?"

At the same time, the one in the front beside the driver had regained his senses. He was now in a squatting position on the vehicle's right front door. He was getting ready to climb out through the driver's side window after the driver, who was already in the process of climbing out. But upon hearing those questions asked by the guy in the back, he stopped and said to him, "Come on now, you idiot! Don't you know who that was?"

"No, not really," the third guy replied.

The second guy told him, "It's that neon-green creep on the front page of yesterday's newspaper! I don't know too many neon-green people, do you?"

"No," he answered.

So then, the one up front said, "Well, come on, let's waste him, all right? Grab your machine gun."

"All right, I'm coming," the guy in the back responded.

By this time, the driver had gotten up and out of the overturned armored truck. Looking around for the Green Phantasm, he said, "All right, you neon punk, I'm gonna—"

Before he could even finish what he was saying, or spot the Green Phantasm, the Green Phantasm teleported over to where he was standing on top of the driver's side of the truck. Once there, the Green Phantasm immediately restrained the criminal by using both hands to grab hold of his machine gun. The Green Phantasm said, "You better watch it with this thing, pal."

"What!" exclaimed the surprised thug, "Why you—"

But before he could continue, the Green Phantasm punched him in the nose and mouth with a right crossover. This momentarily dazed him and allowed the Green Phantasm to seize his machine gun and throw it to the ground.

This made the crook even angrier. So once he could clearly see the Green Phantasm again after being dazed, he started to throw a straight right, saying, "All right, now I'm gonna—oof!"

The Green Phantasm had used his left hand to catch the bad guy's right forearm. As he was doing that, he used his right elbow to strike the crook's nose. He was still stunned by that when the Green Phantasm delivered a side kick that sent him sailing a bit before he finally landed on the ground.

Next, the Green Phantasm followed up by jumping down to the ground, where the bad guy was getting back up onto his feet and regaining his senses. Green Phantasm said to him, "Listen, pal, I want you to know one thing."

"Oh yeah? What's that?" he asked.

"I'm the Green Phantasm, you got that? Green Phantasm," said the Phantasm.

"I got it all right," the thief replied. However, he was still mad at the Phantasm. So he attempted to throw yet another right-hand punch at him. The Green Phantasm pushed the blow aside with his left hand. Immediately following, he punched the culprit in the abdominal area with a right uppercut. Then, he followed up on it with a left uppercut. That caused the thug to fall to his hands and knees.

The Green Phantasm looked down with pity at the crook, who was now holding his stomach in pain. He said to him, "You all right, buddy? Come on. Let me help you up." The Phantasm held out his right hand to allow the guy to take hold.

At first, the criminal was not too proud to accept the favor. He took hold of the Green Phantasm's right hand with his. Then, the Green Phantasm supported him until he was standing upright again. "Hey, buddy," said the Green Phantasm, "you okay?"

"Yeah, I'm all right," answered the criminal.

"That's good," said the Green Phantasm. "Now, you ought to listen up, because there's something I should tell you."

However, the crook was too obstinate to learn from the Green Phantasm. So, before he had a chance to say anything, the bad guy tried throwing a right hook. The Green Phantasm dodged by ducking under the blow. Immediately, he grabbed the guy by his left arm and whipped him backward into the bottom of the overturned armored truck. He then fell forward and landed facedown.

All the while the Green Phantasm had been busy dealing with the first of the three, the other two had been getting themselves ready to fight. They had now climbed out of the truck. From atop the driver's side, they were ready to open fire on the Green Phantasm.

Meanwhile, the Green Phantasm was trying to figure out what to do next with the first thug, who had been keeping him busy. For a couple of seconds, the Phantasm looked up and away. When he did, he managed to catch a glimpse of the other two, who were now aiming for him. Right after he caught a glimpse of them, he stopped and said, "Huh!" Then, he turned his complete attention to the two guys who were about to start shooting. The Green Phantasm thought, *I've got to do something quick.*

Fortunately, he quickly thought of a strategy. The Green Phantasm just decided to use the same technique he had used two nights before in both of his heroic deeds. He would take the form of a shapeless, neon-green projectile and travel along a serpentine path, knocking away both of the crooks.

The Green Phantasm charged and released himself. He shot forward toward the one he saw on his left. The first one he struck was knocked away as the Green Phantasm started a U-turn. Upon completing the U-turn, he knocked the other guy back too. Both bad guys were hit; they fell backward off the truck and lost hold of their machine guns before they even had a chance to fire at the Green Phantasm. After hitting the second of the two, the Green Phantasm made yet another U-turn. This propelled him forward again like he had intended at first. This put him on the roof side of the overturned truck, where the other two rogues now were. Then, Green Phantasm used his hovering ability to descend down to the ground after reappearing as himself.

Once the Green Phantasm was standing on the ground again, he walked over to the two creeps who were still recovering from being catapulted. The one to the Phantasm's left said, "There he is! Let's get him!" At that, he began walking aggressively toward the Green Phantasm with both fists in front of his face and a chip on his shoulder. When he made it over to the Green Phantasm, he got ready to throw a left hook. However, the Green Phantasm used his right hand to push both of the guy's fists to the right. As the Phantasm was finishing that, he countered the bad guy with his own left hook. This stunned the crook for a few seconds. After that, the Green Phantasm launched a straight right with all he had. He pegged the culprit in the very center of his chin. This caused the thug to go flying backward until he landed head and shoulders first faceup on the ground. The guy was so stunned and dazed that he was even hallucinating.

While the Green Phantasm was reveling in his success, the other criminal to his right approached. He was now very near. The Green

Phantasm noticed him in barely enough time to duck and avoid a right crossover. Immediately after ducking, the Green Phantasm hit the guy in his midsection with a right uppercut. This temporarily dazed him so that the Green Phantasm could get in another punch. This time, it was a right uppercut to the very middle of his face. This made him stumble backward into the overturned armored truck. He was lying on the ground facedown along the truck's length. Understandably, he too was dazed and hallucinating.

Next, the Green Phantasm just stood by, watching and waiting to see what the two criminals would do next. Within one minute, the first of the two to get knocked down finally managed to get back onto his feet. He went to help his partner recover too. Once the Green Phantasm saw that the two of them were recovered, he said, "Hey, you guys all right?"

In response to that, the two criminals just looked at him, rolled their eyes, and shook their heads in disbelief. Just like the only other one in that group of three, they were too stubborn even to think about getting friendly with the Green Phantasm. So the two guys looked at each other one more time. At that, one of them glanced toward the Green Phantasm for a second. Then, he made a fist with his right hand and placed it in the palm of his left hand, saying to his partner, "Let's fix this no-good neon freak."

"Yeah!" the other one said in agreement. Then, immediately, they both stormed toward the Green Phantasm with anger in their faces. As they were getting close, they both put their fists up like they were ready to fight.

This looked like a real good opportunity for James Clifton to utilize the skills he had developed as an amateur boxer. As the Green Phantasm, could he battle two opponents simultaneously at this very moment?

Well, whenever the Green Phantasm noticed the two ruffians closing in on him, he put up his dukes as well. Then, the one on his left tried to start things off by throwing a right jab at the Phantasm. But the Green Phantasm ducked to avoid it and then landed a left hook on the right side of the bad guy's jaw. This stunned him so that he staggered momentarily. The Green Phantasm used this opportunity to focus on the other guy.

Just as the Phantasm turned his attention to the guy on his right, a big straight right was headed at him. He ducked in the nick of time to avoid being hit. While returning to an upright position, he delivered a right uppercut to the bad guy's stomach. He immediately followed it up with a left hook to the guy's right cheek. This caused him to turn to his left, staggering in a bent-over position.

Meanwhile, the thug to the Green Phantasm's left had recovered from being stunned by the left hook. He started winding up his right arm for a big straight right. As he launched the big blow, the Green Phantasm quickly noticed and reacted by stooping and landing a left hook on the bad guy's rib cage. Immediately afterward, the Phantasm followed up with a right uppercut to the underside of the crook's jaw. This made him fall back down so that he was again lying faceup on the ground. But this time, he put his hand on the right side of his rib cage, which hurt from the left hook. He just lay there breathing rapidly in panic, holding his right side. At that, the Green Phantasm halted so that he would not hurt the guy too much.

But then, the other one to the Phantasm's right started heading toward him to throw a straight right. But in due time, the Green Phantasm noticed him. While the thug was delivering the punch, the Green Phantasm pushed his right arm aside. That very instant, the Phantasm grabbed hold of his left arm and whipped him face-first into the roof of the armored truck. Next, the Green Phantasm got just a little carried away and threw a right jab to the base of the criminal's skull.

As for the thug, this chain reaction nearly knocked him unconscious. He had already been staggering backward after hitting his face on the truck the first time. Then, before he knew what was happening, he fell backward to the ground. He hit his face the second time while being punched on the back of his neck and head. The guy was now lying face up, severely stunned and seeing all kinds of hallucinations.

The Green Phantasm was starting to get a little carried away, so he stopped to get ahold of himself. That was because he noticed the two guys lying helpless on the ground and did not want to beat them up too much.

However, the other member of the threesome, who had driven the armored truck, was now on the same side of the vehicle as everyone else. During the past few moments that the Green Phantasm had been busy with the other two, the driver had managed to regain control. He had been given enough time to regain his senses, get back on his feet, find his machine gun, get it ready, and make it over to the other side of the overturned truck. He was now prepared to dispose of the Green Phantasm.

Fortunately, while the Green Phantasm was watching over the two fallen criminals, he managed to notice the other one who was now to his far right. It was just in time too. The scoundrel was aiming at the Phantasm, about to pull the trigger.

Knowing he had practically no time left, the Green Phantasm came up with a strategy within a split second. He would head straight at the culprit in the form of a shapeless, radiating mass. Within just another split-second, he quickly energized and launched himself. In less than one more second, in his projectile form, that the Green Phantasm shot smack into the bad guy and went on to drive him backward into the first building at which this straight shot ended. Upon hitting the wall with the crook in front of him, the Green Phantasm reappeared as himself. The thug who had just been smashed against the building just fell forward unconscious. He was out cold.

The Green Phantasm then went back over to check on the other two men. By the time he had made it back over to them, one of the two had crawled over to reclaim his gun. He was now standing upright again. Upon seeing that, the Green Phantasm said, "I'd better stop him before he does any damage."

So, the Green Phantasm quickly teleported over to the crook before being spotted by him. Immediately after reappearing directly in front of the bad guy, the Green Phantasm used both hands to grab hold of the gun before the rascal even saw him.

When the thug felt something pulling on the gun, he said, "Hey! What the—" Then, he looked up at the Green Phantasm and said in surprise, "Oh! Why you—"

The Green Phantasm interrupted and said, "Yeah, you better watch it with that thing, pal."

The criminal uttered nervously, "How did you do that?"

But before the Phantasm could answer, he noticed something else he had to resolve. The other crook was running up behind him. He quickly thought of something to do. Since he and the first of the two were still holding on to the gun, he pulled on it to sling the first thug in an arc and backward into the one sneaking up behind him. With the first guy surprised and distracted for a few seconds, the Green Phantasm yanked the gun away and tossed it about fifteen feet to his left.

Upon turning his attention back over to the two culprits, he met the first one in front of him with a left jab to his right eye. Momentarily, the thug used both hands to hold his eye.

At once, the Green Phantasm went to work on the other creep, who attempted to throw a right jab followed by a left. However, the Green Phantasm dodged them both and hit the left side of the thug's rib cage with a right hook. Then, he followed it up with a left hook to the guy's temple. But the Green Phantasm stopped before he overdid it. That was because the one he had just hit was really groggy and in pain. He was leaning forward with one hand on his right temple and the other on the left of his rib cage, and he was whimpering.

Shortly thereafter, the other one to the Green Phantasm's left was feeling a little better. Having just taken his hands away from his right eye, he went toward the Phantasm, trying to deliver a right hook. At the same time, he said angrily, "Why you son of a—*Ow!*"

The Green Phantasm had caught his right arm and twisted it. Then, the Green Phantasm put his right elbow up by the guy's right temple and just used that elbow to hit him there. In the instant of impact, the Phantasm let go of his right arm. At that, the criminal began to stumble toward his partner, and he placed his left hand on his right temple.

Next, the crook on the Phantasm's right felt a little better and went to consult his partner next to him. He said, "Look, man, we gotta waste this guy."

"Yeah, we do," his partner said in agreement.

"Well, I suggest we both take him at once," said the one to the right.

At that, the one to the left shook off his pain and dizziness. He said, "Yeah, let's do that."

The one to the Phantasm's right said, "Ready?"

"I'm ready," said the thug to the left.

"All right," said the other one, "*now!*"

Just as they were both turning to attack simultaneously, the Green Phantasm grabbed their heads and smashed them together. He repeated that two more times. That knocked them both unconscious. So finally, all three criminals were lying on the ground out cold.

After all that, the Green Phantasm went to the nearest pay phone. He once again dialed 911. Once the operator answered, he said, "I need to report something on the corner of Tenth and Spring Garden. It's an overturned truck that had been hijacked. Three guys are lying unconscious nearby. It's the same armored truck that was headed up Tenth Street and evaded those four patrol cars. Fortunately, it didn't get too far."

"Do you know how it got turned over?" asked the operator.

"Well," answered the Green Phantasm, "I can't say that I do. But I did notice the overturned truck and the three lying unconscious around it. I just thought I'd let y'all know."

"Who is this?" asked the operator.

"I'm just a friend," answered the Green Phantasm, "but right now, I gotta get going." At that, he hung up.

Once he hung up, the operator asked herself, "Is that the same 'friend' who called a little earlier?"

In the meantime, the Green Phantasm went off looking for any other kind of mischief or crime that needed to be stopped. He was once again hovering far above downtown Philadelphia, as he had been doing earlier. While doing so, he thought some things over. He said, "Well, I don't know if I should've made that truck fall over. It feels like vandalism. But at least I stopped those rascals. I just didn't know how else to stop that armored truck. I'm afraid somebody's going to want to know how it got turned over. So maybe I need to figure out another way to stop a moving vehicle. Of course, I may need to confess what I did in this incident. After all, I can't keep running from my problems, because eventually, there will be too many of them. I might need to take some time to think about all this heroism. It's a responsibility."

After that, the Green Phantasm just continued searching. He sighed a couple of times and continued what he was saying. "I guess I want to say another thing too. I wouldn't recommend this task to anybody. That's mainly because it's so dangerous. A person could get killed doing what I'm doing. I mean like, with that group of three that I just dealt with, there were a couple of moments where I was fixing to die. I'm talking about the two times where two of them, and then one of them, was aiming a machine gun at me, ready to fire. If I'd have waited just a couple more seconds, I'd have been dead. I don't think I want to have anyone come with me to fight crime, especially not someone who doesn't have the powers I have. I mean, it's just that if they were to get killed, I'd feel like it was all my fault and I would never forgive myself. That's another reason I don't want to tell anybody who I am."

The Phantasm smiled and said, "But you know what? There's plenty of good things that come out of it too. I mean, of course I thought those two young women I rescued the other night were worth risking my life for. Also, with those two groups I stopped tonight well, at least I stopped them before they did any further damage or destruction. Of course, although I may have done a little damage to the truck, maybe I'll do something different next time. But, the only other thing I want to tell myself right now is that when I'm dealing with these groups of people like I did tonight, I probably need to be more careful and more watchful."

The Green Phantasm ended up above Buttonwood Street. Before he was there too long, a small pickup truck sped below him, headed west. He also heard the faint sound of a young woman's scream coming out of it. At that, he quickly teleported straight down to get a better look, for screaming often meant trouble. Shortly upon making it to the ground, he spotted two young men in the cab with a young woman sitting between them. Upon seeing that, the Green Phantasm said, "Oh no, I don't like what I'm seeing one bit. Those must be kidnappers. I got to hurry up and stop them."

The driver was about six feet tall, weighing around 180 pounds. He was wearing a white T-shirt and a black bandana. His head was shaved except for one long braid of hair hanging down in the back. He also had a mustache and a goatee. His partner on the passenger side was only about five feet eight inches in height and weighed 190 pounds. He was bald and dressed completely in black.

But the young lady who was captured was only about five feet four inches tall; she weighed about 110 pounds. She had blond hair that fell below her shoulders. She was wearing a white sleeveless blouse, a white skirt, and pair of high-heeled pumps. Understandably, she was afraid for her life, not knowing about the help she would receive momentarily.

The Green Phantasm decided to try a different strategy than he had tried with the armored truck. Before too long at all, he thought of something. This new game plan would involve him taking the form of a shapeless projectile.

The Green Phantasm was now ready to fire himself. At once, he charged up and shot himself straight along Buttonwood Street. That put him ahead of the small truck. Once there, he made a U-turn and shot back the opposite way. He only ended up landing and reappearing in the open back of the pickup. Also, just before reappearing as himself, the Green Phantasm had smashed right through the truck's windshield and rear window, leaving them completely shattered and gone.

All three in the front seat panicked at the crashing through of a bright-green flash, followed by the thumping sound in the open back. The short guy on the right looked around in all directions, yelling out, "What was that?" He had a sustained look of surprise on his face.

The driver had lost control and swerved left and right a couple of times. But then, he looked in his passenger side's mirror and noticed that the Green Phantasm was squatted down in the back. He then said to his partner, "Hey, man, you know what that was? It's that neon-green freak in the paper."

"It is?" asked his partner.

Then, the driver replied, "Yes, it is, you idiot! He's in the back of my truck!"

"Oh, is that right?" asked his partner.

"Of course that's right," answered the taller guy. "Now shoot him! Get rid of him! He put out my front and rear windows!"

"You got it, boss," replied the short guy on the right. Then at once, he pointed his revolver outside of where the rear window had been. But as soon as the Green Phantasm saw him getting ready to shoot his gun, he teleported diagonally to end up directly behind the young hoodlum. The young man had only managed to fire three shots when the Green Phantasm used his right hand to grab the guy's right wrist. Then immediately, the Green Phantasm used his left hand to take the gun and throw it out onto the street.

The young man was no doubt very surprised. "Hey!" he exclaimed. "Why you—Whoa!" The Green Phantasm was using both hands to grab the guy by both arms and pull him out of his seat, through the rear of the cab, and into the open back. Of course, the Green Phantasm had tightened up every part of his anatomy while radiating brighter in order to station himself against the rush of the wind from outside. The Phantasm only pulled him from the cab and threw him back toward the tailgate. While lying across the truck, the young ruffian was looking stunned, saying,

"Oh my God, how'd you do that?" He was no doubt wondering how the Phantasm had managed to evade those gunshots and throw him to the very rear of the truck.

In response, the Green Phantasm answered, "That's simply because I'm the one and only Green Phantasm. I'm the Green Phantasm, got that?"

The troublemaker said, "The Green Phantasm?" He was more than likely unwilling to believe either what had just happened or what he was seeing and hearing. Understandably, just like everyone else the Green Phantasm had encountered, this young man had never seen anyone or anything like him before.

The other two in the cab had received a big surprise whenever the guy on the right was suddenly lifted out of his seat. Both the driver and the young lady in the middle had cried out, "What?"

Then, the driver had gone on to say, "What happened?" After that, he turned his head backward to see over his right shoulder. However, he could not find a sign of anything besides his rear window gone and a vague image of his partner all the way against the tailgate. He could not see the Green Phantasm standing directly behind him out of his field of vision. So then, in a panic, he kept shifting his attention rapidly between the road in front of him and what he could see over his right shoulder. At the same time, he was asking, "What's happening? What's going on here?"

Within the next minute, the bad guy received a bigger fright. It was no doubt from the Green Phantasm, who was grabbing hold of both of his arms. Then, the Green Phantasm, who of course was bracing himself against a great rush of wind, pulled the driver out of the cab and threw him backward into the tailgate, where his partner already was.

The short bald one of the two said, "That guy's the Green Phantasm."

"All right!" his angry friend yelled. "So it is. So what?"

As soon as the Green Phantasm had removed both troublemakers from the cab, he teleported in order to reappear seated in the driver's seat. Then immediately, he slammed on the brakes, making the pickup screech to a sudden stop. The truck had now made it to Broad Street. The force of the sudden stop catapulted the two hoodlums up to the front of the open back. The beautiful, innocent girl up front was being projected too. But fortunately, the Green Phantasm grabbed hold of her and stopped her before she even hit the dash. The Green Phantasm then said, "I gotcha. Are you all right?"

Unfortunately, she was too scared and confused to answer. Since the Green Phantasm could sense that, he told her, "It's gonna be okay. I'm here to help you."

She let out a sigh of relief. Without a doubt, she was more than likely very happy and relieved to see the two kidnappers pulled away from both sides of her and a hero now in place of one of them. However, the poor girl was still a little too worried to say anything.

The Green Phantasm said, "But listen, I got to go take care of these two creeps, all right?" Immediately, he got out of the cab. He was now trying to prepare himself emotionally for another fight. He even put up his two fists.

The two kidnappers were now even angrier than before. The leader of the two said, "All right, I don't know how he managed to do this to us, but we're gonna make him pay. Let's put this freak away for good."

At that, he got up and jumped out the back of his truck, ending up on his feet in the middle of the road on the driver's side. He was now face-to-face with the Green Phantasm. Immediately, he pulled out a fifteen-inch-long fighting knife and held it up in front of himself, saying, "All right, you retarded neon freak, you've really made me mad. It's about to be all over for you." With the knife in his right hand, the thug moved toward the Phantasm, trying to swing it at his midsection. However, the Green Phantasm stepped back to avoid being slashed. The culprit advanced toward him again, this time trying to stab the Green Phantasm in the Adam's apple. But the Green Phantasm ducked under it. When he did, he threw a right uppercut to the guy's abdomen. This slightly dazed him for a few seconds. The Green Phantasm took his knife from him and tossed it aside. Then, he used his right hand to pin the bad guy's head against the side of the truck. At that, he hit him with a left crossover between his nose and mouth. This stunned the thug, and he staggered forward.

The Green Phantasm suddenly noticed that the guy's partner was about to join in too. This motivated the Phantasm to hurry up and finish off the leader. So he once again pinned the guy's head against the side of the pickup. But this time, he turned his head toward the front of the truck.

Then, he nailed the guy's jawbone with a big straight right. This snapped his neck and knocked him unconscious.

The Green Phantasm immediately turned his attention to the short guy. The young man tried to launch a big straight right, but the Green Phantasm caught his arm and threw him backward into the truck's open door. Then, the Green Phantasm took off his hat and placed it on the driver's seat. Finally, he delivered three consecutive head butts to the thug's nose, rendering him unconscious as well.

With the two guys unconscious on the ground, the Green Phantasm went to tend to the young woman, who was still in the cab. First, he untied her hands from behind her back. Afterward, he helped her out of the truck while saying in a friendly tone, "Come on; it's okay."

The young woman threw her arms around the Phantasm, giving him a sustained hug. She said through her tears, "Thank you so much. I thought my life was over. I was so scared. Thank you." Still crying, she would not let go. The Green Phantasm just let her hold on to him and cry all she wanted.

After a few minutes, the girl stopped crying and wiped away her tears. At that, she said to the Green Phantasm, "Thank you so much for saving my life."

"Oh, no problem," replied the Green Phantasm.

"You know," said the young girl, "I wish there was something I could do to repay you."

"Oh, it's all right," said the Green Phantasm.

"Well, anyway," she said, "who are you?"

"Well," began the Green Phantasm, "I'm... uh... uh..." Then, he exhaled heavily, not knowing what to say.

"What's wrong?" asked the concerned young lady.

The Green Phantasm hesitated because he was about to say his real name, which of course was James Clifton. He had to stop himself from giving away his identity. He finally said to her, "Oh, nothing's wrong, nothing at all. I'm the Green Phantasm."

"Oh, wow!" exclaimed the girl happily. "The Green Phantasm! That's a good name for you. Even what you did seemed unreal. It's good to meet you."

"Well, thank you," replied the Green Phantasm. Then, after a moment of silence, he said, "Look, we need to call for help. I'll notify the police at once."

The girl grabbed his right arm and pleaded, saying, "No, please, Mister Green Phantasm, we don't need them, not as long as I got you."

The Green Phantasm removed both of her hands and said, "I have to call them. It's the right thing to do. We have to report this to them." He was saying this because even as the Green Phantasm, Clifton wanted to stick to what was right and would not go against the law.

"Oh, all right," the young woman said, somewhat disappointed.

The Green Phantasm retrieved his hat from the driver's seat of the truck. Then, he went to the nearest pay phone. Not knowing what else to do, he dialed 911 again; he wanted to get help there as soon as possible.

The operator answered, "Nine-one-one emergency?"

"Yes, ma'am," said the Green Phantasm, "I need to report something over on the corner of Broad Street and Buttonwood. It's a pair of kidnappers who were in a pickup truck."

"Where are they now?" asked the operator. "Do you know?"

The Green Phantasm sighed and said, "Yes, I do. They're still on that same corner. Their truck is stopped and parked, and they're lying unconscious on the driver's side of it."

Then, in a firmer tone of voice than she had used in the earlier two calls, the operator asked, "Now, do you know who did that to them? I mean, someone has called here two other times tonight with guys lying unconscious. You sound just like the same one who called before. Other than that, I heard a rumor that there was someone involved called the Green Phantasm. I can't help wondering if it's he that I'm speaking to. I mean, have you anything to do with him?"

"Well, perhaps," answered the Green Phantasm. "But I can't talk anymore right now. I gotta go. Just get some help out here fast." At that, he hung up.

He went back over to the young woman he had rescued. He said to her, "Look, I just made the call for you. The police should be on their way. Right now, I gotta get going. Someone else may be in trouble as we speak. Take care now." At once, the Green Phantasm began to hover and then drifted away.

However, before he was too far off the ground, the girl cried out to him, "Wait!"

Sympathetically, the Green Phantasm came back down and said, "What is it, sweetheart?"

She took hold of his right hand and forearm and begged, "Please don't leave me. I don't want you to go. I feel so much safer with you around."

That gave the Green Phantasm an idea. He smiled and said, "I'll tell you what. I'll stand by until the police make it here. I'll go nearby and stay there, and I won't leave until you make it through this and get a ride home. I promise I won't abandon you. I mean, after all, I feel somewhat responsible for all this. I'll be around. Don't you worry."

Feeling a little better, the young lady smiled and said, "Okay."

At that, the Green Phantasm crossed Buttonwood Street to the nearest building and ascended to hover above it. Then, of course, he let himself down onto the roof. From there, he waited, keeping watch until the Philadelphia police arrived. Fortunately, the two kidnappers were still lying on the ground unconscious. The Green Phantasm just wanted to stand by in case the two hoodlums were to regain consciousness, and he had to come to the girl's aid again.

Fortunately, two patrol cars drove up to the scene within a minute. At once, the officers tended to the two knocked-out kidnappers as well as the lovely innocent victim. As soon as the officers began handling the situation, the Green Phantasm shot off in a southwesterly direction.

Very shortly thereafter, the Phantasm was hovering approximately above the intersection of Market and Eighteenth Streets. Before looking for anything else, he took a little time to think about what he had just gone through. He said, "You know, so far, every time I've stopped a criminal or troublemaker, it's given me something more to think about. For one thing, being a superhero was at one time fun to think about, but I guess it's more serious than I thought. I mean, I now realize more than ever that it's a heavy responsibility. Regardless of that, I've got to do it. After all, I would like Philadelphia to be a safer place for everyone as well as myself. I don't know a better way to help to do that than to assist in the prevention of crime. Of course, like I said, it's a heavy responsibility. I'm even risking my own life doing it, and I need to be real careful as far as that goes. I also need to be careful regarding the ones I save and protect like with the pretty blonde I just came to the aid of in the incident with those two kidnappers."

The Green Phantasm paused for a moment and then said, "You know, speaking of that incident, I'd like to think a little on that too. Now of course, I'm not a hundred percent sure I should've smashed through both the front and rear windows of that pickup. It feels like destruction of property. But at least I didn't make it fall over like I did the armored truck. All I did was break the windows. But maybe I could've done something different. But anyway, at least I don't feel too much guilt knowing that those psychos were kidnappers, especially with the way they were inexcusably mistreating that blameless, sweet, defenseless little girl. Oh, what a shame, you know? That just made me think of something else. Even as serious and risky as this task is of being a hero, I think perhaps the people in Philadelphia need me. For instance, I'm not sure the police would've been notified in time to save that poor girl. What if I hadn't been there for her? If she'd have gotten killed or seriously injured, I'd have never forgiven myself." At that, the Green Phantasm fell quiet with a sad look on his face. He remained that way for about two minutes.

But then, after that, he began to smile again, saying, "But you know what? At least there's some good thoughts I have pertaining to what I've been talking about. I perceived that the young girl had confidence and faith in me. I mean, she didn't want me to call the police because she had more trust in me. Even after I made the call, she didn't want me to leave her because she obviously put her trust in me. That made me feel good, knowing I was trusted, needed, and appreciated. That gives me pride in my heroism." After saying that, the Green Phantasm looked up into the sky in different directions, with a sustained smile.

Within a moment, however, he said, "Oh well, I guess I need to move on and see what else I can find. But before I do, I just want to say one more thing. So far, I've probably made quite a few mistakes while trying to be heroic. But at least I've saved a few lives. Hopefully that's what matters more. But anyway, I guess it's time to move forward. Here I go. Let's see what I can find here." So, still hovering above Market and Eighteenth, the Green Phantasm began drifting eastward above downtown Philadelphia, searching for anyone or anything that needed his aid.

The Green Phantasm's search did not last long. While gliding a few hundred feet above the ground, he eventually found something that caught his eye. A woman was walking north on the east side of Broad Street. She was only about five feet two inches tall, weighing about 105 pounds. She had blond hair that went to just below her shoulders and green eyes. She was wearing a short-sleeve blouse, a skirt, and casual slip-on pumps. She was around forty-two years of age. At the time of the Phantasm spotting her, the little lady had not made it too far north of a subway station near City Hall.

As the Green Phantasm paused to observe her, he said, "Well, what do you know? That looks like a really nice lady right there. Of course, I can't quite tell. She's either in her midthirties or just becoming middle-aged. Oh well, I've never been a professional at determining anyone's age. At least I think she's cute."

Another reason that the Green Phantasm was watching this particular woman was that a subway station was not too far behind. Of course, terrible things had happened to people in subway stations, he knew. James Clifton did not want anything to happen to this innocent lady from someone coming out of the station. So, as the Green Phantasm, he stayed where he was and kept watching her.

Eventually, the woman made it north of Cherry Street; she kept heading north. At the same time, someone was coming up out of a station around Race and Vine Streets. It was a young man about six feet two inches tall and 260 pounds. He had shoulder-length, wavy, dark-brown hair and brown eyes. He was dressed completely in black, including a black jacket, a pair of gloves, and a bandana, as well as a black patch over his right eye. He also had earrings in both ears. Upon reaching the top of the stairs, he was putting away a nine-millimeter semiautomatic pistol and looking around to make sure no one was watching.

The woman the Phantasm had been observing was getting close to that same station. Although she was not looking directly at the guy who was coming up, she noticed him putting away something from the corner of her eye and suspected it to be a deadly weapon. Upon noticing, she stopped, gasped, turned around, and began walking fast south.

Unfortunately. the mischievous young ruffian noticed her sudden change of direction. At that, he turned around and saw her walking quickly away from him. He said, "Aw, shoot, she must've seen what I did!" At once, he started running after her.

Once the little woman sensed someone running up behind her, she sped up and began running too. But unfortunately, she was not as fast as the guy behind her.

Fortunately, the Green Phantasm had so far seen everything that was going on. He said, "Oh no, this doesn't look too good. I'd better drift on down just in case something's going to happen." So then, the Green Phantasm descended downward until he touched the ground. He ended up at the northeast corner of the intersection of Broad and Arch Streets. He then hid himself around the corner of the nearest building so he could spy on the situation.

But next, when the small, desperate woman had almost made it to the corner at Arch Street, he suddenly caught her by the hair and threw her down to the ground. The ruthless thug was two and a half times her size. At once, he used his left hand to take out his nine-millimeter and his right foot to turn her and lay her in a faceup position. He said to the poor woman in a threatening manner while holding her at gunpoint, "Hold it, little lady! Don't you dare say a word or make a sound! If you say anything or scream, I drill you. You got it? Now look, we're going into the subway, you and me. First of all, let me have your purse." Understandably, the frightened, innocent sweet lady was shaking and breathing nervously. Afraid for her life, she cooperatively began to hand over her purse.

Of course, in the meantime, the Green Phantasm was not at all happy with what he was witnessing. He had anger and tension building up inside of him with each and every move that the bad guy made. So then, before the guy even got ahold of the woman's purse, the Green Phantasm shot two consecutive laser beams. The first one hit the guy's wrist, pushing his left hand off to his left and pointing the gun away from the unfortunate victim. The second beam hit the bad guy's knuckles on his left hand. This made him lose his grip and drop the gun. Immediately, he tried to shake the pain off his burning knuckles. A few seconds later, he looked to his right, angrily muttering, "I don't know who did that, but now I'm gonna—"

While he was reaching for the gun, he had dropped, the Green Phantasm suddenly teleported and reappeared directly in front of him. Then, of course, they were face-to-face. The Phantasm went on to rebuke him, saying, "All right, creep, this has gone far enough! You ought to be ashamed of yourself."

"Oh," said the troublemaker. "So that was you, huh?"

"You bet your life it was," answered the Green Phantasm.

"Well," the hoodlum said, "I suppose you're that neon-green moron in yesterday's newspaper. But I suggest you move on before I slash your radioactive carcass from one end of this town to the other."

"You know," responded the Phantasm, "maybe I would, but I won't have this. I mean, bullying this helpless, innocent lady who's not even half your size? Not while I'm around. Now I'd like to kindly suggest that you change your ways. You can't keep going through life like this."

It was the goodness in James Clifton that made him try to handle the situation that way. Either as himself or the Green Phantasm, he liked to give people a chance before using a lot of physical force. James did not enjoy hurting others. However, he would do so when he was given no other choice. A lot of the crooks that the Phantasm would try to deal with had too much pride in themselves to take advice, but he still cared enough to try to be fair.

This troublesome scamp that the Green Phantasm was trying to handle was just as stubborn as the rest of them. Unfortunately, the culprit just took offense and became angrier at being advised. He made both hands into fists and gnashed his teeth while glaring at the Green Phantasm. Then, he said, "All right, that's it! You asked for it! Now you're gonna get it!" At that, the thug used his right hand to take out a thirty-five-inch-long machete, which he held out in front of himself and pointed toward the Phantasm.

Upon seeing that, the Green Phantasm shrank back with a look of surprise. No other knife pulled on him up to that point had amounted to that. He thought to himself, *Whoa, gosh! For some reason, these knives get bigger and bigger with every creep I gotta face.* This instant of surprise gave the bad guy a chance to strike at the Green Phantasm. He swished the machete to his left, trying to cut him, but the Green Phantasm took a couple of steps and leaned back to avoid getting slashed.

The middle-aged female victim had gotten up and stepped away once the Green Phantasm had gotten between the two of them. She was now about twenty feet behind the Green Phantasm. She was no doubt very relieved and probably admired the goodness and bravery of the Green Phantasm. But at the same time, she was worried for him as he was being attacked with a machete. She was so grateful for his coming to the rescue, and she hoped he would win.

The Phantasm had temporarily shrunk back because he was overwhelmed by the size of the knife and did not think about anything else. But before too long, he managed to catch a glimpse of his radiating hands. That gave him a reminder. It made him think to himself, *What am I doing? I forgot for a moment that I had these powers. I don't have to be afraid of that machete. Here I go.* At that, the Green Phantasm stopped to charge up for his next move.

At the same time, however, the big bully had just finished swinging his machete to his left. He was now about to swing it back across and even managed to begin the rightward swing. However, it proved to be futile; it was too late for him.

This was because the Green Phantasm took his form as a shapeless radiant projectile. No handheld weapon could stop him then. So, even when the thug was in the middle of a swing, the Green Phantasm launched himself directly at his center mass. Within a split-second, the bad guy was squashed against the fencing around the subway station's entrance, and the machete flew out of his hand. The creep was propelled and crushed with such force that he was rendered unconscious. He wound up lying facedown after falling forward.

The Green Phantasm walked back toward the corner to check on the kind woman who had been threatened. Once there, he asked her with sympathy, "Are you okay?"

She just threw both arms around his midsection, giving him a really big hug. "Oh, thank you so much!" she told him. "Thank you Mister… um, um."

"Green Phantasm," he said. "I'm the Green Phantasm."

"Oh," she replied, "well, thank you, Green Phantasm."

"Sure, no problem," said the Green Phantasm as he hugged her in return.

After their hug, the nice lady used both hands to take hold of the Phantasm's left hand. She wanted to further express her gratitude. She continued by saying, "You know, that was a brave thing to do. That was also good the way you handled it. You're amazing, and you're such a nice man. I wish I could do something for you in return."

"That's all right," said the Green Phantasm. "You've done more than enough already. I just like to know I'm appreciated."

"Well," the woman said, "I appreciate you very, very much. You sure you don't need anything?"

"Well, thanks," answered the Phantasm, "but I'm fine. I just hope you are too. Do you need me to call the police?"

"No," said the woman. "I got it. I'll call them on my cell phone." At that, she took her cellular phone out of her purse. She called the Philadelphia police and told them where she was and what had happened. After that, she hung up and turned her attention back to the Green Phantasm. She said, "You know something? Now that I've met you, I'd like to get to know more about you."

The Green Phantasm heard the sound of a siren from a patrol car getting near, and he wanted to leave before being spotted. He told the lady, "Look, ma'am, I really appreciate your kindness, and I wish we could talk some more, but I've got to get going. Someone else may need my help."

He had a guilty feeling as well as an ashamed look on his face. Sadly, he said, "I'm terribly sorry to end this so abruptly. Good-bye, and take care of yourself, okay?"

"Well, all right," answered the disappointed lady.

All at once, the Green Phantasm took the form of a projectile and whizzed over to the subway entrance and down the stairs. He finally reappeared as himself at the bottom of those stairs. He went on to tell himself, "Well, I just thought I might zoom on down into the subway. I mean, it's not only because I didn't want to be seen by the cops; it's also that I saw that psycho coming up out of here. It reminded me that terrible things have happened down in subways. So I thought maybe I'd check the subway to make sure there were no such happenings or anything. Let's see here."

The Green Phantasm started looking around in every possible direction. However, no one at all was anywhere in sight. He decided to go over to the tunnel to his right to see what he could scope out. While he was running over to it, he occasionally peeked over his left shoulder to make sure he was in no danger.

Finally, the Phantasm made it to the tunnel. Once there, he did one more thing before going into it. He slowly leaned forward and looked both ways. When he saw that the coast was clear, he hopped down onto the nearest railroad track. He walked down the tunnel, watching his back as he went.

The Phantasm stopped when he was about thirty feet into the tunnel. He flattened himself back against the wall. For the next five minutes, he stayed there trying to watch and listen for any sign of trouble or danger. The Green Phantasm finally decided to move on since he could not sense anything amiss.

Once he began to press on, he heard the rising sound of an approaching train. He stopped and looked all around in panic. He said, "I'd better be careful. I got smacked by one the other night."

Fortunately, the train he heard was approaching the station he had just left from the other tunnel. The Green Phantasm realized this when he saw the shine of the headlight getting closer and closer. However, he wanted to get going before someone saw him.

He quickly charged himself up, getting ready to shoot himself as a shapeless projectile again. Once charged, he unleashed himself and wound up a quarter of a mile down the track. He repeated the process until he finally saw something up ahead. It was the station at Spring Garden. The Green Phantasm had come to within about one hundred fifty feet of it. Since he was that close, he just ran up to it.

Once there, he took a quick look around the station for anyone who needed to be helped or stopped, but he had the same luck as at the station from which he had just come. No one whatsoever was present as far as the Phantasm could see. He said, "Well, what do you know? There ain't much going on in the subway tonight. I guess I'll get back above ground."

The Green Phantasm went on up the steps. That put him back along Broad Street. Once above ground again, he took a quick look all around to see whether anything bad was happening. He found no sign of trouble, so he just started running north, passing a few streets. He continued until he got to Wallace Street. The Phantasm stopped there once he heard something east of him in the distance.

The sound was coming from the part of Wallace Street between Tenth and Eleventh Streets. It was the combined sound of a lot of yelling and carrying on of some teenage high-school dropouts. The Green Phantasm said, "I wonder who that is and what they're up to."

He shot himself over to the intersection at Twelfth Street. He reappeared between Eleventh and Twelfth. That got him a better look at the situation. The source of all the commotion turned out to be a gang of six teenage boys who had dropped out of school in the tenth grade. They were of somewhat various sizes with the largest being six feet tall and weighing two hundred twenty pounds. They all had different hairstyles popular with gangsters and wore different street clothes. Some even sported tattoos, earrings, bandanas, and other such articles. This gang of teens was running over to a seventy-two-year-old man who was using a cane. The man was dressed in a suit and tie; he even wore a few beautiful rings.

The six young gangsters managed to surround the rather elderly man by the time he had reached the northwest corner at Broad and Tenth Streets. When he noticed he was surrounded, he said, "Hi, fellas, can I help y'all with something?"

"Yeah," one of the teenagers said. "I want those rings you're wearing."

"Excuse me?" the old man asked.

Then, another boy said, "I want some money from you." At that, every one of them held out an object that he could use as a weapon. Two of them each had a pocketknife. One had a baseball bat. Another had a slingshot, but the other two just put up their fists.

Seeing that he was about to be attacked, the man in the middle said, "Wait a minute, guys. What are y'all doing?"

But before any of them could take a step toward the man, the Green Phantasm teleported and reappeared right next to the helpless old man.

When the boys saw him suddenly appear, they all shrank back in surprise. "Whoa! Who is that?" asked one of them.

The friend to his right said, "Didn't you hear about some neon-green guy in the paper? That's gotta be him."

Next, the Green Phantasm took a few seconds to think to himself, Okay now, these are minors. Perhaps I should try not to be too rough with them.

After that, he addressed them, saying, "All right, guys, what's going on here? What are y'all trying to do to this poor old man, huh? Can't y'all see how weak and helpless he is?" At that, they all just looked around at each other, shrugging their shoulders and shaking their heads.

Continuing, the Green Phantasm asked them, "And what are y'all doing out and about like this on a school night? Are any of you even in school?"

The biggest boy answered by saying, "Well, why does that matter to you? Why are you asking us that?" Other than that, none of them said anything.

The Green Phantasm could then perceive that they were dropouts. He went on to say to them, "Oh, so you all did quit school. Well, I want to say something as your friend. I honestly believe that all of you need to straighten yourselves out and go back to high school. There's not much hope for people like you. Without a high school education, it's a lot harder to obtain a very good job. If I were one of you, I'd turn my life around and get back in school. Do y'all read me?"

Upon hearing that, all six of them began looking at each other, shaking their heads, and muttering. Then, they all said together, "Boo!"

After that, one of them said, "Let's get him!" At that, the ones with weapons held them up again.

The Green Phantasm quickly charged up both hands as well as all ten fingers. He was preparing to fire laser beams in different directions.

He fired four individual small beams that knocked the weapons out of the hands of four of the boys. When that happened, all the shocked teenagers halted and gasped with expressions of surprise. "How'd he do that?" one of them asked.

So, while they were all in a state of shock, the Green Phantasm utilized that moment to set up a force field around himself and the old man he was protecting. This was for his next trick. Just before the bottom of the force field's sphere was formed, he said, "Watch your feet, old-timer." At that, the man lifted up one foot at a time to allow the force field's outer layer to pass underneath. The Green Phantasm was slightly hovering.

By then, the gang of six teenagers had gotten over the surprise they had received. They were ready to try something different. The four who had dropped their weapons went and retrieved them. The biggest boy said, "You guys ready? Let's close in on 'em."

They all went running toward the two men in the middle. However, every one of them collided face-first with the force field that they could not clearly see. They were all nearly knocked out and were severely stunned. They all fell back and landed faceup on the ground. One of them even said, "What hit me?" Every one of those boys was no doubt dazed and confused.

Another one said, "I don't know what or how, but it's something he did that hit all of us."

The Green Phantasm took down the force field.

After a couple of minutes of lying around stunned, the six gangsters finally regained their senses. However, they stayed down on the ground, because they were now too scared of the Green Phantasm. One of them said desperately, "You're not gonna kill us, are you? I tell you what. I quit, okay? I admit defeat."

"Yeah," agreed another, "we don't want any more trouble."

Finally, the biggest boy said, "Look, I now know that we have no chance against you. I'll do anything you say."

"Well, that's good," replied the Green Phantasm, "That's really good. Well, guys, I'll tell y'all what I'll do. I won't do any more harm to y'all right now since you're still only teenagers. I just want you all to think about what just happened, and I suggest you let this be a lesson to you. Maybe that'll help you all make better decisions from now on. But right now, there's just one thing I want you to do for me."

"Sure, anything," one of them said.

"All right," said the Green Phantasm, "very well. I want each and every one of you to run along home right this minute. Just get up and go home, all right? Now go! Scram! Get outta here!"

"Come on, let's go," one of them said desperately. At once, that entire group of youths scurried south along Tenth Street; they kept on running without looking back.

Next, the elderly man looked toward the Green Phantasm and said to him, "By George, that was a miracle if I ever saw one. Thank you, young man."

"Oh, it's nothing," replied the Green Phantasm. "I just want this city to be safer and more peaceful."

"You know," said the man, "I do too. What's your name, son?"

"Green Phantasm," answered the Phantasm, shaking hands with the old man.

"Pleased to meet you," the man said to him.

"Well," chuckled the Green Phantasm, "same here, but right now, I gotta get going. There's no tellin' what might be happening where. I'm sorry to rush off like this. Just take care of yourself, old-timer, and be careful. It's a rough city."

"All right," the man replied. "You too."

The Green Phantasm charged himself and shot straight up. He reappeared hovering a few hundred feet above the ground. While remaining afloat, he said to himself, "Well, let's see. I think it is getting rather late, and perhaps I should call it a night. Maybe I will. But before I do, I think I'll head southwest for a moment to scope that out before I wrap it up for tonight."

The Green Phantasm shot himself as a projectile over to the intersection of Pine and Eighteenth Streets. Upon reappearing there, he descended to the ground. That put him on the west side of Eighteenth Street.

Next, the Green Phantasm looked all around for any bad signs before moving on. Then, he jogged over to the intersection at Seventeenth Street. He also stopped for a moment to look all around there. Finally, the Phantasm just kept on running north on Seventeenth Street.

He ran on past a few streets as he was headed north. However, as he was passing Walnut Street, he heard a voice yell out, "There he is!"

Upon hearing that, the Green Phantasm stopped and said, "Wait a minute. What? There who is?" He walked a few yards south back to Walnut Street. Once there, he looked east down Walnut to see what he could.

But unfortunately, as soon as he had made it back to Walnut, two young men with M-16 machine guns were there to meet him. One of them was ten feet east of him on the north side of Walnut. The other was across on the south side. "Now we got him," said the first one.

"Hold it right there!" yelled the other one from across the street.

These two young men were about average-sized, no more than five feet ten inches tall with an average build. They were aged twenty-three and twenty-four. Other than just ordinary black jeans and work boots, they were both wearing light green T-shirts. The T-shirts had large, thick, black capital letters printed on the fronts and backs of them. The T-shirt of the one closest to the Green Phantasm read, "WASP KILLER." The shirt of the one across the street read, "HORNET KILLER." On the left-hand side of the front of both shirts, a small, black logotype said "X-Termination." Other than that, they both had on light-green masks that completely covered their heads except for openings for their eyes and mouths, which were lined with black. Each mouth's opening was shaped like an extended upside-down trapezoid, and each pair of eye openings was shaped like a pair of rhombuses that slanted away from one another.

Caught in a state of panic, the Green Phantasm was not certain what to do. But on his first impulse, he became a projectile and shot himself with a right turn back around the corner. He still did not know the best solution to his predicament. The only idea the Phantasm came to have was to put up a force field so that he could at least protect himself from gunfire. He did just that.

In the meantime, both Wasp Killer and Hornet Killer, as he dubbed them, were slightly shocked by the Green Phantasm's sudden disappearance. "Where'd he go?" asked Wasp Killer.

"Well," answered Hornet Killer, "I almost couldn't see him, but I think he took a right, right there."

"Oh, he did?" asked Wasp Killer. "Well, let's go see what we can find. We just got to get rid of this guy like the boss told us. I mean, this is the guy, right?"

"Of course it's him," Hornet Killer answered. "How many guys can there be that radiate neon-green light?"

"You're right," agreed Wasp Killer. "Let's put his neon lights out. Come on!"

At that, they both began to run toward the corner. But before they had even taken three steps each, the Green Phantasm came hovering and floating back around. He had enclosed himself in a force field and was elevated two feet above the ground. He moved slowly along Walnut Street. The two bad guys stopped themselves once they saw him hovering by.

"Whoa," said Wasp Killer. "Check it out."

"Yeah," said Hornet Killer in agreement. "There he is. Let's waste him." At once, they both opened fire on the Green Phantasm. They were persistently and determinedly firing round after round after round. However, the bullets only bounced off the outermost layer of the force field.

After a couple of moments, the gunfire stopped. The Green Phantasm was halfway between Seventeenth Street and Sixteenth Street. Wasp Killer and Hornet Killer just stopped shooting and looked at each other in confusion. Wasp Killer said, "Man. I don't understand this. I mean, with all the ammo we just went through, we're not getting anywhere with this. I can't understand why nothing's happening."

"Well," responded Hornet Killer, "perhaps he's got something protecting him, like… I don't know… a force field or something perhaps. Maybe that's why none of these bullets are getting to him. But whatever the case is, I ain't gonna keep wasting my bullets on him. We just might have to think of another way. I mean, we have to take him down somehow. We just gotta eliminate him."

Wasp Killer said, "Yeah, but if what you suggested was true, this is a force field we're dealing with. Now what can we do?"

"Well," answered Hornet Killer. "Let's just try and think about it. We're gonna get him somehow."

"I guess you're right," replied Wasp Killer. "I mean, after all, we just gotta take care of him."

"Yeah," said Hornet Killer, "we can't go back to headquarters until it's done, all right? Now let's see here." They both kept looking all around while racking their brains, because they were both very puzzled. How did they expect to penetrate the force field when all those bullets could not go through it?

While those two villains were busy thinking hard and concentrating, the Green Phantasm was thinking too. He was trying to come up with a way to take this twosome out. Finally, the Phantasm decided to try something while Wasp Killer and Hornet Killer were not paying full attention to him. He slowly began to retract his force field, making sure they did not notice. The Phantasm was going to give those two rogues a surprise attack.

Within another minute, the force field was finally down. The Green Phantasm was still afloat, like when he had come back around the corner, but now without a force field.

In the meantime, Wasp Killer was becoming a bit discouraged. "Look, man," he said to his partner, "I don't know about this. I mean, what if there's no way to take him down?"

"Now look," Hornet Killer told him. "Let's not give up hope just yet. There's no tellin' what we might figure out. Maybe we'll catch him in a weak state of mind or something. Who knows? There just has to be a way. We'll figure it out."

The Green Phantasm just chuckled softly and whispered, "You fools, I have taken off my force field." He paused for a few seconds and said, "Well, here goes."

Having said that, the Green Phantasm shot down to appear in front of Hornet Killer. This no doubt caught him by surprise and scared him. While he was shocked, the Green Phantasm grabbed hold of his machine gun and used it to sling him backward into Wasp Killer. Both guys staggered a little bit from the impact and nearly fell.

While the two bad guys were trying to regain their balance and refocus, the Green Phantasm quickly teleported to the right side of both of them. Just as the two men regained their senses fully, the Green Phantasm used both hands to grasp both of their guns and point them up overhead. At the same time, Wasp Killer and Hornet Killer were struggling to regain control. "Hey, let go!" they were both shouting.

The Green Phantasm put up his defense mechanism; he tightened up every part of his anatomy, radiating brighter and becoming able to stand against anything. As he was doing that, Wasp Killer and Hornet Killer were having a harder time trying to pry their machine guns loose, for the Phantasm was becoming less movable.

Wasp Killer was becoming frightened. When he saw that the Green Phantasm's radiation was getting brighter and brighter, he began to shrink back in fear. "What's happening?" he cried. "I can't do anything! I can't even budge him anymore! What'll I do?"

Anyhow, although Hornet Killer was having trouble too, he was still just as determined. "Oh, come off it!" he told Wasp Killer. "We can still take him." He gave a good hard kick to the Green Phantasm's shin. But it was not at all effective. "Ah, shoot!" he muttered. After that, still pulling on his gun, which was immovable, he threw a side kick to the Phantasm's midsection as hard as he possibly could. However, it did not even move the Phantasm a single millimeter. "Dang it!" Hornet Killer yelled in frustration. "I can't believe this!"

But next, the Green Phantasm finally yanked the two guns out of their hands. That very instant, he tossed the weapons back behind himself. The Green Phantasm loosened up again, with his radiation falling back to normal.

The Green Phantasm was now forced to fight Wasp Killer and Hornet Killer, for they were no doubt mad about having their guns taken away from them. First of all, Hornet Killer marched with his fists up and then threw a left hook. The Green Phantasm ducked underneath it and used a couple of his own hooks to hit him on both sides of the rib cage. It was very painful for Hornet Killer. So he stepped away for a moment while holding on to his ribs.

The Green Phantasm had to turn his attention to Wasp Killer because he was throwing a big, straight right, which the Phantasm barely evaded by swaying to his left. While dodging, the Phantasm threw his own left hook, which hit Wasp Killer in the kidney area. This definitely made him stagger backward while holding the right side of his lower back. The Green Phantasm shrank back in pity for a moment. In fact, he stopped what he was doing completely to look on as both of the culprits were still suffering from the painful blows they had received. Although both guys had tried to kill him, his good conscience kept him from being too rough with them.

After a couple more minutes, Wasp Killer and Hornet Killer were feeling good enough to try to battle the Green Phantasm once more. At once, they both went running toward him. The Green Phantasm took off his hat. As the twosome was getting dangerously close, the Green Phantasm met Hornet Killer with a head butt. Hornet Killer put his hand on his hurting and bleeding nose. Wasp Killer tried to throw a couple of punches but missed. The Green Phantasm caught one of them and head butted him too.

Both bad guys paused momentarily, gently holding on to where they had been head butted. They started looking toward the Green Phantasm with angry faces. They finally removed their hands from their faces, ready to fight the Phantasm again.

However, the Green Phantasm could sense that they were going to come at him again. Before Wasp Killer or Hornet Killer had a chance to advance, the Green Phantasm used each hand to grab one of them on the back of his head by his mask. Then, immediately, he repeatedly smashed their faces together, knocking them unconscious.

Before the Green Phantasm went to try to phone the police, he took a moment to examine the two that he had just taken out. He could not help focusing his attention on the large print on their shirts that said, "WASP KILLER" and "HORNET KILLER." He said, "You know, that reminds me of something. In the subway the other night, weren't there a couple of other guys I dealt with, like Ant Killer and Roach Killer or something? Along with these two, those all sound like insecticides. That's kind of a strange coincidence. I wonder if they all know each other."

The next minute, the Green Phantasm noticed something else. He continued, "Now, what's that say? That small print on both of them says, uh… Is that X-Termination? Hmm, X-Termination, huh? Oh, I get it. It sounds a lot like *extermination*. In fact, insecticides are used in extermination. How silly of me. You know something else? I wonder if the four are all part of this X-Termination, whoever they are and wherever they are. I guess they're a secret organization perhaps. Well, I guess that's twice I've dealt with them, and it hasn't even been half a week. Well, they must be stopped. I've got to find their hideout wherever it is and put all those jerks out of business. They'll all go from X-Termination to 'X-terminated.' Oh yeah, I'll see to that."

After that, the Green Phantasm paused to try to decide what to do next. "Let's see now," he said. "I guess I should notify the police. However, I would also like to make one of these creeps tell me where their headquarters are. But, I guess I knocked them out, didn't I? Heh, looks like I noticed too late, that is the term *X-Termination*. But I'm gonna get to the bottom of it somehow. I'm not giving up hope. Well, anyway, I guess it's time for the unpleasant duty of calling the police. Here goes."

But before the Green Phantasm even made it three yards, he heard something. It was the sound of a patrol car's siren. He stopped to listen. Shortly, he saw the glare of all the flashing colored lights, as well as the headlights, which were all lit up. The car was coming from the east.

The Green Phantasm finally made a decision. He told himself, "Oh well, it looks like they're already coming. I better jet and let the cops handle their business." The Green Phantasm shot straight up to about two hundred feet off the ground. After reappearing there, he shot on toward his subdivision. Once he was above his subdivision, he hovered until he was directly above his backyard. At once, the Phantasm disappeared into a teleportation beam that went straight through his bedroom window.

He reappeared standing in his bedroom. That very minute, he teleported out of his Green Phantasm outfit, and it just collapsed onto the floor. He switched off his neon radiation. He was once again just James Clifton. Without his suit on, James was now in a white T-shirt, underwear, and socks. He put his Green Phantasm outfit inside his closet.

It was now close to 9:00 p.m. James knew he would have to get to bed soon; he had to go to work in the morning. He said, "Well, well, it's certainly been a heck of a night, protecting the streets as the Green Phantasm. It's been educational, exciting, and adventurous. I might even say it feels rewarding. But of course, I may need to be somewhat more careful with it. Other than that, I need to forget about it for right now and get ready for bed so I can go to work in the morning."

Next, James went downstairs to have a snack before bed. He got himself a slice of chocolate cake and a glass of milk. Afterward, he went upstairs and brushed his teeth. Then he finally went over to get into his bed.

Before lying down, James sat on his bed and thought one last time about the crime-fighting he had done all evening. "Oh man," Clifton said happily, "I got to admit; all this heroism gives me pride in myself. I mean, when I think about all those lives I saved and the troublemakers I put out of work... But there's still one thing I can't help thinking about. It's that name *X-Termination*. I mean, just the name alone sounds frightening. Of course, extermination is usually applied mainly to insects, rodents, and other pests. However, to exterminate means to destroy completely. Plus, I would think that an organization like that would want to exterminate, or should I say 'X-terminate,' something a lot more than small pests."

James paused for a moment, and then he continued, "And another thing, I know I kind of came close to being killed a couple times tonight. That taught me to be more careful, which I may really really have to do when dealing with X-Termination. I mean, I can't help remembering how tough those guys were to deal with when I had to save Amanda the other night. Also tonight, Hornet Killer and Wasp Killer seemed so determined to destroy me when they came at me with all that machine gunfire. There's no telling what else they might do. Somebody's got to stop them for sure.

I just got to get to the bottom of it all and put them out of business before it's too late. I for one will stop at nothing in order to do just that."

But the next minute, he decided, "Oh well, I'm off to bed. I've got to get to work in the morning. I'll see what I can do." James Clifton then turned off his lamp and lay down to go to sleep for the night. That put an end to a big evening of protecting the streets of Philadelphia as the Green Phantasm.

CHAPTER SIX

Enter Doctor XT and X-Termination

It was after 11:00 on Tuesday night. The criminals Wasp Killer and Hornet Killer were being brought into Philadelphia's city jail to be imprisoned. Finally, the police officers escorting the handcuffed troublemakers made it to the cell into which the two were to be kept. "Here you go, guys," one of the officers said. Of course, the two had already telephoned their headquarters to notify their boss that they had been arrested and brought to jail.

The cell into which Hornet Killer and Wasp Killer were being put already held four other guys. Two of them were Ant Killer and Roach Killer, who had tried to hurt Amanda Taylor two nights before. The other two were Clyde and Carl, from whom James Clifton had to save Kathryn Brown that same night. All six were about to be in there together.

Next, Wasp Killer and Hornet Killer were inside the cell with their handcuffs removed, and the barred door slid shut and locked behind them. Ant Killer addressed them, saying, "What's up, guys?"

"Nothing much," answered Wasp Killer.

"So," said Roach Killer, "he got y'all too, huh?"

"What do you mean?" asked Wasp Killer. "The Green Phantasm or whoever that is?"

"Well, yeah." Roach Killer sighed. "I mean, I don't know too many other guys that can zoom by in a neon-green flash of light that I can barely see."

"Look, you guys," said Hornet Killer, "it's definitely the same guy who fouled up our plans both times, okay? Now let's all quit moping, all right? I've called headquarters already. Someone will be here shortly to bail us out. Nobody will be able to stop us again after that. So let's all stop griping, because we're getting out of here. We'll be back in business. So please, chill out, all right?"

"Okay," responded Ant Killer.

In the meantime, Clyde and Carl had been listening to all of them talking. Clyde said, "Hey, you guys, y'all know something? I think that guy y'all talking about is the same one who messed up our plans the other night. You see, my partner Carl here said something about some neon-green dude that night. I just didn't believe him at the time. But now, I've been hearing more about this guy, and I'm starting to believe it now."

"You know something?" said Roach Killer to Clyde. "I'm sure it is the same guy. It's gotta be. I mean, I've never heard of this punk before in my life, and already that's twice this week he done messed with us. Heck, you guys too? It's him all right, the Green Phantasm."

Clyde and Carl looked at each other nodding in agreement. They looked back toward the four members of X-Termination. Clyde addressed them saying, "Hey, excuse me, you guys, I was just wondering, whenever y'all's ride arrives to bail y'all out and pick y'all up, is it possible for us to come with y'all?"

At that, the four X-Termination members just looked at each other shrugging their shoulders.

Clyde continued by saying, "I mean, after all, I know you're all mad at the Green Phantasm, and so are we. Carl and I want to help y'all bring him down. Other than that, none of us want to serve time in prison."

Clyde narrowed down his focus to Wasp Killer and Hornet Killer. He said to them, "You two know what else? Your other two partners here told us all about the cool place y'all have thirty miles west of here. They also told me about the great life y'all are living. We have no family to turn to like you guys. And like I said, we want to help you get rid of this Green Phantasm. So I'm asking you, can we please come along and join your organization, please?"

At that, Roach Killer looked around at all his peers asking, "Well, what do y'all think? I mean, why not?"

Then, Hornet Killer said, "You know, maybe we ought to. I mean, they seem really interested, and they seem to like us. Besides, we wouldn't want anyone else to find out about our organization."

"Yeah!" the other three all said in agreement.

Then at once, Hornet Killer turned back to Clyde and Carl, saying, "All right, you two, if the one picking us up agrees to it, y'all can come with us."

"Yes!" exclaimed Clyde in excitement.

"Yes!" agreed Carl.

At around 11:45, someone finally showed up to bail out the X-Termination members. He himself also belonged to X-Termination. His name was Anselm Nielsen. He was a black man. He was seven feet tall and weighed around 650 pounds. He was dressed in a tan fedora hat and trench coat. He also wore sunglasses. Nielsen had just driven up in a white stretch limousine.

So next, Anselm Nielsen went to the front desk. The officer asked, "Can I help you?"

"Yes," answered Nielsen, "I came to bail out the guys in, uh, that cell right there." At the same time, he was pointing to them.

The officer took a look back at the cell to which he was pointing. He asked, "You talking about the one with those six guys, four of them with masks?"

"Yes, sir," Anselm responded. "I came to get, um, all six of them."

"Okay," said the policeman, "That will be twelve thousand dollars."

"Yes, sir," Nielsen told him. "You got it." At that, he gave the officer the money for bail.

Next, the officer said to him, "Wait here, I'll get them for you." Then immediately, he went to the cell and said, "Okay, men, you got a friend here to pick you up. Come on, let's go." At that, he opened the cell to let them out. Clyde, Carl, and the four guys in X-Termination followed him back to the front desk.

Upon reaching the front desk, where Anselm Nielsen was waiting, Ant Killer said, "What's up, Anselm? Thanks for coming to get us. It's good to see you."

"Mm-hmm," Nielsen replied seriously.

"Yeah, man," said Wasp Killer. "Thank you so much for bailing us out."

"All right, guys," he told them, "let's go. The boss wants to see all of you."

"Well," said Roach Killer, "what are we waiting for?" They were all following Nielsen out to the car.

"You know something, Carl?" asked Clyde. "We're free."

"Yeah, free!" exclaimed Carl.

Shortly, everyone was outside. Eventually, they were led to his limousine.

"Whoa," said Carl, "a limousine ride, cool."

Nielsen opened the door that was farthest back on the vehicle's left side, and everyone got in at his signal. Then, all six of them sat down inside the limo. After that, Anselm Nielsen closed the door behind them and went to the front to get in and start the vehicle.

While Nielsen was starting the limousine and letting it warm up, the X-Termination crew in the back was telling Clyde and Carl where they were going and all about life with X-Termination.

"So anyway," said Clyde, "where exactly are we headed?"

"Well," said Ant Killer, "we're going to our headquarters of course. It's about thirty miles west of here. It's a great place. There's all you want to eat and drink, a big game room, a weight room, a basketball court, and a swimming pool. Plus, you get your own room."

"Wow!" exclaimed Carl. "I can't wait until we get there!"

Then, Roach Killer told them, "Now, of course, we all have part-time work to do, but at least it's only part-time."

"But you know what?" asked Wasp Killer. "At least on your days off, you get to have all the fun you want. And, even after you get off on your workdays, you get to enjoy yourself."

"Well," said Clyde, "at least it's a better life than prison."

"Look, you guys," Hornet Killer told everyone, his tone serious. "Before we worry too much about any of that right now, I think we need to see what the boss wants first."

"Oh, all right," replied Ant Killer.

"Yeah, all right," said Wasp Killer.

From that point forward, the pair of hoodlums and the four X-Termination members kept talking and getting to know each other a lot better. They all continued talking for the rest of the ride to X-Termination's hideout.

The place to which they were all headed was the site of an abandoned, shut-down chemical plant. It had been made over into the home, office, and workplace of X-Termination.

The man who started it all was fifty-two-year-old John Perry Perone. He stood about six feet tall weighed about two hundred pounds. He was white and both bald and clean-shaven. John Perry Perone headed, directed, and funded X-Termination.

Perone code-named himself Doctor XT; XT stood for X-Termination. He also claimed himself to be an XTE, which stood for X-termination engineer because of how he chose to utilize the knowledge and experience he gained in engineering and technology.

John Perone was originally from the neighborhood of Society Hill in downtown Philadelphia. He attended high school at Philadelphia High School. He was always the best in his class in every kind of math and science. He even graduated high school by age ten. His parents were no doubt extremely proud of him.

Immediately after high school, John Perone enrolled at Pennsylvania State University at University Park. There, he majored in electrical engineering and studied computer engineering as a minor. In addition, he would also peer into many other kinds of engineering in any way he could. In less than three years, John Perone earned a bachelor of science degree in electrical engineering. Immediately afterward, he progressed on to graduate school. By the time he turned seventeen, he had achieved his PhD. His parents were no doubt amazed and impressed. A PhD before age seventeen? Way to go, Doctor John Perry Perone!

However, even as happy as Perone had made his parents, relatives, and teachers, he had also been up to other business, about which none of them ever knew. No one ever knew his real motive for going into electrical engineering. It was for selfish reasons. In spite of his amazing intelligence, he also had the same sorts of feelings and desires as any other young child. For instance, he was understandably not too happy with the control and supervision of parents and teachers. Therefore, he wanted to hurry through school and college so he could break free and become his own guardian and supervisor as soon as possible. Also, like a lot of young children, Perone tended to want nearly everything he saw. Another reason for going into engineering was to be able to discover or invent a way to obtain anything and everything he possibly could. However, no one but John himself knew the real reason for his shooting through his education so quickly.

John Perone did a few other things on the side. Many young kids throw a tantrum when being restrained from something they really like. John felt the same way. For that reason, he wanted to learn every way he possibly could to eliminate or elude any who tried to stop him from obtaining what he wanted.

For example, by the time Perone had finished his first year of college, he had learned and mastered ways to pick pockets and remove articles without being detected or noticed. Often when John would find someone or something disagreeable, he would provide a distraction by pretending to be friendly or cooperative, and then he would cunningly take what he wanted from the person's pockets and remove watches and other jewelry. No one even knew he had robbed them. Most victims never knew anything was missing until it was too late. By this method of outwitting others, John Perry Perone made good extra money and acquired some nice things.

Another thing that Perone had always studied, even in childhood, was martial arts and self-defense. By the time he was a ten-year-old high school graduate, he had become a black belt in Shotokan karate. After that, John continued to pick up other techniques of self-defense and offense that, though simplified, were effective. He preferred to utilize those kinds of moves when no one was around to watch and when he was sure that no surveillance cameras were present. These moves included attacking pressure points and other sensitive parts of the body, defending himself against knives and handguns, and even handling multiple attackers. Of course, this too he all learned for selfish reasons—definitely for no one else's benefit.

By the time that John Perone had acquired his bachelor's degree in electrical engineering, he had gained enough knowledge to produce anything electronic and computerized. The ambitious John Perry Perone invented himself a handheld electronic device that could detect and deactivate any security cameras or alarm systems that he came across. He also came up with a computerized device that he could install within ATM machines. This device would gather information from people's ATM cards, including their passwords. John could then use all the data and information to produce duplicate ATM cards and therefore perform transactions with everyone's bank accounts. Perone also studied locksmithing on the side. He would not stop until he knew everything there was to know about being a locksmith. With all of these skills, John Perone acquired thousands, sometimes tens of thousands of dollars, on a daily basis, whenever he felt up to it. Some days, he would even go outside Philadelphia to other towns or cities. Amazingly, no one ever knew of even one act of theft or one break-in that he committed—at least no one ever knew it was Perone. If people did show up or happened to be present, John would either render them unconscious or kill them.

So then, with all the money that he had obtained secretly, he moved out of his parents' house while still in graduate school. He had his own dream home designed and constructed in the city of Camden, New Jersey. His parents did not fully understand how he could suddenly afford a nice big place of his own, but they were extremely proud of all that their son John had accomplished.

Even after earning a PhD, John Perone did not choose to teach electrical engineering because he was not interested at all in educating others; he was only concerned with what he could obtain for himself. So instead, he became an ATM technician, to service and repair ATM machines. Although he had told his employer he was interested in helping others, he really wanted to use the position to acquire other people's money for himself. John probably figured he could make more money this way than from being a professor. He installed his computerized devices on any ATM machines on which he worked. In addition, he would even steal from the company for which he was working.

While John Perone was working as an ATM technician, he reenrolled at Pennsylvania State University. This time around, he majored in industrial engineering and studied mechanical engineering as a minor. He also read and learned a lot about chemical engineering in some of his spare time. Of course, even while furthering his education, he was only thinking of himself. John wanted to obtain a lot more than what he already had. For example, he wanted to put a chemical plant out of business and make the facility into his own place of business one day. That was the reason he had gone into industrial engineering. He wanted to have his own place to produce and manufacture whatever he wanted.

After earning a PhD in industrial engineering by age twenty-four, John Perone got a job as a process operator at a company called D and J Chemicals. For the first three months of his employment, the company was constantly losing money. Upper management, along with the owners, were wondering why. Of course, it was really because John Perone was embezzling money in every possible way he could. Shortly thereafter,

Perone acquired a position in upper management by claiming he could solve the problem. But within a month, D and J Chemicals was closed down and out of business. Because of the selfishness and greed of one John Perry Perone, everyone else was out of work. He finally had the opportunity that he wanted. Unfortunately, no one but John Perone himself knew who was responsible for D and J going out of business.

Shortly after D and J Chemicals was no longer in business, John Perone bought the plant and the area it occupied. He used the millions he had at the time, which no one knew how he had acquired. Perone then began planning to have the facility remodeled into his very own place to live, enjoy himself, and do business. It was located about thirty miles west of Philadelphia along US Highway 30. It was set back from the highway on the north side, with a three-mile gravel road leading to it from the highway. At the point at which the gravel road met the highway was a roadblock. No other signs were left up to guide anyone to the facility.

However, at the end of the gravel drive, there were nearly twelve acres of land that John Perry Perone had purchased. For him, this was the beginning of his very own secret organization, which he decided to call X-Termination. To *exterminate* meant to destroy completely, and that was exactly what Doctor John Perone would do to anyone or anything that stood in the way of whatever he was trying to accomplish. Of course, he would require anyone working for him to help him do that. Perone's main goal was to obtain all the money, possessions, and privileges he possibly could. He would "X-terminate" anyone or anything inside or outside of his organization that hindered that. The created word *X-terminate* was the main one in the vocabulary of Perone and his employees. According to them, if anyone or anything was destroyed by one of his devices or methods, it was "X-terminated."

X-Termination's headquarters happened to be a set of buildings, lots, structures, and other areas that took up approximately twelve acres, which had formerly been occupied by D and J Chemicals. Furthermore, of course, Dr. John Perry Perone, or Doctor XT, had gotten all these new buildings and structures erected in place of anything belonging to D and J Chemicals that stood in the way. These new things included, but were not limited to, a great big manufacturing area, a building north of that which served as living quarters, a recreational building, a wide-open space for vehicles to park and fuel up, and so forth. The entire area owned and run by Doctor XT, except for the front and east-side entrances, was surrounded by a rectangular steel barrier. Each and every side of it was forty feet high and ten feet thick.

At the end of the three-mile drive was a gravel parking lot. The lot was right in front of the gate to the great big steel barrier into X-Termination Headquarters. This way in and out happened to be a set of double doors. Each of the two doors was an inch-thick sheet of glass that was protected on both sides by horizontal and vertical steel bars. Both doors had to be pulled open from outside.

On each of the two sides of the double doors was a check-in window to a small room. Each of the two rooms measured eight feet wide by twelve feet long. Inside each room was a square table with two chairs, for one or two people either to eat or play a game. Each room also held a television set mounted above the check-in window. This allowed the one on duty to watch television when he had nothing to do. Otherwise, a couple of other things were at the other end of each room. One of them, of course, was a door to enter or exit the room. The other was a security camera mounted above the door.

Between the two rooms and beyond the double doors was a hallway the length of the rooms. On each side of the hallway was a wall that had a rectangular sheet of glass, which separated the hallway from the room. Each rectangular sheet of glass was horizontally set and had the same height as the check-in window out front. At the other end of the hallway on the inside was a metal detector and a second set of double doors that looked just like the first. Both sets of double doors were locked by means of electromagnets, which could be turned on and off by remote control, allowing the doors to be pulled open.

Just beyond the front entrance/exit was a huge open outdoor area for vehicles. The area measured about four hundred by four hundred square feet or 160,000 square feet. The ground was concrete. X-Termination's vehicles could be parked, worked on, or fueled up there by fuel pumps, which were on the big area's north end.

The south and east sides of the area were bordered by parts of the great steel barrier of X-Termination Headquarters. The east side of the big parking area had the only other way through the steel barrier to get in and out of X-Termination Headquarters. It was a one-hundred-foot-wide garage door that was centered within the parking area's eastern border. It could be raised and lowered electrically, so that trucks or other vehicles could pass through it. The other two sides of the open parking area were bordered by sheet-metal walls, which were almost as high as the thick steel barrier. The north wall had one regular hinged door with a doorknob. This door was centered within the north wall. People could simply open it, walk through, and close it. The eastern half of the north wall also had a one-hundred-foot-wide garage door that was raised and lowered electrically. The parking area's western sheet-metal wall had two powered garage doors that were each one hundred feet wide as well.

On the other side of the pair of garage doors, was the most important part of X-Termination Headquarters for Doctor XT. It was the manufacturing area, where manufacturing and all other important work took place. It also happened to be the same part of headquarters as Doctor XT's office, his laboratory, and the main control room. The manufacturing area took up the same amount of space as the area just east of it—about a hundred sixty thousand square feet. Both the south and west sides were bordered by the steel barrier that surrounded all of X-Termination Headquarters. Both the north and east sides of this area were also bordered by sheet-metal walls. While two garage doors could be opened and closed on the east side, only one was centered on the north wall. Immediately on each side of the only garage door on the north wall was an ordinary hinged door that anyone could open by turning the knob.

Most of the manufacturing area was covered by a shelter. This shelter consisted of a square of sheet metal that was 365 by 365 feet, or 163,225. This square metal roof was supported by fifty-five-foot-high steel posts at all four corners. This shelter protected a lot of things from rain, including all the manufacturing equipment and a humongous acid vat. About two-thirds of the area underneath the shelter had various machines used for production, as well as stainless-steel tables. Another significant device in the area was a moving overhead electromagnet. It traveled about the underside of the shelter's roof and could be lowered and raised to move heavy metal objects from one point to another within the manufacturing area.

Perhaps the largest object on the ground of the entire area was the huge X-Termination Acid vat. This enormous container was one of the few things that Doctor XT had kept over from the company he had driven out of business. He had reinforced the inside and outside of it with the same kind of steel that made up the great steel barrier surrounding headquarters. The cylinder-shaped acid vat was two hundred feet in diameter and fifteen feet high. The southernmost point of it was seventy feet from the interior of the steel barrier's south wall. The westernmost point of the vat was forty-five feet from the interior of the west side of the great steel barrier.

The acid vat was filled up most of the way with a substance called X-Termination Acid. This acid, which Doctor XT had invented and produced himself, was one of the most powerful inorganic acids known. It was a bright, greenish-yellow liquid. X-Termination Acid was so powerful and effective that even a tiny drop could consume the entire hand of an average human being. Other than steel and a few other metals, practically anyone or anything with which the acid came into contact would be reduced to nothing but a stream of vapor and in some cases, also a small heap of ashes. After repeated experiments in his laboratory, Doctor XT hijacked numerous tank trucks that carried the chemicals he needed until the X-Termination Acid vat was nearly full.

X-Termination Acid was one of various weapons that Doctor XT and his employees used to "X-terminate." In order to remove any and all evidence against himself, Doctor XT often dropped people or things into the X-Termination Acid vat to "X-terminate" them. Nothing would be left of the victim except a surge of vapor that would drift up and away. Anything else would be submerged beneath the acid if not consumed by it. Several former X-Termination employees had been eliminated this way, because they had landed in jail, been identified, or jeopardized X-Termination some other way. Doctor XT preferred to "X-terminate" them so that they could never lead back to X-Termination, which could be overtaken or put out of business.

The four other major features of the manufacturing area included a gas chamber, a control room, Doctor XT's office, and his laboratory. Three of these rooms were accessible by going up a flight of stainless steel stairs. The one room that was below the other three was Doctor XT's laboratory. The staircase was four feet wide, and ascended twenty feet from the ground at a forty-five-degree angle. It had an iron guardrail on the side opposite the steel barrier.

At the top of the stairs was a stainless-steel-plated balcony. It was ten feet wide and ran along the west side of the manufacturing area at twenty feet above the concrete ground. The balcony was 165 feet long—one end at the south side of the great steel barrier and the other end at the gas chamber. Like the stairs, it had a guardrail on the side away from the steel barrier. It was supported from below by many iron poles along each side. They were assisted by crossbars and other iron bars that ran diagonally. Each and every one ran either lengthwise or crosswise with the balcony.

The only other feature connected to the balcony was a four-foot-wide stainless steel platform that ended above the X-Termination Acid vat. Five feet before the gas chamber was a four-foot-wide opening in the balcony's guardrail from which the platform extended. The platform was forty-five feet long with guardrails along both sides and was supported from below until it extended above the acid vat. The end of the platform, which was above the acid, had no kind of railing, so that the unfortunate victim could be forced over the edge and plunged into the X-Termination Acid.

At the north end of the manufacturing area's balcony was one of two doorways to the only gas chamber at X-Termination Headquarters. This square chamber was ten feet by ten feet, or one hundred square feet. It was established directly above the southernmost part of Doctor XT's laboratory and was centered along the western side of the manufacturing area with the X-Termination Acid vat. The western and eastern walls of the gas chamber were made from the same hardened steel that surrounded all of headquarters, and these walls were each one foot thick. The open northern and southern sides could be sealed shut by ten-inch-thick glass doors that slid upward from below. Both the stainless-steel floor and ceiling had built-in vents spaced throughout that could be opened and closed. This allowed X-Termination Gas to enter through the floor and exit through the ceiling, which was fifteen feet above the floor.

X-Termination Gas was a poisonous substance that Doctor XT had created. He composed it in a huge container in his lab below. It had the form of a light-purple mist and was so toxic it would instantly kill anyone who came into contact with it or inhaled it. If Doctor XT ever had trouble forcing an exceptional victim toward the big acid vat, he might lure them into the gas chamber, where he would trap and kill them with X-Termination Gas. The only protection from X-Termination Gas was special gas masks that Doctor XT had created and provided for all of his employees and himself. X-Termination Gas was another substance, in addition to X-Termination Acid, that was used to "X-terminate."

On the north side of the gas chamber was the master control room of X-Termination Headquarters. It measured ten feet by twenty feet, making it two hundred square feet, and it was fifteen feet from the floor to the ceiling. This room allowed Doctor XT to monitor and control several aspects of X-Termination. For instance, he could monitor practically anything by means of his own video surveillance system, which he had installed extensively throughout X-Termination Headquarters and in all X-Termination vehicles. He could also activate, control, or deactivate any vehicle or other device that he had invented from there. The control room was another way to the X-Termination Acid vat.

Perhaps the most important thing in the control room was the built-in network of thirty-two computers along the west wall. It was the very item that Doctor XT used to monitor and control everything. The most visible and obvious components were the thirty-two display monitors that were permanently embedded within the stainless-steel wall. They were evenly arranged in four horizontal rows of eight monitors each. Each screen measured twenty-four inches diagonally. Each and every monitor could be used to display past or present footage from any surveillance camera. A monitor could also function as a radarscope to determine the geographical location of anyone or anything within X-Termination Headquarters. It could display any sort of output that Doctor XT needed to see.

Just below the thirty-two monitors was a stainless-steel panel that ran along the same wall and was inclined at a forty-five-degree angle. This panel had everything necessary for the computer network's input, including sixteen built-in keyboards, as well as numerous other buttons, switches, and levers. The operation of each keyboard could be switched over to either of two computers. Doctor XT could also type a special code into any computer and then press a big, round green button to make it perform the function for which he had programmed it. Doctor XT had hundreds of different codes consisting of various combinations of letters and digits. Amazingly, he had memorized every single one of the codes that were used to activate, control, or deactivate anything that belonged to X-Termination.

A horizontal row of eight side-by-side rolling chairs were set before the big input panel to enable people to sit before it. Any individual who sat in any of the chairs would see before himself both an upper and lower keyboard on the panel, as well as a vertical row of four monitors on the wall. The upper keyboard could be used to produce output for either of the two upper monitors, and the lower keyboard could be used likewise for either of the two lower monitors. To the right of each keyboard was a switch that could be used to change the keyboard's operation over from one computer to the other. This entire scenario was repeated exactly at each and every one of the eight stations along the west wall of the control room.

The east wall of the control room consisted of practically nothing but one large sheet of tinted glass. This allowed whoever was in the control room, usually Doctor XT, to oversee the entire manufacturing area. The only other thing within the control room's east wall was a doorway that was five feet north of the gas chamber. It could be opened or shut by a sliding glass door, and on the other side of it was another platform that extended above the X-Termination Acid vat. This platform was exactly like the one south of the gas chamber.

North of the control room was Doctor XT's primary office. His office was the same size as the control room. Of course, in order to enter his office, it was absolutely necessary for one to pass through the gas chamber and the control room. The six-foot-wide doorway to XT's office was centered within the separating wall. This doorway was opened and closed by a pair of sliding doors that could be brought together and pulled apart only by Doctor XT. Each of the two doors consisted of a sheet of frosted glass that was completely surrounded by a steel frame.

The interior of Doctor XT's office had a stainless steel ceiling but had walls made of mahogany. XT's office also had a hardwood floor, most of which was covered by a fancy rug. Doctor XT had several pieces of furniture in his office. The two most important to him were his very large and ornately carved mahogany desk and the deluxe leather rolling chair that he put with it. They were positioned at the center of the north end of his office so that he could sit at his desk and face the entrance to his office. Doctor XT also had eight smaller leather-padded chairs in his office that did not roll and faced his desk in two side-by-side rows of four each. The only other major furnishings were two console tables that were each stationed before a mirror on the south wall on either side of the double doors.

Like many other people, Doctor XT used his office for important functions, such as record-keeping, clerical work, and private meetings, but XT also used this office as a special place for engineering and designing new inventions, as well as any possible changes to current devices or accessories of his. For that reason, he had a personal desktop computer in his office, as well as an extra-large laser printer, which was stationed on the floor directly to the right of his desk. In addition, he did the majority of his computer programming in that office. Most of the time, Doctor XT himself was the only one in his office, and he had complete control over whoever else could go into it.

The only other place within the manufacturing area that was very important to Doctor XT was his laboratory. It was located directly below his office, control room, and gas chamber and took up the combined area of all three of them, which were twenty feet above the floor of the laboratory. Unlike the three rooms above, the inside walls of the laboratory merely consisted of ordinary unpainted plaster wallboard. The inside top of the room was just an ordinary plaster ceiling. The only entrance and exit was a hinged aluminum door within the northern wall, which could be opened by turning a stainless-steel doorknob.

Like a lot of laboratories, Doctor XT's lab was a place at which he did his scientific work, including investigations, experiments, tests, and other tasks. The western and eastern walls each had stainless-steel tables all along them. Each table had both a top surface on which to do work and a lower shelf for equipment storage. All of the tables had various scientific instruments and apparatuses that included beakers, Bunsen burners, flasks, test-tube racks, microscopes, mechanical and electronic scales and other measuring tools, and many other devices. Also, mounted on the western and eastern walls above the tables were several storage cabinets in which Doctor XT kept lots of chemical substances.

Doctor XT used this room for the manufacturing of the chemical substances he invented and created himself, the two most important of which were X-Termination Acid and X-Termination Gas. Some of the scientific work that XT did in his laboratory was also a determining factor in the development of certain other devices and machinery he created.

Doctor XT normally worked by himself in his lab, but occasionally, he brought in from one to a few of his X-Termination employees to assist him.

One other significant feature of Doctor XT's laboratory was a huge machine stationed in the south end of the room. It was the X-Termination Gas generator, which was used to produce and contain X-Termination Gas. It was a sixteen-sided stainless-steel-plated structure that ran all the way from the floor to the ceiling of the southern part of the laboratory. This machine measured seven feet wide from one side to the side directly across from it and was perfectly centered with the gas chamber above. For safety purposes, Doctor XT always operated this generator either from the control room or by means of a computerized device that he wore on his left forearm.

In order for this gigantic generator to produce X-Termination Gas, Doctor XT had to connect eight cylindrical containers to the machine's interior. This was accessible by opening any or all of eight hinged stainless-steel doors on eight of the sixteen sides of the machine's exterior. The cylinders that were connected to the machine contained various poisonous gases and poisonous liquids. Each cylinder was connected by two rubber hoses, one for intake and one for exhaust, to the X-Termination Gas generator's main storage tank on the inside. This cylindrical steel tank was five feet in diameter and the exact same height as the generator's exterior. The bottom eight feet of the inner tank was divided into eight separate compartments, each sealed at the top by a vent that Doctor XT could open and close. Above all the compartments was the upper chamber of the inside of the storage tank, which was undivided. Poison gases and fumes from poison liquids would come from the eight lower compartments and blend together in the upper chamber to form X-Termination Gas. Finally, the very top of the upper chamber, which was also the bottom of the gas chamber above, had vents within it that could be opened to let X-Termination Gas into the gas chamber to poison the unfortunate victim.

For safety purposes, Doctor XT and anyone assisting him often wore gas masks when working in his laboratory. But they always made sure to do so when tampering with the X-Termination Gas generator in any way, shape, or form. Of course, this was for protection from any possible escaping poisonous gases or fumes. Although Doctor XT was away from the generator when operating it, he would have to go over to it when making any kind of repair or changing out a compressed gas cylinder.

The northern half of X-Termination Headquarters took up the same area as the southern half but was entirely different. First of all, it was not divided into two quarters the way the south half was divided by the sheet metal wall between the parking area and the manufacturing area. Secondly, the ground in the northern half of headquarters had more to it than just concrete. It had grass, bushes, and trees but still had concrete walkways. Also, the northern half of X-Termination Headquarters was possibly more enjoyable than the southern half, for it had three large buildings within it. The one farthest west served as living quarters for Doctor XT, his top three officials, and everyone else employed by him. East of that was an amusement center that served as an arcade, a pool hall, and a few other things. Finally, the building that was farthest east in the northern half was a gymnasium that had a basketball court, a weight room, and a swimming pool inside.

The one structure that was completely within the northwest quarter of X-Termination Headquarters was a large two-story building that was like a hotel or an apartment building. Doctor XT provided it as living quarters for himself, as well as everyone employed by X-Termination. The northern and western sides of the building were each ten feet from the inside of the corresponding part of the big steel barrier that surrounded all of the headquarters. This residential building was thirty feet high from the ground to the roof. It also measured two hundred ten feet long from the south side to the north side. From the western to eastern side, it was 160 feet wide. The outside of the building was made of bricks, and the rooftop was a flat concrete surface.

This building in which Doctor XT and all of X-Termination resided had a total of thirty suites within it. Each of the two stories had two hallways that ran from south to north, making a total of four hallways. At each end of each hallway was a set of double doors, making a total of eight sets. On each side of three of the hallways were four suites, each of which had two bedrooms, a bathroom, a kitchen, a living room, and a dining room. The hallway on the west side of the bottom floor was different from the others, for it only had six suites, three on each side. Although the two suites on the northern end of that hall were like the other twenty-four in the other halls, the other four in that one hallway were different. Each of those four was one and a half times the size of each of the twenty-six two-bedroom suites. Each of these four suites had an additional bedroom and bathroom and were inhabited either Doctor XT or one of his three highest-ranking officials.

The number of bedrooms in each suite was intentional. Most of the men who worked for X-Termination had two bedrooms; that member of X-Termination was able to use one room as his bedroom in which to sleep and the other as a game room, hobby room, or for whatever he so desired. However, Doctor XT and his top officials each had three rooms; one of the extra bedrooms was to be used as an office. Of course, the office in the suite of Doctor XT was secondary to the one he had in the manufacturing area.

Another feature of the residential building was a pair of staircases on the outside of each hallway that led to the next level or story of the building. This made a total of sixteen stainless-steel-plated staircases altogether. Starting five feet outside each set of double doors on the ground level were two sets of stairs, one on each side of the doors. From that point, the two staircases slanted up and away from each other and ended on the second story's outside balcony. Each of the four pairs of staircases from the second floor were just like the ones on the bottom, but they started immediately outside the double doors. They also ran against the building's outside wall and led straight to the roof.

The next building east of the living quarters was the X-Termination Amusement Center. It was a twenty-foot-high building that took up ninety thousand square feet, for it was three hundred feet long by three hundred feet wide. It was located at the very center of the northern half of X-Termination Headquarters. All of the outside walls were covered entirely or almost entirely by brown sheet metal, and so was the roof. In the very middle of the amusement center's north side was a swinging door that could be pulled open to enter the kitchen. Fifty feet from the building's west side along its south side was a pair of tinted glass double doors that could be pulled open to enter the game room and dining area. From the double doors to the southeast corner of the building ran a continuous series of tinted glass windows.

Inside the X-Termination Amusement Center was a mirrored ceiling, a stainless-steel wall, and a black-and-red checkered ceramic floor all throughout the game room and dining area. Along the inside of the west wall was a bar. From behind this bar, alcoholic beverages and soft drinks could be prepared for anyone who wanted them. This bar was part of the dining area that extended fifty feet from the wall. The entire dining area was bordered by a guardrail along its eastern side, because the floor of the dining area was three feet above the floor of the game room. All throughout the dining area were a lot of stainless-steel high-top round tables. At each table were four round-topped, stainless-steel stools with black leather cushions on top. Several of the same exact stools were lined up before the bar as well. At the halfway point along the guardrail was a five-foot-wide set of steps that led down to the gaming area.

The gaming area took up the majority of the X-Termination Amusement Center. The first things east of the dining area were twelve pool tables. They were all lined up lengthwise in two north-to-south rows of six each, practically from one end of the gaming area to the other. Outside of the twelve pool tables were twelve high-top tables just like the ones in the dining area. Each table was adjacent to one of the pool tables and had four stools with it, also as in the dining area. Just east of the pool tables were two air-hockey tables and two foosball tables. In the northeast corner of the gaming area were attractions that would be found in a casino. This included three east-to-west rows of electronic video poker machines and slot machines. South of that were four poker tables, a craps table, a blackjack table, and a roulette table. Throughout the rest of the gaming area were lots of upright coin-operated video games like those in an arcade.

The only other two major features inside the amusement center were a pair of restrooms in the northeast corner and a kitchen throughout the rest of the north side's inside. Other than that, Doctor XT, as well as his high officials and other employees, often went to the amusement center when off duty. The number of men in the X-Termination Amusement Center at any time varied from a couple of them to all of them. All of Doctor XT's enlisted employees would take turns cooking in the kitchen and serving drinks.

The only other building of X-Termination Headquarters was a gymnasium. It was centered within the part of headquarters' northern half that was east of the amusement center and had a basketball court, a swimming pool, and a weight room inside. This fifty-foot-high athletic building measured 150 feet wide by about 300 feet long. The four outside walls were made of mason bricks, while the roof was made of sheet metal. The eastern and western sides each had three sets of glass double doors that could be pulled open to enter the building.

Inside the eastern and western sides of the gymnasium was a twenty-foot-wide hallway that also served as a lobby and ran all the way from the northern to the southern ends of the building. Neither the walls nor the floors of either hall had a fancy design, but couches and chairs sporadically lined the walls. This allowed the X-Termination members to sit down either to relax or watch any of the television monitors that were mounted overhead. Across from the three sets of glass doors that were along the outside of each hallway were four more sets of one or two doors each that led from the hallways to the bigger rooms in the middle of the gymnasium. The two northernmost sets of inner double doors would each lead into either end of the basketball court. South of those double doors in each hallway was a single-hinged door that could be pulled open in order to enter the bath and shower area. Finally, two more sets of inner double doors in each hallway could be opened so that one could go from the hall to either the weight room or the room that had the swimming pool.

The northernmost room of the gymnasium was about one hundred feet wide. It ran across the northern end of the building from one hall to the other. The most important and obvious feature of this room was a regulation-sized basketball court, which of course was ninety-four feet long by fifty feet wide, with all the other ordinary dividing lines throughout it. Of course, a backboard and basket were suspended above each end of the court. On each side of the basketball court were wooden bleachers in which people could sit either to rest or watch others play.

South of the basketball area were the restrooms and showers. This room ran from one hallway to the other and was forty feet wide. The flooring and the walls were completely covered with brightly colored ceramic tiles. Lining this shower and bath area were a countertop that had several built-in sinks, several urinals, and many enclosed toilets along the south wall. Across the room along the north wall were many shower stalls. Along the middle of the shower and bath area were two rows of wooden benches on which the X-Termination employees could sit to rest, change clothes, or do any other desired activity.

Located south of the shower and bath area were the weight and exercise room and the room with the natatorium, or indoor swimming pool. To the west was a forty-foot-wide weight and exercise room. It ran all the way from the shower and bathroom to the south end of the entire building. The inside walls of this room were completely covered by mirrors that all ran from the floor to the ceiling. The only two exceptions were on either end of the west wall for the sets of double doors, which opened onto the hallway.

Stationed along the north wall, as well as two-thirds of the east and west walls, were various benches, racks, and machines for different weight-lifting exercises. Halfway along the east wall were two low, wide platforms for performing deadlifts and other exercises that did not require any special rack. Along part of the west wall were a couple of horizontal racks that held dumbbells. Beside each and every bench, rack, and machine was a short, upright rack that held the weighted disks that could be added to barbells. Along the third of the west wall that was in the room's south end were several electronic machines for aerobic exercise, such as treadmills and exercycles.

Throughout the rest of the south end of the room were various leather punching bags. Four small speed bags hung from a platform that was mounted on the east wall. Centered between the east and west walls were three heavy bags of different weights, suspended from the ceiling by a chain.

The only other feature of the weight room were two rows of wooden benches centered between the east and west walls. They practically ran from the north to the south end of the room, with the exception of the punching bag area.

The only other big room of the gymnasium was the one in which the swimming pool was stationed. The inside floor and walls consisted of fine concrete, but the walls were painted sky blue. Two sets of double doors on the ends of the east wall allowed entry from the east hallway.

Centered within this vast room was the most important and obvious feature, which was a long, rectangular swimming pool. The pool measured one hundred twenty feet long by thirty feet wide. It was only three feet deep at the shallow north end, and thirteen feet deep at the deep south end. The entire inside floor and walls of the pool were covered with ceramic tiles of various bright colors. Stationed at the deep end of the pool were two diving boards. The one to the east was only elevated four feet above the ground. The other one west of it was twelve feet above the ground. Surrounding the swimming pool on all sides were lots of plastic tables and chairs.

That was practically all of the features of the place that Doctor XT had planned out and had constructed for his employees and himself. It was none other than the place he had named X-Termination Headquarters. He had built up some of it before employing anyone. He had made X-Termination employees work with him to build the rest of it. Doctor XT had even created his own methods of channeling electricity and plumbing into his headquarters. Also, to provide unlimited television for everyone in X-Termination, Doctor XT had modified and programmed three large satellite dishes that he ordered stationed atop the living quarters building, the recreation center, and the gymnasium.

At age thirty-eight, after having run X-Termination for fourteen years, Doctor XT began hiring for his organization. His very first employee was a man named Anselm Jerad Nielsen. Of course, this just so happened to be the one who was bailing the six men out of jail. Given his overwhelming size, Nielsen was one of the world's strongest men and was by far the largest and strongest employee in X-Termination. Doctor XT had even made Anselm Nielsen his premier associate.

Anselm was now thirty-eight years of age, and had now been in the employ of Doctor XT and X-Termination for fourteen years. He was originally born and raised in a residential area in North Philadelphia. Although that particular area had some poor residents, it did not change how big, strong, and tough Anselm Nielsen turned out to be. Fortunately for him, a lot of his physical size and strength had come from being genetically gifted. He was somewhat bigger and taller than his father, who was somewhat bigger and taller than his father, and so on. Every generation had continued to get taller and taller until Anselm finally became the first Nielsen to make it to seven feet tall. However, he was an only child with no siblings.

Even though he did not receive as much from his parents as some children, Anselm was still determined to make something of himself. All throughout his childhood, Anselm was always much bigger than anyone else his age. This size advantage motivated him mentally, emotionally, and physically by raising his self-esteem. For instance, although not the most intelligent of people, he still managed to finish high school with a grade point average close to a B.

In addition, Nielsen had another achievement that was perhaps greater than what he had managed academically. It was his athletic prowess. The largest part of this achievement was in football. Nielsen earned a lot of recognition in the sport after becoming an all-American in high school. Anselm played various positions on both the offensive and defensive lines. By that time, he had gotten close to his final height of seven feet and already weighed over five hundred pounds, making him the largest high school football player in the United States. Nielsen's incredible size and strength made him practically unstoppable as a lineman. Because of the part he played, his team never lost a game.

Anselm Nielsen received an athletic scholarship to Pennsylvania State University. He was not sure what he wanted his major to be, so he just went into general studies. Also, of course, football was tougher in college than it had been in high school. Still, Anselm excelled in college football much as he had in high school, making the team tough to beat. He was both an offensive and defensive lineman and became an all-American.

Eventually, at age twenty-two, Nielsen earned a bachelor's degree. After graduating from Pennsylvania State University, he was recruited to play football professionally. However, he only continued playing for two more years. It all ended when Doctor XT met him and recruited him.

Up to that point, Nielsen had never had the desire to join a criminal organization or do anything illegal. However, that changed forever when he received some persuasion from Doctor XT, who went up to meet him after a home game at Veterans Stadium. Doctor XT had developed an idea while watching the powerhouse Nielsen had been on the football field in a game. Like a lot of other observers, this mad doctor was very impressed with Nielsen's effectiveness while playing either offense or defense. Whenever Nielsen was a defensive lineman, Doctor XT no doubt admired the way he would penetrate the opposing offense in order to sack the quarterback or at least cause a loss of yardage. Even on offense, Nielsen would hold off so many players on the opposing defense that his fellow running back or receiver would usually make an easy run to a touchdown.

Doctor XT thought to himself that perhaps this huge, powerful behemoth could somehow help him speed things up in order to get more done.

Even though Nielsen had not had any prior interest in being a criminal, Doctor XT was quite persuasive. For instance, he offered him a lot more money than he had been earning by playing football, and the money he had been making was the primary reason he was playing. In addition, Nielsen was impressed by the fact that Perone had been running X-Termination for fourteen years prior to that point without ever getting caught in the act or being found guilty of any crime. Then, whenever Doctor XT explained to Nielsen about his amazing abilities, as well as the technology he had developed, Nielsen came to feel very confident that he would not get caught or found guilty either.

Another major factor that got Nielsen interested was the opportunity to become bigger and stronger, as well as various ways to utilize his size and strength. Anselm Nielsen had always taken an interest in increasing his physical size and strength, which was a reason that he had competed as an amateur in powerlifting in addition to playing football. Doctor XT offered to help him become bigger, stronger, and tougher. XT even created an anabolic liquid formula that would help Nielsen gain physical strength while improving his muscle and fat composition. As a result, Nielsen eventually gained over a hundred pounds of body weight while all of his weight-lifting abilities increased dramatically.

Doctor XT even helped Anselm to become a more aggressive and effective fighter. This ability, in addition to his tremendous size and strength, made him nearly unstoppable. For instance, big Anselm was able to win a fight against a group of six police officers if he had to. Ten people were usually necessary to either hold him in place or pin him down to the ground. The fact that Doctor XT was backing him made Anselm Nielsen even more unstoppable. However, although Nielsen was tougher and more unstoppable than he had ever been before in his entire life, Doctor XT was still clever and cunning enough to subdue him.

Being the premier associate of X-Termination gave Anselm far more pride than anything else he had done in all of his life. Of course, one reason was that he was making far more money working for X-Termination than he had made doing anything prior to that. Also, he saw this position as the greatest and most interesting opportunity ever to utilize his tremendous size and strength. In addition, after having been with X-Termination for fourteen years, Nielsen believed more than ever before that no law enforcement organization would ever apprehend him or deprive him of all the freedom and pleasures that he had obtained by working for X-Termination. Anselm was convinced more than ever that being an official of X-Termination was the ideal job for him. However, even as prosperous as Nielsen had become, he had also become corrupt and depraved, much like Doctor XT was.

Within two years of employing Anselm Nielsen, Doctor XT had given his premier associate a code name, D.D.T., which was derived from the insecticide dichloro-diphenyl-trichloroethane, or DDT for short. As a code name for Nielsen, however, the three letters stood for *devastating destructive titan* because that was what Anselm often proved to be to any people or things that would stand in his way during an assignment. For instance, he often left innocent victims injured with a lot of broken bones or dead of a broken neck. Anselm would also often damage or completely destroy a door, fence, wall, or other object that could possibly obstruct the work of X-Termination. Either as himself or D.D.T., Nielsen did practically all of the destruction to property with bare hands.

Doctor XT even created a logotype for Nielsen's code name of D.D.T. It consisted of all three of the letters stenciled upper-case Roman style. Each of the three letters was followed by a period. Doctor XT also designed and created a uniform that Anselm would always wear in his guise as D.D.T. Both the pants and the short-sleeved shirt were made of super stretch Lycra. The two colors were dark purple and a hue between purple and pink, like fuchsia. A big, dark-purple D.D.T. logotype ran horizontally across the front of the fuchsia shirt, and another ran across the back. A small X-Termination logotype was embroidered above the "T" in dark purple. D.D.T.'s pants were dark purple, but at the top on each side was a fuchsia rectangle. Printed within each rectangle was a dark-purple D.D.T. logotype.

The rest of his uniform consisted of a mask, a pair of gloves, and a pair of boots. His fuchsia mask was made from the same material as the rest of his uniform. It was a pullover mask that concealed his entire face and head. The opening for each eye was shaped like a rhombus, and they were slanted away from each other. The opening for his mouth was shaped like a long, upside-down trapezoid. All three openings had dark-purple trim. Other than that, D.D.T. wore a pair of black-leather weight-lifting gloves and a pair of black-leather steel-toe work boots. Occasionally, he did tasks in his guise as Anselm Nielsen. Whenever he did, he wore a fedora hat, a trench coat over his clothes, and a pair of sunglasses.

Whether it was as himself or D.D.T., Anselm usually had to be at X-Termination Headquarters from Monday to Friday every week. On weekends, he would go to his own dream home in a town called Exton, which was along Highway 30 between Philadelphia and X-Termination Headquarters. Whenever off duty, or driving to or from work, Anselm drove his own personal vehicle, which was a black Chevrolet Tahoe. But on rare occasions, he had to be on duty outside of his normal schedule for a project that was very important to Doctor XT.

As X-Termination's premier associate and one of Doctor XT's top three officials, Anselm Nielsen would at times be put in charge of either all or some of the other X-Termination members. When in charge, he was to be obeyed just as Doctor XT was. Of course, both Nielsen and D.D.T. had a few different ways of being superior to all others in the X-Termination organization. This included physical size and strength, as well as having been employed for fourteen years. However, even with these advantages, Anselm Nielsen was not quite the second in power to Doctor XT, for someone else had been ranking between them in the chain of command for nine years.

The very individual who ranked just below Doctor XT and above D.D.T. was a man named Axel Jerome Axtel. Axtel was an Italian man with black hair and a moustache. He was six feet two inches tall and weighed about 265 pounds; he had a very muscular physique. He was now forty-two years old and had been senior lieutenant the entire nine years he had been with X-Termination. Prior to joining X-Termination, Axtel had owned and run his very own crime syndicate, which was a very big reason that Doctor XT had appointed him as the highest of the top three officials and as the highest-ranked X-Termination employee.

Unlike most others within X-Termination, Axel Axtel was originally from the borough of Manhattan in New York City. Axtel had lived in the neighborhood of the Upper West Side during his childhood and teenage years. He was the oldest of six children. Like John Perry Perone, Axtel had eagerly desired an early education. At the top of his class in math and science, young Axel graduated high school at age twelve. Undoubtedly, he also did not enjoy the control and supervision of parents and teachers and had wanted to break free from that as soon as possible.

Immediately following his high school graduation, Axtel enrolled at the State University of New York in the city of Stony Brook. There, Axel majored in electrical engineering. Eventually, he earned a bachelor's degree by age fifteen. How proud his parents and other family members must have been!

Before long, a good word began circulating around about Axtel's achievement because his family members had told this news to some of their friends, who in turn kept telling others and so forth. The very idea of a fifteen-year-old having a degree in electrical engineering was no doubt very delightful to a lot of people. However, the spread of this message eventually led to something that was perhaps not for the better for Axtel.

Very shortly, a crime boss who was running a syndicate based in Harlem overheard someone talking about Axtel's achievement in electrical engineering at such a ripe young age. He no doubt thought that this Axel Axtel sounded very smart and wanted to find out more about him. So he ordered his men to try to find Axtel.

From that point on, whenever on or off duty, every single member of that criminal organization made absolutely certain to keep his eyes and ears open for any word or clue at all on a certain Axel J. Axtel. One of their efforts was to call every Axtel in the phone book, since Axel himself was not listed. In less than three days, one of those criminals found out where to meet him. It was at a health club, at which Axel had gained a reputation.

So one afternoon, their boss went to that health club, introduced himself to Axel, and invited him to a pub that he owned to talk about a most "wonderful" opportunity. Without hesitation, fifteen-year-old Axel accepted the invitation because to him, it was a possible chance to make a lot more money than he could make doing anything else. It would also allow him to move out of his parents' home. As intelligent as Axel was, he was also very greedy and selfish. He would do whatever he had to in order to acquire anything and everything he possibly could. So he went along with the crime boss to attend this little one-on-one meeting.

This session ended up going well for both of them. The crime syndicate leader was very impressed with Axel Axtel. He greatly admired Axtel's intelligence, personality, and physique, as well as the sort of intentions that he had. Aside from wanting to master electrical engineering, Axel also wanted to become physically bigger and stronger and learn every method of fighting that he possibly could. Another thing this crime boss liked about Axtel was the fact that he truly cared about no one but himself. He figured that Axtel would have no trouble placing the organization's interests above his own, since this ambitious newcomer cared nothing for any family members or so-called friends. Axel immediately joined the family with a warm welcome from his brand-new boss.

Axel still wanted to continue his education and earn a PhD. Fortunately for him, his boss had no objection and in fact wanted him to get his PhD, since it could only make him an even more valuable asset to the syndicate. Every weekday after school, he was involved with the rest of his organization in a lot of illegal activities, including gambling, prostitution, drugs, loan sharking, and other such felonies. Aside from all that, as well as studying for school, Axel utilized the weekends as well as a few nights during the week to lift weights and to train in boxing. In addition, he studied various kinds of martial arts and learned and mastered many other methods of self-defense and disabling others, much as John Perry Perone had.

As Axel continued as a member of the crime syndicate, he became more and more corrupt. After joining them, he remained completely estranged from his family. Within a year, Axel had made more than enough money to buy himself two big things he wanted. One of them was a black Mercedes Benz, and the other was a luxury apartment in the neighborhood called the Upper East Side. Through it all, Axel continued the pursuit of his PhD in electrical engineering. However, he eventually decided to stick to a criminal career rather than teach electrical engineering or even work in the field. Also, before very long, he began to want something else as well.

Axel Axtel was undoubtedly very pleased with the money he was making as a career criminal, which amounted to a lot more than he could ever have made in electrical engineering. As time passed, he kept trying to better himself in every way he possibly could. But by the time that Axel had achieved a master's degree, he seriously began seeking to usurp his crime boss. Even as prosperous as he had become, he was really jealous of his boss, who was making more money than he was. However, Axel did not come up with a game plan for a while, because he was still trying to focus on his PhD.

Finally, Axel Axtel earned his PhD; he was nineteen years old. His crime boss, as well as others, were very pleased with him and his achievement. In addition, he was promoted to be second to his boss in command of the entire secret organization because not only had Axel earned a doctorate, but he had also become greater than everyone in the syndicate in many ways. For instance, he was more aggressive and a better fighter than any of them. He was also faster and more coordinated than the others and the best at handling firearms and other weaponry. Axtel even proved to be the greatest decision maker in the entire organization. These abilities were very obvious when he did more killings and brought in more money than any of his coworkers. He was deemed by his leader as the highest-ranked and most trusted official in the entire secret association.

Regardless of all the honor he was receiving, Axel Axtel himself had a different point of view from everyone else. His ambition of taking over the organization had really grown. To him, this promotion had put him in the perfect position for the opportunity he had been seeking. Axel still despised the fact that his boss was taking in more income than he was and was now more fed up than ever before. Besides, Axel was confident that he could do a better job running the syndicate than his current leader. So, within a few days of being promoted, Axel arranged a one-on-one rendezvous with his boss.

Axel had been offered any kind of celebration he wanted to honor his promotion. But with deceit on his mind, he requested that his boss to get together with him at his apartment on the Upper East Side that Friday evening to discuss a celebration for Saturday. His boss agreed to meet him there.

So then, on Friday evening, after Axel had gone home for the evening, his infamous crime boss came over to meet with him as planned. Axel had his master sit down in the living room. Then, standing before his boss, he finally revealed the real reason for the session. He did not hold back from requesting ownership and control of the organization. The criminal leader denied his request. Somehow, this did not come as a great surprise to Axel, who was expecting a denial. At once, he took out a nine-millimeter semiautomatic pistol and shot his boss right on the spot. Three shots hit the victim above his left eye, and a fourth shot hit him in the throat. It was now all over for the criminal master who had thought Axel to be so loyal and trustworthy that he had never had any suspicion at all that he would meet this sort of ending.

After the merciless shooting and killing of his predecessor, the evil and diabolical Axel Jerome Axtel showed no remorse; he laughed longer and harder than he had ever laughed before in his life. Then, following the assassination, he did not hesitate to proceed to commit yet another depravity. He took the carcass of his deceased master to a big, empty bedroom within his apartment. While in that room, Axel used a chainsaw to cut the dead victim up into many chunks. Following that, he used two other kinds of powered sawing machines to cut the chunks into smaller pieces. Finally, the wicked and corrupt young Italian just gathered all the bloody pieces of his former boss's corpse and clothes. Little by little, he kept flushing them down different toilets in his apartment until he was through to make sure that no one would know about the murder, and that the police would never find the victim. Afterward, Axel Axtel just snickered and said with a lot of pride, "Well, that takes care of that. It's time for me to take over. Ooh, I just love the sound of that!" At that, he emitted a very loud and uncontrolled villainous laugh.

Of course, once his former superior was gone, the devilish Italian American put himself in charge of the crime syndicate he had joined just four years earlier. He decided to rename it after himself. He called it AJA Incorporated. Axel was determined to do better than his predecessor and to make his new business much greater than it had ever been prior to his takeover. He even did a little research on other crime syndicates, like the Mafia for instance, to see what their crime bosses did right and wrong, for he wanted to be the perfect crime boss. Axel was tougher on his men than their former boss had been. This motivated many of them to produce greater results. He also made certain to put away any of his workers who either revealed any secrets to outsiders or did not measure up to his standards. The qualities Axel Axtel possessed—seriousness, aggression, toughness, cruelty, lack of mercy, and other such attributes—caused his employees, police officers, and a lot of others to be too scared to cross him.

Of course, Axel was merely concerned about himself and how his men could benefit him.

AJA Incorporated proved to be a successful venture for Axel. He continued to run it from the hideout in Harlem. However, he took the belongings of his predecessor and kept what he wanted for himself. Whatever he did not want, he sold. For many years, Axel managed to run his organization without getting apprehended by the police because he was much too clever and cunning for them and was always careful to leave no evidence at the scene of a crime. Other than that, he was never overtaken or brought down by anyone who worked for him. He continued running AJA Incorporated until he was thirty-three years old. Soon after that, Axel, along with all of AJA, underwent a tremendous change.

That major change occurred on a fateful evening, during which Axel Axtel and AJA Incorporated met none other than Doctor XT and X-Termination. Both organizations happened to be hitting the same building—the T & A Bank in New York City. Axel had showed up first with two of his men. A few minutes later, Doctor XT had arrived with his humongous premier associate D.D.T. and four other men. Both groups were looking to raid and clean out the bank.

After Axel parked his Mercedes Benz two buildings away, he led his two assistants to a set of double doors at the building's rear. Then, while they were trying to decide how to break in, a voice from behind yelled out, "Hold it right there! Freeze!"

At that, the three of them turned around to face six men, five of whom had guns pointed at them. They were the five masked men that Doctor XT had brought with him. Upon seeing this, Axel and his two employees raised their arms straight up in submission. One of Axel's men mumbled, "Who are these guys?"

"I don't know," replied Axel.

"All right, you three," Doctor XT told them, "what do you think you're doin' here?"

In reply, Axel said, "Well, who are you people, and what are y'all trying to do to us?"

"Look, pal," Doctor XT began, "you better listen to me, and listen good, you got that? We are X-Termination, and we're sure as hell not called that for nothing. You see, right now, we're trying to get in there and clean out this bank, and that, my friend, is what we do to anyone who gets in our way. We 'X-terminate' them, you follow me?"

The somewhat relieved, Axel Axtel responded by saying, "Oh yes, of course, I see exactly what you mean. We didn't know you were coming here. We were going to do the exact same thing. We would never try to stand in the way of you people, honest. In fact, we think so much that what you are doing is a very very great idea. Isn't that right, gentlemen?" Axel's two men nodded affirmatively.

Doctor XT was pleased to hear what Axel was telling him. "Well then," XT began to say, "since you put it that way, the three of you just step aside and let us show you how it's done, all right?" Axel Axtel and his two guys said nothing and complied. Then at once, Doctor XT ordered his five men to proceed. "All right, men, move on in and get it done." At that, big D.D.T. broke the doors open with a side kick followed up by a front kick. Immediately following that, he led the other four men into the building.

Still standing forty feet back from the doors, Doctor XT pointed to Axel Axtel and yelled out, "Hey, you!"

Axel turned his head toward XT and said, "Who, me?"

"Yeah, that's right," replied Doctor XT. "I'm talking to you, man. Come over here. I wanna talk to you."

"Oh, you do?" asked Axel as he began walking over.

"I sure do," Doctor XT answered. "You just might be the one I'm looking for, you know that?"

"What now?" said a confused Axel Axtel as he stopped walking momentarily. He did not know what Doctor XT had meant by that.

But then, Doctor XT went on to tell him, "Come on, man, what's the problem? You don't think we could help each other? I sure as hell do."

Upon hearing that, Axel looked all around momentarily and then said with a huge, hideous grin, "Why yes, of course we could." He then continued advancing toward Doctor XT.

Once Axel had made it over to him, Doctor XT said, before starting their discussion, "By the way, I'm Doctor XT."

In return, Axel told him, "My name's Axtel—that's Axel Jerome Axtel. So what's up, Doctor XT?"

From that point, XT and Axel proceeded with their discussion. Doctor XT went on to tell Axel about himself, as well as the running of his organization called X-Termination. Axel told XT a lot about himself as well, including his takeover of the crime syndicate that he had renamed AJA Incorporated, as well as his early PhD. Both of these corrupt leaders were very impressed with the other.

Axel, in particular, found a lot about X-Termination to be impressive. One of those things was definitely the person who owned and ran it. Although Axtel was somewhat afraid that he had finally met someone tougher than he was, he was still amazed at how Dr. John Perone had started it all and had been running X-Termination for nineteen years up to that point. Another thing Axtel greatly admired was X-Termination Headquarters. He was no doubt impressed with the very large facility that was surrounded by the steel barrier and located away from Philadelphia and any major highways. At being told of this, he wished he could have a place like that instead of his hideout in the middle of Harlem. Axel also greatly admired the huge, gigantic powerhouse called D.D.T., as well as the most nifty and ingenious inventions of Doctor XT.

The only downside that Axel could see was the one obstacle that would obstruct his takeover of X-Termination. This was the difficulty in removing the one and only XTE of X-Termination, Doctor XT himself. In consideration of how clever and witty Doctor XT was, as well as his outstanding production of technology, Axel knew that it would be so much more difficult to overtake Doctor XT than it had been with his own predecessor. However, two more positive points practically made up for all that as far as Axel was concerned. Axtel was totally convinced that he would be able to make a lot more money by joining X-Termination than by running AJA Incorporated. Also, he figured he would be much less likely to get caught or arrested by the police if he were with X-Termination. So, at the end of the inspiring discussion, Axel and Doctor XT shook hands, and XT said to his new addition, "Welcome to X-Termination."

That very weekend, Axel Axtel and his men got everything they wanted from the hideout in Manhattan. They abandoned it and relocated to X-Termination Headquarters immediately. AJA Incorporated had now merged with X-Termination. However, Axel still kept his apartment on the Upper East Side of Manhattan, to which he would go on most weekends.

Although Axel did not gain complete control over all of X-Termination, he did manage to obtain what was perhaps the very next best thing. Almost immediately upon being recruited, Axel Axtel became X-Termination's senior lieutenant. With the exception of Doctor XT, everyone else was to be obedient to Axtel as they would be to XT himself. This even included premier associate D.D.T. Axel Axtel came to be directly below Doctor XT in the chain of command of X-Termination.

Doctor XT had his reasons for making him second in command. XT had no doubt been greatly impressed with Axel in order to recruit him. Although Doctor XT had recruited quite a few other men since Anselm Nielsen, none of them were any match for Axel Axtel. While admiring the great leadership that Axtel had developed, Doctor XT also found fewer flaws with him than with any other X-Termination member. With the exception of Doctor XT himself, Axel was the greatest decision maker and the toughest fighter in all of X-Termination. Like Doctor XT, he could outwit and subdue big D.D.T. Doctor XT was also amazed to learn that Axel had never been apprehended by the police while running AJA Incorporated.

Like Anselm Nielsen and everyone else employed by Doctor XT, Axel Axtel had a code name. Since XT thought that zapping was a powerful and effective way to exterminate, he decided to give Axel the code name of Zapper. His outfit was made of the same material as D.D.T.'s, but it had different colors and designs. Both Zapper's shirt and pullover mask were a bold, bright yellow. On the mask, the opening for each eye resembled a small black lightning bolt. Both lightning bolts were slanted downward and inward toward each other. Two black lightning bolts also formed the design for the mouth's opening. However, they were slanted at a smaller angle, and their bottoms actually touched one another. Zapper's yellow shirt had a small black X-Termination logo stitched onto the same spot as the one on the front of D.D.T.'s shirt. The only other design was the logotype for Zapper, which consisted of all capital letters, with each line of each letter in the shape of either one or two black lightning bolts. The six letters began in the other upper corner and slanted downward with the last letter down below the X-Termination logotype. The Zapper logotype also read the same way on the back of the shirt. Zapper's pants were black. Down the outside of each leg ran a tapering yellow lightning bolt design that began wide at the waist and came to a point just a few inches below the knee. Sewn within each of the two yellow bolts was a vertical downward spelling of Zapper's logotype. Each stylized letter was above the next one and slightly tilted to the right. Otherwise, Zapper had the same kinds of work boots and weight-lifting gloves as everyone else.

Whether as Zapper or himself, Axel Axtel had special privileges given to him by Doctor XT that no one else in X-Termination had. Of course, as the highest-ranked official, he was always the very first choice to take charge of a group. In some cases, he was put in charge of all of X-Termination if Doctor XT was to stay at headquarters instead of going along. Axel was also the highest paid X-Termination employee, earning more even than D.D.T. In addition, whenever Doctor XT held a meeting for X-Termination, Axel would stand beside him and even do some of the speaking. Perhaps the greatest privilege Axel Axtel received was that of being named the first to inherit and take over X-Termination at the end of Doctor XT's reign, which was no doubt due to all the trust and confidence that XT had in both Zapper and the one and only Axel Jerome Axtel.

However, one other official in X-Termination would occasionally gripe about his special privileges. That individual was D.D.T. Nielsen's having been with X-Termination longer than anyone else who worked for Doctor XT undoubtedly gave him a great feeling of seniority. Therefore, he was quite shocked and frustrated at the way Axel Axtel was to come aboard and suddenly become so much more prosperous than he was, for he had been with Doctor XT for five years before Axel's arrival. Anselm just had to live with Doctor XT's arrangement for Axel and himself.

XT ranked Axtel above Nielsen for a number of reasons. One was that Axtel had previously run his own evil organization, which gave him more leadership experience. It also implied that Axtel was a better decision maker and was better at getting people to work together, as well as coordinating many tasks simultaneously. Axtel was also faster and more aggressive than Nielsen, as well as cleverer and more cunning. It was very little wonder that Doctor XT placed Axtel above Nielsen.

So, for the entire nine years of working together at X-Termination, both Zapper and Axel Axtel retained placement in the chain of command that was below Doctor XT and above all other X-Termination employees. XT even taught Axtel some self-defense and fighting techniques that he did not know. Axtel turned out to be not only the highest-ranked but also the toughest individual in X-Termination other than Doctor

XT himself. However, two officials were ranked equally just below him. One of them was of course the premier associate D.D.T. The other was X-Termination's junior lieutenant.

The junior lieutenant of X-Termination was a twenty-six-year-old man named Nicholas Devin Jarrett. Jarrett was a white man but had somewhat darker skin than most other white people. He stood five feet seven inches tall and weighed an extremely solid and muscular 235 pounds. He also had medium-brown hair and brown eyes. Nicholas Jarrett had been with X-Termination for three years, having been the junior lieutenant for most of that time. Jarrett had more physical strength than anyone in X-Termination other than Anselm Nielsen. He had the most strength in proportion to his body weight. However, in spite of his big, thick build, Jarrett was still one of the fastest people of X-Termination.

Nicholas Jarrett was originally from West Philadelphia. As the youngest of three children, he stayed there for all of his life until he went away to college. From elementary school through high school, Nicholas did not do quite as well academically as either John Perone or Axel Axtel, but he still had a grade point average close to an A and graduated high school at age seventeen.

Also, where he fell short academically, he more than made up for athletically. In all four years that Nicholas Jarrett played football for his high school team, he was ranked as the number-one player in the United States. When playing offense, Jarrett was a running back. On defense, he was a defensive back, particularly a cornerback. Nicholas Jarrett was by far the strongest, fastest, and most coordinated player on the entire team. In all four of his high school years, he was deemed their most valuable player.

The position that Jarrett preferred was cornerback on defense because he felt that playing on defense was more important. The object was to keep the opposing team scoreless in order to have a one-sided game. Nicholas Jarrett was practically flawless as a cornerback. On each and every play, he always ended up doing one of three things, whether it was immediately tackling the opposing running back or receiver, sacking the quarterback, or intercepting a pass and making a touchdown for his own team. He was outstanding as a running back as well. Jarrett never got tackled and almost always scored a touchdown. But on a few occasions, he was forced to run out of bounds. Anyone who observed Jarrett thought him to be the most unstoppable player they had ever seen.

Right after high school, seventeen-year-old Nicholas Jarrett enrolled at Pennsylvania State University in University Park, Pennsylvania, where he had received an athletic scholarship. He decided to major in chemical engineering. While receiving an education at Pennsylvania State, Nicholas proved to be a real dominant football player like he had been in high school. Of all the players in the United States, Jarrett was one of the fastest running and one of the strongest for his size. No other team had the one and only Nicholas Devin Jarrett, for no other player was able to combine power and speed the way Jarrett did. Much as he had done in high school, Nicholas Jarrett proved to be the best player in the nation on both offense and defense. He always managed to yield a one-sided game and leave the opposing team scoreless.

By the time Nicholas was twenty-one years old, he had finally achieved a bachelor's degree in chemical engineering. He had two options before him as to what he would do next. Jarrett could either further his education in chemical engineering or play football professionally. For the time being, Nicholas chose to play professional football. He also decided that if he did not always want to play football, he would go on to pursue a master's degree and eventually a PhD in chemical engineering. But whatever the case, he was still proud to hold a college degree that no one could ever take away from him.

Following his graduation from Pennsylvania State, Nicholas Jarrett played football professionally until he was twenty-three years old. His two years of playing came to an end in very much the same manner Nielsen's had. This took place one fateful evening following a home game at Veterans Stadium. X-Termination's top two men met Jarrett after that game. The two men were none other than John Perone and his senior lieutenant Axel Axtel.

Perone and Axtel had no doubt been very impressed with what they had seen of Nicholas Jarrett. Jarrett was the most flawless and unstoppable football player that XT had seen since Anselm Nielsen. Doctor XT and Zapper no doubt admired how Jarrett was always too fast or too strong to be tackled; they were also impressed by his most perfect pursuit of the opposition. When Perone and Axtel consulted with Jarrett, they found out some other interesting things about him as well. Besides playing football, which was Jarrett's foremost athletic activity, he also excelled as an amateur in boxing, powerlifting, and bodybuilding. Both Perone and Axtel agreed that Jarrett had the qualities they were seeking and that he could amount to a true asset to X-Termination.

On his part, Nicholas Jarrett found the idea of joining X-Termination to be very interesting. Of course, he had never before had any intention of committing a crime or doing anything corrupt. However, he found what Perone and Axtel had to say to be very impressive and persuasive. Just like anyone else who became a part of X-Termination, Nicholas found this offer to be the greatest money-making opportunity he had ever encountered. In addition, Nicholas found it to be a more interesting challenge than anything else he had ever done. Even though he had reached the top in college and professional football, he knew it would be tougher to become number one in X-Termination. But Nicholas loved a challenge. Of course, two big obstacles stood in his way—the officials called Zapper and D.D.T. But even if he could not overtake either of the two, or Doctor XT, he would still be acquiring much more money than he would doing anything else. So, with little hesitation, the ambitious youth named Nicholas Devin Jarrett accepted the offer and joined X-Termination.

Shortly upon becoming an employee of X-Termination, Jarrett was named junior lieutenant. Doctor XT greatly admired Jarrett's quality of determination, as well as his ability to be fast and aggressive. John Perone and Axel Axtel even taught Jarrett self-defense and fighting techniques which he picked up and mastered relatively quickly. Nicholas Jarrett turned out to be a tougher fighter and a greater leader and decision maker than practically anyone else in X-Termination, except for Doctor XT and Zapper. Jarrett's ability to put together speed, aggression, and great strength for his size enabled him to manhandle even people who were more than twice his weight. Therefore, even Anselm Nielsen had to think twice before messing with Jarrett. Perone, Axtel, and many others in X-Termination agreed that no other individual deserved to be junior lieutenant as much as Nicholas Devin Jarrett. Jarrett himself felt very honored to be X-Termination's junior lieutenant.

Like all other X-Termination members, he also came to have a code name and a brightly colored uniform. But unlike anyone else, his code name and outfit were very similar to Axtel's. First of all, his code name was Zinger. That was because like *Zapper*, *Zinger* had six letters, began with "Z," and ended with "er." The words *zap* and *zing* possibly had at least one common definition. Otherwise, like with Axtel's code name of Zapper, the six letters of the Zinger logotype were all capital letters that each had the necessary number of various black lightning bolts to form them.

Zinger's uniform was nearly identical to Zapper's. His pullover mask was exactly like Zapper's. The rest of Zinger's uniform consisted of the same colors and material as the one that Zapper had and only had a few minor differences. On the front and back of Zinger's yellow shirt, the six letters read diagonally upward. Therefore, the black X-Termination logotype on the shirt's front had to be placed in the other upper corner. Zinger's pants also looked a lot like Zapper's but with one difference. Each big yellow lightning bolt contained a vertical upward spelling of Zinger's logotype. Each stylized letter was below the next one and slightly tilted to the left. Finally, of course, Zinger had the same kinds of work boots and weight-lifting gloves as Zapper and everyone else in X-Termination.

As Zinger or himself, Nicholas Jarrett was sometimes chosen by Doctor XT or Zapper to take charge of a group. Of course, whenever in charge, he was to be obeyed as Doctor XT, Zapper, and D.D.T. were. Although Jarrett did not have all the special privileges that Axtel had, he was usually the first choice to drive or pilot the main vehicle that X-Termination used as transportation for a mission. Also, even though Axtel was next in line to inherit X-Termination after the end of Doctor XT's reign, another matter was still up in the air. It was the question of who would be next in line after Axtel—Jarrett or big Anselm Nielsen. However, everyone who was ranked above and below Nicholas Jarrett was more than happy to have him as junior lieutenant. So far, he had not fouled up on any assignments or fallen short in any way of Doctor XT's expectations.

Unlike Doctor XT or the two other top officials, Jarrett did not have his own home away from X-Termination Headquarters. Understandably, he had not established one by the time he had joined X-Termination at age twenty-three. Even up to the current time, he still had not given the matter much serious thought, no doubt because he was always busy with X-Termination. So the only home Nicholas now had was his suite in the residential building at headquarters. However, Jarrett did have his own personal vehicle, which he had bought while playing football professionally. It was a sports utility vehicle, namely a red Hummer H3. But for some reason, Nicholas only left X-Termination Headquarters occasionally to have a fun time out and about on a weekend or after getting off duty for an evening.

The individuals who were code-named D.D.T., Zapper, and Zinger were distinguished from all the rest of X-Termination as the three high officials. They were superior to everyone else in many ways. For one thing, each of the three had a much greater quality of leadership, even Zinger, who had been with X-Termination for a shorter time than some of the other members. Also, Nielsen, Axtel, and Jarrett were more intelligent and cleverer, as well as being better fighters than all the rest of X-Termination. Another manner in which those three officials were superior was perhaps not as important. D.D.T., Zapper, and Zinger were much bigger and stronger physically than those who were ranked below them in X-Termination. Some of the employees were slightly taller than Zinger, but he was heavier and had more muscle mass.

Ranked below the three officials were sixteen other individuals altogether who were also in the employ of Doctor XT and X-Termination. Four of them were currently being retrieved from jail by Anselm Nielsen, namely Ant Killer, Roach Killer, Wasp Killer, and Hornet Killer. Other than those four were twelve individuals who had been code-named by a relatively new code-naming system that XT had introduced shortly before Nicholas Jarrett's arrival.

Doctor XT had always derived his employees' code names from terms that pertained to exterminating. Besides the four Nielsen was bringing back to headquarters, certain former employees had been given such code names as Mousetrap and Rat Bait. Those individuals, who were no longer with Doctor XT, had been put away, or as XT would phrase it, "X-terminated," because they had either landed in jail or fallen short of the requirements of an assigned task.

The twelve individuals who were currently at X-Termination Headquarters with Doctor XT, Zapper, and Zinger had been code-named under Doctor XT's newer system. Each of the twelve had a code name that consisted of a capital letter followed by a hyphen and then a one-digit number. In order to get the letters for the names, Doctor XT used the terms for four major kinds of pesticides, namely insecticides, herbicides, fungicides, and rodenticides. Those four pesticide terms were divided equally among the twelve men, three of whom were named for each one.

For each kind of pesticide, the three individuals were ranked from first down to third. At the end of each code name was a number from one to three that indicated the rank of that person. For example, those named for insecticides consisted of I-1, I-2, and I-3. For herbicides, they were code-named H-1, H-2, and H-3. Therefore, the "fungicides" were called F-1, F-2, and F-3. Last but not least, the three rodenticide individuals were R-1, R-2, and R-3.

These twelve men also had uniforms that were all the same design. They consisted of a tight-fitting pullover mask, a short-sleeve shirt, and pair of pants and were made from the same material as the uniforms of Zapper, Zinger, and D.D.T. All of their pants were solid black. However, the shirt and mask of each man was a certain one of four different bright colors, depending on the kind of pesticide after which he was named. For I-1, I-2, and I-3, the color was light blue. The shirts and masks of the herbicide employees were light green. For F-1, F-2, and F-3, they were white. Finally, the shirts and masks of R-1, R-2, and R-3 were pink. Horizontally across the front and back of each and every shirt, the X-Termination employee's code name was sewn on as large black figures. A small black X-Termination logotype was also sewn in the same upper corner as it was on the front of Zapper's shirt. On each mask, the three openings for the mouth and eyes were trimmed in black and were shaped like the openings on D.D.T.'s mask. Otherwise, they all wore black leather work boots and weight-lifting gloves.

These twelve X-Termination workers were originally from a few different cities and towns in Pennsylvania; some of them were from Philadelphia. A lot of their other statistics had variation as well. For example, the men were of a few different races. They also had different fields of study in college, but were all cleverer and more intelligent than the average human being. Also, all twelve of them were great fighters, although of course each one knew a few different and unique fighting and self-defense techniques. A couple of other factors that varied among them were age and physical size. A few were younger than Nicholas Jarrett, while a couple of others were almost as old as Axel Axtel. These twelve men also varied in height and body weight. However, none were as tall as Axtel. Nor was any one of them even as heavy as Jarrett.

In addition to all of those statistics, each and every single X-Termination individual had previously been involved in some athletic activity or other business in which he had performed outstandingly. That was how Doctor XT had taken notice of them. Then, of course, XT met, talked with, and recruited each of them in a very similar manner to which he had done with Nielsen and Jarrett. Also, much like with Nielsen and Jarrett, none of them had ever given any serious thought to becoming part of a criminal organization prior to that meeting. But then, of course, they had found what Doctor XT told them about X-Termination to be very persuasive. So these different individuals joined X-Termination for different reasons. But one major incentive motivated every single one of them. It was the opportunity to make thousands of dollars per day. They also were more and more corrupted as they continued to be part of X-Termination.

The top two people in X-Termination were also the two who were most different from everyone else. John Perone and his senior lieutenant Axel Axtel were not only the two toughest in X-Termination, but they were also the only two who had met one another at a crime scene and merged together. Perone and Axtel were perhaps the two most depraved individuals of X-Termination as well. After all, they were the only two to graduate high school at a very young age, which also permitted them to be corrupted at a young age.

Every individual in X-Termination cared primarily about himself, but Perone and Axtel were the two who cared least about other people— whether they were part of X-Termination or not. Even as much as John Perone, or Doctor XT, provided for his employees, he was only doing so to make a lot more money for himself. Whenever any of his men went on a mission and brought back loot worth hundreds of thousands of dollars, or a couple million, the mad, selfish doctor kept more than 60 percent of it for himself. Worse than that, XT always made sure to "X-terminate" any or all who displeased or betrayed him. It was immediate "X-termination" for any employee of his who landed in jail, failed very badly on an assignment, caused him a great loss, revealed secrets to outsiders, or tried to leave X-Termination or turn against him. The evil and corrupt villain called

Doctor XT merely cared about very little besides himself or what his men could do for him.

Another way that Doctor XT was different from everyone else in X-Termination was the type of uniform he wore. He did not wear stretchy spandex material like everyone else. The main part of his uniform was a black trench coat. It had a small white X-Termination logotype embroidered on the same upper corner on the front of his coat as on most other employees' shirts. On the other upper corner, his code name of Doctor XT was also embroidered in white. Immediately below that was his self-proclaimed title of XTE, which was also in white. Other than that signature trench coat, he just wore a white T-shirt and a pair each of jeans, work boots, weight-lifting gloves, and sunglasses.

Doctor XT was also the only one who had created the X-Termination logotype. Of course, it appeared on most of the employees' uniforms, as well as many of his inventions. It was usually black but took on a different color in a couple of exceptions. The logo featured an enlarged capital X that was followed by the remaining letters, which were all capitalized. The word *TERMINATION* appeared as if it were being projected from the very middle of the X. It started out very tiny at the beginning T and gradually expanded until it reached the last N, which was still within half of the size and height of the X.

Axel Axtel probably ranked second to his boss in not caring about others. He truly did not care about John Perone or anyone else within X-Termination. After Axel had been recruited by Doctor XT, the four men he had brought into X-Termination with him eventually became "X-terminated." But Axel shortly put that behind himself since he was more interested in the fact that joining X-Termination was making him more prosperous than ever. Axtel undoubtedly found X-Termination's operation to be much more impressive and interesting than the operation of the organization that he had taken over and renamed AJA Incorporated. But even though Axtel was always given a bigger share of X-Termination's loot than any other employee, his share still looked very small when compared to the lion's share received by Doctor XT. This made Axel Axtel very jealous of his master. Therefore, the corrupt, greedy Italian was secretly determined to eliminate Doctor XT in order to receive that great big pile of money for himself. However, Doctor XT was not only cleverer, more cunning, and harder to deceive than Axel's former crime boss; he also had the technology that Axel's predecessor lacked. So, even though Axel Axtel had been the highest-ranked and most-trusted X-Termination employee for nine years, he still had yet to find a way to overtake Doctor XT to take control of X-Termination.

As much as each X-Termination employee desired to somehow acquire more money, he was still happier with his job at X-Termination than he would have been with any other job. Doctor XT always paid different amounts to different men of his, but even the least significant individual within X-Termination always got paid at least a few thousand dollars per day. What other job would have paid him that much? Besides, each and every individual working for X-Termination was willing to do anything for excellent pay. So everyone in the employ of Doctor XT was very content with his job though he still had the desire to earn a much greater share of the loot.

The overall operation of X-Termination was very well organized, with organized work schedules for everyone. The normal hours of operation of X-Termination ran from 10:00 a.m. to 10:00 p.m. from Monday to Friday. The schedules of employees normally fell within those hours. Some people within X-Termination worked the full sixty hours every week. Certain others only worked eight hours per day, which amounted to forty hours per week.

Those who were on duty for sixty hours per week included Doctor XT himself, as well as D.D.T., Zapper, and Zinger. A few others who always worked all sixty hours included R-1, H-1, I-1, and perhaps a couple of others. Coincidentally, the individuals whom Doctor XT chose for this schedule happened to be more dominant than the rest of X-Termination's staff. This was undoubtedly because the men who were smarter, faster, and better in other ways than the others were the ones Doctor XT wanted to utilize more often. The X-Termination employees who usually worked only forty hours per week included F-3, I-3, and H-3, as well as a few others.

The more dominant men who always worked sixty hours weekly were the ones more often chosen by Doctor XT to venture out and about from X-Termination Headquarters to handle the much more dangerous tasks than working at headquarters. This was probably because such individuals as Zapper, Zinger, D.D.T., R-1, and a few others were thought by Doctor

XT to be less likely to foul up, or get caught by the police than the less-dominant X-Termination individuals. Those dangerous, risky tasks that took place away from X-Termination Headquarters were done for such purposes as acquiring more money and supplies for X-Termination, as well as destroying anyone or anything that Doctor XT wanted "X-terminated." The number of people who went out on a mission varied from a minimum number of four to a maximum of all of X-Termination. On occasions on which only four were on an assignment, the quartet included Zapper, Zinger, D.D.T., and R-1, who were therefore always involved in every dispatched assignment.

Otherwise, those deemed as the lesser employees of X-Termination sometimes got to go along on an assignment. But these lesser individuals, including F-2, F-3, I-3, H-3, and certain others, spent more time working at headquarters than the other men who were ranked above them. For instance, all throughout X-Termination's hours of operation, any two of those men were always on duty in the two booths at the entrance to X-Termination Headquarters. Of course, they would take turns. Any other X-Termination employee who was on duty but not in one of the booths or tagging along on a mission, was doing some other work throughout headquarters. For example, he might work in the manufacturing area, helping with the manufacturing, production, or maintenance of any of Doctor XT's inventions, or assist Doctor XT in his laboratory. Otherwise, they were to help clean up or maintain other parts of X-Termination Headquarters or maintain and repair X-Termination vehicles.

Sometimes, the higher-ranked X-Termination employees participated in work that was done at the headquarters. But that was whenever they finished a little early or had a slow day in business away from the facility. Also on those occasions, the officials Zapper, Zinger, and D.D.T. would supervise work that was done at X-Termination Headquarters. Of course, this always took place for only a small percentage of the hours that they were on duty. Likewise, the lower-ranked men in X-Termination usually went along on missions for only a small percentage of their hours on duty.

Doctor XT himself occasionally went along with his men on an assignment. XT did this especially when he felt that a mission was of the utmost importance to him. Even when Doctor XT was not out and about with his men during X-Termination's business hours, he was somewhere in the manufacturing area at X-Termination Headquarters. It was either in his office, the control room, his laboratory, or the great big outdoor part of the manufacturing area. He was always working on creating new inventions, upgrading current inventions, making schedules for himself and his employees, supervising the men who were working at headquarters, or monitoring the progress of those who were out on an assignment. When Doctor XT did not accompany his men on a mission, he had his senior lieutenant Zapper take charge. Also, of course, whenever Doctor XT was present for a mission and they had to divide into two groups, he led one group and Zapper led the other.

Furthermore, whenever going out on business required more groups, other officials besides Zapper took charge of a group. For instance, when a third separate group was formed to go off in a different direction, Junior Lieutenant Zinger often led that group. Even the colossal premier associate called D.D.T. sometimes took command of a group. However, one reason D.D.T. was not made a group leader as often as Zinger was that Zinger was a better decision maker and coordinator than he was. Another reason behind this was that big D.D.T. was often needed to break open or destroy any of various obstructions that hindered X-Termination's tasks. So he often went along with the group that needed his strength the most, but sometimes, he destroyed obstructions for every separate bunch of X-Termination's men.

Also, on rare occasions, X-Termination divided into more than four groups. In this case, a group of employees would have to be formed separate from Doctor XT or any of the officials. In either case, the individual code-named R-1 was the first choice to be yet another group leader. If one or two more choices had to be made, they would be H-1, and then I-1. However, even R-1 was hardly ever needed to direct an extra group. Of course, he was the top choice for those rare occasions because he was better in many ways than everyone else in X-Termination besides Doctor XT and his three high officials. With the exception of those above him, he was smarter, tougher, more aggressive, faster, and a better leader than all the others.

Whenever X-Termination ventured out on a mission, they did business differently depending on what they were trying to accomplish and whether it was during the day or after dark. For instance, they dressed a certain way and used a certain means of transportation that was determined by when they journeyed out. They also performed specific kinds of tasks in daylight and certain others at night. In addition, more X-Termination employees got involved in crimes that were committed at night.

When X-Termination went out and about before sundown, each X-Termination member wore ordinary dress clothes topped off by a fedora hat, a trench coat, and a pair of sunglasses. That was exactly how Axtel, Jarrett, and Nielsen dressed for daytime operations, instead of wearing their Zapper, Zinger, and D.D.T. outfits. So did everyone else. The means of transportation for going out in the daytime was a white stretch limousine that was personally owned by Doctor XT.

The crimes X-Termination committed between 10:00 a.m. and sunset were ones that involved less violence and destruction than those they would attempt at night. This was undoubtedly because all the daylight from the sun increased their chances of being noticed and identified by more eyewitnesses. Therefore, not even one half of X-Termination normally went out during the day. Also, of course, they only attempted thefts that gave them little or no possibility of being spotted by outsiders. As a result, the loot obtained by X-Termination in the daytime was nowhere near what they would capture at night. Fortunately for them, both Doctor XT and Zapper had the ability to disable surveillance cameras so that their actions would not be recorded. However, X-Termination only stole from banks and ATM machines when few or no people were around to see them. Other than that, the only stores X-Termination raided in the daytime were small stores in small towns. Of course, they always left the scene after gathering the desired money and supplies and "X-terminating" anyone else who was present. In the stretch limousine, X-Termination did not travel as far as they would at night and usually stayed within a fifty-mile radius of headquarters. Another thing X-Termination almost never did during the day was utilize the physical destructiveness of big D.D.T. to break down doors or other obstructions.

Although the white stretch limousine was usually driven during the day, it was used on rare occasions at night to go and bail X-Termination employees out of jail. That, of course, was what Anselm Nielsen, the one called D.D.T. was currently doing to retrieve Ant Killer, Roach Killer, Wasp Killer, Hornet Killer, and those two outsiders. Since it was Perone's personal vehicle, he usually drove it home on weekends, and some nights drove out and about in it for fun after X-Termination's business hours.

Those were the only major uses for Doctor XT's limousine besides normal use during X-Termination's daylight hours.

In the evening, X-Termination switched to a different business mode. From later in the evening to 10:00 p.m., the men of X-Termination committed crimes that were much more violent, destructive, and exciting than those that they committed in daylight. Of course, Axtel, Jarrett, and Nielsen went out and about in their Zapper, Zinger, and D.D.T. outfits. Therefore, the rest of X-Termination who went with them wore their masks as well as the uniforms that exhibited their code names. The means of transportation at night was a rocket ship designed and produced by X-Termination that Doctor XT named the X-Terminator 4000. Depending on how many X-Termination employees went along on an assignment, they journeyed out in either one or two X-Terminator 4000's.

The work X-Termination did at night usually involved more people and was always faster paced than the work they did during the day. Obtaining a much greater loot during hours after dark required getting more done in a shorter period of time. X-Termination usually divided into two or more groups. Sometimes, the two X-Terminator 4000's even went off to invade two different states. Whenever that was underway, Doctor XT led one ship and Zapper led the other. Other times, if Doctor XT did not leave headquarters, and the two X-Terminators stayed in the same city, Zapper of course, took charge of one ship, and he put Zinger in charge of the other. Whether one or two rocket ships were used for a mission, the people within a ship often divided further into a couple or a few smaller groups to rob different buildings on the same street or block simultaneously.

X-Termination's nighttime operations involved a few other differences in strategy than their daytime tasks. For instance, like during the day, Doctor XT or Zapper would disable the surveillance cameras and alarm system on whatever building or structure they were about to plunder, but at night, XT or Zapper often had to disarm up to several buildings and/ or other things simultaneously. Whenever any people or things stood in the way of the loot that X-Termination was trying to seize at night, those merciless fiends completely destroyed, or "X-terminated," them with either weapons or devices they carried by hand or artillery that was mounted on an X-Terminator 4000.

Another thing that was very different in their operations after dark was the use of D.D.T.'s destructive force. During the day, Anselm Nielsen seldom used his own strength and power to break down or break open anything. But at night, in his guise as D.D.T., he practically punched or kicked open a door or other obstruction at every stop X-Termination made. This was to save time. For example, D.D.T. broke open ATM machines at night, because that technique allowed X-Termination to seize a lot more cash more quickly than they did during the day. In order to get money from ATM machines during the day, X-Termination just used ATM cards that they produced from stolen information to get a little bit of cash at a time. Of course, that method would take longer. D.D.T. would always break down doors, windows, or other obstructions to every bank, store, or other building that X-Termination hit. This allowed more X-Termination members to run in and out more quickly and simultaneously.

Another thing X-Termination sometimes did besides raid buildings was take over trucks after "X-terminating" the driver. Whenever a desired load was too much for X-Termination members to carry in their arms or bring into their rocket ship, one or two of them would hijack a truck that was carrying the desired type of freight. Whether the truck was carrying chemicals, food supplies, money, or whatever else X-Termination wanted or felt they needed, the assigned X-Termination employees would apprehend the truck and drive it back to X-Termination Headquarters. Once the truck was emptied, X-Termination would take it somewhere away from headquarters and abandon it. They also used the hijacked trucks to transport the necessary chemicals to fill the X-Termination Acid vat. Another use for this strategy was obtaining large quantities of iron and steel. Other than that, X-Termination occasionally raided trucks for other reasons as well. This was something X-Termination did more at night; they rarely ever attempted it during the day.

One big reason that X-Termination did much riskier jobs in the night was that they had masks and the darkness of night to decrease the possibility they would be seen and identified. However, they usually worked so fast together that they managed to leave the scene of a crime before anyone had a chance to try to stop them. But on rare occasions, a couple of X-Termination men wound up being surrounded by policemen, who were holding them at gunpoint. Even when that happened, X-Termination always somehow managed to "X-terminate" them. Up to the present, X-Termination had always been too clever and too high tech for anyone to stop them.

The X-Terminator 4000 was a very unique rocket ship that Doctor XT invented within a year after recruiting Junior Lieutenant Nicholas Jarrett. Doctor XT designed the X-Terminator himself and ordered his men to assist him in producing two of them. The X-Terminator 4000 rocket ship was propelled by rocket engines both on land and in the air. It seated up to eight people, including the pilot, and featured two types of mounted artillery.

The total length of the X-Terminator 4000 was about thirty-five feet, while the complete width was twenty-nine feet. The width and height of the main fuselage was about fifteen feet. The height of the ship reached seventeen feet from the ground to the top of the roof when the landing gear was applied. But at the rearmost and highest point of the nine-foot-long fin at the fuselage's rear, the total height was as much as twenty-two feet. The main fuselage was rounded off at the front but had rocket engines at the rear. On each side of the fuselage was an attachment shaped much like it that was only seven feet tall and eighteen feet long. Each attachment also had a rocket engine at the rear, as well as a rear fin that was five feet long and three feet high at its rearmost and highest point.

The outermost exterior of the X-Terminator 4000 was made of light aluminum, which had been painted white. The only exceptions were the bottoms of the fuselage and the two attachments, which were made from the same kind of steel as the barrier that surrounded X-Termination Headquarters. Printed horizontally on the outer side of each attachment to the fuselage was the X-Terminator 4000 logotype. It was of the same style and format as the X-Termination logotype, but each figure within it was purple with blue trim on all edges and corners. Both of the ship's X-Terminator 4000 logos lit up when all the lights were turned on. A much smaller black X-Termination logotype was printed on each side of the nose of the fuselage, just below the tinted windshield.

The X-Terminator 4000 also had many other brightly colored lights on its exterior, which were lit at night. The majority of them were royal blue, but a couple of other colors were also used for a few lights at the ship's rear. Starting at the rear of the fuselage and the two attachments were three ten-inch-wide lights in a row that completely encircled them. The lights at the very rear were red; just in front of those were purple lights. Finally, the color of the foremost ten-inch-wide encircling light was royal blue. Some royal-blue lights encircled the ship horizontally. Each one was a one-inch-wide strip. One strip was lit where the steel base met the white exterior on the fuselage and the two attachments, which were three feet up from the ship's very bottom. On each attachment was another strip of blue light three feet above the bottom one. On the fuselage, horizontal strips of royal blue light ran above and below the windshield to the ship's rear on both sides. A fourth strip also ran seven inches above that, but instead of being a solid line, it was dashed. The only other lights on the X-Terminator's outside were red rotating beacon lights on the peak of each rear fin.

At the very rear of the X-Terminator 4000 were most undoubtedly rocket engines, which provided thrust to propel the ship forward. The fuselage had one big rocket engine built into its rear, as did each attachment. Surrounding each of the three big engines was a round steel barrier that extended by a foot from the very rear of the X-Terminator 4000. The outer edge of each barrier was six inches inside the outer edge of the rear of the fuselage or attachment, and each barrier was eight inches thick. The built-in rocket engines were almost immediately inside the barriers. The middle engine within the main fuselage was the largest of the three, but they were all practically proportional in regards to the ship's portion in which they were installed.

Two other kinds of parts at the X-Terminator's rear helped steer the rocket ship. One, was a movable rudder that was attached to each rear fin, making a total of three. The other was a pair of movable attachments that had a total of eight smaller rocket engines. Connected by vertical hinges on each side of the circular barrier that surrounded the fuselage's rocket engine was a vertical steel holder with a vertical row of four much smaller rocket engines. Each holder was twelve feet tall by three feet wide. However, the very rear of each holder was vertically convex. This made it three feet deep at the top and bottom and five feet deep at the middle. Of course, mounted inside each framed holder from top to bottom were four rocket engines, which provided the X-Terminator 4000 with additional thrust to that of the three much larger engines. Vertical hinges allowed the eight smaller engines to be turned left or right to help steer the ship while the thrust of the three primary engines was temporarily decreased.

The X-Terminator 4000 had eighteen small engines built into the base of the fuselage to provide lift. This enabled the rocket ship to hover, stay afloat, and take off and land vertically. The steel base of the fuselage had eighteen circular openings to allow the eighteen engines to exert force down and away from the ship to provide lift. The engines and openings were arranged in three rows of six that each ran from the front of the X-Terminator to the rear. Each hole was trimmed by a light-purple ring of light that lit up with all the other lights on the vehicle.

The X-Terminator 4000 had landing gear to enable it to travel along the ground. The landing gear was very unique and made the X-Terminator a half-track vehicle, with a pair of wheels at the front for steering and two caterpillar tracks toward the rear. The steel base of each attachment to the fuselage had a long pair of steel doors that would open away from each other and retracted inside the attachment. Then, a mechanism that had an endless iron belt would extend downward and lock into place, which allowed support and movement on the Earth's surface for the X-Terminator 4000. Immediately below the tip of the nose of the fuselage was another pair of double doors that opened and retracted for the pair of front wheels to extend outward and lock into place. Each tire was four feet in diameter and two feet thick. Both of the wheels were turned to aid in steering the X-Terminator. Even when the X-Terminator 4000 was driven on the ground, it was still propelled forward by the rear rocket engines. With the landing gear extended, the ship could still hover in midair, which it sometimes did temporarily to take sharp turns or evade vehicles or other obstructions.

In order to get to the X-Terminator's inside, one or both of two sliding doors had to be opened by Doctor XT, one of his top officials, or R-1. On each side of the X-Terminator 4000's fuselage just behind the tinted windshield was a door that was retracted to the inside of the vehicle and slid backward to be opened. Doctor XT or one of his four highest-ranked employees had to punch in a code on an electronic keypad to unlock and open one or both of the doors. Then, by computerization, the designated door or doors shifted inward and slid backward. At that, Doctor XT and other X-Termination members could climb into the X-Terminator by means of a short stepladder that was extended and lowered from below either door.

The inside of the X-Terminator 4000 housed seats for eight, as well as the controls and instruments at the front. Up front were two captain's seats made of black leather for the main pilot and the copilot. Behind them was a seat similar to those but wide enough for three people. Behind them was another three-person-wide seat.

In front of the two captain's seats were all the controls and instruments for flying. Most of them were just like those found in many other types of aircraft. They included two control wheels, two pairs of floor pedals, and a throttle lever in the middle. Of course, other devices included an altimeter, a tachometer, a gyrocompass, and two kinds of speed indicators. Doctor XT had installed some additional equipment as well. For instance, two overhead video display monitors were installed for the two people sitting in the front. This was an alternative to trying either to see through a tinted windshield or rely on the navigational equipment. A rearview display monitor was mounted between them to serve the same purpose as a rearview mirror. Another feature Doctor XT added was a switch above the throttle lever to switch on or off the control wheel and rudder pedals to the right so that either one or both people in the front could fly the X-Terminator. Usually, only one individual piloted so that the other person up front could operate the artillery. But occasionally, the pilot used assistance from a copilot.

Two other major features beneath the exterior of the X-Terminator 4000 were the tanks located behind the cabin. One contained a modified formula of kerosene fuel that was used to power all of the rocket engines of the ship. The other big tank contained X-Termination Acid, which was used in the artillery.

The other major features of the X-Terminator 4000 were two kinds of built-in artillery. On each side of the fuselage was a ray gun that fired a stream of burning acid. Inside each attachment was a rocket bomb launcher. First of all, attached to the fuselage on each side, as well as to the adjacent attachment so as to be stationed between, was a fifteen-foot-long cylinder eight inches in diameter. Each cylinder had white aluminum skin on the outside and a hollow steel tube on the inside. X-Termination Acid was forced through each steel tube by internal pressure each time a shot was fired. At the front round opening of both the tube and the cylinder, the stream of acid was ignited and heated electrically. Finally, when the projected stream of burning acid hit someone or something, it usually consumed that person or thing entirely, leaving only a pile of ashes in the person or object's place and a surge of vapor that was whisked away. Even with very large objects, at least a large chunk would be completely disintegrated. One of the few substances resistant to ignited X-Termination Acid was hardened steel.

Inside each large attachment to the X-Terminator 4000's fuselage was a rocket bomb launcher. At the upper front of each attachment was a door that was drawn inward and lowered to create an opening through which to fire a rocket bomb. The inside rocket bomb launcher discharged a rocket-propelled nuclear atomic bomb whenever someone inside the X-Terminator's cabin pressed the necessary button after a target was set for that launcher. One or both of the rocket bomb launchers could be used for any desired purpose that X-Termination had. Of course, the atomic bomb used for ammunition was designed by Doctor XT. Each bomb was shaped like a three-dimensional oval that was fifteen inches long and ten inches wide. The front half of the aluminum outside was red while the rear half was white. On the rear was a small rocket engine that was radio-controlled and surrounded by an outer circular steel barrier. The inside of each attachment to the X-Terminator 4000 was able to store twelve of these bombs. However, X-Termination rarely used these bombs for anything, although the heat and radiation from one of them affected people and things within a mile of the center of the explosion. These rocketed atomic bombs immediately exploded on impact.

One other thing that Doctor XT had produced and attached to the middle bottom rear of the fuselage was a Pennsylvania license plate. It was just below the bottom of the barrier that surrounded the huge rocket engine. The figures on the plate read, "XTRMN8R." Both X-Terminators had one.

Doctor XT also invented other weapons and devices for all of his men and himself to use. One of them was a ray gun that he called the X-Termination Ray. It was a new replacement for semiautomatic pistols. They were made for everyone in X-Termination so that each individual had his own. Doctor XT decided to produce and utilize them because they made less noise and left less evidence than a semiautomatic pistol whenever a shot was fired. In addition, they always destroyed the victim much more quickly.

The X-Termination Ray was a handheld small-scale version of the kind of ray gun that was mounted on the X-Terminator 4000. The overall length was no more than one foot, and the widest point was about an inch and a half wide. The complete exterior was made of aluminum that was painted white, while the interior consisted of hardened steel. Above the pistol-style grip was a six inch-long three-dimensional rectangle. In front of that was a cylinder-shaped barrel that was three-fourths of an inch in diameter. The foremost half of the barrel was twice that diameter, namely an inch and a half. Printed on each side above the grip was the name of the device, which of course was "X-Termination Ray," and the letters were all black. The word *X-Termination* took the form of its logotype, but the word *Ray* was printed in normal letters. The entire outside of the enlarged cylinder on the front end of the barrel was equally divided into three colors that would light up. From back to front was a series of one-inch-wide surrounding lights, with the rearmost one being blue, the foremost red, and the one between purple.

Like the ray guns on the X-Terminator, the handheld X-Termination Ray discharged a long, narrow surge of burning X-Termination Acid when fired. X-Termination Acid was stored inside the rear of the ray gun. When the trigger was pulled, a shot of acid was forced through the barrel by internal air pressure. Just before the acid left the barrel of the gun, it was heated electrically and ignited. Finally, when the flaming acid connected with the person or thing at which it was aimed, it completely consumed its target, leaving only a small heap of ashes and a surge of smoke that would be whisked away. If the target was a large wall or other object, a hole or crater was formed by X-Termination Acid consumption. Even then, a pile of ashes was left over. In some cases, a few pieces of unconsumed metal were included in the pile since hardened steel and a few other durable metals could stand up to X-Termination Acid. That was why hardened steel was used to contain the acid inside the ray guns and in the large vat back at X-Termination Headquarters. Also, at the end of every X-Termination member's shift, his X-Termination Ray was refilled with acid, and the electrical heater at the front of the barrel was hooked up for a recharge.

Each and every X-Termination employee had a holster on either side of his utility belt to hold his X-Termination Ray.

Doctor XT did not create any grenades or other handheld explosive devices for any of his men because of the danger of them either being burned or hit by debris in an explosion. However, he did invent and produce X-Termination Gas bombs. They were designed to unleash the same light-purple poisonous gas that was used in the gas chamber at headquarters. The outside of each gas bomb was an aluminum sphere that was half red and half white. On the inside was compressed X-Termination Gas. Each X-Termination Gas bomb came open and discharged its gas upon landing after being thrown or dropped. At hitting the ground, or whatever place a bomb landed, the two halves of the outer sphere were pushed apart by a half inch. At that, the light-purple poisonous gas rapidly escaped and expanded. These gas bombs were often used in situations in which X-Termination was surrounded by too many people on whom to use their X-Termination Rays. This gas almost immediately killed any or all who inhaled it. But, to protect his men, Doctor XT provided his special gas masks. Each X-Termination Gas bomb was three inches in diameter, and each utility belt was designed to hold five of them. Doctor XT also produced some much smaller gas bombs that he only kept and used for himself.

Besides the X-Termination Ray and the X-Termination Gas bomb, Doctor XT also created a few other devices that he did not provide for everyone. For instance, he produced only two of one kind of apparatus, which were only for his senior lieutenant Zapper and himself. This was something he had invented before starting X-Termination. But shortly after recruiting Axel Axtel, he named it the Mega Zapper 2000 and made a second one for him. The Mega Zapper 2000 was a handheld stainless-steel instrument that measured approximately five inches long by three inches wide and was three-quarters of an inch thick. It was designed to discharge a programmable surge of electricity for any of a few different purposes.

The face of the Mega Zapper 2000 had a small video monitor and a keypad below. The video monitor allowed either Doctor XT or Zapper to see what was before him so he could choose a target at which to aim. The keypad allowed one of them to punch in a code to program the surge of electricity before it was charged and released. So either XT or Zapper had to select an object on the video screen by moving a cursor and then locking it onto the desired target. At that, he only had to type in the letters and/or digits for the necessary code. Finally, a large button at the bottom of the keypad had to be pressed to charge and unleash the surge of electricity toward the people or things at which it was aimed.

The Mega Zapper set off a few different varieties of electrical surge for a few different purposes and had a few different effects on people. The Mega Zapper served as yet another backup technique for the X-Termination Ray and X-Termination Gas bombs. Whenever Doctor XT or Zapper figured they were about to raid an area that was more dangerous than usual, one of them temporarily stayed behind while everyone else went ahead. Then, whenever the rest of the X-Termination team was surrounded by too many policemen or other individuals to allow them to draw a weapon, either XT or Zapper fired a surge of electricity that traveled around to electrocute the outsiders they felt the need to eliminate. This sort of electrical surge could be preset with the necessary voltage either to kill or render them unconscious. Doctor XT or Zapper occasionally used the Mega Zapper 2000 on X-Termination employees for still another purpose. This was to revive them after they had somehow been knocked unconscious.

The Mega Zapper 2000 was also used on such things as locks, alarm systems, and security cameras and had the ability to detect those things. Before approaching a building that had video surveillance, Doctor XT or Zapper always detected the closest camera with the Mega Zapper 2000. Then, he would program and unleash a surge of electricity that would hit and blow out that camera and afterward traveled throughout the entire network of video cameras for the building to disable them all. As a result, security cameras seldom caught a glimpse of any X-Termination individuals or their vehicle, which they strived to park out of the view of security cameras. In addition, the Mega Zapper 2000 was also often used to detect and disable any electronic alarm systems or locks. No building was ever safe from Doctor XT and X-Termination. Finally, both Doctor XT's and Zapper's Mega Zappers were recharged after each and every mission.

Doctor XT had also invented two kinds of instruments that he reserved for himself. One was a miniature computerized device that he wore on his left wrist secured by a three-inch-wide wristband. Centered on top of the black wristband was a black metal square surface with a video display monitor and a keypad below. It served as a miniature portable one-screen version of the control room that overlooked the manufacturing area at the headquarters. Doctor XT could use this wrist computer for any of the purposes of the control room. Of course, a single screen only allowed him to see one thing at a time. But he could change the screen display anytime he wanted and could utilize this wrist device from any place on Earth that he so desired.

The control pad on his left wrist was yet another reason that no one in X-Termination, not even Axel Axtel, had been able to overtake him. Just as with the control room, this control pad could be used to activate, control, or deactivate any machine that Doctor XT had invented. Therefore, for instance, even if all of his employees were to band together to destroy him, Doctor XT would be able to punch in a code that could shut down all weapons except for his at any time or place. However, XT still disabled everyone else's weapons occasionally just to protect himself. He was also able to use this pad from anywhere to trap someone inside the gas chamber. He was even able to make an X-Termination vehicle turn around if someone tried to escape. This very small control pad helped to make Doctor XT unconquerable.

He knew a couple of things pertaining to his wrist pad that no one else knew, including its secret codes. Another thing no one else knew was that Doctor XT kept an extra computerized wrist pad in his office as a backup. Either control pad could be used to activate, deactivate, or track down the other.

Doctor XT invented one other ingenious device that he kept entirely to himself. No one else inside or outside X-Termination was aware of it at all, not even Axtel or Nielsen. It was a stainless-steel disc with a center made of silver alloy. At less than half of a millimeter in diameter, this disc was practically microscopic. Doctor XT had produced hundreds of thousands of them in his laboratory, and he kept the unused discs in his office. He was planning on making more of them in the future.

These tiny discs reflected radio waves from the built-in radar system of either the manufacturing area's control room or his wrist computer. They were sometimes used to track down property or employees of X-Termination. To make tracking possible, Doctor XT attached these discs to many belongings of both X-Termination and the employees. Each object had at least several of them. Every vehicle of X-Termination and every employee's personal vehicle had a few hundred discs installed. Whenever his men were asleep, not present, or not looking, Doctor XT installed the discs in their X-Termination uniforms and weapons, as well as many of their personal articles of clothing and some of their other belongings.

The alloy in the center of each miniature disc had a varying percentage of pure silver. Doctor XT made certain that the reflective discs implanted within a specific object had the same or the most similar silver composition. That allowed him to program all the radio waves he sent out at a time to track one specific person or thing. In order to do so, XT only needed to type in the necessary code on either his wrist pad or a keyboard in the control room. This in turn created dots of light that indicated the person or thing he was seeking regardless of the location on Earth. The radio waves Doctor XT dispatched could travel anywhere.

Doctor XT undoubtedly found these discs to be very useful. For instance, he could locate any lost equipment if necessary. On other occasions, these small discs worked wonders for him. On two occasions, an employee who had failed him attempted to flee by leaving the United States. But of course, using his radar system, Doctor XT secretly followed his betrayer, finally caught up with him, and "X-terminated" him. Because the unfortunate victim did not know anything about the invention of these discs, he was no doubt in great shock and surprise, unable to figure out how on earth Doctor XT had managed to find him. Both times this happened, even Nielsen, his premier associate, was indescribably amazed, for he was also unaware of this invention. Even when Doctor XT wanted to "X-terminate" someone who was not trying to escape, he utilized the radar and the reflective discs to be absolutely certain he would not lose him.

John Perone was so fortunate to have created these miniature discs. After all, they were very helpful to him by making tracking no trouble at all. He was always able to find anyone or anything that had been lost. These discs were also another reason that no one in X-Termination had been able to overtake him. He was able to know exactly where his men were at all times. Also, of course, no matter how hard an employee tried to escape, these tiny discs ensured he could not leave X-Termination without being "X-terminated."

X-Termination was now more unstoppable and a much greater threat to society than ever before because of the contributions that Doctor XT had made to his organization, including the substances and pieces of equipment he invented, the people he employed to work for him and/or help him run X-Termination, and all the strategies he concocted to achieve his desired goals. Although different X-Termination employees had different personal goals set before themselves, the main goal of John Perone was to acquire all of the desired wealth and luxury that he could, whether legally or not. In order to do it, he was willing to "X-terminate" anyone or anything that stood in his way.

Most of everyone in X-Termination desired great wealth, luxury, and pleasure as well. This helped make them assets to Doctor XT and X-Termination. Though they all had somewhat different goals and ambitions, each individual was no doubt impressed with how well put together and tough to conquer X-Termination was. Besides, up to the present, no X-Termination employee had heard of another job that would pay nearly as much as X-Termination did.

While all X-Termination employees had remained loyal to the organization, they all had different lives outside their on-duty hours with X-Termination. Some had their own homes to which to retreat on weekends, away from headquarters, including Axel Axtel, Anselm Nielsen, and a few others. But Nicholas Jarrett and the rest of X-Termination only had their suites in the living quarters building at X-Termination Headquarters. Most of those at X-Termination, including Doctor XT, his three high officials, and over half of the rest of the company had neither wives nor girlfriends due to lack of interest in the opposite sex. Of course, the few who had girlfriends kept their X-Termination jobs secret and lied, claiming to do something different. But other than that, no one in X-Termination stayed in touch at all with any of his family members. Some employees spent their free time at X-Termination Headquarters while off duty, while others left headquarters to have fun elsewhere.

Perhaps the most ambitious X-Termination member besides Doctor XT himself was the senior lieutenant, Axel Axtel. Even up to the present, he still did the business he had done before with his own organization, AJA Incorporated. However, he only tended to it on weekends when he went home to New York because he was making a lot more working for Doctor

XT than from doing his own business outside of X-Termination. So his takeover of X-Termination was a much greater desire of his than bettering his own company, but he still had not found a way to conquer Doctor XT.

Though Axel Axtel had yet to gain control of X-Termination, he had more reason to be ambitious than anyone who was ranked below him. Not only was he second in command to Doctor XT, but he also ranked second in other ways. Of course, Axtel was X-Termination's toughest and deadliest individual apart from XT himself. He was also the second best decision maker, for he had never made a decision that backfired up to the present. Axel Axtel was also the hardest to overtake next to Doctor XT. He may not have had the wrist computer or reflective discs of Doctor XT, but he was very alert and still had the Mega Zapper 2000. Although Axel Axtel apparently had no hope of eliminating Doctor XT, his ultimate desire to own and run X-Termination never went away.

Anselm Nielsen was another individual who went home on weekends to the town of Exton. At least for the time being, Nielsen intended to remain a part of X-Termination. Although he had some interest in running the organization, two major obstacles stood in his way: Doctor XT and Zapper, who were both ranked above him. Understandably, a part of Anselm Nielsen would always be frustrated, because after he had worked for Doctor XT for five years, Axel Axtel had suddenly walked in and immediately received better pay, a higher position, and certain other privileges that he had never received. However, although Anselm was superior to all other X-Termination employees in physical size and strength and length of employment, he still had not found a way to conquer either Doctor XT or Zapper. In spite of that, he was still determined to remain loyal to X-Termination, for he could think of no other way to acquire all the money, pleasure, and freedom he was getting from him.

Nicholas Jarrett was one of those who only resided at headquarters. He had not yet established his own home away from X-Termination Headquarters, so for the time being, he remained there even on weekends. Of course, he sometimes liked to go out and about while off duty. He intended to obtain his own home someday.

Just like everyone else in X-Termination, Nicholas Jarrett intended to remain loyal to the organization. Even though he too had an interest in taking over X-Termination, Jarrett chose to be content with his position for the time being. One reason was that he had only been part of X-Termination for three years, a significantly shorter time than certain others. Jarrett also did not have the level of frustration Anselm Nielsen did. Nielsen's dispute did not apply to Jarrett. However, like Nielsen, Nicholas Jarrett had both John Perone and Axel Axtel standing in his way of running X-Termination. In addition, another matter that was still up in the air was whether Anselm Nielsen or Nicholas Jarrett would be the successor for Axel Axtel in taking charge of X-Termination. Whatever was eventually to come for Jarrett, however, he was more than determined to be everything he possibly could be for X-Termination.

Of the rest of the employees, some of them only resided at headquarters while others had homes away from headquarters. Also, of course, whenever they were off duty, they often spent their free time at any of the big buildings in the northern half of X-Termination Headquarters. But sometimes, they went to a fun spot away from headquarters. Otherwise, every employee was very happy with his job with X-Termination. Each individual felt that he was getting everything he could possibly want and more, even though some sort of desire for more money always existed. One disadvantage for each of them was the apparent unlikeliness of advancement or promotion. Not one of them felt that he was prepared to challenge any of the three high officials in any way, not even R-1. So the positions of the sixteen X-Termination individuals ranked below D.D.T. and Zinger always remained constant. However, they were all determined to retain their employment with X-Termination and achieve as much as they could.

Life in X-Termination was undoubtedly a great one from the point of view of Doctor XT and everyone else there. However, this operation was not great for any of the innocent citizens in Pennsylvania or the surrounding states. Their lives and possessions were in grave danger. In addition, X-Termination was already an increasing threat to the United States' government. For instance, they occasionally raided the Federal Reserve Banks in Philadelphia and New York City. Doctor XT was looking to increase the number of people in his organization in order to expand his operation geographically. He was planning to invade Washington DC very shortly. In turn, this would put the entire United States in much greater danger. Following domination of the United States, Doctor XT wanted to invade other countries in the world as well.

A few rare occasions had involved one or two X-Termination employees getting arrested, but no organization or individual had ever come close to putting the X-Termination organization away altogether. One reason was that even those individuals who had been arrested ended up being set free and then "X-terminated" by X-Termination. Other than that, people in X-Termination almost never slipped up because of how well they worked together. However, X-Termination employees of the past did not amount to those of the present, and neither did Doctor XT's creations and technology. So perhaps it was a hopeless quest for any ordinary person or organization to put X-Termination out of business. Therefore, someone with supernatural, superhuman powers and abilities would be needed to stop X-Termination. Maybe the Green Phantasm would have to be the one to do it. After all, he had just gotten four X-Termination individuals put in jail.

It was now close to midnight. Anselm Nielsen was arriving back at X-Termination Headquarters in Doctor XT's limousine. Of course, riding with Nielsen were the six men who had been bailed out of jail: Ant Killer, Roach Killer, Wasp Killer, Hornet Killer, and the two outsiders named Clyde and Carl.

Upon his arrival, Nielsen parked and shut down the limousine. Then, he got out and let the others out as well. Once all six men were standing outside before Nielsen, he told them, "All right, you guys, follow me." So big Anselm began walking toward the set of double doors of the front entrance to headquarters, and the others proceeded to trail behind him.

Anselm unlocked the first pair of doors and let the six individuals enter before him. Afterward, he relocked the doors. Then, he repeated that procedure with the second set of doors. After all that, Anselm pointed toward the open garage door to the manufacturing area, which was south of the other garage door, and said, "Go that way into the manufacturing area." At that, they all advanced toward the manufacturing area.

Once the six men had entered the manufacturing area, they halted and turned to face toward their right. This was because standing to their right were the twelve X-Termination employees who were ranked below Doctor XT and his three high officials. R-1 was standing out front. That very moment, R-1 pointed to the stairs along the south wall and said to the six men, "See those stairs over there? Go on up them stairs, and it'll take you straight to the boss. He's waiting for you." Upon being told that, the six individuals nodded and then began walking toward the stairs.

Once they were more than halfway up the steps, R-1 said to the other eleven with him, "All right, guys, let's go follow them." At once, led by R-1, all twelve of them began making their way toward the stairs as well. This was no doubt part of a game plan that had been put together by Doctor XT.

Meanwhile, Doctor XT was waiting in the control room with two of his officials, Zapper and Zinger. Momentarily, the four members from jail, along with the two outsiders, were turning right to walk along the west wall's balcony toward Doctor XT, Zapper, and Zinger. When Zinger noticed them coming, he said to Doctor XT, "Um, excuse me, boss, but I think that's them."

At that, XT and Zapper turned and took a look. Zapper said, "Well, well, so it is, isn't it?"

"All right, men," said Doctor XT. "You know what to do, right?" Zapper and Zinger both nodded affirmatively. "Good. Let's go." Doctor XT began walking from the control room toward the platform above the X-Termination Acid vat. He had Zinger to his left, and Zapper to his right, both walking with him.

Doctor XT, Zapper, and Zinger shortly met up with the six men from jail at the beginning of the south platform to the acid vat. Once both groups stopped before each other, Doctor XT said, "So, what do we have here, huh?"

"Uh, Doctor," Roach Killer began to reply. "Thanks for gettin' us out. We greatly appreciate it."

"Oh, so you do, huh?" said Doctor XT. "Well, you shouldn't have gone there in the first place, you know."

"I know that," replied Wasp Killer. "But we couldn't handle him. His powers were just too much for us."

"Whose?" asked Doctor XT.

"The one that got us in jail," answered Ant Killer, "that, um, that guy that shines with bright-green light."

"You're talking about the Green Phantasm, right?" asked Zinger.

"Yes," responded Hornet Killer. "That would be him."

Doctor XT turned his attention to Clyde and Carl and asked them, "And just who the hell are you two lunkheads?"

At that, Clyde told XT, "I'm Clyde, and this is Carl. You see, that Green Phantasm freak, he ruined our plans and got us put in jail too. We just happened to be in the same cell as these guys. But we're glad we did, because now we're out and we'd like to join your organization." Zapper and Zinger laughed at that.

Doctor XT said to Clyde and Carl, "So, you would, huh? I bet you would, but unfortunately, it's not that simple."

"Why not?" asked a confused Clyde.

"You don't get it, do you?" said Zapper. "You already screwed up."

"But how?" Carl asked. "We haven't even joined your organization yet."

"What do you mean, how?" Zinger said to him. "You got yourself in jail already; you know that."

"Yes," Doctor XT said, nodding in agreement with his two lieutenants. "That is so true, Zapper and Zinger." XT refocused on the six guys from jail and told them, "You know, it's bad enough that you couldn't handle that freak, but I mean, getting put in jail? We just can't have that." Doctor XT received no argument from anyone. So he continued by saying, "So, now that you've been lame enough to wind up in jail, you're no good to this organization. I wasn't hoping it would come to this, but it has. Y'all ready, Zapper and Zinger?"

Zapper and Zinger drew their X-Termination Rays along with Doctor XT. Of course, they pointed them at the six unlucky victims. Hornet Killer, Wasp Killer, Ant Killer, and Roach Killer began walking along the platform toward the X-Termination Acid vat. However, Clyde and Carl decided to try something different. They began to turn around and run away, but they did not get far; almost immediately, they halted because the other twelve X-Termination employees were standing before them holding them at gunpoint also. "Where do you idiots think you're going?" asked R-1.

"Yeah, you're not going anywhere," said I-1.

"And don't think about climbing over the guardrail," added H-1, "because we'll 'X-terminate' you right on the spot."

Finally, R-1 told Clyde and Carl, "So, go down the platform with them or get 'X-terminated' right here."

At that, Clyde and Carl just went on to follow the foursome toward the acid vat. Then, one by one, all six victims stepped off the platform's end and plunged into the X-Termination Acid. Finally, nothing was left of them except for streams of vapor, which blew away.

After that, Doctor XT said to R-1 and the other eleven employees of his, "All right, men, nice job; that's it. Just go on back about your business." So they all walked off and left the manufacturing area.

Next, Doctor XT turned his attention back to Zapper and Zinger. "Well," he said to them, "I just did what I had to do, you know?"

"You certainly did," replied Zapper.

"Of course," Doctor XT continued. "After all, now that they've been caught and put in jail once, the police are now searching for them. I can't risk the police finding them. I mean, it's not that I think the police could actually bring us down; I just prefer not to take the time to deal with them. You see, I don't like to waste time or money on anything, you know."

"Right," said Zinger.

"Oh well," Doctor XT said. "Now that that's done, no need to worry about them anymore, especially since there's something else I'm worried about more."

"Is it what I think it is?" asked Zapper.

"You better believe it," Doctor XT answered him. "It's the Green Phantasm. He put four of my men into jail in these past two nights. No one's ever done that to us before." Agreeing with XT, Zapper and Zinger both shook their heads.

Doctor XT then continued by saying, "You see, I understand that he gave off glowing, neon-green light. Other than that, Ant Killer and Roach Killer merely caught a glimpse of a flash of green light that whizzed by at lightning speed. Then, Wasp Killer and Hornet Killer failed to gun him down because their bullets did not get to him. Does this guy have special powers that no one else does?" Zapper and Zinger just shrugged their shoulders and shook their heads in confusion.

"Well, I know this much," Doctor XT told them. "So far, no one's gone far enough to put us out of business, and I'd like to keep it that way. However, if this guy is as uncontrollable as they said he is, then there's a slight possibility that if anyone could stop us and shut us down, he could.

So we're gonna go after him and 'X-terminate' him. I'm sure we'll find a way. We'll do whatever we have to do."

Very shortly, Zinger came up with an idea. He noticed an article on the front page of a copy of the *Philosophy of Philadelphia* that he had set down between two of the keyboards in the control room. It was about the company for which James Clifton worked, Ace Nuclear Supply. They were having their fiftieth anniversary celebration that Wednesday night at the Fairmaine Hotel. So then, Zinger picked up the paper and said, "Excuse me, Doctor XT and Zapper? I just had an idea."

"What is it, Zinger?" Doctor XT asked him.

Holding up the newspaper and pointing to the article, Zinger went on to tell them, "That company Ace Nuclear Supply is having a party tomorrow, or I guess that would be tonight since it's after midnight. Do you suppose that if we went there, somebody there could possibly—"

Before Zinger could say anymore, Doctor XT interrupted and said, "Why, Zinger, that's not a bad idea. A lot of great people ought to be there. One of them ought to know who the Green Phantasm is. They're either gonna tell us or all get 'X-terminated.' "

"Why, of course," said Zapper. "And y'all know what I think? I think it's possible that one of those lowlifes there just might *be* the Green Phantasm. Way to go, Zinger."

"All right, all right," Doctor XT told them. "That settles it. We're gonna go there, and we're gonna find out the identity of this freak. Here's what I want: I want you two to pass the word along to D.D.T. and to R-1 and H-1. I want all six of us to be armed, loaded, and ready to go a half an hour before."

"You got it, boss," replied Zapper.

At once, turning his attention to Zinger, Doctor XT said, "And, Zinger, have an X-Terminator 4000 fueled, filled, and ready to go."

"Yes, sir," Zinger responded. Then, with his right thumb up, he told Doctor XT, "We will all be ready."

"Very good," Doctor XT said. "And that's it. We are adjourned. You two may go about your business." At that, Doctor XT went to his office and Zapper and Zinger proceeded to leave the manufacturing area.

X-Termination's main goal now was to find and destroy the Green Phantasm. That would take some emphasis off X-Termination's normal operations, but Doctor XT wanted the Green Phantasm "X-terminated" so that they could continue business as usual. This might be quite a challenge for the Green Phantasm, since this was the first time anyone had been this determined to annihilate him. They would be undoubtedly tougher to overcome than any other criminal or troublemaker the Phantasm had been compelled to face so far.

CHAPTER SEVEN

X-Termination Crashes the Party

It was now almost 5:30 p.m. on Wednesday evening. James Clifton was home after another day of work at Ace Nuclear Supply. This was the night of Clifton's employer's fiftieth anniversary celebration. James still had to get ready, pick up Amanda, and get to the big party at the Fairmaine Hotel, which was on the north side of Spruce Street between Twenty-Second and Twenty-First Streets.

Once James arrived home, he went upstairs to his bedroom. He placed his briefcase on his desk and stopped to think for a moment. James said, "Well, I guess I need to get ready. I mean, I still got to go and pick up Amanda, right? Right! So I better change, clean up, and all that other good stuff at once."

James began taking off his tie. As he was untying it, he mumbled to himself, "Man, I'm, uh, I'm sure looking forward to that party tonight. What a real nice place they picked for it. It ought to be great. Who would want to pass up something like this? I mean, I'm sure Eric and Scott are still gonna go for sure."

James now had his tie off and was beginning to unbutton his shirt. However, he stopped himself. He said, "Wait a minute. What did I say? Eric and Scott! You know, that reminds me, I haven't talked to Scott since Sunday. Oh man, how could I remember Eric and not him? I'd better give him a quick call before I do anything else. I hope they're both still coming."

Immediately, James picked up his cell phone and dialed the number of his good friend Scott MacNicholl. After a couple of rings, Scott answered his cell phone and said, "Hello?"

James replied, "Hey, Scott, it's me, your good friend James."

"Hey, James," Scott said in response. "What's going on, man? What's up?"

"Well," James replied, "I'm glad I caught you. How are you doing, my friend? Is everything all right?"

"Well, yeah," Scott answered, "I'm making it."

"Well, anyway," said James, "I just thought I'd give you a call and check up on you. I haven't talked to you since Sunday, and I'm sorry. I didn't want to simply wait until tonight before speaking to you again. I'm sorry if I seem to have forgotten you."

"Well," said Scott. "I guess it's okay. For the last couple of days, work's been a bit rough for me too. After all, I haven't called you either."

"Perhaps," James said understandingly. "But, um, look, Scott, I just want to be honest and sincere, okay? You see, Scott, here's one thing that happened. After I got off work Monday, I, uh, met up unintentionally with this young girl that, um, I went to have a cappuccino with. That kind of made me forget to call you that evening. I'm really sorry, Scott. I shouldn't have let that happen."

"Oh, really?" said Scott. "Well, uh, look, James, I can understand a little bit, but at least you called me now, and I appreciate it."

"Well, thanks, Scott," replied James. "But there's still something else I think you should know."

"What is it?" asked Scott.

"First of all, Scott," James said, "I feel terrible about what I did to you Saturday morning in the mountains. I mean, the way I got mad with you and pushed you. I shouldn't have done that. After all, I've got my faults too, and I really should not have handled it that way."

"Oh, that?" Scott responded. "Look James, we're past that. It's all right. I shouldn't have done what I did either. I had no good reason to throw water on you."

"Yeah." James sighed. "But, look, Scott, there's still a little more to it. There's something I haven't told you."

"Oh, come on, James," Scott pleaded. "I don't understand what you're trying to say. I mean, what's the problem?"

"Well, Scott," James answered somewhat hesitantly, "it's like, I was having a dream when you woke me up. It was about that same young that I had a cappuccino with. You see, Scott, I had actually met her Friday evening just before I met up with you and Eric. That's what had made me run a little late and drive past Eric's house when I had come to pick y'all up. She was on my mind. But now, it just so happens that she'll be my date tonight at the party. I'm sorry I didn't let you know sooner."

"Wow!" Scott said, a little surprised.

"Look, I'm sorry, Scott," James pleaded. "I admit, I allowed her to make me lose control at first, but eventually, I got ahold of myself, because I knew it would be wrong to let her come between us. I'm really sorry about everything."

At that, James and Scott both took a moment to think things over silently. But then, Scott said to James, "Anyway, James?"

"Yes, Scott?"

"I just want to say, thanks for telling me the truth."

"Oh sure," responded James. "I'm happy to do that. Thanks for taking it so well. Hopefully, we're still friends, right?"

"Absolutely," answered Scott. "So anyway, James?"

"Uh, yeah?"

At that, Scott asked, "So, like, what's her name?"

"All right then," answered James. "Her name is Amanda Taylor. She's a loan officer at a company called Stanley Financial."

"Wow," replied Scott. "That sounds interesting. She sounds great."

"Thanks," said James. "But, um, look, Scott, I'll introduce us all at the party."

"That'll work," Scott said agreeably. "I'm all for that."

"Well, okay then," said James. "But look, Scott, I'd really like to talk with you a lot more, but I've got to get a move on. I still have to pick up Amanda. But you have to admit, even with the hurry I was in, I still cared enough to give you a call."

"In that case," Scott said, "thanks, I appreciate that."

"Oh, anytime," replied James.

"Well," said Scott, "I guess I'll see you at the Fairmaine Hotel in a little while?"

"You certainly will," he answered. "I'll see you then. Bye."

"All right, bye," replied Scott.

They both hung up.

James continued taking off his work clothes. After that, he went to take a brief shower. Next, of course, he put on another shirt, tie, and pair of pants to wear to the gathering at the hotel.

Then, James said, "All right! Now then, at least I've gotten dressed for the party. I guess I ought to call Amanda to make sure we're still good to go. But I think I might grab a quick snack first." So James went downstairs, fixed himself a glass of milk, and ate a banana.

Immediately after finishing his snack, James rinsed out his glass and placed it in the kitchen sink. He then went on to pick up his cell phone and dial Amanda Taylor's cell phone number.

After a couple of rings, Amanda answered and said, "Hello?"

"Hi there, Amanda," James said. "It's me, James Clifton."

"Well, hi, James," Amanda addressed him sweetly. "Whatcha doin'?"

"Well, uh, Amanda," James began, "I just wanted to call and let you know that, um, I was just getting ready for that party tonight—you know, the one I invited you to?"

"Uh-huh," answered Amanda.

"Well," said James, "I just wanted to let you know that I'm ready, and I'm about to come and meet you. Are you still coming?"

"Why, yes," Amanda answered affirmatively.

"Great!" replied James happily. "I would now like to say ahead of time, thanks for coming."

"Oh, sure!" Amanda responded graciously.

"Okay then," said James. "But anyway, Amanda, other than that, how is everything? Everything okay?"

"It sure is," answered Amanda. "What about you?"

"Well," answered James. "I got to tell you, it couldn't be better. Thanks for asking."

"Sure," replied Amanda.

"But look, Amanda," James said, "I'll be right over in a few minutes. I look forward to seeing you."

"I look forward to seeing you too," she said.

"Okay," said James, "Bye."

"Bye," she said. So then, they both hung up.

Before much longer, it was 6:10 p.m. James finally got into his Suburban and began heading over to Amanda's apartment complex in

Lawndale. However, on the way there, he stopped at a flower shop to get her some flowers. He picked out and put together six carnations in a vase, some white and some pink, and added a bundle of lilies to them. After that, he continued on his way.

Then, at just a little past 6:30 p.m., James finally made it to Amanda's place. He parked near her apartment, took the vase of flowers he had bought, and went up to her door. He gently knocked and waited.

Then momentarily, Amanda Taylor opened her door. She was wearing a black sleeveless dress, black hosiery, and some black pumps with elevated heels.

"Hi," James Clifton addressed her.

"Hi," she said in return. At that, they hugged each other.

"So, um, Amanda," said James, "how you feeling this evening?"

"Oh great, wonderful," Amanda answered. "How are you?"

"Well," James began saying. "First of all, I'm really happy to be here right now. Other than that, I'm feeling good enough to say this. I've been thinking about you since we had a cappuccino the other day. So I've got in my left hand a way of showing it." He extended the vase of flowers toward her.

Amanda looked surprised as she took the flowers from him. "Oh my gosh!" she exclaimed happily. "What pretty flowers!" She took them inside and set them down in the middle of her living room. Then, she went back to James Clifton. Upon returning to him, Amanda said, "Oh, James, you're a real sweetheart." At once, she gave him a thank-you hug and planted a kiss on his right cheek.

"Oh, no problem," James said, not knowing what else to say. "Happy to do it."

"Thank you so much," Amanda told him.

"You're very welcome," James replied.

Immediately following that was a moment of silence. But after a moment of that, James finally said, "So, um, Amanda?"

"Yes, James?"

"So, um," James began slowly and calmly, "you ready to go?"

"I sure am," she said sweetly. "I just need to get my purse. Do you mind?"

"Not at all," answered James. He stood and waited as Amanda went to get her purse. She quickly returned to the front door. At that, she stepped outside and closed the door behind herself.

James put out his left hand for her to take and hold and said, "Shall we?"

"We certainly shall," answered Amanda. She took hold of his left hand. At that, they walked toward his Suburban. Once there, James opened the passenger's door for Amanda. Once she was in, he closed it behind her. Finally, he got into the driver's side and started his truck. Then, he backed out of the parking spot he had taken and started heading toward downtown Philadelphia.

While en route downtown, he started up a conversation with Amanda. "So, Amanda," began James, "did you have a good day at work?"

"Yeah, I did," she said doubtfully. "It was a little busier than usual, but I got through it."

"Man," replied James, "Sounds like everybody's busier than usual."

"Really?" she asked. "Why? What do you mean?"

"Oh, nothing much," he answered. "It's just, uh, we kind of have a major project this week. Other than that, one of my friends says he's busy too. That's about all. Of course, as you may also understand, there's been a bunch of talk about that new guy in town. You know, the Green Phantasm?"

"Oh yes, your friend!" Amanda replied with enthusiasm. "A bunch of us have been talking about him too. Oh my, that guy saved my life! I wonder what he's doing right now as we speak."

"Oh yeah, right." James sighed and rolled his eyes.

"Oh, come on, James," Amanda pleaded with compassion. "I don't mean to upset you. I just want to meet him and thank him. He risked his life to help me, and I feel that I owe him a little something for that. Can't you understand, please?"

Then, calmly and kindly, James said, "It's all right. It's quite all right, Amanda. I understand. I don't like to forget people who do me favors, especially one like that. I completely understand how you feel. It's perfectly okay. I still trust you."

"Aw, thank you, James," Amanda said smiling. Then, she gently patted his right cheek.

"No problem. Anytime," he replied agreeably. "If you like, I still think I could arrange for you to meet him. Maybe a little later this week perhaps? We'll see about it, okay?"

"Okay," Amanda answered. Then, she said, "Well, I won't bother you anymore about it right now. We can see about it later."

"Okay," said James, "That sounds good."

"But right now," Amanda told James, "let's just go and have a great time together."

"Sounds like a great idea," James said in agreement. "Let's do that."

After that, a couple of moments of silence went by. James finally decided to say something else. "Excuse me, Amanda?" he said.

"Yes, James," she replied. "What is it, baby?"

At that, James said, "There's, uh, just perhaps something I ought to tell you."

"Really?" asked Amanda. "What's the matter?"

"Well," James answered slowly, "I just thought of something I should've thought of before. It's from when I invited you to the celebration tonight. I didn't think of this then, but I just now figured that you might've had a few friends or relatives you'd have liked to come too. Maybe I should've tried to see if you wanted some passes for them too. I'm really sorry."

"It's okay, James," said Amanda.

"Well, all right," he replied. "I'll try to make up for that next time around."

"Okay," Amanda said agreeably.

"But you see, Amanda," he told her. "There's still a little more to it. I'm just trying to be honest and sincere. You see, I gave a couple of passes to two of my friends, and they'll be there. I just wish I'd have opened that opportunity to you too. I'm really sorry I didn't think of it. But, um, anyway, since you were open, honest, and sincere concerning how you felt about what's-his-name, it made me think about it. I didn't mean to be so selfish."

Amanda was still sympathetic about it all. She said, "Well, thank you for being honest. Maybe I can trust you after all. I'm sure it'll be all right."

"Thank you, Amanda," James said.

"Sure," she replied.

James and Amanda soon arrived at the Fairmaine Hotel. James parked his truck and turned it off. Next, Amanda and James got out and walked toward the front entrance holding hands. It was now 6:55 p.m.

The Fairmaine Hotel was a large building. It was located not too far from Schuylkill River Park. That night, a lot of Philadelphia police officers were guarding and maintaining order at that hotel.

Very shortly thereafter, James and Amanda made it to the front door. He said to the officer who was checking everyone, "Good evening, Officer."

"Good evening, sir," replied the officer.

"I'm with Ace Nuclear Supply," said James, "and she's with me."

Then, James said softly to Amanda, "Let's, uh, show him our passes." At that, James and Amanda both took out their passes and showed them to the policeman.

"Thank you both," the officer said. "Enjoy yourselves."

James and Amanda then walked toward the big dining room where the celebration was taking place. The dining room had anything and everything one would expect to see at a fancy club. All the servers were wearing suits and bowties. A big chandelier hung from the middle of the ceiling. Every table was covered with a big white tablecloth and was set up completely with everything necessary for dining. The room had a lot of ornately designed structures, as well as expensive pictures on the walls. Two other features included a bar that extended down one side of the whole room and a band in another corner playing jazz music. Finally, it had a very large buffet that was set up on several tables that were lined up together so that everyone could get in line to serve themselves.

When James Clifton and Amanda Taylor arrived, several people were already there, including most of the employees of Ace Nuclear Supply and their guests. Also, as it happened, James's two close friends had already made it there.

James and Amanda walked slowly across the big dining room. They remained side by side, holding hands and looking around in all possible directions. Both were looking for a good place to sit. However, James was also on the lookout for anyone he knew. Here and there, he recognized people with whom he worked, but he had not yet seen Eric or Scott. As the two of them were walking and looking around, James said, "So, Amanda, how do you like it?"

"Very much," answered Amanda. "Thank you for bringing me, James. Of course, I've been to a few nice restaurants, but they weren't like this. I have to admit, it's my first time here."

"Well," said James, "I have to tell you the truth; it's my first time here too. Even if my company's held some banquets here before, this will be the first one I've been to. And another thing, someone must've put up a bunch of money to have this establishment built. However, even though owning it can be nice to think about, I might be better off without it. I mean, there's other things in life I'm interested in more than this."

"Yeah, you're right," Amanda replied, nodding in agreement.

But then, just momentarily, when he and Amanda had made it two-thirds of the way across the room, James finally spotted a vacant table with four chairs. It was about eight feet ahead of him. "Hey, um, Amanda?" said James.

"Yes, James?"

Pointing to the table, he said, "Uh, I see a vacant table right in front of us. Is it all right if we sit there?"

"Okay," answered Amanda, "Sure, this is fine." So then, they walked up to it. As soon as they got there, James first tended to Amanda like a gentleman would. He pulled back a chair for her, allowing her to be seated first. Then, he helped make sure she was settled in, after which he sat down himself. He was seated on Amanda's right-hand side. They were both facing the end of the room at which the band was playing in one corner. "Thank you, James," Amanda told him.

"No problem," he replied. "Anything for you." At that, they looked into each other's eyes for a few seconds. After that, James started looking around to his right.

All of a sudden, something caught his eye—or two somethings actually. He thought he saw his two friends, Eric and Scott. James looked their way a little longer and realized that it was indeed Eric Thomas and Scott MacNicholl. They were standing thirty feet away from him, at the end of the buffet that was closer to the bar. They were to the right of his field of vision when he looked at the room's back wall. Upon spotting them, James said softly, "Oh my goodness, it's them."

Amanda asked, "What's the matter, James? What is it?"

Then, James turned back toward Amanda and said, "Oh, uh, nothing much, Amanda; I, uh, I just noticed the two friends of mine that I said I had given passes to, so they could come too. You remember how I mentioned something about that earlier?"

"Oh yeah," she answered, "I remember. That's right, you did."

"Okay then," replied James, "but, um, look Amanda, could you please give me a second?"

"Okay," she answered calmly.

"Thank you," James told her. He stood up and directed his attention toward Eric and Scott. He waved his arms from side to side so they would notice him.

Eric thought he saw someone looking their way trying to get someone's attention. He said, "Hey, Scott, do you see what I see? I wonder if that guy's trying to—Wait a minute… Is that James?"

Scott said, "Let me see. Who are you talking about?" He then tried to look in the direction in which Eric was pointing. Of course, they were both trying to find him among all the people in the room. Scott finally spotted their friend James, the one waving his arms at them. So then, Scott said to Eric, "It is! It is James! Come on!"

When James Clifton saw them both looking at him, he gave them the signal to come his way. At once, Eric and Scott started walking over. Shortly, they made their way over to James's table. "How you doing, James?" asked Eric.

"What's going on, James?" asked Scott.

Clifton was shaking hands with them one at a time. After that, Clifton addressed them in return, saying, "Hey, guys, glad y'all made it here. Thanks for coming."

"No big problem, James," replied Scott, "this is one of the coolest places I've ever been. Thanks for inviting me."

"Well," Eric said agreeably, "I got to admit, that goes for me too. Thank you, James."

"You're both welcome," James told them kindly and calmly.

"So, James," said Scott, "if you don't mind me asking, who's this?"

"Oh, her?" responded James. "Well, uh…" Before continuing, James turned to Amanda and asked her quietly, "Do you mind if I introduce us all?"

"Not at all," she answered agreeably, "I'd be happy to meet your friends."

"Thanks, Amanda," James whispered to her. "All right, guys," James said to Eric and Scott, "this is Amanda Taylor." Then, as he pointed to Eric and Scott, James said to Amanda, "Amanda, this is Eric Thomas and Scott MacNicholl."

Eric and Scott took turns shaking hands with her. As Eric went first, he said, "Hi, Amanda, how are you?"

Amanda smiled and said, "Hey," as she returned the handshake.

Then, it was Scott's turn. He addressed her, saying, "Hey, Amanda, I'm Scott."

As they shook hands, she said in response, "Hi, Scott, how are you doing?"

"Oh, everything's fine," answered Scott. "Thank you."

"Well, guys," Amanda said to both of them, "it's nice to meet you two."

Eric addressed James, saying, "Excuse me, uh, James, you think it would be possible if we…"

Not fully understanding, James just got a confused look on his face and slightly shook his head in confusion.

But then, Scott spoke up and said, "You see, James, what I think he's trying to say is, is it all right if we join y'all?"

"Oh, that," answered James. "Well, uh, that's if Amanda doesn't mind. How do you feel, Amanda?"

"I don't mind at all," she gladly answered. "Take a seat with us, guys."

"Why, thank you," replied Eric.

"Oh yeah," said Scott in agreement. "Thanks, Amanda. Don't mind if we do, huh?"

Scott sat down at Amanda's left-hand side. Then, Eric sat between Scott and James.

James turned to Amanda and said to her softly, "Are you sure you're okay with this?"

"Absolutely," she answered. "They've been your friends for a long time. We just gotta open up to them."

"Well," a somewhat amazed James responded, "in that case, thanks, Amanda, I appreciate your sacrifice. Maybe we'll have more time alone when we get together another time. I mean, there's always next time, right?"

"There you go," Amanda said in agreement.

So then, turning his attention back to Eric and Scott, James said to them, "All right, guys, well, I'm not sure where to start, but as I was saying, this, of course, is Amanda Taylor…"

"Uh-huh," replied Eric.

"Right," replied Scott.

"Well," continued James. "She's a loan officer at um…"

"It's all right," Amanda interrupted. "I'll handle this, James. Anyway, Eric and Scott, like he just said, I'm a loan officer. I work at Stanley Financial. I've worked there for five years since achieving my accounting degree."

"Man, that's wonderful," replied Eric.

"Yeah, that's great," said Scott. "That's a heck of a lot more than I can say."

"Oh really?" asked Amanda. "So, what do you guys do?"

"Well," said Eric, "I work at an electric company. I'm an advanced electrician."

"That's really good, uh, Eric," Amanda told him. "So, what about you, Scott?"

"Uh, well," Scott answered with a somewhat disappointed look, "you see, Amanda, I tried going to college to do, uh, something great, but, um, it didn't turn out to be for me. So I'm in the freight business. I'm a dispatcher at a trucking company. It's too bad I'm not as great as either you or James."

"Well, that's all right, Scott," Amanda told him. "That's still good."

"So, Amanda," said Eric, "where'd you go to school for accounting?"

"I went to the University of Pennsylvania," she answered him.

"Well, anyway, Amanda?" said Scott.

"Yes, Scott?" she answered him rather happily and cheerfully.

"Um, where'd you go to high school?" asked Scott.

"Actually," she told Scott, "it was in New Jersey."

"That's interesting," said Eric. "Is that where you're from originally?"

"It sure is," Amanda answered with a smile.

A waiter appeared at their table. He had two goblets of water on a circular tray. "Good evening," he greeted them. "I brought your water."

"Thanks," James said. "But, look, could you bring us two more please? These two guys will be sitting with us."

"Certainly, sir," the waiter responded. Then, he went off to get the drinks.

They resumed their conversation. Eric said to Amanda, "So, Amanda, I guess you've already gotten to know quite a bit about our friend James Clifton here. I don't know if he told you, but—"

Amanda interrupted. "Let me tell you, okay? James Clifton got a PhD at twenty-three. Within a couple years after that, he became chief engineer at Ace Nuclear Supply."

"Wow, that's really good," said Eric.

"Yeah," said Scott in agreement, "not bad, Amanda."

But then, Eric said, "Hey, um, Scott?"

"Yeah?" Scott replied.

"Look, Scott," Eric said to him. "You, um, ready to go over to the buffet and get something to eat?"

"Sure," answered Scott. "Come on; let's go." At that, they both got up and started over to the buffet, taking the dinner plates that were provided for them. But before getting too far, Scott stopped and looked back at James and Amanda. He said, "Are y'all coming too?"

James answered by saying, "We'll be right there."

After Scott went on toward the buffet, James rotated in his chair to face Amanda. When she detected the interest he was showing, she turned to face him in return. They were then seated face-to-face. They looked into each other's eyes for a moment. Following that, James said softly and calmly, "So, um, Amanda?"

"Yes, James?" she replied slowly and softly.

Continuing in a calm and peaceful manner, he said, "Well, um, look, I'm just asking you this to make sure once more. Is, uh, everything okay with you?"

"I don't see why not," she softly replied. "How about you?"

"Well," answered James, "of course, uh, everything's, um, great. But it's even better since you're here with me."

"Why, thank you," replied Amanda.

"Anyway, Amanda?" said James.

"Uh-huh," she replied.

"I was just thinking," said James, "since I introduced you to my two best friends, it made me wonder something."

"What's that?" asked Amanda.

"Well," James began to say, "do you have, uh, a lot of friends?"

"It's hard to say," answered Amanda, "But I know I have a couple of real close friends like you do with these two guys. I don't know for sure if they include the people I work with. Otherwise, I'm not a hundred percent sure."

"Oh, that's all right," James told her. "I just started to wonder something from when you told me a moment ago that you had a couple of real close friends. Was that the two that were with you when you got off the subway train Sunday night?"

"How do you know about that?" she asked.

"Oh yeah," answered James. "Well, the Phantasm came over and told me when he whizzed around the corner to meet me."

"Okay," she said.

"So," said James, "how are they doing? Is everything okay with them?"

"Yes," answered Amanda, "everything's great. Their names are Erin and Michelle. I think I told you about them the other day."

"All right," he said. "You know something? You sure did, didn't you? I see." James paused for a moment and then said, "So, Amanda?"

"Yes, James?" she replied.

"If you don't mind me asking, what are you doing this weekend?" asked James.

"I don't know yet," she answered.

"That's okay," said James. "Would you rather talk about it later?"

"Yeah," she said. "I think so."

James said, "Well, anyway, you about ready to go get something to eat?"

"Sure," she answered. At that, they both got up. However, as they were getting ready to walk to the buffet together, something caught Amanda's attention, for she had looked around a little bit upon standing up. Among everyone in the room, she noticed in the distance Mark Thompson. Of course, he was the doctor that she had met Monday afternoon after James had dropped her off. Dr. Thompson was between the dining room entrance and the end of the room with the bar. At the moment, he was standing around talking and laughing with a few friends.

So then, as Amanda kept looking Thompson's way, James said, "Amanda, what's going on? Is there something wrong?"

"No," she answered. "Not really."

"Well, what is it?" James asked nicely.

Amanda answered, "Oh, um, James, could you please come with me for a minute?"

"Sure, no problem at all," he answered agreeably.

At that, Amanda took hold of his left hand. Then, she walked on, leading James over toward Mark Thompson. "So, Amanda," James said happily, "where are you taking me, if I may ask?"

"Oh," she replied, "he's, uh, kind of a new friend of mine. I just want to take a minute to introduce you to him."

"Oh, okay," James said agreeably. "I don't mind that at all. Any friend of yours is a friend of mine. How's that sound?"

"It just sounds wonderful, James," answered a pleased and happy Amanda.

Finally, Amanda and James made it over to Dr. Thompson. Upon getting there, Amanda addressed him, saying, "Hey, excuse me, Mark?"

"Huh?" replied Mark Thompson, looking around to see who had called him. But shortly, he looked behind himself and noticed her. At that, he said, "Oh, Amanda, it's you. Good evening. How have you been?"

"I've been good," answered Amanda. "How about you?"

"Oh, great," answered Dr. Thompson. "I can't complain."

"Well," said Amanda. "I just thought I might say hello for a moment."

"Well, thanks, Amanda," he replied. "I appreciate that. So is this him? Is this James Clifton?"

"Yes," Amanda answered nodding. "This is James Clifton." She turned to James and said, "This is a new friend of mine, Dr. Mark Thompson."

Clifton and Thompson shook hands, and James said kindly, "It's nice to meet you, Dr. Thompson."

"You too, Clifton," Dr. Thompson said in return. "I've heard a lot about you."

"Oh, really?" asked James.

"Yes, James," Thompson responded. "I heard about you through a friend of mine who works for you. Then, of course, Amanda told me a little bit about you. So anyway, I understand you got a PhD at twenty-three. And now you're chief engineer at what, twenty-five?"

"That's right," James told him.

"That's outstanding," Dr. Thompson said. "I'm very very proud of you, young man."

"Thanks, um, Mark, or Dr. Thompson," James said hesitantly. "Which one should I call you?"

"Whichever you like," he answered. "Do you prefer James or Clifton? What do you prefer?"

"Either one's fine," answered James. "So anyway, um, Doctor, what do you do? Wait a minute. I just said it, didn't I? You're a doctor."

"Yes, James," replied Thompson. "I practice family medicine. I have an office in downtown Philadelphia. In fact, I'll even give you my card. Here you go."

"Thank you," said James as he took the business card from the doctor. "It's certainly great to have a doctor around."

Dr. Thompson added, "And, if you ever need anything, just give me a call."

"Okay," replied James agreeably. "I'll see what I can do."

"Well, anyway, you two," he said to them, "thanks for stopping by. I hope you two have a good time tonight. Take care of yourselves."

"You too, Mark," Amanda told him.

"Yeah," said James, "have a good one. I'll see you around, Dr. Thompson."

At that, James and Amanda walked off together back toward the buffet. But James stopped Amanda for a moment. He said, "So, Amanda, what do you say we do now?"

"Well, James," she answered, putting her left hand on his right cheek, "I say we get back to whatever we were doing."

"Well," James said a little nervously, "I think we were, uh, uh…"

Before James could continue, Amanda moved her face extremely close to James's. Suddenly, she kissed him on the lips. They exchanged a few more kisses. Immediately after that, Amanda was smiling and chuckling. She pointed toward the buffet with her left hand, saying, "Let's go. Come on, James."

"All right," James replied with a smile. At that, they joined hands once again and started walking toward the buffet together. However, as they were passing their table, James realized something. He saw that their dinner plates were still on their table; they were empty-handed. James stopped Amanda and himself for a moment. "Amanda," he said.

"Yes, James," she replied.

"Well," James said, "seeing that we're going to go and serve ourselves, I think we might want to get our plates. I mean, I think it might be hard to fix our dinner without them."

"Oh, of course," Amanda said, shaking her head and rolling her eyes. "How could I forget something like that?"

"Well," said James. "At least you're no worse off than me. Heck, I overlooked it too." At that, they both laughed. Then, they just walked back over to their table.

But then, as soon as James and Amanda retrieved their plates, something else happened. As they turned to go toward the buffet, they wound up face-to-face with James's two great friends, Eric and Scott. They were just getting back from the buffet with their dinner. "Whoa," said Eric, "what's going on, guys?"

"Yeah, I'll say," said Scott. "Talk about perfect timing. Where y'all been?"

James answered, "Oh, uh, it was nothing. Amanda just introduced me to a friend of hers. It just suddenly happened; that's all. We didn't know he was here until she saw him. But anyway, now that that's over, we're all about to sit down and eat together, and continue our visit. After all, it's this group of four that I came to be with."

"Okay," Scott replied, nodding his head in contentment. "That sounds fair enough. Thank you, James."

"No problem," he said.

"You know what?" asked Eric. "That goes for me too. Thank you for everything, buddy. You really are a great friend."

"Thank you too, Eric," James told him. "I appreciate that a lot. Well, anyway, guys, we'll be right back."

"All right," said Eric and Scott, who sat back down in their seats as James and Amanda continued on toward the buffet.

As they were walking, Amanda sweetly said, "Oh, James, that was really great of you."

James replied kindly, "Well, thank you, I mean, I try to be that way. I just can't help wondering if it's really you who warms my heart and makes me that way."

"Oh, James," Amanda said, a little embarrassed but happy. "That's real sweet. I've never met anyone like you before."

"Really?" asked James. "Well, I've never known anyone like you either." At that, they gave each other a kiss but then moved on.

Back at their table, Eric and Scott had just begun to eat their food. However, before they had gotten too far into it, the waiter had stopped back by, bringing them their water. He offered them something to drink in addition to water. They both requested iced tea. James and Amanda were busy fixing their plates at the buffet.

The time was now approaching 7:30 p.m. So far, the night at the banquet was going great for James. After all, he was in a fancy, spacious, and luxurious dining room with those he cared about; how could it not be wonderful? But unfortunately, the enjoyment of the evening was not going to continue for very long for Clifton and his friends because of someone else who had arrangements to be there as well although he really was not invited and would more than likely not be too welcome. But he was there for his 7:30 appointment like he had planned.

In the meantime, the man was arriving at the hotel with his group. It was none other than Doctor XT and five of those who worked for him in X-Termination. They were all in the process of landing their X-Terminator 4000 somewhere west of Twenty-Second Street. The others who were with Doctor XT included his three highest officials, namely D.D.T., Zapper, and Zinger. Doctor XT had also picked two other young men to come along. The two selected ones for the evening happened to be H-1 and R-1.

Doctor XT had Zinger land the X-Terminator 4000. Everyone then got out of it. At that, Doctor XT secured the vehicle. But then, he gathered all his men together to review the plan briefly. "All right, men," he hollered out, "everybody pay attention! This is the last time we're gonna go over this, all right?" Then, each and every one of them nodded in agreement. "Okay then!" shouted XT. "Now look here, you guys, I'm sure you all know what the plan is. We split up and meet at the dining room. Once there, we hold everyone up, and then, one of those sorry, pathetic losers will tell us who the Green Phantasm is and how to get to him. Heck, one of those pathetic imbeciles might even be the Green Phantasm. At a great party like this, why not, right? Right! Okay, men, any final questions before we proceed?"

Somehow, nothing but silence came from the group; perhaps no one had a question. So then, Doctor XT went on to tell them, "All right, let's move it. Let's get a move on! Zapper, you take Zinger and D.D.T. around the back through the kitchen. H-1 and R-1, y'all come with me."

Next, as they began to separate, XT said one last thing. "Now just lookie here, everybody, if anyone makes any attempt to get in our way or interfere, just 'X-terminate' them, y'all know what I mean?"

"Yeah!" everyone eagerly yelled in agreement.

"All right," replied the Doctor. "Let's go." At that, the group split up into two subgroups of three. Each subgroup proceeded as planned. Doctor XT's squad went around to the front entrance. At the same time, Zapper, Zinger, and D.D.T. went on toward the back door of the kitchen.

Next, as Doctor XT was walking toward the front of the building with two of his employees, he said to them, "Look, you two, I need y'all to handle this. I'm trying to stay focused for my speech in the dining room. So y'all got this, huh? Can I count on y'all?"

"Oh yeah," answered H-1, "We can handle it."

"Yeah," R-1 said affirmatively. "You got it, boss!"

"Well, good," Doctor XT told them. "We're almost there. So go on, you two. Get right on it."

Shortly after that, the three of them reached the front, where two police officers were tending to the front door. Doctor XT stopped about ten feet from the door and centered himself with it. He then signaled his two men to step forward and get him inside. Following that, the doctor just kept still and silent with his arms crossed in front of his chest. He was no doubt trying to let his assistants take care of the two police officers without getting involved. H-1 was to his right, and R-1 was to his left.

H-1 and R-1 then stepped forward to converse with the two officers who were watching the entrance. "Good evening, gentlemen," said one of the officers.

"Good evening," said H-1.

"Can I help you with something?" asked the officer.

"We're here for the party," R-1 answered.

"Well, do you have your passes?" asked the officer.

"Yeah," answered H-1. "We have our passes."

"Okay," replied the police officer. "We need to see them please."

R-1 told the policeman, "I don't think you want to see them."

The other police officer told them rather firmly, "Look, you guys, it doesn't matter if we want to see them or not. The fact is we have to see them; otherwise, you don't get in. Now, either you let us see your passes, or you get outta here!"

"All right," replied H-1. "Whatever you say."

"Yeah," said R-1. "That suits us fine."

Now, of course, the passes to which H-1 and R-1 were referring were actually blasts from their X-Termination Rays. However, the unfortunate police officers did not know that and were about to meet their doom. H-1 and R-1 each took out his X-Termination Ray. Then at once, they each fired a shot at one of the police officers. As a result, the two officers were reduced to nothing but two short heaps of ashes.

Finally, Doctor XT gave them a tiny bit of praise. He said, "Nicely done. Now, come on; let's move it." At that, the three of them proceeded into the building.

But within less than a minute, a woman who was leaving the building happened to notice the two little piles of ashes as well as the threesome leaving them behind. She stopped and turned to look at them. Seeing the two heaps and no officers on duty like earlier, she figured out what they were. She cried out in horror, "Oh no! What have y'all done?"

With no mercy or pity, R-1 just turned around and aimed his ray gun at her. He snapped at the woman, saying, "Shut up!" Then of course, she had a look of great horror, for she was understandably very frightened for her life. But R-1 just blasted her too, leaving her as a third heap of ashes. After that, he went on toward the dining room with H-1 and the doctor.

Meanwhile, the other threesome, which consisted of Zapper, Zinger, and D.D.T., had made it to the door to the kitchen at the back of the building. Once they spotted it, Zapper summoned both Zinger and D.D.T. before approaching it. "Hey, you two," he said to them, "come see."

Zinger and D.D.T. stopped to listen. Zapper went on to say, "Now, look, here's what we'll do. D.D.T., you go and break that door open. Zinger and I will hide behind this garbage container and cover you. So, if anyone tries to stop you, don't worry. We got your back, okay? Trust me."

"Okay," replied D.D.T.

Zapper and Zinger went to hide behind a big garbage container that was only yards away from the back door.

Next, D.D.T. went up to the door and prepared to strike at it. However, a Philadelphia police officer happened to be walking by and noticed him. The officer called for backup; he thought this huge masked man could possibly mean trouble. The officer went up to D.D.T.'s left side. He asked D.D.T., "Excuse me, what are you doing back here?"

In response, D.D.T. just took one glimpse at the officer, but at the same time, he just scoffed, shook his head, and rolled his eyes. Immediately after that, he delivered a really powerful front kick to the door, adding an enormous grunt and growl. As a result, the bottom half of the door was severely dented.

Upon the deliverance of that huge and powerful kick, the police officer pulled out his handgun and pointed it at D.D.T. He yelled, "All right, you, freeze!" In addition to that, five other police officers ran up to the scene and pointed their guns at D.D.T.

"Hold it right there!" shouted one of the five who were there for the requested backup.

Another officer hollered out to the enormous titan, "Turn around and put your hands up!"

Upon hearing the approaching footsteps and the commands yelled out at him, big D.D.T. finally turned around to look attentively at what was behind him. Of course, he noticed that he was completely surrounded. He even became a little afraid and put up his hands as told.

Once he was turned around with his hands up, the officer who had first spotted D.D.T. said to him, "You're under arrest, big tough guy. We're taking you in. Just do as we say!" However, although D.D.T. was obeying them, he gave a funny look to all the officers around him. That funny look meant, "I don't think so. I've got my own backup."

Of course, that just so happened to be the case. Zapper and Zinger, who had been hiding, were just getting ready to come to the aid of their partner. Zapper whispered to Zinger, "You go on the far end of them. I'll stay on this end. You know what to do, right?"

"I sure do," answered Zinger.

"All right," whispered Zapper. "Come on. Let's go."

Zapper and Zinger proceeded as planned. Both sneaked out of hiding and ended up standing several feet behind the policemen, with Zinger to Zapper's far left. Of course, at the same time, all six policemen were closing in on big D.D.T. However, since D.D.T. had noticed Zapper and Zinger in the background, he only got a big grin and chuckled a little bit. This was because he knew that those police officers were going down.

Zapper and Zinger aimed for the officers who were on the two far ends of the group of six. Then at once, Zapper and Zinger each fired his X-Termination Ray at his designated target. As quick as a flash, the two outermost police officers became heaps of ashes.

Immediately after their sudden disappearance, the four remaining officers each suddenly turned and looked at one of the piles of ashes and gasped in horror. "Oh no!" one of them cried, "What happened?" While they were still in a state of shock, those four policemen heard a cackle coming from behind them. At that, they all looked back to see two more masked men, Zapper and Zinger. That wicked laugh had no doubt come from Zapper. Upon seeing those two, all four policemen pointed their handguns at the duo.

D.D.T. got out of his submissive position, and attacked the two officers in the middle. Of course, since big D.D.T. had previously been able to handle four ordinary people at once, this would not be too big of a problem for him. He grabbed those two by their necks and suspended them in midair, letting the poor officers dangle while he squeezed with his huge hands.

Once D.D.T. had elevated those two unfortunate policemen, the other two officers quickly turned to look. But once they turned, Zapper and Zinger blasted them, reducing them to ashes. The only two officers left over after that were those being strangled by D.D.T.

Zapper said to D.D.T., "That's good. Set them down." D.D.T. carelessly threw them to the ground with a growl.

The two police officers were dazed and confused from having landed hard on the ground. Once they regained their senses, they were in a state of panic, not knowing what to do. That was because they saw D.D.T. coming from one way and Zapper and Zinger coming from the other way.

But then, Zapper stopped D.D.T., saying, "Okay, big guy, that's good. You did enough. Thanks, we'll take it from here." At that, D.D.T. stopped and stayed where he was.

Still afraid and intimidated, the two police officers in distress begged and pleaded. One of them said, "Oh please, please, don't kill us. We'll do anything."

In reaction to that, however, Zapper just smiled and cackled. "Ah, ha, ha, ha, ha, ha, ha!" Then, of course, Zinger and D.D.T. both grinned and chuckled too. Zapper finally told the two officers who were lying on the ground submissively, "So, you'll do anything, huh? That won't be necessary. Ready, Zinger?"

"Ready," answered Zinger.

"All right," said Zapper. "Fire away!" At that, Zapper and Zinger both fired their ray guns and reduced the two remaining policemen to two more heaps of ashes.

Right afterward, Zinger said, "That wasn't so bad, heh!"

"Of course not!" Zapper exclaimed, smiling with pride. "That wasn't such a chore now, was it?"

"No!" replied both Zinger and D.D.T.

"Oh well," said Zapper. "Come on. We got no time to lose; let's go. D.D.T., break open the door and get us in."

"You got it," replied D.D.T. At that, the behemoth charged toward the back door. Even once he made it to the door, he did not stop until he broke it off, sent it flying, and got inside the kitchen.

Once D.D.T. was inside, the chefs in the kitchen stopped their work. They turned to look at him and gasped in terror at the huge masked titan. One chef, who was just coming out of a walk-in cooler, ran back in to hide.

Zapper and Zinger came from behind D.D.T., holding out their X-Termination Rays. The entire kitchen staff became even more afraid and remained motionless, not knowing what to do. Zinger was on D.D.T.'s left, and Zapper was on his right.

Shortly, Zapper said, "Okay, boys, let's waste 'em." At that, Zapper and Zinger shot and eliminated two of them. At the same time, D.D.T. roared and charged forward as if he were going to attack. Consequently, the whole kitchen staff panicked and ran. They all scurried out of the kitchen, headed for the building's front entrance.

Doctor XT and the two rogues with him were right by the huge dining room waiting to meet up with D.D.T., Zapper, and Zinger. H-1 asked, "So where's D.D.T., Zapper, and Zinger?"

In reply, R-1 said, "Don't worry; they'll be around any minute. They're coming."

Just as R-1 had finished speaking, the three of them sensed something. They heard the sounds of voices and footsteps of something or someone getting nearer. Without a doubt, it was the stampeding of the kitchen staff, who had been frightened by Zapper, Zinger, and D.D.T. As smart as Doctor XT was, he could tell that it was the doing of his officials, who had obviously made it into the kitchen. However, H-1 asked, "What's that?"

"You idiot!" scolded XT. "Can't you figure it out, huh? Isn't it obvious? It's the work of my three highest associates, you moron! Now let's prepare to open fire, come on!"

Doctor XT, H-1, and R-1 all took out their X-Termination Rays. Then at once, they all pointed them down the hall, in the direction from which the sounds were coming. Momentarily, all of the chefs appeared. Once they saw XT, H-1, and R-1 aiming for them, they stopped running and gasped with a look of terror. Then, the diabolical trio just fired their guns and eliminated three of them. Understandably, the rest of the kitchen staff became even more frightened and further stressed.

<hr>

Shortly, to make matters worse, the trio of D.D.T.. Zapper, and Zinger appeared. The unfortunate victims were no doubt more terrified than ever now that they were trapped between the two evil trios. One of them even cried, "What do we do?"

All the members of X-Termination were so corrupt and devilish that they had no mercy or sympathy for those poor kitchen workers. Zapper just let out another evil cackle, going, "Ah, ha, ha, ha, haaaa!"

"Now we gotcha!" Zinger added.

"Yeah!" D.D.T. said in agreement.

Then, all six X-Termination members blasted away until every last one was eliminated. At the end of it all, they were nothing but little piles of ashes. It was too bad for them all; what a shame. But then, without any kind of feeling of guilt or regret, Doctor XT just told his crew, "Well, at least that's done and out of the way. Let's get on with the plan. Come on, this way, everybody." So they all went to the dining room's entrance.

The chef in the kitchen who had retreated back into the cooler was still hidden. But after a few minutes, when he heard no more commotion in the kitchen, he took a small peek to make sure it was safe. Upon cracking the door open to see that no one was still around, he came out and closed the cooler's door behind him. That very instant, he ran out through the doorway where D.D.T. had knocked away the back door. "I gotta get outta here!" he cried out. "They'll kill me! I've got to call the police. Everybody's in trouble." After that, he ran to his personal vehicle and went home for the night. He was the only kitchen employee who got away safely. All the others were "X-terminated."

In the meantime, Doctor XT summoned all of his men to go over their game plan one last time. "Okay, men, listen up!" XT commanded. "I'm sure you all know what we're gonna do. But I'll go over this one more time for you. First of all, D.D.T., you go in there ahead of us and knock away several tables to give us some room. The rest of you will stand along either side, and you will all use your X-Termination Rays to hold back everyone in the room. Now of course, uh, D.D.T., you'll use yours too, you know." D.D.T. nodded in agreement.

Doctor XT said, "But anyway, look; once D.D.T. clears us a space, he will go forward to the center of the arc you five will form. Now, Zapper and Zinger, you two line up along the left. H-1 and R-1, you two take the right. Everyone must keep quiet and keep their hands up. If anyone tries to escape or tries anything at all, 'X-terminate' them. We're gonna give everyone one minute to divulge the secret of the Green Phantasm. If no one confesses, we put on our gas masks, and I'll give them a dose of X-Termination Gas. Everybody got it all down, huh? Y'all follow?"

"Yeah!" the other five all shouted in unison.

"Okay then," said the doctor. "Let's move on in. D.D.T., get right to work. You other four, go in right behind him, and line yourselves up the way I told you. All right now, *go!*"

Then, suddenly, big D.D.T. stormed on into the dining room at XT's command. Out of those in the room, quite a few turned to look at the huge masked gargantuan titan. Even James Clifton was distracted by D.D.T., and he stared at the big behemoth, wondering what would happen.

Just before X-Termination was about to hit the dining room, all of the Ace Nuclear Supply people and their guests had been enjoying themselves, eating, talking, and so forth. James had been having a good time with Amanda, Eric, and Scott. But at this point, those who were distracted by D.D.T. were somewhat afraid and suspicious. James was looking more and more fearful every second. He even whispered to himself, "Oh my goodness, that shirt says D.D.T.? I can't quite tell, but does his upper left say X-Termination? Oh my! I think DDT is a kind of insecticide. But this guy looks like he wants to destroy something much more than insects. I wonder what he's about to do." Of course, big D.D.T. was just trying to figure out which tables to smash or clear out of X-Termination's way.

While James was staring at D.D.T. with a fearful expression, Scott noticed and became concerned. He asked his good friend, "Hey, James, what is it? What's going on?"

Eric heard Scott and even asked James himself, "Hey, uh, James? What's the matter, man? You all right? What's wrong?"

Once Amanda heard Eric and Scott, she turned toward him and became concerned herself. "James," she said softly and sympathetically, taking hold of his left hand. "Hey, James, what's the matter, baby? What is it?"

"Well, you see," James began to answer, "I just noticed something, and I'm just wondering—"

James was interrupted by big D.D.T., who roared while using his right hand to knock over the table nearest to his right. Fortunately, no one was at the table. However, practically everyone in the room stopped and turned to look his way, gasping in surprise. People at tables near D.D.T. got up and backed away in panic. Understandably, everyone was frightened by the huge masked monster. The three who were with James finally understood what was bothering him, for they too were in fear of the titan called D.D.T. The band stopped playing.

D.D.T. just continued his rampage by smashing to smithereens another table to his left. All the guests became more afraid and continued backing away. As he kept up the demolition, everyone just backed up farther and farther.

A small percentage of the people were somewhat close to the dining room's entrance and had an idea. They began to try to sneak out behind D.D.T. But that option was not available to them, for they had another obstacle—the other four X-Termination members, namely Zapper, Zinger,

H-1, and R-1. Before anyone made it through the doorway, the evil quartet appeared, holding out their X-Termination Rays, and they were ready to fire.

"Oh no, y'all don't!" R-1 told them.

"That's right," declared Zapper. "Everybody put your hands up. Now, get back in there! Move it!" The victims cooperated.

The foursome just went on in behind them. At the sight of those four masked figures pointing their ray guns, everyone in the dining room went into fear and panic mode. They all backed up and bunched together against the other three walls. The people were trying to stay as far away from X-Termination as they could. A lot of screaming and other commotion was taking place.

D.D.T. had now knocked over and smashed about ten tables. Shortly after his four teammates appeared in the dining room, he too drew his X-Termination Ray. All five X-Termination members formed a semicircle, like they had planned. Starting from the left end and going clockwise, the order was Zapper, Zinger, D.D.T., H-1, and finally R-1.

"That's enough, everyone!" shouted Zapper. "Quiet now!"

"Yeah," said Zinger. "Everybody shut up!"

Then, big D.D.T. said, "All of y'all shut your mouths before I blast y'all!"

X-Termination's strong words had little or no effect on all the noise that everyone was making. For one thing, the majority of all those in the room were in a state of panic, not knowing what to do. Furthermore, those commands to quiet down were not sufficient to override all the screaming and commotion. So, even though no one could exit the dining room, X-Termination was having no luck achieving complete silence throughout the room.

However, in the midst of all the chaos and commotion, James was trying to figure out a way to put a stop to X-Termination's plot. With his powers as the Green Phantasm, he knew he had a way to stop them, but he was not quite sure how to go about it without being seen transforming into the glowing, radiant hero. So, while he was trying to figure out a way to do it, he went over to a nearby table and crawled under it. That way, people would not see him make the transformation. He hated to abandon the ones he cared about, namely Amanda Taylor and his two best friends, but he knew that either he or someone else had to stop the villains and save everyone, including his friends. So James Clifton once again activated the radiant source within himself and was radiating neon green like before. For the time being, he stayed crouched under the table until he came up with a strategy for saving everyone.

The depraved, evil, villainous Doctor XT entered the dining room. As he was making his way through the doorway, he swiped the microphone from the hostess's station. The doctor was preparing to make his announcement while his five men were still holding everyone hostage. Finally, he spoke into the mic. "All right, everyone, silence, before we 'X-terminate' you! Quiet, everyone! Knock it off!" At that, everyone stopped and became completely silent. "That's good," said XT. "Now, everyone, put your hands in the air. Get 'em up where we can see them, and don't try anything." All the guests complied with Doctor XT's demands.

Doctor XT started his announcement. "All right, everybody, now hear this and hear it well. Y'all know why I'm here? This is why: I'm looking for that ignorant troublesome rascal that y'all call the Green Phantasm. As great a company as Ace Nuclear Supply is, one of you pathetic peons has to know who he is and how to find him. Hell, I'll even bet one of you is him. So here's the deal: either you reveal the secret of the Green Phantasm to me, or I 'X-terminate' you all right here and right now. You have exactly one minute. Now come on, tell me! Come on out, you energized radioactive green phony! Where are you, huh?"

All the people in the room became more afraid and terrified than ever, thinking they were about to be killed. Without a doubt, none of them knew what to say or do. That was of course with the exception of James Clifton. While Amanda, Eric, and Scott were afraid for their lives, like all the other guests, they began to worry about James because they did not know where he was. They were unaware of his true identity.

But in the meantime, James was preparing to take action. "Well," he said, "I've got to do something quick. They only have one minute until they die." He looked at his right hand and got an idea. He was about to let Doctor XT know that the Phantasm was present. He charged his right hand and lifted up the edge of the tablecloth just enough to aim for H-1 and R-1. All at once, James fired two consecutive laser beams, knocking the ray guns out of their hands. After that, he just let go of the tablecloth and stayed hidden.

When those laser beams suddenly knocked the guns out of the two guys' hands, everyone, including X-Termination, turned and looked that way. "Hey!" H-1 yelled in surprise.

"Who did that?" R-1 said as they both bent down to pick up their ray guns.

While H-1 and R-1 were distracted, a few of the guests on their end of the holdup tried to scurry out of the dining room. However, Doctor XT managed to stop them by holding out his X-Termination Ray. "Hey, where do y'all think y'all going?" he asked them. At that, those few stopped, sighed in disappointment, and went back into the crowd.

Doctor XT made a different announcement, for he was now sure that the Green Phantasm was in their midst. Using the microphone, he said, "All right, Green Phantasm, show yourself! Get on out here! We know you're in here. If you're not out of hiding in five seconds, we will 'X-terminate' both you and the society here defending you. Now come on out before everybody dies."

At that, James said to himself, "I will do just that." Fortunately, he quickly thought of a way to get out from under the table as well as save everyone's lives. So at once, he started charging himself up, preparing to launch himself once again as a shapeless projectile. He set himself up a circular path along which he would zoom at lightning speed knocking away every X-Termination member. He would first send Doctor XT flying. Then, he would advance to R-1's end of the arc formed by the other five. From there, he would upset each and every man along the semicircle by whizzing counterclockwise. Within two seconds of charging, he finally released himself. He sped along his preselected path. Along this path, he struck Doctor XT first, R-1 second, and finally Zapper last. The impact of that lightning-fast, shapeless radiating mass caused each man to be catapulted straight up and land in either a faceup or facedown position. When they all hit the floor, their X-Termination Rays slipped out of their hands.

After striking the last intended target, James reappeared right outside the dining room in the hallway. However, he did not stay in the same spot for long so he would not be identified. Once James reappeared, he took a quick glimpse at his success and then moved on. He teleported a few more times until he made his way out the front entrance of the hotel.

Back in the dining room, while X-Termination was temporarily dazed and confused from falling, one man in the whole room had an idea. He figured that while the bad guys were distracted, this was everyone's one and only chance to hurry and make it out alive. He figured it was now or never. So he yelled to everyone, "Come on! Let's run out of here before they rise back up! Come on! Run for your lives!"

Everyone else in the room heeded the suggestion. After all, they were indeed desperate to get away and save their lives. Everyone—guests, waitstaff, and band members,—stampeded out of the dining room, and then eventually out of the front of the building. X-Termination received no opportunity to regain control over the fleeing crowd. Every individual in the big dining room made it out alive.

In the middle of the rush, Amanda Taylor was looking for any familiar face she could find. Unfortunately for her, she did not know where James was. She could not find him and even thought that he had abandoned her. She said, "Oh no! I gotta find someone who can take me home. Why did James do this to me? What a jerk! He ran out on me. Oh, I'll never trust him again. He left me for dead. But right now, I gotta get home somehow."

But then, within another minute, Amanda spotted her new friend, Dr. Mark Thompson. He was about to climb into his vehicle. Amanda sprinted over to him. She yelled out to him, "Hey, Mark! Mark! Excuse me, Dr. Thompson?"

When the doctor heard someone calling, he looked around to see who. He spotted Amanda running toward him. "Amanda!" he said in surprise. "This is quite a surprise. What's wrong?"

"Oh, Mark," Amanda pleaded desperately, "listen, I hate to bother you, but I have no way to get home. Is there any way I could get a ride from you?"

"Why, certainly," he answered. "It's no problem. I just can't help wondering, where's James?"

"Oh, forget James Clifton," answered Amanda. "He's a real jerk, a real creep. I don't know how I let him trick me into going out with him. He ran out on me. He abandoned me."

"Now, come on, Amanda," advised Dr. Thompson. "I don't think he's as bad as all that. I mean, as great of a guy as he is, he probably had a good, honest reason to do what he did. I'm sure he didn't mean to—"

"Please, Mark," interrupted Amanda, "I really need to get home right now. Can you please take me there? I'm sorry."

"It's okay," replied the doctor. "Go ahead and get in. I'll, um, take you home. It's not a problem."

"Thank you so much," Amanda told him sweetly with a smile. She immediately got in, and they started on their way to her apartment.

In the meantime, James was preparing to go back into the dining room to face X-Termination. As soon as he had teleported out of the hotel, he had sped off as a shapeless projected mass and finally teleported into his bedroom through the window he had left open. Once in his bedroom, he got out his Green Phantasm suit. Then, he teleported out of his dress clothes and into his superhero outfit, once again becoming the Green Phantasm. As quick as a flash, the Green Phantasm hurried back to the hotel.

Next, once the Green Phantasm was back at the hotel, everyone had already gotten into their vehicles and driven off. But the Green Phantasm teleported his way back to the dining room, for he wanted to prevent any further destruction on the part of X-Termination.

While the Phantasm was on his way to the big dining room, all six X-Termination members were regaining their senses. Each one also reclaimed the X-Termination Ray that had flown out of his hand. Then, they all started looking all around the room.

"Man, what happened?" asked H-1.

"Where'd everybody go?" asked Zinger.

"Oh, come off it!" rebuked Doctor XT. "This is the Green Phantasm's doing; y'all know that."

At that, Zapper said, "Why, that glaring, glowing, radioactive neon creep! He'll pay for this!"

"Yeah!" roared D.D.T. in agreement.

"Yeah, that's right," said XT. "We're gonna get him somehow. We'll bring him down. I've already got another game plan. I may have underestimated him this time, but I've already got another way to seek him out and destroy him. We'll do it tomorrow night."

"That sounds great, Doctor," said R-1. "But I just can't help wondering where he is right now. Do you really think a hero like him would do this to us and then just flee the scene like a coward?"

"You know, R-1," XT said to him, "you've got a good point there. After all, any so-called hero in his right mind would come right back to face us. He may actually be around as we speak. But who can really tell if he's in his right mind or not? Well, whatever the case may be, since we're here anyway, let's see what we can find here for ourselves; come on."

"You know what, Doctor?" asked Zapper. "You're right, but we'll definitely get him by tomorrow. Ah, ha, ha, ha, ha, ha, ha, ha, haaaa!"

However, the Green Phantasm had been standing right outside the dining room listening to their conversation. He went on and told them from the hallway, "And you all know what? I guess I'm in my right mind after all."

At hearing that, they all turned and looked anxiously toward the dining room's entrance. "Where'd that come from?" asked H-1.

"So, he is still here after all," said Doctor XT.

"I dare you to come out of hiding!" Zinger shouted to the Green Phantasm.

"Where are you, you radiant-green flashing freak?" asked R-1.

"We'll put your lights out!" shouted D.D.T.

At that, the Green Phantasm teleported over to Doctor XT, reappearing right behind him. At the time, the doctor was at the center of the semicircle that had been formed by the other five, and all of X-Termination was facing the dining room's entrance. Then, in the instant that the Phantasm reappeared, he told XT, "I'm right here." That sudden reappearance surprised and startled everyone. So, of course, they all turned and looked toward the Green Phantasm.

Doctor XT turned around to face the one behind him, but it was with the intention to eliminate the Green Phantasm. However, the Green Phantasm caught his right arm and held it to the side to stay out of the line of fire of his X-Termination Ray. At the same time, he briefly read the doctor's coat and went on to say, "Hi, Doctor XT, the XTE; I'm the Green Phantasm." Then, before Doctor XT had a chance to attack, the Green Phantasm delivered two right uppercuts, one to XT's abdominal area and another to his jaw. Doctor XT fell forward, but still kept hold of his ray gun.

But unfortunately for the Green Phantasm, before he could inflict further punishment on XT, he noticed something else. Doctor XT's five men were about to close in on him with all of their X-Termination Rays aimed at him.

"Let's get him!" yelled Zapper. At Zapper's command, all five ganged up, making the radius of their arc smaller and smaller as they progressively drew closer to the Green Phantasm.

However, before they reached the Phantasm, he moved out of their way. Fortunately, with the pyxorium fused with his nervous system, he could react and move as quickly as he could think. Within a split-second, the Green Phantasm had teleported, reappearing behind big D.D.T. "Hey!" all five of them yelled, looking around in all different directions.

"Here I am!" the Phantasm hollered out. The other four turned and looked toward D.D.T. However, before big D.D.T. could turn around, the Green Phantasm drove his left knee into the back of the huge titan's left thigh. That caused big D.D.T. to stumble backward, almost falling.

But then, the Green Phantasm turned him around. Immediately, he used his left hand to hold off D.D.T.'s right arm, which of course had an X-Termination Ray in the hand at the end of it. The Green Phantasm took off his hat and repeatedly head butted D.D.T. in the face. This severely stunned D.D.T. Then, following the series of head butts, the Green Phantasm took the ray gun from his right hand, threw it away, and finally took D.D.T. by his right arm, slinging him toward the tables he had smashed and knocked over. As a result, D.D.T. tripped over one of them, falling forward. Upon hitting the ground, he rolled over and lay dazed and helpless, still holding his hurting, bleeding face.

Doctor XT had now gotten back up onto his feet and was no longer dazed. He was in the very center among the other X-Termination members with whom he was lined up side by side. The entire quintet was preparing to open fire with their X-Termination Rays.

Fortunately, the Green Phantasm noticed this in the nick of time. He quickly put his hat back on and started his next maneuver. He once again took on his projectile form. With the way X-Termination was lined up, the Green Phantasm was able to whiz along an oval-shaped path, returning to his starting point. All five of them were projected upward like earlier in the evening, and once again, they landed on the floor, losing their grips on their ray guns.

Upon reappearing as himself, the Green Phantasm took several steps back until they were all within his field of vision. He could see D.D.T. to his left and everyone else to his right. Next, the Green Phantasm charged up both of his hands just to be prepared to open fire if absolutely necessary. The Green Phantasm was on top of the situation and had X-Termination within his control.

But then, while Doctor XT was trying to get back up onto his feet, he looked toward the Green Phantasm. Seeing that the Phantasm was prepared to fight, the doctor stayed on his hands and knees and looked at him continuously with fear.

When the Phantasm saw XT looking at him, he said in a firm and straightforward manner, "All right, let me tell you something, Doctor XT! This time, you've really gone too far!"

"Oh, uh, really?" asked Doctor XT nervously. After that, the other X-Termination members turned and looked at the Green Phantasm with fear in their eyes as well. After all, they had all been hit so quickly and suddenly that they could not tell what had hit them or how. So now, seeing that they were all afraid, the Green Phantasm was about to lecture them and try to teach them a lesson. He pointed his right index finger at them and began to utter his first word. However, he stopped because he heard something.

It was the sound of a lot of footsteps approaching, accompanied by yelling. "It's the police! We know you're in there!" In fact, about fifteen policemen had come to put a stop to the massacre and destruction being caused by X-Termination. They had been alerted by the chef from the kitchen, who had earlier eluded Zapper, Zinger, and D.D.T.

Once the Green Phantasm heard the sound of the officers approaching, he paused to think of what to do. But very shortly, he had an idea. He whispered to himself, "Well, maybe I better get out of the way and let the police handle their business. Then, perhaps after they arrest X-Termination, I'll admit my involvement to them. At least I saved a whole bunch of people's lives. But I guess a real hero should be honest. Other than that, I can't just keep running from the police. Even if they don't appreciate me at first, maybe they'll eventually have faith in me. But right now, let me get out of the way."

So, the Green Phantasm went out into the hallway, where he remained for no more than a split second. Before too long, the police officers, who had come to arrest the troublemakers, finally appeared near the dining room. However, the Green Phantasm managed to teleport above them in the form of a long, narrow neon-green beam of radiation. Then, he appeared behind all the police officers for only about a split second. After that, he teleported his way out of the building.

When the Green Phantasm had teleported the first time and reappeared, one policeman had perceived something. He thought that he had heard some sort of whizzing sound behind him. The officer looked behind himself for a few seconds but was unable to find what had made that noise. At that, he had just shrugged his shoulders and returned his thoughts to arresting the ones causing trouble.

Meanwhile, in the dining room, Doctor XT had also heard the police approaching. He was getting ready to use one of his backup plans against them. He had now recovered from being knocked around by the Green Phantasm. He was motivating his men to pull themselves together and duck down behind some dining room tables. "Come on, everyone," he commanded, "down behind the tables!" They all obeyed.

On the way, H-1 noticed the X-Termination Ray that belonged to D.D.T., which the Green Phantasm had thrown aside. "Yo, D.D.T.!" he said.

D.D.T. stopped and asked, "What's up?"

"Your X-Termination Ray's over there," answered H-1.

"Thanks," replied D.D.T. and continued running toward whatever dining room table he could find.

Next, when all the X-Termination members were situated on the other side of a table, Doctor XT hollered out another command. "All right now, gas masks on!" he yelled. They all put on their special gas masks at XT's command.

Within seconds, all of the police officers who had hurried down to the dining room entered and bunched together. They positioned themselves in front of the dining room's entrance and drew and held out all of their handguns. The police could not clearly see X-Termination, for they were hidden. However, one of them yelled out, "All right now, we know you're in here! Come on out of hiding with your hands up! All of you come on now! Move it!"

Ignoring the officer's strong words, Doctor XT proceeded as planned. He got out four capsules that would emit X-Termination Gas. First, XT switched on two of them and tossed them both toward the cops. They landed on the floor behind the police officers, where they rolled into their upright positions and within two more seconds began releasing light-purple fumes.

None of the police officers were able to leave the dining room alive, because the X-Termination Gas spread so rapidly that within two seconds of emission, a huge light-purple cloud had formed between the cops and the dining room's entrance. Within a matter of seconds, nine out of fifteen officers were coughing, gagging, and even falling to the ground dead.

The six remaining police officers turned around to see what was going on. They were understandably shocked and surprised horribly at seeing their nine teammates lying dead, as well as the thinning vapor that had killed them.

"Oh my God!" one horrified officer said. "What happened?"

"I don't know," whimpered another in panic, "but we better step back before it gets us too." The six who were left over started walking backward slowly, winding up among the smashed tables.

However, before they could back up much farther, Doctor XT switched on two more X-Termination Gas bombs. He placed them both in front of the table behind which he was hiding. Both of them gave off X-Termination Gas, which caused the last six policemen to fall down and die. Finally, the X-Termination Gas fumes were progressively fading as all fifteen Philadelphia policemen were scattered near the room's entrance dead. At the same time, Doctor XT had taken out two more bombs just in case he would need them. He saw that all the police officers were dead, so he decided to move on. "All right, everybody," XT addressed his crew, "come on; let's go. Out the back, let's move it. Keep your masks on until we get outside." At that, everyone followed Doctor XT out of the dining room. On the way, each individual reclaimed his X-Termination Ray. Then, they all proceeded on through the kitchen and out the back door. Once outside, they all removed their gas masks.

Finally, all six of them ran back to the X-Terminator 4000 and got back into it. While Zinger was starting the X-Terminator and preparing to shove off, Doctor XT exclaimed, "Why, that cursed Green Phantasm! He made me waste time and money on his neon, radioactive no-good self! We're gonna get him and before tomorrow is over. But right now, it's back to headquarters. I'm gonna go over my plan with everybody." At last, Zinger flew off and headed back to X-Termination Headquarters with everyone.

Meanwhile, the Green Phantasm was slowly walking around in the front parking lot. While he was waiting to go back in and explain some things to the police, he could not help noticing something. Even while he was the Phantasm, he saw that the entire parking lot was practically empty, with only his Suburban and some patrol cars present. At that, he said, "Well, it looks like at least everyone got away safe; I'm just worried about Amanda. I sure hope she's okay. Even though I saved a lot of lives, I feel like I ran out on her. Well, as soon as I get home tonight, I'll call her at once. I wonder how she made it home anyway. Well, perhaps Eric and Scott brought her. I guess I can trust them."

The Phantasm turned toward the front door. He decided, "Well, maybe I should go inside and make sure everything's okay. The cops have been in there for over ten minutes. They should've been able to handle it. After all, I managed to get those jerks under control, but I just want to be sure they got it. Here I go." So then, he proceeded on to the front door to go in.

Then, when the Green Phantasm made it to the door, he stopped momentarily, for he noticed two little piles of ashes. He said, "Whoa, what happened here? I don't know where those ashes are from, but weren't there a couple of policemen at the door when I came up to get in?" He thought about it for a few seconds and then said in shock, "Oh no! This must be the work of X-Termination. They must've done this to force their way in. Those crazy fools! I better get to the dining room right now. They may be too high-tech for the police to handle."

The Green Phantasm immediately ran on toward the dining room. But, even before entering the big room, he once again stopped momentarily because he had stumbled upon several more heaps of ashes. "Oh no!" he exclaimed. "Several other people got killed too! Have they lost their freakin' minds? Those jerks just gotta be stopped! I'm going to see to that right now!" Right away, the Green Phantasm ran on into the dining room.

When the Phantasm made it into the big room, he could not believe his eyes. He was horrified like never before in his life. X-Termination was gone, and the fifteen police officers were all lying there dead. "Oh my

God!" the Green Phantasm yelled. "What have you done, Doctor XT? And as for me, how could I let this happen?"

The Green Phantasm had a guilty conscience. He went on to say, "Regardless of what they've done, what have I done? This is all my fault. If I hadn't become the Green Phantasm and tangled with his men in the subway and on the streets last night, they wouldn't have come here looking for me. And just now, I should've stuck around to make sure they got apprehended. This is all my doing. I let them get away. Oh no!" Upon saying all that, the Green Phantasm knelt down on his left knee. He used his right hand to take off his hat and hold it. Next, he made a fist with his left hand and sadly lowered his head forward, placing his left fist against it. The Green Phantasm remained in that position and wept for a few moments.

However, although he felt guilty about all that had happened, he was determined to put an end to X-Termination, for he knew that someone had to stop them. After a few minutes of weeping, the Phantasm stopped, wiped away the few remaining tears, and stood up again. Next, he put his hat back on, made a fist with his right hand, and placed it in his left palm. James Clifton had just gone from being sad to being angry. For the next minute, he continuously inhaled and exhaled with anger. Then, he muttered, "Man, those psychos! Just who in the world do they think they are? I know I can't bring back the ones they've already killed, but I've got to prevent further damage. Those stupid, foolish morons! They ruined my evening with Amanda and my two best friends! And then they massacred all those good people! Those perverted sons of the devil are gonna pay for that. I'm gonna find their place of business, shut it down, and put an end to their game! X-Termination will become 'X-Terminated.' Doctor XT, the so-called XTE, or X-Termination engineer, will become an 'X-terminated' engineer. Oh yeah, I'll make sure I see to that." Finally, he just slowly ran back out the front of the building.

It was about 8:45 p.m., and James Clifton figured that he might as well go home for the night. He said, "Oh well, I guess I've done all I can for tonight. Perhaps I'll just get on home, eat one more time, and get ready for work in the morning." So at that, he hovered into the air and zipped on toward home, where he changed out of his Green Phantasm suit and back into his dress clothes. Then, of course, he zoomed back over to his

Suburban. Once there, James hid in his vehicle's shadow and switched off his neon-green radiation. Of course, after that, James got into his truck and started for home.

At the same time, over at Amanda Taylor's place, Dr. Mark Thompson was in the process of dropping her off. Finally, Thompson had arrived in front of Amanda's apartment. He parked and turned off his truck. At that, she told him sweetly, "Oh, Mark, thank you so much for bringing me home."

"Oh, no trouble at all, Amanda," he replied. "Just hold on; I'll, uh, come over and let you out." He got out and walked around to the passenger side, where he opened the door for Amanda.

She climbed on out and shut the door. She gave him a big hug. At the same time, she said, "Thank you so much."

"Like I said," he told her, "it's no problem. Of course, I'm really sorry about everything that happened tonight."

"Listen, Mark," Amanda addressed him kindly. "You wanna walk with me to my door?"

"Sure," he answered agreeably. So then, Mark Thompson and Amanda Taylor walked together up to her front door.

Once they got there, Amanda said, "Look, Mark, I don't know if I can thank you enough for what you did tonight. I feel I owe you for this."

"It's okay," replied Mark. "Don't worry about it. I just did it because I care, that's all. You don't have to do anything. I know you appreciate it."

But then, Amanda said, "Well, yeah, but, I'd like to know something: are you busy this Saturday night?"

"Why, no," he answered.

"Well," she replied, "I don't mean to be too forward, but how would you feel about doing a little something?"

"You mean with you?" he asked.

"Mm-hmm," answered Amanda nodding.

"Well," answered Mark hesitantly, "I'd like to, but are you sure it's a good idea? I know you probably have a lot on your mind right now."

"Oh, it's okay," she told him. "Don't worry about it."

"All right then," he replied. "That sounds great. My only other concern is, if you don't mind me asking, what about James Clifton?"

"Listen, Mark," said Amanda, "I understand your concern. I know he seems great and wonderful to you. He did to me too. Just like you, he was nice to me for a while. He seemed to care about me the way you do. Tonight, he even brought me flowers when he picked me up. Perhaps the greatest thing about James Clifton, which I haven't told you, is that he happens to be close friends with the Green Phantasm."

"Oh, really!" responded Mark, amazed.

"Yes." Amanda sighed. "The Green Phantasm is the same one who saved my life in a subway station Sunday night, and he saved a lot of people's lives at the party this evening. On top of that, James had even talked about arranging for me to meet him."

"That sounds fantastic," Mark told Amanda. "So, maybe that's why he appeared to run out on you. Maybe he had to go tell the Green Phantasm."

"But that's impossible!" replied Amanda. "He wasn't gone long enough for that. The Phantasm was there not even five minutes after James disappeared on me. Someone else must've notified him. Other than that, I wonder how James got away while everyone was at gunpoint. Oh well, no use worrying about it now. Another thing too is, although he was going to introduce me to the Green Phantasm, I'll just have to meet him some other way. Well, I'm through with James Clifton. He doesn't care about me. Let's just forget about him."

"Now, Amanda," Mark said kindly, "are you sure about that?"

"Positive," answered Amanda. "Now let's just forget everything bad that's happened and have a good time Saturday night, okay?"

"You got it," he answered happily.

"I'll see you then," said Amanda. "Thanks again for bringing me home." At that, they hugged each other. "Good night, Mark," she said.

"Good night, Amanda," he replied. "Take care." They parted company. Amanda went inside, and Mark started on his way home.

A little after 9:00 p.m., James Clifton finally arrived home. He pulled into his garage, closed the door behind him, turned off his truck, and went inside. Once inside, he stopped for a second and said, "Oh man, what a night!" while shaking his head in disbelief.

He marched upstairs to his bedroom. Once there, he threw his keys onto his dresser, and then he sat down on his bed, exhaling in frustration. "Man, man, man," he muttered, "what an amazing evening this has turned out to be! It started out so lovely and wonderful, but then all of a sudden, everything went berserk, and that brought about such a horrible ending. I don't know whether to blame myself or Doctor XT of X-Termination. Of course, he was the one who crashed the party, but if I had not taken up being the Green Phantasm, maybe he wouldn't have come there looking for me. Other than that, I probably should've let Amanda know I had to retrieve the Green Phantasm, but I don't see how. When X-Termination came in and held everyone hostage, I didn't have time to do anything but hide. At least that's what I think… uh, I don't know. Then finally, it was that so-called doctor who killed all those cops. However, I could have possibly stayed to prevent it, but I let them die. I definitely feel somewhat responsible for all that's happened tonight." At last, James Clifton hung his head forward. For the next few minutes, he felt too guilty to say a single word.

But after those few minutes, James suddenly had a thought. "Well, anyway," he said, "I guess at least I oughtta call everyone to make sure they're okay and to let them know I am. I know what; I'll make a quick call to Eric and Scott, and then I'll call Amanda." James immediately dialed Eric Thomas's number on his cell phone.

After a couple of rings, Eric answered. "Hello?"

"Hi, Eric," said James. "It's me."

"James?" replied Eric. "Oh, thank God! I take it you're okay. Am I right?"

"Yes," James answered. "I am, and I'm at home right now. Do you know if Scott's all right?"

"Of course I do," Eric told James. "I got us both home."

"That's great; that's… wonderful," James replied, "but what about Amanda?"

"Well," Eric uttered rather reluctantly, "I hope so. I really don't know."

"You don't know!" said a somewhat surprised James. "So you mean that you and Scott didn't get her home?"

"We sure didn't," answered Eric.

"Oh, all right," James said. "Well, thanks, Eric. It's good to know you and Scott are okay, but right now, I need to try to get in touch with Amanda."

"Okay, no problem," said Eric.

"All right, well, take it easy," James told Eric. "I'll be in touch real soon, all right? All right, bye, Eric."

"Bye, James," replied Eric. At that, they both hung up.

Next, James dialed Amanda Taylor's cell phone number. After a few rings, she answered. "Hello?"

"Amanda," James said to her, "it's me. It's James, James Clifton."

Unfortunately, she was not happy to hear from him. She responded by saying, "What! Oh my God!" That very instant, she hung up.

"What! Ah, come on!" griped a shocked James Clifton. Then, he tried calling her again but only received the very same result. She hung up on him again.

At that, James just threw his cell phone onto his bed and shook his head in confusion and disbelief. "Oh man!" He sighed, shaking his head. "Well, at least she's alive, but apparently, she doesn't want to talk to me. Maybe she thinks I abandoned her. Of course, it's not like I really did that. Oh well, I'll just have to straighten this out somehow. But supposedly more than that, I need to stop X-Termination. But anyway, I guess I'll just eat and get ready for bed for now."

From that point, James just fixed himself one last meal, got himself ready for bed, and hit the sack for the night. That was the end of the night that X-Termination crashed the party.

CHAPTER EIGHT

X-Termination's Aerial Attack

It was after 11:00 p.m. on Wednesday night. Doctor XT was back at X-Termination Headquarters along with everyone else who had accompanied him to create a disturbance at the hotel. He was about to summon everyone in X-Termination to gather together in the manufacturing area for a meeting. The purpose of this meeting was to go over with everyone his newly constructed plan for the pursuit and destruction of the Green Phantasm.

In the meantime, all the various X-Termination members were in different locations throughout X-Termination Headquarters, engaged in different activities. For instance, F-2 and I-2 were on duty at the entrance. With nothing to do, I-3 was in the same room with I-2, playing cards. At the same time, Zapper, Zinger, and D.D.T. were all over in the weight room pumping iron. R-2, R-3, and H-2 were all in the big game room playing pool. All of the other members were in their bedrooms, either watching television or preparing to go to sleep.

Doctor XT was about to address the entire facility from his control room over his PA system, so that everyone in the headquarters would definitely hear. He said to himself, "All right, it's meeting time. I'm gonna call everybody right now." XT pressed the necessary button and spoke into his PA system, saying, "Attention! Attention, everybody! At this time, we are having a meeting in the manufacturing area. I need every last one of you here this minute. Now, come on! Move it! This is the doctor speaking. Let's go!"

Upon hearing the announcement, every single X-Termination member stopped what he was doing in order to proceed to the manufacturing area. D.D.T., Zapper, and Zinger put down their weights. I-2 and I-3 set down their cards. R-2, R-3, and H-2 put a stop to their pool game. Those watching television in their rooms turned off their sets. Everyone was now moving toward the manufacturing area.

Within the next few minutes, all of X-Termination was proceeding into the manufacturing area through the north and east sides. Doctor XT was standing twelve feet from the X-Termination Acid vat facing northeast. He said to everyone, "Come on, everybody; gather around. I need you all to listen up and pay attention." At that, all fifteen X-Termination workers grouped together facing Doctor XT. However, a few were still murmuring among themselves. Doctor XT clapped his hands twice saying, "All right, knock it off! Quiet down and listen up!" They all complied immediately. It was completely silent.

Doctor XT began his meeting. He said, "Okay, everybody, we shall start our meeting. I'm sure a few of us know what this is about, but this pertains to all of you. That's why I called you all here. Each and every one of you peons needs to make sure you fully understand exactly what your part is in this game plan. You know why? Well, hear this, and listen really, really good. If you fail me, you all get 'X-terminated.' So I suggest you all pay full attention and make doggone sure you know exactly, precisely what you are to do. You all follow me so far?" Everyone nodded and murmured affirmatively.

Before continuing, XT addressed his top official apart from himself, Axel Axtel, also known as Zapper. XT said to him, "Zapper!"

"Yes, Doctor?" replied Zapper.

"Come stand up here with me," commanded Doctor XT. "You and I will both be speaking at this meeting. Come on up."

"Yes, sir, boss," responded Zapper. At once, he went up and stationed himself left of Doctor XT. XT and Zapper were now facing the rest of X-Termination.

"Now, as I was saying," continued Doctor XT, "this concerns each and every one of you. So, before you resume whatever you were in the middle of doing, you'd best be absolutely, positively certain you fully understand everything about your part in this scheme. Your life depends on it. If the Phantasm doesn't kill you first, I will." Upon finishing that, Doctor XT assumed a serious expression on his face and looked around at each and every one of those who were in attendance. He was trying to show that he meant business. No one even dared to try any backtalk.

Doctor XT continued by saying, "Anyway, I'm sure by now, you've all heard of this new freak in town called the Green Phantasm, right?"

"Right," everyone in attendance answered.

"So," continued the doctor, "what I'm about to go over is my plan to bring him out and dispose of him. Every one of you will be needed for this. It will be tomorrow evening. You all know why?" They all did nothing more than look around at each other, shrugging their shoulders and murmuring in confusion. This was because none of them really knew the best possible answer.

Not having received a response, XT turned to Zapper, saying, "Zapper, tell 'em. Explain to them about why and what we've already been through."

"Heh, heh, heh, heh," chuckled Zapper, who was about to begin. He went on to say, "All right, you pathetic imbeciles, I'll explain it to you. Hear this, and hear it well. I'm sure a lot of you are aware of some of the trouble the Green Phantasm caused us. You know, by tampering with Ant Killer, Roach Killer, Wasp Killer, and Hornet Killer? That turned out to be wasted time and money for us, didn't it?"

"Yeah!" everyone answered, nodding in agreement.

"Besides," continued Zapper, "they all allowed for that neon freak to put his nose into our business. So for that, we 'X-terminated' them. That's because, you see, whether they meant anything to us or not, they allowed themselves to become a danger to this organization. We can't have any of that. So we 'X-terminated' them, along with those two outsiders, Clyde and Carl. That takes care of that. However, that so-called 'Green Phenon', or what-the-heck-ever, is just as accountable as they are. Because he has found out about X-Termination, he could put us out of business. That's not good, is it?"

"No," everyone answered in unison.

"Of course not," replied Zapper. "So, you all know what we must do?"

At that, all of the members who were attending the meeting looked around at each other grinning, chuckling, and nodding affirmatively. It was just as if they all knew the answer to the question. Some of them even made fists with their right hands and put them in the palms of their left hands.

"Well, well, well," said a pleased Axel Jerome Axtel, "it appears you all know what we must do. I mean, man, I like this kind of determination and enthusiasm. Although you all know and understand, I'll say it anyway. I say we eliminate, destroy, annihilate, and 'X-terminate' this no-good, disrespectful, foolish, radioactive, shining dumbbell! What do y'all say to that?"

"*Yeah*!" everyone shouted wildly and excitedly.

"Let's do it!" shouted Zinger.

"Let's get him!" exclaimed I-1.

"Yeah!" they all yelled one more time.

"All right, all right," Zapper said signaling everyone to quiet down. "Then that's exactly what we'll do. But, I just want to say one more thing before I turn this meeting back over to Doctor XT. A few of you probably already know about this, but I want to let all of you know. Now, of course, you all know how earlier this evening, Doctor XT, myself, as well as four others invaded that hotel trying to seek out the Green Phantasm. But you see, before then, we did not know everything he was capable of. So we just happened to underestimate him a little bit. Before we even had a shot at him, he already knew we were there. Well, that's the wrong way to go with the one we're dealing with. With someone as clever and quick as him, we need to catch him off guard, by surprise. We cannot allow him a single chance to plan anything out. Otherwise, we'll be humiliated and defeated. So, I'm pretty certain that Doctor XT himself has a plan to do just that. So at this time, let's give him our full, undivided attention as he goes over it with us. Doctor XT, please."

"Thank you very much, Zapper," XT said to him. "So, you all understand now? Huh? You all see why you're all needed for this and why it's tomorrow night? Can one of you tell me?"

While raising his hand, Zinger hollered out, "Yes, Doctor, I think I know! I might be able to tell you!"

"All right, Zinger," Doctor XT said to him, "tell us about it. Explain."

"Very well," Zinger began. "You see, Doctor, and everyone else too, of course, here's why you need us all, okay? That's the first thing I'll tell all of y'all. Like Zapper just said, I think the reason we're all needed is to make absolute certain that this neon creep does not get a single opportunity to do anything to us. The more of us there are against him, the less chance he has to plot against us. Don't y'all get it? More of us can distract him more, so that way, he'll have less time to set up an attack. Furthermore, having every one of us involved is the best way to make sure of that." Upon hearing this, everyone surrounding Zinger looked around at each other, nodding in agreement.

Zinger continued, "I just wanna say one more thing. The reason it must be tomorrow night is that we must eliminate, eradicate, 'X-terminate' this freak as soon as possible. So now, back to you, Doctor XT."

"Thank you, Zinger," said XT. "That was very well put. It's obvious you were paying attention after all. Otherwise, I now presume that we've all come to an understanding. Therefore, I can go ahead and present my plan in full. However, if there's any questions before I start, ask now before I lay it on the line for you."

Doctor XT waited and looked around at everyone momentarily. But they all appeared confident and ready. So the doctor proceeded. He said, "All right now, at this time, I will tell you all what you are to do. First of all, Zapper, you're gonna supervise this whole thing. You wanna show you can take over when my time comes to an end? Well, this'll be a great chance to prove it. I'm trusting you, Zapper. I'm counting on you. You're my number-one guy, right?"

"Right!" Zapper answered with a snarl and a sneer.

"All right!" XT replied. "Zapper, among you three top lieutenants, two of you will hide and wait, and one of you will act as lookout. Other than that, there's not much more to worry about. The other twelve guys will bring him right to you."

"Yes, sir, boss," replied Zapper.

"All right," replied Doctor XT. "Now Zapper, among D.D.T., Zinger, and yourself, two of you will hide in the construction site on that new street that's east off Sixth Street, just south of the downtown area. One of you will station himself on a nearby building. From atop whatever building you select for a lookout, the one of you at that station will keep the other two informed, say when to fire, and so forth. But anyway, Zapper, I'll let you decide whose station is whose. After all, you will be handling this mission."

"Yes, Doctor," replied Zapper. "I'll take care of it all. Ah, ha, ha, ha, haaaa!"

"Excellent," XT said to Zapper. "And now, as for the rest of you, this is your part of this game plan. Listen up, R-1, F-1, H-1, and all the rest of you. Now, didn't you all hear me tell Zapper that you twelve would bring the Phantasm to them?"

"Yeah, yeah, we heard you," some of them said. They were all nodding.

"Good," said Doctor XT. "Here's what you twelve will do. Each and every one of you will be flying one of my XTV500 ships, my latest creation. Of course, the main purpose, as you all know, is to 'X-terminate' the Green Phantasm. Destroy him in the air if you can. I say it that way because I have not overlooked one other possibility. This guy can perform and create some things in the form of radiation. So perhaps he can possibly put on a force field to protect himself. Therefore, if he encloses himself inside a force field, you will keep firing at him, progressively moving him toward the spot where two of my top officials will be waiting. Y'all with me?"

"Yeah!" all twelve said in unison.

"All right," said Doctor XT. "I got one more thing to explain to y'all. There is also the possibility that the Phantasm may not take down his force field until the twelve of you back off. That's why I arranged for two men to hide at the construction site. If the twelve of you have to stop shooting and fly off temporarily, those two men will dispose of him at once, when he takes off his force field. Of course, that's when the other guy watching everything tells them. But like I said, get him in the air if you can. But if you can't, he'll get 'X-terminated' one way or the other. Everybody follow?"

"Yes, sir," answered H-1. "We gotcha."

Doctor XT then said, "I have just one other thing to say before I close out this meeting. The time to head out is 7:00 p.m. I strongly suggest you all make sure your XTV is filled completely with fuel, acid, compressed air, and rocket bombs. Other than that, just group yourselves in whatever way Zapper tells you. If you have any questions or need to know more about what to do, get with Zapper. He's going to take it from here. That concludes this meeting. Everybody just go on about your business."

"Okay!" shouted D.D.T. excitedly.

"Yeah!" yelled F-2. "We're gonna blast that radiant freak."

"We gonna nuke him," said I-2.

"Y'all know what?" asked R-1. "Most of all, we will 'X-terminate' him."

"Yeah!" everyone excitedly yelled in unison.

"All right, that's enough," declared an irritated Doctor XT. "*Quiet!*" Consequently, all the commotion subsided. "That'll be all for now," XT told them. "I'm going to my office. All of you get back to your business. Anything else you need, get with Zapper. That's it, good night, everyone." At that, Doctor XT turned to his right and headed for his office. Everyone else turned and headed back to where they had been before the meeting.

Seconds later, Doctor XT addressed Zapper. He turned around and said, "Zapper!"

At once, Zapper stopped and turned around. He replied, "Yes, Doctor?"

"Come see," commanded XT. "I need one last word with you."

"I'm coming, boss," responded Zapper, who started walking toward Doctor XT. Then, he met up with XT and said, "Yes, Master, what's up?"

"Listen to me, Zapper," Doctor XT said seriously. "You do realize that I am depending on you, correct?"

"Absolutely correct," answered Zapper, nodding affirmatively.

"All right," replied XT. "So then you're absolutely positively sure that you can and you will handle and manage this game plan?"

"No problem whatsoever, boss," responded Zapper. "This plan is completely foolproof. I will see to it that the Green Phantasm is completely devastated, eliminated, and 'X-terminated.' It will be done. You have my word."

"Great!" Doctor XT said firmly. "But, I just want to make sure you understand one more thing. If by some chance anything goes wrong, I will hold you responsible along with everyone else. I will make sure you all go down together. Do you understand that? Huh? Are we on the same page?"

"Absolutely," Zapper responded affirmatively. "I fully understand and accept those terms."

"Very well then," said Doctor XT. "From this point forward, it's in your hands. I do not want to hear anymore until it's done. Right now, I have to go to my office to get some work done. Like I told you, you're in full charge of this, so destroy him! I'll talk to you tomorrow night. Now go! Get him!" At that, XT and Zapper parted company.

Once they had left each other, Zapper headed back to the weight room, where he had been training with Zinger and D.D.T. As he entered, Zinger and D.D.T. were just about to resume their training. However,

Zapper called out to them, "Zinger! D.D.T.!" They both turned and looked toward him.

Zapper went on to tell them, "Look, you guys, you know we're all shoving off at seven tomorrow evening, correct?"

"Yeah," answered D.D.T. and Zinger together.

"Okay," said Zapper. "But listen; I'll need everyone to meet me in the big vehicle area at six thirty, okay?"

"Okay," replied D.D.T. and Zinger.

"Now, look," continued Zapper. "I would like all three of us to go around and let everybody know, vehicles' area six thirty. Can y'all help me with that?"

"Yeah, no problem," D.D.T. answered.

"We sure can," said Zinger.

"And just one more thing," added Zapper. "Let's all make sure that all their XTV ships are filled up."

"You got it," replied Zinger. Both Zinger and D.D.T. were nodding affirmatively.

"All right then," said Zapper. "Let's get back to what we were doing." The three of them resumed their weight training, just as everyone else resumed their previous activities.

These XTV ships that both Doctor XT and Zapper had mentioned were a new kind of vehicle that Doctor XT had designed and had produced by his crew. The name and model was XTV500. XTV stood for X-Termination Velocity. He had just chosen 500 as the model number.

The XTV500 was, of course, a special, unique kind of aircraft that Doctor XT had designed himself. It was driven and kept afloat by XT's very own variety of rocket engines. Other than that, it was shaped similar to the orbiter of a space shuttle system but was much smaller and had delta wings. In addition, the XTV500 was made for one person and was equipped with two kinds of artillery. It could also reach speeds of over three thousand miles per hour.

The XTV500 was about twenty feet long and had a total wingspan of sixteen feet. The top of the roof came to be seven feet off the ground whenever the XTV500 was settled along the earth with its landing gear activated. However, the fin at the rear added another three feet to the total height.

The XTV500 had a fuselage with a tube shape that came to a rounded-off point at the nose. However, the top and bottom surfaces were flat, while the left and right sides were convex, from the cockpit all the way to the tail end. The total width of the fuselage was six feet. But the top and bottom surfaces were each four feet wide. The total height of the fuselage was five feet from its bottom surface to its top. The rear fin was shaped like a right triangle. It was five feet in length with the highest point at the rear.

The delta wings of the XTV500 started about eight feet back from the plane's very nose. They went practically all the way to the tail end of the fuselage. Just like on the wings of other airplanes, these wings had ailerons to make the XTV500 bank while turning.

The outermost exterior of the XTV500 was made from the same materials as the X-Terminator 4000. The bottom half of both the fuselage and the wings consisted of the same hardened steel. The exterior above was made from light aluminum that had been painted white. Printed above each wing on each side of the fuselage was the logotype for the XTV500. It had the same purple-and-blue color design as that of the X-Terminator's. However, the six figures were all in row that was completely upright and slanted. They were slanted to the right on the left side of the plane and to the left on the other side. These logos were actually made to light up whenever all other lights were turned on as well.

The XTV500 also had other brightly colored lights on the exterior, which of course, were lit at night. They were patterned and colored just like the ones on the outside of the X-Terminator 4000. Like the X-Terminator, the XTV500 had four strips of royal-blue light that encircled it horizontally. The lowest one was along the entire boundary between the steel bottom and the white aluminum top. The next two strips up were lined up with the top and bottom of the front windshield, as were the ones on the X-Terminator. Finally, of course, the fourth strip of blue light was a dashed line just inches above the windshield, much like the one on the X-Terminator 4000. The XTV500 also had two other kinds of lights that many other airplanes had. The outer tip of each wing had a red navigation light. The very top of the rear fin had a red rotating beacon light. In addition, the entire rear of the fuselage was surrounded by three colored strips of light, like the rear of the X-Terminator. Each of these strips, however, was only eight inches wide, but they were blue, purple, and red, from foremost to rearmost, just like the X-Terminator's.

At the rear of the XTV500 was a big rocket engine that provided thrust to propel the plane forward. This rocket engine was exactly like the main one at the X-Terminator's rear but was much smaller in order to fit into the rear of the plane. Another difference from the X-Terminator was that the XTV only had one large rear engine instead of three. But that one rocket engine did have a circular steel barrier surrounding it that extended inches from the plane's rear.

To help steer the XTV500, two other parts were located at the plane's rear. One was a movable rudder that was attached to the rear fin. The other was a pair of movable attachments that was similar to the pair at the rear of the X-Terminator 4000. However, these steel holders were only three-fourths of the height of the ones of the X-Terminator, and they each only held six engines instead of eight. But they were connected by vertical hinges on the outsides of the fuselage's big rocket engine; they could be turned left or right to help steer the plane.

The XTV500 had yet another feature that was similar to that of the X-Terminator 4000. That was a multitude of small rocket engines that were built into the base of the fuselage to provide lift. They were used for most of the same purposes as the ones on the X-Terminator. This also implied that no long runway was needed since vertical takeoff and landing was possible. However, the XTV500 only had ten instead of eighteen. The ten engines and the ten round openings ran in two front-to-back rows of five along the XTV's bottom. Each opening was trimmed by a light-purple ring of light.

The XTV500 also had landing gear that enabled it to rest or move along the ground. But it was not much like the X-Terminator's landing gear. Instead, it was merely an arrangement of tricycle landing gear that a lot of other planes had. For each of the three pairs of wheels, a pair of steel double doors had to be opened and retracted inside in order for the respective pair of wheels to extend outward and lock into place. One of those pairs of steel doors was centered under the very nose of the plane. The other two were each off to the fuselage's left or right side underneath one of the two wings.

In order for the pilot to get inside of an XTV500, one of two sliding doors had to be opened. The pilot had to punch in a code on an electronic keypad to gain access. That in turn caused the sliding door to retract inward and slide toward the plane's rear. Then, of course, the pilot had to climb into the cockpit and seat himself.

In front of the pilot's seat inside the cockpit were all the controls and instruments that were used for flying. Most of them were just like those found in other types of airplanes: a control wheel, a pair of floor pedals, and a throttle lever. Of course, other devices included, but were not limited to, an altimeter, a tachometer, a gyrocompass, and two kinds of speed indicators. Doctor XT had also installed some additional equipment, as he had with the X-Terminator 4000. He had two kinds of overhead video display monitors installed. One was an alternative to looking through an unclear windshield or to using navigational equipment. The other served the same purpose as a rearview mirror.

The XTV500 also had two other features in common with the X-Terminator 4000. They were two tanks that were located beneath the plane's exterior behind the cockpit. Just like with the X-Terminator, one contained kerosene fuel and the other, X-Termination Acid. But they had to be smaller than those of the X-Terminator 4000, since the XTV500 was a smaller vehicle.

The XTV500 rocket plane also had the two kinds of artillery that the X-Terminator 4000 had. Of course, this included the pair of ray guns that fired burning acid, as well as the pair of rocket bomb launchers. One of the two ray guns was located above each wing along the fuselage. The ray guns were exactly identical to the ones of the X-Terminator. Below each wing along the fuselage was a steel tube that was a little over a foot in diameter. Each tube was practically as long as each wing and housed eight rocket bombs. Whenever the front of a tube was opened, a radio-controlled rocket bomb shot forth and continued soaring until it exploded upon impact. These two kinds of artillery were operated by two pistol-grip levers inside the cockpit.

Finally, another feature of the XTV500 rocket plane was perhaps unnecessary. At the middle bottom rear of the fuselage was a Pennsylvania license plate. The figures read, "XTV500." Each XTV had one.

6:30 on Thursday night. James Clifton had made it home after another day of work at Ace Nuclear Supply. After work, he had spent a little time at a bar with his two best pals, Eric and Scott. But now, he was upstairs in his bedroom.

"What do you know?" James said to himself. "It's the end of another day. Of course, there's still Friday left and at last the weekend." But then, he had a second thought and said, "Well, I don't know; I mean, it just doesn't seem the same after last night. I mean it's like, X-Termination just decides to show up and ruin everything. Everything was going great for me at first. We were all having a wonderful time. Best of all, I even had Amanda there with me. But then, I had to leave her in order to—"

Suddenly, he remembered something that made him stop and think for a moment. "Wait a minute," he told himself. "You know, that reminds me, I haven't seen Amanda since I disappeared on her last night. I know I had to do what I had to do, but I still feel guilty about leaving her and abandoning her. I'd better get in touch with her."

At that, James took out his cell phone to give her a call. He dialed her number and waited for her to answer. Shortly, she answered her phone and said, "Hello?"

"Hey, Amanda, it's me," James eagerly replied.

"Who is this?" Amanda asked skeptically.

"Amanda, it's James, James Clifton," he told her.

"*What?*" Amanda exclaimed unhappily.

"Amanda, please," James said kindly to try to calm her. "Just let me—" However, Amanda had hung up. "Oh my God," said a frustrated James. "Doggone it, Amanda. Why'd you have to cut me off like that?" At that, he looked down and shook his head in disbelief. He said, "Somehow, I'm gonna have to find her and straighten everything out, because obviously, she's too upset with me."

James had another thought. "And another thing," said James. "I also can't believe that I let X-Termination, or whatever those lunatics are called, get away last night. I had them right where I needed them. I never should've left the scene; I should've realized how tough and how cunning those guys were. I haven't felt that stupid in a long time. I could've put a stop to them right then and there probably. But they're still at large, and it's all my stupid fault. They already raided that banquet looking for me. I wonder what those nutcases are gonna try to do now."

Shortly, he was going to find that out. Back at X-Termination Headquarters, all individuals who were employed by Doctor XT were in their final stage of preparing to shove off on the very important assignment given them—the major task of taking down and destroying the Green Phantasm.

Zapper was standing in the southeast corner of the open area at X-Termination Headquarters, which was for vehicles. He was waiting for every last X-Termination member to gather before him. At the same time, Zapper had Zinger standing to his right-hand side and big D.D.T. to his left. Then very shortly, Zapper, Zinger, and D.D.T. were finally face-to-face with the assembly of all twelve X-Termination workers ranked below them.

First, Zapper softly mumbled to Zinger and D.D.T., "All right, you two, did y'all do as I asked? Did y'all help see to it that everyone prepared for this mission?"

"Yes, sir," Zinger whispered affirmatively in reply.

"We sure enough did," answered D.D.T.

"Good," said Zapper. "I'm about to go over the strategy with them now. I suggest you two pay attention." Both Zinger and D.D.T. nodded in agreement.

"Listen up, everybody," Zapper said to the other twelve. "I'm gonna explain to y'all how to go about this chore of bringing down the Green Phantasm. But first, have you all prepared your XTV500 planes like Zinger and D.D.T. told you?"

"Yeah," many of them murmured, nodding.

"Oh, you have?" asked Zapper. "Are you saying that you're all fully stocked on fuel and ammo—acid and rocket bombs?"

"Yeah!" everyone yelled enthusiastically.

"Great!" Zapper exclaimed back at them. "So, I presume you'll have no problem handling your part of this arrangement."

"None whatsoever," replied R-1.

"Of course not," said H-1.

"Why should we?" questioned I-1. Behind them, R-2 and I-2 looked at each other and nodded in agreement.

"All right, that's enough," Zapper told them. "Just listen to me, and listen good. Each and every one of you lunkheads needs to know your part in this task, all right?"

After pausing for a few seconds, Zapper continued, "The twelve of you are gonna group yourselves the way I tell you and stay that way so you don't get all out of whack, you know what I'm sayin'?"

"Yeah," they all murmured and nodded.

Resuming his instructions, Zapper went on to say, "This is what you're gonna do: You're gonna form three rows that each go four across. I'm gonna tell each one of you your positioning. Now listen carefully."

First, Zapper pointed to H-1, saying, "H-1, you will be the farthest left on the front row. That's your spot. That'll put you on the very front left corner. Just make sure you maintain that position whenever y'all stick together. You got that, H-1?"

"Yes, sir," H-1 answered him affirmatively.

Secondly, Zapper used both hands to point to both H-2 and H-3. He told them, "Now, H-2, you will position yourself behind H-1. That'll put you at the far left of the second row. And, H-3, you will station yourself behind H-2. That's gonna place you all the way to the left of the third and last row. So both of you keep yourselves in line behind H-1 and stay in order. Is all of that fully understood?"

"Yes, sir, boss," H-2 responded.

"No problem," said H-3.

Zapper directed his attention to I-1, saying to him, "As for you, I-1, you will be on the front row to H-1's right. Make sure you stay that way so that you can all cooperate."

"Yes, sir; you got it," replied I-1.

"Very good," said Zapper, who then addressed I-2 and I-3, telling them, "All right, I-2 and I-3, listen up, you two blockheads. First of all, I-2, you will be in the middle row behind I-1 and to the right of H-2. Make sure you don't forget and that you hold on to that spot. Is that clear?"

"Yes, sir, Zapper," answered I-2. "I will make sure to do just that."

"Excellent," said Zapper. At that, he turned to I-3 and said to him, "And, I-3, you, of course, will set yourself up behind I-2 and to the right of H-3 on the back row. Can you handle that?"

"Yes, Zapper," I-3 responded. "I will stay in that very spot."

"Great," said Zapper. Next, Zapper turned to R-1. "R-1, you will be in the third plane on the very front row. You'll be on the right-hand side of I-1. Can you handle that?"

"I most certainly can," answered R-1.

"Very good, R-1," Zapper said in reply. Zapper spoke to R-2 and R-3. "All right now, R-2 and R-3," he addressed them, "from what you've already heard me tell the others, you probably have a good idea where you'll be flying along with everyone else."

"I'm sure we do," said R-2.

"Yeah, I think we do," said R-3, nodding in agreement.

"Well, it sounds like you do," Zapper said to them. "But I'll tell you for sure anyway. R-2, you will get behind R-1 and to the right of I-2."

"Roger," R-2 replied.

"And, R-3," continued Zapper. "You will fly behind R-2 in the back row, right of I-3."

"Gotcha," R-3 responded.

Continuing his instructions, Zapper focused on the remaining three X-Termination employees. "And now, F-1, F-2, and F-3," Zapper said to them. "You all probably know where you'll be in the grouping, I presume."

"That I do," F-1 responded most anxiously and positively. "I'm gonna be at the far right of the front row, with R-1 at my left."

"Not bad, F-1," said Zapper. "Just maintain that spot, you knucklehead."

"Yes, sir," replied F-1, refusing to talk back.

Zapper continued, "Last of all, F-2 and F-3, that's fool number two, and fool number three."

"Yes, Zapper?" they said in succession.

Still having fun insulting them, Zapper asked them disparagingly, "Do you fools even have the slightest idea as far as your part in all this?"

"Well, sure," F-2 answered hesitantly. "I'm gonna be behind F-1, right?"

"Enough!" snarled Zapper. "What about you, F-3?"

"Yes, Zapper," F-3 responded calmly. "I think I'm gonna be all the way to the right of the last row, behind F-2, and right of, uh, R-3. Is that correct?"

"All right, all right, all right," Zapper said to all twelve in attendance. "So you all know your placement. But now, each and every one of you derelict dorks better shut up and listen. The three of us are going to lead you to Philadelphia by means of an X-Terminator 4000 that you are to follow. Whenever we get there and pull away from all of you, you are to search and tear apart the city to bring out the Green Phantasm. Is that understood?"

The twelve all answered in unison, "Yeah!"

Zapper resumed his instructions to them, saying, "And one other thing, if y'all have to expand in any direction, that's fine as long as y'all get the job done in an orderly, timely manner. But when you're all bunched together, make doggone sure you're in the order I gave you and assigned you."

"Okay," some of them replied, nodding.

Finally, Zapper delivered the last part of his instructions as to what the twelve in the XTV500's were to do. "Last of all," he commanded them, "you are to destroy him in the air if you can. However, if he does put on one of his force fields, you will use the ray guns on your planes to maneuver him over to a hiding place where Zinger and I will be waiting. I will direct you to it over the two-way radio."

"Hey, no problem, Zapper," said H-1.

"Yeah, no sweat," said I-2.

"I'm sure we're all gonna work together on this," declared R-2.

"That we will," R-1 said in agreement. "And, Zapper, we'll let you know what happens. That's whether we 'X-terminate' him ourselves, or he puts on the force field."

"Excellent," said Zapper. "And now, everybody, get into your XTV500's and start up your engines. Let's go and 'X-terminate' the Green Phantasm!"

"Yeah!" everyone yelled simultaneously as they all began heading to their XTV500 rocket planes.

Next, Zapper said to Zinger, "Zinger, go fire up the X-Terminator 4000."

"Yes, sir! You got it, Zapper," Zinger happily replied to Zapper's command. "Let's get going, man. Let's do it!" Zinger then headed toward the X-Terminator.

Zapper turned to D.D.T. and told him, "And as for you, D.D.T., go get into the ship with Zinger, all right? I'll be right there."

"You got it, boss," replied D.D.T., who at once obeyed and followed Zinger.

Zapper did one last thing. He briefly walked among all of the XTV500 rocket planes in order to make sure they were all running. Finally, he entered the X-Terminator 4000 and sat down to the right of his junior partner, Zinger, who usually flew an X-Terminator 4000. "You ready to take flight, Zinger?" questioned the masked senior lieutenant.

"You bet," Zinger answered positively. "I'm ready when you are."

"Well, get going," Zapper commanded him, "and make sure everybody else is following behind, all twelve of them."

"No problem," Zinger said in reply. At that, Zapper closed the door to his right and locked the vehicle. He utilized the engines on the bottom of the X-Terminator to make it ascend vertically. Shortly, the other twelve X-Termination members began doing the same thing with their XTV500's. Within a couple of moments, Zinger was well above the big steel barrier that surrounded headquarters, with the X-Terminator 4000 and of course Zapper and D.D.T.

Zinger began flying forward slowly. While doing so, he checked to make sure that everyone else was following behind. He did so by looking at a display monitor that was mounted overhead between Zapper and himself and served the purpose of a rearview mirror.

Shortly, all of the XTV500 planes appeared above the steel barrier. At that, all twelve of them went on to follow behind their three leaders. "Okay, Zapper," said Zinger, "everything's looking good so far. They're all behind us, every one of them." Each and every pilot made certain he was in his designated position among the pack. Fortunately for X-Termination, the twelve were grouped exactly as they had been instructed. For instance, H-1 was at the very left front, with I-1 to his right. F-1 was at the right front of the entire dozen. The rearmost row of four had H-3 on the far left, and F-3 on the far right.

The entire crew continued following the head threesome of Zapper, Zinger, and D.D.T. In response to what Zinger had assured him, Zapper asked, "So, they're behind us, aren't they?" He glanced at the monitor himself and then went on to say, "Well, not bad, not bad. Good observation, Zinger."

After that, Zapper picked up the receiver of a two-way radio on which all those in the vehicles could talk to and hear everyone else. He then addressed the twelve men who were flying the XTV500 rocket planes, saying, "All right, everyone, not bad so far. I just wanna know this: Are y'all with us? Are you all ready to head for Philadelphia?"

"Yes, sir, you know we are," answered R-1 over the radio.

"Roger," said I-1 in agreement.

"Yeah, man, that's a ten-four," assured H-1. After that, a few others gave positive responses to Zapper's questions.

Finally, Zapper told everyone over the radio, "Very well then, let's all shoot off toward Philadelphia!"

Each masked follower happily and excitedly yelled to himself, "Yeah!"

At the same time, Zapper said to Zinger, "All right, Zinger, start soaring toward Philadelphia, on the double!"

Then, as Zinger began to accelerate rapidly, he said to Zapper in reply, "Right, Zapper, you know I will, man. Here we go!" With that, he continued on zooming east toward Philadelphia with the other twelve following behind. The X-Terminator 4000, with the three masked officials, as well as the pack that was being led, came to be over two hundred feet above the earth, flying at over three hundred miles per hour.

It was 6:55 p.m. James Clifton still had the same two things on his mind that he had griped about a little earlier: X-Termination and Amanda Taylor. But at the moment, he was thinking and wondering primarily about X-Termination. He was pacing back and forth from one end of his room to the other.

James was saying to himself, "You know, I wonder what I ought to do now. I know I let them get away last night. Maybe I should be out looking for them. However, I don't know where their hideout is, where they come from, or none of that. On top of that, they could be anywhere right now for all I know. I may not be the best to be able to spot them, but I guess I got to try to do something rather than stay here and do nothing." At that, James stopped pacing and stood centered with his bed, both hands on the footboard. He tried to think about how he might perform differently this time as the Green Phantasm.

While James was standing there thinking, all thirteen X-Termination vehicles were approaching Philadelphia from the west. From the X-Terminator 4000, Zapper addressed the twelve who were in the rocket planes over the two-way radio to deliver his final instructions before releasing them. "All right, everyone, listen up. Do y'all read me?" Zapper said to them.

"I read you loud and clear," responded R-1.

"Yes, sir," answered I-1. "Go ahead, Zapper."

"All right," Zapper told them. "First of all, everybody slow up for a moment. I'm gonna go over something before I release you into the city." Every X-Termination pilot slowed down his XTV500 by reducing the thrust of the rear engines. Likewise, Zinger slowed the X-Terminator.

Zapper continued, "And now, hear this, you fools, and hear it pretty damn good! Zinger, D.D.T., and I are about to pull away and find a spot to wait at. As soon as we fly away from you, you are to storm in and raid all of Philadelphia. The object is to drive out the Green Phantasm from his secluded spot, wherever it is. You may use your artillery to destroy what you have to, but just find him. Have y'all got that so far?"

Many of them answered over the radio with different responses, such as "Yes, sir," "Roger," "Ten-four," and so forth.

"Great," Zapper said in return. "And once you bring him out of hiding or whatever, destroy him with your artillery if you can. Otherwise, just bring him over to Zinger and myself. I will tell you all over the radio where we will be hiding and waiting. But for now, go seek out that freak and destroy him. We're pulling away, so go, now!" At that, Zapper told Zinger, "To the lower right, Zinger." Zinger obeyed and pulled the X-Terminator to their right and downward so that they were out from in front of the whole pack of rocket planes.

Then, all at once, the entire dozen began to zip in an east-northeast direction across Philadelphia. Momentarily, they came to be very close to the Delaware River. They were passing above James Clifton's house.

Clifton heard the rising sound of the soaring craft. He stopped concentrating for a moment to go and find out what was making the sound. Then, sure enough, he saw something like he had never ever seen before in his life. It was the entire swarm of XTV500's. James definitely could not remember when he had ever seen such a thing; it was a pack of twelve rocket planes with blue and purple neon lighting. James was temporarily amazed by what he was seeing, and he no doubt found it all difficult to believe. "Whoa, man," he said to himself, "I wonder what's going on with that."

Besides James, a lot of other Philadelphians also stopped to look at the brightly lit rocket planes. However, James Clifton was preoccupied by what he felt was more important. He finally decided, "Oh well, I don't have time for that now. I gotta worry about how I'm gonna stop X-Termination. I'll just have to catch my break another day." At that, he turned away from the window and walked away.

Meanwhile, in his XTV500, R-1 went on to say to all of his teammates, "All right, everybody, has anyone seen any sign of the Green Phantasm by any chance?"

"Not I," answered I-1.

"Certainly not me," said H-1.

"Nor I," H-2 said.

"Me neither," F-1 replied along with them.

"All right, never mind," R-1 told them. "Just slow it up for a minute."

"Come on now; what are you trying to do?" asked R-2.

"Just slow it down, all right?" R-1 replied sharply. "We're gonna do something to try to bring him out." Everyone else just nodded in agreement and slowed down.

R-1 got back onto his radio and said to one of his teammates, "Hey, R-3, you copy?"

"Yes," R-3 answered, "I read you loud and clear, R-1. Whatcha got?"

"Look, R-3," R-1 went on to say. "This is what I need you to do, all right? I need you to lower your plane slightly below the rest of us and unleash a rocket bomb. Just shoot it at anything you want; it doesn't matter."

"All right, R-1, you got it, man," R-3 replied. "It's a roger." Upon saying that, R-3 slightly decreased the lift to his XTV500 until he was clearly below his eleven accomplices. He selected the first building he saw on his targeting screen. Then, he unleashed a rocket bomb from the plane's right wing. This bomb landed about one fifth of a mile east of the Northeast Philadelphia Airport, causing a major explosion that turned the heads of everyone nearby.

Back at James Clifton's home, he too heard the faint sound of an explosion in the distance. "What was that?" he asked himself. He ran up to the window and then looked all around to try to find the source of it all.

Meanwhile, in the XTV500 rocket planes cruising along up above, R-1 addressed all of his coworkers over their radio, saying, "Okay, everybody, I don't see any sign of the Green Phantasm. Does anyone else by any chance?"

All the other pilots answered with different responses, such as "No," "Not me," and "I didn't see anything."

In conclusion, R-1 said to them, "Well, well, apparently, that didn't bring him out. Here's what we'll do. Let's everybody turn around and shoot back across Philadelphia for another attempt." So the entire dozen turned around and started soaring back toward the west end of Philadelphia.

Unable to find a clue immediately, James began turning away from his window. However, as soon as he had turned around, he began to once again hear the rising sound of soaring rocket planes. "More planes?" he stopped and asked himself. "I wonder why there's so many out tonight."

Out of curiosity, he looked back momentarily just for a quick glance out the window. As he was turning his head forward again, he exclaimed, "What? No way!" He had perceived something with neon lights headed toward him. James ran back over to his window for another look. Of course, he once again saw the twelve XTV500 rocket planes flying overhead. But this time, they were headed in the opposite direction. "That's really weird," said James. "It was strange enough to see them the first time, but why are they headed back the other way? They didn't cause that explosion, did they?"

From his rocket plane, R-1 commanded the two men to his left and right, telling them, "All right now, I-1 and F-1, each one of you fire a rocket bomb and aim it anywhere. Just fire one."

Within seconds after leaving James Clifton's field of vision, I-1 and F-1 obeyed, and each of them unleashed a rocket bomb. Consequently, the two bombs landed and exploded in Fairmount Park.

In turn, the sounds reached James, who then became even more afraid and began to panic. "Oh no!" he cried. "I bet they did make that explosion, plus the two that just took place! Oh God, please tell me this ain't happening!"

Next, James noticed the swarm of planes whizzing past him again; this time, they were headed east, much as when he had seen them the first time. Within seconds, at the command of the one called R-1, all of the XTV500's spread out sideways so that I-2 and R-2 could open fire. Finally, I-2 and R-2 each fired streams of burning X-Termination Acid from both ray guns mounted on their planes. Each shot hit a house that was in the nearest subdivision east of James Clifton's. Both houses became reduced to very little besides two big heaps of ashes and splinters. Everyone who had been in the houses was now dead.

Whenever Clifton saw them fire the shots, he made a quick decision. "You know what?" Clifton said. "I'm gonna have to hold off on X-Termination for now and stop those planes. I don't know exactly how, but I'll only be able to take them as the Green Phantasm. Well, anyway, no time to lose; somebody's gotta hurry up and stop them." At that, James ran and took out his Green Phantasm suit. Immediately, he switched on the supernatural source within himself and teleported from his work clothes into the Phantasm's outfit.

Then, as the Green Phantasm, James teleported outside his bedroom window and reappeared hovering above his neighborhood. At the same time, the X-Termination rocket planes were bunched together again; they slowed down, as the pilots planned their next maneuver. The Green Phantasm teleported until he was hovering in midair about a tenth of a mile behind them. They were all located up above the Delaware River, southwest of Holy Family University.

The Green Phantasm had only one idea. It was something that he hoped would at least distract the bad guys from further destruction to the city. He began preparing all ten fingers to combine their powers to produce one colossal laser beam. Finally, the Green Phantasm finished charging both hands and unleashed one giant-sized neon-green beam, which finally hit the rear of I-3's plane, pushing his plane forward into the rear of I-2's XTV500. Immediately afterward, the Green Phantasm slightly reduced his hovering power to descend slowly below the planes, so he could see what they might do.

Whenever I-2 felt the bump from behind, he said in shock, "What was that?" He looked into his rearview display monitor and saw what had hit him. At that, he picked up his radio receiver and yelled at his teammate behind him, "Hey, watch where the hell you're going, I-3! What's the matter with you, butthead?"

I-3 responded by telling I-2, "Lighten up, jerk! I didn't do nothing, all right? Something pushed me from behind. Now shut your face!"

Of course, R-1 heard them arguing. He signed on to the two-way radio and said to I-2 and I-3, "Hey, guys, guys, guys! What's going on back there, huh? What's the problem?"

"That numbskull behind me just hit me," answered I-2.

"Don't listen to that lying prick," said I-3. "Something hit me from behind and pushed me into him! I just couldn't see what it was."

"Listen up, you two," R-1 told them. "Why don't y'all just pay attention and stay focused, all right? That way, y'all won't keep having that problem, and we can all work as a team on our next movement. Y'all okay with that, huh?"

"Yeah, I am," answered I-2.

"Me too," responded I-3.

"Good," said R-1. "Now let's continue preparing for our next maneuver."

Soon enough, the Green Phantasm could see that he had not provided too much of a distraction. So he decided to try something else. He ascended back up to the height of the rocket planes. But this time, he teleported to reappear several feet to the right of the pack, staying the same distance behind them. Once again, the Phantasm began charging his hands. This time around, he would fire a bunch of smaller laser beams, instead, from all of his fingers. The Green Phantasm released five green laser beams from his right hand. He fired them at a slight angle toward his left so that they would pass in front of F-1.

As a result, F-1 noticed the neon laser beams coming from behind on his right and reacted by swerving to his left. "Yikes!" he yelled to himself. "What was that?" While maneuvering to his left, F-1 nearly collided with R-1.

R-1 noticed in the nick of time and slightly swerved left himself to avoid a collision. "Oh my God!" R-1 exclaimed. "What is everybody's problem tonight? First, it's I-2 and I-3, and now F-1." He picked up his radio receiver and addressed his coworker to his right, saying, "This is R-1 to F-1, do you read me?"

"I read you loud and clear, R-1," answered F-1. "And I'm glad you called me too."

"Well, that's good," said R-1. "And now I want you to tell me something, F-1. What in the devil is your problem? You almost hit me on the right, freak one."

"Let me tell you something, R-1," began F-1. "I don't have a problem, and besides, I wasn't trying to hit you. I was dodging some shots that were being fired at me. It was lasers, bullets, or something. I mean, someone or something must've been shooting at us from behind."

"Wait a minute," interrupted I-3. "That's not the same thing that pushed me from behind, is it?"

R-1 told everyone over the radio, "All right, just calm down, everybody. We're getting ready to turn around again. Then, we'll try to see what's going on, all right?"

In the meantime, the Green Phantasm was preparing his next tactic. He went on to teleport to his left so that he wound up centered behind the pack of planes. The Phantasm dropped slightly below them. He was planning to fire laser beams from all ten fingers again. But this time, the beams would slant upward at about a thirty-degree angle. The pilots out front would then see green laser beams coming up and out from below them.

Very shortly, the Green Phantasm opened fire and repeatedly discharged laser beams from all of his fingers. As he was constantly shooting from behind, some of the X-Termination members began to take notice. First of all, H-1 became startled and exclaimed over the radio, "Hey, what the hell! Someone's shooting from underneath us!"

Secondly, I-1 said over the two-way radio, "You're right, H-1. Somebody or something sure as heck is."

Then, R-1 addressed H-1 and I-1, saying, "What are you talking about, guys? I mean, exactly—well, what do you know? Someone is firing green laser beams our way, aren't they?" Of course, R-1 had now noticed as well.

In reply, H-2 said, "Hey, excuse me, R-1, you don't suppose it's, um… um…" But H-2 could not remember the name "Green Phantasm."

H-1 signed on and said in agreement, "Yeah, I was wondering the same thing too, R-1. You think maybe, uh oh geez." H-1 could not think of the hero's name either.

I-1 got onto the radio next and said to R-1, "You know, R-1, they're probably thinking the same thing I am, aren't they?"

In response, R-1 told them firmly, "All right, guys, just can it, you lunkheads! Of course it's him! Of course it's the Green Phantasm! Who else would dare to tangle with the likes of us and has green lasers? Tell me that, you knuckleheads!"

But then, R-3 interrupted and said over the radio, "Hey, excuse me, R-1, I just thought I'd let you know that it's him all right. I see him in my rearview monitor."

"Oh, you do?" replied R-1.

"Yeah, me too," said I-3.

"So do I," F-3 told them.

This was because the Green Phantasm was now hovering centered directly behind them. R-1 finally told everyone else in the planes, "Well then, what are we waiting for? Let's all turn around and take this neon freak out." At that, the pilots in the XTV500's pulled forward a little farther and turned their planes around, after which they all bunched together once again in their assigned order.

Whenever the Green Phantasm saw that they were turning around, he utilized his teleportation ability to relocate himself west by about three-fourths of a mile. That put him afloat above the part of town called Torresdale. The Phantasm then made certain that his hands were charged and ready for discharging neon-green laser beams.

The XTV500 planes were now reorganized, and the pilots were looking anxiously for their victim. Of course, they were now heading west. They shortly began accelerating gradually. While accelerating west, I-1 signed onto the two-way radio and said to everyone else in the other planes, "All right, I know he's gotta be around here somewhere. Where'd he go, huh?"

"Yeah," said F-1. "Where's he at?"

But then, within a few seconds, I-1 began to see an increasingly obvious trace of neon-green light. He signed on once again and asked all of his X-Termination coworkers, "Hey, do y'all see what I see?"

"What do you see, I-1?" asked H-1.

"Yeah, what is it?" questioned I-2.

"Well," answered I-1, "I don't know if I'm seeing things, but I'm seeing some sort of bright-green light flashing up ahead. Do you all think that's from that Green… uh, whatever he's called?"

At the same time, the one called R-1 recognized the image ahead as well. He was able to discern that it undoubtedly had to be the one and only Green Phantasm. He told everyone else over the radio in a straightforward manner, "Yes, yes, yes, all right? Of course it's the Green Phantasm! Now everyone prepare to open fire." They all made sure that their targeting was ready for use.

Next, R-1 addressed H-1, telling him, "Okay, H-1, this time it's our turn. Let's you and I each fire a rocket bomb at that freak. You with me?"

"I copy, R-1," replied H-1. "Just let me know when."

"All right," said R-1 back to him. "Now!" At that, R-1 and H-1 each unleashed a rocket bomb from his plane's left wing, which of course was aimed for the Green Phantasm.

In the meantime, the Green Phantasm noticed the two projectiles headed toward him. "Oh my goodness," he said to himself, "I better try to get rid of them." He utilized both index fingers to fire two green laser beams. Whenever the two rocket bombs were nearly two-thirds of their way to the Phantasm, they were each touched and set off by a laser beam.

As soon as the two midair explosions had occurred, F-2 asked anxiously over the radio, "So, uh, did that do it?"

"Yeah," said F-3. "Did we get him?" They were about to find out.

The Green Phantasm teleported to reappear another three-quarters of a mile to the west. Then, he was once again facing the oncoming pack of XTV500 rocket planes. "All right," said the Phantasm to himself, "just try that again, I dare you."

Meanwhile, the XTV500s were now getting past the point at which the two bombs had been blown up by the laser beams. Therefore, they were about one mile east of the Green Phantasm. Everyone in the planes was searching for any possible sign of the radiant hero that they were all pursuing. An anxious I-1 went on to say over the two-way radio, "Well, I don't see anything left of him. But anyway, I hope we got him though. If not, I wonder where he went this time."

Shortly, something caught H-1's eye. It was yet another increasing flash of neon-green light up ahead. He signed on and said, "Hey, um, guys, I'm sorry to tell y'all this, but I don't think that did it. Look up ahead everybody."

At that, everyone began to focus on H-1's observation. Within two seconds, some of them noticed it as well, including R-1. So next, R-1 said to all of his accomplices, "Well, what do you know? He must've stopped those two bombs somehow. But anyway, he's got what's coming to him. I just want to know one thing. Are you all thinking what I'm thinking on this next one?"

"Well," responded R-2. "I am if it's what you're thinking."

"Yeah, me too," I-2 said in agreement.

"All right, never mind that now," R-1 told them. "Just do what I say, all right? Now, we're all going to have to fire at him at the same time.

Each and every one of us will unleash not one, but two rocket bombs. Can everybody handle that?"

Several of them responded over the radio with different answers, such as "Yes, sir," "No problem," "You got it," and so forth.

Continuing his instructions, R-1 went on to say, "Very good, men; now, H-2, I-2, and everyone in the middle row just continue flying forward at your current altitude. Everyone in the front row with me shall rise up above them. Finally, as for those in the back from H-3 through F-3, you will station yourselves below everyone else. Does everyone know what they are to do?"

They all took turns responding over the two-way radio, "Yeah!"

"Great," replied R-1. "Now branch out like I said and get ready."

As they all continued cruising west, H-1, I-1, R-1, and F-1 all increased the lift provided by the engines on their planes' bottoms in order to elevate above H-2, I-2, R-2, and F-2. At the same time, H-3, I-3, R-3, and F-3 all decreased their planes' lift to descend below everyone else.

Next, R-1 signed on to the two-way radio and told everyone, "All right, not bad, and now, everyone, target the Green Phantasm. Each and every last one of us will unleash two rocket bombs. Oh yes, that makes twenty-four total. We shall see if he can stop that."

Then, after giving everyone a few seconds to fix his targeting system on the Green Phantasm, R-1 asked all of his teammates over the radio, "So, is everybody ready?"

Many of them then responded alternately over the radio, "Ready!"

"Excellent," said R-1. "Now, when I say 'fire,' you will all fire at once. And now, here it goes: ready… aim… fire!" At that, every pilot complied, and twenty-four rocket bombs went soaring straight toward the Phantasm. They were discharged from about half of a mile away from him.

Upon seeing the bombs heading his way, the Green Phantasm became confused, wondering which one to shoot at first. He was determined to stop them somehow before they did any damage to anyone or anything else. But shortly, the rocket bombs came to be within a quarter of a mile of the Green Phantasm. He did not have enough time to set all of the bombs off with laser beams. He came up with only one other idea. "Oh shoot," he muttered. "I only got one choice." So finally, the Green Phantasm began using laser beams to form a force field that would shield him from too much impact, being burned, or anything else that could have been fatal.

Fortunately, the Green Phantasm managed to complete the force field in the nick of time. The twenty-four rocket bombs from X-Termination came in contact with the force field. As a result, they all began to explode.

In the meantime, R-1 and a few others noticed the bombs were beginning to go off. So R-1 commanded everyone else in the planes, telling them, "All right, everyone put on the brake at once, okay? Let's hold off for a minute and see what happens." They all decreased their thrust to significantly slow their planes.

"Do you think we got him?" H-3 asked over the radio.

"We'll find out soon enough, H-3," R-1 told him in reply. "For right now, just halt like everyone else."

"Okay," said H-3. They all held back to avoid the force emitted by the combined explosion.

But at the same time, the bombs' explosive force propelled the Green Phantasm's force field toward the west. Unfortunately, although the Green Phantasm was being cushioned by his force field, he could not stop himself from being catapulted by the expanding force that was pushing him. "Oh my God!" he exclaimed in panic. "What'll I do here, huh? I'm having a tougher time with this than I did with X-Termination."

The Green Phantasm did not know that the men in the rocket planes actually were part of X-Termination. Speaking of which, after waiting for a moment, R-1 told the rest of the crew, "All right, everyone, let's proceed forward to try to determine how he ended up. Let's go!" Finally, they all put their rocket planes back in their original arrangement and went soaring west. They would soon find out that the Green Phantasm was still afloat, even after the explosion had projected him another half of a mile west.

Very shortly, the XTV500's came to be within two-thirds of a mile of the Phantasm. R-1 told everyone over the two-way radio, "Now listen; if anyone sees a sign of that neon-green creep, let us know. He's gotta be around here somewhere."

Momentarily, two of the pilots on the front row began to see something. It was an increasingly bright, flashing speck of neon-green light. F-1 signed on and said, "Excuse me, everyone; this is F-1. Do y'all see what I see?"

"Are you talking about that flash of green light?" questioned I-1.

At the same time, R-1 noticed too and said to everyone, "So, it's still him all right, isn't it?"

"Yeah," responded H-1. "It still is, and he's still afloat somehow. I just wonder how, because I thought we hit him."

"We'll see," answered R-1. "I got another idea. F-1, prepare your ray guns to fire a double stream of acid."

"Yes, sir," replied F-1.

The Green Phantasm was trying to figure out his next move as the planes were drawing closer to him. "Man," he told himself, "there's gotta be something I can do about those airplanes and the sleazeballs flying them. However, I better keep this force field on until I figure it out. But anyway, let me try something here." So then, the Green Phantasm increased the lift that was coming from the soles of his feet. He was hoping to perhaps rise above the pack so that they could pass under him. But unfortunately for the Phantasm, this attempt was cut short.

The XTV500 rocket planes soon came to be within a fourth of a mile of the Green Phantasm. As they kept getting closer, F-1 used his plane's pair of ray guns to fire two streaks of burning X-Termination Acid. Fortunately, the Green Phantasm himself did not get burned or consumed. However, the fired shots hit the outside of the force field and drove the Phantasm about fifty feet west. In reaction, the Green Phantasm stopped ascending, for he was shocked. Then, he cried, "Oh no, what was that?"

F-2 of X-Termination said over the two-way radio, "Hey, he's still afloat."

"So he is," said R-1. "Well, let's try to find something out here. I-1, fire two shots at this freak."

"Yes, sir," replied I-1. He complied and fired two consecutive blasts at the Green Phantasm. Just as previously, they connected with the force field and forced the Green Phantasm west in midair. This time, he was propelled well over one hundred feet.

"Oh my God," groaned the Green Phantasm. "They're shooting some kind of lasers or something from their planes. That's what that was. It's a good thing I got my force field on. I just gotta stop 'em somehow. But how? That's the question."

Then, while the XTV500's were closing in on the Phantasm once again, I-2 raised a question over the radio, "What's happening here? I thought we hit him."

"Yeah, me too," said I-3. "Why didn't those shots destroy him?"

"You know," replied I-1, "I think there's a reason for this. I just can't remember, um…"

H-1 signed on and told everyone, "I think I might see what I-1's getting at. Didn't XT and Zapper tell us something like, uh, you know, um, um… oh geez, what was that thing he would, um…"

R-1 picked up his receiver and said to everyone firmly, "Yes, yes, yes, all right? Of course that's what it is! He obviously put on one of those freakin' force fields. That's what he did, okay?" In response, the other eleven just remained silent and nodded in agreement.

Next, R-1 continued by telling all of them, "Now listen up, everyone; here's what we'll have to do. We can't 'X-terminate' him in the air as we would like. But, although he has a force field on, all we can do is keep him under control. However, this will require everyone's cooperation; that's *everyone*, okay? Can y'all work with me?" Many of the pilots then gave affirmative responses one at a time.

After that, R-1 resumed his instructions, telling everyone, "I'm gonna explain to y'all how we're gonna do this. We're gonna expand. I'll tell every single one of you how and where you will position yourself. Other than that, we will all take turns firing at the Phantasm to keep him in our sights. Is that clear?"

Most of the XTV500 pilots took turns enthusiastically answering, "Yeah!"

"Very good," replied R-1. "And now, I will give us our positions. I-1, you and I shall remain centered up front."

"Got it," declared I-1.

Next, R-1 told the other two who were in the front row, "H-1 and F-1, you two each move aside from us by about the width of one of these planes. H-1, you go a plane's width to your left. F-1, you do the same thing to the right."

"Yes, sir," each one of them responded over the radio.

After that, R-1 instructed the pilots who were in the middle row, "As for you guys behind us, you'll all spread out to make us eight wide. I-2, you will shift to your left and fire from between H-1 and I-1. R-2, you'll do the same thing from between F-1 and myself."

"Roger," replied I-2.

"You got it," said R-2.

"H-2," continued R-1, "you will move to the left of H-1. And, F-2, you will be at the other end, to the right of F-1. That'll open us up to eight wide. Are we all clear so far?"

"That we are," answered H-2.

"Me too," answered F-2.

"And finally," said R-1, "here's what you guys in the back will do. I-3 and R-3, you two rise up and fly above the rest of us. H-3 and F-3, you two get below all the rest of us."

At that, the four at the rear gave different responses, such as "Got it," Ten-four," and "Yes, sir, R-1."

"Great," R-1 said eagerly, "now, everyone, take your positions." At that, each and every XTV500 pilot changed his position in order to take his part in the formation. Very shortly, the new formation was complete. It now consisted of one side-by-side row of eight planes. Other than that, two were above it and two were below.

R-1 signed on and said over the two-way radio, "Very good, everyone. Now, this is the deal: We're gonna try to keep the Green Phantasm in sight and in front of us. And as we move him forward, we will stay close. We can't afford to lose him. We can't risk him coming up with a new game plan. There can't be any letup whatsoever. Everybody understand?"

More than half of the other eleven answered over the radio in agreement. Those who did not just nodded with a thumbs-up in agreement.

Next, R-1 continued by telling the rest of the crew, "Now, listen, I-1, myself, and those centered with us will propel him forward while he's centered where we need him. F-1 and F-2, you two will manipulate him to the left to either keep him in line or to change the direction we move him in. H-2 and H-1, y'all will do like them, but move him to the right whenever needed. Y'all will all do so as necessary by firing and hitting his force field on the necessary side. Do you all follow me so far?" H-1, H-2, F-1, and F-2 each answered affirmatively.

"Very good," replied R-1, "and now, this is for I-3 and R-3. If Green Phantasm happens to rise too far up, one of you shall shoot his force field along the top to knock him back down in line. Can y'all handle that?"

"Yes, sir," I-3 and R-3 each answered.

"Good," said R-1. "And at last, H-3 and F-3, if the Phantasm goes too far to the bottom, hit the bottom of the force field to put him back in line."

"Yes, sir," replied H-3.

"No problem," said F-3.

"All right," replied R-1. Then, he added, "And look, this is for the last four I spoke to. If it gets too tough for y'all, guys like H-2 or F-2 can temporarily shift up or down to help y'all, all right? Now, I hope we can all work together on this. We'll keep him in our sights until Zapper tells us where to bring him. Let's just make sure to keep this creep under control and in line. Any questions?" No one signed on with a single question, so R-1 assumed that they all understood what to do.

As they were getting dangerously close to the Green Phantasm, R-1 told the other eleven pilots, "All right then. Well, there's no time to lose. Let's continue working on him right this second."

On the other hand, the Green Phantasm managed to notice that the XTV500 pilots of X-Termination had temporarily ceased firing at him. So he decided to try once more to evade them somehow. "Well, I wonder why they quit," the Phantasm said to himself, "Well, anyhow, maybe I better get out of their way while I can. Maybe I'll figure out some other way to conquer them." Upon saying that, the Green Phantasm increased the lift that was applied by his hovering ability. This made him begin to ascend vertically.

Unfortunately for the Phantasm, X-Termination's R-1 noticed him trying to get away. He communicated over the two-way radio to R-3, saying, "Hurry up, R-3, stop him! Don't let him get away!" R-3 slightly ascended his XTV500 and fired two streams of burning acid that hit the upper right of the Green Phantasm's force field. At the Phantasm's point of view, this was the upper left. This forced the Phantasm back down in front of the pack. However, the Green Phantasm was not quite centered perfectly with the flock of planes. R-1 commanded R-2, saying, "Come on, R-2! Knock him back to the center." At that, R-2 used his pair of ray guns to hit the Green Phantasm's force field slightly right of the very center. This practically centered the Green Phantasm perfectly among all of the XTV500 rocket planes.

R-1 went on to tell his teammate R-2, "Good work, R-2." After that, R-1 told everyone over the radio, "All right, everybody; well, it looks like we got him where we want. Let's just make sure we keep him like this until Zapper tells us where to bring him. Everybody copy?" Many of the other pilots then took turns answering to indicate that they had received and understood the message.

From that point on, the XTV500 pilots continued to keep the Green Phantasm within their control and directly in front of them while flying around above Philadelphia. For the majority of the time, the Phantasm's force field was being pushed through the air by one of the rocket planes around the middle of the row, which was eight-wide. The one that would push him the most would be either I-1 or R-1. On occasion, whenever the Green Phantasm would try either to rise or drop from in front of I-1 or R-1, someone—H-3, I-3, R-3, or F-3—would shoot at the force field to knock him back in line. Other than that, different pilots would fire at the Phantasm to manipulate him whenever they all decided to change direction of flight.

While X-Termination had everything going their way, the Green Phantasm was in a situation that was not in his favor. Evidently, the X-Termination members in the XTV500 rocket planes had him within their control completely and were knocking him about like a pinball. The Green Phantasm saw no way out of his unfortunate predicament. Two of the only things in his favor were the protection provided by the force field and prevention of further destruction to people or property in Philadelphia.

So, while still shielded by the force field, yet unable to move about freely, the Green Phantasm was saying to himself, "Oh man, I can't believe this is happening. I don't know what they're trying to do to me, or where they're bringing me. It's a good thing I've got this force field. I mean, I don't know what I'd be right now without it. I sure wish someone could tell me what to do, because this looks extraordinarily bad. No one, not even X-Termination, has been this tough for me to deal with. Oh my God, I hate this."

Meanwhile, X-Termination's top three officials—Zapper, Zinger, and D.D.T.—had been cruising about the southern part of Philadelphia in their X-Terminator 4000. They were in search of a spot at which they could hide and wait to destroy the Green Phantasm.

Finally, they found a construction zone located about half of a mile south of downtown Philadelphia. The new street ran from west to east and intersected Sixth Street on the east side. Of course, an orange and white barricade had been erected to keep everyone off the new road. But other than that, various commercial buildings were still under construction.

Whenever Zapper saw this from the X-Terminator 4000, he told Zinger, "All right, Zinger, this place looks good. We'll tell them to bring him here. Once they do, we'll 'X-terminate' him once and for all. See that street up there on your left under construction?"

Zinger happened to be headed south, flying thirty feet above Sixth Street along with Zapper and D.D.T. This new street was now a little over a tenth of a mile before them to their left. Shortly, Zinger could see it himself and responded, "Yes, Zapper, I see what you're talking about."

"Good," said Zapper, "now take a left there." At that, Zinger did as he was told. He turned left in midair, so that he came to be above the barricaded street.

But then, Zapper gave Zinger another command. He told his junior partner, "Zinger, land in front of the first site on your right." At that, Zinger landed and parked the X-Terminator 4000 directly in front of the first building on their right-hand side. Right after that, Zapper said, "Nice job, Zinger; this is where we'll hide and where we'll have them bring us the Phantasm."

"Yes, sir," replied Zinger.

Zapper turned his attention to big D.D.T., saying, "And as for you, D.D.T., you're gonna go two buildings down on your left-hand side. That's where you'll station yourself and keep watch over what's going on over here. You'll tell us things over the radio, like when the Green Phantasm makes it here and when he takes down his force field."

"You got it, man, no problem," D.D.T. told him in reply.

"And I might suggest a couple of other things," Zapper added. "First of all, park another two buildings down from where you'll be stationed. That way, no one will see the vehicle in front of your site and become suspicious. And another thing, whenever you're leaving or returning to the X-Terminator 4000, have a couple of gas bombs ready in case you need to use them."

"Yes, sir," D.D.T. responded affirmatively. "Good idea, boss."

"Well, I'm glad you understand and agree," Zapper told him. "Now get going. There's no time to lose. We gotta get that Green Phantasm 'X-terminated.' "

"Right," replied big D.D.T. "Yo, man, I'm on it." At that, the masked gargantuan closed up the X-Terminator 4000 and took off once Zapper and Zinger hopped out of it.

Next, Zapper told Zinger, "Come on, Zinger, let's retreat to our spot." Zapper sprinted over to the hiding place that he had chosen for Zinger and himself, with Zinger following behind. They were on their way to hide inside of a large bank building that had not been under construction for very long. First, they darted up a set of five steps that lacked a very steep incline. Then, they got to the platform at the top of the steps. From there, Zapper and Zinger went on through a doorway that was designated for a set of double doors. Finally, they hid behind the very same wall that consisted of that doorway. That front wall of concrete blocks was the only part of the building above the foundation, which was now much taller than either one of them.

D.D.T. had finally parked the X-Terminator 4000 four buildings down on the other side of the street. Before exiting the vehicle, he put on his gas mask. Then, he took two gas bombs from his utility belt. Of course, he was planning to use them to make certain that no one could see him or come near him. Finally, D.D.T. climbed out of the X-Terminator 4000 and closed it.

According to Zapper's instructions, D.D.T. now had to go back to the third building to his left, since he had parked by the fifth building to his left. D.D.T. activated and hurled a gas bomb to about the halfway point in the distance he had to run. Shortly, the bomb began emitting a cloud of light-purple X-Termination Gas. At the same time, D.D.T. ran toward the site to which he was assigned. Once he was around two-thirds of the way there, he threw and landed another gas bomb at the front entrance of the building. This caused even more gas to come out and expand.

The building toward which D.D.T. was running was a nearly finished three-story office building. Once D.D.T. made his way over to it, the powerful masked behemoth growled fiercely while he completely broke open and tore off the entrance door with his bare hands. Once inside, he took a staircase to the roof, since no elevators were yet up and running.

Before long, D.D.T. was on the roof of the office building. That, of course, was the point from which he would keep watching across the street to his right in order to keep Zapper and Zinger informed of the status of the Green Phantasm. He took his handheld two-way radio from his belt to make sure it was ready for use. Then, the big man walked up to the inside of a four-foot-tall concrete barrier that surrounded the roof of the building. D.D.T. went to the corner that was ahead to his far right. Finally, as he began watching to his right, he said to himself, "Well, I guess that's where them guys gonna bring him. And, um, I guess I gotta let Zapper and Zinger know what's goin' on and when to shoot him. Oh well, it looks like they needa get him over here."

From Zapper and Zinger's hiding place, Zapper looked out through the front doorway and managed to spot something far ahead in the sky. It looked like a group of fighter planes with a flash of neon-green light in front of them. Zapper was no doubt wondering anxiously whether the objects in the distance were what he thought they were. So he said to Zinger, "Well, well, I sure hope that's what I think it is. It looks like they might have him. Check it out, Zinger; you think that could very well be our men with that freak under control?"

"Well," Zinger replied, "uh, let me see what you're talkin' about, Zapper." At that, he stood immediately to Zapper's left and took a look for himself. Then, whenever Zinger spotted the same thing as Zapper, he said, "Well, I'll be damned, Zapper; I think it is."

"Well then," said Zapper. "What do you say we find out for sure?" Zinger just nodded in agreement. After that, they went back into hiding. That very moment, Zapper put his handheld radio on the same channel as that of the two-way radios that were installed in all the XTV500's. He signed on and said into his radio, "R-1, this is Zapper, do you read me?"

The planes Zapper and Zinger were seeing far away just so happened to be the twelve XTV500 rocket planes that were being piloted by the other twelve X-Termination employees. They were now above Temple University driving the Green Phantasm west-southwest. So R-1 replied over the radio, "Yes, sir, Zapper, I read you loud and clear. Go ahead."

"Well, R-1," said Zapper, "I think I might be seeing you in the distance, and it looks like y'all have the Green Phantasm out in front of you. Have you got him under control?"

"Oh yes, we've got him all right," R-1 answered happily. "We all had to work together to apprehend him, but now, we've got him trapped in front of us. He may have a force field on, but he can't get away from us. Other than that, I guess he can't keep that force field on forever."

"Excellent!" Zapper happily exclaimed. "Great job, R-1, and everyone else who can hear me."

Zapper went on to tell R-1 over the radio, "Now listen to me, and listen good, R-1. Zinger and I have found a hiding place where we are waiting. That is where y'all will bring the Phantasm to us. I will give you the location. Are you ready?"

"Ready," R-1 responded.

"All right then," Zapper told him. "You know where Sixth Street runs south, right?"

"Absolutely," R-1 answered.

"All right," continued Zapper. "About half of a mile south of South Street is a new street being constructed, with commercial buildings being put up as well."

"Okay," replied R-1.

"Now, look, R-1," said Zapper. "Zinger and I are on the east side of Sixth Street. We are hiding in the first building on the right-hand side. You won't see us, because we'll be behind the front wall, which is like the only wall that is near completion. Just place the Green Phantasm at the top of the set of steps that leads to the front doorway. Then, whenever he takes off his force field, Zinger and I will 'X-terminate' him. Have you got that?"

"Yes, Zapper," R-1 told him affirmatively. "I think I do understand. We will bring the Green Phantasm to the spot you just described. So we just leave him in front of the doorway, and you and Zinger will take care of him from there?"

"That's right," replied Zapper. "Now just concentrate on getting him to us. D.D.T. will be watching from another building, and he'll tell us what's going on and when to fire. Just worry about your part of this deal, all right?"

"All right," R-1 responded. "No problem, Zapper. We're on our way. He'll be right there."

"Excellent," said Zapper. "Great job. We'll be waiting."

"Ten-four," R-1 answered.

Zapper said to Zinger, "Well, what do you know, Zinger? It looks like that thing in the distance is what we thought after all."

"Yeah," Zinger replied in agreement. "After all, it's very unlikely that any other group of twelve planes would have one big flash of neon-green light out front. What are the chances of that?"

Zapper changed his radio back over to the same channel as the radio of their monster-sized premier associate D.D.T. He signed on, saying, "Come in, D.D.T. Do you read me?"

Big D.D.T. responded over his radio, saying, "Oh yes, Zapper, I read you. What's going on, man?"

"Look here, D.D.T.," Zapper told him. "About the twelve guys in the planes, you know they're gonna bring the Green Phantasm our way, right?"

"Yeah, man, I know that," D.D.T. responded.

"All right then," continued Zapper. "Now, it's like this. They have now apprehended him, and he's within their control. They'll have him over here any minute now. Zinger and I need you to keep your eyes peeled and keep us informed on when he gets placed in front of the doorway we're behind and when he takes off his force field. You cannot be a second too late. This is our one and only chance to 'X-terminate' the Green Phantasm once and for all. Do you understand this, D.D.T.?"

"Yes, I understand," D.D.T. answered.

"Are you absolutely positive you understand?" asked Zapper. "We cannot afford to have a single thing go wrong. If the Phantasm escapes, we will never recapture him. So if there's even the slightest detail you don't understand, you sure as hell better tell me right freakin' now! We all got too much to lose over this."

"Look here, Zapper," D.D.T. told him over the radio. "How you think I'm gonna screw up on this, huh? My life and my career is on the line, just like yours and Zinger's, all right? I want that freak 'X-terminated' too; I mean, just after how he done humiliated us all last night, including me, man! I know and understand exactly what I got to do here, all right? There ain't gonna be no letup whatsoever on my end, because I ain't even giving this bright-green punk a split second, okay? I'm gonna tell you exactly when to shoot, I promise. I'm gonna make sure you know; now trust me."

"Sounds great," Zapper told him in reply. "Now just keep strictly on the lookout and make sure you tell us immediately!"

"You got it!" D.D.T. responded most affirmatively.

After signing off, Zapper told Zinger, "Make sure you're ready, Zinger."

"You betcha," said Zinger. "I've been ready to dispose of this creep for a while now. I'm with you a hundred percent on this, completely focused. Nothing or no one's gonna change that, I promise."

While continuing to hide and wait, Zapper let out a snicker right after Zinger finished speaking.

Meanwhile, in the XTV500 rocket planes, R-1 was about to go over another game plan with all of the other pilots. The twelve of them had nearly moved the Green Phantasm to the west city boundary of Philadelphia. They were now up above the part of the city called West Philadelphia. The XTV500 pilots were all going to have to change the direction in which they were moving the Green Phantasm, and R-1 was going to explain to them how they were to make the transition.

They were traveling in a west-southwest direction. R-1 was planning on flying south by east for a change, but still with the Green Phantasm out in front of them all. So R-1 said to everyone over the two-way radio, "All right, listen up, everybody! Y'all hear me?"

Many of the pilots responded, confirming that they could hear and understand him. R-1 continued by saying, "Good, and now, you all understand where Zapper said to bring the Phantasm, right?"

Many of the XTV500 pilots took turns saying "Yeah!" to show that they understood.

"Very good, men," R-1 told them. "Now, we're going to have to change the direction we are flying in, and I'm gonna need you all to work with me as a team to make this change. I'm going to explain what needs to be done. Is everybody ready for this?"

At that, many of the others in the planes gave various affirmative responses over the radio.

"All right," continued R-1, "We're gonna have to change our flight direction completely. But at the same time, we also have to maintain control of the Green Phantasm." The other eleven all nodded to themselves in agreement.

R-1 continued his instructions by saying, "So, while some of you make the direction change, the rest of us will keep the Green Phantasm in line. Everybody follow that so far?" They all then responded one at a time, assuring him that they understood.

Then at once, R-1 addressed five of the other pilots, "Now, this first set of instructions is for R-2, R-3, F-2, and F-3. The five of you better pay close attention to this."

"Yes, sir, R-1," some of them replied.

"Now look, you guys," R-1 told them. "Right now, we are flying west-southwest. You five will be the first to change direction to south by east toward the construction site where Zapper and Zinger are hiding. While you all swing around in one cloverleaf to reposition yourselves, the rest of us will slow down and keep the Phantasm in line. Then, once you're all facing the direction you need to be, we're gonna let y'all take him under control for a moment. After that, the rest of us will come and catch up to you. Then at last, we'll all work together again in controlling the Green Phantasm, just in a different direction than we are now."

R-1 asked the other eleven, "Now, does everyone understand, and are we ready?" To that, they all gave the most positive, eager, and enthusiastic responses they could over the radio. R-1 said, "Great! All righty then, when I say 'now,' the other six will slow up along with me, and you five I instructed will make your move. And finally of course, us seven will catch up to you."

One last time, the other eleven pilots took turns telling R-1 either "ten-four" or "roger" to assure him that they were fully understanding and prepared.

Finally, R-1 began giving his command. "All right, you guys," he uttered over the two-way radio, "here we go! Ready *now*!"

Right away, R-1, H-1, H-2, H-3, I-1, I-2, and I-3 decreased the thrust of the rear rocket engines of the XTV500's. This of course slowed down their planes. At the same time, the other five men in their planes began making a continuous right turn. While they were trying to make the necessary loop they needed to, the other seven, who were now going very slowly, were occasionally firing a shot to control the force field that contained the Green Phantasm.

From within his force field, the Green Phantasm was able to observe the transition through which the X-Termination pilots were going. When he noticed that seven planes had really slowed down and that the other five had pulled away, he asked himself, "Well, what on earth are they doing?"

Then, when he saw the grouping of five rocket planes turning right, he said, "I wonder where those guys are going and what they're up to."

Right after that, the Green Phantasm put those thoughts aside and asked himself, "More importantly, what am I gonna do now? I mean, I guess I gotta do something different, and I guess it will require getting out of this force field. I can't do a whole lot from in here." But shortly, the Phantasm suddenly had one thought. He thought about possibly decreasing the driving force of his hovering ability to start descending toward the earth. He wanted to do that so he could figure out another way to try to take down the XTV500's. However, he could not descend very far.

As the Green Phantasm began to drop toward the ground slowly, he looked up and noticed something coming from the north side of him. It was the five rocket planes being flown by R-2, R-3, F-1, F-2, and F-3. They were headed straight toward him. "Oh, now what?" asked the Green Phantasm.

From a quarter of a mile back, R-1 noticed that the other five had nearly completed their loop. He signed onto the radio, saying, "All right, listen up, you five; can y'all get him from there? Need me to move him over just a bit?"

R-2 signed on and replied, "It's okay; we got him."

"Good," said R-1. "Just keep him in line for a moment. We're all fixing to come up and join you."

R-2 said to F-3, who was still flying at the bottom of them, "F-3, he's trying to go down. Hit him a time or two. Don't let him get away."

"Roger," replied F-3, who then fired two consecutive shots at the lower half of the Phantasm's force field. This knocked the Green Phantasm forward a little while forcing him back to the center of the bad guys' path. Right after that, those five men in their planes once again caught up with the Phantasm and regained control of him, propelling him forward in front of them.

Whenever R-1 noticed this, he told the other six pilots who were cruising with him, "All right, you guys with me, let's rejoin them, and help push that creep like we were before. Only this time, we gradually bring him downward, and then we finally leave him where Zapper told us. Y'all got that?" Those six took turns responding affirmatively over the radio while nodding to themselves.

"Great," R-1 replied. "Now, there's no time to lose. Let's get going and catch up to 'em." At that, all seven of them immediately increased the thrust in their XTV500's to speed back up. At the same time, they all began turning their planes left and kept turning until they were soaring in the same direction as the other five. Soon after that, all twelve rocket planes were together once again in their eight-wide formation, with I-3 and R-3 flying above and H-3 and F-3 below.

While being pushed, the Green Phantasm asked himself, "What are they doing now? Are they taking me somewhere? If so, where?"

At this point, the Green Phantasm still did not know that the men flying the planes were employed by X-Termination. He also did not know what they were trying to do to him or where they were trying to bring him. Plus, unfortunately for the Green Phantasm, the game plan of X-Termination was so far working out the way they intended. He could not maneuver out from in front of the XTV500's, and he was now headed right toward Zapper and Zinger, who of course were waiting for him. Could this be the end for James Clifton and the Green Phantasm?

While all that was taking place, someone was heading south along Sixth Street. That someone just so happened to be Amanda Lee Taylor. She was in her Ford Explorer and on her way to visit her parents.

While on her way, Amanda drove by the construction site in which Zapper and Zinger were hiding, which was to her left. While still waiting for the Green Phantasm, the ruffian called Zinger briefly put his head outside the building's front doorway to see what was going on. But then, Zapper reprimanded him, saying, "Zinger, get back in here, you fool! D.D.T.'s gonna tell us what's happening!"

"Oh, sorry, Zapper," replied Zinger. That very second, he withdrew back behind the wall.

"Never mind," said Zapper. "Just act when he and I tell you."

Zinger just replied by nodding.

However, when Zinger had peeked out of their hiding place, Amanda had just caught an unclear glimpse of it at the far left of her field of vision. As she continued driving, she turned her head to her left for a few seconds, exclaiming, "Oh my God, what was that?"

Next, as Amanda was trying to put her eyes on the road again, something in her driver's-side mirror caught her attention. In reaction, she slowed her vehicle down to see what it was. "Well, I wonder what that is," she said to herself. Amanda continued to examine the neon-green glowing object in her mirror; she finally decided, "Oh my gosh, that must be the Green Phantasm?" At that, she pulled her Explorer over and parked on the side of the highway to her right.

After that, Amanda got out of her Ford Explorer and stationed herself directly in front of it. She then looked continuously back at the Green Phantasm to try to figure out what he was doing. Shortly, Amanda also noticed that a swarm of planes were following him and shooting at him. It looked like something was constantly forcing him in the same direction of the rocket planes. So then, becoming a little worried, Amanda Taylor said sadly to herself, "I wonder what's happening to him."

Out of confusion, Amanda began looking around in all possible different directions. Momentarily, the bank building across the highway that was under construction came to be centered in her field of vision. Suddenly, she remembered the vague image of a masked man's head that she had perceived moments earlier. So then, Amanda looked at that building curiously and said to herself, "Wait a minute; I don't know who or what that was that I thought I saw a few minutes ago, and I can't even think of it right now. But there's just a little something familiar about— well, was that a man with a black-and-yellow mask on?"

Within a moment, Amanda only came up with one idea. She said, "You know, I don't know what's actually happening to Green Phantasm or who or what is hiding over there. I also don't know what the chances of this is, but could there be a connection by any chance?"

Finally, Amanda decided, "Well, maybe I'll sneak over to see if I can find out anything. I don't know what I'll find out, but hopefully, it's worth a try." At that, she began sprinting across the street toward the construction site.

But then, after a few steps, she stopped herself because she had another idea. Amanda said to herself, "I better bring something along in case I need it." She was referring to a softball bat that she was carrying inside her Explorer. Amanda quickly ran back over to retrieve her softball bat. She once again began running toward the site.

Shortly, Amanda came up to the west wall of the incomplete building. She began trying to find a way to sneak up and spy on anyone hiding inside. Before too long, however, she had an idea. Since Amanda had seen a masked figure looking out of the front of the building, she decided to go closer to the rear to try to see what she could of whoever was in hiding there and what he was up to.

Amanda went to a spot along the west side of the project, which was a little over two-thirds of the way from the bank building's front to its back. That particular part of the west-side wall was three and a half feet high from the building's foundation at the time. When Amanda peered over that concrete block construction, she immediately spotted two men to her far left. They were dressed in yellow and black. Within a few seconds, she figured out exactly who they were: two of those guys from X-Termination.

"Oh my God!" Amanda softly exclaimed to herself. "That's two of the guys who invaded the party last night, isn't it? At least I know who this is now. They were all there looking for the Green Phantasm, weren't they? Maybe they do have something to do with this."

Zapper went on to say to Zinger, "All right, Zinger, they're gonna have him here any second now. You ready for this?"

"Heh, am I ready for this?" replied Zinger. "Believe me, man, I've been ready for this. But somehow, it, uh, just, it just seems a little too easy though. Ah, but what the heck! Nevertheless, we're gonna do it. Oh yes, we're gonna 'X-terminate' the Green Phantasm." As he finished saying that, he kept nodding affirmatively.

"Great," Zapper told him. "Now, as soon as D.D.T. tells us, we're gonna take this freak out. Stay ready, Zinger."

Amanda understood exactly what was going on. "Oh no!" she cried in panic, "What am I gonna do? I can't let this happen. I gotta do something, but what?" After a few seconds of silence, Amanda said, "Maybe I should call the police. But no, that won't help. They're about to kill him any second. What can I ever do to stop them?"

Amanda desperately looked all around for a solution until a few things caught her attention and gave her an idea. She discovered some pallets full of bricks and concrete blocks to her left. When she took a look at them, as well as the bat in her right hand, she figured she could possibly utilize those things to somehow break up the misdeed of Zapper and Zinger. At the same time, she also had another thought. She softly uttered to herself,

"You know, I just can't forget what the Green Phantasm has already done for me. I'm talking about how he saved my life in the subway Sunday night, and the way he saved all those lives, including mine, at the banquet last night. Besides, it's unfair for him to have to face all these people by himself, and I really want to meet him and get to know him. So I think I ought to step up and help him. After all, I owe it to him."

She set down her softball bat for a moment. At that, she used her right hand to pick up a brick. Then at once, Amanda hurled the brick at the thug who was closer to her. It was Zinger, for he was on the same side of the front doorway as she was.

Consequently, the thrown brick hit the middle of Zinger's upper back and landed behind him on the concrete foundation of the building. Whenever Zinger felt something hit him, he looked back to his right and exclaimed, "Hey, what was that?"

"What was what, Zinger?" asked Zapper.

Zinger then turned toward him and said in response, "I don't know, Zapper. That's what I'm trying to figure out. I coulda sworn something just hit me from behind."

Zapper told him, "Listen, Zinger, I don't see anybody or anything back there. Maybe you backed into something, all right? Now just stay focused on what we're doing, all right? Now there."

"All right," replied a somewhat frustrated Zinger. "Fine, anything you say, Zapper." After that, Zinger scoffed and shook his head in disbelief. He just put all of his attention back on the Phantasm.

But next, Amanda decided to try something slightly different. This time, she used both hands to seize two bricks to cast at the younger of the two masked culprits. So then, with all her might, Amanda slung the brick that was in her right hand. It struck Zinger's lower back.

Zinger reacted by turning around and yelling, "Hey, what the—" But, whenever Zinger was looking back to see what was attacking him, another thrown brick was flying toward him, for Amanda had immediately followed up with that one as well. "Dang it!" Zinger hollered as he barely managed to duck in time to avoid it. Zinger now knew that someone was indeed throwing something at him after all.

Zapper then turned to him and said, "Look, Zinger, I don't know what your problem is, but—"

"No, no, no, you listen to me, Zapper," interrupted Zinger. "I ain't got no problem, all right? I'm not just imagining things either. I happen to know that some idiot is throwing bricks at me. You know how I know that? I'll tell you. There were a couple of times that I felt something hit me. But that third time, I saw a brick flying at me. It almost hit me too." Zinger pointed out two of the bricks, which were now scattered on the building's floor, and said, "Look at that, Zapper. You see those bricks? I know somebody threw 'em from somewhere, and I know it wasn't you or me."

"All right," replied Zapper. "All right then, Zinger, I see your point. Look, just go 'X-terminate' them real quick, and get back over here, all right? Hurry up."

"You bet," Zinger responded as he sprinted back toward the spot from where the bricks had been thrown.

When Amanda heard Zinger coming, she squatted down in her hiding place and got a few things ready. She quickly placed several bricks, a couple of concrete blocks, and her softball bat in front of her. She finally picked up a brick to throw at Zinger and surprise him.

Zinger went up to the rear end of the west wall of the building. While pointing his ray gun forward outside the short, incomplete wall, he said, "All right, you imbecile, where the hell—*Hey!*"

Amanda had thrown a brick to knock the X-Termination Ray from his hand, which caused him to drop it outside the wall.

At that, Zinger turned to his right to see who had done that. However, he did not obtain a good look. The first thing he saw was another brick flying toward him. It was dangerously close. Of course, Amanda had thrown that one as well. Fortunately for her, that brick proceeded to nail Zinger square in the face. "Oof!" the culprit grunted as the impact dazed him.

Right after that, Zinger tried to shake off the dizziness. But before he could fully regain his senses, something else was headed his way. It was the heavy end of Amanda's bat. She was swinging her softball bat left-handed. At last, she successfully connected it with left side of Zinger's head. "Oh!" Zinger grunted, as he became even more dazed than before and collapsed forward on the three-and-a-half-foot-high wall. Zinger's head and arms were then hanging outside the wall.

Very shortly, Zinger tried once again to recover, but before he could, Amanda used her bat to hammer Zinger on the crown of his head. This nearly rendered him unconscious. So finally, Amanda used both of her hands to violently twist Zinger's head and snap his neck. This caused him to fall unconscious inside the wall.

Shortly after that, his senior partner called out to him, "Hurry up over there, Zinger. I think he's almost here."

After getting no response, Zapper looked back over his left shoulder. He was no doubt surprised and shocked at seeing the unconscious Zinger lying on the concrete. "Zinger! What happened?" he cried.

With no response coming from Zinger, Zapper ran over to him. As he was running over, he muttered to himself, "Man, this freakin' job's almost finished! Why does something just have to go wrong now because of that? I don't believe this!" Upon making it over to the unconscious Zinger, Zapper sighed heavily, shook his head in disbelief, and began reaching for his Mega Zapper 2000 with his left hand. He was going to use it to revive Zinger.

However, before Zapper could retrieve his device, something surprised him. His X-Termination Ray was unexpectedly knocked out of his right hand. The shocked Zapper of X-Termination exclaimed, "Hey, what the—"

Although Zapper did not know it, it was a thrown brick that made him drop his ray gun. Before Zapper could finish his exclamation, something else hit him in the face, making him yell, "Oof!" It was a huge concrete building block that Amanda had used both hands to sling at him. Zapper was now very dazed and staggering.

While Zapper was still dazed, a desperate and determined Amanda Taylor leaped over the wall, taking her bat with her. Once inside, she quickly approached Zapper and swung her bat left-handed to land a blow to his abdominal area. "Oh!" hollered Zapper, as he bent over with both hands on his midsection.

Immediately afterward, Amanda followed up with a right-handed swing that struck his lower back. He cried out, "Ah, what's happening?" He still did not know what was hitting him.

Amanda swung her bat once more, to hit Zapper on the back of his knees. This caused the masked villain to fall to the ground.

While Zapper was lying faceup and helpless on the concrete foundation, he caught a glimpse of Amanda while trying to recover from his dizzy spell. At that, he said to her, "So, you're the one who—"

Zapper now knew that someone was indeed attacking them. But before he could finish what he was trying to say, Amanda landed a very painful blow. She delivered a very sharp, powerful kick to Zapper's genitals. "Oh, ow, ow, ow!" Zapper cried out in pain, while placing both hands on his crotch.

Right after delivering that kick, Amanda walked over to Zapper to try to land another hit. She then stood to the left of Zapper's head and got a right-handed grip on her softball bat. She swung it down low into Zapper's crown. As she was swinging, Amanda yelled to him, "Shame on you!" This, of course, was in reference to what they were trying to do to the Green Phantasm. This blow severely stunned Zapper, who now sensed practically nothing; he only hallucinated.

Next, Amanda stomped to Zapper's left side and kicked his jaw very hard with her left foot. While delivering the stomp, she shouted, "And your partner too!" Amanda was referring to Junior Lieutenant Zinger, whom she was condemning as well as Zapper. Her left-footed stomp wrenched the neck of the stunned Zapper and knocked him unconscious. "Thank God that they're both out," said a much-relieved Amanda Taylor.

Amanda turned her attention to the X-Termination Ray that she had earlier caused Zapper to drop. She then had a thought. "I better destroy it," she said. "I don't want for anyone else to get their hands on it." She immediately began continuously hacking away at it with her softball bat and smashed it up as much as she could.

All of a sudden, Amanda heard another sound. It was the voice of someone trying to get through on Zapper's two-way radio. Upon hearing that, she rushed over to the left side of Zapper's belt, where the radio was located. She did not want to risk anyone else finding out what was going on. Amanda just took the handheld radio from Zapper's utility belt and smashed it to bits as well.

After repeatedly hammering the radio, Amanda decided to try something different. She retrieved the concrete block that she had slung at Zapper earlier. She finally threw it down onto the radio as hard as she could. This caused the concrete block to break into several pieces.

One of the pieces of concrete flew over and slightly nudged the head of the unconscious Zinger, causing him to begin regaining consciousness. Shortly, Zinger groaned and began uttering, "Oh man, what... what's going on? What's happening?" He kept looking all around until he could see clearly. Once his vision was cleared up, he used both hands to try to push himself up again.

In time, Amanda looked around and noticed that Zinger was trying to raise himself up again. He had already made it to his hands and knees. She quickly picked up her softball bat and dashed over to him. Zinger then looked up and saw her standing before him. He began to say to her, "Oh, it was you, huh? Who do you think you're—"

But suddenly, Zinger became afraid and gasped in fear because Amanda was preparing to swing at him. She swung her bat and nailed Zinger on the left side of his head above his ear. This blow dazed the young thug and caused him to collapse back down to the ground. "Oh, no, you don't!" Amanda told Zinger, who was now lying face down. Then at last, she gave him one big stomp to the back of his head and neck, knocking him out once again.

D.D.T. was still trying to contact Zapper over the radio. He was trying to get in touch because the twelve in the XTV500 rocket planes were now extremely close to their destination. But of course, the big guy was having no luck getting through because of all that Amanda had done. Not having received any response, D.D.T. said to himself, "Man, I don't know why they ain't sayin' nothin' to me. But I sure enough hope they hear me, that's for sure."

The men in the XTV500's were preparing to drop off the Green Phantasm. R-1 told all the other pilots over the two-way radio, "Okay, let's all slow up our planes and extend him out front some more." At that, they all decreased thrust to slow their rocket planes dramatically and began opening up the distance between themselves and the force field that contained the Green Phantasm.

Then, R-1 delivered his next command. "All right, everybody, you're doing fine," he told them. "But this next instruction is especially for H-1, H-2, and H-3, maybe even I-2 and I-3. So listen up, especially you men I just named." In response, they all confirmed that they were listening.

R-1 continued by saying, "All right then, that bank building ahead on the left is where we are to drop him off, all right? It's where Zapper and Zinger are waiting. As we're approaching the building, we will slightly turn left. You men to the left of our formation will shoot at his force field in any way you have to in order to set him down at the top of those steps in front of the doorway."

"No problem, we got this," H-1 told him in reply.

"Yeah, we sure do," said H-2 in agreement.

"Good," said R-1. "Get right on it." So then, as they were still getting closer, everyone in an XTV500 began making his plane turn slightly left. Of course, at the same time, the five designated pilots kept shooting and manipulating the Green Phantasm's force field until they finally got him exactly where they wanted. "All right, nice job, men," R-1 said, commending them.

While this was happening, D.D.T., who was still looking on from his station, made another attempt to radio Zapper. "Yo, Zapper," said D.D.T. over the radio, "do you read me?" D.D.T. received no answer from Zapper but still went on to say over the radio, "Well, anyway, I just wanted to tell you that the guys in the planes just dropped off the Phantasm. He's still got his force field on. I'll let you know when he takes it off."

Some of the XTV500 pilots were wondering what to do next. The one called I-2 signed onto the radio and said, "So, anyway, um, shouldn't we notify Zapper and Zinger?"

"No, no, no," R-1 said to him. "D.D.T. has that end covered. Don't y'all remember?"

"Oh yeah, he sure does," replied I-1.

"Yeah, that's right," said H-1.

Then, R-1 went on to tell everyone, "All right, everybody, it looks like we did our part. Zapper, Zinger, and D.D.T. should have it from here. Anyway, we better take off now. The Green Phantasm may not even remove his force field until we go. Besides, why don't we take ourselves a break? I say we resume our original formation and slowly and peacefully cruise east." Everyone else agreed. Then, of course, the twelve pilots turned their planes to their left until they were facing east. From there, they repositioned their XTV500's so that they were once again in three rows of four. Finally, of course, they went on coasting east.

Meanwhile, a confused Green Phantasm was now trying to figure out what was going on and what to do from that point. "Well, I wonder what just happened," he said to himself. "I mean, at first, they were knocking me around, and now they just left me here. I wonder why they did that."

Having said that, the Green Phantasm became silent for a few seconds, shaking his head in confusion and disbelief.

But then, the Phantasm said, "Oh well, whatever the case may be, I still gotta stop 'em somehow. I guess I'll take off my force field since I can't do much to 'em from inside of it." At that, he began retracting his force field and kept doing that until it was gone. "There," said the Green Phantasm, "now I got to see what I'll try to do next to stop those planes."

At the same time, D.D.T. had noticed the Green Phantasm taking down his force field. He tried to notify Senior Lieutenant Zapper. "Hey, hey, yo, Zapper, come in please, man," said big D.D.T. while trying to get through to him. At receiving no answer, a worried and frustrated D.D.T. muttered, "Oh man, I hope he can hear me." But then, D.D.T. signed back on to his radio and said, "Look, Zapper, if you can hear me, the Green Phantasm just got out of his force field. So *now*!" Then, watching anxiously, D.D.T. was thinking to himself, *Is he gonna get him?* Of course, although D.D.T. did not know it, Zapper and Zinger were unable to attack, because they had been knocked unconscious by Amanda, who was making sure to keep them that way. So the Green Phantasm did not get "X-terminated."

The Green Phantasm was now ready to set out after the XTV500 rocket planes once again. He went on to teleport from atop the bank building's staircase to the rooftop of the building directly across the street being constructed.

Just as the Green Phantasm was beginning to teleport, Amanda happened to glance back and notice a flash of neon-green light. She knew that it had to be him. She turned around and ran toward the building's doorway. At the same time, she shouted, "Green Phantasm, wait!" But by the time Amanda had made it to the doorway, she was too late, for the Phantasm had already teleported. However, she just went back to watching over Zapper and Zinger, so as not to allow them to regain consciousness.

Meanwhile, from where D.D.T. was stationed, he saw the Green Phantasm disappear and at first did not know what to think. But then, he just said to himself, "I don't know, man; I mean, I guess they got him. Hopefully, they did. If so, great, man. I'm sure enough glad this is over. I just need someone to tell me what to do next."

The Green Phantasm was actually perched atop another building. So then, from the point to which he had just teleported, the Phantasm searched throughout the sky for any sign of the twelve XTV500 planes. Within ten seconds of searching, he spotted a pack of planes coasting east. "Well, I wonder if that's them," he said. Right after that, the Green Phantasm took the form of a shapeless, radiating projectile and began shooting over to another spot to get a closer look.

As the Phantasm whizzed on by, D.D.T. caught sight of him from his station and said, "Hey, what was that?" Then, very shortly, the Green Phantasm ended up hovering in midair up above Independence National Historical Park in downtown Philadelphia. Whenever D.D.T. saw the neon-green figure turn up in the distance, he realized something. "What? No way!" cried big D.D.T. "They ain't destroyed him at all, man!"

Next, D.D.T. tried again to contact Senior Lieutenant Zapper. But, of course, he could not get through, for Amanda Taylor had rendered him unconscious and destroyed his radio. So instead, D.D.T. changed his radio over to the same channel as that of Junior Lieutenant Zinger and tried calling him. When Amanda heard someone trying to reach Zinger, she just took his radio and smashed it up too. Finally, the conclusion D.D.T. reached was, "Oh well, I don't know why I can't get 'em. Maybe they're telling the others how to recapture him." Although D.D.T. did not know for certain, he guessed that Zapper and Zinger were talking with the XTV500 pilots about regaining control of the Green Phantasm. So he just went on and waited until he was told what to do next or until the Green Phantasm was brought to the designated spot again.

But in the meantime, the Green Phantasm was getting a closer and better view of the planes he had spotted moments earlier. He managed to perceive twelve rocket planes that looked just like the planes that had gained control and knocked him all around earlier. In fact, they were actually indeed the XTV500 planes of X-Termination. "Yep," said the Green Phantasm. "It's them all right. Let's see; what shall I'll try this time?" In his XTV500 rocket plane, the one called R-2 was saying to everyone else over the two-way radio, "Listen, everybody, I've already had the break I need. I'm tired of coasting around. I want some more action. For instance, I say we turn and fly northeast into the next town outside of Philly and we destroy all the buildings we can, and see if we can, I don't know, find something nice to claim and bring home. I'm anxious to see what we can do with these planes. What do y'all say? Anybody up to it? Anybody wanna go northeast and bombard the next city?"

"Sure, I'm up to it," replied I-2.

"Yeah, me too," answered I-3.

"I'm feeling up to it too," added F-2.

Then, R-2 finally asked R-1, "What do you say, R-1? Feeling up to some action?"

R-1 gave in and told R-2 over the radio, "Well, okay, why not? We've already gotten the job done. Besides, who knows? Doctor XT might become proud of us. So y'all ready to turn to the northeast and blast off?" Many of them responded in agreement. "Very good," said R-1, "let's go, now!" At that, all twelve of them turned their planes to their left until they were headed northeast. At once, they all began accelerating rapidly. However, they were not aware that they were not going to get very far.

The Green Phantasm was perched atop Independence Hall, and the twelve XTV500 planes were about a mile northeast of him, high above the Delaware River. The Green Phantasm was preparing to fire a big shot at one of them. "Let's see what this does," he said to himself. He was charging in preparation to unleash the largest, most powerful laser beam possible, which of course would combine the power of all ten fingers. He was aiming this beam at the plane of H-2, who of course was in the middle of the outer left of the pack.

So then, from Independence Hall, the Green Phantasm fired his colossal laser beam. Just as H-2 was beginning to pull away with everyone else, the beam smacked his plane on the left rear. This pushed the plane upward a few feet and turned it completely around, leaving H-2 face-to-face with H-3. The upward diagonal force of the beam had raised him slightly higher than H-3. This all took place before H-2 even knew what was happening.

Once H-2 was turned around, his XTV500 went on soaring southwest, in the opposite direction of the other eleven. As soon as H-2 began taking off in that direction, he destroyed H-3's plane in the process, although not intentionally. The top of H-3's XTV500 was torn up by the steel base of H-2's XTV500.

H-3 ducked forward just in time to avoid being hit or killed himself by the oncoming plane. Afterward, he looked up again and exclaimed,

"Hey, what the hell was that?" However, a lot of damage had been inflicted to the top of the fuselage of H-3's XTV500. The front windshield had completely shattered, and the cockpit's roof had completely ripped off and flown away. The top of the fuselage was completely stripped of its outer aluminum skin, and the vertical fin was even knocked off the rear. As far as internal damage, the tanks of fuel and X-Termination Acid had been impacted, and fluid had rapidly leaked out of the bottom.

Soon, the leaking fuel and acid was ignited by the plane's rocket engines, starting a fire that traced its way back to the big tanks. Momentarily, this triggered a major explosion. "Oh no!" cried H-3 when he knew that his plane was about to blow up. Then, all of a sudden, a gigantic spring below H-3's seat catapulted him out of his XTV500. It was an automatic ejection spring that was normally compressed underneath the seat but would automatically project the pilot out through an opening in the roof if something went wrong with the plane. This opening was made by a hidden pair of double doors that slid apart to come open. Also, the colossal coil spring had one end bound to the cockpit's floor and the other end attached to the bottom of the seat.

Whenever H-3 was ejected and falling toward the earth, he knew he would have to utilize his parachute. He opened it and continued descending slowly as he watched his XTV500 rocket plane disintegrate completely into smithereens. "Dang it!" he muttered in anger and frustration. "How the hell did all this happen? Why did H-2 do that to me?"

Very shortly after that, H-3 was getting ready to make his landing on Interstate 95, not too far northeast of downtown Philadelphia. The Philadelphia City Police had been observing his descent, and a few cars were headed north on Interstate 95 to meet him. Each car had two officers inside.

The X-Termination employee called H-1 had noticed the explosion in his rear display monitor. He turned his attention to it and then asked himself, "What was that? And where are H-2 and H-3? I don't see 'em. I hope that wasn't one or both of them that exploded." Immediately, H-1 signed on to the radio and said to all the other pilots, "Attention, this is H-1. We gotta slow down, everybody. Everyone, slow down, please. H-1 and the other nine that were still with him reduced thrust until they were all coasting slowly again.

At that, R-1 signed on and asked, "What is it, H-1? What's going on?"

"Well," H-1 began to answer. "I'm really worried about what I'm seeing in my rearview monitor. I mean, a moment ago, I hardly caught a glimpse of perhaps an explosion or something, and now, I don't see H-2 or H-3 behind me."

"Are you sure?" R-1 asked H-1.

"Absolutely," replied H-1. "I'm looking right in it, and I don't see either one of their planes behind me."

"Well then," said R-1, "let's have them tell us themselves."

In the meantime, H-3 was making his landing on the interstate. Upon touching ground, he found himself face-to-face with the police cars, which were stopping before him. Within a matter of seconds, they all got out of their cars and aimed their guns at him. "Put your hands up! You're under arrest!" shouted one of them. Seeing that he was outnumbered, H-3 just complied. Following that, all six police officers closed in on him and removed his parachute. One of them even put the handcuffs on him while another cop disarmed him. Finally, of course, H-3 was taken away to jail. As for the exploding XTV500 rocket plane, the debris from it landed about a quarter of a mile north of where H-3 had landed.

H-2 had been flying southwest above downtown Philadelphia. After a moment of flying by himself, he had looked up and around to discover that the other eleven were no longer grouped with him. However, he did realize either that the Green Phantasm had turned him around or that his XTV500 had damaged the top of H-3's. H-2 said to himself, "Geez, I wonder where everybody went. Oh well, I guess it doesn't matter too much now that we got the job done. I just don't know how or why they suddenly disappeared on me. But anyway, I guess I'll spend some leisure time alone until I'm told otherwise."

R-1 tried calling H-2 over the two-way radio. H-2 had been so caught up in his own little world for the past few moments that he was not paying attention to everything that H-1 and R-1 had been discussing. Soon, he heard R-1 trying to reach him. After R-1 tried a few times, H-2 signed on and said to him, "This is H-2; go ahead, R-1."

"H-2," said R-1. "H-1 tells me you're not behind him."

"Well," replied H-2. "Uh, no, I'm not. I mean, what happened to all of you? We were all together one minute, and now I find that I'm flying solo. Where'd y'all go?"

"Listen, H-2," R-1 told him. "Ten of us are still together. We're still heading northeast. But then, we slowed it down because H-1 said that you and H-3 aren't behind him anymore. Do you know anything about H-3?"

At that, H-2 slowed his plane and answered, "No, I don't."

"And another thing," added R-1. "H-1 also said a little something about a possible explosion behind him. Do you know anything about that?"

"I have no idea," H-2 answered.

For a couple of seconds, R-1 shook his head in confusion and then asked H-2, "So anyway, H-2, where are you right now?"

"Me?" H-2 replied. "Well, I'm—" H-2 cut himself off suddenly because he realized something. He was taking a look all around at his surroundings to discover that he was heading in the opposite direction after all. So H-2 told himself, "Oh God, I don't know how, but I did fly away from them after all, didn't I?"

Next, H-2 signed back onto the radio and continued addressing R-1, "Anyway, R-1, I don't know how, but I'm flying over South Philadelphia. I got the Delaware River to my far left, and I see the Philadelphia International Airport way up ahead."

"All right, H-2," R-1 said to him. "I don't know what kind of a stunt you're trying to pull, but you need to quit playing these games, turn your butt around, and get back here pronto. You got that? Now come on!"

In response, H-2 signed on and said, "Let me tell you something, R-1; I ain't tryin' to play no games, all right? I honestly don't know how I happened to go the other way; I just did! But look, I'm turning around, okay? Now quit accusing me, shut your stupid face, and keep it shut!" H-2 was no doubt infuriated by the way R-1 had accused him. However, he just turned his plane around and began soaring northeast to try to catch back up with everyone else.

R-1 became even angrier himself whenever H-2 mouthed off to him. However, he decided to set those feelings aside because he knew he had better things to tend to than quarreling with H-2. So R-1 just said to everyone, "All right, everyone, we've found out about H-2. Now, let's see about H-3." He tried to reach H-3 over the radio, saying, "H-3, come in please. Do you read me, huh? Can you hear me, H-3?" After that, R-1 tried a couple more times only to receive no response.

R-1 tried asking all of the other pilots, "Okay, does anyone else know what's going on with H-3, by any chance?" Most of the other XTV500 pilots only gave negative responses, for none of them knew. Other than H-3 himself, no other X-Termination member, not even H-2, knew that H-3's plane had exploded or that he had been arrested.

The Green Phantasm was trying to figure out how to stop the rest of the XTV500 rocket planes. He was still perched atop Independence Hall. The ten planes that were still together had now slowly moved a little farther northeast of downtown Philadelphia. The Green Phantasm was asking himself, "So, what kind of technique should I try this time?" He kept thinking of different abilities that he had until he came up with an idea.

"Say, I know what I'll try next," the Green Phantasm said. As he had been trying to think of something, he eventually remembered the method he had used Tuesday night whenever he had taken the form of a projectile, shot forward alongside a pickup truck, taken a U-turn as a projectile, and smashed through the truck's windshield. He decided to use the same sort of technique on one of the planes on the front row to get inside the cockpit.

The XTV500's were now a little over two miles northeast of the Phantasm. The Green Phantasm began preparing to teleport. Suddenly, he took on the form of a teleportation beam and traveled to his desired location. The Green Phantasm reappeared as himself about a hundred feet behind the pack of ten planes, but slightly to the left of I-1, I-2, and I-3. Of course, he was using his hovering ability to stay afloat.

Immediately, the Green Phantasm once again became a projectile and shot straight ahead. Finally, he took a U-turn to his right and wound up inside I-1's cockpit after crashing through the plane's windshield. This no doubt caught I-1 by complete surprise. He was too stunned to say or do anything.

At the same time, H-1 had barely noticed a flash of bright-green light coming from the far right of his field of vision. This caused his head to turn. "Whoa, what was that?" he asked himself. Then, he signed on to the radio and said, "Excuse me, R-1, this is H-1 here. I'm worried that we might be under attack. I just saw a big speck of bright light appear to my right and go away. At least I thought I did."

"Really!" said R-1 in reply. "Well, maybe we are. I don't know who or what, but after what's happened with H-2 and H-3 and what you might've just saw, we better stay on the lookout. So, everybody, keep your eyes peeled and keep watch in all possible directions."

Meanwhile, inside I-1's plane, the Green Phantasm was trying to persuade him to change his ways. "Look, I-1," the Phantasm said, "I know you don't believe it, but yes, it's me. I'm the Green Phantasm, and I'm gonna get right to the point. I don't know how long you've been with, uh, hmm, X-Termination? Well, anyway, I gotta tell you, it's a rotten way to live. You can't keep living a life like this. There's no real bright future in it. One day, you'll be sorry you killed all those innocent people. Are those really the kind of memories you want? Maybe you should think about that. Well, anyway, we gotta shut this thing down. Believe me, it's for the best."

But I-1 was too proud to listen. So, when the Green Phantasm turned around to look at all the buttons, controls, and instruments, I-1 pulled out his X-Termination Ray with his right hand. Fortunately, the Green Phantasm noticed in the nick of time. As soon as he noticed, he immediately used both hands to push I-1's right arm aside while keeping himself out of the line of fire from the X-Termination Ray.

During the struggle, I-1 managed to fire three shots. Although they did not hit the Green Phantasm, they still hit, disintegrated, and consumed most of the equipment in the cockpit. No instruments or gauges were left, and the control wheel fell to the floor. All this destruction caused the plane to stop running, and it began falling to the earth.

All this misfortune temporarily distracted I-1 from the Green Phantasm, who still knelt toward him in his lap. This allowed the Phantasm to take away his ray gun and throw it to the floor. "Oh no," I-1 whimpered to himself. This was because he now knew that his XTV500 was plummeting toward the earth.

At first, the Green Phantasm wondered what was wrong with I-1. But then, he too looked around and realized what was happening. At that, he told I-1, "Well, it looks like we'll have to jump ship."

In response, I-1 snapped, "I don't care! Just get out, you stupid freak!" Not having any other choice, the Green Phantasm just became a shapeless projectile and shot back out through the spot where the now-shattered windshield had once been. Afterward, I-1 jumped out as well and parachuted the rest of the way down.

Once I-1's XTV500 had begun falling, I-2 asked himself, "Hey, what happened to I-1?"

R-2 was wondering the same thing. I-2 and R-2 were no doubt surprised at the sudden unexpected disappearance of I-1 and his plane.

After having shot out of I-1's rocket plane, the Green Phantasm just reappeared above it as himself. While hovering in midair, he set his sights on the nine planes that were still cruising above him. I-1's broken-down XTV500 finally landed about a mile and a half east of Temple University. I-1 eventually landed nearby his plane, only to be arrested by the Philadelphia police. The Green Phantasm just teleported upward to reappear behind the remaining XTV500 rocket planes.

At the same time, one of the pilots was coming up behind the Green Phantasm. It was H-2, the one who had unintentionally flown off in the opposite direction earlier because the Green Phantasm had fired at him to turn him around. H-2 was now about to be within three-fourths of a mile of the rest of the pack after having soared all the way back. H-2 was able to recognize them, and he said to himself, "Good, it's them. Let me catch back up to them."

But then, H-2 noticed something. "Well, uh, I don't know if I'm seeing things correctly, but it looks like a couple of them are not there," said H-2. Then, he saw another thing that made him wonder. He asked himself, "Now, am I just hallucinating, or is something producing a flash of green light?"

Shortly after that, H-2 had drawn a quarter of a mile closer and was able to see everything more clearly. He even noticed that the bright-green light was in the form of a person, which could have only meant one thing. "Oh my God, I don't believe this," H-2 said shaking his head in disbelief. "I don't know how, but it's... it's the Green Phantasm, isn't it?"

H-2 also figured out something else. "You know something else?" he asked himself. "I betcha that punk's the one who done spun me around. I knew I hadn't done it. But anyway, it makes perfect sense now, and he's gonna pay for this."

H-2 advanced almost another fourth of a mile and noticed something else. "Well, it looks like something happened to a couple of them after all. I know they were looking for H-3, and now it looks like something happened to either H-1 or I-1 up front. But what the hell am I thinking? I bet the Green Phantasm did it. Oh well, it's time to make that neon creep pay. Here goes."

Upon making that determination, H-2 began preparing both ray guns and rocket bomb launchers. At the same time, he thought to himself, *Hopefully, he hasn't noticed me. So I'd better blast him before he does.* Very shortly, H-2 had his targeting system set on the Phantasm. He only had to unleash both streams of burning acid and two rocket bombs.

The Green Phantasm had been making preparations of his own. He was about to become a shapeless projectile, shoot forward, make a U-turn, and crash in on I-2. At once, H-2 pushed the necessary buttons and fired all of the shots from his plane. However, that was going to turn out unsuccessful for H-2 because the Green Phantasm was launching himself forward as well, as a radiating, shapeless, projected mass. Then, of course, as a projectile, the Green Phantasm began turning right and went on to complete a U-turn. Finally, of course, the Phantasm darted through and completely demolished I-2's windshield, after which he reappeared in his regular Green Phantasm form.

Although the Green Phantasm had made it into I-2's cockpit, neither he nor I-2 was going to get a chance to say or do anything to the other because I-2's XTV500 was about to blow up from the combination of fired shots that H-2 had intended for the Green Phantasm. One of the acid beams caused one of I-2's rear rocket engines to blow. Then, within the next couple of seconds, the two rocket bombs exploded; the one on the left completely blew up I-2's left wing, and the bomb to the right destroyed the plane's entire rear end.

These two explosions caused I-2 to be ejected from the cockpit. The Green Phantasm projected himself up and out of the plane too. Then, he hovered above the other planes, letting them pass under him as he began contemplating his next move. As for I-2, he went on to parachute toward the ground. Very shortly, one colossal explosion of I-2's XTV500 took place. The big interior tanks of fuel and acid that had both leaked fluid ended up catching on fire.

A very startled I-3 quickly veered to his left to get around the explosion that had taken place in front of him. "Holy shoot!" he yelled to himself.

This explosion also distracted R-2 and R-3, who abruptly looked to their left, asking, "Whoa, what was that?"

In the meantime, H-2 was now caught up with the other pilots again. He too had witnessed the explosion of the XTV500 of I-2. H-2 went on to say to himself, "Oh no, I didn't blow him up, did I? Well, hopefully, at least I got the Green Phantasm. I can't wait to tell them. I hope they'll be as proud of me as I am, heh, heh, heh." From there, H-2 just continued cruising with the other eight remaining planes. Unfortunately for I-2, he landed in a spot about a mile and a half north of where I-1 had landed. Of course, he was arrested too. The pieces of his blown-up plane had hit the ground in various places.

The Green Phantasm was now ready to crash in on another pilot. The XTV500's had passed him by about an eighth of a mile. However, the Green Phantasm now had his sight set on I-3's plane. So then, the Phantasm finally unleashed himself in his projectile form once again. Very shortly, he smashed through I-3's windshield to reappear inside the cockpit after having made another U-turn as a projectile.

I-3 was no doubt as shocked and surprised as I-1 and I-2 had been at the Green Phantasm's sudden breakthrough and appearance. "What!" cried the shocked I-3. "It can't be! No way!"

"Oh yes," replied the Green Phantasm. "It's me, the Green Phantasm. I presume you weren't expecting me, were you?"

I-3 went on to tell him, "So, you must be the one who just caused that plane to—"

"No, no, no," interrupted the Green Phantasm. "I did not blow up the plane in front of you, okay? I don't know how, but as soon as I busted into the cockpit, it just got blown up right on the spot. I have no idea who did it, but that's what happened."

"Yeah, right," I-3 replied sarcastically, refusing to believe him.

"I'm not lying, I-3," declared the Green Phantasm. "And I'm also not gonna lie about this. We need to shut down this plane." At that, I-3 shook his head in disbelief and disagreement, but the Green Phantasm went on to tell him, "Believe it or not, it's for the best. In fact, I'm about to do it right now."

He began reaching back with his left hand. Then, of course, as he was doing that, I-3 began reaching for his X-Termination Ray with his right hand. The Green Phantasm managed to perceive this, and suddenly, he put both hands up to stop I-3. Finally, the Phantasm took away I-3's ray gun and tossed it out of the plane through the opening from the shattered windshield.

The loss of his X-Termination Ray infuriated I-3. As a result, he began to throw a straight right punch toward the Phantasm. While doing so, he muttered, "Why, you son of a—"

Unfortunately for I-3, the Green Phantasm caught his fist. Then immediately, he retaliated with his own straight right that connected with the very center of I-3's chin. This snapped I-3's neck and rendered him unconscious. However, the Green Phantasm and the person within him, James Clifton, felt guilty. "Oh no," he said to himself sadly. "I didn't mean to do that."

The Green Phantasm turned around to try to figure out how to land and shut down the plane. James Clifton did not know very much about the operation of any kind of aircraft. So, as the Green Phantasm, he just kept randomly pressing buttons and pulling switches and levers until the XTV500 just stopped functioning altogether. Finally, of course, the plane just shut off and began falling toward the earth.

Once the fall had begun, the Green Phantasm grabbed the unconscious I-3 and jumped out of the plane with him. Then, the Phantasm activated his hovering ability to bring himself and I-3 down to the ground safely. I-3's rocket plane ended up making a crash landing about a half of a mile south of Allegheny Avenue, northeast of Dropsie University. But at last, the Green Phantasm brought I-3 down to the spot at which I-2 had just been apprehended by the police. Then, of course, the Phantasm handed I-3 over to them too.

In response, one of the police officers on the scene of the arrests of both I-2 and I-3 said, "Thank you, Green Phantasm, thank you."

In reply, the Green Phantasm said to them, "No problem. I just gotta try to stop those other planes."

"Be careful, Green Phantasm," another officer told him.

Next, the Green Phantasm teleported upward to reappear behind the eight XTV500 planes that were still cruising above. The one of them to which he was now contemplating putting a stop was the plane of H-2. H-2 was one of the only two pilots remaining on the far left of the pack;

the other was H-1. The Green Phantasm still did not know that H-2 was the one who had attempted to put him away just moments earlier, but instead destroyed I-2's plane. However, the Phantasm just began charging in preparation to become a shapeless projectile once again and crash in on H-2.

H-2 was still under the impression that he had destroyed the Green Phantasm. He was thinking to himself and trying to come up with a way to tell the others about his so-called accomplishment. "You know," H-2 said to himself, "I really wish there was some way I could tell everyone that I 'X-terminated' the Green Phantasm. I'm just afraid that if I tell them what really happened, they'll think I blew up I-2, or whoever exploded."

H-2 suddenly had an idea. "I know," he said happily. "I'll just tell everyone that after he spun me around, I shot at him and finally managed to blast him to smithereens. Yeah, that's what I'll do. That way, I get to be the one who 'X-terminated' the Green Phantasm." But of course, H-2 had another thing coming.

Before the eight rocket planes even came to be a couple hundred feet from the Green Phantasm, the valiant, determined, and radiant hero crashed in on H-2 as a neon-green projected mass. Of course, the Phantasm had shot straight past the right side of H-2 and taken a sudden U-turn to his left. Finally, of course, after crashing through and shattering the windshield, the Green Phantasm returned to his regular form.

What a tremendous shock this had to be for H-2. In fact, the thug was too stunned to finish saying anything. "No way!" he cried in panic. "It can't… it just can't… How can…? I thought, I mean, you're supposed to be— "

"Thought what, huh?" the Green Phantasm asked him. "What am I supposed to be? Destroyed? Blown to bits? Is that it?"

"Well…" H-2 slowly murmured.

"Well, what?" the Green Phantasm urged.

Still not knowing what to say, H-2 began to utter, "You see, it's just that, um, moments ago, I, uh…"

The Green Phantasm figured out one possibility. He said to H-2, "Wait a minute, what did you do moments ago? Was that you who blew up that other plane a few moments ago, by any chance? I mean, did you try to shoot at me and hit that plane instead?"

H-2 could not think of any other response, so he just replied, "Well, yeah, I guess so."

Nodding in agreement, the Green Phantasm told H-2, "I guess so too. That must be why it blew up once I busted in."

Unable to refute the Phantasm, H-2 just nodded and nervously said, "Yeah."

"Oh well, no matter," said the Green Phantasm. "I guess we're past all that now. What I gotta do now is shut down this plane and all the other ones too."

That caused H-2 to go from being afraid to being angry. "Oh, no, you don't!" he muttered at the Green Phantasm.

"Oh, yes, I do," the Green Phantasm said in reply. "And if you don't cooperate, you're going to jail just like the last guy I just got finished with. Now, tell me what to do to turn this off." However, nothing but silence came from H-2. So the Green Phantasm finally declared, "Fine, I'll just have to figure this out myself. Whether you know it or not, it's for the best. I promise you that."

This attempt at persuasion only made H-2 even angrier. So then, he reached down toward the right side of his belt to draw his X-Termination Ray as the Green Phantasm began turning around. But then, the Phantasm turned toward H-2 again and prevented him from taking the ray gun from its holder. Finally, the Green Phantasm took the X-Termination Ray from him and threw it out of the plane through the opening made by the shattered windshield.

As a result of that, H-2 really lost control of himself. While he was trying to deliver a big right jab, the Green Phantasm caught his right wrist and held it. "Why you—" H-2 growled as he then tried to throw a left hook. But the Green Phantasm pushed that attempted blow aside.

Finally, after all that, the Green Phantasm let go of H-2's right wrist to allow him another chance to be cooperative. However, H-2 just tried to hit the Green Phantasm with another big right jab. The Green Phantasm pushed that big blow aside and retaliated with his own straight right to H-2's chin, knocking the bad guy unconscious.

Next, the Green Phantasm decided to follow the procedure that he had used after punching out I-3. He just shut off H-2's plane, threw H-2 over his right shoulder, jumped out with him, and used his hovering ability to bring H-2 and himself down toward the ground. H-2's XTV500 crash-landed north of I-3's, close to Wyoming Avenue. The Green Phantasm brought the unconscious H-2 to the same spot he had brought I-3. Once again, the police thanked him and wished him well.

Not long after H-2's plane had begun falling, H-1 noticed that no planes were behind him any longer. So he signed on to the radio and said anxiously, "R-1, R-1, come in, R-1. Do you read me?"

"What is it, H-1?" replied R-1.

"Look, R-1," said H-1. "I'm really starting to think we are under attack. I still don't know what happened to H-3 earlier, and now, I don't see H-2 behind me either. I don't know what it is, but there's gotta be something that someone's trying to do to us."

"All right," R-1 told H-1. "Maybe you're right. Maybe there is. Let me see if I can call H-2 on the radio."

"Okay." H-1 sighed.

R-1 signed on and tried a few times to call H-2. But, of course, he received no answer. "Oh, dang it!" R-1 muttered to himself. "I think H-1's right. I know H-2 somehow went astray earlier, but I can't figure out where he is now. I don't know who or what it is either, but something's definitely going on here."

R-1 was absolutely right. Something was going on. That pack of rocket planes was now reduced from twelve to seven. They were nearly past the part of Philadelphia called Logan. The Green Phantasm was on his way to catch back up with them.

Eventually, the Green Phantasm came to be hovering almost a hundred feet behind the remaining seven planes. "So," he said to himself, "I wonder which one I'll try to stop next. You know, I might try something a little different now. After all, I got… what's that, seven? I guess there's seven planes left that need to be put out of commission, and I got to do it before they start going again to destroy the city."

Next, the Green Phantasm centered his attention on the plane being flown by R-3. He was floating behind R-3's left, getting ready to shoot himself into the cockpit as he had with many of the other XTV500's. "Here I go," declared the Phantasm, after which he unleashed himself once again as a shapeless projected mass of neon-green radiation. Then, of course, he shot straight ahead, made a U-turn to his right, and broke through R-3's windshield. The Phantasm was now face-to-face with R-3.

"What!" cried R-3. "No way, it can't be!"

"Oh yes," replied the Green Phantasm. "It's me all right. I'm the Green Phantasm."

Still unwilling to believe his eyes, R-3 went on to utter, "But… that's impossible. I thought you were, uh, I mean, you're supposed to be…"

But the Phantasm interrupted and said, "What, destroyed? Is that it?"

Too afraid to say much, R-3 began uttering, "Well, uh…"

But then, the Green Phantasm just told R-3, "Oh well, never mind that. I ain't got time for that. However, what matters now is that I gotta shut off this plane and all the others too."

"Oh no," argued R-3. "I don't think so. You got that wrong, you neon-green airhead." At that, R-3 began to try to draw his X-Termination Ray.

But, just as he had done previously, the Green Phantasm put a stop to this attempt. While doing so, he said to R-3, "Forget it, R-3. Don't even think about it." Then, of course, the Phantasm just took the gun away and tossed it out of the plane. "You won't be needing that anymore," he told R-3. "Not where you're going."

Of course, this infuriated R-3, as it had the other X-Termination members. R-3 began throwing a straight right punch while muttering, "Why you—"

But, also as before, the Green Phantasm caught and stopped his right arm. "Look, R-3," the Phantasm told him, "I don't have time to fight. Do you have a parachute?"

"Yeah, so what?" R-3 rudely replied.

"Good," said the Green Phantasm. "Just make sure to use it." Then all of a sudden, the Phantasm momentarily activated his invincibility. During that moment, he slung R-3 by his arm out through the opening from the shattered windshield. Consequently, R-3 fell from his plane toward the earth.

The Green Phantasm switched off his invincibility. That same moment, he peered down from the plane to make sure R-3 would be able to use his parachute. Very shortly, his parachute opened, and he continued his slow descent.

Next, the Green Phantasm looked around for any controls that could possibly activate the XTV500's artillery. Soon enough, he spotted two pistol-grip levers, one on each side of the seat. Each of them had a button on the front and one on the top. The Green Phantasm went on to grab hold of the two levers. He pressed the button at the front of each of them, which was like a trigger.

Pressing both buttons caused burning acid streams to be projected forward from both ray guns. One stream hit the rocket engine at the bottom right of the rear of R-2's plane, causing that engine to explode. The other stream of burning acid consumed a large portion of R-2's left wing. "Hey, what was that?" exclaimed R-2.

Next, the Green Phantasm compressed the big round buttons atop both levers. This caused both rocket bomb launchers to launch one bomb each. The two bombs hit both of R-2's rocket bomb launchers, leading to multiple explosions, which included the blowing up of both of R-2's wings, as well as each and every single rocket bomb.

R-2 got ejected through the roof of his plane. Shortly, he began falling toward the earth and ended up parachuting the rest of the way. As R-2 was descending slowly, one colossal explosion completely blew up his entire XTV500; the fuel and acid tanks had ignited.

At this humongous explosion, both F-2 and F-3 gasped in fear and veered off to their right to avoid being hit by debris. R-1 noticed the explosion in his rearview display monitor. "What the hell?" he exclaimed.

This even caused H-1 to turn his head to his right and mumble to himself, "Whoa, what was that?"

At the same time, the Green Phantasm was looking to avoid being impacted by the explosion. Once he noticed the great big explosion taking place, he immediately started trying anything he could to shut down R-3's XTV500. Under stress and despair, the Phantasm kept pressing every button and pulling every switch and lever he possibly could. Finally, the plane stopped running in time and began falling straight down. Of course, as it was falling, the Green Phantasm shot out of it and hovered in midair.

R-3 had ended up landing slightly north of Chew Avenue, and R-2 had hit the ground nearly a quarter of a mile north of him. Of course, nearby R-2, R-3's rocket plane landed, as well as the debris left over from his own blown-up plane. R-2 and R-3 were apprehended by the Philadelphia police, much as the previous five pilots had been.

Only five XTV500's were still coasting up above. They were the planes flown by H-1, R-1, F-1, F-2, and F-3. R-1 had come to realize that neither R-2 nor R-3 were behind him any longer. "What!" R-1 exclaimed. "Now, what happened? Let me make sure."

R-1 signed onto the two-way radio and made a few attempts to address R-2 and R-3. But of course, he received no response from either of them. He realized that something had happened to them too. This made R-1 more furious than ever. "That does it!" R-1 growled to himself. "I mean that really does it! Whoever that punk is that did all this, I dare him to show himself right now! I'm gonna make damn sure he pays for all this!"

The Green Phantasm teleported upward to reappear within a hundred feet behind the five rocket planes that were still in the air. He positioned himself to hover in a straight line behind R-1. One thing the Phantasm did not realize was that these XTV500's had display monitors that served as rearview mirrors. The Green Phantasm had now unintentionally disclosed himself to R-1, who spotted him in his monitor.

"Well, what do you know?" R-1 said to himself. "If it isn't the Green Phantasm! I don't know how, but it must've been him. I just thought Zapper and Zinger were gonna—oh, never mind. We just gotta waste this neon freak. We gotta 'X-terminate' him."

❦

Immediately, R-1 signed on and addressed his four remaining teammates over the radio, "This is R-1 calling; y'all read me?" The other four replied affirmatively. "Good," continued R-1. "I just found something out all right, and y'all won't believe it, but it's the Green Phantasm that's in our midst. I don't know what went wrong back at the site, but he's the one who took down a bunch of us. I just spotted him behind me."

Upon hearing this, H-1, F-1, F-2, and F-3 all had trouble believing their ears at first. However, they chose to accept what R-1 was telling them, for none of them could think of any other possibility behind all the sudden disappearances and strange happenings.

H-1 was thinking to himself, *So it's the Green Phantasm, is it? Is that so? Well, I thought for sure that Zapper and Zinger had him "X-terminated."*

I don't see what could've happened to them. But if R-1 says he saw him, then I guess it's true. He must still be at large. I just wonder where he is now. From the look of things, we gotta get that radioactive creep.

While F-3 was having similar thoughts, he was also saying to himself, "Well, I don't see the Green Phantasm. I wonder where he is." Although F-3 was not aware of it, he was just about to stop wondering.

Suddenly, the Green Phantasm crashed through F-3's windshield in his projectile form. F-3 went directly from a state of wonder to one of shock. After reappearing before F-3, the Green Phantasm told him, "Yes, it's me, F-3. I'm the Green Phantasm." F-3 was too stunned to reply. However, the Green Phantasm continued by saying, "Anyway, I'm gonna need you to get out of the way. I need to borrow your plane."

These words of the Green Phantasm made F-3 angry. He muttered, "I don't think so!" At the same time, he began drawing his X-Termination Ray. But before he could target the Phantasm, the gun was ripped away from him and thrown out of the plane.

Immediately, the now angrier F-3 threw a big straight right punch. But the Green Phantasm pushed that blow aside and countered with a right crossover to F-3's nose. The Phantasm did not punch extremely hard this time, only enough to daze F-3 slightly and make his nose bleed.

The good conscience of James Clifton moved him to ask F-3, "Are you all right?"

But F-3 just kept glaring at the Green Phantasm with no answer. The Green Phantasm could see that F-3 was still burning with anger and began to lecture him. "Look, F-3," said the Phantasm, "I know you're still mad, but it's only fair that I let you know something, all right? I honestly don't think you can take me, because I already punched out many of your teammates. Besides, you may not understand this either, but I gotta do this. It's for the best. So you'd best get out of here and parachute toward the ground."

F-3 went from looking angry to looking puzzled. He was no doubt very unsure of what to do, for he was between the devil and the deep blue sea. F-3 did not want to be hurt by the Green Phantasm or end up becoming "X-terminated" by his boss, Doctor XT. But then, the Green Phantasm yelled urgently, "Go on!" That made F-3 more afraid so that he obeyed the Green Phantasm.

The Green Phantasm then set his sights on the plane in front of him, which was being flown by F-2. While trying to aim for F-2's plane, the Green Phantasm was saying to himself, "Well, at least F-3 came to his senses. I wonder what F-3 means though. Is it Fool Number Three? I'd have to say that's what he is for working for X-Termination and for trying to help take me down. I wonder who that is in front of me. Is it Fool One and Fool Two by any chance?"

Next, the Green Phantasm tried to use the plane's control wheel to veer slightly right. However, he finally managed to move the XTV500 right by stepping on the right rudder pedal. Finally, the Phantasm got F-3's plane lined up so that the center of it was in line with the outer right of F-2's right wing. Then, all at once, the Green Phantasm unleashed a rocket bomb from the launcher on the left wing.

As a result, the entire rear of F-2's plane was blown up, causing F-2 to be ejected from the cockpit. He proceeded to parachute toward the earth. The first major explosion at the rear of F-2's plane led to an even bigger explosion that completely blew the XTV500 to smithereens. Fortunately for the Green Phantasm, he now knew how to steer an XTV500. So, whenever he noticed the explosion in front of him, he immediately steered around it to the right to avoid being impacted.

The Phantasm was not the only one whose attention was aroused by the explosion. The three remaining pilots out front sensed it as well, including F-1, who had seen F-2's plane explode in his rearview display monitor. At once, R-1 signed on and said over the two-way radio, "All right, what just happened? Did another one of our planes explode?"

"Yes, it did," replied F-1. "It was F-2's. I just saw it in my monitor."

"Oh, is that so?" said R-1. "Well, I guess the Green Phantasm did that; he must have. Well, that does it. We can't take any more of this mess. We gotta take that punk out. Let's 'X-terminate' him, all right?" At that, H-1 and F-1 each responded affirmatively.

Although the Green Phantasm was now positioned behind F-1, he had heard R-1 and F-1 talking over the radio. This somewhat worried the Phantasm, for he now knew that they were aware of his presence. "Oh no!" gasped the Green Phantasm. "They know it's me! Oh my God, what are they gonna do?"

R-1 delivered his next command. "All right, H-1 and F-1," he addressed them, "just do as I say, all right? We're gonna have to get back up to full speed. So let's start shooting forward until I tell y'all what to do next, okay?" H-1 and F-1 both gave affirmative responses to show that they had received and understood the message. At that, R-1 commanded them, "Okay, now!" At R-1's command, all three of them ceased cruising slowly and began soaring straight ahead.

In the meantime, both F-2 and F-3 had completed their descent toward the earth. They had landed just north of Philadelphia's city boundary, just north of the part of Philadelphia called Oak Lane. Otherwise, of course, pieces of debris from F-2's XTV500 had landed in various spots all around. Both F-2 and F-3 ended up being arrested.

Meanwhile, up above, the Green Phantasm was still flying the rocket plane that he had hijacked from F-3. While the remaining three pilots were beginning to pull away, the Phantasm suddenly had a thought. *Let's at least see if I can lighten the load.*

Next, he targeted the XTV500 in front of him, which was being flown by F-1. F-1 had not even advanced an entire mile when his plane was hit by a pair of rocket bombs that had been fired by the Green Phantasm. Each bomb completely blew up a wing on F-1's plane. That caused F-1 to be ejected from the cockpit, after which he parachuted toward the ground. Finally, shortly after F-1 began descending, the damage caused by the first two explosions of his plane's wings led to much more. Very much like what had taken place with a few other XTV500's, two trails of leaking fluid from the fuel and acid tanks were ignited, leading to a humongous explosion that blew F-1's XTV500 to smithereens.

The time was now approaching 8:30 p.m., and the Green Phantasm had only two XTV500's left with which to deal. Those two, of course, were the ones flown by H-1 and R-1. The Green Phantasm was still slowly cruising north in F-3's XTV500. Very shortly after the explosion of F-1's rocket plane, R-1 delivered his next command over the two-way radio. "All right, men," said R-1, "start preparing your artillery. We're about to turn around and open fire on the Green Phantasm. At my command, you're gonna turn around and start soaring back the way we came. Then, as soon as you spot that neon-green dimwit, start shooting at him at once. Y'all follow me so far?"

"Yes, sir, R-1, I follow you completely," H-1 answered proudly and affirmatively.

Of course, no response was received from F-1. However, R-1 was much more focused on taking down the Green Phantasm than on why F-1 was not responding. So, whenever R-1 and H-1 were about two and a half miles north of Philadelphia's city boundary, R-1 gave out his very next command. He said over the two-way radio, "All right, let's turn around now!" At that, R-1 and H-1 both began turning their XTV500's around, after which they once again began picking up speed while heading back south toward Philadelphia.

F-1 soon made his way to the ground. Even though he was outside Philadelphia, F-1 was apprehended by the police, much like his accomplices had been. Also, of course, various bits and pieces of his plane had fallen and scattered all around him.

The Green Phantasm was still slowly cruising north while inside what had been F-3's XTV500 rocket plane. It did not take long for R-1 and H-1 to spot it, for they did not even have to go back a whole mile. H-1 went on to say to R-1 over the radio, "Say, R-1, isn't that one of our planes up ahead?"

However, by the time H-1 had finished asking that, the plane had shut off and begun falling toward the earth. The Green Phantasm had shut it down as he had shut down some of the other XTV500's. So, before responding to H-1's question, R-1 said, "Slow it up, you guys, I think the Phantasm might've just done that."

H-1 decreased the throttle and slowed his XTV500 along with R-1. Then, R-1 answered H-1's question by telling him, "By the way, yes, H-1, that is one of our planes." After that, R-1 went on to say, "So, let's see what he's gonna do next."

The Green Phantasm had actually seen the oncoming planes of R-1 and H-1. In fact, that was the reason he had begun putting F-3's XTV500 out of commission. At the same time, the Phantasm was saying to himself, "Man, somehow or another, I just gotta stop those other two that are still left. But I don't know, I guess I'll have to get out of this plane to do it. Well, here we go."

Once the XTV500 had fallen over two-thirds of the way to the ground, the Green Phantasm maneuvered out of it. Of course, the Phantasm once again shot himself along a U-shaped path as a shapeless projectile. This time though, he shot forward, up, and backward to reappear hovering above the falling aircraft.

Immediately after, the Green Phantasm teleported and repositioned himself. He ended up floating in midair about a quarter of a mile behind H-1 and R-1. R-1 immediately noticed the Green Phantasm in his rearview display monitor. "I don't believe it!" R-1 muttered to himself. At that, he signed on to the two-way radio and said, "All right, men, we gotta get going at once. I'll explain; just speed up and keep heading south, now!"

"Ten-four," replied H-1.

R-1 did not know how the Green Phantasm had gone from taking down F-3's aircraft to floating behind them. But one thing R-1 was beginning to realize was that they could not maneuver their rocket planes as quickly as the Green Phantasm had just relocated himself. That was why R-1 had just decided to pull away and try a different strategy.

So next, while heading south back into Philadelphia, R-1 said over the radio, "Look, guys, the few of us who are left are obviously not gonna get him like that. So we're gonna try something else."

While H-1 was flying and waiting, R-1 suddenly said over the two-way radio, "All right, guys, let's start bombing this city. Just keep firing rocket bombs at will. Perhaps if by some chance, he gets hit, gets dazed, and tries to recover, we can blast him and 'X-terminate' him."

"Hey, no problem," replied H-1. At once, both R-1 and H-1 each unleashed two rocket bombs. However, none of the four bombs hurt anyone or destroyed anything because something had set them off before they'd made it too far. Both pilots made another attempt to fire rocket bombs. But, just as before, the four bombs exploded before getting very far. "That's weird," said H-1. "These bombs aren't destroying anything. Besides, they're exploding much too soon. I wonder why."

R-1 was thinking and wondering the very same thing, but all of a sudden, he wondered no more. He had managed to spot something in his rearview display monitor. It was none other than the one they were after, the Green Phantasm. R-1 then figured out something; he had overlooked the possibility moments before. As R-1 and H-1 had been soaring south above Philadelphia, the Green Phantasm had been repeatedly teleporting to follow them. In addition, the Phantasm had fired laser beams to connect with the rocket bombs and make them explode sooner. R-1 suddenly remembered the Green Phantasm having set off their rocket bombs much earlier when the twelve of them were still trying to gain control of him the first time. He now fully understood what was going on. So then, R-1 signed on immediately and began saying over the radio, "Wait, everyone! Hold your fire—"

However, R-1 delivered his command a little too late. He stopped himself from saying anything further because he heard an explosion. It was from H-1's plane. While R-1 was trying to deliver the command to stop firing rocket bombs, H-1 had already begun to release yet another pair of them. At the same time, the Green Phantasm had unleashed five simultaneous laser beams from his left hand. They had all been set by the Phantasm to travel forward under H-1's XTV500 and then out in front of it in order to distract H-1. But somehow, the laser beam to the far left just happened to come in contact with the rocket bomb that had just come out of the left launcher. It caused the bomb to explode and in turn also blew up H-1's entire left wing, as well as a little bit of the fuselage's left side.

This explosion took place while R-1 and H-1 were flying up above downtown Philadelphia. It led to H-1 being ejected from his plane so that he could parachute toward the ground. Shortly, R-1 noticed all this in his rearview display monitor. "Oh no!" cried R-1. "Please, not H-1!" As H-1 continued his descent, the rest of his rocket plane exploded into bits. "Nooooo!" yelled R-1 as he was slowing down his XTV500, approaching South Philadelphia. "No, no, no, no, no!"

In desperation, he signed on to try to reach F-1 over the radio. "F-1, F-1, come in, F-1," R-1 begged frantically. Although no response came from F-1, he signed on again and pleaded excitedly, "Do you hear me, F-1? H-1's plane just blew up! Would you just pick up the damn thing and answer me?"

R-1 still did not know that F-1's XTV500 had been taken down. However, he was just about to find that out for sure. "Oh geez!" R-1 muttered to himself. "I can't believe this; why won't he answer me?"

R-1 tried once again to get in touch with whomever he could over their two-way radio. "Come on," urged R-1. "Somebody talk to me over the radio! Is there any one of you still in flight?"

Receiving no response while continuing to coast into South Philadelphia, R-1 went on to try to take a good look for himself. He thoroughly checked the view behind himself. He even leaned forward and checked on both his left and right to see whether any other XTV500 rocket planes were still flying along with his. But of course, R-1 could not spot any of X-Termination's vehicles or employees. Seeing that he was the only one remaining out of the original twelve, R-1 became frightened and began to panic. "Oh no!" he cried. "What do I do now, man? What do I do about the Green Phantasm, huh? On top of that, what am I gonna say to Doctor XT? He'll… he'll kill me. Yeah, that's what he'll do. I just know it, man."

While R-1 was frantically looking all around in fear, his accomplice, H-1, was landing downtown. H-1 touched ground right around the intersection of Ridge Avenue and Vine Street. Upon landing, he was surrounded by several police officers who had appeared to come from nowhere. Of course, being outnumbered, H-1 had to give up and let them arrest him, especially since they were all holding him at gunpoint. Otherwise, of course, various parts and pieces of H-1's XTV500 scattered and landed all throughout the downtown area south of his arrest.

Meanwhile, X-Termination's gigantic premier associate D.D.T. had heard the explosion of H-1's plane from atop the building on which he was stationed. The sounds in the distance had caused him to begin turning around to his right to look all around for the source of it. "Yo, man, what was that?" big D.D.T. asked himself while looking around at what was up above.

D.D.T. focused his attention on something that caught his eye. He had managed to spot R-1's XTV500 rocket plane, which of course was still slowly cruising south of downtown Philadelphia. Upon seeing one of their rocket planes, D.D.T. was wondering why the twelve of them were not together. He had another idea, he hoped he was right. He suggested to himself that perhaps the twelve of them had destroyed the Green Phantasm, and they were now cruising around slowly and relaxing after all their hard work.

But then, not even a moment later, the colossal masked gargantuan found out it was something entirely different. He knew for sure that the Green Phantasm had not been "X-terminated" after all because he saw the Green Phantasm, who had teleported and reappeared hovering behind

R-1's XTV500. This caused D.D.T. to become much more afraid and to worry a lot more about the other eleven planes. "Oh no!" cried a panicking D.D.T. "This can't be happening, man! What'll I do?" The fear that had just overcome D.D.T. was definitely no big wonder, for this situation did not look good for X-Termination.

Anyhow, up above, the Green Phantasm proceeded to make his next move on X-Termination. From thirty feet behind R-1's plane, he once again took the form of a shapeless projectile. Then, of course, he shot himself out in front of R-1 and made a U-turn that ended inside R-1's cockpit after smashing through the windshield. Finally, of course, the Green Phantasm was kneeling face-to-face with X-Termination's R-1.

R-1 was much angrier than any other XTV500 pilot had been that night. This no doubt had to do with the fact that he was the only one of the original twelve who was still in flight. R-1 also knew that the Green Phantasm had had something to do with what had happened to the other eleven planes and their pilots. So R-1 was understandably more determined than ever to get even and make the Phantasm pay. "All right, that does it!" yelled a most infuriated R-1. "It's payback time for you, you despicable, disrespectful, retarded, radioactive freak!" Immediately after yelling all that out, R-1 pulled out his X-Termination Ray and aimed for the Green Phantasm.

But the Green Phantasm saw that he was about to be shot and knew he had to do something as quick as a flash. So he obeyed his first impulse and got himself out of the line of fire by quickly becoming a shapeless projectile and making a U-turn forward, left, and back to end up hovering behind the left side of the plane.

Inside the only remaining XTV500, R-1 was saying to himself with a little pride, "Well, at least that got him out of my plane. Let's just see what I'll do now." Although he was all alone in this airborne battle, R-1 was still determined to somehow destroy the Green Phantasm. As far as R-1 was concerned, this fight would not be over until it was over.

R-1 suddenly had another idea. "I know," he said to himself. "I'll use the ray guns to destroy the city instead of the bombs. I mean, I know he can't set that off like he can the bombs. Of course, while I'm destroying what I have to to get to him, I just need to watch out for the hiding places of Zapper, Zinger, and D.D.T." At that, R-1 began preparing to use both mounted ray guns and was about to increase the plane's throttle in order to begin soaring again. While getting ready, R-1 told himself, "After all, someone's gotta 'X-terminate' that neon creep, and if I gotta do it myself… well, here goes."

At the same time, the Green Phantasm was determined not to give up and quit either. So he was getting ready to make another attempt to hijack the XTV500 rocket plane of R-1. He had just mistakenly overlooked the possibility of R-1 drawing his X-Termination Ray. Regardless, he would be ready for that this time for certain. So then, the Green Phantasm charged himself up, and once again, in his projectile form, shot forward and made a U-turn. Finally, of course, he ended up in the cockpit, facing R-1 for a second time.

Fortunately, the Green Phantasm made it into the cockpit in the nick of time. Whenever the Phantasm reappeared as himself, the XTV500 had just begun flying south. Of course, on the other hand, this was rather unfortunate for the one called R-1 of X-Termination. "What!" screamed a very frustrated R-1. "You again!" Immediately, R-1 began reaching for his X-Termination Ray with his right hand. However, he had no luck this time, for the Green Phantasm stopped him, took away his ray gun, and threw it out of the plane.

The Green Phantasm was no doubt relieved that he had just disarmed R-1. But unfortunately for the valiant, determined hero, he overlooked yet one other possibility. As soon as the Phantasm had turned back around to resume being face-to-face with R-1, he was dazed and shocked because R-1 had thrown a right jab and landed his right fist between the Green Phantasm's nose and upper lip.

Although the Green Phantasm was stunned and surprised by that blow, he quickly managed to grasp what was happening. So, whenever R-1 tried to deliver a left hook, the Green Phantasm ducked to avoid it. Then, he had to dodge a right hook, which was followed by another left hook. Finally, as R-1 was trying to land a right jab, the Green Phantasm used his left hand to catch and hold R-1's right wrist.

While the Green Phantasm was still holding R-1's wrist, he attempted a left hook. But the Green Phantasm used his right hand to push that left hook aside and return the right jab that he had just received a moment before. This blow of course dazed R-1. So then mercifully, the Green

Phantasm released R-1's right wrist and asked him, "Hey, um, you all right, R-1?"

R-1 was too dizzy and groggy to respond. The Green Phantasm went on to say to him, "Look, I know you're mad right now, I realize that. But believe it or not, this is for the best. You can't keep living this kind of life."

R-1 recovered from his dizziness. All he felt like doing was glaring angrily at the Phantasm in silence. R-1 was too proud of himself and too angry to heed the words of the Green Phantasm. So he just kept trying to take out the Phantasm with more punches. The two of them just continued struggling and fighting as the XTV500 headed south-southwest.

Meanwhile, when D.D.T. noticed R-1's XTV500 continuing to fly off after the Green Phantasm had overtaken it, he decided to call someone over his handheld two-way radio. First, he tried several times to address Senior Lieutenant Zapper. Of course, D.D.T. received no reply whatsoever. Then, since he had had no luck reaching Zapper, he decided to settle for Zinger. But Zinger did not respond either. Both Zapper and Zinger were still being kept unconscious by a certain Amanda Taylor, who was determined not to let up on them and had also smashed their radios.

In addition to worrying about the only rocket plane of theirs that he could still see up above, D.D.T. also began to worry about Zapper and Zinger. He began to think that something must have happened to them—not only had they failed to "X-terminate" the Green Phantasm, but they also could not be reached over the radio. So finally, D.D.T. only knew of one other thing to do. It just so happened to be the last thing he had hoped to end up doing: he had to notify Doctor XT, who of course was back at X-Termination Headquarters.

Although D.D.T. was nervous and afraid, he changed his radio to the same channel as that of Doctor XT. Then, he signed on and said, "Excuse me, Doctor XT; come in please."

Hoping to hear great news, Doctor XT responded and said, "Yes, whatcha got, D.D.T.?"

"Look, man," D.D.T. answered his boss, "I'm afraid that there's a problem."

"What?" exclaimed an unbelieving Doctor XT. "A problem!"

"Yeah, man," D.D.T. replied. "I'm afraid so. I mean, for one thing, the Green Phantasm ain't been 'X-terminated' at all!"

"*What?*" Doctor XT yelled again over the radio as he became even angrier.

"And another thing," continued D.D.T. "I keep on trying to contact Zapper and Zinger, but they ain't answerin' me."

"They're not answering you?" exclaimed Doctor XT. "Are you just now finding this out?"

"Not exactly," D.D.T. answered.

Then, Doctor XT scolded him by yelling, "Why, D.D.T., you big lunkhead, why didn't you go check on them sooner?"

D.D.T. began uttering a response, "Well, I, I, uh— "

"Never mind!" yelled Doctor XT. "Get your ass over there right now, and see what's going on! And then, for their sake as well as yours, you sure as hell better have something good to tell me. Now get going, you great big galoot, *now!*"

"Right away, boss," D.D.T. responded as he started on his way. At once, D.D.T. began running as fast as he could down the stairs to get to the bottom of the office building on which he was stationed. While heading down the stairs, he put away his radio and put on a gas mask.

Meanwhile, the only remaining XTV500 rocket plane was now approaching the Philadelphia International Airport. The Green Phantasm and R-1 were still struggling. But then, the Green Phantasm finally landed a huge straight right on R-1's chin. As a result, R-1 nearly became unconscious and was seeing double.

Then, while R-1 was severely stunned by the punch, the Green Phantasm said to him, "Well, it looks like this is the end of the line, bud. I'm afraid I gotta do this. There's just no other way, man. I'm sorry."

R-1 was still too groggy to hear the Phantasm clearly. But thinking he had heard someone say something, R-1 began uttering, "Wait, uh, what, huh? What?" While R-1 was uttering those words, the Green Phantasm was pressing buttons, pulling levers, and flipping switches trying to shut off the plane. At last, the XTV500 stopped running.

It began falling toward the ground while up above the longest runway of the airport. At the same time, R-1 had now recovered from his dizzy spell. Still angry at the Green Phantasm, he began to say to him, "Why you—"

"It's too late for you," interrupted the Green Phantasm. "I'm afraid you're done for."

"Oh yeah?" replied R-1. But suddenly, he glanced outside and noticed that the plane was falling. At that, he gasped very loudly in fear for his life.

The Green Phantasm suddenly became a shapeless projectile and shot out of the plane. He projected forward, up, and back and ended up hovering above the falling XTV500. Finally, the Phantasm watched from above as the plane landed hard on the runway, with R-1 still inside.

Meanwhile, back on the new street, big D.D.T. had now made his way over to the X-Terminator 4000 that he had earlier parked outside of the building next door to the one out of which he had just run. While running, the huge man had pulled an X-Termination Gas bomb from his belt in case he felt the need to use it. Of course, that was also the same reason he had on his gas mask.

Next, D.D.T. opened the sliding door that was on the left side of the X-Terminator's cab. But before he had a chance to climb in, something unexpectedly occurred. All of a sudden, D.D.T. heard a voice shout, "Freeze!" Then at once, he turned completely around to find himself surrounded by six Philadelphia police officers. They had all suddenly appeared as if from nowhere, and they were all now holding him at gunpoint.

Big D.D.T. immediately extended both arms straight up. While doing that, he dropped the gas bomb from his right hand. The bomb fell to the ground and began emitting X-Termination Gas. Very shortly, the police officers began to collapse and die from inhalation of X-Termination Gas one at a time. D.D.T. just laughed at them all and said proudly to himself, "You see? Nobody can stop X-Termination, *nobody*. And you know what else, if there's somebody over there who did something to Zapper and Zinger, they gonna pay too." At that, D.D.T. just climbed into the X-Terminator 4000, shut the door, and began heading toward the bank building in which Zapper and Zinger had stationed themselves.

Meanwhile, the Green Phantasm was checking on the status of X-Termination's R-1. He soon discovered that R-1 had been knocked unconscious by the hard impact created by the XTV500's crash landing. James Clifton's good conscience caused him to begin feeling guilty about what he had just allowed to happen to R-1. He even began to wonder if this was right to do as the Green Phantasm.

Very shortly, the Green Phantasm noticed that airport security members were headed his way. He decided to let them take care of R-1, while he went on to tend to anyone or anything else that needed him. So the Green Phantasm activated his hovering ability and began gradually ascending straight up. While doing so, he watched a little longer to make certain that airport security had R-1 under control.

At the same time, D.D.T. had now pulled up and parked the X-Terminator 4000 in front of the bank building. Immediately, he opened the left sliding door, jumped out, and stormed toward the building's front doorway. Finally, once D.D.T. had made it to the top of the steps, he stopped to look over the building's interior. The monster-sized rogue absolutely refused to believe his eyes. The very thing he spotted was without a doubt nothing other than Zapper and Zinger being kept unconscious by a certain young lady who held a softball bat. Upon seeing this, he muttered to himself, "What? No way! This can't… man, this can't be…" Before saying anything else, big D.D.T. just emitted one big long growl.

Next, he stormed on in to stop the young woman, but suddenly remembered something. "Oh yeah, that's right," said D.D.T., as he stopped himself from entering. D.D.T. had just realized that he needed to notify Doctor XT of the situation. So then, he signed on to his radio and said, "Come in please, Doctor XT."

"What is it, D.D.T.?" Doctor XT replied.

"Listen, Doctor," D.D.T. said to him, "I'm just calling to let you know what's goin' on."

"Okay," responded Doctor XT. "So what's going on?"

"Look," D.D.T. began, "It's like this. What I just done seen is that Zapper and Zinger are both on the ground knocked out."

Before D.D.T. could continue, Doctor XT cut him off and exclaimed, "What! Knocked out! What do you mean, knocked out?"

"Well," answered D.D.T., "I don't know how, but there's this girl in there, and—"

"What!" Doctor XT yelled, interrupting D.D.T. again. "No freakin' way! God damn it, D.D.T.! There is no freakin' way in hell that you've been with me a hell of a lot longer than anyone else, and this is the best news you can give me!"

"Hey, look—" D.D.T. began to say.

However, Doctor XT was much too furious to let his premier associate say any more. "No, you look!" yelled the most infuriated doctor. "I have had it with each and every one of you! You've all really done it this time. That does it! I mean with fouling up such a simple foolproof game plan, that really does it! I'm coming over there right now! And, unless y'all can still do anything to better the situation before I get there, you three are gonna get it too. Well, good-bye, D.D.T.! I'll see you when I get there." At that, Doctor XT signed off and began storming out of his office toward the other X-Terminator 4000.

Immediately, D.D.T. growled and grunted in frustration. Then, he turned around and glared at the young woman who had evidently dropped in and attacked Zapper and Zinger. "I'll get her for this!" muttered big D.D.T. It was no wonder D.D.T. was angry with her. How could he not be? Amanda's actions were wrecking their entire scheme and also led to the trouble he was now in, along with all the rest of X-Termination.

So, D.D.T. entered through the doorway, drew his X-Termination Ray with his right hand, and pointed it at Amanda. While doing that, he hollered out, "Hey!" Amanda then turned around and gasped in surprise. "Yeah, that's right," continued D.D.T. "I'm talkin' to you, you little slut! Move away from them, now!" At that, Amanda submissively raised both hands while still holding the bat with her right. At the same time, she slowly walked toward the middle of the building's rear. D.D.T. began moving in and drawing closer to her.

Meanwhile, the Green Phantasm was now ready to move on from the airport because he had seen the unconscious R-1 being pulled from his plane. He also noticed a couple of city police cars driving up to the scene. So at last, the Green Phantasm charged himself, took the form of a shapeless projectile, and shot on toward the downtown area. He reappeared floating not too far south of downtown Philadelphia and near the same street on which he had been left by the rocket planes much earlier.

As he was still hovering high above the city, the Green Phantasm said to himself, "You know, I think that's the spot where those jerks dropped me off earlier. I just can't help wondering why they chose that particular spot. I mean, was there something weird going on there or something?"

It just so happened that on the inside of what was soon to be a bank, D.D.T. was now looking down at Amanda, with whom he was face-to-face. She was undoubtedly much afraid for her life, and she could not figure out what to do now. So she kept standing before D.D.T. with both hands in the air.

D.D.T. used his left hand to snatch the softball bat from Amanda and throw it out of the construction site altogether. "No!" screamed Amanda.

Immediately, D.D.T. fired his X-Termination Ray at the rear wall behind her. While doing so, he hollered, "Quiet!"

The burning acid from the ray gun made a very large hole in the wall. Amanda turned around to see it and then let out a very loud scream. She was no doubt terrified of what that blast could have done to her. While Amanda was screaming, big D.D.T. grabbed her left arm and told her, "I told you to be quiet! So you'd better, unless you wanna get it too!" Finally, when Amanda turned around to see the X-Termination Ray pointed at her, she ceased screaming and went into tears.

While all this was going on, the Green Phantasm was getting ready to teleport into downtown Philadelphia. But Amanda's screams reached him in the nick of time. So at once, the Green Phantasm stopped preparing to teleport and turned his head to the right, saying, "What was that? You know, it sounded like it came from… right around that same spot. Well, no time to lose; I gotta hurry up and find and help whoever's in trouble." At that, the Green Phantasm charged himself up and became a glowing neon-green projectile. Then, at lightning speed, he reappeared at the bottom of the steps that led up to the bank building's front doorway.

The Phantasm teleported from the bottom of the steps to the top. Almost immediately upon reaching the top of the steps, he spotted something going on inside the building. The first thing the Phantasm could see was X-Termination's D.D.T. backing away from the rear wall holding someone at gunpoint. "Hey, you!" the Green Phantasm shouted out.

"Say, what was that?" said big D.D.T. as he stopped backing up and began turning his head to look back. But while D.D.T. was turning his head around, the Green Phantasm fired a single laser beam that caused the huge thug to lose hold of his X-Termination Ray and drop it. "Hey!" yelled the surprised D.D.T.

The Green Phantasm said to him, "Yeah, that's right, you big buffoon, I'm talking to you. You'd better watch it with that thing, pal!"

While holding Amanda's right arm, D.D.T. turned himself completely around to see who was trying to confront him. That very moment, big

D.D.T. and Amanda both realized it was the sudden arrival of the one and only Green Phantasm. D.D.T. was too stunned to say or do anything for the moment. Amanda, on the other hand, was no doubt extremely relieved. She stopped crying and whispered to herself, "Thank God."

The Green Phantasm discovered for himself that it was Amanda Taylor who was in trouble. He began to say, "Oh no, Aman—" But he stopped himself so that she would not know his secret identity. However, the Green Phantasm proceeded to point to D.D.T. and tell him in a straightforward manner, "All right, unhand her, you big galoot, now!"

But D.D.T. just glared at the Phantasm and began raising his right fist. The Green Phantasm charged his entire left hand and unleashed a large, powerful laser beam that connected with D.D.T.'s chest and caused him to stumble back and away from Amanda. At that, the Green Phantasm turned to Amanda and said, "Hey, excuse me, uh, Miss, come get behind me." Amanda complied and ran toward the Green Phantasm. Finally, she ended up on the outside behind her hero.

Next, once D.D.T. was standing erect again, the Green Phantasm told him, "Look here, D.D.T., you stay away from her from now on; I mean that. Do you hear me?"

D.D.T. was too angry to answer. He just stormed toward the X-Termination Ray that he had dropped. But he did not make it all the way, because the Green Phantasm teleported to reappear standing between D.D.T and his weapon. "Oh, no, you don't," said the Phantasm to the shocked D.D.T.

Next, D.D.T. tried throwing a big straight right punch at the Phantasm. But he missed because the Green Phantasm had teleported to dodge it. The Green Phantasm then reappeared standing next to D.D.T.'s front right. At first, the huge masked villain muttered, "Where's he at?" Then all of a sudden, as D.D.T. turned to look to his right, the Green Phantasm grabbed his right arm and threw him to the ground. D.D.T. ended up lying faceup, stunned and dazed with his feet toward the unconscious Zapper and Zinger.

Shortly after taking down the massive titan, the Green Phantasm noticed the unconscious Zapper and Zinger, who were lying closer to the bank building's west wall. The Phantasm looked at them with wonder for a few seconds but then went on to his next move against D.D.T. The Green

Phantasm once again took the form of a teleportation beam. He ended up facing D.D.T. while standing at his feet.

Still dazed and confused, the supersized thug began sitting up. At the same time, he was looking around and wondering how he had gotten into that position. Then, D.D.T. suddenly noticed the Green Phantasm standing before him, which made him realize that it must have been the Green Phantasm who had set him down. "Oh, that does it!" big D.D.T. angrily muttered as he began reaching for one of the X-Termination Gas bombs on his belt.

But all of a sudden, the Green Phantasm zapped D.D.T.'s left hand with a single laser beam while telling him, "Don't even think about it."

At that, D.D.T. immediately became much angrier and began to get back up onto his feet. While doing so, he growled at the Green Phantasm, "Why you—"

Something else suddenly took place. Before he was aware of it, D.D.T. was being driven backward by a radiating projected mass. The Green Phantasm had transformed himself. Very shortly, the Phantasm rammed the great big scoundrel backward into the building's east wall.

This made D.D.T. much dizzier and groggier than he had been earlier. So, immediately after the extra hard impact with the wall, big D.D.T. just collapsed to the ground. He wound up sitting on his rear end with his back against the wall. He then continued to see practically nothing but hallucinations before his eyes. D.D.T. had no idea where he was at the moment.

"All right, pal," said the Green Phantasm, who was now standing before the monster-sized X-Termination official.

"Whoa, wait a minute, what the—" D.D.T. uttered while trying to recover from his dizzy spell.

"That's right, I'm talking to you, D.D.T.," the Green Phantasm said.

D.D.T. finally managed to recover his senses. At once, whenever he clearly saw the Green Phantasm, he began trying to get up again. While trying to rise, D.D.T. angrily muttered, "Oh, there you are. Now I'm gonna—"

But then, the Green Phantasm delivered a big side kick that set the huge villain back down. "Oh no, forget it," he said to D.D.T.

This made D.D.T. even angrier. So, right after the Phantasm sat him all the way back down, D.D.T. made another attempt to get to his feet again. This time, the Green Phantasm combined all five of the fingers of his right hand to fire a big, powerful laser beam at him. This forced him backward into the wall, after which he fell straight down onto his rear end again. The aggravated Green Phantasm delivered a side kick with his left foot to D.D.T.'s midsection. Then, he said firmly, "Did you hear me? I told you not to!" Upon saying that, the Green Phantasm delivered a big roundhouse kick to the villain's midsection.

D.D.T. was constantly grunting and groaning in pain while sitting against the wall. In addition, he was stunned and dazed from the blows he had just sustained and was holding both spots at which the Green Phantasm had kicked him.

Next, the Green Phantasm went on to say to big D.D.T., "You getting my message now, D.D.T.? *A*re you? Because you see, D.D.T., I don't think you want to try anything against me."

D.D.T. looked up at the Phantasm. He saw the Green Phantasm's right hand getting brighter as it was being charged and became afraid. "What are you gonna do to me, man?" D.D.T. asked in fear.

"Well, that all depends," the Green Phantasm began. "I don't want to hurt you, D.D.T. But after everything you've tried to do, the least you can do is cooperate with me."

"Oh, really?" replied D.D.T. "Well, what is it that you need me to do, man?"

"First of all," said the Green Phantasm. "I'll tell you what I think D.D.T. means. I don't know what your master meant it to mean, but to me it means dumb, dim-witted turkey."

That caused a look of surprise to come over D.D.T.'s face. No one had ever said anything like that to him before. Also, the big man was embarrassed at being told off in the presence of the girl he had tried to control a little earlier. Amanda Taylor began laughing to herself when the Green Phantasm insulted D.D.T.

"Yeah, that's right," continued the Phantasm. "That's what I think you are, for being a part of X-Termination and for going to work for, uh… what's his name? Is he, uh, Doctor XT or something?"

"Well, yeah," D.D.T. nervously answered.

"Anyway," said the Green Phantasm. "Are you ready to cooperate with me?"

"Okay," D.D.T. responded. "Just, uh, don't kill me. So what is it that you need from me, man?"

"That sounds better," the Green Phantasm replied. "Now, I want an explanation for all this. Perhaps you can tell me what's going on out here tonight. Earlier, I had a dozen planes trying to destroy me. Of course, at one point, they just happened to drop me off right in front of this building. I wonder if you would know anything about that. Would you?" D.D.T. went on to nod affirmatively.

"Oh, really? said the Green Phantasm. "And I would also like to know about what those two masked troublemakers are doing way back there," he said, pointing to Zapper and Zinger, "and how that young woman got caught up in all this. By the way, you'd better leave her alone from now on. You better not touch her or go near her ever again. Do you understand that?"

"Yes, I understand," D.D.T. answered.

"Good," the Green Phantasm said to him. "And now, start explaining everything to me."

"Well," D.D.T. began, "you see, we was trying to, um, destroy, that is, 'X-terminate' you."

"I figured that," said the Green Phantasm. "With the planes and everything, but keep going."

"Okay," D.D.T. continued. "You see, those planes done left you at the front of this here building, 'cause um, Zapper and Zinger over there was waiting behind that doorway to 'X-Terminate' you. You see what I'm saying?"

"Uh-huh," the Green Phantasm responded, nodding.

"But then somehow," added D.D.T., "you done got away, man."

"Okay," said the Green Phantasm to D.D.T. "So I got away. But there's two other things I'm trying to understand too. Now, if Zapper and Zinger were over at the doorway waiting to take me out, why are they now over there lying unconscious? On top of that, how did that girl get caught up in all this? Would you mind telling me that, please?"

"I don't know everything about that," D.D.T. said while trying to answer. "I guess that she must've used her bat to knock them out or something. I didn't see it, honest. All I saw when I came over was the two of them knocked out and her standing over them with her bat. I mean, who knows? I guess um…"

At that, the Green Phantasm decided he had heard enough about what had happened at that site and suddenly felt the need to find out something else. So he cut D.D.T. off by saying, "Enough, enough, all right? I now have something else I want to know even more."

"Oh yeah? What's that?" replied D.D.T.

"Let me tell you something, you dumb, dim-witted turkey!" the Green Phantasm scolded him. "You know what? Of every organization there is in the world, there's definitely one I know of for sure that needs to be shut down. That would be X-Termination, or whatever that sleazy commode is that's run by those crazed psychos and nutcases."

D.D.T. could not believe his ears. However, the Green Phantasm continued, "Anyway, it is now past the time to put y'all out of business like y'all need to be. The place you all belong is in jail. Someone's got to get y'all there if it's got to be me."

It was absolutely no wonder that big D.D.T. did not like what he was hearing. He finally made fists with both of his hands and began to raise them in a threatening manner—but not for long.

The Green Phantasm created an even more threatening gesture. The determined superhero lifted up both of his hands, charged them, and aimed all ten fingers at the masked gargantuan sitting before him. At the sight of that, D.D.T. once again became afraid. He lowered and unclenched his fists. Then, he put up his open hands in a submissive gesture.

The Green Phantasm went on to say to the great big titan, "All right now, I'm ready to get down to business. I'm sure y'all have a hideout or a headquarters somewhere, and you're gonna tell me where it is."

A look of great surprise came over D.D.T.'s face. However, the Green Phantasm continued by saying, "Yeah, that's right, D.D.T. I already took down all of y'all's planes and put them out of commission. So now, your facility is next. It's gonna get shut down too. Oh yes." The Green Phantasm continued charging both hands threateningly. Finally, he ordered D.D.T., "Now start talking." Apparently, the Green Phantasm was now getting his way with that gigantic, monstrous, masked behemoth. But unfortunately for the Phantasm, he would not remain in complete control for very long.

Just as D.D.T. was beginning to speak, another major unexpected event took place. All of a sudden, to the surprise of D.D.T., Amanda Taylor, and the Green Phantasm, the northwest corner of the bank building practically disintegrated. Understandably, this quickly turned the heads of the three individuals who were still conscious. The Green Phantasm was distracted from D.D.T. In turn, the Phantasm stopped charging his hands at the villain and asked himself, "What on earth caused that?" as he was looking wonderingly at the huge opening in the corner way behind him on his left. He was about to find out what the cause was.

What had burned the humongous hole in that corner was a stream of heated acid that had been fired from one of the ray guns of X-Termination's other X-Terminator 4000, which was being flown by none other than Doctor XT himself. Immediately after reducing a large portion of that corner to a few smoldering ashes, Doctor XT landed and parked the large aircraft not very far west of the building.

Then, the evil doctor leader of X-Termination entered through the opening he had created. At once, the Green Phantasm addressed him saying, "Oh, it's you, is it, Doctor XT?"

"Yep, that's right," replied Doctor XT. "So, we meet again, Green Phantasm."

The Green Phantasm said to him, "I should've known you'd be along."

"Oh, really?" said Doctor XT. "And what makes you say that?"

"That, I'm not quite sure about," answered the Green Phantasm. "But there's one thing I am sure about though. Just tell me, was this all your idea? You know, the way you all tried to destroy, or should I say 'X-terminate', me? Was it your idea? Was it?"

"Well, what do you know?" Doctor XT said in reply. "You figured that out, didn't you?"

At that, the Green Phantasm went on to tell XT, "Yeah, I guess I did, all right! And that idea of yours was a terrible idea! And you know what else? I'm gonna see to it that every one of your operations comes to a grinding halt. Someone needs to put you out of business, and from the look of things, I guess it's gonna have to be me. I'm not stopping until you're all put away in jail, just like all of your pilots, whose planes I shut down this evening. You get what I'm sayin'?"

While the Green Phantasm was saying all this, Doctor XT just stood in the center of the building, from which point he looked to his right at the unconscious Zapper and Zinger. Then, he turned and looked toward D.D.T., his premier associate, who was sitting against the building's east wall. At that, he shook his head in disbelief. But for some reason, Doctor XT was not responding to the Green Phantasm.

The impatient Green Phantasm teleported over to stand face-to-face with Doctor XT. Upon reappearing in that location, he shouted to Doctor XT, "Excuse me, Doctor. You hear me talking to you?" But Doctor XT still appeared to be ignoring him.

Doctor XT turned to his right until he was facing his senior and junior lieutenants, Zapper and Zinger. He looked down at the left side of his waist and began reaching for something that he kept in the left half of his utility belt.

Whenever the Green Phantasm saw him reaching under the left side of his coat for something, he yelled out to the corrupt doctor, "Oh no, Doctor XT! Don't you dare! You better not even point that thing in my direction! I'll be ready for you, believe me."

Doctor XT momentarily looked back at him and shook his head. Then, he said to the Phantasm, "Oh please, I'm not as stupid as you must think I am. To run a company like X-Termination, I can't be that stupid. Hell no." At that, XT just turned his attention back over to Zapper and Zinger.

After the villainous doctor turned back around, the Green Phantasm said something in retaliation. He told Doctor XT, "Actually, I think you are pretty stupid. I mean, to run that kind of company, especially with the kinds of intentions and desires that you have in mind, you gotta be one of the stupidest people I ever heard of, if you're not the absolute stupidest."

Somehow, those words seemed to go in one ear and out the other. That was because the doctor would not hold back any longer from what he was trying to do. Doctor XT drew his Mega Zapper 2000 with his left hand. He programmed it quickly and fired two surges of electricity separately at Zapper and Zinger. This caused both lieutenants to begin regaining consciousness. "What's going on here?" said Zapper.

Zinger started groaning and then uttered, "Ah man, what… what happened, man? What's… um, what's happening now?"

"Zapper! Zinger!" Doctor XT hollered out to them. They both turned to look at him. "That's right," he continued. "It's me." Zapper and Zinger looked all around to try to figure out what was going on. However, Doctor XT commanded them, "All right, you two, put your masks on, now!" XT was referring to their gas masks. D.D.T. still had his gas mask on.

While all this was going on, the Green Phantasm decided to try a different strategy. Once again, he took the form of a teleportation beam. This time, he placed himself at the building's front doorway on the north wall. As soon as the Phantasm made it there, he charged and prepared both hands as he put them up and out in front of himself. He then said to all four of the bad guys at the site, "All right now, you all better hold it and listen up!" This definitely grabbed the attention of Zapper, Zinger, and D.D.T., who all turned and looked directly at the Green Phantasm. "Look here, you guys," said the Phantasm. "None of you better try anything against me. I am charged and ready, and I know y'all have seen what I can do. That was last night, I believe. So, if you don't want to get hurt, you better not try anything; I mean nothing whatsoever, nothing."

Zapper, Zinger, and D.D.T. all looked around at each other, nodding in agreement. Then, they all began raising their hands as if they were submitting to the Green Phantasm. He looked around at them nodding in approval, for he appreciated their cooperation.

However, Doctor XT was not in compliance with the Phantasm, unlike his three officials who were still down on the ground in submission. Doctor XT had his back turned toward the Green Phantasm, and he had just put away his Mega Zapper 2000. But then, the Green Phantasm went on to say to the mad doctor, "I'm talking to you too, Doctor XT! You better turn yourself around, pal."

Doctor XT looked back at the Green Phantasm with a hideous smirk on his face. At once, he said, "Well, if you say so, Green Phantasm." He began turning himself around while apparently putting his hands up submissively like his accomplices. Finally, as soon as XT was facing the Green Phantasm directly, he dropped something to the ground from his right hand. The Green Phantasm looked down at the feet of Doctor XT to see what the object was.

Doctor XT had just dropped an X-Termination Gas bomb. While putting away his Mega Zapper 2000, he had also taken out a gas bomb and set it to go off. The bomb began rapidly unleashing X-Termination Gas once it hit the ground. Whenever the Green Phantasm noticed this, he gasped in fear and began trying to figure out what to do next. Doctor XT was laughing very hard and went on to put on his gas mask too. Zapper, Zinger, and D.D.T. began taking down their hands and looked around at each other with all of their thumbs up, for the Green Phantasm had now lost control of them.

The Green Phantasm was still looking all around trying to come up with another tactic against X-Termination. But the light-purple mist of X-Termination Gas continued expanding, eventually hiding Doctor XT and his three men. "Dang it! It's too late!" muttered the frustrated Green Phantasm, for he could no longer see the bad guys.

The Green Phantasm heard Amanda call out, "Green Phantasm!"

Upon hearing this, he looked back over his left shoulder at Amanda and said, "Oh shoot, that's right! I gotta get Amanda outta here." At that, he teleported over to where she was standing. She was at the bottom of the building's front steps. The Phantasm ended up standing to the immediate left of her.

"Well, hi, Green Phantasm," said Amanda. "I'm Amanda, Amanda Taylor."

"Hi, Amanda," replied the Green Phantasm. "Um, listen; I uh, I gotta get us outta here, okay?"

"Okay," said Amanda. "That sounds great. I'm just glad you're here."

"No problem," the Green Phantasm replied. "But listen; I'm about to put a force field around us, so watch your feet. And grab on to me too, because I'm rising up off the ground." At that, he began emitting neon-green beams from all ten fingers to sketch and form the outer layer of the force field. When Amanda noticed this, she climbed up onto the Phantasm and secured herself with her arms and legs around him. Then, the Green Phantasm began utilizing his hovering ability to slowly ascend straight up. Finally, of course, the Green Phantasm completed the force field.

He continued to float away from the site while inside the force field with Amanda. "We need to get away from this place," he told her. "I mean, it's just not safe to be here right now. It sure is a good thing I have this force field to protect us from, you know, X-Termination and that light-purple gas of theirs."

"Mm-hmm," Amanda murmured in agreement while nodding. "I just want to thank you so much for saving me," she told the Phantasm.

"You're welcome," the Green Phantasm responded. "Let's go somewhere else besides here." From that point, they just drifted away.

Doctor XT came out of the bank building followed by Zapper, Zinger, and D.D.T. Very shortly, XT spotted the Green Phantasm, who was hovering up above, along with Amanda. "Well, well," he said. "So there goes the Green Phantasm, huh? And I wonder what that girl's doing with him." At that, he turned to his three men and asked, "Do any of you blockheads know anything about that? Do you?"

"Actually, I think we do," answered Zapper.

"Yeah," said Zinger. "You see, that girl that's with him just happened to drop in on us and give us a surprise attack while we were waiting for the Phantasm to be dropped off here."

"She did?" asked Doctor XT. "Well, just how did she know y'all were in here?"

"Oh, I don't know," Zinger answered. "But for a few seconds, I looked outside the front doorway to—"

"You did!" cried Doctor XT. "Well, no wonder she knew! She saw you poking your head out! And another thing, where are all my XTV500 rocket planes and the men who were flying them?"

"I can answer that," D.D.T. responded. "It's like, the Green Phantasm, he done took them down."

"He did!" hollered out Doctor XT. "Just how do you know this?"

"Well," D.D.T. began answering. "First, I saw the last one or two go down. And the Green Phantasm told me."

"He did?" asked Doctor XT.

"Yeah, he did," replied D.D.T. "That was when he came in here to confront me."

The infuriated Doctor XT, said, "Why didn't..." But he could not bear to continue. Doctor XT was furious with everyone within his organization. The ones with whom he was angriest were the twelve individuals who had piloted the twelve XTV500 rocket planes because they did not manage to recapture the Green Phantasm regardless of how much they had outnumbered him.

Doctor XT told his three masked high-ranking officials, "That's it; the three of you just get in your ship, and get your asses back to headquarters. We gotta get our men outta jail and get all our equipment back. Just get back to the facility, now!" After saying that, Doctor XT jumped into the X-Terminator 4000 in which he had come, started it up, and went soaring back toward X-Termination Headquarters. Zapper, Zinger, and D.D.T. all got into the other X-Terminator and followed behind Doctor XT, with Zinger as the pilot.

It was now after 9:00 p.m. Still inside the force field with Amanda, the Green Phantasm was now descending in front of the Museum of Art in Fairmount Park. Once he made it to the ground, he said to her, "Well, I guess I can take this thing off now," referring to his force field.

He told Amanda, who was still holding on to him, "Just watch yourself, okay? I'm uh, fixing to take down this force field."

"All right," replied Amanda. So all at once, the Green Phantasm spread all ten fingers and began retracting the outer layer of the globular force field. Then, as the force field began fading, it took the form of ten narrow beams that were being reabsorbed through the Phantasm's fingers. Finally, before long, the force field was gone entirely.

"Oh man. What a night it's been for me," said the Green Phantasm.

"Yeah, I'll bet," Amanda responded. "I'll never forget it either."

"Really? Well, I guess not," the Green Phantasm said in to her. Then, he went on to say, "But anyway, I was just wondering another thing. Exactly what happened at that construction site tonight? I mean, I saw Zapper and Zinger knocked out in the far right corner. Other than that, big D.D.T. said that you had a bat, and he suggested that you'd supposedly knocked them out or something. Just how did all that come about anyway?"

"Well," Amanda began. "It all started when I was driving down the main street. Then, I saw one of them looking out of the building, and I saw you getting shot around by all those planes. So I stopped and ran up to the site to see what was going on."

"You did what?" said the Green Phantasm.

"Look," she told him. "I did that because I recognized that guy from the party last night; you know, when those bad guys crashed the party looking for you. Then, I saw you being driven that way. That's why I went over to investigate."

"Yeah, perhaps," the Green Phantasm said. "But, Amanda, you could've gotten yourself killed. Did you realize that when you went over there?"

"But, Green Phantasm," she pleaded. "I was just looking out for you. Then, when I found out what they were trying to do to you, I just couldn't let them do it. Please don't be mad at me, please."

"Amanda, look," he said calmly. "I'm not mad, okay?" After that, he just kept shaking his head, not knowing what to say or do next.

Amanda put both of her hands on the Phantasm's right forearm and asked him very sweetly, "What's wrong, Green Phantasm?"

"Look," he answered. "I appreciate you looking out for me. I just never would've forgiven myself if you'd have gotten hurt, killed, or whatever, you know? Can't you understand that?"

"Yeah, I can," she replied, looking away. "But if I'd have let Zapper and Zinger annihilate you, I couldn't have lived with myself either. Besides, you saved me in the subway Sunday night, and you saved us all at the party last night. I just couldn't forget you for that. Other than that, I thought it was unfair the way they were all just ganging up on you like that. I just couldn't leave you alone to face all them. I just thought I owed it to you to help you."

"I see," said the Green Phantasm, nodding. Then, he told Amanda, "Well, I guess I can't blame you for being worried for me the way I was for you. Other than that, I do appreciate so very, very much how you stood up for me. I just need to explain one other thing."

"What's that?" Amanda asked him.

At that, he put his hands on her shoulders. "Listen, Amanda," he said. "It probably is a real shame what they're trying to do. I agree completely as to how horrible it is what intentions they have against so many innocent people as well as me. I know they're out trying to destroy me. But now that you've gotten in the way of the game plan they had tonight, they may come looking for you too."

"Oh my," she softly exclaimed. "I'm really sorry."

The Green Phantasm took hold of her hands and told her kindly, "Amanda, please, it'll all be okay. I mean, hopefully it will be."

At that, she said, "Well, I just didn't mean to cause a problem."

"I know, I know," the Green Phantasm replied. "I just gotta find them before they find you or me. They just gotta be stopped."

"Anything I can do?" asked Amanda.

"Well," the Green Phantasm began, "all I can say is, just don't go anywhere you don't have to. Once you get off work, that's if you work anywhere, just go straight home and stay there."

"But, Green Phantasm…" Amanda begged him.

"Amanda, please," he told her. "Those guys are out looking for me. I mean, from what you saw tonight and last night, can't you see that?"

"Well, yeah," Amanda answered.

"Look," continued the Phantasm. "Somehow or another, I intend to put those freaks away in prison, where they need to be. But until then, they will eliminate, destroy, and completely devastate anyone or anything that gets in their way. Until either myself or someone finally shuts down their business, no one around here is safe. So, if there's anywhere outside this city you can stay, I suggest you go there. You don't think they know your name, do you?"

"Well, I didn't tell them my name. At least I don't remember," Amanda responded.

"I guess that's good," said the Green Phantasm. "Hopefully, they don't know it."

Then, Amanda put both of her hands behind the Green Phantasm's shoulders and said to him very sweetly, "Well, at least I finally got to meet you."

"Yeah, I guess you did," he said, putting his hands down by his sides.

She affectionately ran her left index finger under the Green Phantasm's chin and then began running her open left hand up his right cheek. While doing so, she told him even more softly, "Now that I've gotten to meet you, I want to get to know you some more."

"Really?" the Green Phantasm replied nervously. "Well, all right."

Amanda lifted up the Phantasm's green hat. Upon removing the hat, she looked confused. She thought his haircut looked familiar.

"What's wrong?" he asked.

"Well," Amanda began. "Um, I… I don't know. It's just that, well, you, uh, kind of you kind of remind me of someone." Although Amanda could not quite remember, the person she was trying to think of was undoubtedly James Clifton. Of course, she was probably too upset with James to want to think about him. However, she finally said, "Oh, never mind," and placed the Green Phantasm's hat back on his head.

She said to her hero, "Excuse me, Green Phantasm?"

"Yes, Amanda?" replied the Green Phantasm.

Then, she asked him kindly, "Would you mind turning off your green light for a little while; that's if you can, would you, please?"

At that, he answered hesitantly, "Well, uh, all right, sure, I guess so."

"Thank you," she replied happily. At that, Clifton switched off his neon-green radiation but remained in his Green Phantasm outfit. Then suddenly, Amanda drew even closer to him, put her arms over his shoulders, and said as sweetly as ever, "Oh, my hero." She began kissing her hero all over his face. She was evidently in love with the Green Phantasm.

However, James Clifton was not sure how to think or feel about that. He enjoyed receiving all the attention, sweetness, and affection from the young woman he loved, even if it was as the Green Phantasm. He no doubt found the experience to be rewarding after the long, hard fight he had just had against the forces of X-Termination. While continuing to kiss the valiant superhero, Amanda began running her hands gently and smoothly all over his body.

Even as much as James loved and enjoyed this, something was troubling him. Not only was Clifton worried that X-Termination was still at large, but he was also concerned that Amanda was into him as the Green Phantasm and not James Clifton. She still did not know that Clifton and the Green Phantasm were one and the same. He did not want to tell her that yet because, even as upset as Amanda possibly still was with James Clifton for apparently abandoning her the night before, he was determined to straighten everything out between her and himself as James Clifton.

However, he finally decided to put those thoughts aside for the remainder of the evening and enjoy the company of Amanda Taylor. Very shortly, he placed his hands on Amanda's shoulders and began exchanging kisses with her. From that point, they continued to hang out in Fairmount Park for a while. Eventually, the Green Phantasm brought Amanda back to her Ford Explorer, where they finally gave each other a good-night kiss and parted company. Amanda went to her home, and James used his super powers for one last thing. As the Green Phantasm, Clifton got himself back home and into his bedroom. Finally, he teleported out of his Green

Phantasm suit, switched off the pyxorium within himself, showered, and ate something before going to bed for the night. That finally concluded the evening of X-Termination's aerial attack.

CHAPTER NINE

The Search for Amanda

It was now after 11:00 p.m. on Thursday night. Anselm Nielsen was arriving back at X-Termination Headquarters in the stretch limousine with the twelve X-Termination members he had just broken out of jail. They were without a doubt the very ones who had flown the XTV500 rocket planes in the attempt to annihilate the Green Phantasm. But of course, their attempt had failed. So now, they were back at headquarters to find out what Doctor XT would say or do.

Anselm parked the limousine just left of the double doors that served as the front entrance. He got out and let the twelve passengers out. After that, he shut the door. Finally, Nielsen ordered them, "Follow me."

Next, big Anselm Nielsen led the twelve X-Termination employees to the double glass doors. Once there, he unlocked and opened both sets. At once, Nielsen pointed to the inside of the doors, saying, "Right this way, guys, and go to the manufacturing area. The boss wants to see y'all." So then, all twelve of them walked on through the doors in random order but single file. After that, they all turned left and walked on toward the manufacturing area. At last, Anselm Nielsen just relocked both sets of double doors, after which he followed everyone to the manufacturing area.

Meanwhile, Doctor XT was waiting in the control room with Zapper and Zinger. Shortly, everyone Nielsen had bailed out and brought back to headquarters entered through the manufacturing area's east side. Before too long, Zinger noticed something and said to his two bosses, "Hey, excuse me."

"What is it, Zinger?" asked Doctor XT.

Then, pointing toward everyone, Zinger answered, "Look over there. It looks like Nielsen brought everybody back."

At once, Doctor XT and Zapper turned and looked in the direction in which Zinger was pointing. "Nice observation, Zinger," said Zapper.

"Yeah, not bad, not bad," replied Doctor XT. But next, XT commanded Zapper and Zinger, "Well all right, men, let's go take care of this piece of business." In reply to that, Zapper snickered briefly, for he knew what they were about to do.

Doctor XT addressed Zinger, saying, "Now, Zinger, you will go around to the other side of them with D.D.T. Other than that, I'm pretty sure you know what to do."

"Well, uh…" replied Zinger, who could not continue speaking, for he was not quite certain as to what XT had in mind.

"Zinger, you fool," reproached Zapper. "Don't you get it? We're about to force them all into the X-Termination Acid, and you and D.D.T. will take control from the other side!"

"All right, all right," Doctor XT told them. "Knock it off, you guys; let's move it." So Zapper and Zinger followed Doctor XT out of the control room.

Anselm Nielsen had just made it into the manufacturing area behind the entire X-Termination crew. Next, he called out to them, shouting, "Hey, guys!" At that, they paused, turned around, and gave him their attention. Then, pointing to his left, Nielsen commanded them, "Go up those stairs to the left, to the balcony above." In response, they all murmured affirmatively to show that they understood.

Everyone went over to the staircase located in the southwest corner of the manufacturing area. Then of course, they all began marching up the steps. They were all no doubt wondering what was going to happen next. Some began asking questions. For instance, I-2 said, "I wonder what the doctor's fixin' to say or do to us."

"I don't know," replied H-2.

"Well," said H-1. "I guess we're about to find out."

"Quiet!" yelled Anselm Nielsen. "Shut up! Just keep it movin'." So everyone just proceeded on up the steps with Nielsen following behind.

Then very shortly, many of the X-Termination members had made the right turn at the top of the staircase and were walking along the west side of the big steel barrier. Up ahead, of course, they could not see much other than the oncoming trio of Doctor XT, Zapper, and Zinger. All three of them had very serious-looking facial expressions. This intimidated some of the crew members. A really worried F-2 whispered to a few other fellow workers, "I don't know about this."

"Me neither," whispered F-3.

"Me neither," whispered R-2.

Then, in a lowered voice, R-1 said to them, "Hey, guys, just hold your horses. We don't know anything yet. Let's just see what Doctor XT tells us, all right?" At that, the others became silent again.

Momentarily, Doctor XT and his two lieutenants stopped a few yards from the platform leading to the X-Termination vat from the balcony. Then suddenly, XT put out his right hand to signal everyone to halt before him. As a result, of course, everyone complied. In turn, Anselm Nielsen stopped behind all twelve of the X-Termination employees.

But next, Doctor XT whispered to Zinger, who was behind him, "All right, Zinger, go take your place."

"Take my place?" he replied. "Why, sure, yes, sir, boss."

"That's it," Zapper happily told Zinger. "Just be ready to draw your ray gun, you know what I mean?"

"Got it!" Zinger answered in a very enthusiastic and affirmative manner. So at that, he went over and stood to Anselm Nielsen's left and was now facing both Doctor XT and Zapper.

Doctor XT and his top three officials were now looking at the group of crew members with serious, earnest looks on their faces. Everyone stationed on the inside of the leaders was no doubt feeling really tense and was very worried about what trouble they might be in. As a result, none of them knew what to say, so they remained completely silent as they all kept looking back and forth between the two pairs of officials who were stationed on both ends.

Finally, within the next minute, Doctor XT addressed them by saying, "All right, everybody." At that, all twelve made complete eye contact with Doctor XT. He continued, "I presume you all know why I've called you here at this time."

"Well, uh…" uttered a rather puzzled I-3.

"Just let me think for a minute," replied H-3.

But then, the one called R-2 sounded somewhat more certain than those two. He said, "Now look, I don't know this for sure, but I do believe that—"

Before R-2 could continue, R-1 took over to finish his statement. "Yeah, yeah," he said very affirmatively, "I know what you're about to say. You're saying you believe that it's about what happened with our aerial attack, where we were supposed to take down the Green Phantasm." After that, R-1 began looking around at all of his associates and asked all of them, "Don't you all think that that's probably what he wants us here for right now?"

In response to that, all of the other crew members began looking around at one another, nodding in agreement and saying, "Yeah."

"All right," Doctor XT told them all. "Enough!" At that, everyone turned their undivided attention back over to XT. Then all at once, Doctor XT began speaking to his entire staff. He started out by saying, "Okay, listen up, you good-for-nothing screw-ups."

Upon hearing that, all of the X-Termination workers developed surprised looks on their faces. They all looked around at one another. Some even said, "What! What's he saying? What's he mean by that?"

The murmuring suddenly came to a stop at the command of two of X-Termination's top officials. "Silence, everyone!" Zapper yelled at the top of his lungs.

"Yeah!" Zinger hollered out in agreement. "Shut up, everybody!" They all became silent again, but they were still somewhat shocked from suddenly being called good-for-nothing screw-ups.

"Thank you, Zapper and Zinger," Doctor XT said before continuing. He went on to tell his crew, "Anyway, as I was about to say, all you losers have no idea what you've put me through tonight. I have just lost a whole, whole bunch of money on the twelve of you, and you've all put my organization in jeopardy. Is there any explanation at all?"

Right away, the twelve crew members began conferring in order to try to figure out what to tell Doctor XT. I-2 asked, "So, what are we supposed to do now?"

"That's what I'm wondering," said I-1. "Are we supposed to tell him what happened?"

"Well, I can't think of another way," said H-1.

"All right," R-1 finally told everyone else, "that's what we'll do. We'll tell him everything. Now. Do y'all need me to do the talking?"

"That's perfectly okay with me," said F-3 without hesitation.

"Me too," said F-2.

"Have at it, R-1," H-3 told him.

"Okay then," R-1 declared. "Here I go." He turned to address XT, saying, "So anyway, Doctor…"

"Yes, R-1?" replied Doctor XT, eager for an explanation.

"It's like this," R-1 began. "You see, at first, we obtained control of the Green Phantasm, and we had him under control, all twelve of us."

"All right," said Doctor XT. "So if you had him within your control, what happened? How the heck did everything go wrong?"

"Well," replied R-1. "That's what I was fixing to get to. You see, Zapper had a plan that he went over with all of us. Although that Phantasm was inside a force field, we still got him where Zapper wanted, so he and Zinger could, you know, 'X-terminate' him. But unfortunately, they somehow never managed to."

"Never managed to?" asked Doctor XT, as he shot an angry look at Zapper, Zinger, and Anselm Nielsen. But then, he turned his attention back to R-1 and asked, "So then, what happened?"

"Well," R-1 started again. "Whenever Zapper and Zinger didn't 'X-terminate' him, he, uh, came after us. Other than that, I don't really know what to say, except that the second time around, he just turned out to be much too nimble for us. I mean, the Green Phantasm just outmaneuvered the XTV500 rocket plane. We've just never ever before dealt with anyone or anything the likes of him. I mean, he just—"

"That's enough!" scolded Doctor XT. "Just cut the crap! Cut it! You know, there's no way you all could not have regained control of him. After all, from what you said, y'all did it the first time. Besides, there's only one of him and twelve of you. Oh, this makes a lot of sense, it really does." He shook his head in disbelief.

After a couple of moments, Doctor XT resumed. He said to his crew, "You know something? All twelve of you numbskulls not only fouled up on such a simple, foolproof assignment, but you have also put the entire organization of X-Termination in major jeopardy. I mean, you derelicts got arrested and got put in jail. There's no telling who all has now found out about X-Termination, you know, like who we are and where we're located. I pay you all exceedingly well, and this is what I get?" At that, he scoffed and once again shook his head in disbelief.

But then, R-1 spoke up and said, "Excuse me, Doctor."

"What is it, R-1?" the angry doctor snapped. "What do you want?"

"Well, you see, Doctor," said R-1, "I just want to assure you that I never told anyone anything about us, not a soul."

"I never said a word about us to anyone either," declared I-1.

"Neither did I," said H-1.

"Me neither," said F-1. "I mean, none of us did. Ain't that right, everybody? We never told anybody anything, did we?"

"No," the eight others answered in unison, while they all shook their heads as well.

"Oh really!" replied Doctor XT. "You're quite sure of that, eh? Well, that's a relief."

I-2 said, "And we're not gonna tell anyone any secrets either, are we?"

"Of course not," answered F-2.

"You know something, Doctor?" said H-1 to Doctor XT. "We're definitely not gonna let anyone find anything out now. We're also not going to court over this. One reason for that is that we're now out of jail. Oh, and I wanna thank Anselm, or D.D.T. there, for getting us out, and I wanna thank you too, Doctor. That wouldn't have been possible if it weren't for you." Upon hearing that, big Anselm Nielsen chuckled.

"But anyway, Doctor," continued H-1, "at least now, we're back where we belong. Now, no one's gonna take us alive. We're not gonna mess up again."

At hearing that, Doctor XT smiled and said, "Well, I trust y'all won't. I'm gonna see to it that nothing ever goes wrong with y'all again."

"Thanks a lot, Doctor," F-3 told him.

"Yeah," said F-2 in agreement. "Thank you so much, Doctor XT."

But then, for reasons unknown to them, Zapper began laughing at what F-2 and F-3 had just said. Zinger and Nielsen also started chuckling. Upon noticing that, R-2 said to his teammate R-1, "Say, R-1, why do you suppose Zapper, Zinger, and, uh, D.D.T. are all laughing? Is there like a hidden meaning or something to what XT done told us, I mean, you know, like a part he omitted?"

"You know," responded R-1. "You've got a point there. I thought it sounded too good to be true. You might be right, R-2. Something about all this does seem peculiar."

The laughter among the three top officials subsided. R-1 and R-2 stopped mumbling along with everyone else. Doctor XT continued with his plan. "Well, well, well," he said to his crew, "you all seem surprisingly grateful and appreciative. It's really great to see that. I'm hoping you still will be grateful after the next phase."

"Hmph, next phase?" asked I-1 wonderingly.

"Well, what do you know?" R-1 asked himself. "There's something peculiar after all."

"All right, men," Doctor XT said to his top three officials, "this is our cue. Let's do it." So at once, Doctor XT, Zapper, and Zinger all took out their X-Termination Rays. Everyone was now at gunpoint. They were all in a state of panic, not knowing what to do. It was no wonder Axtel, Jarrett, and Nielsen had been laughing, for they had known what XT had really been planning.

I-3 and F-3 decided to try one last resort. They tried going to big Anselm Nielsen for a possible way out. Out of desperation, F-3 begged the big man, "Please, big guy, could you please let us by real quick?"

"Yeah," said I-3, "if you let us go, we'll—"

"Forget it," Nielsen told them. "You go nowhere." At that, Nielsen used both hands to push them back into the crowd. Following that, Anselm Nielsen just removed his fedora hat, trench coat, and sunglasses, tossing them behind him onto the balcony's floor. Then, he put on his D.D.T. mask, once again assuming his guise as the one and only D.D.T. of X-Termination. Finally, he drew his X-Termination Ray, so that he too took part in holding everyone at gunpoint.

At the same time, many of them had questions rolling around inside their heads. The one called H-3 even said, "What is going on here?"

"Yeah," said R-2, "Why are you doing this to us, Doctor XT?"

"Ah, shut up," snapped Doctor XT. "Who are you kidding? Did you really think I'd let y'all get away with that? Off course not! Y'all just lost me a fortune on equipment, and y'all couldn't even carry out a simple assignment. So what do I need you all for, huh?" As a result, everyone looked around at one another, not knowing what to say.

Doctor XT went on to say to them, "Also, not only are all you losers no use to me, but now, you could even bring down my company and ruin me. I know you all said you wouldn't divulge any secrets, but I can't take any chances on that. So there's only one other solution."

Next, Doctor XT looked around at Zapper, Zinger, and D.D.T., saying to them, "All right, men, are you three ready? Let's do it!" Immediately, XT shouted to the twelve crew members, "Everybody, move on in! To the acid vat, now!" Many of the X-Termination members began slowly walking along the platform toward the X-Termination Acid vat.

However, in the midst of all the commotion, I-1 tried to entreat Zapper so he could possibly be excused. He desperately begged, "Please, Mister Zapper, is there any way you can—"

"Forget it!" yelled Zapper. "Keep it moving! Just do what the doctor says!"

"Yeah, that's right," Zinger told them. "Now get moving! Whether it's the acid vat or the ray gun, y'all are gonna get it either way. Now get a move on!"

So then, everyone continued walking toward the middle of the X-Termination Acid vat. Then, shortly, not knowing what else to do, each and every condemned X-Termination member just stepped off the platform's end and plunged into the acid. The result was always a surge of vapor, which was all that the X-Termination Acid would leave of each individual.

Then at last, it came time for R-1, one of the toughest and cleverest members, to take his turn plummeting into the X-Termination Acid. He was now standing at the very end of the platform with the vat of acid before him. Behind R-1 was the quartet of Doctor XT, Zapper, Zinger, and D.D.T., who were all still pointing their ray guns his way. Before simply taking the plunge, R-1 decided to try one more time to talk his way out of getting "X-terminated."

R-1 turned around to face the four people he had always obeyed ever since joining X-Termination. From left to right clockwise, he could now see Zinger, D.D.T., Doctor XT, and finally Zapper. He began entreating them, saying, "Listen, I know you've already 'X-terminated' everyone else. I mean, I guess you had to. But I just wanna say one last thing. I've been loyal for quite some time. I was even with y'all when we all disrupted and crashed that party. I just messed up tonight. Is there any way I can get another chance, huh? Is there anything at all that I can do?"

R-1 was not the type to easily give up hope, for he at least had the guts to make one final plea. But would that really make Doctor XT change his mind?

As much as the words of R-1 might have made some people think twice, they had no effect on Doctor XT. He was too corrupt and depraved even to pay a single piece of mind to what R-1 had said. XT could only think of what he desired for himself, and he was still fuming about the loss of all the XTV500 planes—an incident in which R-1 had been involved. Doctor XT heartlessly replied, "Forget it! You're no good to me! Now get it over with!"

Finally, R-1 just stepped backward toward the end of the platform. Then of course, he fell backward off the end and plunged into the X-Termination Acid. Doctor XT and his three highest-ranked associates looked on as the twelfth and final blast of vapor rose up from the X-Termination Acid.

Zinger said, "Well, I guess that's the end of that." Zapper and D.D.T. just nodded in agreement.

But next, Doctor XT told the trio, "Well, anyway, now that that's out of the way, I need to see you all in the control room." He went back onto the balcony and stepped back to the south side of the platform. He then extended his left arm and index finger, pointing toward the control room beyond the gas chamber. Right away, he commanded this high-ranking trio, "Control room now! Get going!"

Upon hearing that, Zapper, Zinger, and D.D.T. turned around to see their master pointing north. Zapper told Zinger and D.D.T., "Well, come on, you two; let's go." At once, Zapper began walking toward the control room with Zinger and D.D.T. right behind him. Doctor XT followed the three of them. All four of them just kept walking until they finally got into the control room.

Once Doctor XT entered the room, he addressed his three men, "Attention, you guys. Listen up!" They all turned around and gave XT their attention. Right away, he said to them, "Now look, you guys, I know that the other twelve did not carry out their part, so therefore, we have now 'X-terminated' those derelicts. But now, I need to hear your side of the story. I wanna know what happened on your end of the deal. What else went wrong? Why did the Phantasm not get 'X-terminated'? Come on now! Somebody needs to talk to me."

Zapper immediately said to his colleagues, "All right, you two, I got this." He turned to XT and began his explanation. "You see, boss, it's like this: We had the Green Phantasm right where we wanted. We had him beaten. But something else unexpected took place that wasn't very likely at all. A young lady came from behind and knocked out Zinger and me with a bat."

Doctor XT asked, "Was it the same lady who was at the scene when I got there?"

"That would be her," he answered, "but all that happened there was, Zinger and I were just focused on what we were trying to take out, which of course was the Green Phantasm. We just should've paid more attention to what was around us as well. We still would've been able to take him."

"Well," said Doctor XT, "at least I can discern two things from what you just said. First of all, maybe those twelve idiots weren't fast enough for y'all. Second of all, that girl had no business interfering. Nobody crosses X-Termination and gets away with it. I say she has some accountability as well. At least I find what happened between you and Zinger more justifiable than those other twelve, who, for some reason, couldn't regain control of just one Green Phantasm. It's not like anybody else dropped in on them."

But then, big D.D.T. spoke up and said, "Yo, excuse me, Doctor."

"What is it, D.D.T.?" XT asked him.

"Well," D.D.T. said. "I feel like I owe you an explanation as well."

"Oh, you do?" asked Doctor XT, curiously.

"Yeah," he answered. "You see, I made sure to do my part, by letting Zapper and Zinger know when the Green Phantasm was in place. I even told them when to fire. When the Phantasm started getting away, I even let them know then what was going on. But all the times I called them and alerted them on the radio, they never even responded; I didn't know why. I figured maybe they were too busy. But eventually, I realized that something could really be wrong. Perhaps I should've acted much sooner. So maybe it's my fault too."

"Well," said Doctor XT, "considering everything else we've just been over, I'll tell y'all what I'm gonna do. I'm going to give the three of you one last chance to bring down the Green Phantasm. But we also need to find this young lady, whoever she is. She put her nose into our business and fouled up our scheme. Therefore, she must go down too, agreed?"

"Yeah," Zapper, Zinger, and D.D.T. replied in unison, nodding in agreement.

"And another thing," Doctor XT added, "it might also be possible that y'all could do better without those twelve other screw-ups who are evidently no good to us. That's another reason that I'm giving y'all this final chance, to verify that."

"Oh yeah," replied Zinger. "Thank you, Doctor XT."

"Hold it," Doctor XT told them. "There's one more thing I should tell you. There is one catch to this. This has to be done by a certain time."

"Oh, it does, eh?" said Zapper.

"That's right," said Doctor XT. "You have two nights to get it done. It is Thursday night now, so you have until midnight Saturday night. By then, I want both the Green Phantasm and this girl found, captured, and 'X-terminated.' I don't want to say or hear any more now. Just notify me when you've caught at least one of them. After all, they seem close to each other. Abducting one of them should lead you to the other one with no problem. But in the meantime, just figure out a way and get it done. Right now, I've got to get back to work. I suggest you three get right on it. If I hear nothing by midnight Saturday night, you three are going down too. Now go!" At that, Doctor XT just walked past them to his office and shut the door.

"Well, you heard him, men," Zapper said to D.D.T. and Zinger. "Let's do it! Come with me, and we'll figure out a game plan." At that, Zapper walked out of the control room, with the other two following behind.

Next morning, at close to 7:00 a.m., James Clifton got up for another day of work at Ace Nuclear Supply. Of course, it was Friday. Somehow, the day started out for James Clifton like another ordinary day. He had breakfast and got dressed and ready for work like usual. Finally, he drove to Ace and reported for work at about 8:00 a.m.

As usual, shortly after walking through the front door, James stopped to talk briefly with the receptionist, Jenna Daniels. "Good morning, Jenna," he addressed her.

"Good morning, Mr. Clifton," she replied.

"So," Clifton continued, "is everything okay after last night? I was just hoping that you weren't too affected by all those planes that attacked the city last night."

"Oh, I'm fine, thank you," Jenna told him. "I thought I heard about one house that got destroyed, but at least it wasn't ours."

"Well, that's good," said James.

"Besides," Jenna continued. "There could've been a lot more damage if it weren't for the one I think we should all be thankful to."

"Really?" asked James. "And who would that be?"

"Haven't you heard?" she asked, somewhat surprised. "The Green Phantasm. Isn't it a good thing he interfered? He saved a lot of lives and prevented too much further damage."

"Oh, of course, him," answered James. "Why didn't I think of that, and especially considering that I'm a close friend of his?"

"You're friends with the Green Phantasm?" Jenna asked curiously.

"I sure am," Clifton answered most affirmatively.

"Wow!" This amazed Jenna. "Could I possibly meet him sometime?"

"I'll see what I can do," answered James. "But right now, I gotta get to my office. You take care, okay?"

"You too," she responded.

From that point forward, James Clifton just went about his job at Ace Nuclear Supply like he had always done on every ordinary day of work. Soon, it was getting close to 5:00 p.m. and time for James to leave work for the day. Since it was Friday, it would have been for the weekend as well. So, at about 5:00 p.m., James said to himself, "Well, I guess that wraps up another week of work. I guess I'll just head for home if nothing else." He walked on out to his truck, like he had always done at the end of the day.

Suddenly, before getting too far into the parking lot, James heard his cellular phone ringing. He stopped walking and answered it. "Hello?" said James into his phone.

"Hey, James, how's it going?" said Eric Thomas.

"Oh, hi, Eric," James replied. "What's up, buddy? What's going on?"

"Not too much, James," Eric answered. "At least it's Friday, and I just got through wrapping up another week of work."

"Well, I won't argue with that, because me too," James told his friend.

"But anyway, James," said Eric, "I was just kinda wondering another thing."

"What's that?" asked James.

"I guess you're aware of the planes that soared through Philadelphia last night?" Eric asked.

"Well, yeah, am I ever!" replied James.

"So," Eric said, "the thing I was wondering is, did anything happen to you by any chance?"

"Well," he began, having to think for a few seconds about how to talk around his involvement as the Green Phantasm, "at least I can honestly say, I definitely did not lose anything from it. Thank you for asking."

"Oh, no problem," Eric replied. "But still, I just can't help wondering, who'd be crazy enough to try to pull a stunt like that?"

"I think I know who," James told him.

"Oh, really?" asked Eric. "Well, who do you think?"

"X-Termination," James answered. "Don't you remember? That's the exact same group of psychos who had the nerve to crash the party Wednesday night. You don't think that could've been them?"

"You know," Eric responded, "you could be right. That makes more crazy stunts I've seen this week than I ever had in years. But fortunately, just like Wednesday night, the Green Phantasm was there. Good thing too, because whoever those creeps think they are, they need to be stopped. Don't you agree?"

James did not hesitate to answer, "I couldn't possibly agree more."

"Well, okay then," Eric said. "But James, I just wanted to ask you another thing."

"Okay," replied James. "What is it?"

"Well," Eric began to say. "Scott's about to meet up with me, and we're going over to that pub called Big J's Bar and Grill on Lombard Street. I was wondering if there was any way that you could meet us there. What do you say, James?"

"Well, I suppose I could," James answered slowly, trying to think about it. "I was about to just head home." But then, he suddenly realized that he could not see any reason why he should not. So, more enthusiastically, he told his friend, "Forget all that. Why not?"

"Great!" exclaimed Eric, who sounded delighted.

"I'll see y'all there," James declared. "I'll get there when I can."

"Thank you so much, James," Eric said happily. "I'll see you in a little bit."

"Okay, bye, Eric."

"Bye, James." They both hung up.

James went over to his Suburban and got into it. At once, he began heading over to Big J's Bar and Grill, where he would hang out with Scott and Eric. At about 5:40 p.m., James parked across the street from the pub. He then went around to the parking meter to put in coins.

But as James was completing this task, something briefly caught his eye. Standing out among everyone else walking along the sidewalk was a group of three men who were all wearing trench coats, fedora hats, and sunglasses. One walked behind the other two; he was a black man, a foot taller, and much bigger than even the second biggest of the trio. The two who were in front of him were white men. The one at the front right looked Italian and was just a little bigger and taller than the one on his left.

At the moment, this threesome was walking on past James Clifton. As they were passing him, he stared at them as though they were unusual. He said to himself, "Now that's something you don't see every day; three men in a group dressed like that. Another thing too is, that the real big one looks about seven feet tall. Something about them just makes me wonder what they're up to. I also even wonder if they're undercover in disguise." James could not believe his eyes, so he shook his head in disbelief.

James immediately received another distraction. A voice called out to him, "James! James, over here!" At that, he took his eyes off the three men and began looking around to try to find whoever was calling his name. The same voice hollered out his name again. This time, the source of the voice added, "Look behind you! We're right across the street from you!"

James complied and looked straight across the street. At once, he found out who had been calling out to him. It was Eric and Scott. They were now waving to him so he would recognize them. "Oh!" called out a relieved James Clifton. "It's you guys! Hold on; I'll be right there!"

James began carefully walking across Lombard Street, looking out for traffic. He finally made it to the other side and happily greeted both Eric and Scott. "Hey, Eric! Hey, Scott! How you guys doing, huh?" he said while shaking hands with them.

"So, James," said Scott, "whatcha been up to since Wednesday night, huh?"

"Well, Scott," James responded, "work's been just the usual. I'm just glad I made it through last night, you know, whenever X-Termination made that aerial attack in all those rocket planes."

"Is that who that was?" asked Scott. "How do you know that?"

"Scott, please," said Eric, "give James a break. He might have other things on his mind." Then Eric turned his attention to James and asked him, "Oh, and speaking of that, if you don't mind me asking, how's Amanda doing?"

"Well, Eric," James began, "she should be okay. I'm pretty sure she made it through last night. I mean, that's what I believe chances are. She just thinks I'm a jerk, because she believes I abandoned her on Wednesday night."

"No way!" said Scott.

"I'm sure you didn't really abandon her," Eric said.

"Of course I didn't," replied James. "I'm just not too sure what to do now."

"Don't worry, James," soothed Eric. "You'll figure something out."

"Yeah," said Scott. "Of course you will."

"Well, anyway," James finally said, "I guess let's go inside. Shall we?"

"Okay," said Eric. So all three friends began to make their way inside.

But shortly, something else caught James's attention. He heard the screaming of a young lady in trouble. He stopped, looked back to his right, and saw what was going on. One of those men in a fedora and trench coat, whom he had seen walk by him moments before, the biggest of the three, was using both of his hands to hold up a young woman with short blond hair. In the big man's clutches, she was squirming, trying to free herself while screaming, "Let go of me! What are you trying to do to me?"

But then, the Italian-looking one said to his partner, "No, no, put her down. That's not her."

The big black man complied. Afterward, he said to the woman, "Yo, sorry, miss; we made a mistake."

"Yeah," said the smallest of the three men, "we thought you were someone else; we're terribly sorry." But the young lady just scoffed at them and stormed away.

The Italian guy told the other two, "Come on; let's keep moving." So they continued walking.

James did not like what he was seeing. He decided to try to get a closer view and possibly see what he could find out about those three.

While James was still looking back to his right, Scott called out to him, "Hey, James, are you coming?"

At that, he briefly turned to Scott and said, "Yeah, I am, just go on ahead. I gotta go back across the street real quick. I'll be right back. All right?"

"All right," answered Eric, who proceeded on into Big J's Bar and Grill, along with Scott.

James began running to try to catch up to the odd-looking trio, who were now a little over two hundred feet ahead of where he had first watched them pass by him. While James was running, he said to himself, "You know, it's strange enough to see those three men together dressed like that, but just what in the world were they doing to that poor girl? Now that, I don't know. For all I know, they could be up to something. So I think I just might go check this out."

A few minutes later, James stopped running when he was about twenty feet behind them. From that point, he kept walking behind them. But at the same time, he kept turning his head to look up, down, and all around in different directions, so that the three men would not think he was trying to follow them.

Momentarily, the unique trio stopped when the shortest one of them said, "Hey, look!"

"What?" asked the other two, who turned to see what he was indicating. He was pointing straight ahead toward a nice-looking young woman who had short brown hair. She was walking toward them.

In the meantime, when those three had stopped, James stopped walking as well. He turned completely around to look away from them. Even while James Clifton was facing away from them, he heard one of them tell his partner, "No, no, no, that's not her." It was the Italian guy who had been walking at the right front of the group.

Hearing that only made James more curious. He turned his head to his right just enough to peek over his right shoulder out of the outer corner of his right eye. While doing that, James asked himself, "Now, what did they say? Not her? I wonder what they mean, 'not her.' Not who?"

But very shortly, the young lady walked past James Clifton's right side, continuing in the same direction he was facing. Clifton watched her walk by for a few seconds and then asked himself, "Is that who they're talking about? I wonder why. I mean, it seems kind of coincidental that she and the one they were manhandling a few minutes ago were nice-looking with a short haircut, kind of like Amanda."

James suddenly became tense and said to himself, "Wait a minute, what did I say? Amanda! Now, I really wouldn't think it's likely, but I guess it is possible. I just hope Amanda's not the one they're looking for. But just in case, I'll follow them just a wee bit further, to see if there's anything else I can find out about them." The three bizarre individuals had just begun walking along Lombard Street once again. James Clifton resumed walking behind them in the same manner he had just done moments before.

Within the next minute, however, the smallest and shortest of the three suddenly said something that surprised James Clifton. While he was walking along behind them, the man told the one to his right, "Look, I'm really sorry, Zapper."

"What!" exclaimed James, who could hardly believe his ears.

The guy on the right front of the little group rebuked his partner, saying, "Shut up! Quiet, you fool! I told you not to use our code names when we're not in our outfits. Don't you get it? There's no telling who might be overhearing us. They might even try to identify us! Now, come on; let's keep moving." So at last, the three odd characters just went about their business.

James could not help wondering about the things he had just overheard. So he stopped walking and stood in one spot to try to figure out who those men were and what they were trying to do. First of all, he asked himself, "Now, did that guy say 'code names'? And before that, did that other one call him Zapper?" James had a couple of additional thoughts about that threesome. They actually had code names, and one of them was perhaps Zapper.

With those two things in mind, James seriously began thinking. He said to himself, "I wonder where else I've heard of something like that. The only other instance I can immediately recall is the three associates of Doctor XT that I encountered last night and the night before. I'm talking about, you know, Zapper, Zinger, and—wait a minute, what did I say?"

At once, James took a moment to try to figure something out. "Now, did I just say Zapper? I think I did. Wasn't one of those guys just called Zapper? I believe so. Another thing too is, it seems coincidental that there are three of them as there were three associates to Doctor XT. Besides, that guy that was called Zapper is a little foreign looking and sounding. So was Zapper of X-Termination! And that shorter guy to the left sounded something like Zinger. Finally, that guy behind them is a big, big black guy, just like D.D.T. was!" Having said all that, James took one last look at the trio as they were still walking and looking around.

Then, James finally decided, "By George, I think I figured it out! That's just gotta be Zapper, Zinger, and D.D.T. After all, I think it seems unlikely I'd find that exact same variety within another group of three, and that's with even one of them having the same code name or nickname. That just absolutely must be who those guys are."

Right after that, he managed to discern something else. He continued, "But I'm also afraid I might've figured out another thing too. I know I said moments ago that the young women I saw them tampering with were good-looking and short-haired like Amanda. Is it possible that they're after her? Of course, I can't really think of what Amanda's had to do with X-Termination, except for last night, when she took out Zapper and Zinger and then came face-to-face with D.D.T. Wait a minute now, you know what? That must be why they'd be after her, and I bet they are too. I mean, on Wednesday night, I think I saw a nice little bit of what they obviously do to those who get in their way, and Amanda got in their way last night. Oh no, it's them, and they're out looking for Amanda. Oh, what have I done?" At that, he momentarily hung his head forward.

It turned out after all, that the trio James had just spotted wearing coats, hats, and shades was actually Axel Axtel, Nicholas Jarrett, and Anselm Nielsen. They, of course, were the same three who were also called Zapper, Zinger, and D.D.T. Clifton was absolutely right, and it just so happened that Axtel, Jarrett, and Nielsen were trying to find Amanda Taylor in order to bring down the Green Phantasm as well as do away with her.

But Clifton soon lifted his head up again. At the same time, he made a fist with his right hand and placed it in his left. "Oh well," he said with determination, "I guess I can't change what's already happened. I'm just gonna have to worry about what I'm gonna do now. I just gotta find Amanda before they do. Well, it looks like tonight, I'm going out again as the Green Phantasm."

James started walking back toward the pub to meet up with his pals, Eric and Scott. On the way, he tried to call Amanda on her cellular phone but received no answer. He just went on inside to hang out with his two friends. Then, the three of them sat down, ate, drank, talked, and enjoyed themselves.

Finally, at about 6:50 p.m., James, Eric, and Scott walked out after paying their tabs. Scott MacNicholl addressed his two friends, saying, "All right, guys, y'all enjoy it? I sure had a good time."

"We sure did," Eric responded.

"That's right," said James.

"Well then," continued Scott," now that we're done with that, I was wondering if anybody wants to go to my house to hang out, play cards and stuff? What do y'all say?"

"I'm all for it," Eric answered him with confidence.

"How about you, James?" asked Scott.

"Well," James began to answer his friend, "I would like so very very much to come over. However, I'm afraid there's a problem that's just come to my attention. You see, it's about Amanda. It's not so much me, I guess, but she's in trouble. That's why I can't make it. I gotta find her."

"Look, James," Scott told him, "I don't understand what you're saying. What exactly do you mean that—"

"Scott, please," Eric interrupted. Then, he turned to James and said, "It's all right, James; I understand. I've known you and trusted you for a long time, and what you told us sounds serious. I'm sure you know what you're doing, and I think you'd better go. I just hope everything turns out okay."

"Well, thank you very much, Eric," James replied, "thanks for understanding."

"Sure, no problem," said Eric. "I'm behind you all the way."

Then, even Scott added, "Yeah, me too. I think Eric was right. I'm sorry, James. You have my support as well."

"Thank you too, Scott," James responded. "Well, anyway, I guess I gotta get going. Thanks for everything this evening. See y'all later, guys."

"Okay," said Eric. "I'll talk to you later."

"All right, bye," said Scott. They all parted company. Then of course, James started on his way home, and Eric and Scott drove their trucks to Scott's house.

Later, about 7:15, James pulled into his driveway and then into his garage. While he shut off his Suburban and got out, he said to himself, "Well, it's a good thing that I've eaten and that I've made it home. I've got a job to do tonight." Of course, James was referring to his job as the Green Phantasm.

James ran upstairs to his bedroom. Once there, he took out his Green Phantasm suit and went to stand by the foot of his bed. He activated the pyxorium in his nervous system and began radiating neon-green light. At that, Clifton turned toward his bedroom door. From that point, he tossed his Phantasm outfit a few feet ahead and teleported out of his work clothes and into his superhero suit. Then, he just had to put on his dark-green boots. Finally, James Clifton was once again the Green Phantasm.

Right away, he just forgot about the work clothes that had collapsed on the floor and went over to his bedroom window. He opened the window and teleported out through it. He then reappeared hovering and floating above his subdivision. While up above, he said, "Well, I guess it's about time, so let's do it. I just need to find either Amanda or X-Termination before they find her."

It was now 7:20 p.m. As the Green Phantasm, Clifton took the form of a shapeless projectile and shot toward downtown Philadelphia at supersonic speed. Shortly, the Green Phantasm reappeared as himself, hovering up above and looking down at the downtown area. He was nearly two hundred feet above, on the lookout for either Amanda Taylor, X-Termination members, or any other sign of trouble.

Very soon, the first thing spotted by the Green Phantasm was a 1969 Dodge Charger headed west on Market Street out of the downtown area, trying to get past the University City area. The twenty-two-year-old driver was in flight from two Philadelphia city police cars. The Green Phantasm decided to go down and help the policemen catch him. Of course, the Phantasm also wanted some help trying to find Amanda, as well as to inform the police that X-Termination was still at large and after her. That was without a doubt an added incentive for the Green Phantasm to come to their aid.

Before the Dodge Charger made it past Drexel University, the Green Phantasm teleported and reappeared a hundred feet ahead on his right. The Phantasm began charging both hands while facing him. Then at once, he combined the power of all ten fingers to unleash the largest, most powerful laser beam he possibly could. The gigantic beam hit the car on the underside in front of the right front tire. This made the entire right side of the Charger come off the ground, making the car tilt to the left by about forty degrees. This gave the Green Phantasm the break he needed for his next move. So immediately, the Green Phantasm became a projectile and shot toward the underside of the car. Once there, he made a sharp turn and shot straight up. This caused the Dodge Charger to overturn completely onto its roof. It finally skidded upside-down until it stopped.

The two police cars pulled up and stopped behind the overturned Charger. The Green Phantasm reappeared and stood in front of it. He immediately charged his hands and kept them that way, for he did not know what would happen next. The police officers got out of their cars and ran up to the driver's side window of the Charger. Both policemen were holding out their guns in case the young man tried to crawl out of the car. The Green Phantasm was watching both sides from the front, for he wanted to make sure the guy would not escape.

Then, one of the police officers yelled to him, "Come on outta there!"

Soon, the young man began slithering facedown out through the driver's window. Shortly after that, he got onto his hands and knees and looked up to see the two policemen holding him at gunpoint.

"Stand up and put your hands on your head!" one of them ordered him.

The young man complied. Finally, the other officer turned him around and cuffed his hands behind his back.

The young man was white, about five feet ten inches tall, and weighed around one hundred eighty pounds. He wore his blond hair short. He was wearing a white T-shirt and blue jeans. The young man was an accused rapist. That was the reason the police had been after him. So then, the police officers just read him his Miranda rights and placed him in the back of one of the cars. At last, the one driving that car took him away to jail.

After all that, the Green Phantasm ran behind the overturned Dodge Charger. To the other policeman, he called out, "Hey! Excuse me, Officer!"

In response, the officer said, "Oh, Green Phantasm, thanks so much for helping us stop this guy."

"Oh, it's not a problem," the Green Phantasm told him, "but, look, there were just a couple of other things I needed."

"What do you need, Green Phantasm?" asked the policeman.

"Well, first of all," the Green Phantasm began, "there's someone in trouble. Her name is Amanda Taylor, and she's a loan officer at Stanley Financial. She's a white young lady that's about five foot nine with an average build. She's got a short haircut and brown hair. She lives in an apartment at Lawndale. Her apartment number is 1-H. You see, there's someone after her."

After the officer finished writing those few facts down on a piece of paper, he asked the Green Phantasm, "So, who is it that's after her? I mean, do you know?"

Without hesitation, the Green Phantasm answered most affirmatively, "As a matter of fact, I most certainly do. You see, that's the other thing I needed."

"Well, then," replied the policeman, "by all means, go on. I'm ready to take it down, so start describing them."

"All right," the Green Phantasm continued. "You see, the one or the ones trying to hunt her down are members of that organization, X-Termination."

The officer asked, "Do you mean the same ones who wrecked the party that Ace Nuclear Supply had at that downtown hotel? And is that also who made the attack on the city from those rocket planes?"

"That's them all the way," answered the Green Phantasm. "But you see, I have a little more information on them that I want the Philadelphia police to have."

"All right, go ahead," the police officer told him. "What else you got?"

"Well," the Green Phantasm responded, "I may not need so much to provide these code names, but I do need to tell you a little more about three certain individuals. First of all, the one called Zapper is about six feet tall, Italian looking, and he's built much like me. He's got black hair and a mustache. Then, there's a white guy with brown hair, who's a couple or a few inches shorter than him. That's the one called Zinger. Now last of all, there's the one called D.D.T. He's a seven foot-tall black guy that's just humongous, bigger than both of the other two put together."

"Is that all?" asked the officer.

"Just one other thing," the Green Phantasm answered, "I just found out today that they're not always in their costumes. I saw them earlier today in fedora hats and trench coats. Fortunately, I managed to overhear them and identify them."

"Thank you," said the policeman. "So, other than that, no vehicle descriptions?"

"Well," said the Green Phantasm, "none other than the one y'all just may already be aware of. That's the hovering caterpillar track vehicle that they must call the X-Terminator 4000. Does it sound familiar to you?"

"Well," said the police officer, "I can't think of it off the top of my head. But perhaps I should take a note of that too."

"All right," replied the Green Phantasm. "Well, anyway, it's a big, powerful white vehicle with caterpillar tracks and a bunch of rocket engines. In blue and purple letters along the sides, it says, 'X-Terminator 4000.' "

"All right," the officer told him. "Thanks, I got it down."

"Now look," said the Green Phantasm once more. "I don't know for sure what sort of vehicle that trio was in when I saw them earlier this evening. However, I just about do know that when they're in their Zapper, Zinger, and D.D.T. outfits, they're in that X-Terminator 4000. But anyway, could you please pass this on to some more police officers? I'm looking for all the help I can get, and as you can see, I'm here to help too."

"You got it, Green Phantasm," the policeman declared to him. "We'll see what we can do. Thanks again for helping us catch this guy."

"Oh, you're very welcome," the Green Phantasm told the police officer. "But anyway, I gotta get a move on. I just hope I find Amanda before those guys do. Or, I wouldn't mind finding them before they find her. Thanks for everything, Officer."

"You're welcome," replied the officer. "We'll get right on it. Good luck, Green Phantasm."

"Thanks, Officer," replied the Green Phantasm. "Well, I gotta shove off now. I got no time to lose. Just be careful, because those guys are awfully clever and cunning. They killed a bunch of policemen the other night. Well, bye, Officer, and thanks again." At that, both the Phantasm and the policeman went about their business.

The Green Phantasm once again became a shapeless projectile and shot himself back into downtown Philadelphia. He placed himself high above like he had been before. While the Phantasm was hovering above and on the lookout, he said to himself, "Oh gosh, I hope I'm not even a second too late. Otherwise, I'll never, ever forgive myself. Oh, Amanda, please tell me they haven't gotten to you yet. Please!"

Meanwhile, someone else was on his way to Philadelphia as well, actually three someones—Doctor XT's top three officials, namely Zapper, Zinger, and D.D.T. They were in an X-Terminator 4000, which was hovering and flying toward Philadelphia, four feet above Highway 30. Zinger was piloting from the front left seat, with Zapper sitting to his right. D.D.T. was sitting behind them. After the attempt they had made earlier undercover with coats and hats, they were now returning to the city in the guises for which they were best known.

While they were en route to Philadelphia and within five miles, Zapper told his two teammates, "Well, you two, as I said before, I know we couldn't do as much as we wanted in disguise earlier. But now that we're in our uniforms again, we can do a whole lot more damage. We'll even 'X-terminate' everyone in our way if we have to. But hopefully, we'll find that girl tonight. You guys ready for this?"

"Oh yeah," responded D.D.T.

"As ready as I'm gonna get," said Zinger.

Shortly, Zapper spotted a gas station up ahead on their left. He ordered Zinger, "Pull up to that gas station there, Zinger. I just can't help wondering if there's some unlikely chance that they'll know something about this. If not, we'll hit 'em up and get something out of it. So let's stop here."

"You got it, Zapper," replied Zinger. Zinger caused the X-Terminator to drift to the left. Then, he pulled up toward the gas station and came to stop about sixty feet from the west side of the store. Finally, in the parking lot, Zinger just landed the X-Terminator with it facing the west wall of the little building. After that, he turned off the engine.

Next, Zinger opened the sliding doors on both sides. Before anyone even had a chance to leave his seat, Zapper commanded, "Hold up, guys! Wait!"

In response, D.D.T. shook his head in confusion while Zinger inquired, "What is it, Zapper?"

"Just wait a minute," ordered Zapper. "I gotta take care of something." Zapper took out his Mega Zapper 2000 and programmed it to detect security cameras. He used his right hand to hold it outside the door on the vehicle's right. While doing that, he pressed a button that caused the Mega Zapper to record a computerized image of the small store and display it on the screen.

Shortly afterward, Zapper retracted his device back inside of the X-Terminator so he could look at it to see where the cameras were located. At once, Zapper perceived eight miniature arrows on the screen, pointing to the placement of different security cameras. He just selected and touched the lowest right of the eight arrows, making it flash, for it was marking the security camera for which he decided to aim. This happened to be the camera closest to him on his right.

Zapper activated a surge of electricity that he was about to discharge into the gas station's security system through the security camera he had designated. He put his Mega Zapper 2000 on the outside of the X-Terminator once again. Right away, he unleashed the surge of electricity he had been charging up. The surge hit and got inside of the targeted security camera, blowing it up and destroying it. This led to a chain reaction, in which the powerful surge of electricity spread throughout the entire surveillance system of the station. In turn, this caused every camera and monitor inside and outside to blow up and stop functioning altogether.

After all that, Zapper said to Zinger and D.D.T., "All right, guys, I believe that did it. Now let's get a move on. Come on! Let's go!" At hearing that, Zinger exited the X-Terminator 4000 on its left side. Zapper got out on the other side, and D.D.T. followed behind him. Finally, all three of them met in front of the vehicle. "Okay, men," said Zapper to his two coworkers, "we're gonna clear out this store. We're gonna try and see if someone here knows where what's-her-name is that foiled our plans last night. However, we're still gonna take all their money and anything else we could possibly need. Just make sure you leave no stone unturned. Can y'all handle that?"

"Yeah," answered D.D.T. "Let's do it."

"This shouldn't be a problem at all," Zinger declared confidently, "especially since you shut off all the cameras. Of course, it's not that anybody could stop us anyway, you know?"

"Sounds great," Zapper said happily. "That's what I like to hear. Come on, you two. Let's move on in. D.D.T., you break in through the back. Zinger, you come with me." Right after that, he secured the X-Terminator 4000. Then, the three of them split up into two teams in accordance with Zapper's orders. Finally, Zapper and Zinger started jogging toward the front door as D.D.T. began running to the back.

Meanwhile, inside the store, two employees were surprised when the security monitors stopped working. They included the manager on duty, who was in the office near the back door counting and sorting out money, as well as the cashier behind the checkout counter. "What's going on?" asked the store manager.

"Oh my gosh!" said the shocked cashier. "What happened?"

The manager began making fruitless attempts to turn the monitors in his office back on. "Oh my God!" exclaimed the manager. "I can't turn them back on. I wonder what caused them to go off." After several attempts to get the monitors going again, the frustrated manager finally declared, "I'm gonna go outside and see if I can find anything."

The manager on duty closed and locked the safe below his desk. Then, he got up and went out of his office, locking the door behind him. Immediately, he turned left and went directly to the back door. Once there, he began using his keys to unlock and open the back door. But unfortunately, that poor manager had another thing coming.

At the same time, big D.D.T. had finally made his way to that very door. Before the manager could fully unlock the door, D.D.T. delivered a front kick with his right foot to the very middle of it. This knocked the door out of whack. It also made the part of the door with the latch hit the manager's right-hand knuckles, making him let go of the keys and shake his hand in pain. A few of the bolts that were securing the door's hinges got pushed halfway out.

After shaking the pain from his right knuckles, the shocked store manager looked up and began backing away. At the same time, he asked himself, "What on earth just did that?"

D.D.T. followed up the first kick with a great big side kick. This completely knocked the door out of its frame and sent it flying. One of the door's upper corners even hit the manager in the face, dazing him and knocking him to the floor. He landed facedown, and the back door landed to his left along the hallway.

Very shortly, D.D.T. stormed on in through the empty door frame. The manager of the store began regaining consciousness, and he got up onto his hands and knees. Then, he turned around, and the first thing he saw was the huge masked powerhouse reaching for him with his great big right hand. "Oh my God!" the frightened store manager cried. "Who are you?"

Big D.D.T. grabbed hold of the man's neck right away. He tightened his grip and lifted the poor guy up off the floor. That very second, the merciless, oppressive D.D.T. turned to his right and pinned his innocent victim against the wall, continuing to press down on his throat and choke the daylights out of him. Of course, at the same time, the manager put both hands on D.D.T.'s titanic forearm, trying hopelessly to remove the hold on his throat. But then, D.D.T. loosened his grip for a few seconds, allowing the store manager to speak. "What are you trying to do, huh? What do you want?" asked the desperate manager.

"Yo, look here, little man," said D.D.T., talking down to him. "We need whatever money y'all have. Where you got some hidden, huh?"

"I can't give you any," replied the manager. This only made D.D.T. angrier, for he was determined to carry out Zapper's orders. He switched hands and used his left hand to choke the poor man. Then, he used his right hand to draw his X-Termination Ray and hold the manager at gunpoint. "All right! All right!" gasped the unfortunate victim. Once again, D.D.T. loosened his grip to let the man speak. Finally, the manager told the huge bully, "It's in that office behind me on my right."

"Excellent," growled D.D.T. "And I need one other thing too."

"What's that?" asked the store manager.

"Who is she? Where is she?" inquired D.D.T. Now, of course, he meant Amanda Taylor. However, the manager had no clue about all that.

So, the only response that D.D.T. received from him was, "I don't know what you're talking about. I mean, where's who?"

This only frustrated D.D.T. further. Upon hearing that unwanted reply, D.D.T. put away his ray gun, and then he said with a snarl, "Look here, I ain't got time for games! I'm trying to find out about that girl that got in our way last night. We was trying to take out that green freak in this city, but she put her nose in our business. Now do you know who I'm talking about?"

The only answer that the manager gave D.D.T. was, "Well, I guess by green freak, you mean the Green Phantasm. But I'm afraid I still don't know anything regarding what she did to y'all or who it was. I'm really sorry."

"Well," replied D.D.T. "I'm afraid 'sorry' doesn't lead us to her. You're just a useless wimp, you know that?" Immediately after that insult, D.D.T. used his right hand to twist and snap his victim's neck, rendering him unconscious. He turned the unconscious store manager around and followed up with a great big right punch to the back of the neck. This broke his neck and killed him. D.D.T. just tossed the dead man onto the floor and then went to break into the manager's office.

Zapper and Zinger had now entered through the store's front entrance. They were standing not too far inside the store, whispering to each other, exchanging ideas about how to handle the cashier.

At the same time, the cashier was thinking to himself, *I wonder who those guys are. What interesting costumes they're wearing!* He finally said to Zapper and Zinger, "Excuse me, can I help you guys?"

Zapper and Zinger looked toward the clerk. Immediately upon turning to look, Zapper said to Zinger in a lowered voice, "Have your X-Termination Ray ready."

"You got it, Zapper," whispered Zinger.

Zapper said to the cashier, "You know, as a matter of fact, you can. We need you to tell us who the young lady is and where and how we can find her."

"I'm really sorry," the guy replied. "I have no idea who or what you're talking about."

Of course, that was definitely not the answer Zapper was looking for, because it would certainly not help him track down Amanda Taylor. So the now angrier Zapper just drew his X-Termination Ray and held the clerk at gunpoint. In a threatening tone, he told the poor man, "I don't have time for this. You're wasting my time! Now open the register and leave it open!" The frightened man opened the drawer of the cash register.

Zapper whispered to his partner, "Give me a hand here." At that, Zinger drew his X-Termination Ray and stood to Zapper's right. He was now assisting Zapper in holding up the cashier. As soon as the unfortunate, innocent victim finally opened the drawer all the way, he put both hands up, seeing that two men were threatening him with guns.

Next, Zapper shouted, "Move away from there, and get out here to the floor!"

"Just do what he says!" said Zinger. Fearing for his life, the cashier kept both hands raised overhead and obeyed Zapper and Zinger. Shortly, he was out in front of the checkout counter with the two masked scoundrels. Zapper still had Zinger to his right, and the cashier was now face-to-face with both of them.

Then, Zapper addressed him, saying, "Now listen to me, you fool, I'm gonna give you a better explanation of what I wanted. So, I better get an answer from you this time. First of all, we're X-Termination, and we were trying to take down the Green Phantasm last night. However, just when we had him where we wanted him, this stupid brunette with short hair attacked us from behind and fouled up our scheme. So do you know her name or where we should go to look for her?"

"Listen," whimpered the cashier, who was more scared now than before, "I sincerely do wish I had the answer for you. I just never ever knew anyone spoiled your plans—honest I didn't. Is there anything else I can do to make up for that? Anything at all? Please don't kill me. I'll do anything you want. Please, Mister Zapper!"

"Well," responded Zapper, "I'm afraid to admit that since you don't have the answer, you're just standing in our way. You see, we're not called X-Termination for nothing. That's what we do to anyone or anything standing in our way, if you know what I mean."

Upon hearing Zapper say that, the clerk managed to discern that they were about to put him away, or "X-terminate" him, as they did to anyone who crossed them. He just began sobbing and said, "Oh no!"

But then, Zapper told him, "However, there's only one other thing you can do for us now."

"There is?" asked the desperate victim. "Great, what is it?"

"Just get out of our way," responded Zapper.

"No problem," replied the relieved employee. "I'll do just that with no problem."

"Excellent," said Zapper. That very second, Zapper and Zinger burst out laughing, for their victim had fallen for their trick without a clue as to the hidden meaning of what they were saying. Shortly, after the laughter subsided, Zapper gave Zinger a pat on the left arm, signaling him to carry out the "X-termination" of the helpless victim. So at once, Zapper fired his X-Termination Ray, reducing the cashier to a heap of ashes. "Well done, Zinger," Zapper told his partner. "Now go clean out the register, and start gathering up anything else we may need. I'll go see about D.D.T." At that, Zapper ran on past Zinger to go check on big D.D.T.'s progress.

In the meantime, big D.D.T. had gathered up all of the cash that had been left out on the desk in the manager's office. He had also taken out and picked up the big, heavy, cast-iron safe that had always been located underneath the manager's desk. The loose cash was now in a pouch on the left side of his belt. So at last, the humongous gargantuan was carrying the big safe out of the office. He turned right out of the office to go meet Zapper and Zinger. Not sure how to get the safe opened, D.D.T. just hurled it straight down the hall.

Zapper had just started up the hallway from the other end. The first thing he saw was the safe flying toward him. Zapper barely noticed it in time to avoid being hit. He turned around and jumped aside as fast as he could. "Yikes, what was that?" he cried.

Zapper heard the safe land just outside the hallway. He turned to look at it and then looked to see who had thrown it. Whenever he saw D.D.T. standing down the hall, he fumed, "D.D.T., you big galoot, watch it, you lunkhead!"

Immediately after that, D.D.T. walked on toward the safe he had just thrown. Once there, he said, "Look, I'm sorry, boss. I was just trying to break it open." Then, the huge titan just picked the safe up again, but this time, he thrust it straight down in front of himself. However, that still did not open it.

Zapper said to D.D.T., "Look here, you go help Zinger gather up what we need, and I'll take care of this safe. I'm sure you collected any other cash lying about, right?"

"You bet I did," answered D.D.T.

"Well done," Zapper told him. "Now, go give Zinger a hand. I got this."

"You got it," replied D.D.T. He started walking around the store gathering up various beverages, groceries, and other things as he went.

Zapper once again took out his Mega Zapper 2000. He targeted the dial for the combination lock on the safe and programmed his Mega Zapper to produce a surge of electricity that would blow up the safe's entire locking mechanism. He then discharged the surge of electricity. Almost immediately, the lock's dial, the disks underneath, and a few other parts came flying off. Zapper was now able to swing open the safe's door with ease, and he did just that after getting a big grocery bag from behind the checkout counter. Finally, of course, he began transferring all the cash from the safe to the bag.

Several minutes later, everyone was ready to depart from the gas station. Zapper had finally cleared out the safe, and the other two had put everything they had gathered in bags. "All right now," Zapper addressed D.D.T. and Zinger, "come on, you guys; let's all get ourselves and the things we've collected over to the X-Terminator. Y'all with me? Come on! Let's move it! There's no time to lose. We gotta find that girl and bring down the Green Phantasm."

"You're right about that," declared Zinger. "The people here may have wasted our time, but at least we got something out of it. But anyway, I say, let's go."

"Yeah," D.D.T. said in agreement.

At last, Zapper walked out through the store's front exit door, and Zinger and D.D.T. followed behind him. A couple of minutes after that, the masked threesome made it back to the X-Terminator 4000. Zapper typed in his secret code on the passenger side door, which caused both doors to come open. Next, Zinger got inside the door on the right side after putting his bags just behind the front passenger seat. While Zinger was inside, both Zapper and D.D.T. handed him their bags, and he put them away.

⚊⚊⚊⚊⚊⚊⚊⚊⚊⚊⚊⚊⚊⚊⚊⚊

Then, Zinger exited the vehicle and tried to walk around to the driver's side. But when he got there, D.D.T. was already in the driver's seat. Zapper, of course, was now in the front on the passenger side. "Hey look, y'all," said D.D.T., "I wanna drive this time. I ain't never gotten to pilot one of these before."

"All right, D.D.T.," Zapper told him. "I'll give you a chance. But, you better do a good job, or it's the last time you'll operate one of these."

"Okay, no problem," replied D.D.T.

So then, Zinger just went back around to the passenger side and got into the backseat. Afterward, of course, big D.D.T. just started up the X-Terminator 4000 and took off, hovering and flying toward downtown Philadelphia. Eventually, D.D.T. got them all to Catharine Street.

Zapper commanded, "Land and park in one of those spaces, next to one of those meters."

D.D.T. parked about halfway between the intersections of Nineteenth Street and Twentieth Street. He was facing east with the vehicle's left side to the north side's curb.

Momentarily, D.D.T. shut off the X-Terminator. Then, he opened both doors. All three of them got out and met in front of the vehicle. But upon meeting out front, Zapper immediately noticed something. The left side of the X-Terminator 4000 had hit and knocked over a parking meter. The endless belt on the left side that helped drive the X-Terminator was now on top of the parking meter's pole, which was lying along the sidewalk.

"D.D.T.!" Zapper said to him. "Would you care to explain that?" At that, Zapper pointed to the parking meter that D.D.T. had begun to roll over. The titan turned to see what Zapper was pointing to.

When D.D.T. noticed what he had done, he said to Zapper, "Oh, that? Well, I just didn't think it was that big of a deal, not a stupid little thing like that."

"Well, D.D.T.," replied Zapper, "I'm not overly concerned about that one little meter either. However, nobody that careless is gonna operate a vehicle on my property. I'm talking about whenever I take over X-Termination. I do have to admit one thing. You're a real powerhouse, and you're extremely valuable to us. But in the meantime, I'm turning this chore back over to Zinger. It looks like it'll be a long time before you drive another X-Terminator 4000. But anyway, there's no time to waste. Let's get moving, so we can find the one we're looking for. Come on!

For a few seconds, D.D.T. hung his head forward, for he was now ashamed, embarrassed, and humiliated. But shortly, once Zapper closed up and secured the X-Terminator 4000, D.D.T. just followed the other two on through downtown Philadelphia. The three of them continued on their rampage to try to find and apprehend Amanda Taylor.

Fortunately, someone else was still venturing through the city and on the lookout as well. It was the Green Phantasm, beneath whose suit was none other than the person of James Paul Clifton. He was once again hovering above downtown Philadelphia, looking out for either Amanda, the work of X-Termination, or any other sign of trouble.

Very shortly, something somewhat peculiar caught his eye. It was an average-sized forty-one-year-old black man wearing a dark-gray trench coat. He was walking east along the north side of Locust Street. The Green Phantasm thought he looked suspicious, because of the manner in which he was looking around in all directions, as if to make sure no one was watching him. So the Green Phantasm continued watching from above in case the man was possibly up to something.

Three minutes later, the guy down below stopped in front of a jewelry store between Sixteenth and Seventeenth Streets. He stood looking at it with interest momentarily. After that, he looked around one more time to make certain he was not being watched. Finally, he proceeded on into the store.

At the same time, of course, the Green Phantasm had been watching it all from above. He finally said to himself, "I wonder what someone like that would want with a jewelry store. I mean, by the way he's looking over his shoulder and all, I think he might be trying to pull something off or something. I don't know what he's up to, but I do know that I don't have a good feeling about it. I'd better go check this out, here I go." So he started on his way down toward the jewelry store.

Meanwhile, inside the store, the black man in the trench coat was walking toward a counter to consult the first sales representative he saw. Once he made it to the glass-covered display counter, the lady behind it said, "May I help you?"

"Yes, ma'am," the man replied. Then, as he was pointing to a ten-karat gold-plated watch that was accented with several diamonds, he said, "I'm interested in that watch right there. May I see it, please?"

"Certainly," she replied. So next, the lady took the watch from among many other items that were on sale and slowly handed it to the man so he could examine it. Then momentarily, she asked him, "Was there anything else you were interested in?"

"As a matter of fact, there was," the one in the coat answered politely "What I would like is for you to clean everything out of the cash register and put it all in a bag for me. I would also like you to put all the other stuff in this case in a bag as well."

Not believing her ears, the surprised woman behind the counter said, "Excuse me, sir? What did you say?"

At that, the man looked at her with anger and told her, "You heard what I said. I told you to empty out the register along with this glass case." That very second, he took a.45-caliber semiautomatic pistol from his right coat pocket and pointed it at the innocent saleslady. "So move it, now!" he yelled to her.

The frightened sales rep was now in too severe of a state of panic to say anything. So she just obeyed the robber holding her at gunpoint. Within ten seconds, the woman managed to dump all of the register's cash into a paper bag, which she handed over to the greedy rogue. Then, she got another bag and began removing each and every item on sale in the display case. "Hurry up!" shouted the crook. At hearing that, the unfortunate woman behind the counter even began sobbing while trying to hurry as fast as she could. Then finally, she handed the bad guy a second bag, which contained every piece of jewelry that had been underneath the glass.

But next, before the thief had even turned around to leave, someone else entered the store. It was the Green Phantasm, who had made his way down to the scene to try to put a stop to any and all mischief. First, the Phantasm began creating a force field for protection, for he could see that this criminal was armed. While still forming the force field, he said to the troublemaker, "All right, creep, whatever you're doing, you'd better cease and desist."

At that, the bad guy turned around and said to the Green Phantasm, "Yo, man, you talkin' to me, fool?"

"I most certainly am," the Green Phantasm answered calmly. "Now, look, I realize that it can be tough to get by, but all these armed robberies are not the answer to your problems. And right now, I need you to put down the gun, or there will be trouble for you."

"What!" cried the robber, who was now angrier and too proud to listen. "I don't believe this," he said shaking his head in disbelief. Then, he turned and pointed his handgun at the Green Phantasm and told the valiant hero threateningly, "I'm gonna blow you away with my forty-five!"

The Green Phantasm had finished making a force field. Immediately after that, the man with the pistol started persistently firing away at him. However, the bullets kept ricocheting off the force field. At the same time though, the sales rep looked away in fear, for she could not bear to watch someone get shot. The efforts of the corrupted scoundrel proved to be futile. However, he still kept firing away until he finished off the clip inside his pistol.

Then, after firing all of the clip's rounds, he paused for a moment to reload. The man was no doubt surprised that the Phantasm was still standing. "Man, shoot!" he muttered. "What in the world's going on here?"

In the meantime, the Green Phantasm was taking down his force field. Right after that, he charged up his hands for his next move.

Finally, the depraved crook had reloaded his semiautomatic. At once, he tried to aim for the Phantasm again. But before he got a chance to fire a shot, the Green Phantasm used his left hand to fire a laser beam that knocked the handgun out of the thug's hand. It landed seven feet to his left on the floor. "Hey, what happened?" the guy asked.

Right after that, the bad guy started to run to his left to try to reclaim his gun, but before he made it all the way, the Green Phantasm teleported and reappeared standing in front of him, with his right foot on the handgun. "What!" cried the shocked criminal. Then, he looked up at the Green Phantasm and said, "Why, you—" But before finishing, he threw a big right punch at the Green Phantasm. But when the punch connected, the Green Phantasm was not affected at all, for he had radiated brighter to become invincible. "Dang it!" exclaimed the frustrated criminal. "What is this guy made of?"

Next, the man in the trench coat began looking into the eyes of the Green Phantasm. They stared at each other steadily for a couple of minutes. At last, the thief made one more attempt to take out the Phantasm. He tried a combination that included a right uppercut to the midsection followed by a left hook. But the uppercut had no effect on the Green Phantasm, for his invincibility was still activated. Immediately after that, the Green Phantasm ducked to avoid the left hook. While doing so, he threw his own left hook to the thug's rib cage. "Oh, ow, ow, ow!" he yelled, putting both hands on his ribs.

Shortly thereafter, the guy looked up at the Green Phantasm with anger. Then, he took his hands away from his ribs and said to the Phantasm, "I'm gonna get you for that!"

"Oh really? You think so?" asked the confident Green Phantasm.

The bad man did not answer, however. Instead, he began to prepare to throw another punch. But before he could begin delivering a blow, the Green Phantasm took the form of a shapeless projectile. That very instant, he smacked the crook, knocking him back several feet, so that he was lying on his back. Then at once, the Green Phantasm just transformed back into himself after only advancing between three and four feet.

The criminal was now severely dazed and shocked, for he did not know exactly what had hit him. As he was regaining his senses, he thought to himself, *I don't know what he did or how, but there ain't no way I can take him. I'm hauling tail on outta here.* Without a doubt, the robber was now afraid instead of determined and aggressive like he had been before. Finally, he jumped up, grabbed the two bags that he had forced the saleslady to prepare for him, and ran for the door.

However, the thief did not make it out of the store because the Green Phantasm got in his way by means of teleportation. Less than two seconds after the Green Phantasm stationed himself in front of the door, he hit the man in the trench coat with a big left jab to the chin. Consequently, the culprit was rendered unconscious when he ran straight into that punch. He fell backward to the floor.

The guy lost hold of the two bags, which went flying back whenever the Phantasm hit him. At that, the Green Phantasm teleported toward the checkout counter and caught them. Then, he handed them back to the saleslady.

The woman was amazed and relieved. "Thank you so much, Green Phantasm," she told him.

"No problem," replied the Green Phantasm. "You better call the police on this guy."

"You're right," she said. At that, she dialed 911, not knowing what else to do. Then of course, she gave them her report before hanging up.

The Green Phantasm then said to the sales representative, "I was kind of wondering one other thing. You may not be the one to ask, but if you don't mind, I'd like to anyway."

"Okay, sure," she replied. "What is it?"

"There's someone I'm looking for," the Green Phantasm told her. "Her name's Amanda Taylor. She's a loan officer at Stanley Financial. I don't guess you've seen her or heard of her, huh?"

"I'm sorry; I can't say I have," the lady told him.

"Oh well," the Green Phantasm replied kindly, "thanks anyway. There're just some guys after her, and I just need to find her before they do."

"Well, good luck," she said. "I hope everything turns out all right, because I appreciate you helping me out. Thank you so much, and God bless you."

"Well, you're welcome," the Green Phantasm told her, "but anyway, I don't have much time for thanks. I gotta get going. Well, good-bye now."

"Bye-bye," the woman said in reply. So then, the Green Phantasm went on out of the jewelry store and continued jogging east along Locust Street. Fifteen minutes later, he stumbled upon something else that aroused his attention.

At the corner of Locust and Ninth Streets, the Green Phantasm spotted a young couple on the other side of Ninth. They were walking back to a parked gray 1995 Corvette ZR-1. The young man was twenty-one years old and six feet two inches tall with brown hair; he weighed about 230 pounds. He was wearing a blue dress shirt and some navy-blue dress pants. The young lady he was with was about five feet six inches tall and weighed around 130 pounds. She had long, dirty-blond hair, and she was wearing a neon-pink T-shirt and blue jeans.

However, the aspect that caught the Green Phantasm's attention was the young man's somewhat wild behavior. The Phantasm thought he possibly could have been drinking. The reason he was concerned was because drunk or drugged people might hurt others as well as themselves. The Green Phantasm took a few moments to watch and see what might end up happening.

While the couple was on their way back to the Corvette, the guy was screaming and yelling very happily and excitedly. He hollered out, "Whoo, yeah, that was great! I had an exciting time! Whoo-hoo!"

At that, his date replied, "Yeah, I had a good time too." She said that gladly but not as excitedly as the man had spoken.

Next, they finally made it back to the car. Once there, the young man went to the driver's side door and placed his left hand on the hood while he used his right to take his keys out of his pocket. Just as soon as he took out his keys, his left hand slipped off the hood and he nearly fell forward. "Oh my God!" he yelled. But he managed to stop himself.

The young woman he was with got in front of him and said, "What's the matter? Are you okay?"

"Who, me? Okay?" he replied. "Of course I am. What are you worried about?"

"Never mind," the young lady responded.

Then, the man tried to use one of his keys to unlock the door. However, he could not turn the key. "Hey, what's wrong with this doggone key?" he asked in frustration. Then, he pulled the key out and took a closer look at it. "I used the wrong one," he told himself. After that, he sorted through them until he found the right one. "Ah, there it is," he said more calmly.

Then, the young man tried to insert that key into the lock, but missed and scratched the outside of his door. After that, he made another attempt but scratched the door again. He then whispered to himself, "Oh man, what is wrong with me tonight?" The problem was that he had drunk a little too much, and his vision was affected by that. So next, he tried a third time to use that same key but dropped his set of keys.

His date was able to discern that he had given himself a little too much alcohol at the bar from which they had just come. At the same time, the Green Phantasm could sense that too from where he was watching. So he stuck around in case they might need his help, for he did not like what he was seeing.

When the guy picked up his keys, the girl he was dating said to him, "Look, I'm really worried about you. I think you've had too much to drink. So we better call it a night. Why don't you let me have the keys so I can drive you home?"

"What?" asked the intoxicated young man. "What are you talkin' about? I ain't ready to go home, and I ain't giving you my keys. We going go somewhere else baby."

"Johnny, please," the young lady pleaded. "I know you're just drunk, but this is for your own good. Now just trust me, okay?"

"Forget all that, sweet thing," he said more firmly. "We're going somewhere we can be alone. Now get in the car on that side."

"That's fine," said the girl, beginning to cry. "If you're gonna be that way about it, you'll have to go on without me. I'm taking another ride home." At that, she began to storm off.

But before she got too far, the man ran after her. He caught up and grabbed her right arm to restrain her. "Where you think you're going, huh? You're going with me! Now come on."

"Ow, Johnny!" the frightened young woman screamed. "Let go! You're hurting me!"

"I can do worse than that," he told her. "You wanna see?" Right after the abusive drunk said that, he punched the poor innocent young woman in the midsection. That made her fall to her knees and really start crying. After that, he began preparing to hit her again. But something stopped him.

Fortunately, it was the Green Phantasm. He had teleported over and grabbed the drunk guy's right arm before he could throw another punch. "Hey, watch it, pal," the Green Phantasm told him.

At that, the guy who was battering his date let go of her and turned around to see who or what was trying to stop him. When he saw the Phantasm, he said, "Hey, man, who in the devil are you? Who do you think you are, huh?" He tried shoving the Green Phantasm. But that proved to be futile, for the Green Phantasm had tightened up inside to become more radiant and invincible.

"I'm the Green Phantasm," the Phantasm replied. "And this young woman here was trying to do the right thing. So you'd better let her go. I'm not just gonna stand back and watch you beat her up."

"Why don't you mind your own freakin' business?" said the violent drunk.

"You know something else?" asked the Green Phantasm. "You got no business beating up on this innocent victim. She has the right to leave you if she wants. And another thing, you really need to change your ways. For those who drink too much or resort to violence, there's not a bright future. So I'd strongly recommend a different route than the one you're on."

At hearing this, the twenty-one-year-old guy took offense and grew angrier. He then threw and landed a big right between the Green Phantasm's eyes. But that proved ineffective since the Phantasm had made himself invincible again.

Right after that, the youth tried throwing a left hook. But before he could connect, the Green Phantasm took the form of a shapeless projectile and smashed the young guy backward into the side of his car. This knocked the intoxicated young man unconscious. Then, of course, the Green Phantasm transformed back into himself. Upon reappearing, he opened the driver's side's door of the 1995 Corvette and put the unconscious youth in the front seat. "There," said the Green Phantasm, "he should be better when he wakes up."

Afterward, the Green Phantasm turned his attention to the poor girl who was on her hands and knees in tears by the front of the car. He walked up to her and said, "Excuse me, miss. Are you okay?"

At that, she looked up at the brave, radiant superhero. When she did, the Green Phantasm gave her a smile and extended his right hand, offering to help her back onto her feet. The relieved young lady took hold of his right hand and lifted herself into an upright position. In the instant that she was finally standing up straight, she threw her arms around the Phantasm, giving him a great big sustained hug. Although the girl was still shedding a few tears, she said to the Green Phantasm, "Thank you so much, Green Phantasm. I hate even to think what would've happened to me if it weren't for you. I even realize what a fool I was."

"Well," the Green Phantasm told her, "I wouldn't say that. I mean, you're not a fool; he is. I even tried talking to him because I don't like to just put someone away without giving them a chance. But he didn't leave me much choice but to take him out."

"Oh well," said the girl. "Anyway, thank you very much for saving my life."

"No problem," replied the Green Phantasm as he began to step away from her.

But the victim of attempted date rape grabbed hold of the Green Phantasm to keep him from leaving. She had her left hand holding his cape and her right hand holding his right arm. "Wait," she said to him, "don't go. Please don't leave me. I'm scared. Please don't leave me here alone."

The Green Phantasm turned back around. He sighed momentarily, for he really wanted to find Amanda more than anything, but he told the frightened young woman, "Well, all right, I won't leave you here. There is someone else I'm trying to find who's in trouble, but I'll stay with you until a taxicab gets here. I know you were thinking about taking one home."

"Thank you," she said to him. "So anyway, who is it you're looking for?"

"Well," answered the Green Phantasm. "I don't know if you know her, but I guess I'll tell you anyway. Her name's Amanda Taylor. She's a short-haired brunette, and she's a loan officer at Stanley Financial."

"Well," said the young lady, "I can't say I know her. But I can say that a well-known live band was playing at the bar I just came from on Eighth Street. A lotta, lotta people were there. I don't know if that'll help or if she's there, but that's about the best I can tell you."

"Oh, that's all right," replied the Green Phantasm. "I appreciate your trying to help. Thanks. I just might go and check it out. Thank you, dear."

"You're welcome, baby," she said in return. "Thank you so much for everything." At that, the girl went and stationed herself directly to the Green Phantasm's right. Then, she wrapped both arms around his midsection. After that, he put his right arm around her to make her feel more secure.

A few minutes later, a taxi passed right by them. As it passed, the Green Phantasm put out his left hand to signal the cab. At the same time, he shouted out, "Taxi!" The taxi came to a stop.

After that, the young girl let go of her hero and started running toward the cab. Just before getting in, she turned around to say one last thing to the Green Phantasm. "Well, good-bye, Green Phantasm," she told him sweetly, "and thanks again for everything."

"All right, bye-bye," replied the Phantasm. "Now take care of yourself, and keep out of trouble." At that, the young lady got into the taxi, and it drove her on home.

The Green Phantasm continued searching for Amanda Taylor. He kept running east along Locust Street. He was headed toward the bar the young woman had suggested. The Phantasm was still feeling tense, for he was uncertain as to whether he would find Amanda in such a big city. However, he kept heading toward Eighth Street, for he had no other bright ideas at the moment. "Oh gosh," said the Phantasm rather sadly, "I don't know if this idea will work, or any idea for that matter. One thing I do know is, if I don't find her before something happens to her, I'll never ever forgive myself, no way."

James Clifton was feeling both ashamed and discouraged. But just when he was beginning to think all hope was lost, he heard a somewhat familiar voice as he approached the corner of Locust and Eighth Streets. "Wait a minute," said the Green Phantasm. "Who's that? I don't know if that's really her, but let me just check to make sure."

He ran up to the west side of the intersection. When the Phantasm looked around the corner of the last building before Eighth Street, he saw something he wanted to all right. On the other side of the street was Amanda Lee Taylor. With her were her two friends, Erin and Michelle.

Michelle said to Amanda, "Are you sure you don't want to go anywhere else with us tonight?"

"I'm positive," answered Amanda. "It's been a long week for me. I've been through a lot, and I've got a lot on my mind. So I'm just gonna take the next cab home. We'll have more fun next time."

"All right," said Michelle. "Well, thanks for coming out this evening, and take care of yourself, okay?"

"Okay," replied Amanda.

"Well, have a good night," said Erin.

"All right, bye," said Amanda.

"Bye! Good night," Erin and Michelle said. At that, they left Amanda and went back to Michelle's vehicle.

After Amanda's two friends had left her, the Green Phantasm started to run over to her but stopped himself momentarily. "Wait a minute," he said to himself. "Maybe this ain't the best idea. I think I'll go talk to her as James Clifton." The Green Phantasm quickly zoomed back home, where he got out of his suit and into some ordinary dress clothes. After that, he whizzed back to the spot where he had found Amanda and switched off his radiation.

After doing all that to return to his guise as mere James Clifton, he began running toward Amanda. He called out, "Amanda!"

At that, she looked all around to try to spot the one calling her name. Then very shortly, she saw James Clifton running toward her. "Oh my

God," she said. "It's... well, I hate to say it, but it's, uh, James Clifton. I can't believe he tracked me down like this. What does he want with me?"

James made it over to Amanda and told her, "Oh, Amanda, I'm glad I found you. Thank God you're still all right."

"*What?*" exclaimed Amanda. "Glad you found me! What were you doing looking for me anyway? I can't believe you, James."

"I had to come out looking for you," he told her. "It's extremely important."

"Extremely important?" asked Amanda.

"Yes," answered James Clifton. "It most certainly is. You see, there's someone after you."

"Oh, someone's after me, huh?" she replied. "Yeah right, the only one after me right now is you."

"Amanda," James said calmly. "Look, I didn't mean me, all right? I was actually talking about... X-Termination."

"Oh, X-Termination," Amanda said critically. "I wonder who you think you are to be telling me this after what you did to me the other night. After the way you set me up, I wonder what you're trying to do to me this time. How can I possibly trust someone who just disappeared on me, leaving me to die?"

"Amanda, come on, please," James pleaded. "It's not like that at all. You see, it was the Green Phantasm who—"

"Oh God, James, please! Give me a break!" Amanda snapped. "First, you're trying to frighten me with some nonsense about X-Termination, and now you're trying to lie to me about the Green Phantasm? I'm sure he told you those guys were after me, just like when you ran and told him about the holdup at the party the other night." She just shook her head at James in disbelief.

"As a matter of fact," James told her, "I did. That was why I left you the other night—"

"Enough!" Amanda interrupted. "By the way, James, I no longer need you to introduce me to your friend, because I've met him already. I met him last night when he was there to save me from D.D.T. and then Doctor XT. Otherwise, as you might know already, he saved all those lives, including mine, at the party last night. As impressive and wonderful as he is, I don't see how he could possibly befriend a jerk like you. And I guess I might tell you something else too. Tomorrow night, I've got a date with someone else that's obviously more caring than you, James Clifton."

"Oh, really?" replied James. "Is it by any chance Dr. Mark Thompson?"

"Wow, good guess," Amanda responded sarcastically, pretending to be impressed.

"Well," James began to say. "I know this is probably important to you, but I strongly suggest you don't do that or even go out anywhere."

"Shut up, James!" yelled Amanda. "It's bad enough you tracked me down, but now you're trying to take control of my whole life? Oh my God, stay away from me from now on, and don't you ever come near me again!" As she finished saying that, she began backing away from him.

But then, James said to Amanda, "Amanda, look, there's just one last thing I really, really need to tell you. I seriously believe that it will definitely make you understand everything."

"Oh really?" Amanda said harshly, continuing to glare at him.

"Yes, I'm positive," Clifton replied affirmatively. "I just need you to listen to one last thing. After that, I'll leave you alone and never bother you again, if that's still what you want. So could you please just let me say one more thing?"

"Oh, all right," she said doubtfully, while rolling her eyes, "I guess I'll listen to just one more thing. So what is it?"

"Okay, Amanda," he began, "I'm about to let you know the truth. I've never told anyone this before, and I still don't intend to. But because of how much you really mean to me, I'm gonna go ahead and tell you. You see Amanda, I'm—"

But right then, a taxi pulled up right in front of them, and James did not get to finish what he was about to say. "I gotta go, James," Amanda told him, for she was more interested in getting home than staying around to listen to him. She just stormed on toward the cab without even looking back or saying "Good-bye." Finally, she got in and shut the door, and the taxi took her on home.

James was very frustrated. How could he not be? After he had finally found Amanda, she had only become angrier with him than previously. Besides, now that they had parted company, he would have to try to find her again. James had been about to tell Amanda that he himself was actually the Green Phantasm. As risky as it may have been to tell her that, it was the only way he could think of to undo the tension between them. However, a taxi had showed up before James could tell her the truth about the Green Phantasm and himself.

As frustrated and upset as he had now become, he was not even in the mood to use his powers as the Phantasm to get home. He just kept waiting for the next taxi to come along.

At the same time, someone else was ready to turn in for the night as well. It just so happened to be X-Termination's masked trio of Zapper, Zinger, and D.D.T. They had been on a rampage all evening and were now walking back to their X-Terminator 4000. At the moment, they were walking west along Catharine Street toward their vehicle, which was parked on the north side of it.

As they were walking along, Zapper said to his two teammates, "All right, you guys, I say we call it a night. If we didn't find her tonight, we'll find her tomorrow."

"Okay then," replied Zinger.

"Yeah," said big D.D.T.

Whenever they made it to Nineteenth Street, Zapper stopped and commanded Zinger and D.D.T., "Listen, guys, you two go on ahead of me. I'll stay back here and cover you."

"Yo, man, what are you talkin' about, huh? What are you saying?"

"Trust me, D.D.T.," Zapper told him. "Just move on toward the X-Terminator. I gotcha covered, all right? Now go!"

"Let's just go, D.D.T.," said Zinger. "I'm sure he had a good reason to tell us that. If I know Zapper, he knows what he's doing. Now, come on; let's go."

Zinger and D.D.T. just proceeded on over to the X-Terminator 4000. Upon making it over to their vehicle, Zinger said to D.D.T., "Well, D.D.T., let's get on into the X-Terminator."

"Okay," replied D.D.T. At that, Zinger went around to the driver's side door and D.D.T. to the passenger's side.

But before they had a chance to open the doors and get in, something suddenly came up. Both Zinger and D.D.T. were surrounded by police officers, who appeared as if from nowhere. "Hold it right there! Freeze!" they all shouted at the two rogues.

Both Zinger and D.D.T. turned around. Each one of them was surrounded by four officers who were pointing their guns at them.

"Both of you put your hands up!" yelled one of the police officers. D.D.T. and Zinger both complied.

Meanwhile, Zapper was working on the backup plan that he had in mind. From the east side of Nineteenth Street, he had managed to see all the police officers holding up his two men. He had his Mega Zapper 2000 out and was programming a surge of electricity to take out the eight officers who were holding Zinger and D.D.T. at gunpoint.

Zapper unleashed a powerful surge of electricity that followed the path for which it had been set. The surge started with the policeman farthest back on Zinger's side of the X-Terminator 4000. The programmed electrical surge shocked and knocked that officer out and then traveled in an arc, taking out the remaining officers one at a time. Within a few seconds, all eight police officers were lying on the ground unconscious.

After that, Zapper went running toward his partners. As he was getting close to them, he yelled to them, " 'X-terminate' them, you fools!" At that, D.D.T. and Zinger took out their X-Termination Rays and began firing at the unconscious police officers, reducing them to heaps of ashes until that was all that was left of them.

Something else of which the devilish threesome was unaware was also taking place. In addition to the eight annihilated police officers was also a ninth police officer. A black female officer had been hiding behind the X-Terminator 4000, backing up all of the other officers.

Just as Zinger and D.D.T. had finally finished off all the other officers on the scene, the remaining officer peeked around to the driver's side of the X-Terminator. She was horrified when she saw what now remained of those four policemen. At that, she gasped and jumped back behind the vehicle. The female officer tried to sneak out on D.D.T.'s side. But unfortunately for her, D.D.T. was standing on that side behind his victims. Whenever the lady noticed that, she once again leaped back behind the X-Terminator 4000.

Just as she was disappearing behind the X-Terminator, big D.D.T. caught a glimpse of movement. "Hey, what was that?" he asked himself. At that, he walked on toward the rear of the X-Terminator to find out who or what it was that he had just barely noticed.

D.D.T. finally made his way to the X-Terminator 4000's rear. Once there, he found the hiding female officer. Whenever she looked up at the huge masked gargantuan behemoth with whom she was now face-to-face, she went into a panic and screamed hysterically.

D.D.T. did not try to attack or harm the woman. Instead, he put away his X-Termination Ray. Then, he said to her nicely, "Hey, baby." That was no doubt because he was attracted to her.

In reaction, the officer stopped panicking and thought, *Oh my God, what is with that guy?*

In the meantime, Zinger had just started up the X-Terminator 4000 and was getting ready to shove off with Zapper and D.D.T. Zapper was now running up behind D.D.T., trying to get his attention. He was repeatedly shouting, "D.D.T.!" But D.D.T. was so infatuated with the attractive officer that he almost did not hear Zapper calling him.

Even when Zapper made it over to the rear of the X-Terminator, D.D.T. still did not notice, for he was too distracted by the woman. Zapper saw what was holding D.D.T.'s attention. At that, he took out his Mega Zapper 2000 and gave the officer a zap of electricity, which rendered her unconscious.

Next, when D.D.T. saw her collapse to the ground, he exclaimed, "Hey, who did that?" He looked back on his right and saw Zapper standing behind him. "Aw, Zapper, what did you do that for?" asked D.D.T. "Why did you—"

"Enough, D.D.T.!" yelled Zapper. "Zinger's waiting on us! Now let's go!"

Zapper took out his X-Termination Ray and was about to fire it at the now-unconscious police officer. But before he could shoot his ray gun, D.D.T. said, "No, don't do that, Zapper! I like her. Don't disintegrate her."

At that, Zapper put away his X-Termination Ray and said in response, "Okay, fine, D.D.T., if it'll keep you in your right senses. Now let's get a move on! Come on!"

Finally, D.D.T. and Zapper got into the X-Terminator 4000. Then of course, the diabolical threesome began heading back to X-Termination Headquarters. While they were in flight, Zapper said to Zinger and D.D.T., "Well, guys, although we didn't find her tonight, we'll find her tomorrow. It'll be Saturday, so she definitely oughtta be out there somewhere. However, we say nothing to XT. He does not want to hear anything until it's done." They just continued on until they eventually made it back to headquarters. The time was now close to 11:00 p.m.

At the same time, James Clifton was at home sitting on his bed. He had a lot on his mind. How could he not? He had once again located Amanda before X-Termination did, but she was now angrier with Clifton than she had been before. James felt guilty about it all. He could not help wondering whether he would be facing this crisis if he had not become the Green Phantasm. He also wondered whether Amanda would be in danger if not for that.

A guilt-ridden and depressed James Clifton sat for a while and hung his head forward. He said to himself, "Oh man, why is all this happening? I thought it would be great being the Green Phantasm. I had no idea it would put me under this much pressure. But, I've already made my vow and officially accepted my position as the Green Phantasm. I mean, I've already got everyone counting on me, and I can't turn my back on them. I guess neither a real man nor a real hero would do that. Of course, I've got no way of knowing if I'll find Amanda before those scumbags do, but I'm gonna try. I'm definitely not giving up. It's like I just said; a real hero doesn't just back out on his word, does he? No, of course not, and neither will I. But I'm still scared of what's gonna happen. If they capture Amanda and destroy her, I'll never forgive myself, never."

James burst into tears as he hung his head down even farther. He was uncertain about finding Amanda in time but too determined to give up. He was too upset to go to sleep or even eat anything. He just sat on his bed for hours and hours with nothing but a guilty conscience for company. At least the search for Amanda was not yet over.

CHAPTER TEN

Amanda Gets Captured

It was now past 2:00 p.m. on Saturday afternoon. James was just waking up. It was undoubtedly the latest he had slept in a long time. Of course, all the worry about Amanda Taylor and X-Termination had put him under so much stress that he had had a tough time going to sleep. In fact, it was almost 6:00 a.m. when James had finally fallen asleep.

But even now that James had awakened, he was still stressed about everything that was going on. Immediately upon waking, he felt the impulses of fear and worry return, causing him to panic. "Oh my God!" he cried. "What happened? Did I fall asleep? What's going on, huh? What time is it now?" Then, James looked at the digital alarm clock on his nightstand and saw that it was 2:21 p.m. "*What*?" he cried in panic. "Two twenty-one!" At that, James jumped out of his bed and ran over to the mirror above the sink just outside his bathroom. "Oh no!" exclaimed Clifton. "How did I let myself do this? Now, they're gonna—"

James stopped himself, for he suddenly realized that he was losing control of himself and that his present attitude would not help anything. He told himself calmingly, "Okay, okay, calm down, James Clifton; just get ahold of yourself. This kind of behavior is not gonna get you anywhere. So, just, uh, calm down, okay?" Right after that, James took a couple of moments to catch his breath.

After pausing for a couple of moments, a calmer James Clifton said, "Okay, now that I've calmed down some, I need to try not to be emotional but be logical and reasonable about all this. Now let's see, before last night, Amanda was angry with me. But then, I found her, and she possibly became angrier with me. Now, on top of that, I overslept this morning.

But wait, I can't change what's already happened. The only thing worth worrying about is what I'm gonna do now."

James stopped to think momentarily. He had an idea. "Well," he said, "here's what I'll do first: I'll try to call Amanda on her cell phone. She may not be overjoyed to hear from me. But I just want to be sure that she hasn't been found by X-Termination. So here I go."

That very second, James began punching in Amanda Taylor's cell phone number. After a couple of rings, Amanda answered her phone. "Hello?"

James was so relieved to hear her voice.

"Amanda," James said in reply, "it's me… It's James, James Clifton."

"James?" Amanda responded with revulsion. "What do you want with me, huh? What are you trying to do to me?"

"Amanda, please," James told her calmly. "I'm not trying to do anything to you, okay? I'm just happy they haven't gotten to you yet."

"Haven't gotten to me!" Amanda snapped. "Who hasn't? X-Termination?"

"Well, yeah," James answered still remaining calm, "that's exactly who—"

"Forget it, James Clifton!" Amanda yelled to him. "You're just trying to frighten me to win me over, aren't you? Well, let me tell you something. I'm not the least bit afraid, okay? Besides, I still don't know who you think you are to tell me that and to try to run my whole life! But one thing I do know is, I never want to see you or talk to you again. Good-bye!" At that, Amanda ended the call.

"Oh man," said a somewhat disappointed James Clifton, "That really went well. I knew she wouldn't be extremely happy, but I didn't expect that. Regaining her trust may be easier said than done. But I've got much bigger things to worry about right now." He paused for a few moments in silence.

After those few moments, James said to himself, "Well, I guess I better not try calling her again just yet or going by her place. I mean, she's already upset with me, and I don't want to make matters worse. I just need to make sure X-Termination doesn't get to her. After all, someone's just gotta stop those guys. I guess I can resolve my problems with Amanda later, although I wonder where she's going tonight."

After a couple more moments of silence, James said, "Well, it looks like I'm going back out tonight as the Green Phantasm. After all, it's a better idea than just going as James Clifton. At least that way, I can hover up above for a bird's-eye view. That'll be a better way to spot Amanda, any X-Termination members, or any other sign of trouble."

But all of a sudden, James realized something else. "You know what?" he asked himself. "I never ate or took a shower last night after I got home. Of course, being the Green Phantasm's quite a responsibility, and it's got me under a lot of tension. But I can't go through life like this. So, before I head out as the Green Phantasm, let me shower and get something to eat." At that, he began walking toward his bathroom to take a shower.

But on the way to his bathroom, he had another thought. "You know," Clifton told himself, "before I do any of that, I need to call my friend Eric. Even though he was understanding and considerate enough to let me go about my business, it may be best I let him know what's going on. So I'm gonna go ahead and call him. Here goes."

James dialed the number of his best friend, Eric Thomas, waiting for him to answer.

Shortly, Eric said, "Hello?"

"Hi, Eric," James responded happily, "it's your good buddy, James Clifton."

"Oh, hey, James," Eric said in return, obviously glad to hear from him. "How's it going? Is everything all right?"

"Well, at least so far," James answered him. "Thanks for asking."

"Oh, really?" asked Eric. "I wonder what you mean by 'so far'. Is there something you're worried about?"

"Well, Eric," responded James, "I don't know how you asked the right question, but you did. In fact, that's what I was getting at. It's also why I left you and Scott yesterday evening. As much as I appreciate your consideration and understanding, I think it's probably best if you knew what was really going on. After all, I'd probably be under more tension if I kept trying to hide it. So if you please, just let me explain, okay?"

"Okay, no problem," said Eric. "I'm all ears."

"All right," he began, "well, anyway, Eric, the reason I went on home for the evening was because of Amanda Taylor."

"Oh, Amanda," replied Eric. "Is there a problem with you and her? I mean, Scott and I never meant to come between you two."

"No, no, no, please, Eric," James pleaded, "it's got nothing to do with you and Scott, nothing like that at all. The other night, I think she was delighted to meet y'all. But you see, Eric, Amanda is in danger."

"In danger?" asked Eric. "What kind of danger?"

"Well," he answered, "there's someone after her. Remember those guys who crashed the party the other night?"

"Yeah, I think I do," replied Eric. "You're talking about that organization called X-Termination, I suppose."

"Exactly," said James.

"So," said his friend, "I guess you're saying that they're after her. Well, I wonder why they would be, and if you don't mind me asking, how did you find out?"

"Well," James began, "you remember how, while we were walking into the bar, I had to run across the street to see something?"

"Yeah, I think I do."

"Well, you see, Eric," James continued, "I had seen three guys walking along in hats and coats. I thought that looked odd, so I figured I'd go check 'em out. But then, I followed them for a short distance and overheard them. That's how I found out who they were and what they were up to. It was then that I knew that it was three X-Termination members, Zapper, Zinger, and D.D.T. I also realized that they were looking for Amanda."

"Really?" Eric said in reply to all that. "Well, I still can't help wondering why they're after Amanda. I mean, when they broke and busted in the other night, weren't they after the Green Phantasm?"

"Actually, they were, and they still are. But after Wednesday night, it was Thursday, the next night that X-Termination unleashed another scheme to take down the Green Phantasm. I'm talking about the one with all those rocket planes."

"Oh yeah, that one," replied Eric. "Well, what about it?"

"You see, Eric," James continued, "on that one, Amanda interfered and fouled up their game plan. That's probably why they're looking for her. Besides that, I guess, in turn, they want that to lead them to the Green Phantasm."

"Well," said Eric. "I hope she'll be all right. Have you seen her or heard from her?"

"I'm glad you asked," James said, "because at least they still haven't gotten her yet. But I saw her last night and talked to her just before I called you. However, unfortunately for me, Eric, she's upset with me."

"Really?" asked Eric. "I wonder why."

"Well, it's like this, Eric," said James. "At the banquet Wednesday night, she thought I'd abandoned her, when I really went to find the Green Phantasm to save everyone there. I tried to tell her that, but she wouldn't believe me. Then, I only made her angrier when I found her last night and when I called her moments ago."

"I'm sorry to hear that," Eric said with sympathy. "Well, at least I believe you. But you must be going through a lot right now."

"Yeah," replied James in agreement, "I am under a lot of tension. But the Green Phantasm and I are trying to do something. We're trying to find either Amanda or X-Termination before they find her."

"Well, good luck to you both," his friend said. "I sure hope it all ends well. The only other thing I want to say is, could you please keep me updated?"

"You got it, Eric," said James. "And thanks a lot."

"No problem," he replied.

"Just one other thing," said James.

"Whatcha got?"

"Do you know what Scott's doing right now, by any chance?" James asked his friend.

"It's a good thing you asked, because he's here. He stayed over last night. Wanna talk to him?"

"I'd be delighted to," James responded. "Put him on."

So after that, Eric went to find their other good friend, Scott, and gave him the phone so he could talk to James. Shortly, Scott was saying, "Hello?"

"Hey, Scott," James responded. "It's me, James Clifton."

"Oh, well, uh, what's going on, James?" Scott asked him.

"Not much…" James started to say. "Well, actually, a lot."

"A lot?" asked Scott. "No way, man. What's wrong?"

"Well," answered James, "first of all, I kinda feel bad about going on home yesterday evening. So I thought maybe I should explain."

"Sure, James," replied Scott. "Go ahead."

"Well, you see, Scott," he began, "it was about Amanda, you know, the one I was with at the party the other night?"

"Oh yeah, her," said Scott. "So what are you saying?"

"Well," continued James. "I'm saying that she's in trouble. The secret organization called X-Termination is out trying to find her. She got in their way Thursday night, so they're after her for that. So right now, the Green Phantasm and I are trying to find either Amanda or X-Termination before they locate her and capture her."

"Really?" Scott asked. "You serious?"

"Yes, Scott," James answered somewhat firmly, "I'm afraid I am serious. I never ate, showered, or anything last night. I even overslept this morning. That's because Amanda's not only in danger, but she's also angry and upset with me."

"Wow!" Scott said in reply to all that. "But look, pal, I'm sure it's all not as bad as it seems. Philadelphia's a big city. I don't know what their chances are of finding her. But I guess you gotta do whatcha gotta do. After all, I don't guess I'd want to take the chance if I was you. Well, I hope everything turns out all right; I think it should."

"Well, thank you, Scott," James said happy with his friend's reaction. "The only other thing I want to say is, I've explained everything to Eric. If you want to know more, you can ask him."

"All right, thanks," said Scott. "But can I ask just one more favor?"

"What's that?" asked James.

"Just keep in touch," answered Scott.

"I promise I will," he told him, "but anyway, Scott, I'm afraid I gotta get going. I still have to eat and take a shower and stuff."

"All right," Scott replied. "Well, thanks for calling us. I guess I'll let you go now. Well, bye, James."

"Okay, I'll get back in touch soon. Bye," James said. After that, they hung up.

James went on to take a shower. After that, he put himself together a very heavy breakfast, since he had missed supper the night before.

Finally, by the time he was finished with all of that, it was almost 4:30 p.m. "Well, what do you know?" he asked himself. "It's almost 4:30 already. Time's really flown by this afternoon. Well, anyway, I guess I'd better get ready to head back out as the Green Phantasm."

So, James Clifton rinsed off his glasses and dishes and put them in his dishwasher. After that, he went up to his bathroom to brush his teeth. Finally, he began getting undressed so he could get into his Green Phantasm suit.

Shortly, James took out his superhero's outfit. Of course, in order to prepare to make the transition once again, he activated the pyxorium in his nervous system. Then momentarily, James Clifton was emitting bright neon-green radiation. Last, he teleported into his outfit and was once again the Green Phantasm. "All right," he told himself, "let's go get 'em."

At that, Clifton teleported out through his bedroom window. Like previously, he reappeared hovering a few hundred feet above Philadelphia. Just as always, the Green Phantasm was on the lookout for anyone who possibly needed his help. Of course, the two things he was undoubtedly hoping to find more than anything else were Amanda Taylor and X-Termination. However, he saw no immediate sign of either.

But then, after gazing over the city for a few minutes, the Phantasm heard a faint scream somewhere in the distance. "What was that?" he asked, as he began searching for the source of it.

Before long, he discovered the source of the commotion. He spotted a woman running south along Twentieth Street, between Green and Spring Garden Streets. She had two rogues chasing after her.

The Green Phantasm descended to obtain a better look at the situation. The victim turned out to be a woman who appeared to be in her midthirties; she was about five feet six inches tall and had blond hair. She weighed about 120 pounds and wore a white sleeveless dress with flowers on it.

The troublemakers pursuing her happened to be two young white men in their early twenties. The slightly older one was six feet two inches tall, weighing about 190 pounds. He had short, curly blond hair and had on a black trench coat, a white T-shirt, and a pair of blue jeans. The younger guy was six feet tall and 185 pounds. He had long black hair, which he was keeping in a ponytail. He was dressed in some light-colored blue jeans and a matching jean jacket.

At the moment, the two men were in hot pursuit of the helpless, innocent lady, and they were catching up to her. The slightly younger guy with the ponytail was holding a fighting knife in his left hand. He was to the right of his partner. The other scamp to their left called out to her, "Hey, come back here, baby! Where you going?"

The desperate woman was running for her life. "No!" she sobbed as they were getting closer.

But shortly, as she approached the intersection at Buttonwood Street, one of the guys chasing her grabbed hold of her left arm. It was the slightly taller one with blond hair. He then stopped himself as well as the intended rape victim. At once, the frightened woman turned around and screamed to him, "What are you doing? Let go of me!"

The other thug got in front of her and held her at knifepoint. The lady who was now in great danger turned back around and gasped when she saw the knife that had been pulled on her. Still in tears, she pleaded for her life, saying, "What are y'all doing? I'll let y'all have whatever y'all want. Just don't kill me, okay? Please."

The one holding out the knife smiled and said, "Are you kidding? You're what we want." At that, he brought the knife progressively closer and used his right hand to start lifting up the bottom of her dress. "Let's see what you got," he told the woman, who was now even more frightened and crying her eyes out.

But all of a sudden, the knife flew out of the young man's hand and landed on the ground, several feet to his left. "Hey, what happened?" the surprised troublemaker asked looking around for what had caused him to lose the knife.

Now, of course, the one who had shot the knife from the scamp's hand was none other than the Green Phantasm. The Phantasm was now descending straight toward the ground on the side away from the projected knife. Upon making it to the pavement, the Green Phantasm told the two thugs, "Hey, I did that, all right? Now let her go."

At that, all three of them turned to look at the radiant neon Green Phantasm. "Oh, it's you, huh?" said the one in the trench coat, with curly blond hair.

"Yeah," said the other one with the ponytail, "that's who knocked the knife out of my hand." Upon saying that, he began running over to retrieve his knife. However, the Green Phantasm fired another laser beam to send the knife another ten feet away. "Man, I don't believe this!" fumed the frustrated thug.

"Yeah," said the other guy, "let's blow this freak away." At that, they each took out a nine-millimeter semiautomatic handgun. But before either culprit could aim for the Phantasm, he fired two large laser beams with his already charged hands. In order to unleash these two beams, he had combined the power of five fingers for each one. In turn, each powerful neon-green laser beam projected one of the bad guys back by over ten feet. Consequently, they both ended up lying faceup on the ground. The guns even flew out of their hands whenever they landed.

Right after that, the younger guy with the long, dark hair, who was now understandably very much afraid, said in a panic, "Oh my God! I don't know how he did that, but I can't take him. I'm gettin' outta here, man!" Immediately, he sprang to his feet in desperation and began running north along Twentieth Street.

Just as he was scurrying off, the other guy, who was a couple of years older, began to say, "Wait a minute! Where are you going? There's no way I can—" But it was now too late for him to say any more, for his partner had by then run over a hundred feet away. Since he did not think he could face the Green Phantasm alone, he just decided, "Oh, what the heck! I'm getting out of here too; forget this." At that, he too got up and ran behind his friend.

However, the Green Phantasm did not try to stop them. Since he was much more concerned about saving Amanda from X-Termination, he just let the guys go. But the lady he had just helped was still thankful to him for saving her. She ran right up to the Phantasm and took hold of both of his hands, saying, "Thank you, um…"

"Green Phantasm," he told her kindly. "I'm the Green Phantasm."

"Oh, well, thank you so very much, Green Phantasm," she continued. That very instant, the woman gave him a great big hug to further express her gratitude.

"No problem," replied the Green Phantasm. But then, after the hug, he said, "Look, we gotta get you some help. I've got to notify the police somehow."

Fortunately, a patrol car just so happened to be passing by them along Hamilton Street. Just before the car made it to the scene, the Green Phantasm said, "Oh good, there's one." That very minute, he went over to Hamilton and put up both hands to get the cop's attention.

"Well, what do you know?" said the officer. "It looks like the Green Phantasm. After how he helped the city two nights ago, I'll stop anything for him. Let's see what he needs." The policeman pulled over and got out.

The officer walked up and said, "Good evening, Green Phantasm. What can I do for you?"

"Well, thanks for stopping," answered the Green Phantasm. "There's been a situation here. This lady here just got attacked by two young men. Fortunately for her, I was here to stop this thing. But I let the two clowns get away though."

"Oh, you did?" asked the officer.

"Yeah, I'm afraid so," the Green Phantasm responded. "But you should find a knife and a couple of guns nearby, because I disarmed them when they pulled those weapons. I can also describe the two guys."

"Okay, go ahead," said the officer, who took out a miniature notepad and got ready to write.

The Green Phantasm went on to say, "Well, one of them was about six foot two. He had curly blond hair, and he was wearing a long, dark coat."

"All right," replied the policeman.

"Now, the other one was a couple of inches shorter than him," the Green Phantasm continued. "And he had long, dark hair in a ponytail. He also had on some jeans and a jean jacket. I believe that's about all I got."

"All right, thank you," replied the police officer as he finished writing down everything.

"But anyway, Officer," said the Green Phantasm, "I might've tried to stop those guys, but I've got something else to worry about right now."

"Oh, really?" the officer said in reply. "I understand."

"Yeah," the Green Phantasm said, "it's that organization called X-Termination. But perhaps you're already aware. I mean, I told another officer that they were still at large and that they're after this young lady named Amanda Taylor."

"Oh yes," the officer responded, "I think I have heard."

"But look," the Phantasm told him, "just be careful around them, or should I say *extremely* careful? After all, they've already massacred all those policemen at the hotel on Wednesday, not to mention at least several others. Other than that, I hate to think who else they might've already taken the life of as well."

"Then you probably don't want to hear this, do you?" said the policeman.

"Hear what?" asked the Green Phantasm.

"Well," the officer continued. "We lost nine people from the force last night."

"No way!" exclaimed the Green Phantasm.

"I'm afraid so, although I hate to say it," the police officer told the Phantasm. "Nine of us surrounded the vehicle of theirs that you had described to us. But then, those X-Termination members must've somehow killed them all and then taken to flight in, um, it was their… what was it?"

The Green Phantasm let out a sigh and told him, "It was their X-Terminator 4000."

"Oh yes, that," replied the officer, "but anyhow, all nine of them had gotten slaughtered. Eight of them were nothing but heaps of ashes."

"That's X-Termination all right," the Green Phantasm whispered to himself as he looked away. He turned back toward the police officer and said, "Well, anyway, I gotta get going. I don't know what else to tell you about X-Termination, except to be super extremely cautious. That's because they seem really, really clever and cunning. But somebody's gotta put them out of business, if it has to be me."

"I agree with you a hundred percent," replied the policeman.

"I'm sure you do," responded the Green Phantasm. "But for now, I think this woman here needs some assistance. I'll let you get back to her. Thanks, Officer."

"Thank you, Green Phantasm," the officer said in return. At that, the Green Phantasm shot up above and resumed his search for Amanda, as well as X-Termination.

Shortly after he resumed, he said to himself, "Man, now I know for sure that they've gone too far. But why do I feel like this all my fault? I mean, perhaps if I had not given the police that information, they might've not surrounded that X-Terminator only to get themselves annihilated. I somehow feel like I'm responsible for all those lives being taken. Something tells me I gotta settle it all tonight, no later. After all, I know one life I don't want taken is that of Amanda Taylor. Anyway, I guess all this moping's not gonna get me anywhere. I better get a move on." So, from that point, the Green Phantasm continued his search for the one he loved.

At the same time, someone else was venturing through Philadelphia as well. Without a doubt, it was the trio of X-Termination's three highest-ranking officials other than XT himself. Zapper, Zinger, and D.D.T. were heading north on Broad Street, approaching a dance club called Remington's Dance Club. Their X-Terminator 4000 was parked nearby.

While Zapper was leading his two associates toward the nightclub, he said to them, "All right, you two, we're gonna knock off this dance club here. Y'all ready to do what y'all do best?"

"Yeah!" shouted D.D.T. and Zinger simultaneously.

"Very well," Zapper said in reply. "Let's do this."

But then, Zinger said to Zapper, "Hey, um, Zapper, by any chance, are we gonna—"

Somehow, Zapper knew what he was about to say. So before Zinger could finish, Zapper said, "No, Zinger, probably not. We gotta focus on locating that tramp who fouled up our scheme, and we've only got tonight to do it. There's no time to massacre everybody."

"All right," Zinger responded. "Anything you say."

Before reaching the entrance, Zapper commanded D.D.T. and Zinger to stop, saying, "Hold it, you guys; let me take care of something first."

The threesome was standing a little over fifteen feet from the front door to the club. The very moment in which they had all stopped, Zapper took out his Mega Zapper 2000. He was no doubt about to disable the video surveillance system.

Momentarily, Zapper selected the security camera for which he would aim. It was farthest toward the right of his field of vision. From Zapper's point of view, it was located at the club's right front corner.

Zapper programmed his electronic device to send an electrical surge to shut down that particular security camera and then spread throughout the entire video surveillance system to completely deactivate it. Once the surge was unleashed, Zapper, Zinger, and D.D.T. allowed a few moments for all of the cameras to go down. Finally, Zapper told Zinger and D.D.T., "Okay, men, I believe that takes care of the cameras. Now, you two take care of the bouncer. Go on."

Zinger looked to D.D.T. and said, "You heard him, big man; let's move. Come on." D.D.T. just emitted a grunt and a growl and followed Zinger.

Whenever Zinger got to be around seven feet from the entrance, he stopped and said softly to D.D.T., "Go take out that bouncer; I gotcha covered."

So then, D.D.T. went on up to confront the bouncer. He was very big and tall as well, though not quite like D.D.T. He was a six-foot-nine inch white man and weighed about 450 pounds. Perhaps Zinger had an interest in seeing the two big men face-to-face.

D.D.T. proceeded to face the bouncer. First, he tried to walk on by to enter. But the bouncer, who was to his right, grabbed his right arm to restrain him. "Hold it, big fella," he said. "I need to see your ID, and I need you to remove your mask for a moment too."

"Look, man," D.D.T. told the bouncer, "you better let go and stay outta my way."

"Listen, tough guy," the bouncer said firmly, "there's no way you're barging in here like this. If you even try to storm on through, the rest of security, as well as myself, will throw you out and turn you over to the cops."

D.D.T. broke free, turned right toward the bouncer, and used both hands to squeeze the bouncer's big neck. He then told him, "Yo, man, I don't think so. I most certainly… won't?"

All of a sudden, the bouncer vanished, and all that remained was a heap of ashes on the ground. Zinger had drawn his X-Termination Ray and disposed of the man. D.D.T. looked around, "I wonder how—oh, that's how." He finally noticed Zinger with the ray gun and discerned what had to have happened.

At that, Zinger said, "See? I told you I had you covered." In response, D.D.T. nodded.

But then, that very moment, Zapper came up and told them, "All right now, I see y'all took care of that. Now, let's get moving! There's no time to waste, so move it, you fools, and keep your eyes peeled."

"Yo, keep my eyes peeled?" asked D.D.T. "Is it for, uh, um…"

Zapper scolded him, "You know who we're looking for, you lunkhead! Now keep a sharp lookout, you big galoot!"

The masked trio proceeded on inside. They thoroughly searched out every area and every room for Amanda Taylor. They even checked any ladies' restrooms.

Later, when Zapper was certain they had covered every part of the club, he said to Zinger and D.D.T., "Well, guys, that's gonna do it here. Now let's move on."

"Well, you got it," replied Zinger. "Of course, I ain't sure we oughtta go the same way we came in. I mean, there's no telling who might've gone to check out the scene of the bouncer's demise. Then again, it's not that any of them would be able to stop us anyway, you know."

D.D.T. asked, "So how y'all suppose we gonna get outta this place?"

"What do you mean how?" Zapper asked him in disbelief. Immediately, he pointed to an emergency exit door. At the same time, he told D.D.T., "There's an exit, you buffoon. Can't you see that? Now go on, break it open, and let's get a move on."

At once, D.D.T. shook his head in disbelief. But he also proceeded to charge into the door and force it open.

Unfortunately, this set off an alarm. D.D.T. and Zinger started to look around to see whether they had drawn any attention. However, Zapper sharply commanded them to push on. "Forget about that, you peons," he told them. "Let's move out! There's no time to worry about that. We got bigger things to deal with. Now go!"

"You heard him," said Zinger. "Let's go." At that, Zinger exited the building.

"Yo, man, I'm going," said D.D.T. Then, he just followed behind Zinger. Zapper brought up the rear.

Once all three of them were outside the back of the club, D.D.T. asked, "So which way we gonna go now?"

"There!" Zapper responded. He was pointing straight ahead at a high fence made of vertical wooden planks.

"I wonder what he means by that," D.D.T. said in confusion, for he did not understand why Zapper was directing him straight toward the fence.

Zinger said to his huge partner, "Uh, D.D.T., I could be wrong, but I think he might want you to break through the fence."

"What!" D.D.T. complained. "Now, what's up with that? Why do I always gotta be the one to break something open?"

"Listen, D.D.T.!" snapped Zapper, "You want a shot at taking over X-Termination? If so, you'll do what we need you to do! After all, we can have you replaced, you know. Is that what you want? It's your choice. If not, you'll get us through that fence right now! Now go on. Do it! I ain't got time for this!"

So D.D.T. let out a tremendous roar as he used his huge right foot to kick a big hole in the wooden fence. Then, he used both of his fists to enlarge the opening that he had already begun to form.

Zapper said, "Nice. Now let's proceed."

D.D.T. and Zinger walked on through the fence with Zapper following behind.

But now, X-Termination's evil masked threesome happened to be on someone's property. It was a run-down and abandoned storage center. Like a lot of storage centers, it consisted of long buildings that all had units accessible by garage doors. But the previous owner and operator had been driven out of the business. The property had since then been bought and taken over by a twenty-eight-year-old man named Maxwell Parkerson. He was five feet ten inches tall, white, and weighed around 340 pounds. He had long, dark hair; a beard; and tattoos on both forearms. He was wearing a black T-shirt that had his initials "MP" spray-painted on the front in white. He also wore blue jeans.

But for some reason, Maxwell Parkerson made the storage center a place of refuge for friends of his and any other people who were in need. Parkerson would rent out a storage garage unit for an extremely cheap price to someone who could not afford his own place to live. His tenants included people who had been kicked out of their homes, as well as some high school dropouts, people living in poverty, and other individuals with whom no home owner or employer wanted to interact. However, Maxwell himself lived and worked in his own office, which had all the utilities he needed. Of course, some of the tenants did bad things. But Maxwell did not mind as long as they paid to be on his land.

Now that the X-Termination officials were at the old storage place, Zapper commanded his two men, saying, "Go on ahead, and go through to the other side. I'll be right behind you." So, of the four buildings on the entire piece of property, Zinger and D.D.T. began walking between the first two they saw to their left.

Maxwell Parkerson was standing before the first building with five friends, taking a cigarette break with them. But shortly, one of them said,

"Hey, Max, there's someone walking by right there. I don't think they live up in here; check them out."

At that, Maxwell turned to see where his friend was pointing. He saw the two masked men, Zinger and D.D.T. and called out to them, "Hey, you two, y'all need something? I make the deals here. What brings y'all to my turf?"

In response, D.D.T. and Zinger stopped and turned left to see who was talking to them. They saw Maxwell Parkerson standing before them. That very moment, D.D.T. said to Parkerson, "Yo, man, we are X-Termination, and we just lookin' for somebody."

"Listen, you two," Parkerson told them, "I don't know who it is you think you're looking for, but if you need anything, you come looking for me. It's like I told you two; I'm the one that makes the deals here; y'all got that? Now what are y'all doing on my land, huh? What do y'all want?"

"Listen, man," said Zinger, "here's what's going on. Like he said, we are X-Termination. We're the ones who sent out those planes the other night, to try to bring down the Green Phantasm, remember?"

"Oh yeah," Maxwell answered. "So that was y'all?"

"It certainly was," answered Zinger, "but that's not the point; this is. This young lady interfered with our plans that night. She has short dark hair. We're trying to find her and, in turn, take down the Green Phantasm. Have you seen either one of them?"

"Look here, pal," Maxwell told Zinger. "We don't care what your problem is. The fact is, you're trespassing on my property. There's a price to pay for that. Plus, if you want any information from me, there's a charge for that too. So now, for your presence and the request you've made, it's gonna cost y'all. How much money you two got on you?"

"Yo, man," said D.D.T. to Maxwell Parkerson, "we ain't paying your no-good behinds diddly-squat. So if y'all ain't got nothin' for us, you better get outta our way."

"He's right," Zinger added. "We're not called X-Termination for nothing. So I'd step aside if I were you."

"Oh yeah?" replied a now-angry Maxwell Parkerson. "Well, you two are really asking for it. We're gonna make y'all pay for this somehow. Come on, everybody! Let's get 'em!"

At that, D.D.T. and Zinger looked at each other in confusion. Then, they looked back toward Parkerson, still wondering what was about to happen.

Momentarily, ten people who were dwelling at the run-down storage center came up and began surrounding Zinger and D.D.T. They were all different sizes, although not one of them was as heavy as Maxwell Parkerson. They also wore various types of clothes and hairstyles; some had beards, tattoos, piercings, jewelry, and more. Nearly each and every one of them was holding out either a knife, bat, or other item to use as a weapon. Then, they all began closing in on the masked duo. Zinger and D.D.T. were now looking all around, trying to figure out what they should do.

But all of a sudden, to everyone's surprise, six of the ten who were closing in unexpectedly collapsed to the ground unconscious. The other four stopped and turned to look at those six, for they were no doubt in shock. Maxwell Parkerson and his five friends were surprised as well. Even Zinger and D.D.T. were wondering what had happened. As they began looking for the source, Zinger said, "Now, I wonder how—oh, I see." Zinger had managed to figure it out.

The one who had made those six guys collapse was Zapper. Whenever D.D.T. and Zinger had gone up ahead, Zapper had stayed by the fence's opening, in case he would be needed with his Mega Zapper 2000. It was a good thing he had done that, because apparently, he had just been needed to take down some of those who were outnumbering them. Just like on other occasions, he had programmed a powerful electrical surge to zap the ones who were targeted.

Whenever Zinger saw Zapper holding out his device, he pointed that out to his gigantic partner, D.D.T. Then, they both thanked Zapper with two thumbs up each. But Zapper's expression remained serious. He then went on to put away his Mega Zapper, make a fist with his right hand, and put it in his left, while nodding affirmatively. He was commanding Zinger and D.D.T. to take out the remaining four who had surrounded them.

Zinger understood that and gave an affirmative nod in return, after which he shouted, "Right!"

D.D.T. roared out in agreement, "Yeah!"

Zinger drew his X-Termination Ray. That very instant, he turned around and zapped the man who was all the way to the right. That reduced him to a heap of ashes, turning the head of the man who had stood to the right of that victim. "Oh my God!" he exclaimed at the sudden annihilation of his friend.

Next, D.D.T. used both of his hands to grab the other two men by their necks. With a grunt and a growl, he rammed the crowns of their heads together and rendered them unconscious. Next, D.D.T. slammed the guy in his right hand down. After that, he killed the one in his left hand by breaking his neck. Then, he just dropped that victim to the ground as well.

Out of the ten who had previously encircled D.D.T. and Zinger, only one was still standing. However, he was now twenty feet back from the unbelievable masked pair, for he had backed away in fear for his life.

Shortly, Zinger began firing his X-Termination Ray at the six guys Zapper had taken out. He zapped one man into a pile of ashes. At that, he said, "Yeah, let's 'X-terminate' them." Then, he fired a shot at another victim, reducing him to ashes as well. At the sight of this, Maxwell Parkerson and his five friends ran around the building to hide in a garage unit on the other side, for they were no doubt afraid and horrified. The remaining individual who had taken part in surrounding the two masked culprits earlier just took off and ran as fast as he could.

But, before Zinger or D.D.T. did any further damage, Zapper came along and said to them, "All right, guys, let's get out of here. Come on, let's move it!" In response to Zapper's command, Zinger and D.D.T. followed behind him.

Anselm Nielsen always enjoyed using his great strength and power to damage people and things. Therefore, he seized practically every opportunity. So, while following behind Zapper and Zinger, the humongous, colossal titan inflicted some major damage on two storage units to his left. First, he combined both hands and charged into a closed garage door, while putting forth a powerful shove. This left an enormous dent in the garage door and knocked a pair of wheels out of the two runners. He moved over to the storage unit next to it, which had its garage door raised up. Big D.D.T. reached up and grabbed the bottom of the door with both hands. That very instant, he pulled the door out of the runners completely and slung it to the ground. Finally, he just continued following Zapper and Zinger to the other side of the abandoned storage center.

As the troublesome threesome leaving, Maxwell Parkerson came out of his hiding place. He crept around the end of the building in which he had been hiding and watched X-Termination leave. As they were on their way off, Zapper said, "All right, you two, we're gonna knock off a couple of gas stations, and then we'll hit that Italian restaurant on Columbia Avenue called Castelano's."

Parkerson managed to hear all that Zapper had just said and said to himself, "Is that so? Well, that ain't my biggest concern. The fact is, those jerks killed some people of mine and tore up my land. I don't know who or how, but somebody's gonna pay the price for all this."

It was now after 6:00 p.m., and the Green Phantasm was hovering up above Philadelphia, trying to find either Amanda Taylor or X-Termination. Before long, he managed to spot something. It was a couple of police cars with flashing lights, parked at the club that the three X-Termination members had hit a little earlier. "Hmph," said the Green Phantasm, "I wonder what that is. Well, it looks serious, so I'll go down and check it out. I wonder if it was X-Termination by any chance. If so, I'll hopefully be able to catch them and stop them. So here I go."

The Green Phantasm became a shapeless projectile and shot down toward Remington's. He ended up reappearing at the entrance. He went up to one of the investigating police officers and said, "Hey, excuse me, Officer. What happened here?"

"That's what we're trying to figure out," he answered. "First of all, the video surveillance system went out somehow. Other than that, I can't help wondering if the jerk who made that happen is also the same jerk who did that over there."

At that, the Green Phantasm turned to see what the policeman was pointing to. He then noticed the pile of ashes at the doorway. At the sight of it, the Green Phantasm gasped and said, "Oh no, it was X-Termination. They were here."

"X-Termination?" asked the officer. "Is that the guys you gave us the information on?"

"I'm afraid so," the Green Phantasm told him. "But look, although I reported that they were still at large, I think maybe I'll have to be the one to stop them."

"Come on now," said the police officer. "What makes you say that?"

"Listen," answered the Green Phantasm, "those guys have already killed a whole bunch of police officers. So it's true that they've got to be stopped. But I just think it may be too dangerous for y'all to try to deal with them. Something tells me that the one to take care of those punks may have to be me. Even if that is so the case, so be it. In fact, I better get moving right now so I can find them. Just, um, make sure and play it safe, okay?"

"All right," replied the officer. "Whatever you say, Green Phantasm. We greatly appreciate your help. Thank you."

"No problem," said the Green Phantasm. "Here I go." At that, he entered the building and went searching for X-Termination. While the Green Phantasm was venturing through the club, everyone there turned and looked in wonder at him, for someone who emitted such bright neon-green light was not an everyday sight. Since a lot of people were apparently showing interest in him, he would occasionally ask, "Have y'all seen any guys come through here with masks and brightly colored outfits?"

He would receive different responses like, "I think maybe I did. I don't know. "; "Perhaps, but I wasn't paying attention"; or "I could have. It's possible." But then eventually, one individual told him, "You know, I believe I did see three guys who fit that description, but I never saw them go back through to the front. So they could still be in here somewhere."

"Thank you so very much," the Green Phantasm responded most gladly. "That's what I needed to hear." After that, he continued searching for the diabolical threesome.

Eventually, the Green Phantasm finally made it to the emergency exit door that the three men had used to escape earlier. However, he still could not see any trace of them. So he said to a security member of the club, "Excuse me; there's three individuals I'm looking for with brightly colored costumes and masks. They're members of X-Termination. Have you, by any chance, seen them or even noticed anything unusual in here tonight?"

"I'm not sure," answered the security guard, "but a while ago, somebody opened that exit door right there. However, there was really nothing wrong. It was either an error, a false alarm, or something."

"Thank you," the Green Phantasm told him.

"Sure," responded the security guard.

So then, the Green Phantasm paused to try to figure something out. "Let's see," he told himself. "For some reason, I haven't found 'em yet. But I think someone told me that he never saw them go back toward the entrance, right? I mean, of course, if I were them, I wouldn't either, considering that one of them must've used his ray gun to shoot the bouncer, or whoever was by the door. So I guess they didn't go back out the front."

Then momentarily, he continued, "But wait, didn't that guard just say that somebody opened that door when nothing was wrong?" All of a sudden, he figured it out. "By George, that's it!" he exclaimed. "They must've gone through that emergency exit to escape. Why else would someone open it if there was nothing wrong?"

At first, the Green Phantasm did not like the idea of going through the door and creating another false alarm. But momentarily, he decided, "Well, there's a lot worse things to worry about right now than false alarms. Besides, I gotta find those guys, and I don't have any time to lose." So the Green Phantasm just exited through the emergency door. Just like he thought would happen, the alarm went off.

Next, once the Green Phantasm got outside the back of the building, he began looking all around and asking himself, "I wonder which way they went from here." Before long, he noticed the big hole in the wooden fence ahead of him. So then, the Phantasm said, "Now, I wonder how that big hole got into that fence. I mean, it would probably take someone or something really big and powerful."

All of a sudden, he had a thought. "Wait a minute," the Green Phantasm said. "Did I say big and powerful? I did, didn't I? Why, they could've used big ol' D.D.T. to bust through that fence. Let me go check that out to see if I can find anything else as well, especially since I think they might've gone that way." The Green Phantasm teleported over to the fence, where D.D.T. had broken through so he and his two teammates could pass.

Once the Green Phantasm came out of the teleportation beam as himself, he put one foot on the other side of the hole in the fence. After that, he bent over and maneuvered his upper body through the hole too, so he could look around the storage area for any damage that X-Termination could have caused. Some of the first things that the Phantasm noticed were six victims lying between the first and second buildings. Of course, each victim was on the ground either dead or unconscious. "I wonder if they did this," the Green Phantasm said to himself. "I mean, it's a possibility. I better go get a better look at this."

So immediately, the Green Phantasm began running over to the scene of X-Termination's massacre. Another thing the Phantasm noticed was the person of Maxwell Parkerson standing nearby with his five closest friends. They were all grieving over all of the loss and damage that had been sustained that evening. As the Green Phantasm approached the scene, he recognized three piles of ashes, to which three other victims had obviously been reduced. That to him was a definite indication that the X-Termination officials had passed through the run-down storage area. "Yep," he told himself, "they were here all right."

Next, the Green Phantasm went to talk to Maxwell Parkerson. "Excuse me, sir," he said to Parkerson.

Maxwell turned around and replied to the Phantasm, "Well, just who do you think you are, huh? And what are you doing on my property?"

"Well," the Green Phantasm began, "um, first of all, I'm the Green Phantasm, and I—"

"Hold it right there," Parkerson interrupted. "I'm Maxwell Parkerson, and I own and control this piece of land you're on. But anyway, you say you're the Green Phantasm, huh?"

"Well, that's right," replied the Green Phantasm.

"Well then," continued Parkerson. "I guess you're that guy they were talking about while they were here a little earlier."

"You mean those members of X-Termination?" asked the Green Phantasm.

"See? He knows them," said one of Maxwell's friends.

"I do see," Maxwell replied to his friend in agreement. "And y'all know something else? I don't know why I didn't think of this before, but I think I've found the one who we're gonna make pay the price for everything they've done to us."

"Wait a minute," the Green Phantasm pleaded. "What are y'all talkin' about?"

"What are we talking about?" Parkerson said to the Phantasm. "Take a look around you, ya' radiant green fool." Then, pointing to the injured and slaughtered victims lying about, Maxwell asked the Green Phantasm, "Can't you see that?"

"Why, yes," the Green Phantasm answered. "It's quite evident they did that."

"You're doggone right they did!" Maxwell told him firmly. Right after that, he pointed out the two garage doors that had been destroyed by the one called D.D.T. and told the Phantasm, "You see that? Look what they did to my doors!"

The Green Phantasm took a look and said to Parkerson, "Look, I'm really sorry about all the damage."

But before he could continue, Maxwell Parkerson told him, "Yeah, I bet you are sorry, and you know something else? You're about to become even more sorry."

"More sorry?" replied the Green Phantasm. "Come on, Max; what do you mean?"

"Look, man," said Parkerson, "we'll get to that in a minute. First, let's get down to business. For one thing, you're on my land, and there's a charge for that. And another thing, somebody's gotta pay for all this destruction to my property. So I'm asking you, Green Phantasm, how much money you got on you?"

"Listen," the Green Phantasm began to answer. "I'm in my superhero costume, and I don't have any money on me. The only reason I'm here is because I'm trying to track down X-Termination. I mean, they were obviously here earlier, and—"

But Parkerson would not let him continue. "All right," Maxwell interrupted, "that's it! I don't know why you're looking for them, but I do know that if it weren't for you, they wouldn't have come through here and done all this destruction. I mean, it was you they came here looking for. So, since you have no money and you haven't stopped those guys before they wrecked my land, we're just gonna make you pay the price another way."

"Maxwell," pleaded the Green Phantasm. "Wait a minute. Please listen to me."

"Shut up!" scolded the angry owner of the storage center. He went and got a megaphone from his office nearby, which was in the first building. At once, he spoke to every tenant of his over the megaphone, saying, "Attention, everyone! We got a trespasser here by my office. I need everybody's help to take him out. Come on! Get over here!"

"Hold it now," begged the Green Phantasm. "What's going on?"

But, before he could receive an answer from Maxwell, a lot of people who dwelt in leased-out storage units began coming in from all sides to surround the Green Phantasm. One reason that a lot of tenants were willing to help was that most of them had also become friends of Maxwell Parkerson, in addition to merely being tenants. Anyway, as they all continued to close in on the Phantasm, Maxwell yelled to everyone, "Come on; let's waste this freak! Go on! Get him!" Even the five close friends who had been next to Maxwell joined in on the mob. Many of those attacking the Phantasm carried such items as knives and clubs or sticks with which to hammer him. Over twenty-five people were involved.

But just before the attackers could inflict their first strike, the Green Phantasm found himself a way to escape from the center of it all. He noticed a gap among all the people on one side through which he could teleport. That would place him closer to the wooden fence into which D.D.T. had knocked the big opening. So the Phantasm just teleported out from the midst of it all and ended up by the wooden fence.

Everyone in the crowd gasped in surprise when the Green Phantasm apparently disappeared into thin air. Then, they all began looking around, trying to figure out what had happened. "Hey, what happened?" asked one of them.

"Yeah; where'd he go?" asked another.

Right after that, Maxwell Parkerson asked everyone, "What's the problem, huh? What's going on?"

But that very minute, the Green Phantasm said to Parkerson, "Listen, Maxwell, I know you're upset about the damage, and I'm sorry I didn't find those guys sooner. But this is not going to solve the problem."

Upon hearing that, Maxwell and everyone else turned around to face the Green Phantasm. "Whoa!" they all said in unison, for they were in shock at seeing him near the fence without knowing how he had gotten there.

Maxwell Parkerson shook his head in disbelief and muttered to himself, "I don't know how he managed to sneak over there, but I do know that we're gonna get him!" Right after that, he told all of his lessees, "Come on, everybody! Let's annihilate this radioactive creep once and for all." They all began to close in on the Green Phantasm once again.

While they were drawing closer, the Green Phantasm looked toward Maxwell Parkerson, who was to the left of his field of vision. He then tried begging, "No, Max, wait! Please, wait!"

However, while the Green Phantasm was begging and pleading fruitlessly, some of those coming toward him were preparing to throw knives at him. The Green Phantasm noticed in the nick of time, when a knife began flying at him. "Holy shoot!" he exclaimed, after which he teleported a few feet to his right to avoid the knife, which flew by and landed in the fence.

As soon as the Phantasm relocated, a few more attackers prepared to unleash their knives. "Oh shoot!" muttered the Green Phantasm, "Doggone it! This really sucks!" So this time, the Green Phantasm teleported himself forward to turn up behind the whole group of attackers. "Where'd he go now?" one of Parkerson's men said regarding the Phantasm's sudden disappearance.

But shortly, another guy managed to notice his reappearance and shouted, "There he is!" At that, they all began to turn around to face the Phantasm yet another time.

This time around, the Green Phantasm was charging his hands in preparation to unleash an enormous green laser beam. Just as everyone began to draw closer to him, he unleashed the largest and most powerful beam he possibly could. In turn, this sent twelve people soaring backward toward the wooden fence. They were the twelve individuals who had been to the left of all those the Green Phantasm could see. This no doubt astounded and overwhelmed the remainder of the pack. They all turned their heads and gasped in complete shock as their twelve teammates landed on the ground.

After that, all of those who were left standing made another attempt to surround and take down the Green Phantasm. As they began moving toward the glowing, radiant hero, one of them yelled, "Let's spread out more!" They began to widen out.

However, before the group of young men could expand by very much, the Green Phantasm put a stop to their scheme. His hands were still charged with radiant energy. He produced and discharged yet another gigantic neon-green laser beam that had the combined force of all ten fingers, as had the previous beam. This, too, sent a large number of attackers back toward the fence, so that everyone the Phantasm had hit ended up lying on the ground before the tall wooden fence.

Somehow, the Phantasm missed one individual, who was now left standing between both groups of attackers that had been knocked over and stunned by huge laser beams. This gangster looked toward the Green Phantasm, smiling and chuckling. "He missed me, heh, heh, heh," said the proud young hoodlum to himself. Then, he drew a twenty-six-inch-long machete to cast at the Phantasm.

As the young man was preparing to hurl the machete, the Green Phantasm muttered to himself, "Doggone it, that crazy fool! What's he trying to do, kill me?" Then, while the machete was flying toward him, he took the form of a shapeless projectile and hurled himself at the individual. The Green Phantasm proceeded to force his opponent backward into the fence. In fact, it was right next to the spot through which D.D.T. had broken earlier. Unfortunately for landowner Maxwell Parkerson, this made the big hole in the fence even bigger.

Whenever the Green Phantasm and his combatant connected with the fence, the young rascal went right through it and ended up lying on his back on the other side of the fence. On the other hand, the Green Phantasm just went from a shapeless projectile back to his normal form and was now standing before the enlarged hole in the fence.

The youngster who had hurled the machete was now on the other side of the fence, lying faceup on the ground, groaning and whimpering in pain and fear. His back was hurting from having broken through the fence, and he was seriously dazed from the enormous blow inflicted by the Green Phantasm. "Oh my God," the young man said while weeping, "what's happened to me? What's going on?" From that point, he just continued shedding tears.

The Green Phantasm walked through to the other side to see whether the guy was okay. "Hey, guy, excuse me," the Phantasm said to him. "Are you all right?"

At that, the fallen thug looked up at him and cried in panic, "Oh no!" Then, he put his hands in front of his face submissively and exclaimed, "What are you gonna do to me, huh? Please don't kill me! Please don't!"

"Hey, hey, hey, hey, hey, hey, hey," the Green Phantasm told him calmingly, "I'm not going to kill you, okay? Now calm down. I'm just asking if you're okay."

"Oh, all right," said the somewhat relieved guy on the ground. "Well, I don't know, Green Phantasm. My back hurts, and right now, I'm feeling embarrassed, humiliated, ashamed—"

Before he could continue, the Green Phantasm told him, "Yes, you really should be. I'm sorry you're hurting like this right now, but you tried to kill me with that machete. I possibly could've killed you in self-defense, but fortunately for you, I don't desire to be a killer. I only ran you through the fence. You need to learn to make better decisions."

"Listen," whimpered the one lying on the ground. "Just leave me alone, okay? Go away, please! I don't want anymore. Just leave me alone!"

"Okay," replied the Green Phantasm, "anything you say." The Phantasm just went back through the hole in the fence. He decided to let the one who had just been lying at his feet alone, because his good conscience prohibited infliction of further damage and he had more important matters to pursue.

The Green Phantasm was again on the property owned and run by Maxwell Parkerson. He was now going to try to resolve any problems he may have still had with Maxwell and his tenants. After stepping back through the hole in the wooden fence, the Green Phantasm teleported and turned up standing before the crowd that had attempted to subdue him. Many of them were back on their feet, and the Green Phantasm was prepared to strike if necessary.

"All right, everybody!" the Green Phantasm told them all. They all gave him their undivided attention. "Listen up, okay? I'm sure you're all mad right now, but I assure you, I didn't come here for this. I'm not looking for any trouble, all right? I only came here looking for X-Termination. Y'all know that, right?" However, the Phantasm received no answer because the ones to whom he was speaking knew that he was right but were too ashamed to answer him.

But then, the Green Phantasm continued by saying, "Well, I do believe y'all do know that. But look, I don't want to hurt anybody here, y'all got that?" At least some of them nodded affirmatively. But at the same time, Maxwell Parkerson, who was still looking on, shook his head and scoffed in disbelief.

The Green Phantasm continued telling everyone, "All right, and now, I got one last thing to say. I don't mean to sound arrogant or immodest, but I think it's only fair I let you all know something. Whatever you're thinking about doing next, you'd better just forget it. I've been through tougher than this already, and I honestly do not believe that y'all stand a chance taking me out. Now you see, I promise you that I don't want anyone to get hurt or any further damage done any more than you do. So, if you all seriously do not want that either, I strongly suggest y'all break this up and get back to your business." After finishing what he had to say, the Green Phantasm just became silent and stood by to see what Parkerson's men would do next.

For a couple of moments, they all stood around looking at each other and trying to decide what to do. But very shortly, one of them decided, "Look, I don't know about y'all, but I'm going back to my home. There's just no way to take this guy; at least I don't see how. So I'm going, okay? I'm going. Excuse me please." At that, he walked off and went back to the storage unit in which he was staying.

Another said, "You know, I think he might be right. I don't know how the Green Phantasm did what he did, but I don't stand a chance against him. So I'm with that guy." He too began walking off.

After that, the remaining tenants of Maxwell Parkerson did a little murmuring among themselves. Then finally, they all began leaving the scene, no longer willing to face the Green Phantasm.

At seeing them all walk off, Maxwell Parkerson said to them, "Wait a minute, guys! What are y'all doing? Come on; what's wrong with all of you?"

But then, the Green Phantasm answered, "I don't think there's anything wrong with them, Maxwell. I think they all finally came to their senses, and I'm proud of them."

Parkerson stood around for a few moments in silence, not knowing what to say. Then, he turned around and ran. This was because he did not think he could defeat the Green Phantasm either, and he wanted no further damage done to his property. Finally, Parkerson went into one of his storage units to hide from the Green Phantasm.

At last, when nearly everyone had gone back to their business, the Green Phantasm turned around to try to talk to Maxwell Parkerson. But of course, Parkerson had taken to flight. However, the Phantasm managed to catch a glimpse of him as he was entering one of the units to his left.

So then, the Green Phantasm began running between the first two buildings to try to find Maxwell. "Hey, Maxwell!" he called out to him. At last, he found him in the very next storage garage unit after passing the two that had earlier been damaged by D.D.T. of X-Termination. Maxwell was standing all the way in the rear left corner with his back to the Phantasm.

Next, the Green Phantasm took a step inside and said, "Hey, Maxwell."

At that, Parkerson peeked behind himself but then looked away and put up his hands in a submissive gesture. "Please, Green Phantasm," he said in a panic, "what are you gonna do to me?"

The Green Phantasm told him calmly, "Come on, Max. Please relax and put your hands down, okay?"

"But after what I tried to do to you, you'll kill me," Maxwell replied.

"No, Maxwell," said the Green Phantasm, "I'm not going to kill you or do anything to you, so calm down."

Maxwell turned completely around to stand face-to-face with the Green Phantasm. "Okay, okay, okay," he said repeatedly while trying to calm down.

The Green Phantasm went on to say, "Listen, as I was telling everybody else, I'm not here to hurt anybody or anything. I'm just here trying to find X-Termination. Now, by any chance, do you have any clues as to where they went from here?"

"Look, man," answered Parkerson, "what if I don't wanna say anything, huh? What are you gonna do to me then?"

"Maxwell, look," the Phantasm told him. "I won't make you talk about it if you don't want to. I mean, that's quite fine; you don't have to, all right? I've got better things to do right now than stand here and argue anyway. But I just thought I might let you know one other thing. If you don't tell me anything, and I don't ever find them, they could very well pass back through here and do some more damage and even kill some more people. I didn't think you'd want that, but if you do, that's perfectly all right with me. I'll just go ahead and let you go. So just have a nice evening, okay? Bye." At that, the Green Phantasm began walking away.

But then immediately, Parkerson said to him, "All right, all right, wait! You're right, man, I see your point. Now would you please let me tell you what I know?"

The Green Phantasm stopped, turned around, and said, "All right, that's better. Now, what did you find out? Did you hear them say anything at all?"

"Well," answered Maxwell. "It's like this: I heard them say just a little something as they were leaving. I thought I heard one of them say that they were gonna knock off a couple of gas stations and then that Italian restaurant on Columbia Avenue."

"Do you mean Castelano's?"

"Yeah, that," responded Maxwell Parkerson. "And that's all the information I have."

"All right, thank you," the Green Phantasm told him. "That ought to help. I appreciate this, Max. Thanks again, and have a good night. I gotta get going."

"Anytime, Green Phantasm."

So next, the Green Phantasm used his hovering ability to rise and hover above Philadelphia once again. While hovering, the Green Phantasm said to himself, "Man, I don't know exactly why or how, but something tells me I gotta settle everything tonight. I guess that's because of everything X-Termination's done and everything I'm going through right now. It's got me feeling so tense that I can't stand another night of it all. So I've gotta not only find Amanda before they do, but I've got to put them out of business before the night is over. Yes, it absolutely has to be tonight." At that, the Phantasm nodded affirmatively.

Then, he began trying to think about what to do next to try to locate either Amanda Taylor or the X-Termination members who were looking for her. "All right," said the Green Phantasm, "what now? Where should I try to go from here? I don't know, but I hope that what Maxwell told me is true; I mean, what he said about them hitting two gas stations and then that restaurant on Columbia. Wait a minute now; that's a real nice place there. I wonder if Amanda is there by any chance."

But then, he decided, "Well, I don't know about that either. But I do know that X-Termination is going to hit there. So I can catch them there, make them tell me where their hideout is, and put an end to their operation once and for all. Of course, I don't know what two gas stations they're going to, and I feel really sorry that I won't be at either one to stop them. But I do know where Castelano's is. I just need to try to get there before they do, and I hope I'm not too late. So, I better get going right away. Here I go."

It was now past 7:00 p.m., and the Green Phantasm began making his way over to Castelano's Italian Restaurant on Columbia Avenue. With the speed at which he could either teleport or project himself, it did not even take him close to a minute to get over there.

Once there, the Green Phantasm began looking around for any sign of X-Termination. The Phantasm carefully teleported and sneaked around to every side of the building to make certain that they had not made it there yet. But somehow, he did not even spot a single trace of Zapper, Zinger, or D.D.T. So finally, once the Phantasm was certain he had looked everywhere on the outside, he said, "Well, from what I can see so far, it looks like they haven't gotten here yet. So hopefully, I beat 'em here."

The Green Phantasm told himself, "I just hope Amanda wasn't at either of those gas stations, even though I don't know—wait a minute. Speaking of her, I wonder if she's here or not. I guess I'd better make sure."

So, the Green Phantasm began running around to look in every window upon which he came to see if he could spot Amanda Taylor. While searching, he declared, "Oh man, I hope for sure she's not in here. If she is, I gotta do something." He kept looking for Amanda.

All of a sudden, at the second window to which he came, he spotted something that caught his eye. However likely or unlikely it was, the Green Phantasm saw Amanda Lee Taylor seated at a table dining with her date, Dr. Mark Thompson. "Oh no!" exclaimed the Green Phantasm, "What'll I do now? I gotta get her out, warn her, or at least… I don't know, try something." The Phantasm was now nearly in a state of panic, for he was worried about Amanda.

After a couple of moments, he said, "You know, at least it's a good thing I found her before they did. Thank goodness for that! But still, I hate for her to be in the midst of it all when those guys come and raid the place. Now what am I gonna do?"

After trying to think of a solution, he only came up with one idea. "Well," he said, "I probably oughtta not go through there as the Green Phantasm. I might draw too much attention or produce too much excitement. I guess I'll just go in as James Clifton. She may not be happy to see me, but this is the best way I know of to get her out of X-Termination's way. After all, I don't wanna risk anything else happening to Amanda after Thursday night. So I'll just hurry home, get out of my suit, and zip back over here as James Clifton. Then, I get myself a table so I can get in here." At that, he used his powers to rush home at lightning speed.

Once James made it to his bedroom at home, he got out of his Green Phantasm suit and put on some dress clothes. Then, he shot back over to Castelano's. Whenever he made it there again, he went and hid behind the big garbage container behind the restaurant and deactivated the pyxorium within himself. That made him stop emitting neon-green light, and he became like an ordinary man again. Finally, James walked back around to the front entrance.

Upon making it to the front, James went inside. At once, the hostess at the front desk asked him, "Can I help you, sir?"

"Yes," he answered. "I'd like a table please."

"Right this way," replied the young lady. At that, Clifton followed her until she stopped at a square table with four chairs. "Here you are," the hostess told him.

"Thank you," said James. Then, she left him.

Right afterward, James looked all around for Amanda, but could not find her right away, for the restaurant was very, very crowded. After a matter of seconds of looking around, James just sat down at his table and tried to think of what to do next.

While Clifton was sitting and thinking, his waiter came along and brought him a glass of water. "Your water, sir," he said. "Would you care for something else to drink?"

"Oh, thanks," responded Clifton as he took his water, "and um, I'll, uh, need a few more minutes to think about it."

"You got it," the waiter told him. "I'll be back." He turned and walked off.

Next, James looked at the glass of water and thought, *You know, perhaps I should drink some water and cool down, so I can keep ahold of myself.* So he drank up half the glass.

But then, after he had calmed down a little, something unexpected happened. Someone passed in front of James, and he looked up to see that it was Amanda Lee Taylor. She was on her way to the restroom. "Good!" James happily exclaimed to himself. "It's Amanda. I'll try to catch her on the way back."

Once Amanda was past James, he began to get out of his chair. But as James was getting up, his waiter approached him and said, "Excuse me, sir; have you decided on anything?"

As soon as James stood up, he turned around and said, "Oh, uh, I… I, uh, gotta go to the bathroom. I'll be right back."

"No problem," replied the waiter. "That'll be fine."

"Thanks," said James. After that, he went toward the restrooms. He stood near the men's room, waiting for Amanda to come out.

Several minutes later, Amanda Taylor came walking out of the ladies' room. Immediately, James approached her. "Amanda," he said to her.

In reaction, Amanda halted before him and gasped with a surprised look on her face. Not knowing what to say, she uttered, "Oh my… what the… James! James Clifton?" Amanda could hardly believe her eyes. So she looked away from James and pleaded, "Will somebody please tell me this isn't happening?"

"Listen, Amanda," James told her calmly, "I know you're extremely upset with me and you're probably not wanting to talk to me right now. But it's really a good thing I found you. I mean, this is very, very important."

"Yeah, right!" Amanda snapped in reply. "It's just like when you found me last night, you pervert!"

"Amanda, please," James begged. "I know what you think, but I promise you that it's not what it looks like, okay? You gotta listen to me, because your life depends on this. You're in terrible danger."

"James, please!" Amanda told him with a snarl on her face. "I suppose you're about to tell me about X-Termination, right? Answer me, James? Is that right?"

"Okay, fine, I'll answer you," James replied, "even though you may hate me for this. Yes, Amanda. I'm not lying about this, okay? I found this out from the Green Phantasm. He was trying to track them down, and he managed to find out that they're coming here tonight. In fact, I think they're probably gonna be here soon. So I suggest you hurry up and leave; please, I'm begging you, for both of our sakes."

But Amanda just looked down, sighed, and shook her head in disbelief. "Oh, James!" She sighed. "Oh my God, I can't believe you. I mean, you tracked me down last night, and you found me here tonight. On top of that,

I'm here with Mark Thompson, and you're making that up, all because you're jealous. You'll say anything to tear me away from him, won't you?"

"Amanda," James said still rather calmly, "I'm telling you, you're wrong about me."

However, this only made Amanda angrier. "That does it, James!" yelled Amanda. "It is completely and officially over between you and me! I never want to see you or talk to you again! Have you got that, huh? Have you?"

James was hesitant to say yes because, although he understood what Amanda had said, he also knew that she did not understand him correctly. So he merely uttered, "Well, um… I mean, I, uh…" James did not know what to say.

But a really furious Amanda Taylor did not have the patience to wait for an answer. "That's it, James!" she snapped. "Just stay out of my sight from now on, and have a nice life!" At that, she began to storm on past him.

"Come on, Amanda," James begged and pleaded. He used his left hand to grab and hold her right arm. "Please don't give me that," he added.

Amanda turned to James and yelled at the top of her lungs, "Let go of me, you freak!" That caused a lot of people to turn their heads to see what she was yelling about.

Trying once more to calm her, James told Amanda, "No, no, no, you gotta listen to me."

Amanda refused to calm down and listen. In turn, she went on to scream out, "Help! Help me! Somebody get this creep off me!" That brought about even more attention.

Shortly, even the restaurant manager rushed to the scene and said to James and Amanda, "Hey, excuse me; is there some trouble here?" When that happened, James just let go of Amanda and turned toward the manager.

Before James could utter a single word, Amanda exclaimed, "You're freakin' right there is!" Then, pointing to James Clifton, she yelled, "That's the trouble! That is! Yeah, I'm talkin' about that perverted, overrated creep right there!"

"Hold it! Hold it!" said the restaurant manager while trying to calm her. "Just calm down and tell me what's going on here."

Somewhat calmer, Amanda went on to tell the manager, "I'll tell you what's going on here, okay? This guy's been stalking after me, trying to track me down for the past few days, and now he finally found me here tonight. I'm trying to tell him to leave me alone, but he won't. The fact is, I'm really here with someone else, and he knows that too." At hearing all this, James sighed and shook his head in disbelief, for he was misunderstood, and Amanda was possibly giving the manager the wrong idea.

Immediately afterward, the general manager turned to Clifton and asked, "Young man, is this true?"

Not sure what to say, James just hesitantly began by uttering, "Well, yeah, but—"

The manager replied, "Okay, so it's true then."

A somewhat frustrated James Clifton began to say, "Yes, but you don't understand!"

"Enough!" the restaurant manager declared firmly. "I don't have time for this, all right? Now I'm going to have to ask you to leave. You're not gonna come in here and harass my customers. Now get out!"

However, James tried pleading once more, saying, "Please, sir, please don't do this to me! Could you please just—"

"I said get out, now!" yelled the manager. "If you don't leave immediately, I'm calling the police." At that, Clifton just began walking toward the front door in order to leave, for he did not want to get into any trouble with the police. As he was leaving, the manager told him one last thing, which was, "If I ever catch you hanging around here again, I'm putting out a restraining order against you. So don't you ever come back to Castelano's again!"

Once James was outside the building, he stopped, hung his head forward, sighed, and shook his head in disbelief. "I don't believe this," he said to himself. James Clifton was no doubt ashamed, embarrassed, and humiliated. Not knowing what else to do, he just began walking away from the restaurant. He did not attempt to fight back, for he did not want to make matters worse between the restaurant and himself.

James was walking east along the north side of Columbia Avenue. As he was walking, he was saying to himself, "Man, man, man, I've never felt so foolish in all my life. I never would've thought that being a hero would come to this. I don't know what to do now. I mean, I'm now banned from this restaurant. Of course, I had already kind of figured that Amanda wouldn't be happy and that this wouldn't be a great idea. Why didn't I listen to myself?"

After a few moments of silence accompanied by grief and discouragement, Clifton said, "Well, I guess there's nothing more I can do or say now. Even if I could do anything, what difference would it make? After all, Amanda wants nothing more to do with me. But still, I sincerely do love and care about Amanda Taylor. I just hope she leaves the place before those guys get there. But regardless, I guess she doesn't need me anymore. After all, what would anybody want with a screw-up like myself anyway? I don't think I'd want anything with that. Oh well, I might as well go home."

Clifton just proceeded to the corner of Columbia and Broad Street. Once there, he just stood and waited for the next taxicab to come along. Poor James Clifton was undoubtedly so upset that he was in no mood to activate or utilize his powers as the Green Phantasm. So, once a taxi drove his way, he signaled it to stop, after which he took a ride home.

It was soon 7:30 p.m. At that time, a large, powerful vehicle pulled up near Castelano's Italian Restaurant. The vehicle was none other than an X-Terminator 4000. The three men in the X-Terminator were Zapper, Zinger, and D.D.T. This corrupted, diabolical masked trio had finally arrived at the restaurant in order to attack it as planned and hopefully locate and abduct Amanda.

Zinger parked directly in front of the restaurant, on its side of Columbia Avenue. However, he put the left side of the X-Terminator 4000 toward the curb. At once, Zapper, Zinger, and D.D.T. got out of the X-Terminator and secured it. "All right, you two," Zapper said to his two accomplices, "let's go. Follow me." So then, Zapper began walking toward the entrance with Zinger and D.D.T. following behind.

After advancing a few yards, Zapper commanded Zinger and D.D.T., "Hold it! Stop where you're at!" At that, they complied, and Zapper himself halted as well. Then, he told his partners, "Let me disable the surveillance cameras, all right? Now don't move." Zapper took out his Mega Zapper 2000 and sent a powerful electrical surge into the very first camera he spotted. In turn, the surge traveled throughout the entire chain of security cameras and caused all of them to blow up and stop working completely.

Right afterward, Zapper said to his colleagues, "All right now, let's go!" Zapper began moving toward the front door with the other two following behind. Shortly, whenever they reached the restaurant's entrance, Zapper gave orders to his two associates, telling them, "All right, you two, the cameras are down. Now let's spread out and see if we can spot this young lady."

"You got it, boss," said big D.D.T. in reply.

"I'm on it," said Zinger.

"Very well," Zapper said to them. "Now get movin', and keep your eyes peeled. Thoroughly check every window, every opening you come across, all right?" Then, Zapper pointed to his left, saying, "D.D.T., you go that way." Pointing to his right, he said, "Zinger, go the other way." Finally, he gave his men one last order. He said, "If either of you finds anything, holler at once. Now, are we clear on all this?"

"Yeah," answered both D.D.T. and Zinger simultaneously while nodding affirmatively. "Right!"

"Well," said Zapper. "What are y'all waiting for? Get going, now!" At that, both Zinger and D.D.T. complied immediately.

Within a matter of seconds, Zinger and D.D.T. each made it up to the very first window to which he could come. However, the search did not take very long. It was not even one minute into their reconnaissance when Zinger thought he might have found the lady for whom they were looking. It was indeed Amanda Taylor, who was walking back to her table. He just examined her for a few more seconds to try to make sure he was seeing the very same face he had seen two nights before. He even asked himself, "Now, am I sure that's her?"

At last, Zinger could see no reason why the one he spotted could not be the one for whom they were hunting. "I guess that must be her," he decided. "After all, the likeness is amazing and remarkable. Let me call Zapper and D.D.T." So next, Zinger yelled out, "Zapper! D.D.T.! Come quick!"

Within a couple of seconds, they both appeared as if from nowhere. "Whatcha got there, Zinger?" asked Zapper.

"Yeah," said D.D.T. "What's going on, man?"

"Well," Zinger told them, "y'all may correct me if I'm wrong, but I think I may have found her."

"Found her?" asked Zapper. "Do you mean the one who foiled our scheme the other night?"

"Yeah, perhaps," answered Zinger, "come here and let me show you." Zapper and D.D.T. surrounded Zinger to try to see her.

Zinger pointed to Amanda, saying, "Y'all see that girl in the red dress and the dark-brown hair?"

"Well," Zapper uttered as he was trying to see for himself. "Well, what do you know?" He finally said once he spotted her, for he too was able to recognize her. Then, he turned to Zinger and said, "Good work, Zinger."

"Yeah, we got her," D.D.T. said in agreement while nodding and smiling. Then, he chuckled to himself.

Zapper immediately stepped back several feet and summoned Zinger and D.D.T., telling them, "Zinger! D.D.T.! Get over here now!" Shortly, they stood side by side before Zapper. "Now hear this," he said. "This is what we're gonna do: D.D.T., you go through the back door to the kitchen and make sure she doesn't escape."

"You got it," replied D.D.T.

Zapper continued, "And, Zinger, you and I will go through the front door."

"Yes, sir," answered Zinger.

"All right now!" said Zapper to Zinger and D.D.T. "We're all clear on what to do, right?"

D.D.T. and Zinger nodded and said, "Yeah."

"Very good," Zapper said in reply. "Just one more reminder: The security cameras are down. So don't worry about getting caught on video; not that anyone can stop us, you know? Now, D.D.T., get moving to the back door. Once there, go on in and annihilate and 'X-terminate' anyone who tries to stop you or stand in your way. Can you handle that?"

D.D.T. just chuckled and uttered in, "Mm-hmm, you know I can, oh yeah."

"Excellent," Zapper told him. "Now start heading back there now!"

D.D.T. began marching around to the back door.

Once D.D.T. had parted company with Zapper and Zinger, Senior Lieutenant Zapper decided to do one other thing. He wanted to notify someone of the progress they had made in locating the young woman who had fouled up their scheme to destroy the Green Phantasm. The individual to be informed was the only X-Termination official ranked higher than Zapper. That, of course, was John Perone, alias Doctor XT, the very individual who owned, ran, and funded all of X-Termination.

Zapper told Zinger, "Zinger, before we proceed, I need to call the doctor real quick. I think he might like to know about this." At that, he alerted Doctor XT on his two-way radio. "Doctor, come in please. This is Zapper calling."

From his office, Doctor XT answered and said, "What is it, Zapper? You must have some good news for me. Whatcha got?"

"Well, Doctor," answered Zapper. "I just thought you may like to know that we found her."

"That's great," replied XT. "This better be the one who fouled up our plan the other night. I presume that's who it is."

"That's her all right," declared Zapper. "We found her at Castelano's Italian Restaurant on Columbia Avenue."

"No matter," said Doctor XT. "Just bring her out, and go to the top of the Comcast Center building on Seventeenth Street. I'm gonna meet y'all there."

"You are?"

"Of course," answered Doctor XT. "I'm so proud of you that I'm not gonna make you finish this job without me. I've got us a game plan. With that young lady, we can lure the Phantasm and destroy him. Just make sure the Green Phantasm shows up there by nine. You know how to make sure of that, don't you?"

"Yes, Doctor," Zapper responded. "You know I do."

"Very well," Doctor XT said to Zapper. "I'll be atop that building in about one hour. Just make it all happen."

"Yes, sir," Zapper replied affirmatively.

After that, Zapper told Zinger, "All right, let's go on in and bring her out. Move it." At that, Zinger followed Zapper to the entrance.

The gargantuan behemoth called D.D.T. was in the process of breaking and entering through the back. Normally, a person would have to pull the back door open from the outside. However, D.D.T. delivered a powerful front kick accompanied by a roar, so that the door was bent up and forced to the kitchen's inside. All of the door hinges nearly broke off completely as well. But D.D.T. just went inside, tore off the door altogether, and tossed it outside.

D.D.T.'s sudden break-in aroused a lot of attention. All of the kitchen employees stopped what they were doing to look toward him. "Who on earth is that?" murmured one of them. Then, they suddenly became more afraid when D.D.T. drew his X-Termination Ray and growled at them. Everyone in the kitchen gasped in panic, and they all submissively put their arms and hands straight up overhead, fully extended.

"Yeah, that's right," growled D.D.T. as he held them all at gunpoint. "Nobody move."

Shortly, a waiter entered the kitchen to retrieve an order. As he was walking through the kitchen, he said, "I'm looking for—"

Suddenly, he stopped talking and halted when he noticed D.D.T. holding up everyone in the kitchen. He was now in a state of panic, not knowing what to say or do. But he nervously began to utter, "I… was… just gonna…"

D.D.T. just snarled and fired his ray gun at the waiter. Of course, the stream of burning acid completely burned and consumed the unfortunate, innocent victim, leaving a mere heap of ashes. One reason D.D.T. did this was that he was frustrated at someone walking in on him. Another was that he did not want that waiter to walk back out and inform anyone else of his presence.

Regardless of D.D.T.'s motives, everyone else who had seen the horrible tragedy gasped in horror. One chef scurried behind a stove to hide from the humongous masked villain. "Oh my God!" he whimpered to himself. "I don't wanna risk getting shot myself!" Finally, he squatted down.

At once, D.D.T. turned his attention back over to all the kitchen employees. "All right, y'all," he said to them, "I'm D.D.T. of X-Termination, and I'm looking for that girl that got in our way the other night. I know she's in here; I done saw her. Somebody tell me who she is, and where she's sittin', huh? What do y'all say?"

"I'm sorry," answered one of the chefs. "I don't know her."

"Me neither," responded another. "I wish I could help you out, I really do."

D.D.T. shook his head in disbelief. He then told the kitchen staff, "Man, y'all are useless." That very minute, he opened fire on each and every one of them, reducing them to heaps of ashes one at a time. But somehow, in the midst of it all, another chef managed to run and hide behind the stove where the one chef was already hiding. "What are we gonna do?" he asked the first chef there.

"I don't know," replied the other chef. "We might figure something out. Just keep quiet, or he'll hear us." The second chef just nodded in agreement. Unfortunately though, they were the only two kitchen employees left, for D.D.T. had now finished off the rest of them.

After destroying those helpless victims, D.D.T. proceeded to cause further destruction. He began the rest of his rampage by delivering a side kick to a table on his left. This caused the table and everything on it to crash to the floor.

D.D.T. came to a stove on his right. It was the one behind which the two chefs were hiding. D.D.T. jumped up and kicked over a large iron pot of boiling soup. As a result, the scorching-hot soup spilled from the pot onto the second chef who had gone into hiding. That caused the chef to scream hysterically, for he was undoubtedly burned very badly by the soup from the pot.

D.D.T. heard the screaming and said, "Hey, what was that?" Then, he went to look around the end of the stove to his far right to see who was screaming. Whenever the other chef who had not been burned sensed the huge man coming, he scampered off to hide somewhere else.

But when D.D.T. found the one who had been screaming, he looked down at him and said to him, "Yo, man, you go nowhere from here. Heh, heh, heh, gotcha."

At that, the helpless victim rolled over onto his back and submissively put his hands in front of his face, begging and pleading desperately, "No, please, please, don't hurt me! Don't kill me, man, please!"

D.D.T. put away his X-Termination Ray, after which he bent down and grabbed the chef by the neck with his left hand. Immediately, D.D.T. picked his victim up off the floor and used both hands to snap and break his neck. At last, the ruthless titan just dropped the now dead chef onto the floor. After that, D.D.T. proceeded to cause further destruction to the kitchen and the things in it. At least one chef managed to evade big, bad D.D.T. and escape. But of course, several others were now piles of ashes, and one was lying dead of a broken neck.

Zapper and Zinger had entered through the front. Upon their entry, they turned heads and aroused the attention of many customers as well as restaurant employees. That was likely because masked men in colorful costumes were not commonly seen in public, particularly not in a fancy Italian restaurant.

The hostess at the front desk tried asking Zapper and Zinger, "Can I help you guys?"

But the masked duo just ignored her and kept walking farther into the restaurant. "Come on, Zinger," Zapper said to his partner, "let's find her and take her out of here. Of course, you know what to do if somebody bothers us, right?"

"I sure do," answered Zinger. " 'X-terminate' 'em."

"Very good," replied Zapper. "Now keep your eyes peeled, and leave no stone unturned."

"You got it, Zapper," Zinger told him. From that point, he continued following Zapper, and they both kept looking all around.

But momentarily, having noticed them wandering, the restaurant manager walked up to them and said, "Excuse me, guys, y'all need help with something?"

"Step aside!" Zinger rudely replied.

"Guys," the manager rebuked them, "I'm not going to have y'all wandering and roaming about my restaurant. If that's all you're here for, I'm gonna have to ask you to leave before I call the police."

"Well, well," said Zapper. "So you're trying to stand in our way, are you? Haven't you heard? We're X-Termination, and you know what we do to those in our way, don't you?"

"That's it; I'm calling the police," declared the frustrated manager of the restaurant.

At that, he turned and started walking toward a telephone. But as he was walking away, Zapper told Zinger, "Take care of him, Zinger." At once, Zinger drew his X-Termination Ray and fired one shot at the manager, changing him to ashes. That turned the heads of a lot of customers, who gasped in horror. In turn, nearly everyone at the restaurant looked to see what had happened.

At that, Zinger held up his X-Termination Ray and said to everyone who was looking on, "Yeah, that's right. That's what happens when someone decides to cross us or get in our way. If anyone else tries to stop us, they'll get it too. Now stay back!"

———◇———

Next, about three people tried to run out through the front door, but Zapper shot them in quick succession with his X-Termination Ray. This, of course, reduced them to three piles of ashes. A lot of people cried out in horror over that tragedy as well. Then, they all kept murmuring in panic, for they were not certain what to do.

Momentarily, Zapper dashed over to the front door, where of course, the three heaps of ashes now were. He then yelled, "Silence, everybody! Quiet!" Those who heard him cooperated, for they did not want to become ashes as well.

Zinger strolled farther into the restaurant while holding up his ray gun. He tried to help quiet all the people in the restaurant by yelling to them, "Shut up, everybody! Yeah, y'all heard him! Everybody, shut your mouths!" From that point, all the noise subsided until silence was the only thing coming from every customer and employee in the dining area.

"Excellent," said Zapper regarding the complete silence. "All right now, nobody move. I got an announcement to make."

Immediately, Zapper began by saying, "This is why we're here tonight. Two nights ago, we were plotting to 'X-terminate' the Green Phantasm. But all of a sudden, this foolish young lady decided to attack Zinger and myself from behind, fouling up our scheme. So we're here looking for that young lady. Oh yes, we know she's in here. So somebody either tell me where she is or have her come out to me at once. You have one minute before I 'X-terminate' you all. Do y'all hear that? One minute."

Zapper told his junior teammate, "Zinger, start going around and looking for her, and go ahead and put on your gas mask."

"Roger," Zinger responded, after which he began roaming about the restaurant in search of Amanda. At the same time, he held out his X-Termination Ray, in case he felt the need to use it.

Shortly after Zapper announced his threat and dispatched Zinger, one young man approached him and said to him, "Hey, excuse me, um, Zapper? Is that your, uh, name?"

"Yes, yes, yes," Zapper responded irritably. "What do you want? Do you know something about this girl or what?"

"Come on please, Zapper," the young guy begged nicely. "You can't just hold us all responsible for this."

"Enough!" snarled an impatient Zapper. "Do you know who this young lady is or not?"

"Well, no," the guy answered slowly and reluctantly.

"Eh, then what good are you?" Zapper replied. At that, he just gave the young victim a blast from his X-Termination Ray, which left another heap of ashes.

In reaction, everyone who saw the horrible occurrence briefly gasped in horror and just became silent again, for none of them intended to become victims themselves. However, the now "X-terminated" victim had been accompanied at Castelano's by his fiancée, who not only gasped in horror but screamed out, "Jonathan!" Right after that, she even ran up to the remaining ashes, got down on her hands and knees, and kept crying her eyes out. Then, the young girl looked up toward Zapper and screamed at the top of her lungs, "How could you do that to him, you dumb ugly freak?"

At once, the merciless, unyielding masked fiend just took out his Mega Zapper 2000 and shocked her with a surge of electricity. This caused the young woman to fall unconscious.

Dr. Mark Thompson and Amanda Taylor were still at their table, trying to figure out what to do, like everyone else in the dining room. This was no doubt on account of the possibility that Zapper was about to massacre every individual present. "Mark," said Amanda quietly.

"Yes, Amanda?" he replied.

"We gotta do something."

"I agree," Thompson uttered softly in return, "but I don't know what to do right now. One of them might kill us if we try anything."

"You don't understand," Amanda told Dr. Thompson, "it's me they're after. I interfered with their plans the other night. They're trying to find and capture *me*."

"What!" a very surprised Mark Thompson exclaimed, whispering, "No way! I can't believe what you're saying. Will somebody please tell me it's not true?"

"Mark, please," Amanda begged desperately. "Isn't there anything we can do at all? My life's in danger here! Please, Mark, they're gonna capture me and kill me!"

"All right, all right, all right," Thompson responded. "I believe you, okay? I guess there ought to be some way out of this predicament. This just isn't my area of expertise, but I'll try to think of something."

While Mark Thompson was racking his brains, a frightened Amanda Taylor said, "Oh, I don't know. But what I do know is, the other night, while they were waiting for the Green Phantasm, I sprang out of hiding, and hit them with—"

"Amanda!" exclaimed Thompson, for she had given him an idea.

"Yes, Mark," she responded. "What is it?"

"That's it!" he answered. "You just made me think of something. I don't know how great of an idea it is, but I have a plan."

"You do? What is it?"

"Well, you know how you just said that you sprang out of hiding and hit them?"

Amanda nodded and said, "Uh-huh."

"You see, Amanda," he continued, "that's what we're gonna do. Whenever Zinger comes by here, we're gonna attack him from behind, knock him out, and try to sneak out through the back."

"Well, all right," Amanda said in reply. "I'm just a bit worried about everyone else in here. I hate to just let them all die."

"I understand, and so do I," Mark told her, "but I have a feeling that they're just going to kill everyone no matter what. That's whether they manage to capture you or not. So, for that reason, I'm not letting them take you."

"Maybe you're right," Amanda said to him. "So anyway, let's do this. I've taken out that creep before, and I feel ready to do it again. Okay, Mark, how are we gonna do this?"

"Here's what we'll do," answered Mark. "I'll need you to hide yourself underneath the table."

"Why you want me to do that?" Amanda questioned him.

"Because," he explained, "it's the best and safest way to hide us both, so he doesn't notice us before it's too late for him. I'll tell you when to jump out and help me take him out."

"All right, all right," Amanda replied. "Just tell me when, okay?"

"You got it," he said, "now get on under there." At that, Amanda lifted the tablecloth and crawled underneath the table. She stayed down on her hands and knees, waiting for her cue. At the same time, Mark squatted down, hiding and waiting for Zinger to walk by.

While Amanda was waiting under the table, she began having second thoughts about James Clifton. She said to herself, "Maybe I made a mistake. I mean, James was right about X-Termination coming after me. Besides, we sure need the Green Phantasm right now. I should've thought about that. You know, maybe James Clifton is not such a bad guy after all. I just can't understand why he abandoned me the other night."

Then, after a few seconds of silence, Amanda went on, "Other than that, I really like the bravery of Mark Thompson. But I'm still worried for him, because he doesn't have the powers that Green Phantasm has. I only wish I hadn't blown off poor James. If something happens to Mark, I'll never forgive myself. Even as mad as James might have made me, I feel terrible about the way I scolded him, got him put out of this place, and caused him so much hurt and humiliation. He may never want to talk to me or see me again after that, because I don't think I'd want to either. I just hope I get through this somehow." After that, Amanda remained silent, for her guilty conscience allowed her to say nothing further.

But shortly, Zinger made his way over to the table behind which Thompson was hiding. As Zinger began walking past, Mark suddenly sprang up and grabbed him from behind with both arms. Then immediately, he used his right hand to grab hold of Zinger's right forearm, because he was holding the X-Termination Ray in his right hand. At once, he raised up Zinger's arm to point the ray gun straight up. Then, he called out to Amanda, "Now, Amanda, now!"

A very surprised Zinger was trying to figure out who was holding him from behind and why. "Hey, what the… Who's doing this?" he exclaimed. "What's going on here?"

At the same time, Amanda sprinted out from under the table at her cue. She appeared in front of Zinger, who at once recognized her and understood why he was being restrained from behind. "Oh, it's you, huh?" he said. "So that's what this is all about."

Next, Zinger focused on the one who was holding him back, saying, "All right, you retarded freak, you better turn me loose!" Unfortunately for Dr. Thompson, the person of Nicholas Jarrett was stronger than he was, and his experience with X-Termination had made him tougher as well. Thompson knew he would not be able to hold on to Zinger for very long. So then, determined to seize Amanda, Zinger used his left hand to pull Thompson's left arm away. That very second, he turned around to try to regain control of his X-Termination Ray. "You better let go of my arm!" he commanded Mark Thompson.

While those two were struggling, Amanda was trying to figure out a way to take out Zinger. Momentarily, she suddenly had an idea. She took a vase of flowers from a table that was at her rear left. She drove the bottom of the vase into Zinger's crown. That caused him to become dazed. Zinger said, "Oh my God, what hit me?"

After that, she regripped the vase around its top, holding it upside down. Then, she clubbed Zinger over the top of his head. This caused the glass vase to shatter but also dazed Zinger further and made him fall to his knees. Amanda then used both of her hands to twist Zinger's head and neck violently, which made him collapse onto the floor unconscious. Everyone who saw that happen gasped in amazement. Mark Thompson commended Amanda, saying, "Thanks, Amanda, good job."

"Sure, no problem," Amanda replied.

Meanwhile, when Zapper noticed the people near that scene gasping in amazement, he asked, "What's going on back there?" He began taking a few steps closer, hoping to obtain a better look at the situation.

As soon as Zapper had moved forward several feet, four people tried to sneak out behind him. However, he noticed them attempting to escape. At that, he quickly turned around and told them, "Oh no y'all don't!" Immediately, he shot them all with his X-Termination Ray, reducing them to four more heaps of ashes.

While Zapper was distracted, Mark Thompson said to Amanda, "Come on, let's go out the back."

"Okay," responded Amanda, for she was undoubtedly desperate to evade the hands of X-Termination. Right away, Mark began sneaking toward the kitchen with Amanda following behind. They both remained bent over so that Zapper would not spot them.

Big D.D.T. was still on a rampage throughout the kitchen, causing more and more destruction. The entire kitchen area was a disaster all over, as if an earthquake and a tornado had hit. Very shortly, Dr. Mark Thompson went on down a very short passageway that led from the dining room to the kitchen, with Amanda following him. They also had to go through a swinging door to enter the kitchen area. That door was halfway down the short passage.

When Mark and Amanda set foot in the kitchen area, they paused and gasped in fear upon seeing the huge masked troublemaker called D.D.T. Mark Thompson whispered to Amanda, "Quick, get back before he spots us!" That very instant, they both dashed right back into the little passageway.

While they were hiding from D.D.T., Mark said quietly to Amanda, "Just stay behind me, and I'll tell you when it's okay."

"All right," she whispered in reply.

Mark Thompson used his left eye to peek around the corner before him to his right. He was watching to see when D.D.T. would look away completely so they could sneak by him. D.D.T. paused for a moment to look around and smile at everything he had destroyed. Then very shortly, the humongous rascal began walking away from Mark and Amanda to go and check for anything else he could possibly knock down or demolish.

Mark finally told Amanda, "Okay, now's our only chance. Just tiptoe right behind me. See that doorway ahead to the left?"

"Uh-huh," Amanda softly answered.

"Good," he told her. "Come on now. It's now or never. Let's sneak on outta here." At that, Mark Thompson began slowly and carefully tiptoeing toward the rear exit where D.D.T. had torn off the door much earlier. Of course, Amanda was following behind him.

However, once they had gotten two-thirds of the way to the door, something else suddenly happened. A couple of moments after Mark and Amanda had gone through the swinging door to the kitchen, seven other individuals went through after them. They had no doubt managed to notice Mark and Amanda's attempt to escape and decided to follow behind.

But then, all those others who were trying to follow their footsteps caught sight of something that was to their far right. It was none other than the huge titan called D.D.T., who was still destroying more and more equipment. At the sight of the humongous masked villain, they all gasped and screamed in panic.

Big D.D.T. stopped and said, "What! What in the world was that?"

At the same time, this got Mark's attention as well. He suddenly stopped and turn around to see what was making that combined sound of gasping and screaming. Then, he not only noticed the others who were trying to escape, but also D.D.T. getting ready to turn around. He began to panic as well but fortunately, figured out another plan to evade D.D.T. in the nick of time.

Ahead of Mark and Amanda was a prep table that D.D.T. had knocked over. With no time for anything else, Mark told Amanda, "Quick, down behind this table, now!" Immediately, he leaped behind the table, taking Amanda with him. From that point, they both remained hidden on their hands and knees.

D.D.T. was now turned all the way around and saw the other people who were trying to sneak out behind Mark and Amanda. While they were trying to scurry out, D.D.T. drew his X-Termination Ray and shot the one in the lead, reducing him to ashes. Everyone who had followed him stopped and gasped in horror. Next, D.D.T. fired a shot at another, producing another heap of ashes.

After that, everyone turned to look at him. He was pointing his ray gun at them. Threateningly, D.D.T. growled to them, "Yo, where y'all going, huh? Y'all ain't goin' nowhere!" At that, he fired his X-Termination Ray at the wall behind the innocent victims. The burning acid consumed a huge chunk of the wall, leaving a hole that was between four and five feet in diameter.

In reaction to this, the five who still remained turned and ran back into the dining room. D.D.T. ran up behind them to make sure no one else would try to escape. Whenever Zapper saw the five individuals returning to the dining room in a state of panic, he said to himself, "That's it, D.D.T.! Don't let anybody get away."

In the meantime, Mark and Amanda were still hiding behind the overturned table. While D.D.T. had his back turned to them, Mark quietly told Amanda, "Hurry, Amanda, run on outta here while he can't see us. Go now. I'll follow after you." Amanda obediently sprang up and scurried out through the back doorway.

Shortly, Thompson jumped up and began running out behind Amanda. But as he was trying to escape, something else went wrong. After the five hostages had gone back into the dining area, D.D.T. found another opportunity to destroy something. Whenever the swinging door swung back toward him, the huge titan grasped it with his left hand and completely ripped it off at its hinges. Then, big D.D.T. let out a roar as he turned around and threw the door toward the back exit.

Just as he was exiting the building, Mark looked back one last time to make sure he would get away safely. But unfortunately for him, the swinging door had been hurled toward him. He noticed this in the nick of time and jumped backward to avoid being hit. "Yikes!" he yelled as he dodged the flying door.

Unfortunately, hollering something out did not help Mark Thompson. In fact, it turned out to be a mistake because D.D.T. heard him and then turned around to try to find whoever had yelled. "Hey, who said that?" D.D.T. asked. However, he could not see anyone right away because Mark was hiding around the corner at the end of the wall to D.D.T.'s left. D.D.T. started walking slowly toward the kitchen's exit.

Thompson heard him coming and muttered to himself, "Oh no, I should've kept my big mouth shut! What on earth have I done?" He was no doubt very much afraid without knowing what to do.

Suddenly, Amanda came up to the doorway to check on him. "Mark," she said. He turned his attention to her. Amanda asked him, "Are you coming?"

Thompson just, "Listen, just go, Amanda. I'll figure something out somehow. It's you they're after, not me. Now get going, and don't worry about me. Save yourself, all right?" At that, Amanda just began running away, occasionally looking back to make sure that Mark would somehow get away safely.

But then, very shortly, Mark finally had enough of hiding and waiting. So he decided to try something else. He began tiptoeing slowly and carefully out of the building. But all of a sudden, before he made it outside, a large chunk of the back wall disappeared on his right. This left behind nothing but vapor as well as two small heaps of ashes inside and outside the kitchen. It was the result of a shot fired from D.D.T.'s X-Termination Ray.

In reaction, Mark stopped and turned around only to find himself at gunpoint. "Freeze!" D.D.T. commanded him. He just complied and submissively extended both arms overhead.

Big D.D.T. told Mark Thompson, "I ain't lettin' you go anywhere. Now get over here!" Obediently and cooperatively, Thompson placed both hands on the crown of his head and began walking back along the same wall he had sneaked along to try to escape. Finally, he stopped when D.D.T. told him, "Right there! Now, look at me and don't move." At that, Mark turned to his left so that he was face-to-face with D.D.T.

While still holding out his X-Termination Ray, D.D.T. growled in a threatening manner, "All right, you little wimp, you know who we're here for. Now you better tell me, where is she?"

Thompson nervously responded, "I-I, uh, I don't, uh, know who or where she is; honest, I don't."

D.D.T. grunted in frustration. After that, he put away his X-Termination Ray. Mark was temporarily relieved and began taking his hands down. But all of a sudden, D.D.T. grabbed hold of his neck with his right hand. "You are so useless, you know that?" he told him. Thompson was too afraid to try to say or do anything.

At the same time, D.D.T. kept tightening his grip on his neck to strangle him. This huge villainous titan was even plotting to break his victim's neck to kill him. He went on to tell the poor doctor, "I'm gonna snap your neck like a stick of balsa wood." Upon saying that, D.D.T. placed his left hand on top of Mark's head in preparation to break his neck.

But, before D.D.T. could begin to twist with his left hand, he became startled. He had felt something striking his right knee. This made D.D.T. temporarily remove his left hand, so he could see what had hit him.

Most unexpectedly, the source of that blow to his left knee happened to be Amanda Taylor, who had delivered a front snap kick. When Amanda had begun fleeing at Thompson's command, she occasionally looked back to make sure that he would get away. Upon seeing him in the clutches of D.D.T., Amanda had gone back to help him, for she did not want Mark to die.

Fortunately, Amanda had managed to find a four-foot-long piece of steel pipe lying in front of a big trash container just outside the back of the restaurant. She had taken it with her upon finding it, for she had planned to use it for the next big blow after the kick to the knee.

So then, even though D.D.T. had noticed Amanda, it was too late to avoid the next lick. The piece of pipe was already being swung at him in a similar manner to that of a baseball bat, except for being aimed higher up. Very shortly, D.D.T. was clubbed on the upper right side of his head. This dazed the huge scoundrel so that he lost hold of the victim he was strangling and staggered back a couple of steps.

At the same time, Mark fell to his hands and knees. At once, Amanda went over to help him recover so that he could escape with her. While nudging him to try to bring him to his senses, Amanda said to him, "Mark, are you okay? We gotta get out of here! Come on, Mark!"

Then, he regained his senses and said, "Oh my goodness, what's happening?"

"Mark, it's me," she responded. "I just set you free, all right? Now let's go, come on."

Then at once, Mark got up onto his feet and said to Amanda, "Amanda, I can't—" But then, he saw D.D.T. trying to regain his senses and said, "Never mind, let's get going. Come on!"

Amanda tried to strike D.D.T. with the piece of pipe a second time. While she was swinging the pipe, Thompson told her, "No, Amanda, don't worry about... uh, him?"

Unfortunately, Amanda's second attempt to clobber the huge villainous titan failed. Big D.D.T. suddenly recovered completely and grabbed hold of the piece of pipe with his right hand. Amanda gasped in surprise. At the same time, Mark scoffed in frustration.

Upon catching the pipe with his right hand, D.D.T. used his left hand to grab Amanda by her right arm and pull her closer to him. He then looked down and growled to her, "So, it's you, huh? Heh, heh, heh, I gotcha, baby."

At that, the terrified Amanda Taylor screamed hysterically. But that shortly ended as D.D.T. threw down the pipe piece and gave her a powerful chop with his huge right hand at the lower back of her neck. This rendered her unconscious. Finally, D.D.T. just let her collapse onto the floor.

At seeing that, Mark pointed his right index finger at D.D.T., saying, "Why, you big bully, how dare you do that to her! You'll never get away with this! I oughtta—"

But then, D.D.T. turned his attention to Mark, who began to shrink back when looked down upon by the vast behemoth. D.D.T. growled in frustration and said to Thompson, "So, you lied to me, huh? You knew where she was, didn't you?"

Mark, on the other hand, was too afraid to know what to say or do. He just continued slowly to back away from D.D.T. Momentarily though, he began to utter, "Well, uh, you see, um—" But all of a sudden, Mark turned and looked back to his lower left because he had backed into the prep table behind which he had hidden a little earlier and nearly fell backward over it.

But then, before Mark knew what was happening, D.D.T. had grabbed him by his right arm to stop him. Then, all at once, the huge masked troublemaker roared as he made a fist with his right hand and pounded Mark on the back of the head in a downward motion. This sprained poor Mark Thompson's neck, as well as made him collapse to the floor unconscious. Both Amanda Taylor and Dr. Mark Thompson were now lying unconscious at the hand of big D.D.T.

Next, D.D.T. picked up both victims and slung them over his shoulders to carry them to Zapper. Amanda was over his left shoulder, and Mark Thompson was over his right. At once, the huge villain began making his way toward the dining room entrance and exit, where Zapper was waiting.

Once D.D.T. entered the dining area, a lot of people turned their heads toward him and gasped or exclaimed in surprise. Many of them were intimidated by the colossal masked thug and felt sorry for the two unconscious victims who were being carried by him. One man said, "Oh no, what has he done to them?"

"Yeah," said another bystander in agreement. "I wonder what they're gonna do to them now."

But suddenly, as D.D.T. was looking all around while walking toward Zapper, he noticed something to his left. It was Zinger lying unconscious. Big D.D.T. did not believe his eyes. So he stopped to get a better look and mumbled to himself, "Hey, what happened to Zinger? I don't believe this, man."

At the same time, Zapper was wondering what all the excitement was about. So he shouted out, "Hey, what's going on back there?" At that, Zapper began walking toward the disturbance to see what was creating it.

As soon as Zapper had walked nearly twenty feet, two customers at the restaurant attempted to sneak out through the front exit. But just as they were making their way through the door, Zapper noticed them. In quick reaction, he turned around and shot both victims, reducing them to ashes. "Oh, no, y'all don't!" Zapper said for everyone else to hear. Consequently, no one else dared to try to escape.

Then, momentarily, Zapper got close enough to discern that his enormous accomplice was the center of attention in the back of the dining room. He called out to him, "D.D.T., what's going on back there, huh? What are you doing?"

At once, D.D.T. turned his attention from Zinger to Zapper. He then began walking closer to Zapper. He said, "Oh, hey, boss, I was just trying to figure out what was up with Zinger."

"What! Zinger!" exclaimed Zapper. "What in the devil are you talkin' about?"

"Well," answered D.D.T. "He's laying on the floor right over here."

"*What?*" fumed Zapper.

"Somebody must've done that to him," continued D.D.T. "I don't know."

For a few seconds, Zapper looked down and shook his head in disbelief. Then, he told his gargantuan associate, "Never mind that now. So I see you caught her, eh?"

"I sure enough did," replied D.D.T., "and this guy I got here, he was trying to help her, but—"

"No matter," said Zapper, "Just bring those two fools outside the front door. I'll take care of Zinger. Now get moving, all right? Go on."

"You got it, boss," D.D.T. responded. At that, he went toward the front entrance and exit so he could get out of the restaurant.

As soon as D.D.T. was outside, Zapper put on his gas mask to prepare for what he was about to do. That very minute, he took a gas bomb and tossed it over to the front door. At once, it began emitting purple X-Termination Gas. As the gas continued to spread more and more, a great panic came upon the customers and employees toward the front.

Some of them began collapsing onto the floor dead of X-Termination Gas inhalation. Others tried to maneuver toward the kitchen area.

Before anyone made it too far, Zapper dashed over to the kitchen's entrance ahead of them. Once there, he placed another gas bomb where the swinging door to the kitchen had once been. Of course, X-Termination Gas began to be discharged from that one as well. So now, no one was able to escape the dining room without dying of gas inhalation. That was with the exception of Zapper and Zinger of course, who had on gas masks.

Once the second gas bomb had been stationed, Zapper darted over to assist his junior associate, Zinger. Immediately, Zapper took out his Mega Zapper 2000 and programmed it to revive his partner. At last, he gave Zinger a slight zap of electricity to bring back his consciousness.

As a result, Zinger became conscious again. For a few seconds, he looked around while still lying down and said to himself, "Whoa, man! What just happened?" Then, he got to his hands and knees, took another look around, and said, "What's going on here?"

At that, Zapper said to him, "Get on up, Zinger. This is Zapper here."

"*What?*" replied a shocked Zinger. "Zapper!" At once, Zinger got back onto his feet. Then, he turned toward Zapper and said, "Zapper, look, man, I can explain, all right? I came upon Amanda, I mean, the girl we were looking for. The guy she was with tried grabbing me from behind. But then, I figured out their game plan, and I had that guy under control. I just don't know. I, uh— "

"Never mind," interrupted Zapper. "D.D.T. caught those two fools and brought them outside."

"Oh, he did?" asked Zinger.

"Of course," answered Zapper. "Now let's get out of here. Keep your mask on until we get out."

"You got it," replied Zinger. At that, they both ran toward the front door to exit the restaurant.

While Zapper and Zinger were on their way out, everyone else inside was panicking more than ever because of the expanding X-Termination Gas. They were all afraid for their lives. Many of them tried lying down or anything else they could think of to stay out of the purple mist. However, no one managed to make it out of the dining room alive. What a massacre on the part of X-Termination!

While running behind Zapper, Zinger called out, "Hey, Zapper!"

"What is it, Zinger?"

"Well, I may have already told you this, but her name's Amanda."

"Oh, really!"

"Yeah," answered Zinger. "I managed to discern that when the guy she was with called it out, and I didn't forget it either."

Zapper then told him, "All right, not bad, Zinger. But for right now, let's get outside. Once we're out, you can confront them if you want to."

"Sounds good," Zinger said in reply. Shortly, Zapper and Zinger were outside the front door of Castelano's Italian Restaurant, where D.D.T. was still holding the two unfortunate victims.

Once outside, Zapper and Zinger removed their masks, and Zapper ordered D.D.T., "All right now, D.D.T., lay that guy on the ground. We need to have a few words with him."

"Heh, heh, heh, you got it," D.D.T. responded with a grin. At once, he put the unconscious Mark Thompson onto the ground so that he was lying faceup at everyone's feet.

Then, Zapper told D.D.T., "Very good." After that, he turned to Zinger and said, "Just a minute, Zinger, I got something to say to him first. Then, you can have at him."

"Okay," replied Zinger.

Zapper once again took out his Mega Zapper 2000, which was still programmed to revive someone who was unconscious. He used it on Mark to make him regain consciousness. As soon as Thompson was conscious again, he gasped in great surprise and exclaimed, "Oh my God, where am I? How did I get here?" Then, Mark looked for a moment at the three masked ruffians and asked them in fear, "Who are y'all, and what are y'all trying to do to me?"

Zapper knelt down on his left knee at Thompson's left-hand side. "Well, well, well, what have we here?"

"What have we here!" he replied. "Well, I'm, uh, Dr. Mark Thompson. Who do you think you are, and what do you think you're doing, huh? You better not hurt the poor girl, you hear me?"

This made the X-Termination officials angrier. "Shut up!" shouted Zapper, while Zinger drew his X-Termination Ray and held Mark Thompson at gunpoint.

In turn, Thompson gasped in fear and said desperately, "Never mind, I'm sorry! Just tell me what you want from me, okay? Just don't kill me."

"Well then," Zapper said to him. "Now that you've asked, I'll tell you. I've got a message that I want you to deliver."

"Okay," Mark said calmly, "go on. I'm… I'm listening."

"All right," continued Zapper. "You see, Thompson, I'm sure you know about this guy called the Green Phantasm, right?"

"Yeah," answered Thompson. "I've heard of him."

"Good enough," said Zapper. "But anyway, the Green Phantasm will come along very shortly. When he does, you are to tell him to come and meet us at the top of the Comcast Center building by nine. Have you got that?"

"Yes, sir," he politely answered. "Got it."

"Excellent," replied Zapper. Then immediately, he stood back up and turned his attention to Junior Lieutenant Zinger. "So, Zinger," said Zapper, "you got something you want to say to him too?"

Zinger nodded and declared affirmatively, "I got something for him all right. Oh yeah, I owe him one."

"Then have at him," he told him.

"I will," replied Zinger, as he was putting away his X-Termination Ray. Zinger knelt down at Thompson's right-hand side. Then immediately, he began glaring at Mark Thompson and pointing his left index finger in a threatening manner. "All right, punk," he said angrily, "what kind of stunt were you trying to pull in that dining room, huh?"

Mark nervously responded, "What are you talking about?"

This only aggravated Zinger further. He used his right hand to begin strangling Thompson. At the same time, he fumed more angrily than before, "You know what I'm talking about! You know what you and Amanda did to me! Stop pretending you don't know! I don't have time for these games!"

"Okay, okay, okay," Mark Thompson begged and pleaded. "I'm sorry, man. You're right, I do know. I'm sorry, Zinger."

At that, Zinger removed his right hand from Thompson's throat and said more calmly, "And another thing, do you have any idea who we are, huh, do you?"

"Yes, Zinger," Thompson answered, "you're, um, you're X-Termination, right?"

"Yeah, we are," Zinger responded. "But you really don't know us very well, do you?"

"Um, no, I really don't," he answered.

"No, I didn't think so," Zinger said in reply. "Now, of course, as you said, we're X-Termination. For some reason, Dr. Thompson, everyone else in that restaurant besides you seemed to know and understand that nobody but nobody ever crosses X-Termination."

"Oh, uh, really?"

"Yeah, really," Zinger responded, "and you know something else? We ain't called that for no reason. I mean, that's what we do to anyone who gets in our way. Oh yeah, we 'X-terminate' them. And right now, it's amazing how the tables have turned on you and me, isn't it?"

"It certainly is."

"Well," said Zinger, "it's time for you to pay." At that, Zinger made a fist with his right hand and landed a big jab between Mark Thompson's nose and upper lip. This seriously dazed Dr. Thompson. Next, Zinger used his left hand to turn and hold down Thompson's head. Then at once, he landed another big right jab on the right side of Thompson's jaw. This knocked Dr. Mark Thompson unconscious.

After that, Zapper told Zinger, "All right, that's good, Zinger." At that, he stood up and turned his attention to Zapper, waiting to be told what to do next.

Zapper said, "All right, you two, let's get on out of here. We got to go meet the doctor atop Comcast Center. Zinger, you go fire up the ship. Now come on; let's go."

So, at Zapper's command, the diabolical threesome went running for the X-Terminator 4000. They all flew off with Amanda Taylor in their clutches. The unconscious Mark Thompson was left lying in front of Castelano's. Although he had made a heroic attempt to save Amanda, he ended up proving unsuccessful against X-Termination. Of course, one possible reason was that he was no Green Phantasm, as Amanda had suggested earlier when having second thoughts about James Clifton.

Speaking of James Clifton, the young bachelor was sitting in his bedroom on his bed. It was now 8:20 p.m. Clifton was hanging his head forward in misery. He had feelings of regret and humiliation from being blown off by Amanda and from being expelled from Castelano's. James felt much too ashamed to have a single idea of what to do now.

But then, after sitting silently for a while, James finally uttered a few words to himself. "Man," he said, "I don't know this for sure, but this feels like the worst night of my life. What good thoughts are there at all to have? I mean, that's especially with getting myself kicked out of that restaurant. Well, I guess the only good thing might be that I didn't get put out as the Green Phantasm." After that, James scoffed, shook his head, and said sarcastically, "Yeah, sure, I suppose I should feel fortunate that I got kicked out as James Clifton and not the Green Phantasm. Yeah, right."

But all of a sudden, those words of sarcasm gave James an idea. "Wait a minute!" he exclaimed. "What did I just say? Is it what I think I said?"

He paused momentarily, after which he said more happily, "You know what? I do believe it is. I may have gotten expelled as James Clifton, but not as the Green Phantasm! Therefore, although I can't go back to Castelano's as James Clifton, I can—oh, never mind. Other than that, I don't think anybody knows I'm the Green Phantasm. But anyway, I've got X-Termination to take care of, don't I? Man, I can't believe all this misery made me forget that." He shook his head in disbelief.

However, now that James's mood had been lifted, he had a more positive view of the situation he was facing. In fact, he had one other positive idea as well. He said to himself, "And you know something else too? At least I got put out for trying to help someone, you know. I guess that's better than if I'd done something horrible. So maybe, well, just maybe, this situation's not quite as bad as it looks. Besides, if I really am a good guy, I should be able to somehow make everything right again." At that, Clifton nodded to himself with a smile.

But next, James decided, "Well, anyway, I got something else to do right now. I've got to once again become the Green Phantasm. That's because I need to get over to Castelano's Italian Restaurant, where I can hopefully intercept those creeps before they do any further harm to anyone or anything. I just hope I'm not too late. More than that, I hope nothing's happened to Amanda. So what am I standing around for? Here I go."

Once again, James ran to retrieve his Green Phantasm outfit. Then right away, he activated the pyxorium in his nervous system and took on the blinding neon-green glow that he always had as the Phantasm. Next, he zipped himself into his suit by teleporting. "All right now," said James, "once again, I'm the Green Phantasm! Well, there's no time to lose. Let's get going." So as the Phantasm, James teleported out through his bedroom window. After that, he became a shapeless projectile a couple of times until he ended up above Castelano's Italian Restaurant.

Then, as the Green Phantasm was using his hovering ability to slowly descend toward the ground, something caught his eye. It was the unconscious Dr. Mark Thompson, whom X-Termination's Zinger had knocked out moments ago. So the Green Phantasm asked himself, "What happened to that guy on the ground?" Then, he answered himself, saying, "Well, I need to make sure the restaurant's okay. Maybe then, I'll go help that guy."

Finally, the Green Phantasm landed in front of Castelano's. He briefly turned around and said, "Hang in there for a moment. I'll be right there, okay?"

When the Green Phantasm looked forward at the restaurant, a look of surprise came over his face, for he could not believe his eyes. One of the first things he could see was some leftover X-Termination Gas. Some of it had already escaped. "Oh my God!" exclaimed the Green Phantasm. "That looks like their gas!"

The Phantasm sprinted up to get a better look. The next thing he noticed only made him more horrified. "Oh no!" he cried at the sight of it. The Green Phantasm had seen the countless innocent victims scattered throughout the entire dining room of Castelano's, lying dead from the X-Termination Gas.

The Green Phantasm now realized that he was too late to stop X-Termination from invading the restaurant. How guilty he felt now! He turned, looked away from the restaurant, and hung his head forward, shaking it in disbelief. At the same time, he sadly said to himself, "What have I done? How could I have let this happen? I can't believe I—" But, the Phantasm could not bear to say any more.

After a few moments of silence, the Green Phantasm began saying to himself, "Well, it looks like X-Termination did hit this place after all, just like they said they would. I mean, who else would this be the work of? I've had it with those jerks! After all, I'm looking at a whole lot more innocent people slaughtered by them; yet, I feel completely responsible. Of course, they're the ones who committed this massacre. But on my part, I let it happen when I could've prevented it."

With the emphasis that the Green Phantasm was putting on his own faults, he was actually angrier with himself than any of the X-Termination officials. He scoffed and muttered to himself, "Dang it, dang it, dang it! Out of all my screw-ups!"

After that, both Clifton and the Phantasm made a transition from a fit of anger to a state of tears because of another thought they had. "And you know what else?" sobbed the Green Phantasm. "Most of all, I hope Amanda was not affected by this killing. I sure hope with all my heart, soul, and strength that she was gone before those no-good peons got here. Because otherwise, I don't know how I'll ever live the rest of my life. I mean, you know, with all the hurt I've already caused the poor girl, and I certainly hope and pray that there's not this too. Please, God, no."

But then, the Green Phantasm made his crying subside and said, "Well, I know she's the one they were after. So I just need to make sure she's alive and okay. I sure hope she is."

The Green Phantasm asked himself, "But, how am I gonna do that? I don't know if I should try to call her or not. I mean, she was here with that, uh, doctor friend of hers that she introduced me to. That's like, Mark Thompson or somebody, right?"

Then, all of a sudden, the Green Phantasm remembered something. "Wait a minute," he told himself. "That's not him lying on the ground behind me, is it? I didn't take a good look, but I guess anything's possible."

At that, the Green Phantasm ran over to the unconscious victim so he could examine him more closely. Once there, he gently picked up the poor guy's head and turned it so that he could see the face better. Finally, the Green Phantasm concluded, "Oh God, I think maybe it is. It looks a lot like the Mark Thompson I remember. I need to try to revive him to see if I can find out anything."

The Phantasm suddenly had a thought. He said, "You know what? Maybe I'll try to do this as myself. After all, I don't want to excite this injured victim too much by being the Green Phantasm. Besides, something tells me I should talk to him as James Clifton. So I'll be right back."

At once, the Green Phantasm teleported upward. Upon reappearing, he projected himself back toward his home. Shortly, the Phantasm ended up in midair near James Clifton's bedroom. At that, he teleported through the window into his room.

Once James was in his room, he teleported out of his Green Phantasm suit. But he did not put it away, since he figured he would probably need it later that night. James picked up his regular dress clothes and zipped into them. He retained his neon-green glow so he could quickly transfer back to the scene of X-Termination's devastation.

Immediately, Clifton teleported out through his window again and started on his way back to Castelano's. Whenever he appeared above the place, he teleported to a secluded area behind it. Once there, James Clifton switched off the activity of the pyxorium within him. At that, he ran around to the front of the restaurant as himself.

As soon as James spotted the unconscious Mark Thompson, he dashed over as fast as he could. Once Clifton made it over to Thompson, he quickly dropped to his knees and started yelling as loudly as he could, "Mark! Hey, Mark! Dr. Thompson, can you hear me? Come on, Mark! Are you okay, buddy?" At receiving no response, James made two fists, gnashed his teeth, and grunted in frustration, "Oh, God, come on!"

But James soon calmed himself down and began trying something different. He placed his hands on Thompson's shoulders and began gently shaking him. In a concerned tone, he begged and pleaded, "Hey Mark, look, man, just say something, all right? I'm begging you, Mark, just say anything at all, please." But James still received no answer, and he began to panic wondering what to do.

Momentarily, he tried yet another strategy. He wanted to try to revive Thompson by using CPR. So he gently tilted back Mark's head and blew into his mouth to try to restore his breathing. Then, all of a sudden, he heard a grunt and a groan. He immediately stopped what he was doing to see if it was Mark Thompson making those sounds.

Thompson began muttering, "Oh, oh my, oh man." He was apparently trying to recover.

Happily, James said to the victim, "Mark, you all right? Thank goodness you're alive."

"*What?*" said Mark Thompson as his eyes began to open. "Who said that? What's happening?"

"Calm down, Mark," James said kindly."It's James, James Clifton. You remember me?"

"Why, James Clifton?" asked Thompson. At once, he looked to his right and saw James kneeling before him. Thompson was perhaps a bit surprised to see him there, but then he told him, "I don't know why or how, but I sure am glad to see you."

In return, James said, "I'm happy to see you too."

"So, what brought you back over here?"

"Well," answered James. "I was told that X-Termination was gonna hit this place, and it looks like they did. But you see, Mark, this could've been prevented. I actually knew earlier that they were going to strike. However, I got so upset that I forgot about that and didn't tell the Green Phantasm. He's the only one I know who could've stopped this. But I was just too careless, thoughtless, negligent, and irresponsible. You can go ahead and say it. I'm a screw-up, aren't I?"

"Oh, come on, James," Thompson told him sympathetically. "You're not as bad as all that. In fact, there's something I need to tell you too. You see, I tried to save Amanda. But those guys were too clever and too tough for me. So I failed, and I only got her captured. It's my fault too, James." At that, James looked away, scoffed, and shook his head in disbelief. Whenever he did that, Mark told him, "Look, I'm sorry, okay? I know you care about her a lot. I know you do."

"Come on, Mark," James said to him nicely. "Calm down, all right? Look, it's not your fault, and I appreciate what you tried to do. You see, I'm sorry too, Mark. I feel completely responsible. I should've told the Green Phantasm, and he should've been there for y'all. But anyway, we'll just have to figure out what to do now. So first of all, is there anything at all you could tell me that might help me find her? Did you pick up any details at all from those guys?"

"Well, as a matter of fact, I did."

"Okay," James replied gently, "go ahead; I'm listening."

"But you see, they left a message that they wanted me to give to the Green Phantasm."

"That's great!" James exclaimed more happily. "Just tell it to me, and I'll give it to him."

"Oh, you will?" said Mark Thompson. "Why, thank you, James. Now listen, they told me to tell the Green Phantasm when he came along to go and meet up with X-Termination at the top of the Comcast Center building by 9:00 p.m."

"Okay, thank you," James said in reply. "I'll make sure to tell him that."

"Thank you too, James," said Mark. "I knew you weren't such a bad guy."

"Well, I hope I'm not," replied James. "I'm definitely not Mr. Perfect. Are you all right, Mark? Are you gonna make it?"

"Well," Mark Thompson responded, "I don't know, I'll have to see if I can—" As he was trying to get up, he suddenly stopped himself and yelled, "Ow! Ow, ow, ow!"

James became worried and cried out, "Mark, what's wrong? You gonna be all right? What's the matter?"

"It's my neck," whimpered Mark Thompson in pain. "I must've sprained my neck."

"Oh my God," said James. "X-Termination must've done that to you."

"Yeah, they did."

"I gotta get you some help," James told him. "I wonder if there's a way I can—"

But then, James heard a faint sound in the distance. It was the sound of police sirens. He was pausing momentarily to see if those police cars were actually on their way to the scene.

Very shortly, several Philadelphia police cars turned and appeared before him. They all pulled up and parked, leaving their lights flashing. Every police officer got out and ran toward James Clifton and the fallen victim, Dr. Mark Thompson. "Hey, what's going on here?" one of them asked as they all completely encircled Clifton and Thompson.

"Listen," James began, "I just got here, but I can tell y'all what happened. I was stopping to help this guy, but I don't mind tellin' y'all what I know."

"All right," said another policeman. "What do you know? Any idea who did this?"

"As a matter of fact, I know who did this," he answered affirmatively while nodding, "It was members of that group, X-Termination."

"X-Termination?" asked a third officer wonderingly.

"I'm positive," responded James.

"Oh yeah," said another policeman. "They raided that anniversary celebration of Ace Nuclear Supply a few nights ago."

"Yeah," James said in agreement, "and they took that fleet of rocket planes to flight to try to destroy the Green Phantasm."

"The Green Phantasm!" exclaimed still another police officer. "That's it! They're the ones he reported to us."

"Exactly," declared James. "They massacred everyone inside, and they left this man out here on the ground."

When all of the officers looked down at him, he said, "Yeah, my name's Mark Thompson. I was eating here with this girl named Amanda Taylor. I tried to get us both out to save our lives. However, they beat me really bad and knocked me out. I don't know if I can get up, because my neck hurts too much. Worst of all, they kidnapped Amanda Taylor."

"Amanda Taylor!" exclaimed one officer. "Isn't that the one who—"

"Yes," interjected another, "that's who the Green Phantasm said they were after."

Next, they all began turning their attention back toward James Clifton. When he noticed this, he told them, "By the way, I'm James Clifton. That's... James Clifton. I guess I should've said that earlier. I'm sorry."

Immediately after that, he paused for a few seconds and then said to the police, "And there's another thing I think I should say too. Somehow, I think the Green Phantasm's gonna have to be the one to stop them. I mean, those guys are just too dangerous for y'all to handle. After all, they already slayed all those policemen at the banquet the other night. I just didn't think about that, and neither did he before he reported those guys to you."

This caused all the police officers to murmur among themselves in confusion. At that, James continued by saying, "And another thing; somehow, I think he's gonna have to find them and put them out of business tonight. After all, I bet he can't stand anymore of this killing by them, because I know I can't." Many of the policemen looked at each other and nodded in agreement.

Finally, James said, "So, I think I need to get going so I can notify the Green Phantasm. I just want to tell y'all to be careful, because I think there's still some of their poisonous gas left inside the building. Other than that, I think this guy lying in front of us needs some help. So be careful with him. Anyway, I think I need to go ahead and take off. I wish I could help y'all more."

"All right, thank you, Mr. Clifton," one of the officers told him.

"No problem," he said in reply. "Have a good night. And, Mark, I'm sure it'll be all right. You'll get through this."

"Thanks, James," Thompson told him.

"All right, here I go," said James as he began running around to the back of the restaurant.

While James was running, he was saying to himself, "Man, they really, really did it this time. Those crazy lunatics killed all those innocent people, and they abducted my favorite person of all. I just can't let them hurt poor Amanda for anything in the world. Neither can I let them do anymore killing. Just like I was telling those cops, it's gotta be tonight. I'm not stopping until those mad, crazy buffoons are in jail, all of them."

James finally made it to the same hidden spot in which he had arrived a little earlier. Once there, he declared, "I have taken control of them once before, and I'm fully prepared to do it again." At that, James activated the acquired source of power within himself and lit up a radiant neon green. He told himself, "Here I go again. I better hurry home and change." So at once, he teleported to above Castelano's Italian Restaurant. Immediately, he became a shapeless projected mass and shot himself toward his home.

When James shot through midair up above, one shocked policeman said, "Well, I wonder where that came from. Was that the Green Phantasm?"

A second cop added, "If so, that James Clifton guy sure didn't waste any time."

Within a few seconds later, Clifton ended up inside his bedroom once again. This time, of course, he was about to get back into his Green Phantasm outfit and resume his role as the one and only Green Phantasm. As soon as James made the transition once more, he boldly declared, "All right, I gained control of those jerks the other night, and I'm fully prepared to do it again." Then, the Green Phantasm made a fist with his right hand, which he placed in the palm of the left, and said with confidence, "It's time to pay up, Doctor XT. You want me? Well, you sure asked for it this time. Here I come."

Without hesitation, the Green Phantasm shot out through the window and ended up hovering above downtown Philadelphia. He was then looking for the Comcast Center building on Seventeenth Street, and very shortly, he spotted it. However, he could not see very well who was atop it, for a huge billboard was posted at the very front of it.

Next, the Green Phantasm shot toward Comcast Center. He then reappeared as himself, hovering in midair face-to-face with the building, about two stories below the roof. Then, the Phantasm looked up and said, "Here I come. Oh yes, this is it." So he began ascending upward to have a rendezvous with X-Termination.

But suddenly, after rising a couple of yards, the Green Phantasm stopped himself because he'd had a thought. He told himself, "Wait a minute. This could be too dangerous for me to just shoot on up here like this. So perhaps I'd better do something just to be on the safe side."

Before too long, the Green Phantasm had a good idea. "I know what," he said. "Why don't I put a force field around myself? I mean, for all I know, they could all open fire or someone could possibly jump me from behind. But this force field should be able to protect me from all that. Well, here we go." So finally, the Green Phantasm began emitting narrow beams from all ten fingers to form a force field. Shortly, whenever the spherical force field was completed, he continued his ascent toward the rooftop.

Less than a minute later, the Phantasm began slowly rising above Comcast Center. By the time he was fully higher than the building, he could see something all right. The Green Phantasm saw four individuals standing in a line facing him; from left to right, it was: Zapper, Amanda Taylor, Zinger, and finally, Doctor XT. They were all in front of one of the two X-Terminator 4000's stationed on the roof. Amanda was being held at gunpoint by Zapper and Zinger, with XT standing nearby. Fortunately for the Green Phantasm, no one was even aiming at him.

However, everyone noticed the Phantasm right off. XT and his two lieutenants stared at him curiously to see what he would do in order to decide how to go about overtaking and defeating him. "Guys," said Doctor XT to Zapper and Zinger, "I don't think we ought to shoot at him just yet.

He might have one of those force fields on. Just keep on holding Amanda hostage." Zapper and Zinger nodded in agreement and complied.

At the same time, the Green Phantasm moved himself forward toward the four people before him while keeping his force field intact. "Well, well, well," said Doctor XT to the Green Phantasm, "if it isn't the Green Phantasm. I see you made it, huh? Got the message after all, didn't you?"

"You're damn straight I did," answered the Green Phantasm. "So, what's going on here, Doctor XT? What do you psychopaths think you're doing with her? Well, it's definitely something you ain't got no business."

"Is that so?" asked Doctor XT. At the same time, Zapper and Zinger looked at the Phantasm and then at each other as if they were puzzled.

"It certainly is," the Green Phantasm responded. Then, he told the two masked lieutenants, "And I'm talking to you too, Zonker and Ziphead." But Zapper and Zinger just busted out laughing upon hearing that.

In reply to the laughter, the Green Phantasm said, "Oh, so y'all find that funny, huh? Go ahead and enjoy your last laugh, because you may not be laughing anymore after tonight. I ain't quitting until you're all behind bars. On top of that, don't y'all dare hurt that poor woman. That's the biggest freakin' mistake you could possibly make with me. Y'all are gonna let her go. I'm gonna see to that, oh yeah."

"Really!" Doctor XT responded. "All right, I'll make a deal with you. If you can just take off that force field, and walk this way nice and easy, we'll gladly release her."

"You will?" asked the Green Phantasm.

"Yes, we will," replied Doctor XT.

"All right, Doctor," the Phantasm told him. "You got it then. I'll do that for her sake. But I suggest that none of you try anything against me. I know y'all have seen what I can do."

"Tell me about it," said XT in reply.

"And another thing," added the Green Phantasm, "I just thought I might let y'all know something, okay? This right here is the end of the line for you guys. You've really done it to me this time. I'm talking about how you killed all those innocent people at Castelano's, and now, you've put your hands on the one I care about the most. You're gonna set her free and get rid of all your weapons. After that, I'm turning y'all in to the police. I'm not just gonna stand back and watch you crazy lunatics slaughter a bunch of innocent, undeserving victims. It's about to all end right now, because I'm not gonna take anymore."

"He sounds like he means business, doesn't he?" asked Doctor XT.

"Yep," responded Zinger, "That he does."

"I do mean business," declared the Green Phantasm. At that, he began taking down and retracting the force field he had formed. Next, he started walking toward the three X-Termination leaders and of course, Amanda Taylor, whom he needed to rescue from them. As the Green Phantasm was walking, he said to the corrupt threesome, "Look, I'm coming just like y'all want me to. Just don't try anything stupid, y'all got it?"

"Yeah, we hear you," Doctor XT answered him.

Finally, the Green Phantasm went up to talk with Amanda, who had both hands handcuffed together behind her back and stood between Zapper and Zinger at gunpoint. "Green Phantasm," Amanda said to him between sobs, "I'm so sorry. This is all my fault."

"No, Amanda," said the Green Phantasm sympathetically, "I should've been at the restaurant to stop those guys, but I wasn't. It's my fault."

"No," sobbed Amanda, "it's mine. I'm the one who snapped at James in front of everyone. He was probably so upset that he didn't get to you in time. I'll never forgive myself for what I did to poor James. He was just trying to help me. I'm sorry, okay?" After that, Amanda just kept on crying.

On the other hand, even in his guise as the Green Phantasm, Clifton was happy to see how sorry Amanda was about the way she had treated him earlier. After all, he truly cared about her no matter what. The Green Phantasm sympathetically told her, "Look, Amanda, it doesn't matter what's already happened. Let's just get you out of here, okay?"

At once, the Green Phantasm turned to Doctor XT and said to him, "All right now, Doctor, I did what you wanted. Now for your part of the deal." Doctor XT just nodded in agreement.

Then, the Phantasm looked back toward Amanda and said to her, "It's gonna be all right, Amanda. Nothing's gonna come between us now." Amanda felt relieved at that, and her crying began to subside.

But next, Doctor XT shouted, "All right, *now!*"

That caused the Green Phantasm to say to Zapper and Zinger, "Well, you heard him, guys." But Zapper and Zinger just looked at each other and started laughing. This confused the Green Phantasm, making him ask, "Hey, guys, what's so funny?"

All of a sudden, something grabbed the Green Phantasm by the neck and began choking him. This shortly became accompanied by a sustained roar. "Oh my God, what's happening?" cried the shocked Green Phantasm.

At once, the Phantasm found out what was happening. The individual who had ahold of him turned him around and started squeezing his neck with both hands. The source of this great surprise turned out to be the huge masked gargantuan behemoth of X-Termination, D.D.T. "Yeah, now I gotcha!" D.D.T. growled down at the Phantasm.

The Green Phantasm understood everything. This included the reason Zapper and Zinger had been laughing, as well as the hidden meaning behind Doctor XT's deal. After all, XT had not said that D.D.T. would not attack. The Phantasm knew that he was being set up for a surprise attack by big D.D.T. But he got to know too late, for D.D.T.'s gigantic hands were now choking the life out of the valiant hero. This made the Phantasm too dazed to attempt any supernatural abilities.

Upon seeing this, Amanda cried, "Oh no!" Then, she resumed crying, for she was terribly worried and afraid of what would become of her hero.

At the same time, the evil Doctor XT of X-Termination said to himself happily, "Good job, D.D.T." Zapper and Zinger looked at each other, smiling and chuckling.

D.D.T. abused the Green Phantasm further. He went on to use both hands to lift the Phantasm up by the neck. Then, the monstrous titan turned around and ran toward the rear of the billboard that was on the building's top, carrying the Phantasm in a chokehold. Finally, big D.D.T. made it to the billboard and slammed the Green Phantasm backward into it. The Green Phantasm's hat fell off and landed nearby.

D.D.T. just kept the Green Phantasm pressed against the back of the billboard and continued choking the daylights out of him. "All right, punk," said D.D.T. to the Green Phantasm threateningly, "we outwitted you this time. You said the other night that I was a dumb, dim-witted turkey. What do you say now, huh? You still think so? Do you?" To allow the Green Phantasm to answer, D.D.T. removed some of the pressure he was applying to his throat.

The Green Phantasm took a few seconds to catch his breath so he could respond. He was not a hundred percent sure of what to say or do in this predicament. However, above all, the Green Phantasm was still determined to rescue Amanda and put X-Termination out of business. That made him unwilling to back down, for he knew a real hero would not. So the Green Phantasm bravely told the huge, powerful villain, "It's what you are, and what you've always been; you know that."

That response may have shown courage on the part of the Green Phantasm, but it made D.D.T. even angrier. He had been hoping he could force the Green Phantasm to retract the comment he had made two nights before. However, he did not achieve that desired result. So the humongous masked ruffian proceeded to inflict further damage on the Phantasm. D.D.T. lowered the Green Phantasm so that he was standing on the roof. He used his left hand to keep choking the Phantasm. While doing that, he delivered two big uppercuts to the Green Phantasm's midsection. Being punched and choked simultaneously stunned the Green Phantasm so much that his head slumped forward. He was nearly rendered unconscious.

Next, big D.D.T. dragged the Green Phantasm over to the front edge of the rooftop, out in front of the huge billboard. Once there, he stood and held his victim upright at the edge. Then, D.D.T. let go and landed a big uppercut to the underside of the Green Phantasm's jaw. This made the helpless Green Phantasm fall backward off the building. He was plunging toward the ground.

Immediately afterward, D.D.T. chuckled to himself with pride. At the same time, Amanda was crying more than ever. After all, how could she possibly be rescued with her only hope now gone? With the Green Phantasm defeated, Amanda apparently had no way out of her predicament. She appeared to be up the creek.

But after enjoying his triumph, big D.D.T. of X-Termination turned around to face Doctor XT and his two fellow officials, Zapper and Zinger. At that, he raised both fists overhead as a sign of victory. "I did it!" exclaimed D.D.T.

"Really?" questioned Doctor XT. "What exactly did you do, D.D.T.?"

"What did I do!" responded D.D.T. "I defeated him entirely. I knocked him out and sent him fallin' toward the earth. I done totally killed that punk. Oh yeah, he ain't nothin' now but a dead neon freak. He's over with."

"*What?*" exclaimed a frustrated Zapper.

"You did what?" Doctor XT asked angrily.

"Yo, I just told you what I did," D.D.T. answered. "I punched that sucker out and knocked him off this building. There ain't nobody that's gonna survive that."

Doctor XT shook his head in disbelief and then said to D.D.T., "Oh, D.D.T., you humongous, brainless, blithering blockhead!"

"What!" replied D.D.T. "What do you mean by that?"

"I'll tell you what I mean!" yelled Doctor XT. "You had him where we needed him, and then you fouled it up!"

"Come on now," begged D.D.T. "How did I do that?"

"I'll tell you how," said Zapper. "Haven't you seen what he's capable of?"

This only confused D.D.T. further, and it showed on his face. "What do you mean, man?" he asked in confusion, "What are you talkin' about?"

"What am I talkin' about!" exclaimed Zapper. "That guy can hover in midair, you know that."

D.D.T. uttered, "Yeah, but—"

"But nothing!" interrupted Zapper. "If he recovers while falling, he'll use his hovering ability to stop himself. Then, now that he knows our plan, he'll come right back and conquer us. Can't you see?"

D.D.T. now understood Zapper and felt ashamed of himself. He bowed his head and shook it in disbelief at himself. Then, when he looked up at his bosses and his teammate Zinger, even Zinger scoffed at him and muttered, "Man, man, man!"

After that, Doctor XT addressed his monster-sized premier associate, "So, D.D.T., that was a stupid decision you made, wasn't it?"

"Yeah, it was," answered D.D.T.

"And you wonder why Zapper's gonna get this company instead of you, do you?"

"Look, man," D.D.T. said to Doctor XT, "I did what I did because that green punk done called me a dumb, dimwitted turkey. It made me mad when he did that. That's why I did it like that."

"Well, D.D.T.," said Doctor XT, "I'll have to agree with the Phantasm on that. You're certainly not my best decision maker. That's why Zapper's second in command to me, and you're not! You see what I'm saying? That's also why Zapper's going to inherit X-Termination, and *not you!*"

But then, Doctor XT became somewhat calmer and said to D.D.T., "However, D.D.T., you have been with me much longer than anyone else has, and you have been very very useful to us. So I'm giving you one last chance to 'X-terminate' the Green Phantasm. I have another plan already. But it will be entirely up to you to make absolutely certain that you take care of everything. If you fail me this time around, it's 'X-termination' for you, you dumb, dimwitted turkey!"

D.D.T. was shocked to hear his own master insult him just like the Green Phantasm had. However, he nodded in agreement and said in reply, "Yes, Doctor, you got it, man."

"Very good," said Doctor XT. Then, he summoned everyone, saying, "All right, everybody, let's move on out of here. Zapper and Zinger, y'all take the ship y'all came in. Leave the girl for me. I've got some questions to ask her." After that, XT turned to D.D.T. and told him, "All right, you big buffoon, let your empty-headed self ride with Zapper and Zinger. Go on! Get!" D.D.T. just obeyed and went on with them.

Next, Doctor XT turned to Amanda and said to her, "Okay, sweetheart, come along with me. You and I got us a lot to talk about. Now let's go." He then gently grabbed and tugged Amanda's left arm to try to get her to walk with him.

However, she tried resisting and begged the mad doctor of X-Termination, "Come on, Doctor XT, please. Why can't you just let me go?"

Unfortunately for Amanda, Doctor XT just became angrier. This moved him to tighten his grip on her arm and yank her along with him. At the same time, Doctor XT snapped angrily, "Shut up and come with me! I ain't got time for this! Let's go! Come on!" Then, Amanda burst into tears as Doctor XT escorted her toward the X-Terminator 4000. Her situation was apparently going from bad to worse. After all, Amanda knew she was headed to their headquarters, where the Green Phantasm could only be less likely to rescue her.

In the meantime, the Green Phantasm had been plunging toward the street below. After having fallen about two-thirds of the way, he began regaining consciousness. At the same time, the Phantasm uttered to himself, "Oh man, what's going on? What's happening right now?"

He noticed the ground below him, and it appeared to be getting closer to him. "Oh my God!" cried the Green Phantasm. Then, he only had one thought which he quickly utilized in the nick of time. In order to slow and break his fall, the Green Phantasm activated his hovering ability. This created a force that pushed downward from the soles of his feet and put on the brakes for this valiant, radiant hero. He finally stopped less than a yard above the ground.

Right after that, the Green Phantasm just let himself down onto the sidewalk in front of the building from which he had fallen. He took a glance around at his surroundings and only became confused. So he asked himself, "Where am I, huh? And what am I doing here?"

The Green Phantasm became somewhat calmer so he could figure out what had happened to him. He looked pensively at the front of the Comcast Center building and said, "Okay, so I'm down on the ground in front of the Comcast Center. Just let me think back, all right?"

The Green Phantasm went on to utter to himself, "Well, anyway, I think I came to the top of this building to meet up with X-Termination, correct?" After pausing a few seconds, the Phantasm continued, "The next thing I remember is that D.D.T. attacked me from behind and…"

Suddenly, the Green Phantasm figured out what had actually happened to him. "So that's how I got here," he said. "D.D.T. knocked me off. Oh well, no time to lose; I better get back up there fast."

At once, the Green Phantasm became a shapeless projectile and projected himself straight up. He then reappeared as himself, hovering and floating face-to-face with the large billboard at the front of the building. At that, he yelled out, "All right, you guys, I'm still here! Y'all hear me?"

The Phantasm received no response. So then, he hollered, "I'm talking to you, Doctor XT! You guys too, Zapper, Zinger, D.D.T.! You think you've 'X-terminated' me, do you? Well, you haven't accomplished a doggone thing. You hear what I'm saying?" But still, he heard nothing but silence in response.

The Green Phantasm became a bit concerned and asked himself, "What's going on here? I wonder why nobody's answering." Next, he said, "I don't know, but I'm gonna check this out. Here I go."

Then suddenly, he stopped himself and said, "Wait a minute. I don't know what they're up to here. So I better put on a force field just to be on the safe side." So at once, the Green Phantasm began emitting neon beams from all ten fingers in order to form the force field. Shortly, of course, the force field became complete.

So next, the Green Phantasm turned to his right and began moving to the left front end of the billboard. Then, he finally turned to his left to see what was going on behind the billboard. However, the Green Phantasm saw no sign of X-Termination or Amanda Taylor. So he shook his head in confusion and said to himself, "Oh man, this is really weird."

But then, right after that, the Phantasm decided, "Maybe I better get a better look." The Green Phantasm moved forward a couple of yards while staying inside the force field. Immediately after that, he looked to his left to see whether any X-Termination members were hiding elsewhere. However, not a single one of them nor the X-Terminator 4000's were visible.

Next, the Green Phantasm, unable to believe his eyes, really began to panic. He did not know what to do at the moment. He began retracting his force field. At the same time, he exclaimed, "Oh my God, tell me this ain't happening!"

The Phantasm teleported over to the right front of the billboard in order to make certain that no X-Termination members were hiding anywhere. He checked both in front of and behind the billboard but still saw no sign of Doctor XT, Zapper, Zinger, or D.D.T. So then, the Green Phantasm began running back across the top of the building. Shortly, he stopped in the middle and made one more effort to find the bad guys. The Green Phantasm started looking around in all different directions. While doing so, he yelled out, "All right, this is it! Where are you guys?"

However, he received no answer whatsoever. "Come on now, Doctor XT!" the Phantasm continued yelling at the top of his lungs, "Y'all too, D.D.T., Zapper, and Zinger! Do you hear me? I'm talking to you! Come on out of your hiding place! I ain't finished with you yet! And where's Amanda?! What have y'all done with her, huh?"

But after that, the Green Phantasm just waited a few moments to see whether anyone would show. He never saw or heard anyone. That made him very afraid. He began to cry. "Oh no," the Green Phantasm sobbed, "will somebody please tell me this is not happening? It just can't be."

After that, the Phantasm took one last look all around to make absolutely certain that what he thought he saw was really true. Unfortunately, he detected no clue at all as to the whereabouts of Amanda Taylor, or anyone with X-Termination. It was quite evident that the devilish foursome of Doctor XT and his three masked officials had taken Amanda and left. The actual truth in fact was that they had taken the captive Amanda Taylor back to X-Termination Headquarters with them, and both James Clifton and the Green Phantasm were beginning to realize that.

So finally, he removed his hat and mask and dropped them both at his feet. Then, he deactivated the pyxorium within himself and stopped radiating neon-green light because he was feeling much too guilty to want to utilize his Green Phantasm powers.

So next, Clifton knelt down onto his right knee and bowed his head while sadly uttering, "Oh no, what have I done? I really really did it this time." At that, he just kept crying. Eventually, he uttered to himself mournfully, "Poor Amanda, and it's all my fault. I have failed as the Green Phantasm." Poor James just resumed and continued his weeping.

It was no wonder that James Clifton could not stop crying. The one person he loved and wanted to protect was apparently now gone. With Amanda Taylor as his favorite person of all, how could any other heroic deeds performed have mattered to him now? As far as Clifton was concerned, his failure to help and protect Amanda blotted out the greatness of having done so for anyone else. That was also another reason that James had just switched off his Green Phantasm capabilities, because nothing else he could do as the Green Phantasm could undo the abduction of Amanda, who was of the utmost importance to him.

This Saturday night appeared to be the worst night of all for the Green Phantasm. It was also probably one of the worst nights in the life of James Clifton. After all, he could not possibly have had too many other occasions of feeling the kind of guilt and sadness he was currently feeling. Also, as the Green Phantasm, he had just sustained his first real defeat. The only positive thought was that he was still alive. Courage and heroism had possibly helped him survive when his life was on the line at the hands of big D.D.T. However, Amanda Taylor was now captured.

James continued to kneel and weep over the kidnapping of Amanda, until at last, he found it within himself to use his super powers one last time. This was to get himself home. What a horrible night for both James

Clifton and the Green Phantasm. It was probably even more so for the now captive Amanda Lee Taylor, who was undeniably in great danger.

CHAPTER ELEVEN

The Final Showdown

It was after 10:00 on Saturday night. Still in his Green Phantasm suit, James Clifton was back at his house. After having been through a humiliating defeat at the hands of X-Termination, Clifton just sadly walked upstairs to his room. All the while, he hung his head forward heavy with guilt and sorrow. How could he not? After all, he had allowed himself to be defeated by D.D.T. Plus, Amanda Taylor was now gone, and he did not know where she was. Earlier in the evening, he had made it to the restaurant in time to save her, but he then allowed her to be captured by leaving her. How could James possibly forgive himself after all that?

Clifton finally made it upstairs to his bedroom. Once there, he just took off his hat and mask and threw them down onto the floor by his desk. At that, he just sat down on his bed. Poor James still had his head hanging forward, and he started crying. Understandably, it was because of the abduction of Amanda, whom James no doubt loved so much. But now, he had no way of knowing what would happen to her, and he felt that it was all because of his negligence.

James continued crying, not knowing what to do at the time. He said to himself, "What have I done? How could I have let this happen? What kind of a hero am I?"

In fact, James now felt even worse than he had that Wednesday night, when X-Termination had crashed the party and killed all those police officers as well as many others. Even the guilt he had felt late that night was nothing like the guilt he was feeling at the present. "Oh man, poor Amanda," James cried, "and it's all my fault."

James sniffled a few more times. Then, he said, "Man, I thought I'd screwed up the other night at the party. It was already bad enough that I abandoned Amanda that night without saying anything. Then, I really felt bad seeing all those cops die. But I really, really did it this time. I don't know where Amanda is, and I won't be able to find her now. It's true I saved all those people's lives Tuesday night. Then, Wednesday night, I helped all those guests get away safely. But now, it's like none of that matters. I have failed as the Green Phantasm. I'm no hero at all." After that, James Clifton spent the next few minutes crying his eyes out.

Then, James said, "You know, if I hadn't taken up my role as the Green Phantasm, this wouldn't be happening right now. I had no business becoming a superhero. I'm not responsible enough."

But then, James stopped crying and took a few moments of silence to think back over everything that had happened since Sunday night, when the unintended transformation had started it all. All of a sudden, James started to think more positively because he finally remembered what he had done for Amanda at the subway station Sunday night. So rather enthusiastically, James said, "Wait a minute! Now, if I hadn't become the Green Phantasm, those two guys in the subway might have hurt her or killed her. What if I hadn't been there for her? Then, she wouldn't still be alive right now—that's if nothing's happened to her yet. I don't know, maybe it was a good idea. Just let me think." So then, Clifton gave further thought to Sunday, Tuesday, and Wednesday.

Then finally, he said to himself, "Of course, I did make quite a few mistakes Sunday night. But, I learned from them, didn't I? Of course, I did."

Then, James stopped and thought some more. At last, he said, "And you know what else? I made a few errors Tuesday night, and I learned from them, didn't I? I certainly did."

After that, he went on and did even more thinking to himself. A few minutes later, James Clifton told himself, "But of course, I know I messed up pretty bad Wednesday night. I mean, without notice, I kind of walked off on Amanda. Also, I let all those policemen die and allowed for X-Termination to get away. But at least I know where I went wrong, right? Right! Will I make those mistakes again? No way! Well, anyway, at least a few good things came out of all that on Wednesday night. Well, whatever the case is, at least the three most important people to me made it out alive—namely, Amanda, Eric, and Scott. At least I still have them. Whoa, wait a minute. Oh shucks, I forgot; I don't know about Amanda. I hope she's still alive." Upon saying that, James just became silent for the next couple of moments. He murmured, "Now, let me think about tonight. Hmmm."

After a couple of moments, James began saying, "Now, what about what happened tonight? First of all, how could I have just deliberately left and gone home, putting Amanda in danger? Well, I guess I can't go back on that now. I probably need to worry about… what to do now? I mean, I guess they took her to their hideout. But I don't know where that is. Besides, they already outwitted me and defeated me once tonight."

So once again, James became quiet. But this time, he tried a lot harder to think of a good idea, as far as how he ought to go about pursuing X-Termination in search of his one love, Amanda Lee Taylor.

However, James stopped for a moment to try to figure something else out. "Well, first of all," he began, "I wonder what the odds are that they've already killed her. I hate to ask myself this, but if I were Doctor XT, what would I do? Of course, it's hard to think about, because I'm not like him. I'm not a criminal or a killer. I'm trying to be a hero. However, I do believe that it's me they were after. I mean, Tuesday night, Hornet Killer and Wasp Killer were shooting at me. Then the next night, X-Termination broke into the hotel looking for me. Plus, Thursday night, all those rocket planes were shooting at me, with Zapper and Zinger hiding at the construction site, looking to destroy me. So, as I was saying, I believe it's me they're after. So maybe Amanda is still alive. They could be using her as bait to lure me into a trap. Oh man, this is heavy."

James stopped to think a little more. But, he only came up with one idea. So, after a minute, he said, "Well, there's only one thing I know to do. I guess I'll have to call her on her cell phone. It may be what they want regarding how they're setting me up, but it's the only way I'm gonna get to her. I guess I gotta try something. After all, her demise could happen at any moment for all I know."

Meanwhile, at X-Termination Headquarters, Doctor XT had made it back not too long ago. Of course, D.D.T., Zapper, and Zinger had made it back as well. Without a doubt, they were holding poor Amanda captive. How terrified and afraid she must have been at the moment! It appeared to her that she was about to be killed. In addition, it did not appear to her that anyone would find her in time. After all, no one else actually knew the location of X-Termination Headquarters. Anyone could understand how frightened she must have been.

So now, all five of them were in Doctor XT's office above the manufacturing area. Of course, that included Doctor XT, Zapper, Zinger, and D.D.T. It also included the kidnapped Amanda Taylor. She had her hands locked behind her back in handcuffs. Understandably, she was in tears, afraid for her life. XT and Amanda were leaned against the front of his desk. All the others were surrounding them in a semicircle. "Well, sweetheart," addressed Doctor XT tauntingly, "what do you think of my facility? How you like my office?"

Too afraid of what was yet to come, Amanda offered no answer. She just kept sniffling and crying as if XT had not asked her anything.

"No answer?" asked Doctor XT. "Well, at least you still have until midnight. Even if he doesn't come, you and I could still have a hell of a time together. What do you say? Would you care to look around?" However, Amanda just looked away from him with contempt.

"I take that as a no," XT replied. "Oh well, I thought I'd offer to let you have the best time possible, since you found your way here, and it's all going to be over at midnight." Amanda was not in the mood for a good time. After all, she was possibly looking at the end of her life. The only interest she had at the present was the Green Phantasm, who would hopefully make his way over and save her life. It was no wonder she did not care for what the doctor could offer her.

But anyway, X-Termination was awaiting the arrival of the Green Phantasm. They were hoping to dispose of him as well as Amanda. However, Doctor XT still planned to do away with Amanda at midnight, even if the Phantasm did not come. They were betting the Green Phantasm would call her, because Doctor XT presumed he had her number. They had fought for each other on Thursday night. So, for the present, they all continued waiting to hear from the Phantasm.

But then, momentarily, they all heard Amanda's cell phone ringing. Doctor XT said, "Well, I wonder who that could be. I guess I'll release you so you can answer." He got out a key, unlocked the handcuffs, and took them off, but only because he figured it must have been the Green Phantasm calling.

At once, Amanda used her left hand to reach into one of the front pockets of her dress. She took out her cell phone and answered it. "Hello," said Amanda on her phone.

"Amanda," said James. "It's me. It's the Green Phantasm."

"Oh, thank God," Amanda replied so happily, "am I ever so happy to hear your voice! Listen to me, I—"

But Doctor XT would not let her keep talking to him. "All right, that's enough," said Doctor XT, taking away the phone. "I'll take it from here." Then, he said to his three men, "Hold her, will you?" At that, Zapper held her right arm, and Zinger held the left.

Next, Doctor XT got onto the phone to talk to the Phantasm. "Hello, Mister Phantasm," he said. "You know who this is?"

"I sure do all right," James responded. "You're none other than Doctor XT, the X-Termination engineer."

"Well, not bad," said XT. "You know me better than I thought. How would you like to know me even better?"

"That's quite enough, Doctor," Clifton told him. "I think you know why I'm calling."

"Do I?" XT taunted.

"Doctor," James addressed him angrily, "what have you done with her?"

"I'm sorry, say what?" Doctor XT asked, still teasing him.

Even more angrily, James said, "Come on, Doctor. Stop joking around, and answer me! What in the devil did you do to her, and where did you take her? You better tell me!"

"Oh, that," answered Doctor XT, still smiling with pride. "Look," said XT, "I'll tell you how to get here, but you better listen good, pal. I know you're gonna come for her; I already know that. But you better follow my instructions precisely, you understand?"

"Mm-hmm," replied James Clifton.

"All right," said Doctor XT. "I'm about to tell you how to get here, but hear this, and hear it well. First of all, you'd better come here all by yourself. You are not to bring anyone else here or tell anyone where I am. If anyone else shows up while you're here or I find out you told someone about my facility, I will 'X-terminate' your girl right on the spot. So I suggest you keep this all to yourself and show up by yourself. Have you got all that?"

"Oh yeah," James answered affirmatively.

"All right then," continued Doctor XT. "I'll explain to you how to get here, now listen up. You will take Highway 30 west of Philadelphia. My headquarters will be thirty miles west of the city."

"All right," replied Clifton.

"Okay, okay, now listen," the doctor told him. "Here's what you are to look for: it is a gravel drive on the north side of the highway. However, there will be a roadblock at it."

"Oh, really?" James asked eagerly.

"Oh yes," answered XT. "You see, my facility is set three miles back from the highway. If you follow the gravel road, you will eventually come to a huge steel wall. That is not to mention a gravel parking lot with a white stretched limo and some other vehicles out front."

"Oh yeah, I'll find it," James declared with confidence, continuously nodding affirmatively.

"And another thing," added XT. "We will be inside the west half of the big barrier. I'm talking about my manufacturing area. That's where I've got a big acid vat, of X-Termination Acid! Ha, ha, haaa! Other than that, there's a set of steps and a balcony leading to my control room and my office."

"No problem," Clifton said confidently. "I'll find it all with no trouble. You can count on me."

"Well, good," replied Doctor XT. "But look here, tough guy; I got two last things to tell you."

"Okay, what are they?" asked Clifton.

"First of all," said Doctor XT. "You do just like I told you earlier."

"What are you talking about?" asked James Clifton.

"You don't remember?" asked Doctor XT, a little surprised. "It's like I said, you neon-green fool—"

"Who the hell do you think you're calling a fool?" asked an infuriated James Clifton. "Don't you make me come over there and kick your—"

"Hey, hey, hey!" yelled Doctor XT. "You better calm down. Next time you get all crazy and rambunctious, I'm gonna dispose of her right on the spot. So you better settle down, bub."

"All right, all right," James said more calmly. "So anyway, Doctor, as you were saying?"

"As I was saying," continued Doctor XT, "you better make sure you keep your mouth shut about this whole thing."

"Well," replied Clifton, "I guess I don't have any other choice, do I?"

"If you want to keep your girlfriend alive as long as possible," Doctor XT answered, "then, no, you don't."

"Well, you got it then, Doctor," James told him.

"Excellent," replied Doctor XT.

"So what about the other thing?" asked James.

"The other thing?" asked Doctor XT. "Oh yes, of course, that. Well, I just thought I'd let you know, that you have until midnight. That's how long you have to settle this once and for all. Of course, if I don't see you or hear from you by then, poor Amanda's demise will take place. So what do you say? See you by midnight?"

"No problem," Clifton answered with confidence. "I'll be there way before then."

"Sounds great," XT replied. "We'll all be waiting for you. I suggest you get a move on. You only got till midnight, and keep this to yourself like I told you."

"All right, no problem," Clifton said. "I'll see you when I get there. Bye." At that, they both hung up.

Next, Perone just gave the cell phone back to Amanda. Of course, she had been struggling all the while in the clutches of Zapper and Zinger. However, they were too strong for her to break free. But they all allowed her just one moment to put away her cell phone.

After that, Doctor XT gave Zapper and Zinger an order concerning the captive Amanda. Headed out of his office, through the control room, XT directed his two lieutenants, saying, "Come on. Bring her this way."

Zapper and Zinger just obeyed, following their master and leading Amanda by her arms. Finally, big D.D.T. followed behind them all.

Understandably, at the same time, Amanda kept struggling, saying, "What are y'all doing? Let me go!"

Finally, Doctor XT led everyone through the gas chamber and stopped just outside of it. "All right, everybody," XT addressed his crew, "let's stop right here." They all stopped at his command.

Then, Doctor XT addressed Amanda, "Well, well, my dear, I'm sure you know by now that your hero is on his way."

"Yes, I do," Amanda replied nodding.

"Well then," said XT. "I suppose you also know that you only have a short time left."

"We'll see about that," Amanda told him. At that, D.D.T., Zapper, and Zinger all looked around at each other, laughing and shaking their heads in disbelief.

"Well, anyway," continued Doctor XT, "I took that into consideration. So, considering that you only have until midnight, I thought I might place you where you could catch all the fun. I mean, who doesn't like to see a hero meet his doom, huh? Therefore, Miss Amanda, I hate to have you miss out on something great. With the small amount of time you got left, it's the least I can do."

Next, XT addressed Zapper and Zinger while pointing to an upright pole just outside the gas chamber and next to the steel barrier that surrounded all of X-Termination Headquarters. He said to them, "All right, handcuff her to that pole, with both hands behind it. Let her face out."

"You got it, boss," replied Zinger.

"Heh, heh, heh, heh," laughed Zapper. At once, Zapper and Zinger complied accordingly.

"Oh, Doctor," Amanda addressed XT, "you're so depraved, so corrupt, so insane, and so… devilish."

"Am I?" asked Doctor XT, tauntingly. "Well, once I 'X-terminate' the Green Phantasm, I will have all of Philadelphia under my control."

"You think so, huh?" asked Amanda. "You just wait and see." They all just laughed at her. But Amanda had not yet given up hope. After all, it was not over yet, for either herself or her hero. Besides, she strongly believed in the Green Phantasm, for she knew that he could find a way to save her.

Meanwhile, back at his home, James Clifton was getting ready to take up his role as the Green Phantasm once again. He was also trying to think about whom or what he could have to go against and how. Of course, one strong possibility was the huge gargantuan behemoth, D.D.T., the same one who had been used to defeat him much earlier on the building top. Could the Phantasm do better this time around? Besides, what other schemes could the evil Doctor XT have concocted for the final showdown, which would take place at his very own establishment? For once, was the Green Phantasm able and ready to beard the lion in his den? This was very serious indeed.

So James Clifton said, "Well, it looks like there's only one thing to do. Of course, I know I have my doubts about who or what I'll have to face. But other than that, I really love and care so much about Amanda. Therefore, I want to try and save her life, right? Of course, I do. So I guess I've got no choice but to go down there alone like Mister XT wants. Besides, I've only got until midnight. So I guess I better get a move on." Upon saying that, James picked up his Green Phantasm mask and hat and walked over to his bedroom window. Sighing, Clifton said, "Well, here we go, I guess. I'll just have to do what I can."

After that, he took one last moment to think about having to battle X-Termination on their own ground, their headquarters of course. "You know," said a worried James Clifton, "I still can't help wondering what on earth Doctor XT's gonna throw at me this time. Of course, after I took down all those guys in the rocket planes, I don't know what ended up happening to them. Otherwise, I'm pretty darn sure there'll be at least Zapper, Zinger, and whoa, uh-oh, D.D.T. Oh yeah, none other than D.D.T., the very one used to beat me up and throw me off that building earlier tonight. I'm sure I'll have him to deal with. And this time, it'll be at X-Termination Headquarters. They can definitely find a way for him to get me there." At that, James quieted down for a couple of moments. Even though he was a bit worried, he was still determined.

After a couple of moments, Clifton was smiling with a more positive view of the situation. "Wait a minute!" he exclaimed happily, "You know what? There were a couple other times I had to face that big galoot, right? Yeah, there were, and you know what else? Those other times, I outwitted him. Perhaps D.D.T. is a dumb, dim-witted turkey after all. The only other thing I'm wondering is, what happened tonight? How was that encounter different from all the others?"

After looking back and reviewing how all of the encounters with D.D.T. had been the same and different, he finally said, "Now, wait a minute. I think I see what happened. At the party Wednesday night and the construction site Thursday night, I was ready for him. But tonight, he caught me off guard, by complete surprise. I didn't even know he was there behind that billboard. I had no idea that Doctor XT would do something like that. But I will know for next time, right? Right! This time, I will be ready, for D.D.T. or anyone else that so-called "doctor" wants to bring on. I mean heck, for Amanda's sake, I'll face it."

After that, James Clifton was just about to put on his hat and mask and shove off toward X-Termination Headquarters. However, he paused one last time. He said, "I just want to make sure of one more thing. Am I quite sure that I'm ready to do this? Let's see, now. I know Tuesday night, I was in a tough spot with Wasp Killer and Hornet Killer. But I found a way to outsmart them, right? Of course, I did. Then the next night, when Doctor XT and X-Termination were holding up everyone at the party, I figured out a way to stop him, correct? I most certainly did. Plus, I know I'll never forget Thursday night, when a dozen rocket planes were nuking me and blasting me left and right. Although I got knocked around quite a bit, I eventually took 'em all down, didn't I? By all means, I certainly did." Then, he stood there for a moment, grinning and nodding happily.

After that, Clifton said, "Now, I know I might've made some errors, but at least I learned from them, didn't I? Absolutely. Will I make them again? No way! Besides, although some things have gone wrong, and it looks really bad, would a real hero just give up and back out? Of course not! Although I've wound up in some predicaments, I got through them, didn't I? I sure did. So therefore, I can get through this somehow. So what was I fussing and crying about earlier? I mean, with the powers I have, I know for sure that I can find a way to save Amanda and put X-Termination in their place."

So finally, a brave, determined James Paul Clifton put on his Green Phantasm mask and the hat too. That same moment, Clifton activated the pyxorium within himself, which caused him to give off blinding neon-green radiation. Once more, James Clifton was none other than the Green Phantasm. "All right!" he yelled excitedly, "This time, I'm ready for sure. Amanda may have the wrong idea about me, but she'll get to know the truth tonight. Other than that, I will see to it that the XTE, Doctor XT becomes an 'X-terminated' engineer. Truly, I tell you, tonight, X-Termination's going out of business. It's time for the final showdown! Here we go."

The Green Phantasm began charging up, preparing to shoot out through the bedroom window. Then, of course, he released and launched himself as a shapeless projectile. Within a second, the Green Phantasm had reappeared in his human form, hovering above the next subdivision. He was now two-thirds of a mile from his home.

It was about 10:50 p.m., and the Green Phantasm was on his way to X-Termination Headquarters. Still afloat where he had just reappeared, the Green Phantasm said, "Well, I guess I'd better get moving. I've only got until midnight to get down there and go through whatever I have to, to get Amanda out of that terrible place. I got no time to lose."

Then, immediately after that, the Green Phantasm became like a projectile again, and shot himself west toward Highway 30. That same instant, he reappeared just outside of Philadelphia, along U.S. Highway 30.

Before getting too far, the Green Phantasm just wanted to be sure he was going the right way. "All right now," said the Phantasm, "before I continue on, I might wanna… make sure this is the right highway. He did say Highway 30, didn't he? Yes, I do believe he did. Let's see, now."

Upon saying that, the Green Phantasm started jogging westward, looking for a sign that indicated the highway number. Fortunately, it did not even take an entire minute to find a sign, and luckily, the highway number on the sign was 30. "Great," he said, somewhat relieved. "Let's keep moving."

At that, the Phantasm once again projected himself at supersonic speed. This time, he went five miles farther and then reappeared. From that point on, he kept repeating the process, only covering a maximum of five miles at a time along Highway 30. Of course, as he progressed along, the Green Phantasm would check the closest mile marker to keep track of how much of the necessary distance he had already gone.

Then, before too long, when the Green Phantasm had covered most of the distance, he was about to project himself one last time. This final burst of supersonic speed was meant to move him the last four out of the thirty-five miles he was supposed to go. So after the Phantasm finally reappeared in human form, he paused momentarily, looking around for any sign of a gravel path that was blocked off. He even looked back to try to make sure he had not passed it up.

Momentarily, the Green Phantasm began jogging, continuing on westward in search of the gravel roadway. "Anyway," he said while running, "I tried to stop a bit short of the thirty-five miles, just to be sure I didn't pass up my pathway to their hideout. Oh man, I just gotta find it. Amanda, please hang in there, my baby; I'm coming to you." Understandably, the Phantasm was becoming worried and was afraid some of the time because the possibility existed that either he may have passed it up, or he would not be able to find their headquarters. At present, could the Green Phantasm have possibly been exerting himself in vain?

But fortunately, something finally turned up after almost three minutes of running alongside the highway. The Green Phantasm was beginning to feel foolish, in addition to being worried. However, about a quarter of a mile up ahead, he thought he saw something that looked like it could be the blocked-off gravel drive he was seeking. "Well, what do you know?" he asked himself wonderingly. "At least finally, I think I see something. Man, I sure hope that's it. Let me, uh, go check it out." At that, he started sprinting on toward the prospective roadblock. While running, the Phantasm said, "Oh, please let this be it, oh please."

Finally, he made it over to his sighting. Fortunately, what the Phantasm had thought he had seen a quarter of a mile back turned out to fit the description that Doctor XT had given him. He was now at the starting point of a private gravel road that was wide enough to consist of two lanes. Also, right there at the turning point from the highway stood an orange-and-white-striped barricade of the type used for road closures. Of course, without very much doubt, a white rectangular sign with block letters was posted, which said, "ROAD CLOSED."

"Well," said the Green Phantasm. "I hope this is the turning point I'm looking for. It looks like it could be. I mean, this is a gravel drive that I'm at, and this is a roadblock. I just hope it's the right one. Oh well, it probably is, I suppose. I guess I don't have time to waste. I'd better get going."

Upon having said that, the Green Phantasm began charging himself up once again. Before launching himself, he halted momentarily. "Now, wait a minute," he told himself. "The doctor said, um, three miles, didn't he? Maybe I'll just go for two and a half. Hopefully that way, I won't risk running smack into the big steel wall. I'll just advance by two and a half, and then, I'll see what to do from there. All right now, two and a half miles, let's do it!" So, after saying that, the Green Phantasm finished charging up. Then, he once more became like a shapeless neon-green projectile. But this time, of course, he only advanced about two and a half miles like he had planned.

Upon reappearing as a person, the Green Phantasm just paused for a matter of seconds to check out what was up ahead of him. "All right now," he said, "I just wanna, um, make certain I'm going the right way. Let me, uh, see what I can see up ahead." So then, the Green Phantasm put his right hand up to his forehead, so he could focus on his view. Now of course, it was dark, and X-Termination Headquarters was supposedly half a mile away. But fortunately, the Phantasm managed to catch a vague image. He thought he saw some small degree of light, slightly rising above something rectangular and horizontal. Also, in the lower right corner of his field of vision, he thought he noticed a tiny speck of light peeking just above what looked like possibly the front of a car. Could that be what he was looking for?

The Green Phantasm said to himself, "I'm not a hundred percent sure, but it looks like it might possibly be it. Let me get a closer look to be sure." He used his mind to select a spot up ahead, at which he would reappear at the end of a teleportation beam. He set the designated point just a few yards to the left of what he could see around the bottom right. Finally, the Phantasm charged up and became a long narrow beam of radiation. Then, he became like himself at the end of it, within a split second.

Now, upon reappearing, the Green Phantasm went over to the vehicle that he had vaguely perceived from half a mile away. With the light he was giving off, and the source of light he had vaguely perceived a minute or two before, he could get a decent view of the vehicle. Fortunately, it turned out to be the stretch limousine he was seeking. The small source of light nearby happened to be the front entrance to X-Termination Headquarters. Besides that, the huge horizontal rectangular object he had perceived just so happened to be the front side of the great big barrier that surrounded all of X-Termination Headquarters. So the Green Phantasm took one last look at it all just to be sure. Consequently, he could see that he had found the hideout of X-Termination. "This must be it," a somewhat amazed Green Phantasm uttered. "Yes, this is it!"

But then, before making too much more noise, the Phantasm stopped himself. "Wait a minute now," he spoke softly. "I might wanna keep my voice down. If he hears me hollering and screaming out here, there's no telling who or what he might send out after me. But anyway, like I was about to say, I've found you, Doctor XT. Heh, heh, I'm here."

The Green Phantasm then started trying to figure out how he might get inside. "Let's see," he said, "I wonder how I ought to try to get in there. I know there's an entrance right here, but maybe I ought not do that. I mean, people normally go through there, so they could possibly be expecting me to. If that's the case, there's no telling what sort of trap they possibly could've set for me. Well, I don't wanna take any risk I don't need to. So I won't go for that, oh no. But what about another doorway somewhere else? Nah, forget that. They could be booby-trapped, too. Let's forget I ever mentioned any of that."

So then, the Green Phantasm tried to see if he could think of some other method of getting inside. He said, "Now, if I ought not be going through a door, what other possible way is there? The only other way I can possibly think of is to perhaps go over the top of the barrier and go inside from above. But should I actually try to do that?"

But then, the Phantasm had a thought. "Wait a minute," he said more happily. "Maybe that's not too bad of an idea. Maybe that way, I'll go up above, where I can see them without being seen. Besides, I'll get a bird's-eye view of everything. Yeah, that's what I'll do. Let's get ready to shoot on up there."

Before getting started, he had a second thought. "Hold on," he said, "maybe not. They might hear that, and start aiming for me. Maybe I'll do something quieter, like um, hovering. Yeah, that's it! I'll hover my way up. Here I go." At that, the Green Phantasm placed tension on his feet, activating his hovering ability. Consequently, he was slowly and gradually ascending up the front of the big steel barrier.

X-Termination was still inside, waiting anxiously for the appearance of the Green Phantasm. "I wonder where that Green Phantasm's at right now," said Zinger. "I mean, I just can't help remembering the other night, at that party we crashed, he was able to move so fast we almost couldn't see him. Wait a minute; if he can go that fast, do y'all think it's possible he could actually be here right now?"

"Well," answered Zapper. "You could be right, Zinger. It's quite possible."

"But, y'all know what else I was thinking?" asked Zinger.

"What is it, Zinger?" asked Doctor XT.

"Well," responded Zinger. "I also remember how, just before he appeared in front of us, he had been in hiding, listening to us. Y'all don't think he could be doing something like that right now, even as we speak? With his powers and supernatural abilities, I think just about anything's possible. Don't you all agree?"

"You know something?" asked Doctor XT. "You might have a point there, Zinger. Thanks for saying that."

"Holy shoot, that's right!" exclaimed Zapper.

"Yeah!" said D.D.T. in agreement.

"All right then, men," said Doctor XT in a lowered voice, "let's all go ahead and take our places." Then, looking at Zinger, XT made an eye movement at him, signaling him to tell D.D.T. to take his spot.

"All right, D.D.T.," said Zinger at his normal voice level, "why don't you—"

"Quiet, you fool!" Zapper snapped at him in a lowered voice. "Don't you remember what you just told us? He could be hearing us. Now, keep it quiet, you stupid freak!"

"Sorry," Zinger whispered to Zapper. Next, he turned back to D.D.T. and continued by whispering, "All right, all right, go hide right here inside the gas chamber. We'll tell you when to spring out on him, okay?"

"Okay," D.D.T. whispered back.

After that XT summoned both Zapper and Zinger, saying, "All right, you two, let's all stick together like we planned. You two do your thing."

"Come on, Zinger," commanded Zapper. When Zapper said that, both Zinger and he stood on different sides of Amanda, holding her at gunpoint with their X-Termination Rays. Doctor XT just stepped forward in front of them all, looking around for any sign of the Green Phantasm.

The Green Phantasm had made it to the top of the steel barrier's front. It was now after 11:00 p.m. But before elevating his entire body above the top, the Phantasm decided to try something to be sure it was safe. While remaining afloat, he took off his hat and held it straight up overhead, even sometimes waving it from side to side. Fortunately, that did not arouse any sort of response or reaction. The Green Phantasm then ascended just a few more feet, so that his waist was at the same elevation as the barrier's top. Once again, he tried using his hat to see if anyone would notice. But luckily, nothing happened the second time either. So after that, the Green Phantasm just ascended the rest of the way up and perched on the steel barrier's top.

Then, after letting himself down on top of the barrier, the Green Phantasm looked around in every direction he possibly could. Of course, the one thing he was looking for was Amanda Taylor, the young woman he loved so very much. However, he did not see any immediate sign of anyone present. So then, the Green Phantasm told himself, "Well, they gotta be in here somewhere. Now, if I remember right, I think XT told me the west half. So I think I'll go look there." Therefore, he started jogging westward along the barrier's wall.

He stopped when he made it about half of the way across the front of the manufacturing area. Then, the Phantasm made another attempt to find a sign of anyone's presence at all. However, from up above, he could not get the best view possible because the elevated shelter in the manufacturing area blocked off a large portion of what could possibly be seen. With that being the case, the Green Phantasm declared, "Well, I guess I'll have to try something else besides this. I mean this must be the area they're in, because I believe I'm in the west half. I can see maybe a little, but that stupid shelter, or whatever that raised platform is, is in my way. I wonder what else I'll try here. At least I can see the bottom part of some tank or vat, which I guess is that vat of acid, that 'whatchamacallim' kinda said something about. But anyway, let me see."

The Green Phantasm only came up with one other idea. "Well," he said to himself, "perhaps I'll try to see what I can see from the top of that shelter there." So at that, the Phantasm just teleported himself over to the center of the shelter's roof.

"All right now," said the determined Green Phantasm from the shelter's roof, "I oughtta find something this time. Now, didn't he say something about a set of steps and a balcony leading to his control room and his office? Well, I guess there's only one way to find out. I say let's check it and see." So then, he slowly and carefully tiptoed toward the west edge of the shelter's roof.

Once the Green Phantasm had made it over to the roof's edge, he was able to get a better view of what he had tried to see before. He looked around below a little bit, and then spotted something all right. What could the Phantasm have finally seen? Well, it turned out to be exactly what he had been hoping to find. From above, the Green Phantasm was so happy and relieved that he had finally found his one love, Amanda Lee Taylor. However, he could also see three others surrounding her. Without a doubt, this threesome consisted of Doctor XT, Zapper, and Zinger. So now, the Green Phantasm was trying to think of a way to face them and rescue Amanda. Fortunately, she was still alive at present.

The Green Phantasm said, "Great! I finally found Amanda. Oh, I hate to think of the tough time she's been through. This must've really been a rough night for her. First, I upset her at that Italian restaurant. Then, she got kidnapped. After that, she had to see me get defeated at the top of the Comcast Center building. And now, she must be so scared for her life. I just gotta get her out of this place and get her home. I just need to figure out a way to deal with those three jerks. Of course, I don't see that really big jerk, D.D.T. Is it possible they got him hidden somewhere? I don't know; hopefully, I'll be ready for him this time. But right now, let's see what I'll do about these three."

So once again, the Green Phantasm paused for a moment to try to think of a game plan. However, he only came up with one idea. "Well," he said, "there's only one way I know of to go about this. From here, I'm gonna teleport and reappear at the top of those stairs. But, as soon as I reappear, I'll immediately charge up both my hands and all my fingers. That way, I'll be prepared to open fire, in case they decide to try to shoot their ray guns at me. At least I've got ten lasers to counter them with. Of course, even if they don't decide to open fire on me, maybe I'll try to be cooperative. After all, I've got Amanda's life in my hands. Well, I'll see when I get down there." After saying that, the Green Phantasm teleported over to the end of the balcony.

In the meantime, Doctor XT had turned toward his two men, Zapper and Zinger, to go over something with them. "All right, men," he said to his two lieutenants, "this is what we are to do. We are to—"

However, the Green Phantasm had just reappeared in the distance. He now had all ten fingers charged and ready to open fire, in case it was necessary. Doctor XT was paying attention to Zapper and Zinger, with his back to the Green Phantasm. But from another viewpoint, Junior Lieutenant Zinger, who was at Amanda's left, managed to notice. So then, he said to XT, "Excuse me, boss."

"Zinger, please!" Doctor XT told him upon being interrupted. "Would you let me—"

However, Zinger persisted. "But, boss, look!" He used his left hand to point to the Green Phantasm.

"All right," replied XT, "what is it that's got you—" Now, as Doctor XT was asking that, he was turning around to see the thing at which Zinger was pointing. Once XT caught sight of the Phantasm, he interrupted himself, exclaiming, "It's him! Thanks for telling me, Zinger."

At that, Doctor XT paused for a few seconds, after which he said, "All right, you two, stay here and hold her captive. I'll handle this." Amanda sighed with relief.

Then at once, Doctor XT began walking along the balcony toward the Green Phantasm. While he was walking, he began speaking. "Well, well, well, if it isn't the Green Phantasm."

"It's me all right," replied the Phantasm, moving toward XT.

"I see you found your way here," XT told him.

"Of course," said the Green Phantasm. "Anybody could've."

"Is that right?"

"Yes, that's right," answered the Green Phantasm. "I even kept this whole thing a secret, like you told me to."

"So, you did," replied Doctor XT. "That's fantastic; great job, Phantasm."

Then finally, Doctor XT and the Green Phantasm met halfway. They were now face-to-face. The Green Phantasm still had both hands charged and ready to fire. He went on to say to the evil Doctor XT, "All right now, Doctor, so, what about Amanda, huh?"

"Did you say 'What about Amanda?'" asked Doctor XT.

"That's right, Doctor. You heard me right," the Green Phantasm told him. "That's the reason I'm here. I came for Amanda. I have held up my part of the deal. And now, what about Amanda? What do I still have to do for her? I'll do whatever it takes. I'm not leaving this dump unless it's with her, and I will see to that no matter what. Now tell me, Doctor, what's going to happen now?"

"Well there, Mr. Phantasm," Doctor XT responded, "let's just say that I've got plans for the two of you. But you better stay calm and not get crazy. You remember what I said would happen? I said I'd dispose of her right on the spot, didn't I?"

"Yes, you did," answered the Green Phantasm, nodding affirmatively.

Then, pointing back toward Amanda and the two watching her, Doctor XT said, "And I guess you see my two men holding her hostage back there."

"Mm-hmm."

"Anyway," continued Doctor XT. "just make sure you don't get rambunctious. And now, if you wish to reunite with your girlfriend, just follow me this way, nice and easy. Right this way, my friend."

The Green Phantasm started following Doctor XT back to the spot at which Zapper and Zinger were watching Amanda. Of course, the Green Phantasm did not have every bit of trust in Doctor XT. How could he? After all, Doctor XT had tricked him before. Besides, he knew that Doctor XT was looking to destroy him somehow. The Phantasm did not know the entire game plan of the X-Termination crew. So, while following the doctor, he paused for a few seconds. He looked around in every possible direction to make sure no one was trying to attack from behind, above, or anywhere else. Since he could not find anything, he just continued following behind Doctor XT.

Doctor XT and the Green Phantasm finally made it over to the spot where Amanda was handcuffed to the pole. "Well, here she is," XT told the Green Phantasm.

"Amanda!" he exclaimed happily.

"Oh, Green Phantasm," replied a relieved Amanda Taylor, "am I ever so happy to see you! I knew you'd come. I have always believed in you."

Seeing that the two were happy to find each other, Doctor XT said to his two men, "Come on, you two; step aside." At that, Zapper and Zinger lowered their X-Termination Rays and walked over to the other side of the gas chamber's entrance. Then, Doctor XT himself went to stand next to them.

However, before the Green Phantasm went any closer to Amanda, he looked critically toward Zapper and Zinger because they were still holding their ray guns, and the Green Phantasm suspected a scheme. He said to them, "All right, you two, what are y'all thinkin' about doin'? I see those guns. Oh yes, I ain't no fool."

But then, Doctor XT replied, "Oh yeah, you know what? I forgot. Zapper, Zinger, hang 'em up." At that, they put their X-Termination Rays into their holders. Seeing that it was now safer, the Green Phantasm disabled the charge within both of his hands. Then, he turned his attention to Amanda.

"Amanda," he addressed her in a soft voice, so that they could keep their conversation as private as possible, "I'm glad I made it to you. How are you feeling? Are you all right? I know you must be terribly afraid. This evening's been really miserable for you, hasn't it? I know, and it's all my fault."

"Oh please, Mr. Phantasm," Amanda pleaded. "Don't say that."

"No, really," insisted the Green Phantasm. "I know that you were at that restaurant this evening. I just didn't make it soon enough."

"You're friends with James Clifton, aren't you?"

"I am," answered the Green Phantasm.

"Maybe that's what happened," said Amanda. "He came to the place and tried to tell me something. But I wouldn't listen to him. Other than that, I was too mean to him. I must've upset him so much, that he didn't find you in time. I guess you both knew those guys were after me. I'm awfully sorry that I got us into this mess."

"Oh well." The Green Phantasm sighed. "At least he eventually notified me. If not for that, I wouldn't have even found you just now."

"True," said Amanda in agreement.

"You know something?" he asked. "Clifton and I are closer than you think. It's like, we always keep in touch about, you know, everything. He even let me know Wednesday night, when Doctor XT and X-Termination invaded and held up that banquet—"

"Wait a minute," Amanda interrupted. "You mean, he really told you?"

While nodding continuously, the Green Phantasm replied very softly, "Yes, he did. He really did. Yes, Amanda."

"You know something?" she asked, starting to feel ashamed. "James tried to tell me that he had done that. But, I'm afraid to admit, that I was too stupid to believe him. I just didn't see how he told you and got you there so fast. There just didn't seem to be enough time. I may not understand how, but I guess it's true after all. Other than that, I guess if he hadn't done that, I may have not made it out alive. I've been wrong about him. I feel so terrible. I guess I made a real fool of myself, didn't I?"

"That's all right," the Green Phantasm told her. "It's a perfectly understandable mistake."

"Perhaps," said Amanda, "but other than that, whenever he had come after me to try to tell me something, it was obviously really, really important. Otherwise, he might've not gone out of his way to try to find me. I just never thought about it that way. Besides, he is a really, really close friend of yours. I just can't possibly understand how I ever could've been so hard on poor James Clifton. I hope he'll forgive me, but I don't deserve to be forgiven. I can't even find a way to forgive myself." At that, she began crying again. At least she was no longer angry with James. However, the guilt she was feeling for her previous hostility to him was unbearable for her.

The Green Phantasm placed his left hand on Amanda's right shoulder to try to calm and comfort her. He said, "Come on; don't cry, Amanda. It's okay. There's no need to be so hard on yourself. It was all just a misunderstanding. You didn't know before what you do now. Everything'll turn out fine. You'll be able to make up with him."

Easing up on her crying, Amanda asked the Phantasm, "You really think so? Do you honestly think he'll forgive me?"

"Hey," said the Green Phantasm, "I'm so sure of all that, that I'll bet my life on it. You mean everything to James. If I know him, he'll definitely forgive you with no problem whatsoever. Don't worry; I'll fix everything. I'll even get you out of this horrible place." After that, raising his right hand, the Green Phantasm declared, "I promise not to leave here tonight, unless it's with you."

"Oh, Green Phantasm," Amanda addressed him sweetly, "I'm so happy to tell you that you and James Clifton are the two greatest guys I have ever met."

Clifton could hardly believe his ears. He was understandably amazed that Amanda now desired both Clifton and the Phantasm more than any other men she knew. Perhaps now, he could always approach her either way. This even made Clifton wonder if he should go on to tell Amanda that the two were one and the same. However, he just decided to hold off on revealing the secret.

"Oh, gosh, Amanda, you earnestly, sincerely mean every word of that?" At that, she smiled and nodded at the Green Phantasm. "Well, um," he uttered all choked up, "I, uh, don't quite know how to tell you… how, uh, amazed and happy I am to hear you say that. Other than that, I don't know what to say." Then at once, he let out a sigh as if he had been rendered speechless.

"Well, uh, I don't know," Amanda told him.

But then, after a couple of moments of silence, the Green Phantasm said to her, "Well, anyway, the only thing I've thought of is: thank you so very much, Amanda Lee Taylor. I'm sorry if that's not enough."

"Oh, that's all right," said Amanda to the Phantasm, "You can always thank me later. Besides, you're so very welcome, you handsome, heroic hunk of mine."

Those words of Amanda's no doubt choked him up even further. However, the Green Phantasm did not remain in a speechless or paralyzed state for very long because he knew he still had to find a way to set Amanda free. So then, the Phantasm told her, "Amanda, listen; I'm really, really glad we cleared up all our troubles and worries. But right now, I've got to get you out of here. Don't get too afraid, okay? I'll figure out a way. I've just gotta get his keys somehow."

Now, while the Green Phantasm and Amanda were conversing, Doctor XT went on to signal Zinger silently, so that the Green Phantasm would not hear anything and get suspicious. XT was communicating with Zinger by pointing toward the gas chamber and then making another hand signal, which supposedly meant to bring something back out of it. What could X-Termination possibly be up to now?

In the meantime, the Green Phantasm and Amanda Taylor continued their discussion. So now, Amanda asked the Phantasm, "Do you really think you can do it?"

Confidently, the Green Phantasm answered her by saying, "Definitely, I've got very little doubt about it. I'm positive I can outmaneuver and outwit Doctor XT and make him hand over his keys. The other night at the party, I managed to outdo all six of them, to get them under my control. Even on Thursday night, I managed to save you from them. I just made a mistake tonight. But at least I've learned from it. I've taken these creeps before, and I'm able and prepared to do it again."

"That's my hero!" she declared.

"Oh yes," said the Green Phantasm, "nothing's gonna stop me now."

But all of a sudden, something from behind began choking the Green Phantasm. It was D.D.T. again. While the Green Phantasm had just been focused on Amanda, the huge behemoth had come from behind and grabbed his throat. At the same time, D.D.T. let out a roar and said, "Gotcha!" No wonder XT was signaling Zinger. It had been to tell D.D.T. to attack. D.D.T. had been waiting just inside the gas chamber for his cue. But unfortunately for the Green Phantasm, he was once again caught by surprise and under attack. Both Amanda and he were in a state of shock.

While holding the Phantasm by the throat with his right hand, D.D.T. proceeded to slam him backward against the steel barrier and kept on choking him with that huge hand. "All right, punk!" D.D.T. said in a threatening manner. "What I did earlier tonight was only the beginning. But this time, I'm gonna put you down for good. I'm gonna finish what I began on that building top."

At the same time, Amanda and the other X-Termination members were looking on. Amanda was very worried for her hero. Doctor XT, Zapper, and Zinger, however, were all smiling and chuckling. "Well, my dear," said XT to Amanda, "what do you think of your hero now? Since my man D.D.T. accidentally fouled up our plans earlier, I thought it only fair that he get the first shot at destroying him. Since it's almost the end for you too, I just didn't want you to miss out on something great. Isn't this exciting?" However, Amanda just looked up and away from him and scoffed.

Doctor XT told her, "Well, I take it you don't like this. Oh well, don't worry; you won't have to deal with it much longer. After him, you're next."

"Never!" cried Amanda, holding fast to her belief in the Green Phantasm.

D.D.T. continued strangling the Green Phantasm. His victim tried to remove the big man's hand, but D.D.T. was much too strong for him. D.D.T. then tried to make matters worse for the Phantasm by moving him from side to side, rubbing the back of his head, neck, and shoulders hard against the steel wall. The Green Phantasm's hat even fell off. As much as this no doubt made the Phantasm feel more and more dazed, he would not run out of determination.

Next, after rubbing the Green Phantasm against the barrier several times, big D.D.T. just took the stunned Phantasm and threw him down backward onto the balcony. The Green Phantasm was now lying on his back, trying to regain his senses. But before he had a chance to get up, D.D.T. used his left foot to stomp on the Phantasm's midsection.

"Ow, ow, ow, oh!" cried the Green Phantasm, while he placed both hands on his abdomen and began to roll over to his right.

D.D.T. used his right foot to roll the Green Phantasm back into a supine position. Then, the gargantuan used his huge right foot to mash down on the Green Phantasm's abdomen. "Yeeow!" the trapped Phantasm yelled.

Big D.D.T. let up with his right foot for just a few seconds. But then, he stepped back down onto the Phantasm's midsection. This time, he even took his left foot up off the balcony's floor and balanced himself on his right foot, where all of his weight was then centered. This caused the Green Phantasm such pain and discomfort that he could not stand it. The poor Phantasm began gagging and hallucinating and was nearly rendered unconscious.

Then, after several seconds, D.D.T. finally had enough and stepped off the Green Phantasm. He took hold of the stunned Phantasm's left arm and stood him upright, still holding his arm. Shortly, the Green Phantasm had nearly recovered. But when D.D.T. sensed this, he delivered two low blows, one to his abdomen and one to his genital area. The Green Phantasm was dazed once again and started to fall to the balcony. But D.D.T. stopped him and put the helpless hero over his right shoulder to carry him over to the acid vat.

Although the Green Phantasm was in the clutches of the huge and powerful D.D.T., he had still not given up hope. He was determined to save Amanda and would fight anyone or anything to do it. So then, once D.D.T. had made it to the platform's end, the Green Phantasm was beginning to regain his senses. Although he was held in place by D.D.T., he began looking for a way out of his predicament.

But next, D.D.T., who was now looking out over the vat of X-Termination Acid, started changing the way he was holding the Green Phantasm. He placed both hands under the facedown Green Phantasm, putting the left on his chest and the right on his abdomen. D.D.T. then extended both of his arms upward, like in a military press. From that point,

D.D.T. was preparing to toss the Green Phantasm into the acid. "This is it for you, Green Phantasm," he declared.

"Come on, D.D.T.!" shouted Zinger. "Destroy him!"

"Come on, Green Phantasm," cried Amanda. "Do something, please!"

Fortunately, the Green Phantasm heard Amanda calling to him. This no doubt motivated him, for it was a reminder that she was counting on him. But very shortly, with a grunt and a growl, D.D.T. used both arms to launch the Green Phantasm upward and forward toward the middle of the acid vat.

While flying toward the X-Termination Acid, the Green Phantasm fully recovered and thought of something quickly. Before plunging into the acid, the Phantasm stopped himself by activating his hovering ability. He started making himself float both up and back toward D.D.T. Everyone else saw this happen as well.

"That radioactive creep!" griped Zinger.

"Come on, D.D.T.!" urged Doctor XT.

"Ah, shoot!" muttered Zapper.

Amanda, however, was undeniably glad. "Yes!" she exclaimed happily. "Go, Green Phantasm!"

That made the Green Phantasm somewhat happier and less afraid. He was so happy to hear that in fact that he looked toward Amanda and smiled. Then, they were both smiling at each other.

But unfortunately, this pleasant moment did not last for very long, because this distraction allowed D.D.T. to regain control of the Green Phantasm. For some of the time that the Phantasm was afloat and focused on Amanda, his feet were just a few feet above D.D.T. So next, D.D.T. used both of his hands to reach overhead and grab the Green Phantasm's ankles. At that, the huge, merciless titan just slung the hero down onto the platform, making him land on his back.

"Yah!" yelled the surprised Green Phantasm.

"Oh no," said the worried Amanda Taylor, who now had a look of horror and felt sorry that she had messed up her hero's game plan.

As for the Green Phantasm, he was no doubt very shocked and dazed; being unexpectedly slammed into the platform's surface had knocked the wind out of him. "What happened?" he asked in shock.

"Come on!" urged Zinger. "Finish him off, you big dufus!"

The Green Phantasm recovered from his dizzy spell and realized what must have happened. But before he had a chance to do anything else, he looked up only to see D.D.T. towering above him. Then at once, big D.D.T. stomped on his midsection again. Consequently, the Green Phantasm put both hands where D.D.T. had stomped him, holding his stomach, which hurt.

While the Green Phantasm was distracted by that, D.D.T. used both hands to pick him up by the neck and hold him back against the platform's railing that was toward the north. While choking the life out of the Phantasm, D.D.T. said to him, "This is the end of the line for you, Green Phantasm. What do you got to say now? You still think I'm a dumb, dim-witted turkey, huh?"

The Green Phantasm still did not run out of courage or determination. He wanted to be a real, true hero and was not willing to give up very easily. So then, perhaps to D.D.T.'s surprise, the Phantasm responded, "Yes, D.D.T., it's what you've always been, and it's what you always will be, oh yes."

"You just wanna die, don't you?" said D.D.T. to the Phantasm. "Well then, you neon-radiating fool, I'll be happy to oblige."

Upon having said that, D.D.T. threw the Green Phantasm backward toward the platform's floor. This time, he stomped the Phantasm's throat. This put the Green Phantasm into an even worse state of shock and dizziness. It was so much worse that he had all sorts of hallucinations. After that, D.D.T. used his left hand to lift the Green Phantasm up by the back of his neck. Still holding the helpless Phantasm by his neck, D.D.T. stood him upright and delivered three right uppercuts to his upper abdominal area. This no doubt stunned the Green Phantasm even further. After that, D.D.T. let go of his neck and delivered a big right uppercut to the underside of his jaw. This sent the Green Phantasm flying backward several feet, and he wound up lying on his back unconscious.

Meanwhile, Amanda, who had been witnessing all of this, started feeling much guiltier than ever; she wished she had not distracted her hero from his battle when she saw him lying unconscious. "Oh no," she said sobbing, "this is all my fault. If he gets killed, I'll never forgive myself for messing him up." Amanda quite understandably felt this way because it did not look good for the Green Phantasm, who was now in deep trouble.

D.D.T. did one more thing to make sure the Green Phantasm was out. He picked up the Green Phantasm's arms and dragged him back toward the acid vat. Once D.D.T. made it to just a couple of feet from the platform's end, he did one last act of violence to the Green Phantasm. He turned the Phantasm facedown and propped him on railing, so that he was hanging on by his chin. It was a lower railing on the north side. Then at once, D.D.T. used his left foot to mash the Green Phantasm's throat against the railing. He kept this up for about fifteen seconds.

"No, don't!" Amanda cried out to him. "Please let him go, please!" But D.D.T. completely ignored her.

But then, Zapper urged the colossal fighter by saying, "Come on! Just get him over with!"

At that, D.D.T. stopped strangling the Phantasm and began to proceed with disposing of him. He picked him up by his rib cage on both sides. Then, he carried him to the end of the platform.

Luckily, the Green Phantasm began to regain consciousness while being carried. Then, by the time D.D.T. was holding him above the X-Termination Acid, the Phantasm's eyes were completely open. "What's happening? Where am I?" he softly asked himself.

D.D.T. said to him, "Asta la vista, Green Phantasm!"

"What was that?" asked the Green Phantasm, still dazed and confused. "Who said that?" He looked around until he noticed that he was suspended above the acid vat. Then at once, he gasped in surprise.

Before the Green Phantasm could come up with a strategy, D.D.T. released him, and he began falling toward the acid. Not knowing what else to do, the Green Phantasm immediately turned to his right and managed to catch the platform's end with his right hand. However, he could not get a good enough grip to hold on long. His right hand soon slipped off the end of the platform, after which he disappeared underneath it. Within a couple of seconds, D.D.T. heard the sound of splashing acid. Following that, a stream of vapor rose straight up from the acid. It had obviously been made by whatever had made the splash. So D.D.T. looked down over the platform's end and saw no sign of the Green Phantasm.

While looking down into the acid vat, D.D.T. became silent for a few moments because he found it a bit difficult to believe what he was seeing. Could he have actually eliminated the Green Phantasm on his own? At the same time, the other X-Termination members were looking on with much anxiety. But of course, Amanda was looking on with much worry. She even said desperately, "Oh, please tell me he's not gone. If he is, I'll never forgive myself."

But then, after trying for a few moments to make sure his opponent was dead, D.D.T. reached one conclusion. After all, the Phantasm had apparently disappeared over the end of the platform. Other than that, D.D.T. had seen a surge of vapor rise up from below, where he had also heard a splash. Plus, even at the present, he could not see any part of him anywhere. So it looked like the end of the Green Phantasm.

D.D.T. turned and began heading back over to his teammates. But after a few steps, he stopped and raised both arms straight overhead. "Yes!" he exclaimed excitedly. "I did it! I got rid of him! I have 'X-terminated' that neon-green wimp! *Yeah*!"

"Way to go, D.D.T.!" congratulated Zinger.

"Not bad," added Zapper.

"Well," said Doctor XT. "I guess I don't need to get rid of you guys after all, do I?"

"No, I guess not," replied Zapper.

"Well, guys," said XT, "at least you all took care of my greatest headache, the Green Phantasm, and 'X-terminated' him. We're all gonna celebrate later. But right now, let's talk about what to do next. Come with me to the control room. This way, men."

"Come on, D.D.T.!" Zinger called out to the big guy, who had supposedly done away with the Green Phantasm.

"I'll be right there!" D.D.T. replied to him.

"Don't worry, sweetheart," XT told Amanda tauntingly. "I'll be right with you." Then, Doctor XT, Zapper, and Zinger just proceeded on over to the control room.

At the same time, Amanda too believed the Green Phantasm, her hero, to be no more. In the midst of everything, she broke out into tears. How could she not? After all, the one she admired the most was apparently deceased, and it looked like Amanda was about to be killed herself. So, while crying, she said, "This is all my fault. I'll never forgive myself while I'm still alive. I was too mean to James Clifton. I just got the Green Phantasm killed. I probably deserve what I'm about to get. But deep down,

I know I really, truly love them both. They both risked their lives for me, and the Green Phantasm just got himself killed for me. I certainly don't need anyone else. But why did it all have to end this way? Why? Oh well, I'll just have to make the best of the few minutes I've got left." Amanda felt guiltier at the present than ever before in her life. But was the Green Phantasm really gone like everyone thought?

In the meantime, the Green Phantasm was underneath the platform from which he had been thrown. He was holding on to a crossbar under the platform, hanging upright above the X-Termination Acid. Once he had caught onto the platform's end, he swung himself to below it. In the instant that his right hand had slipped, he used his left hand to catch and grab hold of the nearest crossbar. Then, in order to create a splash and a stream of vapor, the Green Phantasm had simply taken off his right-hand glove and thrown it into the acid. So, regardless of what everyone else believed, he was not dead or gone after all. The only thing gone of the Phantasm was his right glove.

While hanging underneath the platform, the Green Phantasm said to himself rather quietly, "Oh man, that was the closest call I had ever received. I thought for sure I was a goner. Well, I guess they all think I'm dead. Good, that's what I want 'em to think. But of course, it cost me a glove. And you know what else? That huge punk D.D.T. just beat the stuffing out of me. I ain't gonna let him get away with that. As soon as I catch my breath, I'm gonna make him pay. Of course, even as much as I wanted them to think I died, I'll bet Amanda's really worried and scared right now, perhaps so badly I can't even picture it. Well, anyway, I just need one more moment to pull myself together. Then, I'll be right there." He kept hanging there, trying to allow for his second wind to come through.

Meanwhile, D.D.T. was walking back and forth along the platform, thinking and talking to himself about what he had just done and how he felt now. "Yo, man," D.D.T. said, "this is both exciting and unbelievable. I guess the boss ain't gonna get rid of me after all. I know destroying that stupid neon freak was the one thing he was lookin' to do. That was the one thing standin' in our way. But I took care of it. Oh yes, it's all thanks to me. Ha, ha, ha, ha!" At that, D.D.T. took a few minutes of silence.

But then, his pride caused him to develop yet another idea. "You know something?" he asked himself. "I wonder how the doctor's gonna reward me. I mean, that neon-green dope was his biggest headache, and I took care of it for him. Now, I think they been saying that Zapper was his number-one man, and he gonna take over X-Termination when XT's reign comes to an end. I ain't sure I agree with that. I done been with XT longer than anybody in this whole facility, and I know we all saw what I just did. The master oughtta reconsider and give me that privilege. Yeah man, I gonna have me a talk with him. Maybe that way, one of these days, X-Termination gonna be all mine, oh yeah. Well, for right now, I'm gonna go join up with my teammates in their celebration." At that, D.D.T. started walking from the acid vat to the control room, smiling with pride.

But of course, from below, the Green Phantasm had been listening to all that D.D.T. was saying. So he went on to say to himself softly, "You know, D.D.T., maybe it won't be all yours after all. Stop kidding yourself. You may not realize it, but you ain't got nothin' done, you big gavone. Nope, you got another thing comin'. Of course, I thought I was gonna die, too. But, I guess it's amazing what one can do in desperation. Well, anyway, it's time to teach him a lesson. Oh yes, I feel revived and ready. Here I go."

Even now, D.D.T. was still slowly walking away from the X-Termination Acid vat, looking around in every direction, smiling and chuckling with pride. But of course, he was completely unaware of the big surprise he was about to receive. At the very same time, the Green Phantasm activated his hovering ability. He moved himself back to the platform's end and at once began ascending straight upward.

At the present, Amanda was still in tears over what she thought had happened to her hero. But she shortly stopped crying because a flash of neon-green light began appearing above the acid vat. Amanda looked out to see that it was indeed the Green Phantasm. He had not been destroyed after all! How happy, relieved, and surprised she was. Amanda reacted with a gasp, followed by a great big smile. She began to say something but decided to keep quiet so that no one would hear her and she would not mess things up any further for the Green Phantasm. "Oh, Green Phantasm," she whispered to herself, "thank goodness."

The Green Phantasm kept hovering until he set himself down on the end of the platform. Then, he looked toward Amanda, placing his right index finger in front of his lips, saying, "Shh!"

"Okay," Amanda uttered silently, nodding her head affirmatively. Of course, she wanted to be as helpful and supportive as possible, so as not to add any additional problems to the ones she felt she had already created.

By this time, D.D.T. was about three-quarters of the way from above the acid to the balcony that was along the great steel barrier. At the end of the platform above the acid vat, the Green Phantasm was getting ready for his next move. He was charging himself, preparing to teleport. So then, he released himself as a teleportation beam and reappeared directly behind big D.D.T., who had been walking very slowly.

D.D.T. stopped momentarily for he thought he had heard a faint sound nearby. "What was that?" he asked himself. He tried looking all around to see if he could spot the source of the faint noise, but he could not.

Amanda was looking on anxiously, wondering what the Green Phantasm was about to do next.

"Surprise, surprise, D.D.T.," the Green Phantasm said tauntingly.

"*What?*" cried the shocked D.D.T., "Who said that?" D.D.T. was freaking out. After all, the three other X-Termination members were in the control room. Furthermore, he did not think it could possibly be the Green Phantasm. How could he not have been frightened?

But then, the Green Phantasm said in response, "it's me, you big galoot." At that, he drove his left knee into the back of big D.D.T.'s left thigh.

"What, whoa!" D.D.T. yelled as he almost fell backward.

Next, the Green Phantasm took the form of a shapeless projectile. He hit the back side of D.D.T.'s left leg making him lose his balance, fly back several feet, and land on his back. Immediately upon striking D.D.T., the Green Phantasm reappeared as himself.

Still lying on his back, big D.D.T., who was now in shock, asked, "What happened?"

But then, the Green Phantasm went over to stand at the feet of the huge behemoth, and D.D.T. noticed him. This motivated him to regain his senses, and he instantly recovered from dizziness. Unwilling to believe what he was seeing, D.D.T. said critically, "No way, it can't be you. This is the devil's work. That's what it is."

"Listen to me, big man," the Green Phantasm addressed him assertively, "you've really gone too far this time. I know you've probably been with Doctor XT for quite a while, but you can't continue like this. You need to change your ways, because sooner or later, someone will put you down. It's not my intention to do that, but I will if I have to. I like to try to give people a chance. So how do you feel about turning over a new leaf?"

"Heh, heh, heh, heh," chuckled D.D.T., shaking his head in disbelief at the Green Phantasm's lecturing.

"I'm telling you," asserted the Green Phantasm. "There's not much hope for people like you, so I suggest you turn around right now."

D.D.T. had too much pride to listen to the Phantasm. So then, with a grunt and a growl, he quickly got back onto his feet. He immediately tried to reach for the Green Phantasm with his left hand.

But of course, the Green Phantasm was ready for him this time. So whenever D.D.T. struck at him, the Green Phantasm ducked under his huge left arm and then retaliated with a right uppercut to the underside of the jaw of the gargantuan. "Argh!" growled big D.D.T., as he stumbled two steps backward, slightly stunned by the uppercut.

While D.D.T. was somewhat dazed, the Green Phantasm teleported over to the balcony, where his hat had previously been knocked off. Once there, he placed it back on and teleported back to the platform to continue facing big D.D.T. He charged up both hands with radiant energy, just in case he would need to fire any laser beams.

D.D.T. soon recovered, and when he did, the Green Phantasm told him, "Look, D.D.T., I really think you oughtta—" But he did not get to finish what he was saying because D.D.T. tried throwing a great big right hook. The Green Phantasm discontinued speaking in order to step back and avoid it. Then, before D.D.T. had a chance to strike at the Phantasm again, he combined the power of all five fingers of his right hand in order to launch a huge bright-green laser beam. This rather colossal beam hit D.D.T. in the center of his face. This time, he was pushed back several steps. Because D.D.T. staggered so much and nearly fell, he placed both hands on the railing to his left, to keep himself standing upright.

Meanwhile, over in the control room, Doctor XT and Zapper both had their backs to the Green Phantasm and D.D.T. But Zinger was facing XT and Zapper, as well as the direction of the platform on which D.D.T. and the Phantasm were fighting it out. All of a sudden, when the Green Phantasm had fired that shot, Zinger thought he saw something. "What was that?" he said quietly to himself, as he tried to get a better look to see what was going on.

Of course, everyone thought that the Green Phantasm had been destroyed. But whenever Zinger took a look to see what had made that brilliant flash of neon light, he saw none other than the Green Phantasm, who had not been reduced to vapor after all. "Oh no," said Zinger to himself, "it can't be."

Doctor XT was still going over his future plans with Zapper and Zinger. But shortly, Zinger interrupted XT, saying, "Excuse me, you guys."

"Zinger!" Doctor XT scolded him. "No interruptions; let me finish what I'm saying."

"But look!" Zinger shouted, pointing toward what he saw.

"All right, what is it?" asked Doctor XT. XT and Zapper turned around to see what Zinger was pointing at.

Upon seeing the Green Phantasm still alive, Zapper exclaimed, "*What?*"

"I thought y'all said he was destroyed," said Doctor XT.

Zinger just shook his head and rolled his eyes in confusion.

"Well, don't just stand there, you two!" shouted Doctor XT.

"Come on, Zinger," Zapper said. "Let's go." So both Zapper and Zinger drew their X-Termination Rays and ran on through the gas chamber. Doctor XT was not too far behind.

In the meantime, while those two were on their way, D.D.T. had just recovered from being struck by the big laser beam. Not knowing what else to do, he just took out his X-Termination Ray. But before he could target the Green Phantasm, he combined the power of both hands to produce the largest, most powerful laser beam that he possibly could. Before D.D.T. even had a chance to fire at the Phantasm, he unleashed the gigantic, powerful neon-green beam. This beam smacked squarely into big D.D.T., forcing the huge, monster-sized scoundrel toward the acid vat. "Aah-nooooo!" he yelled as he was being launched. Finally, D.D.T. ended up above the X-Termination Acid. Then, from that point, he just fell straight down with an enormous sustained scream and plunged into the X-Termination Acid. That was the end of both D.D.T. and Anselm Jerad Nielsen.

Now, while D.D.T. had been driven along the platform, Zapper and Zinger had just made it out of the gas chamber. However, they both stopped before walking onto the platform, because they were too late to come to the aid of their humongous partner, D.D.T., the devastating, destructive titan.

"D.D.T.!" shouted Zinger.

"Noooooo!" yelled Zapper. After that, both Zapper and Zinger were silent for the next few moments. It was tough to deal with the sudden loss of their longtime friend and partner. Jarrett felt toward the big guy like he would have a family member.

"Oh no," Zinger uttered mournfully.

"We'll just have to cope without him somehow." said Zapper.

Because of his good conscience, James Clifton had a guilty feeling about what had just gone down. Even as the Green Phantasm, he walked all the way down to the end of the platform above the X-Termination Acid. Once there, he took off his hat and took a few moments of silence. As much as D.D.T. had tried to kill him, his guilty conscience still caused him to shed a few tears when he looked down and saw no remaining sign of the big man.

James Clifton had a guilty feeling about D.D.T.'s unfortunate ending because when he took on his role as the Green Phantasm, he had wanted to be a hero, not a killer. Therefore, killing D.D.T. or anyone else had never been something that James originally had in mind. In order to stop an attack, he would only apply the minimum degree of force that he felt was needed. Even when James had unintentionally and all of a sudden obtained his powers from the pyxorium on Sunday night, he still did not want to utilize any capabilities for selfish or hurtful purposes. Even just now, when the colossal powerhouse D.D.T. had begun to resort to his X-Termination Ray, Clifton desired, not to kill the big man, but to merely protect himself. It was no wonder that James felt guilty and ashamed about D.D.T. being gone. But all the while, Amanda Taylor, who was still handcuffed to the pole, was proud of the Green Phantasm and admired so very much his goodness, bravery, and heroism.

However, Doctor XT, did not have the same sort of feelings as everyone else. A major reason for that was because his conscience had been ruined by the wicked, corrupt, and selfish desires he had always had from childhood. As a result, he thought very little about the end of his longtime associate, Anselm Nielsen, who was called D.D.T. Perone sincerely cared about no one but himself. He had been merely using Anselm Nielsen for his power.

So, even after all the years of their working together, this sudden, incredible loss hardly mattered to John Perry Perone. Perhaps he would now find another humongous powerhouse to serve the purpose that Nielsen had been serving as D.D.T.

Lacking sympathy for anyone, Doctor XT just stormed out of the gas chamber behind Zapper and Zinger. He was strictly determined to carry out his purpose regardless of what had happened. He hollered to his two lieutenants, "Zapper, Zinger!"

"Yes, Doctor," replied Zinger, when they both turned to look at him.

"What are you two lunkheads doing?" Doctor XT asked them.

"Well, uh…" Zinger responded while trying to think of what to say.

"Never mind!" XT scolded. "Forget about D.D.T. We've got ourselves a neon radioactive menace to 'X-terminate.' Now go on and catch him while he's off guard; hurry up!"

"Come on, Zinger!" ordered Zapper. At that, both Zapper and Zinger began running down the platform toward the Green Phantasm, who was still looking down into the X-Termination Acid vat with remorse.

Now once Amanda had noticed the two men running toward the Phantasm, she yelled to him, "Green Phantasm, look out!"

"Say what, huh?" said the Green Phantasm wonderingly, as he started to turn around. But by the time the Green Phantasm could fully turn around, Zapper and Zinger had already stationed themselves before him and extended their ray guns, holding him at gunpoint. Zinger was standing before the Green Phantasm on his left, and Zapper was facing him on the right. Next, even Doctor XT held out his X-Termination Ray as well, helping his two men hold up the Phantasm.

Upon seeing the bad-looking predicament he was now in, the very first reaction on the part of the Phantasm was none other than a very loud, sustained gasp. The Green Phantasm was overwhelmed and frightened by all of the X-Termination Rays aimed for him. Undoubtedly, Amanda was very afraid and worried for him too. *Oh shoot,* the Phantasm thought to himself. *Why didn't I know better than to turn my back on them? These guys are clever and quick, and this is their turf. I knew when I got here to be careful and watchful at all times. Why didn't I do that just now? Aw shucks, dad blame it! What'll I do now?*

"Heh, heh, heh, heh," snickered Zapper, "We got you pretty well covered, don't we? You annihilated D.D.T., and you're gonna pay for that. You got anything else to say before we 'X-terminate' you?"

No response came from the Green Phantasm, except a continuation of heavy breathing and perspiring from tension. He was understandably too afraid for his life to know what to say or do.

Zapper said to him, "Well, well, Green Phantasm, cat got your crotch? Ha, ha, ha, ha, ha!"

Zapper lowered his voice and whispered to the Phantasm, "Look, I'll tell you what; since it's about to be all over for you, I'll be nice enough to let you know who I really am."

Zapper used his left hand to raise up his mask, just merely enough to show his face. "I am Axel Jerome Axtel," he told the Green Phantasm in a soft voice.

After that, he gently nudged Zinger with his right elbow, saying, "Just, uh, let him know who you are, Zinger."

"Okay," whispered Zinger.

So then, while Zapper was pulling his mask back down, Zinger pulled his up some and showed his face. "And I'm Nicholas Jarrett," he told the Green Phantasm. At that, Jarrett pulled his mask back down.

"And let me tell you somethin' else," Zapper said to the Green Phantasm, still maintaining a lowered voice. "That guy you sent flying into the acid— "

"Uh, D.D.T.?" stammered the Green Phantasm.

"Mm-hmm," answered Zapper. "Was Anselm Nielsen, huh, huh."

"Okay, uh, thanks," the Green Phantasm replied nervously.

"So," Zapper addressed the Phantasm. "How about telling us who you are?"

"Okay," the Green Phantasm answered. "Why not?" So, in an attempt not to further infuriate X-Termination, he cooperatively put his right hand on his mask, preparing to raise it up a little. First, he switched off his neon radiation for a moment. Second, he moved his mask up onto his forehead, so Zapper and Zinger could see his face. After that, he told them, "I'm uh, Clifton, that's James Paul Clifton." At that, he pulled his mask back down and began radiating again.

"All right now," said Zapper. "You now have only ten seconds left of your life. That oughtta give you a little time to say whatever else you got left to say or to figure out how you want to put an end to both James Clifton and the Green Phantasm. Either we can blast you with our X-Termination Rays, or you can join up with the one whom you sent before you into the acid. The choice is up to you. Other than that, any last words? You got ten seconds, starting right… now! Of course, if you try anything stupid, we 'X-terminate' you on the spot. So what do you say now, Green Phantasm?"

So now, James was trying to find a way out of this life-threatening predicament in a hurry. Of course, he was being held at gunpoint by Zapper and Zinger, who were standing before him, and by Doctor XT, from the balcony by the gas chamber. He thought to himself, *Man, I gotta do somethin' quick. I got three men with ray guns to evade. Reappearing in a different spot could be too dangerous. Three guys are more bound to hit me than just one. But of course, what if there weren't—wait a minute, I got an idea.*

At least now, Clifton had found a possible way out. So then, having only three seconds remaining, the Green Phantasm quickly got himself ready and teleported. Before anyone could see what he was doing, he reappeared to Zinger's right but was still in front of him. "Huh!" cried Zinger, when he thought he saw the Green Phantasm relocate as quick as a flash.

Then, before Zinger could turn to aim for the Phantasm, the Phantasm caught his right arm. He then raised it overhead to keep himself out of the ray gun's line of fire. The Green Phantasm was now using both hands to hold up Zinger's right arm. Next, he slung Zinger forward into the railing on Zapper's left. At the same time, he took his X-Termination Ray and then tossed it into the X-Termination Acid.

Now, while the Green Phantasm was struggling with Zinger, Zapper exclaimed, "*What?* You moved!"

Zapper and Doctor XT both positioned themselves to open fire on the Green Phantasm. Zapper, of course, was already standing before the Phantasm, near the end of the platform. But Doctor XT stepped over a few feet until he was barely past Zapper's right-hand side. Both men now had their X-Termination Rays pointed at the Green Phantasm and were now ready to squeeze the triggers.

Fortunately, the Green Phantasm happened to look to his left and notice this in the nick of time. He only had about a second to do something though. Fortunately, he managed to pull something off within a split second. He only had one idea though. Still holding Zinger by his right arm, the Green Phantasm quickly jerked him between himself and the deadly pair of Zapper and XT.

At the same time, Zapper had begun to fire his shot, being followed up by Doctor XT firing his ray gun. The Green Phantasm pulled Zinger in the way in just barely enough time to avoid getting hit. Just as the Green Phantasm was placing Zinger in front of Zapper and XT, the blast from Zapper's X-Termination Ray hit Zinger and began reducing him to ashes. Before he was reduced all the way down to a heap, the blast from Doctor XT hit him as well, speeding up the destruction of the junior lieutenant. Finally, it came to be the end of both Zinger and Nicholas Devin Jarrett. Nothing remained of him but a heap of ashes, which was now in the middle of the platform, just a couple of feet from the end.

The sudden annihilation of Zinger momentarily distracted Doctor XT and Zapper, who could not believe their eyes. Of course, XT and Zapper were now the only two members left in X-Termination. "Zinger!" Zapper cried out in horror.

Although this was another major loss for X-Termination, it was another really close call for the Green Phantasm/James Clifton. If he had hesitated for even another split-second, perhaps he would have been "X-terminated" instead of Zinger. In the meantime, poor Amanda Taylor, who had been looking on, had received quite a scare when XT and Zapper were firing those shots. But after that, she let out a sigh of great relief when she looked up and saw that at least it was not her hero who had been hit by them.

Even though Doctor XT and Zapper were temporarily distracted by the sudden destruction of one of their highest-ranked employees, Green Phantasm knew they were going to turn their attention back over to him. How could he doubt that? The loss of Zinger, in addition to the earlier loss of D.D.T., could only have made X-Termination angrier and more upset. Therefore, the determined Phantasm wanted to hurry up and act while he could. So, while XT and Zapper still had some of their attention on the now departed Nicholas Devin Jarrett, the Green Phantasm charged up his right hand's index and middle fingers. Then at once, he fired a laser beam with his middle finger, knocking the X-Termination Ray out of Zapper's hand. It landed a few yards up the platform toward the balcony. That same instant, a laser beam from his index finger knocked the gun out of Doctor XT's hand. It went flying a few yards farther from the gas chamber, landing on the balcony. In rapid succession, Zapper and then Doctor XT each yelled, "Hey!" as he turned his head quickly toward the Green Phantasm.

After that, Doctor XT tried to run over to retrieve his ray gun. But before he could make it, the Green Phantasm teleported over toward him. He came out of the teleportation beam between XT and the X-Termination Ray. Then, the Green Phantasm surprised Doctor XT with a left jab, into which he ran face-first. "Oh no, you don't!" exclaimed the Green Phantasm, while the shocked, stunned XT stumbled backward. The Phantasm immediately took XT's X-Termination Ray and hurled it into the X-Termination Acid.

In the meantime, Zapper had just made it over to his X-Termination Ray to reclaim it. But before he had a chance to target the Green Phantasm, he managed to take notice and shoot the gun out of his hand. This time, it landed closer to the X-Termination Acid. "*What?* Again!" cried Zapper.

Then suddenly, Zapper made another attempt to retrieve his X-Termination Ray. But of course, before he could, the Green Phantasm teleported to end up standing between Zapper and the ray gun. Just as the Phantasm had done a moment ago with Doctor XT, he knocked Zapper back with a left jab and then tossed his X-Termination Ray into the acid as well.

"Way to go, Green Phantasm!" yelled Amanda.

At the same time, Doctor XT had just recovered from the left jab delivered by the Green Phantasm. He was now angrier than ever. He began muttering, "Why, that neon-green punk has really done it this time! First D.D.T., then Zinger, and now all our freakin' guns! It's time to go on to the next plan, and 'X-terminate' that radiative nuisance for good, and for sure. And why? 'Cause that neon freak has been a much bigger pain than he's worth!"

At that, Doctor XT turned his attention to Amanda, who was still handcuffed to the pole. He took out his keys to the cuffs, went to start unlocking them, and said to her, "All right, babe, we're going to another spot."

"What do you think you're doing?" Amanda snapped.

"Settle down, sweetheart," XT told her. "This time, it's all about to be over for sure. We're just moving to the other side of the gas chamber."

"Oh, is that so?" asked an angry Amanda Taylor.

"You bet it is," responded Doctor XT. "I've got him beat. This time, he's all mine. Now, come on!"

As soon as XT had removed the handcuffs, he used his right hand to lead Amanda by her left arm. She immediately started struggling and screaming. While trying to break free, she cried out loudly, "Let me go! Help! Somebody, help! Let go of me, you dumb, ugly, devilish creep!" However, Amanda did not have much luck trying to break loose from XT's grasp. But Doctor XT was also not having the easiest time possible manhandling his hostage.

In the meantime, the Green Phantasm was still on the platform outside the gas chamber, keeping Zapper under control. But fortunately for Amanda, her screaming and crying for help reached him. So, at present, while Zapper was still stunned by a left hook, the Green Phantasm paused and shifted his attention over to the gas chamber, where Doctor XT was with Amanda. The Phantasm looked for a few seconds and was able to perceive the struggle going on between them. "Oh no, Amanda!" exclaimed the worried Green Phantasm. "I don't know what he's trying to do to her, but I gotta hurry on over there and stop him." So the Green Phantasm began charging up so he could teleport on over.

But Zapper was now recovered from that last blow he had just taken. He was no doubt still determined to do away with the Green Phantasm. However, the Green Phantasm was not paying enough attention and did not see him coming.

The Green Phantasm's attempt to teleport did not end up successful. While charging and getting ready, he said, "Here I go—oof!" Before he could release himself, he was hit and dazed by a big right jab to his left eye from Zapper.

Then, the Green Phantasm shook away the dizziness and got a vision of Zapper. He now knew who had just hit him. But before the Phantasm had a chance to defend himself, Zapper landed a right crossover between his nose and mouth. This punch busted the Green Phantasm's upper lip and knocked him a couple of steps toward the acid vat. The Green Phantasm was now under attack by Zapper. Plus, at present, he was leaning over toward his right, with his right hand holding the top railing and his left hand over his busted lip. "Aw shoot!" the Green Phantasm muttered in frustration.

After that, the Green Phantasm turned back toward Zapper to continue battling him. But unfortunately, a right side kick from Zapper was already headed for him. This kick landed in the middle of the Phantasm's abdominal area, making him fall back and land faceup on the platform. His hat even fell off again. The Green Phantasm was now even closer to the X-Termination Acid vat.

The Green Phantasm tried to get back up, but before he could, Zapper landed a left side kick to the top of his head, knocking him back down. "Dang it!" yelled the Phantasm, as he used his left hand to temporarily hold the spot where Zapper had kicked him.

Zapper used his left foot to mash down on the Green Phantasm's throat, choking him. Zapper said to him, "You ignorant, radioactive son of the devil! You killed D.D.T. and Zinger, and you threw our guns away! You're gonna pay for that; oh yes, you are!"

The Green Phantasm could not reply, because he was being choked. However, he did not fully agree with everything that Zapper had just declared, and he was still determined to get past both Zapper and Doctor XT in order to save Amanda and get away safely. But quite evidently, the Green Phantasm was having a very tough time dealing with Zapper, and now, his dizziness was getting worse every second. In addition, he was now having hallucinations.

Zapper's point of view was not too difficult to understand. Although unintentional on the part of the Phantasm, Axtel had been put through a lot in one night. That included the sudden loss of his two longtime friends and partners, Nicholas Jarrett and Anselm Nielsen, in addition to his powerful, effective X-Termination Ray. All that at once probably triggered his anger, making him much more aggressive. Also, Axel Axtel was the one designated to take over X-Termination at the end of Doctor XT's reign. Even if Perone did not care about the person of Axel Axtel, the privilege of getting to own and run X-Termination someday was an added incentive to do whatever XT wanted. Of course right then, he knew that Doctor XT wanted the Green Phantasm destroyed.

Zapper may have not had the size or strength of big D.D.T., whom the Green Phantasm had battled earlier, but the Phantasm was still having one heck of a time trying to make a comeback against him. Zapper was smarter and faster than D.D.T. Besides, he was the highest-ranked X-Termination official, except for Doctor XT. Therefore, it was not too big of a surprise that Zapper was really difficult to deal with as well.

But anyway, the Green Phantasm eventually had a wide-eyed, open-mouthed expression on his face, indicating that he was extremely stunned. Zapper noticed this and removed his left foot. While the Green Phantasm was still extremely dazed and still seeing many hallucinations, Zapper began lifting him up from the platform. He stood the Phantasm up on his feet and held him by his trunk, having him bent over. Then, Zapper walked him backward to the platform's end, above the X-Termination Acid. Finally, Zapper used both hands to squeeze the Phantasm's neck, strangling him. While maintaining his grip, Zapper said, "All right, Green Phantasm, as you can see, it's all fixing to end for you and your so-called heroship. Got anything left to say?"

Now, of course, the Green Phantasm was not able to say or do anything, because of the tight grip Zapper had on his throat. He was choked up in more ways than one, as Zapper was about to suggest. "What's the matter?" Zapper asked tauntingly. "You, uh, all choked up? Heh, heh, heh, heh!"

Still having received no response, Zapper just continued by saying, "Well, since you have nothing more to say, let me tell you this: I'm gonna take charge of X-Termination one day. I'll do anything I have to to get there. I'll even 'X-terminate' you myself if I have to. I'm not gonna allow some neon peon like you to take that privilege away from me. You understand that, don't you? Of course you do! So downward and in you go! Sayonara, Green Phantasm!" At that, Zapper hit the Green Phantasm in the face with his left knee, knocking him senseless and giving him a nosebleed.

Zapper stood the Phantasm up for a second or two. Then, he delivered a side kick to his midsection. As a result, the Green Phantasm started to fall back into the X-Termination Acid. But with the little bit of consciousness he had left, he managed to notice just in time that he was falling to his doom. This motivated the Phantasm to quickly grab hold of the railing's vertical end on his right. "Dang it!" he muttered as he caught it. "That was another freakin' close call! Got dang it!"

"Oh, shoot!" complained Zapper, for he was not able to dispose of the Green Phantasm as easily as he had thought. He delivered a right side kick to the left of the Green Phantasm's rib cage. This hurt, for it was an area of all skin and bones.

"Ow!" the Green Phantasm whimpered in pain. Right away, he used his left hand to hold the part of his ribs that Zapper had just kicked. But fortunately, he still managed to maintain his grip on the railing with his right, for he had not run out of determination.

"You might as well give it up, Green Phantasm," Zapper said, talking down to him. "Can't you see you're done for?" But the Green Phantasm just shook his head in disagreement.

"Oh," said Zapper, "I take that as a 'no.' Well, how about this?" Upon asking that, Zapper went in to place the ball of his left foot on the knuckles of the Green Phantasm's right hand, which of course, was being used to hold on to the railing. Immediately, Zapper pressed his foot down on his knuckles with a slight clockwise twist to make it more effective.

"Aaaaaah!" yelled the Green Phantasm very loudly. Of course, it just so happened that the knuckles getting mashed were on the hand without the glove. Next, as quick as a flash, the Green Phantasm simultaneously grabbed the railing with his left hand and removed his right. Right after that, he shook his right hand to try to get rid of the pain, although he had abrasions on and around three of his four knuckles.

"Curse you, Green Phantasm!" Zapper said, for he was having a frustrating time knocking the Green Phantasm off the end of the platform. But the Green Phantasm only looked back at Zapper with an angry expression of his own. Zapper continued throwing punches and kicks at the Green Phantasm, who was holding on for dear life.

Now all the while, at the same time that Zapper had been violently attacking the Green Phantasm, another struggle had been taking place in the control room. It was without a doubt the one between Doctor XT and Amanda Taylor. XT had finally managed to drag Amanda all the way to the door of his office. Once there, he handcuffed her to a pole just outside his office, like he had earlier done outside the gas chamber.

"Well, my dear," Doctor XT addressed Amanda, "I just had to move us to a different spot. But that's all right, because believe me; I've got the Green Phantasm right where I want him. If Zapper can't take care of him, I will 'X-terminate' him for sure. One way or the other, he's all mine."

"Hmph," scoffed Amanda, "I don't believe you. The Green Phantasm is at least hundreds, possibly even a thousand times the man that you only hope to be. He risked his life to come down here for me, and he's already made it this far. He's not a rotten cheater like you. I have so much confidence in my hero, that I'll even bet my life on him."

"So," said the overconfident Doctor XT. "You just decided to make a bet you know for sure you'll lose? And you made your life the wager? Well, I'll be happy to oblige. You really want to die after all, no problem." At that, Doctor XT just smiled and chuckled.

But then, he told Amanda, "And just let me be kind enough to share something else with you, since your time's just about up. I care nothing about these freakin' morons workin' for me. I mean, heck, you know there ain't nobody in my organization like me. As far as I'm concerned about Nick Jarrett and dumb ol' Anselm Nielsen, who on earth were they? I'll just get another Zinger and another D.D.T. I'll even call them Zinger II and D.D.T. II, for I'll make doggone certain that they're better than the originals. And as for Zapper here, if he wants to obtain my business one day, he better get this job done. Otherwise, I'll replace him too. Who cares about Axel Axtel, or whatever that stupid name was of that worthless fool? Although I pay them well, the biggest piece of pie is still mine." Upon saying that, he chuckled.

Amanda just shook her head in disbelief. It was not hard to understand why, because she now knew that Doctor XT, the XTE of X-Termination, really cared about no one but himself and that he was really seeking his own advantage. It was no wonder that he had misused his expertise in all the different kinds of engineering. Furthermore, Amanda had figured out something else too. This selfishness was also the reason that XT had cared nothing about the other X-Termination members who had perished. Evidently, the twelve guys from the rocket planes the other night were not around. So she figured XT had destroyed them for not letting him have his way. And just now, Doctor XT had thought nothing of the end of D.D.T. and Zinger. A person had to be extremely selfish and haughty to allow for all that. Otherwise, Amanda could not comprehend how or why anyone could have such bad morals.

With all that in mind, Amanda said to Doctor XT, "Why, you diabolical fiend, you're actually proud of all that? You've completely lost your marbles! You're so insane and so demented! I wouldn't work for you if my life depended on it! You just wait; the Green Phantasm will put you in your place where you belong. XT will come to mean 'X-terminated,' because that's what ends up happening to people like you." At that, Amanda topped all that off with a scoff.

"Listen, babe," Doctor XT addressed Amanda, "you sure got a lot of nerve for someone who's about to die. But if you keep pushing me like that, I'll go ahead and do it now. I've got it all set up. You and him will both be 'X-terminated' for sure, even if Zapper here doesn't get him for me first. But perhaps Zapper will; his life depends on it. Yep, he better get it done." XT just nodded affirmatively. "Let's watch the fun," he said.

So then, both XT and Amanda began looking on as the Green Phantasm and Zapper kept fighting it out. Amanda was a bit worried but confident that her hero could get through this battle somehow. "Come on, Green Phantasm," she said to herself.

On the other hand, Doctor XT said to himself, "Come on, Zapper; you better get it done. You wanna stay alive and run this business one day? Get him 'X-terminated.' If I gotta do it, I'm 'X-terminating' you too. Let's go, Zapper."

Meanwhile, Zapper was still trying to knock the Green Phantasm into the X-Termination Acid by constantly delivering different punches and kicks. The Green Phantasm, of course, was still trying to hang on to save his life. But now, he suddenly remembered the need to hurry and rescue Amanda. Therefore, he would somehow have to end the fight between Zapper and himself quickly. However, Zapper was persistently hacking away at him, not allowing him a chance to set up any of his moves. So the Green Phantasm only knew one other thing to do.

He began tightening up every part of his anatomy. Just like in previous instances, his neon-green radiation became brighter because of the increased activation of radiant energy, and he became invincible. He felt the need for temporary invincibility to get back up onto the platform.

So then, as the Green Phantasm was straining and charging up, Zapper's kicks and punches were becoming less and less effective.

"What in the devil? I don't believe this!" Zapper muttered, whenever one big side kick to the Phantasm's abdomen did not budge him an inch.

The Green Phantasm then turned toward Zapper and began lifting himself back up onto the platform. At the same time, Zapper just continued throwing punches and kicks. However, they proved to be futile, since the Green Phantasm had become completely invincible.

Shortly, the Green Phantasm was finally standing upright, face-to-face with Zapper. He had an angry look on his face. "Oh no," Zapper said to himself, "it can't be. What'll I do now?"

Zapper thought of something quickly. Seeing that his efforts so far had been a fruitless task, and that his X-Termination Ray was gone, he only had one other option. He took out his Mega Zapper 2000. At once, he began delivering a lightning-like blast of electricity to the Green Phantasm. However, the Green Phantasm was still invincible. So, this too, proved to be ineffective.

Then, even while getting zapped, the Green Phantasm took a couple of steps forward. Suddenly, he grabbed Zapper's right wrist and rammed it against the nearest railing. This knocked the Mega Zapper out of his hand, making it land on the platform. Right after that, the Green Phantasm used both hands to grab hold of Zapper's shirt and then throw him backward, making him land faceup on the platform. At that, the Green Phantasm just loosened up his anatomy, and his radiation went back down to normal.

As for Zapper, he was now in a state of shock. He could not believe how the tables had been turned on him. A few moments before, Zapper had kept the Green Phantasm under control. But now, he was lying helpless at the mercy of the Green Phantasm. Being in that position without any weapons, Axtel did not know what to do at the moment. So he just submissively put up his right hand in front of his face, trying to signal the Green Phantasm to stop. "Please, Mister Phantasm," he begged desperately, "you're not gonna kill me, are you? What do you want from me, huh?"

Clifton's good conscience made him halt before Zapper. He did not wish to harm anyone. So he was about to allow Axel Axtel a chance to cooperate. Having calmed down some, he said, "Listen to me, Mr.

Axel Axtel, I don't wanna kill you, all right? I'm not here to hurt or kill anybody, you understand?"

"Why, uh, Clifton," replied Axtel, "I'm afraid that I do not fully understand. What about both D.D.T. and Zinger? You killed them, and that makes me afraid you're gonna kill me too."

"Hold it, Axel," he said. "I'm afraid you're a bit mistaken. You see, with D.D.T., killing him was never what I had in mind. I tried giving him a chance, but he tried to use his ray gun on me. I had no other choice, although I didn't mean to send him into the acid. And as for Zinger, I didn't kill him; y'all did. I was just trying to avoid being shot myself. It was you and Doctor XT who fired the shots that killed him. And right now, with you, I don't wanna kill you, and I really don't want to kill the doctor either. However, I will not sit back and watch poor, innocent Amanda Taylor get killed or mistreated like she doesn't deserve. I came for her, and I'm not leaving, unless it's with her. I don't care what I gotta do to save her. I'm gonna see to it that I do just that."

"So, what are you trying to tell me?" asked Axel.

"I'll tell you this," he responded. "If you don't want any more trouble or for anyone to get hurt, just cooperate with me, okay?"

"And how do I do that?" Zapper asked curiously.

At that, Clifton told him, "I just need you to step aside and let me through. If you do that, I promise not to lay a hand on you."

"But I can't do that," Zapper replied. "My master will—"

"All right," said the Green Phantasm. "Well, I guess I better prepare myself, since you want to do this the hard way. I'm almost ready for you."

"No, no, no, wait!" exclaimed Zapper, who was all of a sudden afraid of the Green Phantasm's powers. "I'll do it; I'll get out of your way. Just, uh, don't kill me, okay?"

"All right," said the Green Phantasm. "Thank you, Zapper."

So at once, Zapper just strolled back toward the balcony that was along the great steel barrier. Once there, he just took a few steps away from the gas chamber, leaving a path for the Green Phantasm.

The Green Phantasm went jogging toward the steel barrier as well. Then, he started to turn right to advance toward Doctor XT and Amanda Taylor. However, he did not make it too far at all.

Although Zapper had apparently cooperated with the Phantasm, he was really up to a new scheme. He had really wanted to allow the Green Phantasm to turn his back on him, so he could attack from behind. The Green Phantasm had had some sort of second thought that Zapper's cooperation was too good to be true. Could someone so desperate and determined have really submitted that easily? By no means, and neither had Axel Axtel.

So then, in the very instant that the Green Phantasm had completely turned right to face the control room, Zapper crept up behind him. Before the Green Phantasm knew what was happening, Zapper had put him in a headlock that he was applying with his left arm. Once again, the Green Phantasm's hat fell off onto the platform. "*What*? What's happening?" he cried in surprise.

"Ah, ha, ha, ha, ha, ha!" laughed Zapper. "Why, you radioactive fool, you were dumb enough to believe that? Why, you idiot, I've got this whole business here in my future, and my life depends on this. You really thought I would give up and back off that easily? Heh, heh, heh, that's what's wrong with you so-called heroes. You're going down, my friend. This time, in you go; come on."

"Darn it! He tricked me!" Clifton muttered to himself, as Zapper began walking him down the platform.

Then, within a few seconds, the Green Phantasm decided, "That's it; I gotta take him out this time." At least he now realized that Zapper was only trying to deceive him. Therefore, he knew he had to knock him out.

So shortly, the Green Phantasm used his left hand to grab hold of a railing to his left. That stopped the advancement toward the X-Termination Acid. In desperation, he jerked his head out of the headlock. "Hey!" yelled Zapper.

At that, Zapper used his right hand to try to regain his hold on the Green Phantasm. However, the Green Phantasm caught his right arm and whipped Zapper forward, making his abdomen hit the top railing that was now on his right, facing the steel barrier. This did not hurt Zapper too much, but it made him somewhat angrier. Of course, the Green Phantasm sort of expected that.

The Green Phantasm began charging himself up for his next move. In the meantime, Zapper was muttering to himself, "I'm gonna get him for this!" So at once, Zapper turned right to come face-to-face with the Phantasm once again. While he was turning, he tried to throw a left crossover with his left fist. But before he could connect, the Green Phantasm unleashed himself as a shapeless radiant projectile. He drove Zapper backward into the steel barrier.

Now, Zapper was in a severe state of shock, not knowing what had hit him. "What was that?" the stunned, groggy Zapper asked while seeing lots of hallucinations flying and floating around him randomly. Then momentarily, Zapper saw a vague image of the Green Phantasm, who was actually standing before him. At seeing that, Zapper obeyed his first impulse and threw a straight right at him. However, the Green Phantasm sidestepped to his own right to avoid it. That same instant, the Green Phantasm threw and landed his own straight right, which hit the left of Zapper's jaw and knocked him unconscious. Zapper/Axel Jerome Axtel was now lying out cold facedown on the balcony.

The Green Phantasm retrieved his hat, which had just fallen onto the platform a few minutes earlier. He was now ready to move on to the next phase, which undoubtedly involved facing Doctor XT in order to save the one person he loved with all his heart, Amanda Taylor. Just as the Green Phantasm had taken out Zapper, Amanda had let out a sigh of relief. Of course, at the same time, she was proud of him and happy that her hero was still alive.

XT was witnessing the Phantasm's progress as well. Doctor XT had other ideas pertaining to the Green Phantasm. At the same time, he could sense that Amanda still believed in the Phantasm. So he turned to her and told her in a lowered voice, "You better not say a freakin' word. I am totally prepared to dispose of this neon peon. He's fixing to go down for sure. Of course, I'll wait until after to 'X-terminate' you. You see, otherwise, he might just go on and zip away. But if you even try saying or doing anything at all, I'll just go ahead and take my chances on that. But in the meantime, watch this."

Upon hearing that, Amanda got a little tenser. That was because she knew she had to keep silent. After all, how could she have been helpful to the Green Phantasm by keeping quiet? She still did not give up hope, for she knew it was still possible for her hero to prevail.

So next, the Green Phantasm had just begun walking toward Doctor XT and Amanda. He stopped just before the gas chamber. From that point, Doctor XT and the Green Phantasm were now looking directly at each other.

"So," said Doctor XT, "if it isn't the Green Phantasm, who else would it be?"

"That's right, Doctor XT," replied the Green Phantasm. "It's me all right."

"Well," Doctor XT said, "I presume you've come for this so-called Amanda?"

"You know it, man," the Phantasm told him. "There's no doubt about it. I just want us to know another thing too. I'm not leaving here unless it's with her."

"Is that a fact?" asked an unbelieving Doctor XT.

"That it is," the Green Phantasm answered affirmatively.

"You really think so, huh?" asked Doctor XT, still in disbelief.

At that, the Green Phantasm nodded and then went on to tell XT, "And I think another thing too. You've gone way too far this time. To plot a scheme like this, you have completely lost your mind. You've already killed all those other countless innocent victims in the past, and now, you're about to kill this desirable, lovely young lady? You crazy, perverted, depraved lunatic!"

At hearing those words, Doctor XT just scoffed, chuckled, and shook his head.

But then, the Green Phantasm continued by saying, "And another thing; I so strongly believe the need for you to be put in your place, that I'm willing to do it myself. But, above all, I will not allow the one I love and care about to perish in an undeserved manner. If I have to put you out of business to stop her from that, that's what I'll do."

"Well, well, well, is that right?" asked XT. "I'll tell you what; if you can just walk over here nice and slowly, you can have her."

"What?" the Green Phantasm muttered to himself, not believing his ears.

Doctor XT took out his Mega Zapper 2000 and held it up to Amanda in a threatening manner. Then, continuing what he was saying, Doctor XT told the Phantasm, "That's right, Phantasm, all you gotta do is walk on over here nice and easy. It's your best bet. But if you use one of your moves, you know, like teleport or project yourself over here, in order to get here, I'll give her a fatal surge of electricity. So you better take your time and go slow. Only then might you two get back together."

"All right, Doctor," responded the Green Phantasm. "Anything you say to keep her alive."

"That's better."

Then, the Green Phantasm began to walk on through the gas chamber. But, before putting his entire body inside of it, he stopped to think about something. Wait a minute, should I really just ease on over there like he wants? I mean, couldn't this be a trap? Because like earlier tonight on the building's top, wasn't that a trap, when he asked me to come on over and talk? It sure was, wasn't it? Besides, this is his home base, where he's more likely to get me. Other than that, didn't Zapper just try to trick me? Well, if I can't entirely trust Zapper, or perhaps Axel Axtel, how much more could I trust the one he works for, that perverted him? So I'd better be really, really careful. Now, let's see here.

So next, the Green Phantasm started walking very slowly through the gas chamber, at the same time looking around in all directions for a single sign of trouble. However, after taking no more than four steps forward, the Phantasm just teleported backward, to reappear back outside the chamber. Once there, he stood there for a matter of seconds to see if any lasers or other concealed weapons would either be released or open fire. But somehow, nothing happened. So then, the Green Phantasm just started over again walking slowly and carefully through the gas chamber.

The Green Phantasm soon made it halfway through the gas chamber. At that, Doctor XT told him, "You're doing fine there; keep it up." Then, that very second, Doctor XT turned his back toward the Green Phantasm.

"Hmmph," said the Green Phantasm curiously. "Now, what's he talkin' about, huh? What's he up to now?"

With his back to the Phantasm, Doctor XT used his right index finger to select and press a button on the control pad that was around his left wrist. "What are you doing?" Amanda asked with much anxiety.

"Watch this, baby!" Doctor XT snickered. Of course, that only made Amanda tenser regarding what was about to happen.

All of a sudden, the Green Phantasm heard something behind him. It sounded as if it could have been a sliding door closing and latching.

The Phantasm instantly looked back to find that something had closed and locked behind him after all. It was a thick, vertical plane sheet of glass that completely sealed off the gas chamber's entrance that he had already gone through to get in. "Uh-oh," the Green Phantasm said as he began to turn back around to move forward. "I'd better—oh no! Don't tell me I'm trapped!"

Another glass barrier was now sealing off the other end of the gas chamber as well. Each wall of glass was about eighteen inches thick. It was almost impossible for even the Green Phantasm to break the glass. He was in a really bad situation. He was now trapped inside the gas chamber. "Oh no!" cried Amanda, who was looking on in a state of terror.

The Green Phantasm decided to try anything he could think of in order to break out of the chamber. "Oh shoot!" the Green Phantasm exclaimed. "I gotta do something. There's no tellin' what's gonna happen to me! I gotta get outta here!"

<hr>

After panicking for a few seconds, the Green Phantasm calmed down just a little and said to himself, "Okay, all right, let's see if this works." At that, he began charging both hands with radiant energy. Next, he combined the power of all ten fingers to create one gigantic, colossal laser beam, which he shortly unleashed, targeting the glass door closer to XT and Amanda. However, this only proved to be a useless technique, for the glass did not even receive the slightest scratch. "Dang it!" muttered a frustrated Phantasm. "It didn't even much scratch it! Doggone it! What am I gonna try to do now, huh?"

After racking his brains for another idea, the Green Phantasm decided, "Well, I only got one other thought so far. Let's see if it works. I guess it's worth a try." Then, the Phantasm started charging up in preparation to project himself against the glass. He released and projected himself toward the wall of glass, in the form of a radiant-neon shapeless projectile. But unfortunately, this too, proved to be futile as the Green Phantasm ricocheted off the glass and ended up reappearing as himself. "Aw man, this is nuts!" fumed the Green Phantasm. "Dang it! Dang it! Dang it! Ah, shoot! Doggone it, this is impossible! I mean, this is just freakin' impossible!" Without much doubt, the Phantasm was now more frustrated than before. Of course, this was not tough to understand, for nothing he had tried to do to break the glass seemed to work at all.

On a brighter note, although rather angry and frustrated, the Green Phantasm was still more than determined to endure what he would have to go through and get Amanda out of that facility safely. Therefore, he would do anything but give up hope. The Phantasm reduced some of the tension he was under and had a second thought. "Well," he told himself, "I may not be able to break the glass, but with the powers I have in my possession, I should be able to get through this somehow. Of course, I don't know what Doctor XT's planning to do to me in here, but I should be able to do something about it."

The Green Phantasm asked himself, "But now, what should I go on and do next? Hmmmmm." At that, he just stood facing Doctor XT and Amanda, doing nothing but thinking. At the same time, Doctor XT was chuckling to himself, for he had noticed that anything the Green Phantasm had tried proved to be futile.

Then, XT walked over to a microphone on the west side of his control room. He programmed his PA system to go to some hidden speakers inside the gas chamber. Doctor XT said over the PA system to the Phantasm, "Well, well, Green Phantasm."

"Yeah, I heard you, Doctor XT," replied the Phantasm. "What are you up to, huh? What in the devil do you think you're doing?"

"You know something?" asked Doctor XT. "You sure got a lot of nerve for someone in your situation. Isn't it obvious, you neon freak? You can't get outta there. I got you right where I want you. It's all over for you now. You're about to be 'X-terminated.' How can you even think to speak to me that way?"

"I'll tell you how," answered the Green Phantasm. "You see, Doctor, this ain't over yet. I'm not giving up, because real heroes never give up! Once I get through this, I'm getting Amanda out of this sleaze pit. Furthermore, if you don't go ahead and stop this, I'm shutting down X-Termination. I'll even see to it that XTE means 'X-terminated engineer.' You may as well just give up now, because you're on your way down. If you don't believe me, just wait and see. What do you say, Doctor XT? Are you gonna stop, or do I have to stop you?"

The Green Phantasm had quite a positive, courageous attitude. However, it only made Doctor XT angrier. He said in reply, "So, you must really want what's coming to you. I can tell, because you're testing my patience! I'll be happy to oblige. Sayonara, Green Phantasm!"

"Sayonara!" the Green Phantasm said to himself. "What's he mean by that, huh? What's he fixin' to do now?"

Shortly thereafter, two rows of vents running along the length of the gas chamber's floor came open. "*What?*" cried the frightened Green Phantasm upon noticing. "Oh no, what's gonna happen now?" At the present, the Green Phantasm was too concerned about what would seep through the vents to think about anything else. He was in too much of a state of panic to activate a defensive capability of his.

A thin mist of light-purple vapor began to appear above each row of vents. With very little doubt, it was X-Termination Gas. Every second, both masses of vapor expanded continuously, as more and more was emitted from Doctor XT's laboratory below. The X-Termination Gas also kept rising progressively higher and higher. Within three seconds of being unleashed into the gas chamber, the X-Termination Gas had reached a level between the Green Phantasm's knees and waist.

All the while, Doctor XT had been causing all this to happen from the control room. The only other thing he had the heart to do was to look all around smiling and chuckling. Eventually, he looked toward the captive Amanda Taylor and said to her, "Well, babe, it looks very much like the end for you both. Of course, you know you're fixing to be next. But otherwise, what the heck, I just thought I might let you see this so you wouldn't miss it. Wouldn't you say that's fair of me, hmm?"

However, Amanda was focused on her hero and was not paying attention to what Doctor XT was saying. So she did not respond. At this, Doctor XT said to Amanda, "Oh, no answer, huh? I take it you don't care too much for this. Oh well, look on the bright side; at least you don't have much longer after this."

Amanda still did not pay any mind to Doctor XT because, even with as much trouble as the Green Phantasm was in, she still held fast to her belief in him. Amanda figured that, with the powers and determination of the Phantasm, he could somehow survive the X-Termination Gas. So then, she said in desperation, "Come on, Green Phantasm, please don't die! You can make it through this! I know you can do it, come on! Don't let it kill you!"

At the same time, as the X-Termination Gas was rising and expanding around the Green Phantasm, he was thinking to himself, I know there's gotta be a way past this, but how? It's too late to put up a force field. Is there some other defense I can—wait a minute, that's it! I only have one chance. There's only one way I can possibly get through this. Here I go.

The Green Phantasm created tension in every part of his anatomy. Of course, like always, he strained himself and held his breath in order to do it. This made him radiate even brighter by applying radiant energy that made him invincible. It was true that straining and holding his breath for a long period might have brought about nausea and even unconsciousness. However, applying the invincibility mechanism was the only way that the Green Phantasm could now prevent inhalation of X-Termination Gas, which was fatal.

So, as Doctor XT kept forcing more X-Termination Gas into the gas chamber, the Green Phantasm just held fast to all of his tightness to try to remain invincible.

From outside the gas chamber, Doctor XT and Amanda could see what appeared to be a blinding flash of neon-green light in the middle of a purple cloud of X-Termination Gas. Doctor XT looked curiously and asked himself, "Hmph, I don't know what's doing that. What's he up to in there?" Without a doubt, Doctor XT could not understand why the Green Phantasm was persistently giving off much brighter light than usual. He began to become afraid of whether this scheme would work.

Doctor XT finally made a decision. "Actually," he said, "I know what I'll do. If this round of gas doesn't 'X-terminate' him, maybe I'll send him another one. Of course, it might be possible that he's immune to my X-Termination Gas. I mean, after all, nothing we've tried has been able to stop him so far. So, if it turns out he's invulnerable to X-Termination Gas, I'll just either try something else or maybe just leave him in there. At least he can't get out, and that's good. Of course, he can't survive in there forever. So, one way or another, I've got him. Oh yes, this is it for you, Green Phantasm." After that, Doctor XT just chuckled to himself.

Amanda, however, had other ideas. Whenever she saw the really bright radiation coming out of the X-Termination Gas cloud, she could tell that the Green Phantasm was trying to fight his way through the surge of gas. She also knew that as long as he was able to radiate, he was still alive. So she still did not give up hope for the Green Phantasm, her hero of all men. She just whispered to herself, "Come on, Green Phantasm. I know you can make it! Don't let it kill you! Please don't die, please! Come on! You can do it! Come on, Green Phantasm!"

Meanwhile, inside the gas chamber, the Green Phantasm was still straining and holding his breath after three minutes now. Side effects including nausea and hallucinations were beginning to occur. However, this did not make the Green Phantasm give up. He was determined that he would endure anything to survive and save his beloved sweetheart, Amanda Taylor. He was in fact, thinking to himself, *I'll throw up if I have to. I just can't let this gas kill me. I just gotta get Amanda outta here! I just gotta!*

Then, after two more minutes, the strain of staying invincible had become much worse for the Green Phantasm. Of course, he was much more dazed than before. Also, he could now see nothing clearly and was receiving many different hallucinations. He even felt as if he was about to pass out. But he still felt the need to keep his anatomy tightened to the fullest because he would rather anything else happen to him besides being killed by the X-Termination Gas.

Next, Doctor XT finally decided to stop putting in more gas and to go on and let it all out. "Well, anyway," he said as he closed off the vents that were on the gas chamber's floor, "let's see what we now have. I can't clearly see what's actually happening, but I'll just clear the gas chamber and then decide what to do from there." At that, Doctor XT opened two rows of vents that were along the gas chamber's ceiling. Then, he switched on some fans, which drew all the X-Termination Gas up through the vents and forced it up and out through a big smokestack up on the roof.

In the meantime, as the X-Termination Gas was leaving the gas chamber, the Green Phantasm was getting closer and closer every second to unconsciousness. The image he was now perceiving kept changing back and forth between a very blurry scene with too many hallucinations and complete blackness. He was not certain as to whether he would survive, but he was determined to give it his best attempt, for Amanda's sake.

Then finally, the last trace of X-Termination Gas ascended upward. But even as this happened, the Green Phantasm lost consciousness and collapsed onto the floor of the gas chamber. Straining every muscle, in addition to holding his breath, had evidently built up too much pressure inside of him. So now, the Green Phantasm was lying faceup and unconscious on the floor of the gas chamber. All of his radiation had even ceased.

Both Amanda Taylor and Doctor XT were looking on as all of this was taking place. Now, Amanda went into tears and sobbed, "Oh no, please tell me this didn't really happen. This is all my fault." At that, she just persistently cried. How could she not? After all, she thought her hero was now dead. In turn, perhaps she was going to die too. Amanda was much too afraid and upset to know what to do now. It appeared completely hopeless to her.

At the same time, the most evil, corrupt, and depraved Doctor XT looked on happily. He had wanted the Green Phantasm to drop dead. So he just proceeded as planned. While smiling and chuckling, he said, "You see? I knew nobody could survive that. Well, it's time to 'X-terminate' him for good. All right now, it's to the acid with this freak."

Doctor XT opened the glass doors of the gas chamber. Then, he went over and grabbed hold of the Green Phantasm's feet. At that, XT began dragging him out of the chamber and through the control room. The Green Phantasm's hat came off at the doorway that separated the gas chamber and the control room. From there, Doctor XT just continued dragging the Phantasm toward the platform that extended from the control room to above the X-Termination Acid vat.

Poor Amanda Taylor was crying more than ever. After all, her hero was now at the mercy of Doctor XT, without any consciousness or radiation remaining. Also, she was handcuffed in place, unable to do anything to help. To her, it was apparently all over for both the Green Phantasm and herself. But was the Green Phantasm really dead, as both Amanda and Doctor XT thought?

As Doctor XT had just managed to make it onto the platform with the Phantasm, something miraculous suddenly took place. Before being dragged too far along the platform toward the acid, Clifton slowly opened both of his eyes. He was now regaining consciousness. At least one thing was for certain. He had not been killed by the fumes of the X-Termination Gas. He had only been unconscious because he had passed out from too much pressure being built up inside of him.

So shortly, as soon as Doctor XT had dragged the Phantasm halfway down the platform, the Green Phantasm jerked his right foot out of XT's left hand while he was not looking. Caught by surprise, Doctor XT exclaimed, "What?" Then, as he was turning to look toward the Green Phantasm, he said, "Why, you—ohhh!" When XT stopped to see what happened, the Green Phantasm drove his right foot into the doctor's genital area. At that, Doctor XT let go of the Phantasm's left foot and placed both hands where he had just kicked him. What a state of shock and surprise XT was now in, for he had thought for sure that the Green Phantasm was dead.

Immediately, the Green Phantasm got right back up onto his feet. While Doctor XT was still distracted, the Phantasm teleported over to the gas chamber to retrieve his hat. Then at once, he put it back on and teleported back over to face Doctor XT.

Amanda suddenly looked up and instantly stopped crying. "Oh, thank God!" exclaimed the ever-so-relieved Amanda Taylor. "He's still okay! I knew you could make it, Green Phantasm! I knew you could! Go, Green Phantasm!"

The Green Phantasm said to Doctor XT, "All right, Doctor, this time, you've really, really gone too far! It's the last straw! I'm getting Amanda outta here. Either that or I'm shuttin' you down for good. I suggest you hand me the cuff keys, 'cause it's the end of the line for you."

Doctor XT looked toward the Green Phantasm. Now recovered from the low blow, he told the Green Phantasm, "I can't believe my eyes. How can this be happening? I knew I shouldn't have got you out of there. With all my wisdom and knowledge, how could I have been so stupid to believe that that gas would work on someone with your super powers?"

"That's enough, Doctor!" the Green Phantasm told him firmly. "It doesn't matter anymore. We're past that now. Just cut the crap, and give me the doggone keys, or else!"

"All right!" replied Doctor XT. "Just stay right there and calm down so I can." At that, the Green Phantasm patiently waited while Doctor XT reached back to his right rear inside his coat to get something.

Doctor XT pulled out what he had been trying to get. Hoping for the handcuff keys, the Green Phantasm began reaching forward to try to collect them. However, the object Doctor XT had pulled out turned out to be a Mega Zapper 2000. "Ha, ha, ha, ha!" laughed Doctor XT, as he was charging it up to give the Green Phantasm a major electric shock.

At the same time, the Green Phantasm began to become suspicious when Doctor XT was laughing. Then, he managed to notice in the nick of time, that it was not a set of keys that Doctor XT was holding out. Seeing that it was another device created by Doctor XT, the Green Phantasm quickly backed up to avoid a shock. He immediately teleported backward to the other side of the control room. From there, he used the index finger of his left hand to fire a laser beam that knocked the Mega Zapper out of Doctor XT's hand. The device ended up landing very close to the platform's end. "What!" cried Doctor XT. "Why, I'm gonna…"

Doctor XT started turning to run and retrieve his Mega Zapper 2000. However, before he even completed two steps, the Green Phantasm had teleported and reappeared behind him. Then immediately, the Green Phantasm used his left hand to grab hold of the collar of XT's coat and stop him. "Oh, no, you don't!" the Phantasm told XT.

At that, Doctor XT turned around and tried to hammer the Green Phantasm with a great big right. But the Green Phantasm dodged, and then he teleported, placing himself behind Doctor XT. "Where'd he go now?" asked Doctor XT.

The Green Phantasm tapped Doctor XT's left shoulder, saying, "Guess who."

Turning around again, Doctor XT said, "Right, I'm—oof!" The Green Phantasm landed a big straight right on his chin. As a result, Doctor XT's head snapped back, and he was dazed and staggered backward.

While Doctor XT was stunned from that punch, the Green Phantasm became a projectile. This time, he only shot himself a few feet, just enough to hit Doctor XT and knock him backward. Doctor XT landed on his back on the floor of the control room. At the same time, the Green Phantasm reappeared as himself, standing by the feet of XT.

He knelt down above Doctor XT's chest, using his knees to pin down XT's arms. "All right, Doctor," the Green Phantasm told him, "this is it, pal. Where are your cuff keys, huh? Just tell me, and I'll get them myself."

"Well," said Doctor XT. "I guess I don't have much choice, do I? After all, I'm no match for you. I mean, isn't it really something, the way you have turned the tables on me? Now, why are you doing this, huh? What are you gonna do to me now? You're not gonna kill me, are you? Whatcha gonna do, huh?"

"Let me explain, all right?" replied the Green Phantasm. "I just want to save Amanda. She does not deserve to die, and I am not going to let you kill her. I'm not leaving here, unless it's with her. I'll do anything I need to to get her away from this condemned, corrupted, and no-good facility."

"All right," replied Doctor XT, "I guess it don't matter if I give them to you or not. I may as well. I mean, you're probably just gonna kill me whether I hand 'em over or not. So why not just go on and kill me like you did everyone else here tonight. After all, it's really what you want, isn't it? I'm sure they're all just better off dead anyway. Furthermore, I guess I am too. Wouldn't you agree? Just go on, Green Phantasm, do it! Take the keys! Get me over with! Take your girlfriend with you! Go on. You know you want that."

"Hold everything, XT," answered the Green Phantasm. "I'm afraid you're mistaken. First of all, I'm not here to kill anyone. I didn't mean to kill Anselm Nielsen, the one called D.D.T. After I tried giving him a chance, he tried to shoot me with his ray gun. I was just defending myself when he died. Then, as for Nicholas Jarrett, or is it Zinger, I didn't kill him; y'all did. It was all three of you holding me at gunpoint. I was only trying to save myself. It was you and Zapper who fired the shots that killed him. And last but not least, regarding Zapper, that's Axel J. Axtel, I—"

"So," interrupted Doctor XT, "you've learned a lot since you've been here tonight, haven't you?"

"If you say so," the Green Phantasm responded. Then, pointing to the unconscious Zapper, he told Doctor XT, "It's all thanks to that guy over there. But anyway, as I was saying, I wasn't gonna kill him either, and I don't think I did. That is although he wanted to kill me. Then, after I gave him another chance, he kept attacking me. So all I did was knock him out. So you see, I'm not a killer like you. Therefore, I really don't want to kill you either. Other than that, I even have a guilty feeling, even though it was you and your crew who killed all those innocent people at the banquet the other night. And on top of that, I feel responsible, although it was Zapper, Zinger, and D.D.T. who killed all those people at the restaurant earlier this evening. At least I'm not proud of all that like you are. Sympathy is one thing I've got that you haven't. That's why I'm holding back from hurting you or killing you, although I think you deserve it."

"Oh, is that right?"

"And another thing," continued the Phantasm. "I really don't think you'd all be better off dead. You would really be better off discontinuing this business and turning over a new leaf. There's no real future in this, for either you or anybody who works for you."

"Oh, but there is," argued Doctor XT. "You make thousands a day. Plus, you get all the freedom and enjoyment that you want."

"Well, perhaps," replied the Green Phantasm, "but I don't see any of your other men out here tonight. I'm talking about the ones in the rocket planes two nights ago. I guess they're all in jail. Certainly, you don't think it's worth that to live this kind of life."

"Actually," said Doctor XT, "they're not in jail."

"They're not?" asked the Green Phantasm. "What do you mean, they're not?"

"You idiot," XT told the Phantasm. "How could you think I'm stupid enough to let them remain in jail, so that they could go to court and tell everyone about my organization? I couldn't allow for that. I have 'X-terminated' them, you fool."

"What?" exclaimed the Green Phantasm.

"That's right!" replied Doctor XT. "I had them busted out and did away with them!"

"No way!" cried the Green Phantasm.

"Why not?" argued Doctor XT. "They couldn't fulfill what I needed them to, not even with a foolproof plan. So why do I need them? They only turned out to be a waste of time and money. So therefore, I'm better off not having them. Besides, I can't let myself get put out of business. That's why I 'X-terminated' them. Then, if I ever 'X-terminate' you, I'll do the same thing to Zapper."

"You'll what?" asked the shocked Green Phantasm.

"That's right," answered Doctor XT. "I'll 'X-terminate' Zapper too. Of course, it's no big deal that you annihilated D.D.T. and Zinger. If they were still around right now, I'd 'X-terminate' them too, for letting you get past them."

"You crazy fool!" yelled the Green Phantasm. "You lunatic, you care about no one besides yourself, don't you? That's why you pay everyone thousands a day. It shuts their minds to the consequences of messing up. And another thing: just because everything doesn't go your way, you're just gonna keep killing everyone in your way for the rest of your life? What kind of future do you call that? This is what I call selfishness taken way too far. There's no real hope for people like you."

"So, what are you saying?" asked Doctor XT.

"Listen," the Green Phantasm told him. "Like I said earlier, I don't want to kill you. Here's what I would like from you: As you already know, I want you to free Amanda. Other than that, I'd really like for you to go to the Philadelphia police and confess to them what you have done. Of course, they may put you in jail, but it's a better way for you to go than this kind of life. Besides, I think you need to be stopped. I'll even do it myself if I have to."

Then, while nodding, Doctor XT said to the Phantasm, "I understand."

"Oh, really?" asked the Green Phantasm. "I don't see how you understand so quickly, but it's good to hear that you do."

"Yeah," replied Doctor XT, "I completely understand why you're doing this and why you're telling me all this."

"Okay," replied the Green Phantasm.

"You see," said Doctor XT. "It's because you have your super powers as the Green Phantasm."

"What do you mean?" asked the Green Phantasm.

"What do I mean!" protested Doctor XT. "Don't you get it? With all your supernatural capabilities, I'm no match for you; you know that. I know that too. That's why I threw everything at you that I did. You saw that I dispatched all those rocket planes, right?"

"Right," answered the Green Phantasm.

"Then tonight," continued Doctor XT, "I had to use the aid of my lieutenants and finally trap you inside the gas chamber."

"Okay," said the Green Phantasm. "So what's your point?"

"You see," XT told him, "all the things you just told me did make some sort of sense. But I don't believe that you truly meant or believed in what you said. I think you only pretended to feel that way because of the powers you've somehow inherited."

"Oh, come on, Doctor," pleaded the Green Phantasm. "I know you know better than that."

"Well," Doctor XT said. "I do have to admit something. It's really amazing and remarkable what you've managed to do so far with your powers. I mean, the other night at the banquet, you really fouled up our scheme big-time. Other than that, you've managed to defeat all of my other men, and they wound up in jail. Then tonight, you made it on through D.D.T., Zinger, and Zapper. Heck, you even survived the gas chamber. And even now, it's down to just me. I got to hand it to you; that's impressive. But you only dare to face all of that because of what makes you the Green Phantasm. Without all that, I bet you wouldn't even dare to stand up to me right now. I honestly think you only appear to fight for what you believe in because of your super powers. You wouldn't even care if not for that, would you?"

"Look," the Phantasm told XT calmly. "You know that's not true. First of all, I did not plan on having these powers; it just happened. But even before that, I've always desired to do the right thing. I've always had the will to do everything I can to make Philadelphia as safe of a place as possible, for myself, and those that I love and care about. That's what motivated me to take up my role as the Green Phantasm. Other than that, we both know a lot of people who care as much as I do, if not more. They're just not as capable as me. But, that does not mean that they don't care. I mean, take Amanda over there, for instance. She's not as powerful or capable as me, but Thursday night, she obviously cared enough to stand up for me, didn't she? So you see, Doctor, with or without my superior powers, I'm still just as caring. Do you understand what I'm saying?"

Unable to object to what the Phantasm had just explained, Doctor XT told him while nodding, "I see your point."

"Okay then," replied the Green Phantasm.

"But just one other thing," said Doctor XT.

"What's that?" asked the Green Phantasm.

Doctor XT told the Phantasm, "So far, everything you've said has made a lot of sense; I got to admit that. I mean, I really can't argue with what you've already told me. But even after listening to all that, I still don't think you would dare to go against me right now, if you didn't have your powers as the Green Phantasm."

"What?" asked the Green Phantasm, shaking his head in disbelief.

"You know," said Doctor XT, "it's quite possible that you were right about my way of life and what I ought to do regarding it. However, at least one thing's for sure. If you were to somehow defeat me in a fight without your supernatural abilities, you'd definitely make a full believer out of me."

"Well," said the Green Phantasm, "I'm not really worried about changing what anyone believes."

"All right," replied Doctor XT. "I'll tell you what: Why don't we have one last fight? This is my proposition: If you can win a fight against me as a normal man without any super power, I'll change like you want me to. I'll discontinue what I do for a living and straighten my life out. I'll even turn myself over to the police and stay in jail for life if I have to."

"Oh, really?" asked the Green Phantasm, who could not believe what he was hearing.

"I mean, come on," Doctor XT told him. "Isn't like, the good guy supposed to be fair? Besides, you said you don't really want to kill me, didn't you? Other than that, you already used your powers to defeat the rest of my organization. Why don't you see what you can do without them, since it's just down to me now?"

"You've got a point there," responded the Green Phantasm, nodding in agreement. At that, the Phantasm got off Doctor XT, so that he could get back up onto his feet.

"You know something?" said the Green Phantasm to Doctor XT. "I think what you've got in mind sounds like a good idea. After all, like you suggested, I hate to just put you away without giving you a chance to change. Also, I would like to show that I really am fair and just. But there's just one other thing."

"What's that?" asked Doctor XT.

"You see, Doctor," the Green Phantasm told him, "I could switch off my radiative, supernatural powers to have one last fight with you. However, I only have one problem with it. Other than my superior powers, I have no other weapons or devices as you have. I don't desire to use weapons like a lot of crooks and killers do. Yet, that's another thing I need my powers for. I need something to defend myself from those that are armed. If I deactivate the radiant energy from within myself, it'll be like you'll be armed and I won't. I don't know what you still have under your coat, or on your belt, or what that keypad thing is on your left wrist. But I do know that those things will make this fight unfair to me. So, if you could at least set your arsenal aside, that would make us even Steven."

Doctor XT sighed for a moment, but then he said, "Well, all right, I guess you got a point there too. Okay, I'll disarm myself, especially since I could still take you." So then, Doctor XT took off his coat and belt and went to set them down inside the gas chamber. While he was over there, he even removed his gloves and sunglasses, as well as the computerized device on his left forearm. All he was now wearing was a pair of work boots, his pants, a white T-shirt, and a wrist wrap on both of his wrists. Doctor XT went back to face the Green Phantasm. "All right, Green Phantasm," said Doctor XT. "I took off all the extras like you wanted. So now, what about your powers, huh?"

The Green Phantasm finally saw no more reason to object. So he told Doctor XT, "Okay, Doctor, I guess fair is fair." At that, James Clifton switched off his neon-green radiation. So now, he was not emitting any bright-green light. He was now like a mere James Paul Clifton, only wearing a Green Phantasm suit.

"All right, Phantasm," XT addressed him. "You listen up. I'm gonna go over this one last time. First of all, if I win, might as well say when I win, I'm going to 'X-terminate' you, then Amanda, and finally Zapper. After that, I'll just start all over." At that, Clifton just scoffed and shook his head in disbelief.

Then, seeing that the Green Phantasm was not very enthused by that idea, Doctor XT continued by saying, "However, if you were to, by some unlikely chance, come out on top, I would not only set Amanda free, but if necessary, put an end to X-Termination, turn my life around, even let myself get put in jail if I have to. Have we got a deal?"

"Deal," confirmed the Green Phantasm. At that, they shook hands in agreement.

Next, the Green Phantasm took off his hat and set it down close to Doctor XT's office. "Now, Doctor," he said while raising his right hand, "just once more, I promise to fight you as an ordinary human being, without using any supernatural abilities as the Green Phantasm. You have my word."

"Good," said Doctor XT. "Now, let's get it on."

But then, before the Green Phantasm began to fight, Amanda interrupted him. "Excuse me, Green Phantasm," she addressed him.

"What is it, Amanda?" he asked her.

"Are you sure this is a good idea? I don't trust him," said a very concerned Amanda Taylor.

However, the Green Phantasm turned toward her for a few seconds and told her, "Don't worry, I got faith and confidence. I can do this."

After that, the Green Phantasm turned his attention back to Doctor XT. Just as he was turning back around, a big straight right was headed toward him. The Phantasm barely noticed in time and quickly jumped to his left. Apparently, the final fight had now begun.

So now, both the Green Phantasm and Doctor XT were standing up facing one another, each one having both fists in front of himself. Next, Doctor XT took a few sidesteps to his left to try to get around the Green Phantasm. But he just turned himself accordingly, to remain face-to-face with Doctor XT. The Phantasm was now facing the doorway that was leading to the acid vat, which was behind Doctor XT.

Then, Doctor XT tried throwing a left crossover at the Green Phantasm. But the Phantasm stepped back to avoid it. After that, the Green Phantasm tried coming back toward XT with a left jab. But Doctor XT sidestepped left to avoid it.

Then at once, Doctor XT tried to duck and throw a straight right at the Green Phantasm's midsection. "Oh, shoot!" he muttered as he jumped backward to evade it.

Less than two seconds later, Doctor XT tried throwing a right crossover while stepping toward the Phantasm. But that very second, the Green Phantasm used his left hand to catch and hold XT's right forearm. The frustrated Green Phantasm then said angrily, "You son of a—" But before finishing, the Green Phantasm landed a right uppercut to the left side of Doctor XT's jaw.

"Oof!" exclaimed Doctor XT, who was stunned by the blow.

The determined Green Phantasm went on to deliver a series of various lefts and rights. Without a doubt, Doctor XT was progressively getting further dazed and stunned with each and every blow. After several punches, Doctor XT finally fell to his hands and knees on the floor.

"Way to go, Green Phantasm!" exclaimed Amanda, anxiously looking on.

Now, the Green Phantasm was about to continue beating up Doctor XT, but before he could resume, Doctor XT put up his right hand, signaling the Green Phantasm to yield. "I can't take anymore!" Doctor XT yelled out. As a result, the good conscience of James Clifton caused him to hold back from delivering any further blows.

Doctor XT began to rise slowly back up to an upright position. While XT was gradually getting up, the Green Phantasm took a few seconds to look around. But unfortunately, this gave Doctor XT the break he needed for a cheap shot; for the Green Phantasm, taking his eyes off his opponent proved to be a mistake. So, while the Phantasm was temporarily distracted, Doctor XT delivered a straight right to his genital area.

All of a sudden, the Green Phantasm became dazed, not knowing what had just hit him. He had been caught quite by surprise. In turn, he bent over while holding on to his genitals and staggering toward the doorway to the platform that was above the X-Termination Acid. "Oh my God!" he exclaimed "What happened?"

Then immediately, he looked toward Doctor XT and caught a glimpse of him. However, he did not have time to avoid getting hit. So Doctor XT landed a right crossover on the Green Phantasm's left cheek. Consequently, the Green Phantasm was seriously stunned and fell to the floor.

Then, Doctor XT used his right foot to roll the Phantasm into a faceup position. At that, XT began repeatedly kicking and stomping away at his rib cage and abdominal area. The Green Phantasm was now in trouble. The tables had been turned on him, and he was apparently not going to receive the break that he had given Doctor XT just moments before.

After having repeatedly kicked and stomped the Phantasm, Doctor XT paused for a few seconds, during which he chuckled and said to himself, "You gullible fool, you were dumb enough to believe me?" Then, at once, Doctor XT kicked him in the face, which nearly knocked the Phantasm unconscious.

So now, the Green Phantasm was so stunned he was seeing nothing but countless hallucinations right before his eyes. This permitted Doctor XT to set up his very next move. He stood the helpless Green Phantasm up in the doorway to the acid vat. The wobbly, staggering Phantasm was about to collapse back toward the floor. But before he could collapse, Doctor XT delivered a side kick to his midsection that sent him flying backward. The

Green Phantasm landed on his back, lying along the platform at about the halfway point between both ends of it.

A rather worried Amanda called out to her hero in distress, "Come on, Green Phantasm!" In turn, this helped the Green Phantasm begin to regain his senses. Before he knew it, he could see clearly again.

But before he had a chance to get up again, Doctor XT used his left foot to mash down on the Phantasm's throat, in order to choke him. The Green Phantasm started becoming dazed again, and before too long, hallucinations, as well as the feeling that he would pass out, occurred as well.

After a few seconds of being choked, the Green Phantasm was once again so stunned that he was almost completely helpless. So, for a second time, Doctor XT stood him up just like before. But this time, it was at the very end of the platform, just above the vat of X-Termination Acid.

Doctor XT tried using his right hand to give the Green Phantasm a slight push. At the same time, he said to the Phantasm, "It's all over for you now. It's time to die, time to be 'X-terminated'! Now let's go."

Somehow, that soft push did not move the Green Phantasm too far at all. Fortunately, the Green Phantasm suddenly got out of his dizzy spell and could sense things clearly once again. So then, Doctor XT tried again to push the Phantasm backward into the acid. But the Green Phantasm used his left hand to push XT's right hand aside. Then immediately, he used both hands to shove Doctor XT backward several feet. Now, Doctor XT was in a state of shock, for he had thought he was in full control. So being shoved like this was most unexpected. It now appeared as if the Green Phantasm was back in control of the situation. But unfortunately, it was not for very long.

Although the Phantasm had just made quite a comeback, he overlooked one thing. Although he could sense everything clearly, he did not manage to notice how close he was to the platform's end. The Green Phantasm tried getting into his stance as a boxer, in order to prepare to continue fighting Doctor XT. Whenever he placed his right foot to his rear, the ball of his foot was at the edge of the platform's end. Within a few seconds, his right foot slipped backward over the edge, causing him to fall back. But luckily, he managed to catch the vertical end of the railing to his right with his right hand. Then, he also placed his left forearm onto the platform's end to help prevent himself from falling into the acid vat.

"Oh no, not again!" cried a very worried Amanda Taylor, who wanted her hero to win the fight and hated to see him in that predicament.

Doctor XT, however, was happy to see things go wrong for the Green Phantasm. So the crazed villain went from being afraid to being proud, for he once again had the advantage. "Hmm, hmm, hmm, hmm," he chuckled. "What a moron, he didn't see that? Heh, heh, now I've got him."

So then, the Green Phantasm tried to lift himself back up onto the platform. But unfortunately, he did not make it very far, for Doctor XT ran over and kicked him in the face. This dazed him for a couple of seconds, so that he fell closer to the X-Termination Acid. The Green Phantasm was now hanging from the platform's end with his left hand holding on to the edge and his right hand holding the lowest part of the railing on his right. At this point, he was afraid for his life, but still refused to give up hope, for he knew that he somehow or another had a way out of that predicament.

Doctor XT was becoming more frustrated. After all, he was so eager to put an end to the Green Phantasm, and this battle was still not over. So then, out of anger, frustration, and anxiety, Doctor XT drove his left heel into the knuckles of the Phantasm's right hand. "Yeouch!" yelled the Green Phantasm. However, he still managed to hang on out of determination.

"Ah, dang it!" exclaimed Doctor XT. Then at that, he once again placed his left heel against the Green Phantasm's knuckles. But this time, he mashed harder and longer, even rotating his heel from left to right repeatedly. This no doubt added more pain to what the Phantasm had already sustained from the first time.

"Ow, ow, ow, ow!" the Green Phantasm shouted repeatedly. The pain in his right knuckles was becoming unbearable, especially since his right hand was the one without a glove. So at once, he placed his left hand on the railing at his right. Then, he removed his right hand from the railing and started shaking off the pain. Unfortunately though, his right knuckles not only hurt but were now bleeding. "Oh no," he muttered. "I'll take out this cheapskate, if it's the last thing I do!"

Right after that, the Green Phantasm placed both hands onto the railing to his right. From that point, he made yet another attempt to lift himself up onto the platform. But before his head even rose above the platform's floor, he found he could not rise any farther because Doctor XT had put his right foot on top of the Phantasm's head to stop him. "Where do you think you're going?" Doctor XT asked tauntingly.

The Green Phantasm snapped, "Where's it look like I'm going?" Upon hearing that, Doctor XT became angrier and stomped the Green Phantasm's crown. This only made the Phantasm fall back down below the platform. However, he still maintained his grip on the railing and did not plunge into the acid.

"The neon freak is getting on my last nerve!" muttered the infuriated Doctor XT. Then at once, he drove his right heel into the Green Phantasm's right-hand knuckles, which of course were already hurting.

"Ow! Dang it, you freakin' idiot!" shouted the angry Green Phantasm. Once again, he removed his right hand from the railing and tried to shake off the pain.

At the same time, Doctor XT began using his left heel to try to inflict pain on the Phantasm's left-hand knuckles as well. Although he kept mashing and rotating his heel against those knuckles, the Green Phantasm was more able to endure that, for he still had a leather glove on that hand.

Eventually, however, even his left knuckles were beginning to hurt too much for him to keep holding on. So then, he once again grabbed hold with his right hand and started shaking his left hand to try to relieve the pain.

Doctor XT once again drove his left heel into those vulnerable, sore, bleeding knuckles. The Green Phantasm was still trying to shake the pain out of his left hand. The pain sustained itself this time in his right knuckles and was only worse than previously. However, he still managed to hang on out of desperation and determination. This time around though, the Green Phantasm became slightly dazed and yelled out even louder than before, "Ow, ow, ow, ow, owwww!" So right away, he grabbed onto the railing with his left hand and removed his right. He not only shook his right fingers and knuckles, but even gently bit down on them this time.

Next, Doctor XT again mashed his left heel into the Green Phantasm's left hand. This time, the Green Phantasm looked up toward XT and told him, "I dare you to try that again. This time, I'm ready for ya."

"Oh, you are?" asked Doctor XT, chuckling and shaking his head in disbelief.

"You bet I am," responded the Green Phantasm. "Just bring it on and see what happens if you don't believe me."

"Well, well, well," said Doctor XT. "You're really asking for it, aren't you? I'll be happy to oblige." So, that very instant, Doctor XT made yet one further attempt to smash the Green Phantasm's left knuckles with his left heel. But before he could connect, something greatly unexpected took place.

By the time XT managed to land his left heel, the Green Phantasm quickly used his right hand to grab onto the pole above where his left hand was holding and at once removed his left hand. As soon as he removed his left hand, the left foot of Doctor XT hit the steel vertical end of the railing. This made XT slightly shocked and dazed, for the steel railing was much harder and stronger than the Green Phantasm's hand. "Whoa, what happened?" asked a surprised Doctor XT.

Before the crazed villain could fully retract his left leg, the Green Phantasm all of a sudden grabbed hold of it. He was now using his left hand to firmly hold the bottom of XT's left leg, just above his ankle. At that, Doctor XT regained his senses and exclaimed, "Hey, what's going on? What's holding my—what?" XT was now looking down to see the Green Phantasm's left hand holding the leg, while the other hand was holding the railing. Doctor XT cried out, "Why you—whoa, no!"

This was because the Green Phantasm tried to sling him by his left leg down toward the X-Termination Acid. Consequently, Doctor XT began to fall forward into the acid vat. But before going over the edge of the platform, he was able to use his right hand to reach over and catch hold of the other railing. Then, instead of plunging into the acid, he swung himself toward the railing on the south side of the platform. Right after that, he caught it with his left hand and was now holding on with both hands while dangling above the X-Termination Acid.

At the same time, the Green Phantasm's right hand nearly slipped off the bottom of the railing onto which he was hanging. But fortunately, he managed to catch hold of it with his left hand to keep himself from falling.

In the meantime, Amanda was cheering for the move he had just made. "Way to go, Green Phantasm!" she shouted to him.

However, Doctor XT was much angrier because of the trick that the Green Phantasm had pulled on him. In fact, he had now lost all of his patience and decided he had had enough. "Aw, dang it!" he yelled, "Why, that—" Before he finished, he quickly pulled himself back up onto the platform.

At the same time, the Green Phantasm was trying to climb up onto the platform and had now placed his left leg on the platform but did not make it any farther. That was because a most infuriated Doctor XT used his right foot to deliver a big side kick to the left of the Phantasm's face. This knocked the valiant hero back toward the X-Termination Acid. The Green Phantasm was once again hanging from the lowest part of the railing by both of his hands. "Oh no, you don't!" Doctor XT angrily shouted at the Phantasm. "You stubborn, ignorant son of the devil! I've had it with you! I'm about to put an end to this right now!"

So then, Doctor XT began running toward his office. When he was almost there, he glanced toward his belongings in the gas chamber for a couple of seconds and quickly said to himself, "Well, I know I said I wouldn't use any of those things. I know what I'll do." Then, he finally darted on into his office.

Upon hearing Doctor XT say those things, Amanda, who was right next to the office, suspected that XT was up to something. She thought to herself, *Oh no, he's about to do something unfair to destroy the Green Phantasm. I gotta try to warn him or something.* So she called to her hero, "Green Phantasm, can you hear me?"

In the meantime, the Green Phantasm had been making yet another attempt to climb back onto the platform. He answered Amanda, saying, "Yeah, I hear you; what is it, Amanda?"

"Listen," she told him. "Just use your powers from here on, okay? This whole thing's just a trick."

At that, Doctor XT began sprinting back toward the Green Phantasm with something in his right hand. It was a steel test tube that contained X-Termination Acid. But at the present, it was sealed off at the top by a cork.

But in response to the advice of Amanda, the Green Phantasm said to her, "I gave him my word. I'm supposed to hold up my part of the deal, whether the other guy does or not." As soon as he had finished saying that, he finally made it back up onto the platform. The Green Phantasm was now down on his hands and knees at the end of the platform and facing the control room.

Unfortunately, the Green Phantasm did not have a chance to get up onto his feet, or maneuver anywhere. In the instant that he looked up, the first thing he saw was Doctor XT standing before him. In a threatening manner, Doctor XT said to the Green Phantasm, "Going somewhere? I think not! In fact, I'm going to end it all for you right here, right now."

The Phantasm was at first a bit puzzled at hearing XT say that, for he did not know how XT was about to just end it all. But then, all of a sudden, he became frightened when Doctor XT held up the test tube above him. Next, Doctor XT used his left hand to take off the cork, in order to prepare to pour the X-Termination Acid out onto the Phantasm.

In a situation such as this one, the Green Phantasm would normally have fired a laser beam to knock the test tube out of XT's hand. But the pyxorium within James Clifton was presently deactivated because of his promise not to use any super powers as the Green Phantasm. However, he did manage to pull off a different strategy.

Out of desperation, the Green Phantasm suddenly made a vertical leap, during and used his left hand to knock the test tube out of Doctor XT's right hand. As a result, the test tube of acid went flying to the left of the Phantasm and landed in the big vat of X-Termination Acid.

This move, however, proved to be more dangerous than using his supernatural abilities would have been because whenever the Green Phantasm knocked away the tube of acid, a small surge came out through the mouth of the test tube and splattered. One small drop contacted and completely consumed the green leather glove of the Green Phantasm's left hand. This no doubt gave the Phantasm quite a scare. "Oh my God!" he cried. Then, he gasped and told himself, "That could've been my hand."

So now, both Doctor XT and the Green Phantasm were really angry at each other. On the part of the Green Phantasm, it was because Doctor XT had just attempted something unfair, and both gloves were now gone. On the other hand, Doctor XT was even angrier now, because he had expected to end this battle quickly and suddenly; yet, another game plan against the Green Phantasm had proved to be a failure.

For a few seconds, Doctor XT was looking to his right after the test tube had been knocked into the huge vat of acid. Fortunately for the Green Phantasm, this would provide the break he needed. Doctor XT began turning his attention back over to the Phantasm. But before he could fully refocus, the Green Phantasm landed a right hook to the back of his left thigh. This surprised Doctor XT and caused him to stumble backward, so that he almost fell back.

Then immediately, the Green Phantasm followed up with a right hook to the back of Doctor XT's left knee. This made XT fall to his left. But at once, he caught and held on to the top of the railing to his left, so that he did not completely collapse onto the platform's floor.

The Green Phantasm was still determined to regain control and win this fight. So, that very minute, he threw a big left jab to the genital area of Doctor XT. This made XT lose his grip on the railing and fall all the way to the floor. Of course, this was because he was now hurting below the belt.

Still angry about everything the villainous doctor had done, the Green Phantasm proceeded to the next step. First, he finally got back up onto his feet again. Then, while Doctor XT was still holding on to his hurting genitals, the Green Phantasm used his right foot to place XT faceup. Then right away, he knelt down above the doctor to pin him down, like he had before they had begun their fight.

The Green Phantasm put his left hand on Doctor XT's throat to choke him. At the same time, he used his other hand to point in a threatening manner. "All right, Doctor," yelled the Green Phantasm, "you've really made me mad this time! What do you have to say for yourself, huh?"

After that, the Green Phantasm delivered a right crossover to his left cheek, saying, "Well, come on! Answer me, you crazed wacko! Answer me!"

As a result, XT went from being dazed to being angry. He was now looking at the Green Phantasm with a snarl. "Don't give me that stupid look, you psychopath!" the Green Phantasm told him, after which the Phantasm hit XT with a right jab in the center of his forehead. Doctor XT was even more dazed from that punch.

Then, before throwing any further punches, the Green Phantasm said to Doctor XT, "Listen to me, Doctor, I just want to uncuff Amanda, so I can get her out of here. Can I have the keys to unlock the cuffs?"

But the stubborn doctor just responded, "No way, I ain't giving those keys to you, you neon-green moron, never!" In addition, Doctor XT just scoffed at the Phantasm.

In reaction to that, the Green Phantasm just squeezed harder with his left hand. At the same time, he yelled, "You better give 'em to me! Come on! Hand 'em over!" Then at once, he delivered a right hook to Doctor XT's temple. "Did you hear what I said?" the Green Phantasm continued yelling. "I said hand over those doggone keys!" At that, he began to throw another punch.

All of a sudden, he restrained himself, when he heard Doctor XT beg and plead, "All right, all right, all right, hold it! Wait a minute; wait just a minute." So Green Phantasm stopped to listen.

"Uh, look," Doctor XT began saying. "You got me, all right? You got me; I give up."

"You do?" asked the Green Phantasm. "Do you really mean what you're saying this time? When you told me a little earlier that you couldn't take anymore, you tricked me. Are you really serious this time? I mean, how serious are you?"

"Yes, yes, of course, of course," answered Doctor XT. "This time, I truly and sincerely do give up. I honestly admit that you win. You have now made a believer out of me. I am fully convinced that everything you tried to tell me is true. So, if you like, you can become the Green Phantasm again."

"Well, good," replied the Green Phantasm. At that, he switched his radiation back on and was once again radiating bright-neon green light. Then, he got back up onto his feet. He then addressed Doctor XT, saying, "Come on, tough guy, get up." So then, Doctor XT stood up as well.

"Well anyway, Green Phantasm," Doctor XT addressed him. "At least now, I can no longer argue with anything you've said to me tonight. For one thing, you really are fair and just after all, and you really do care like you said you do. Other than that, with or without your super powers, you're a better man than me. I also can't argue with the way you held up your part of the deal, can I? Even showing that all that didn't even take super power, did it? Man, you were right about everything."

"Very good, Doctor," replied the Green Phantasm. "But now, what about your part of the deal? What about Amanda?"

"Of course," answered Doctor XT. "I guess a deal's a deal. I'll let you have the keys to set Amanda free. I'll even do whatever else I have to do too. But first, do you mind if I tell you a little bit about myself?"

Then, somewhat doubtfully, the Green Phantasm told Doctor XT, "Well, I don't know, but, all right, go ahead." At that, the Green Phantasm listened with interest.

"All right," began Doctor XT. "Now you see, as you already know, I call myself Doctor XT. XT understandably stands for X-Termination. I'm undoubtedly the one who started X-Termination. Even now, I own, run, and fund the organization, and that's why I call myself that. But you see, my real name is John Perry Perone."

"John Perry Perone, huh?" said the Green Phantasm. "Interesting."

"You see, Green Phantasm," continued Doctor XT. "I'll even tell you why we're called X-Termination. It's like this: Of course, to exterminate means to destroy completely. That is exactly what we will do to anyone or anything that gets in the way of what we want."

"And what do you want?"

"What do we want, you say?" asked Doctor XT. "Well, I simply want for each and every one of us to live the kind of lifestyle we so desire. We just need a lot of money as well as other things to be able to do it. Of course, a lot of people either won't give it to us, or might try to stop us. So we 'X-terminate' them. By 'X-terminate,' I mean to kill or destroy someone or something by our means. Another thing too is, I'm the XTE of X-Termination. That means X-Termination engineer. You see, every single thing you see here, or in our possession, was designed and engineered by me."

"Well," replied the Green Phantasm, "I really don't know what to say, except one thing. I understand wanting the kind of lifestyle you all desire, but about the ones you 'X-terminate,' what about their lives? I mean, have you ever thought about that?"

"Well," Doctor XT said hesitantly. "I guess not."

"I thought not," the Green Phantasm replied, "but does it really seem right to be so selfish and to hurt others in order to get what you want? Besides, what do you think is gonna come at the end of it all?"

"You know," responded Doctor XT. "I got to admit, sometimes there is a little something that doesn't seem right about it. I guess another thing I should tell you is, I graduated high school at age ten, and then I got my first PhD at age seventeen. Of course, I've always wanted every great thing I saw ever since I was a little boy. I guess you could say I was really well educated before I learned better how to control my covetousness. So then, I used the knowledge I had gained to try to obtain everything I wanted. Then, before I knew it, I started X-Termination and eventually influenced others to go along with me and help me. Even as intelligent and inventive as I became, I never really gave much thought at all to the aftermath."

"Well," said the Green Phantasm. "Like I was saying earlier, there's no real future in this. I think you really need to discontinue this business, erase every bad deed you've done, and start a better life than this."

"I guess you're right." Doctor XT sighed.

"Anyway, Doctor," said the Green Phantasm. "Now that you've been considerate enough to share all that with me, I think I'll do a little something in return."

"Oh, really?"

"Uh, yeah," answered the Green Phantasm, "so, uh, let's… come into the control room, so both you and Amanda can hear this." At that, they both walked into the control room. Doctor XT went first and then stood on the other side, across from the Green Phantasm. The Green Phantasm just stopped and stood by the platform. Doctor XT and Amanda turned their attention to him.

The Green Phantasm began by saying, "Look, you two, I'm about to tell y'all something I've never told anybody before. So listen up, all right? This may come as a shock to at least one of you. I'm fixing to, um, show you as well as tell you. So just, uh… watch and listen."

James Clifton switched off his radiation for a moment. While he was deactivated, he went on to remove his mask. Once his mask was removed, a surprised look appeared on Amanda's face, for the identity of the Green Phantasm was now revealed. Doctor XT just looked puzzled and shook his head in confusion, for he did not understand what the Green Phantasm was doing, or why.

James went on to tell both XT and Amanda, "So anyway, um, you two, of course, I may not need so much to tell you this, Amanda. But anyway, Doctor, my name is… Clifton, James Paul Clifton. I am the chief engineer at Ace Nuclear Supply."

"Well, well," replied Doctor XT, "that's very, very interesting, uh, James, uh, Clifton."

"Thank you," Clifton told him. "And let me tell you more about myself. As I was telling you before, I was never looking to obtain these powers I have. It just happened to me by accident; it was completely unintentional. Last weekend, I went on a camping trip with two of my friends. Late, late Friday night, a meteorite struck. Little bits and pieces came off and scattered a little. One of them landed in a nearby cave and combined with a piece of quartz. I decided to call that meteorite material pyxorium."

"Pyxorium?" Doctor XT asked with interest. "Some powerful material. I'd like to get my hands on some and see what I could create with it."

"But there's more," continued James Clifton. "You see, Doctor, Sunday evening, I brought home that green piece of quartz. Then later, I thought I'd lost it, when it actually landed in a glass of water and dissolved. Then, I drank the water, not knowing it was in there. So you see what I'm saying? It was unintentional, but it happened."

"I see."

"Otherwise," added Clifton, "I've always had the desire to do what's right. That's how I intend to use my powers. I want to do everything I can to make Philadelphia as safe as possible. That's why I became the Green Phantasm. Of course, it requires breaking up the works of those who make the city unsafe. Other than that, you know, I didn't kill any of your men, other than D.D.T., whom I was defending myself against. That is because I only want to stop killers, not become one myself, okay?"

"Okay."

"And just one other thing," James Clifton continued.

"What is it?"

"Another thing I've noticed is that you keep this kind of life secret from others. I mean, you did tell me to keep to myself about coming here. Now, doesn't it ever get frustrating to not be able to tell anyone else any of your secrets? I mean, what do you think about that?"

"Well," responded Doctor XT. "I got to admit that it does create tension. It makes me feel the need to 'X-terminate' those who put my business in jeopardy. Other than that, I don't always enjoy having to hide away from the public."

"So, I guess there's no really happy future in what you're doing, is there?"

"Absolutely not."

"All right then," replied James Clifton. Then at once, he switched his radiant energy back on. Then, he put his mask back on his face. Finally, he teleported over to where Amanda was handcuffed to reclaim his hat.

After that, the Green Phantasm said, "All right, Doctor XT, I'm ready to set this young lady free. Can I please have the keys?" So then, the

Phantasm started walking back toward Doctor XT, as the doctor reached into his left front pocket to get out the handcuff keys.

"All right, let's have the keys please," the Phantasm told him. But then, while Doctor XT was trying to hand over the keys, the Green Phantasm had one other thought. He said to XT, "There's just one other thing I was thinking too."

"What's that?"

Then, while pointing toward the gas chamber, the Green Phantasm told the doctor, "You know, since you're now going to turn over a new leaf, I guess you won't be needing that stuff in the gas chamber anymore."

"Well…" replied Doctor XT, after which he paused and looked around for several seconds.

But then, XT finally took a look at the things he had set in the gas chamber, followed by a look toward the X-Termination Acid vat. He quickly developed an idea. "You know what?" he addressed the Green Phantasm, "You're right, I guess I won't be. I tell you what: I'll go uncuff Amanda, and you can go toss those things into the acid."

"Okay," the Green Phantasm answered anxiously. At that, the Phantasm went over to the gas chamber to get the objects that Doctor XT had set inside. At the same time, Doctor XT was on his way to unlock the handcuffs by which Amanda was bound. While he was doing that, he occasionally checked to make sure that the Green Phantasm was doing what he wanted.

Shortly afterward, the Green Phantasm was on his way to the acid vat with Doctor XT's things. In the meantime, Doctor XT had now set Amanda free. He then led her to the other end of the control room, where the gas chamber was.

Meanwhile, the Green Phantasm had now made it to the end of the platform above the X-Termination Acid vat. "Well," he said to himself, "I guess this is the end of X-Termination." At that, he dropped Doctor XT's coat and other belongings into the X-Termination Acid. Then, he watched it all get turned to vapor before his very eyes. "Well, I guess that's that," he said in conclusion. Right after that, he began to turn around to head back toward the control room.

All of a sudden, before the Green Phantasm had turned all the way around, Doctor XT pulled something out from under the wrap on his left wrist. It was a miniature X-Termination Gas bomb. It looked like the ones he normally used when necessary but was only one half of an inch in diameter. As soon as the Green Phantasm was turned back around and headed back toward the control room, the tiny gas bomb was already being hurled toward him.

The gas bomb landed on the platform, about two feet before the Green Phantasm. At once, it began discharging an expanding cloud of light-purple X-Termination Gas. "Oh my God!" exclaimed the surprised Green Phantasm. "What'll I do?" In a state of panic, the Green Phantasm started walking backward toward the end of the platform. Then, he started to step back into the acid vat; the toes of his right foot were still on the edge. At that, he began to fall backward. "Oh no, help!" he cried.

But luckily, within a split second, the Green Phantasm had an idea. He quickly teleported to save himself from falling. He then reappeared nearly eighty feet away from the end of the platform, above the X-Termination Acid. Immediately upon reappearing, he activated his hovering ability to float above the acid vat. The Green Phantasm remained that way momentarily while plotting his next maneuver.

At the same time, Doctor XT was leading Amanda through the gas chamber. She scolded him, saying, "Why, you psychomaniac, how could you do that? You said you'd turn your life around!"

"You weren't listening earlier," Doctor XT told her. "I only said if necessary, and if I have to. But as it happens, I don't have to. But anyway, I got big plans for us. I'm even gonna start things over."

In the meantime, the Green Phantasm noticed Doctor XT and Amanda running through the gas chamber. How understandably angry he now must have been! He had just been convinced that he had won and that Perone was going to discontinue X-Termination. Yet, after all the wasted time and effort on his part, John Perone, Doctor XT, pulled off another stunt that gave the Phantasm a close encounter with suffocation. "Why, that two-faced, double-dealing, double-crossing, dimwitted son of the devil!" fumed the angry Green Phantasm.

Then at once, the Green Phantasm teleported over to the balcony on the south side of the gas chamber. He reappeared before Doctor XT and Amanda Taylor, who both stopped with surprise. "Aha!" said the Green

Phantasm to XT. "I should've known I couldn't trust you. Somehow or another, I knew it was too good to be true."

"Oh really, is that so?" asked Doctor XT in disbelief.

Right away, the Green Phantasm took the form of a shapeless projectile and knocked Doctor XT toward the control room. He then reappeared as himself, standing at the feet of Perone, who was now lying on his back.

First, the Green Phantasm briefly spoke to Amanda, telling her, "Go on down that balcony as far as you can. I'll be right there to get us out of here." At that, Amanda complied and ran to the end of the balcony that was at the top of the stairs leading to it.

Next, the Phantasm pointed at Doctor XT with his right index finger. "And as for you, you stay away from her!" the Green Phantasm told him firmly, "Don't ever let me catch you near her again! I'm getting her outta here, and after that, I'm making sure you go to jail."

"Oh yeah?" asked Doctor XT. "Well, we'll see about that." At that, he got back up onto his feet and went up to the Green Phantasm to try to fight him again. Doctor XT then tried throwing a big straight right. But the Green Phantasm sidestepped it and delivered a right uppercut to his abdomen. XT was now bent over, holding his abdomen with his left hand.

Right after that, the Green Phantasm turned around and began running toward Amanda. But somehow, Doctor XT quickly recovered from being punched and ran up behind the Green Phantasm. XT used both hands to grab hold of the Green Phantasm's left arm. This stopped the advancement of the Green Phantasm and surprised him. "Whoa!" said the shocked Green Phantasm, as he was being pulled backward.

Immediately, Doctor XT began to sling the Green Phantasm by his left arm toward the control room. It just so happened that a continuously expanding mass of X-Termination Gas was now in the control room. "In you go, freak!" said Doctor XT to the Green Phantasm, while slinging him.

All of a sudden, the Green Phantasm once again managed to turn the tables on Doctor XT. As Doctor XT was letting go of the Green Phantasm, he just reached back toward him with his right hand. That very instant, he caught the doctor's right wrist, onto which he held to stop himself. Immediately after that, the Green Phantasm just whipped Doctor XT into the control room.

Doctor XT was now somewhat shocked and dazed because the Green Phantasm had just caught him by complete surprise and also because he was now seeing purple mist before his eyes. "What happened? Where am I?" the stunned Doctor XT asked himself.

Meanwhile, the Green Phantasm took a look around for a few seconds to see that the X-Termination Gas was expanding and spreading throughout the entire manufacturing area. "Oh my goodness," he said to himself, "that's a lot of gas in that one tiny capsule. I'll be damned."

But then, someone suddenly called out to him. It was Amanda. "James! Green Phantasm!" she yelled, "Help me!" Of course, she too had noticed the expansion of the purple gas.

At once, the Phantasm turned and looked toward her. "Oh shoot!" he muttered to himself. "That's right, I almost forgot. I gotta hurry up and save Amanda." He teleported himself over to her. Upon reappearing, he addressed her, "Oh my God, Amanda."

"Oh, James," Amanda replied. "I'm glad you're here; there's gas everywhere."

"Yeah, I know, I know. Listen, I got a plan."

"You do?" Amanda asked anxiously. "Good, what is it?"

"I'm about to put a force field around us," answered the Green Phantasm. "So please, watch your feet, okay?"

"Okay," Amanda responded. So then, the Green Phantasm began sketching and forming a force field.

But all the while, Doctor XT was progressively losing consciousness. His field of vision was constantly darkening. This was because, although he did not know it, he was being weakened by the X-Termination Gas, even though it was a much thinner surge than usual. Even at the present, he was continuously inhaling more and more. Not knowing where to go or what to do, XT had both arms extended in front of himself, while randomly and continuously changing the direction in which he was walking. "What's happening to me?" he cried in panic. "Where's the door? I gotta get outta here!"

Doctor XT finally managed to find a doorway. But of course, it was by feeling around with his hands. Nevertheless, he was relieved to have found a way out of the control room. "At last, I found a way out!" he exclaimed happily. "I better hurry up and get out of this room." So Doctor XT proceeded on through the doorway.

In the meantime, the Green Phantasm had finished putting up the force field that now enclosed Amanda and himself. He was ascending straight up by means of his hovering ability. Amanda was holding on to the Phantasm with both arms wrapped around him. "Here we go," said the Green Phantasm. "Hang on."

As for Doctor XT, it turned out that the doorway he had gone through from the control room actually led toward the X-Termination Acid vat. Unable to see clearly due to the mist of X-Termination Gas, XT kept progressing slowly along the platform with his right hand on the railing to his right. But finally, he made it to the end of the platform. He could now sense the edge through the sole of his left foot. Unfortunately for him, he was not in his right mind, for he was so desperate to get out from amid the poisonous gas. So then, he told himself, "Good, I found the stairs." At that, he proceeded to step off the platform's end.

Suddenly, Perone realized something. He quickly figured out that what he had just come to could not have been a set of stairs. After all, his right hand had been on a railing, none of which was inside the gas chamber. Therefore, he had obviously not gone through the gas chamber. Besides, in order to get to a staircase, he would have had to turn left, which he had not just done. Other than that, the only path from the control room that had a railing alongside it and came to an end was the platform leading to the X-Termination Acid vat. John Perone suddenly realized all that, and said to himself, "Wait a minute, there's no stairs here!" Then at once, he tried to reach backward with his right hand to catch the railing. However, he had already stepped too far forward toward the X-Termination Acid. Perone kept screaming until he finally landed in the acid. Then at once, the X-Termination Acid sublimed his entire body as well as his clothes into nothing but vapor. So that was the end of both John Perry Perone and Doctor XT, the XTE of X-Termination.

The screaming followed by the splash reached the Green Phantasm, who turned and looked. Next, he noticed a cloud of vapor rising above the purple mist of X-Termination Gas. "Oh my goodness," Clifton sighed while shaking his head in disbelief. Then, he became silent for a moment, and kept gazing over the entire manufacturing area, for he had a guilty conscience over the fate of Doctor XT.

Amanda, who was still inside the force field with him, tried to look to see what was troubling James. But then, still uncertain, she asked him, "What is it, James? What's wrong?"

"Oh, uh," he began to answer. "Nothing much. I just didn't intend for it all to end this way. I just have a guilty feeling about the horrible ending for Doctor Perone. Although it's definitely not what I wanted for him, that's what ends up happening to people like that. But at least we still have each other. So let's get out of here, Amanda." At that, the Phantasm just ascended up and over the top of the steel barrier's front wall. Then at last, he descended diagonally toward the point at which the gravel parking lot met the gravel road that led to it from the highway.

Upon landing, the Phantasm took down the force field. Then, James and Amanda took a moment to look back at X-Termination Headquarters. "Well," said James Clifton, "I guess X-Termination's no longer in business. After all, that so-called XTE, John Perone, Doctor XT, or whoever, is now an 'X-Terminated Engineer.' "

"Yeah, I guess so," replied Amanda. "But what about the other guy?"

"Other guy?"

"Yeah," answered Amanda. "The one called Zapper; the one you took out just before you fought XT."

"Oh yeah, him," responded James. "I'll have to see to him later. Right now, the fumes in that place make it too dangerous. The main thing is, I managed to get you out of there alive."

"Oh yes," Amanda replied softly and sweetly. "Thank you so much, James Clifton." At that, she threw her arms around him for a great big hug.

After that, James said, "Well anyway, I'm wondering what I should do from this point. Of course, I might have to notify the police, which could be the right thing to do. But right now, I gotta get you home. I think it's been a long, rough night for both of us. So therefore, we need to get away from this horrible place, and get to the place we call home. So, come on, let's get back to Philadelphia."

But Amanda restrained him, saying, "Wait a minute, James, excuse me. I kinda wanted to let you know something. You see, whenever XT had told you he was willing to turn his life around, he had a hidden meaning to that. He only said 'if he had to,' and that was exactly what he meant. Because then, even after you'd won, he still didn't think he had to. And do you remember when I shouted to you that it was a trick and that you ought to use your super powers?"

"Listen, Amanda," James told her. "I understand what you're saying. I even sort of figured that there was some kind of catch to it somewhere. It's just that I had to keep my part of the deal, whether he did or not. That's what a real hero does. If I stoop to his level, I'm as bad as he is."

"I guess you're right," replied Amanda. "And I guess that means I can trust you."

"Well," said James. "The good guy is always supposed to be fair and just. But anyway, grab on for a ride home. C'mon, let's go."

So finally, Amanda once again held on to her hero. The Green Phantasm activated his hovering ability and started on his way back toward Philadelphia, to bring Amanda back to her apartment. It was now well after midnight.

Then, after about forty-five minutes of hovering through the air, they finally descended and landed in front of the door to Amanda's apartment. At once, James deactivated his radiation, and she let go and got off him. "Thanks again for everything you've done for me tonight," she told him.

"Oh, no problem," James said in reply. "It's no trouble."

"Look, James," Amanda said to him, "I really need to tell you something. I owe you a really big apology."

"An apology?" asked James Clifton, who took off his hat.

"Yes, an apology," Amanda answered. "You see, I didn't realize until tonight, of course, that you and the Green Phantasm are one and the same. It's great to have you both. Other than that, I now feel differently about what you did at the party the other night."

"Listen, Amanda," James said to her, "about that, I really should've—"

"No, no, please, James," Amanda pleaded, "I have realized that if I had been in your shoes, I'd have done the same thing. At least I'm still alive, thanks to that. I just never looked at it that way. How I could've been so foolish, I don't know."

"Oh well," said James, "no need to worry about it now. You just didn't know um…"

"And another thing," Amanda continued. "When you came around town looking for me and you found me, that made me think the worst about you. I couldn't have been more wrong."

"Well, I guess there's another thing I should mention too," added James. "You remember last night, Friday that is, when I found you and was about to tell you something when a taxi pulled up?"

"Mm-hmm," Amanda answered while nodding.

"You see," James continued. "I was about to tell you what you found out tonight, that I'm the Green Phantasm. That's what I was gonna tell you."

"Oh, I see," replied Amanda. "And I also understand that when you were trying to track me down, it was obviously very important. I was just too much of a stuck-up snob to listen; shame on me."

"No, don't say that."

"You know something else?" asked Amanda, "The other night, after you'd fought off all those planes and I'd come to your aid, I knew there was something familiar about you when we spent a little time together. Of course, that and everything else all make sense now."

"Well," said James, "at least we're clear on everything. I guess we both need to get inside right now and get some rest."

"Well, all right," replied Amanda. "But look, if there was anything I could do to show thanks or repay you, I'd—"

"I got an idea," James told Amanda. "What do you say we have breakfast tomorrow morning?"

"Sounds great," Amanda responded. "I'll be more than happy to."

"Okay," said James. "Why don't I pick you up about nine thirty?"

"That's fine," answered Amanda. "I'll be ready then."

"Great, thanks," James replied. "Well, anyway, I guess I'd better be going, so why don't we say good night?"

"Okay," Amanda whispered. Then, James and Amanda gave each other one more hug, which this time they held on to for a couple of minutes. During that sustained hug, Amanda said to James in a soft voice, "Thanks again for everything you've done for me. I feel like I owe you my life."

"Well," said James. "I don't need you to give me that." At that, they both chuckled.

James and Amanda finally let go of each other. Then, they followed up with a good-night kiss. "Oh well," Clifton said to his girlfriend. "I guess that's it. I'm gonna shove off for home now. So good night, Amanda."

"Good night, James," she said in return. At that, she went inside and closed her door.

As for James Clifton, he put his Green Phantasm hat back on. Right after that, he once again activated the radiant energy within himself and was now radiating neon-green light again. Then, of course, he continued teleporting and projecting himself, until he finally ended up in his bedroom.

At last, James switched off his powers and radiation for the night. After that, he took off his Green Phantasm outfit, which of course, no longer included his gloves, thanks to both Doctor XT and himself. He went into his bathroom, where he set his suit on the seat of his toilet. He took a shower to try to wash away all the blood, sweat, and germs and become clean.

After all that, James Clifton finally hit the sack for the night. That was the end of the final showdown.

CHAPTER TWELVE
The Conclusion

It was now 8:30 a.m. on Sunday morning, and James Clifton was waking up. At once, he began reminiscing about the previous night. How could he not? After all, he had just been through the most intense, exciting, dangerous, and frightful night of his life. It was also no doubt one of the most memorable. Besides, he was not fully awake yet. So it was no wonder that he was still thinking a lot about his final battle with X-Termination.

James said to himself, "Oh man, what a night! I've never had a night like that before in my whole life. I've had some wonderful, exciting evenings before, but they all lacked the intensity of this one. And of all my nights as the Green Phantasm, that one took the cake. There have never been so many times I've nearly gotten killed. I mean like, whenever D.D.T. nearly made me plunge into the acid, I barely caught on in time to prevent it. After that, XT, Zapper, and Zinger almost shot me when they had me at gunpoint. Then, there was the gas chamber, where I somehow survived the fumes of the X-Termination Gas. And later, Doctor XT almost made me fall into the acid vat, after which he could've killed me by pouring a little bit on me." At that, he became silent for a couple of moments.

After those moments of silence, James sat up, turned to his left, and placed both feet on the floor. He was still feeling drowsy. So Clifton hung his head forward and said in a tired voice, "Man, man, man, I know I don't drink, and I didn't last night, but this sure feels like a hangover." Right after saying that, Clifton remained sitting upright, but dozed for the next five minutes.

James all of a sudden awakened with a more positive outlook. "But anyway," he said happily, "I may have thought last night was the worst night of my life. However, the pride it made me have in myself came close to making up for that. I think I put X-Termination out of business, which will hopefully make things safer for Philadelphia. Also, at least I managed to save Amanda, although I still feel terrible about what all she had to go through. But, I think I have straightened out all the problems between her and me. At least I hope so." He took a couple of moments of silence, looking all around with a smile on his face.

All of a sudden, while looking all around his room, James noticed what time it now was. It was now 8:43 a.m. "Oh my gosh," a somewhat tense James Clifton said, "you know what? Speaking of Amanda, I'm supposed to meet her at 9:30, aren't I? Yes, I think I am. I'd better get ready."

So then, James went over to the sink to wash his face. After that, he got himself dressed. Then finally, he momentarily took one last look at himself in the mirror and told himself, "I am ready."

He went to exit his room to head downstairs. But suddenly, before getting through his bedroom door, he heard his cell phone ringing. He stopped to answer it. "Hello?" said James into his phone.

The one calling was his very close friend, Eric Thomas. "Good morning, James," said Eric. "How ya' doin' there, buddy? What's goin' on?"

"Oh, hey, Eric," James responded, "what's happening? I just got up not too long ago. What are you up to this morning?"

"Well," answered Eric. "I called you because you're my best friend, and I was rather concerned. No offense, but you just kind of haven't been exactly yourself this weekend. But then, of course, I know you told me and Scott that you had a problem, and that Amanda was in trouble. So I was just sort of wondering, is everything all right? I mean, how's Amanda now? She okay?"

"Oh yes, of course, of course," James responded rather affirmatively. "She is now. Thank you for asking, and thank you for calling. But, um, anyway, I still might just let you know, those guys, X-Termination, who crashed the party the other night, they were after her. Last night, they captured her and took her away to their headquarters. Then, I had to... well, I had to get the Green Phantasm to go and get her out of that place. But now, Amanda is safe at home, and I believe X-Termination is out of business."

"Well, that's good to know," Eric said. "I am glad."

"Thank you, Eric."

"Anytime."

"But anyway, Eric," James said, "due to what Amanda and I have just been through, we're about to go have breakfast this morning."

"Oh, all right," said Eric. "No problem, then. I guess I'll let you go so y'all can enjoy."

"Thanks, Eric," James told his friend, "and thank you again for calling me. So, I'll tell you what, maybe I'll give you and Scott a call later. If you see him or talk to him, could you please let him know that you've talked to me and everything's all right?"

"Will do."

"All right," said James. "Well, thanks again for everything, Eric. But I gotta get going now to go get Amanda. So I'll talk to you later, all right?"

"All right," responded Eric. "Bye, James. You be careful."

"Okay, Eric," James said in reply. "Bye." At that, they both hung up. Then, of course, James started on his way to pick up Amanda. It was now approaching 9:00 a.m.

In the meantime, Amanda was now ready and waiting for James Clifton to meet her at her apartment. She was sitting in a chair in her living room. While she was waiting, she too unexpectedly received a call on her cell phone. She answered, "Hello?"

The caller happened to be Dr. Mark Thompson. "Hi, Amanda," he addressed her. "It's Mark Thompson."

"Well, hi, Mark," Amanda said in reply. "Whatcha doing?"

"Well, Amanda," he answered, "I hope you're all right. Where are you right now?"

Amanda could sense that he was worried. So she told him very kindly, "Doctor Thompson, please, I'm sitting at home in my living room. It's okay; calm down."

"All right, if you say so," he responded. "I just couldn't help thinking about the last I remember of you. I mean, last night—"

"It's okay," Amanda told him. "I completely understand."

"Okay, never mind then," he replied.

"But anyway, uh, Mark?"

"Yes, Amanda?"

"So, how are you feeling right now?" Amanda asked him. "Are you okay?"

"Well," he answered, "I'm glad you asked. I, uh, went to the hospital last night. But the doctors said I'll be fine. Of course, I came to be in quite a state of shock, you know, whenever the big man knocked me unconscious. On top of that, I was under stress about what could've happened to you. But eventually, your ex, James Clifton, came to my aid. He got me some help. I'll tell you this too. He seemed just as worried about you as I was, if not more. He even said he'd have to fetch the Green Phantasm, which was your only hope. Certainly, if that was the case, I was hoping he'd find you and rescue you. But now, it seems evident that he did, and it's just good to know you're safe. Of course, I'm at home too and still recovering. But the main thing is that you're alive and well. It's you I was worried about most of all."

"Well, listen, Mark," Amanda said to him, "that's really sweet of you to say. Other than that, I appreciate everything you've done for me. But there's something I should really tell you."

"There is?" he asked. "Well, then, I guess, by all means, tell me; go ahead."

"Well, all right," Amanda replied. "Now, you see, Mark, even as much as you really care and as kind as you've been, I'm afraid we can't get together anymore."

"Really?"

"Well," continued Amanda. "It's just that I found out the truth about James Clifton."

"You did!"

"You see," said Amanda. "I was wrong about him. After the banquet the other night, I had thought that he was a jerk. But whenever you suggested that he had to possibly find the Green Phantasm, you were right. I've even realized that if I had been him, I'd have done the same thing. After all, a lot of lives depended on that. Right now, you and I are still alive thanks to that. I think we have both James and the Phantasm to thank for that."

"Well, I guess you're right," he told her. "And I guess you know best what you ought to do."

"Yeah," said Amanda in agreement. "I'm sorry to disappoint you. I can tell that both you and James care. I just have more in common with him. I also feel a different connection with him. Then now, I finally realize that it's him I belong with."

"I understand," Mark calmly replied. "I guess you gotta do what you gotta do. I mean, I know you were seeing him before me. But anyway, I still care about you the same, and it's still okay to give me a call anytime you need something."

"Thank you so much for everything," Amanda replied, "and I appreciate you calling. But I guess I better get going, because James is meeting me for breakfast this morning."

"Well, that sounds great," said Mark. "Hopefully, we'll talk again some other time."

"Okay."

"Well, take care of yourself, all right?" he told her.

"You too."

"All right, bye, Amanda," he said at last.

"Bye," Amanda said in return. At that, they both hung up.

After that, Amanda continued waiting for James Clifton to arrive.

Then finally, at 9:25 a.m., he pulled into a parking space in front of Amanda Taylor's apartment. He got out and walked up the steps to her front door. Finally, Clifton gently knocked on the door.

Amanda did not even hesitate to go right up and open her door. "Hi," she addressed him sweetly with a smile.

"Hello, Amanda," James said in return. "Good morning."

"Good morning," she said in response, while slightly chuckling. They gave each other a hug followed by a kiss.

"So, Amanda," said James. "How are you feeling this morning?"

"Well, James," Amanda began, "I can honestly, sincerely tell you that I've never felt so wonderful in my life. At least now, we're no longer in danger from X-Termination. On top of that, I have the greatest guy I've ever met standing before me."

"Why, thank you, Amanda!" James exclaimed happily.

"So, James," Amanda said to him. "How about you? How are you feeling this morning?"

"Well anyway, Amanda," he responded, "I can't remember a time that I was ever as happy as I am now. I mean, for one thing, I'm real happy to be here right now. After all, with you here, how could I not be? Of course, I'm also happy that you're still alive and well, and that you're this happy and cheerful after, you know, after what all I've put you through." At that, he started to look away with a rather unhappy expression on his face.

Then, becoming concerned, Amanda sympathetically took hold of his left hand and said to him, "Oh, James, what do you mean by that? What's the matter?"

But then, James turned back toward her, took hold of her left hand with his right, and said to her gently, "Excuse me, Amanda?"

"Uh-huh?" she replied very pleasantly.

"Uh, may I please step inside for a moment?" James asked her slowly and politely.

"Sure," she answered him. James followed her inside, closing the door behind himself. Amanda went over to sit on her couch and pointed to her immediate left, telling James, "Come sit right here."

At that, he went and sat down at her left-hand side. They held each other's hands like they had done at the door. Then, while they were looking into each other's eyes, Amanda said softly, "So, James."

"Yes, Amanda?" he replied.

"Is there something troubling you?" she asked. "I mean, what's wrong?"

"Well," said James. "It's really nothing that you're not already aware of. Now of course, I still feel lucky to have you in my life, and I'm still happy to be here this morning and to go have breakfast with you this morning. It's just that when I finished telling you how I was feeling this morning, I began to feel guilty again, about, you know, what all you've had to go through during the past few days because of me. I mean, I'm not too proud to admit, it's all my doing. You can just blame it all on me." At that, James just turned his head the other way.

But then, Amanda placed her right hand on his jaw and turned his head back her way. At once, she told James, "James, please, look at me and listen."

After that, she slowly and gently moved her right hand up onto his left cheek. Then, she sweetly told him, "Come on now, James; please stop being so hard on yourself. I put myself in danger."

"You did?" asked James. "Like how?"

Then, Amanda went on to tell him, "Well, like Thursday night, I didn't have to go take out Zapper and Zinger. Besides, even once I did, I let myself get carried away and didn't get out of there sooner. I just didn't want to allow them to destroy you. However, I ended up putting us both in danger whenever D.D.T. and Doctor XT were on the scene. So I guess this is all my fault."

"Now, look, Amanda," James began to say to her. "I really don't think—"

"Excuse me, James," interrupted Amanda. "There's one other thing, too. Last night, when you came to me at the restaurant, I was too foolish and hardheaded to listen. I'm the one who snapped at you to make you go away. So I'm at least as much to blame as you, if I'm not more so."

"Well, perhaps…" James sighed. However, he still had a guilty feeling. So he went on to say, "But still, none of that would've had to take place if I hadn't insisted on becoming the Green Phantasm."

But after that, he began to think about other events and began smiling with a more positive outlook. "However, on a brighter note, at least I think I put X-Termination in their place. I guess they'd still be at large if not for the Green Phantasm. I'm just sorry about everything you had to go through, because you didn't deserve it."

"James," Amanda said calmly, "it's no use worrying about it now. What's now done is done; it's all in the past now."

"You're right," James said in agreement. "I guess the only thing worth worrying about is what I'm gonna do now. What I want to do right now is take us to breakfast."

"Not a bad idea," Amanda said and smiled as they both got up. But then, she said, "Excuse me, James."

"Yes, Amanda?"

"Listen," she told him calmly. "Although everything we've been through is in the past, I still want to tell you, thanks so much for saving my life. Another thing is, I still want so much to show appreciation and gratitude in any way I can. Now of course, I know you said late last night that I don't have to give you my life. However, I think I'd feel better if I drove us to breakfast and I treated us."

"You would?"

"I certainly would," Amanda responded. "There's kind of another reason, too. You treated me Wednesday night; so this time, I'll do the treating. I would prefer that, if it's okay with you."

"It most certainly is." James told her affirmatively.

Then at that, she began walking toward the front door, with James following behind. But she stopped just before the door and turned around. "Look, James," she said, "just another thing. I promise not to tell anyone that you're the Green Phantasm."

"Well, I appreciate that," James replied. "I figured you were someone I could trust. That's why I was willing to tell you Friday night. But let's keep it to ourselves like you said you would."

"Okay," said Amanda. "So, shall we be on our way?"

"That we shall," James answered. "Just lead the way."

"Just close the door behind you if you would," Amanda told James.

James followed Amanda outside and closed and locked the door, like she had asked him to do. It was now 9:40 a.m. Amanda and James both got into her Ford Explorer. From that point, they went on to a place called Lily's, which was in downtown Philadelphia, where they enjoyed having breakfast and talking.

Later that day, James bought himself a new pair of leather gloves, which of course, he made dark green like the ones he had previously had. As a result, he once again had a fully complete Green Phantasm outfit.

Then later on, around 5:30 p.m., he once again activated the pyxorium within himself. Immediately afterward, of course, he suited himself up as the Green Phantasm. Then, as the Green Phantasm, he went out to protect Philadelphia from troublemakers and help out the unfortunate innocent ones who were victims to them.

It appeared as though the Green Phantasm had prevailed over X-Termination. Although X-Termination had managed to "X-terminate" a lot of things, they somehow failed to "X-terminate" the goodness and heroism of the one known as the Green Phantasm. However, Axel Axtel, who was code-named Zapper, was still lying unconscious in the manufacturing area of X-Termination Headquarters. But somehow, James Clifton had been so involved with Amanda Taylor that he had now completely forgotten about Zapper, the only X-Termination member still alive. Therefore, James had still not notified any police force about X-Termination Headquarters.

On a brighter note, Amanda Taylor was safe at home in Philadelphia once again. Fortunately, two others that James cared about were also home safe, namely Eric Thomas and Scott MacNicholl. Finally in conclusion, whenever someone innocent needed saving or the scheme of a troublemaker needed breaking up, the Green Phantasm could always be trusted.

Scott Mark
MacNicholl
age: 24
height: 5'9
weight: 180lbs

Eric Austin Thomas
age: 26
height: 5'10
weight: 170lbs

(James Paul Clifton)
age: 25
height: 6'3
weight: 290lbs

Amanda Lee Taylor
age: 26
height: 5'9
weight: 155lbs

XTERMINATION

(John Perry
Perone)
XTE
age: 52
height: 6'0"
weight: 200lbs.

ZAPPER
(Axel Jerome Axtel)
Senior Lieutenant
age: 42
height: 6'2"
weight: 265lbs

ZINGER
(Nicholas Devin
Jarrett)
Junior Lieutenant
age: 26
height: 5'7"
weight: 235lbs

D.D.T
(Anselm Jerad
Nielsen)
Premier Associate
age: 35
height: 7'0"
weight: 650lbs.

www.ingramcontent.com/pod-product-compliance
Lightning Source LLC
Chambersburg PA
CBHW061848310726
48972CB00004B/935

9 781963 254525